DEAN KOONTZ OMNIBUS

DEAN KOONTZ OMNIBUS

Comprising

Cold Fire,
The Face of Fear,
The Mask

Dean Koontz

HEADLINE

First published in this omnibus edition in 1993
by HEADLINE BOOK PUBLISHING PLC

This omnibus edition was originally published in three separate volumes.
Cold Fire was published in hardcover in 1991 and in paperback in 1991
by HEADLINE BOOK PUBLISHING PLC; *The Face of Fear* was
published in hardcover in 1978 by Peter Davies Ltd and in paperback in
1989 by HEADLINE BOOK PUBLISHING PLC; *The Mask* was published in paperback in 1982 by Coronet Books and reissued in 1989 by
HEADLINE BOOK PUBLISHING PLC.

10 9 8 7 6 5 4 3 2 1

British Library Cataloguing in Publication Data

Koontz, Dean R.
    Dean Koontz Omnibus: "Cold Fire", "Face
    of Fear", "The Mask"
    I. Title
813.54 [F]

ISBN 0-7472-0805-0

Typeset in 11/12 pt Times by Colset Private Limited, Singapore

Printed and bound in Great Britain by Clays Ltd, St Ives Plc

HEADLINE BOOK PUBLISHING PLC
Headline House, 79 Great Titchfield Street, London W1P 7FN

CONTENTS

Cold Fire   1

The Face of Fear   343

The Mask   573

COLD FIRE

Part One

THE HERO, THE FRIEND

In the real world
as in dreams,
nothing is quite
what it seems.

   – The Book of Counted Sorrows

Life without meaning
cannot be borne.
We find a mission
to which we're sworn
– or answer the call
of Death's dark horn.
Without a gleaning
of purpose in life,
we have no vision,
we live in strife,
– or let blood fall
on a suicide knife.

   – The Book of Counted Sorrows

AUGUST 12

·1·

Even before the events in the supermarket, Jim Ironheart should have known trouble was coming. During the night he dreamed of being pursued across a field by a flock of large black birds that shrieked around him in a turbulent flapping of wings and tore at him with hooked beaks as precision-honed as surgical scalpels. When he woke and was unable to breathe, he shuffled on to the balcony in his pajama bottoms to get some fresh air. But at nine-thirty in the morning, the temperature, already ninety degrees, only contributed to the sense of suffocation with which he had awakened.

A long shower and a shave refreshed him.

The refrigerator contained only part of a moldering Sara Lee cake. It resembled a laboratory culture of some new, exquisitely virulent strain of botulinus. He could either starve or go out into the furnace heat.

The August day was so torrid that birds, beyond the boundaries of bad dreams, preferred the bowers of the trees to the sun-scorched open spaces of the southern California sky; they sat silently in their leafy shelters, chirruping rarely and without enthusiasm. Dogs padded cat-quick along sidewalks as hot as griddles. No man, woman or child paused to see if an egg would fry on the concrete, taking it as a matter of faith.

After eating a light breakfast at an umbrella-shaded table on the patio of a seaside cafe in Laguna Beach, he was enervated again and sheathed in a dew of perspiration. It was one of those rare occasions when the Pacific could not produce even a dependable mild breeze.

From there he went to the supermarket, which at first seemed to be a sanctuary. He was wearing only white cotton slacks and a blue T-shirt, so the air-conditioning and the chill currents rising off the refrigerated display cases were refreshing.

5

He was in the cookie department, comparing the ingredients in fudge macaroons to those in pineapple-coconut-almond bars, trying to decide which was the lesser dietary sin, when the fit hit him. On the scale of such things, it was not much of a fit – no convulsions, no violent muscle contractions, no sudden rivers of sweat, no speaking in strange tongues. He just abruptly turned to a woman shopper next to him, and said, 'Life line.'

She was about thirty, wearing shorts and a halter top, good looking enough to have experienced a wearying array of come-ons from men, so perhaps she thought he was making a pass at her. She gave him a guarded look. 'Excuse me?'

Flow with it, he told himself. Don't be afraid.

He began to shudder, not because of the air-conditioning but because a series of *inner* chills swam through him, like a wriggling school of eels. All the strength went out of his hands, and he dropped the packages of cookies.

Embarrassed but unable to control himself, he repeated: 'Life line.'

'I don't understand,' the woman said.

Although this had happened to him nine times before, he said, 'Neither do I.'

She clutched a box of vanilla wafers as though she might throw it in his face and run if she decided he was a walking headline (BERSERK MAN SHOOTS SIX IN SUPERMARKET). Nevertheless, she was enough of a good Samaritan to hang in for another exchange: 'Are you all right?'

No doubt he was pale. He felt as if all the blood had drained out of his face. He tried to put on a reassuring smile, knew it was a ghastly grimace, and said, 'Gotta go.'

Turning away from his shopping cart, Jim walked out of the market, into the searing August heat. The forty-degree temperature change momentarily locked the breath in his lungs. The blacktop in the parking lot was tacky in places. Sun silvered the windshields of the cars and seemed to shatter into dazzling splinters against chrome bumpers and grilles.

He went to his Ford. It had air-conditioning, but even after he had driven across the lot and turned on to Crown Valley Parkway, the draft from the dashboard vents was refreshing only by comparison with the baking-oven atmosphere in the car. He put down his window.

Initially he did not know where he was going. Then he had a vague feeling that he should return home. Rapidly the feeling became a strong hunch, the hunch became a conviction, and the conviction became a compulsion. He absolutely *had* to get home.

He drove too fast, weaving in and out of traffic, taking chances, which was uncharacteristic of him. If a cop had stopped him, he would not have been able to explain his desperate urgency, for he did not understand it himself.

It was as if his every move was orchestrated by someone unseen controlling him much the way that he controlled the car.

Again he told himself to flow with it, which was easy since he had no choice. He also told himself not to be afraid, but fear was his unshakable companion.

When he pulled into his driveway in Laguna Niguel, the spiky black shadows of palm fronds looked like cracks in the blazing-white stucco walls of his small house, as if the structure had dried out and split open in the heat. The red-tile roof appeared to ripple like overlapping waves of flame.

In his bedroom, sunlight acquired a coppery hue as it poured through the tinted windows. It laid a penny-colored glow in stripes across the bed and off-white carpet, alternating with bands of shade from the half-open plantation shutters.

Jim switched on a bedside lamp.

He didn't know he was going to pack for travel until he found himself taking a suitcase from his closet. He gathered up his shaving gear and toiletries first. He didn't know his destination or how long he would be gone, but he included two changes of clothes. These jobs – adventures, missions, whatever in God's name they were – usually didn't require him to be away more than two or three days.

He hesitated, worried that he had not packed enough. But these trips were dangerous; each could be his last, in which case it didn't matter whether he packed too much or too little.

He closed the suitcase and stared at it, not sure what to do next. Then he said, 'Gotta fly,' and he knew.

The drive to John Wayne Airport, on the southeastern edge of Santa Ana, took less than half an hour. Along the way he saw subtle reminders that southern California had been a desert before the importation of water through aqueducts. A billboard urged water conservation. Gardeners were installing low-maintenance cactus and ice plants in front of a new Southwestern-style apartment building. Between the greenbelts and the neighborhoods of lushly landscaped properties, the vegetation on undeveloped fields and hills was parched and brown, waiting for the kiss of a match in the trembling hand of one of the pyromaniacs contributing to the annual, devastating wildfire season.

In the main terminal at the airport, travellers streamed to and from the boarding gates. The multi-racial crowd belied the lingering myth that Orange County was culturally bland and populated solely by white Anglo-Saxon Protestants. On his way to the bank of TV monitors that displayed a list of arriving and departing PSA flights, Jim heard four languages besides English.

He read the destinations from top to bottom on the monitor. The next to last city – Portland, Oregon – struck a spark of inspiration in him, and he went straight to the ticket counter.

The clerk who served him was a clean-cut young man, as straight-arrow as a Disneyland employee – at first glance.

'The flight to Portland leaving in twenty minutes,' Jim said. 'Is it full up?'

The clerk checked the computer. 'You're in luck, sir. We have three open seats.'

While the clerk processed the credit card and issued the ticket, Jim noticed the guy had pierced ears. He wasn't wearing earrings on the job, but the holes in his lobes were visible enough to indicate that he wore them regularly when he was off duty and that he preferred heavy jewelry. When he returned Jim's credit card, his shirt-sleeve pulled up far enough on his right wrist to reveal the snarling muzzle of what appeared to be a lavishly detailed, colorful dragon tattoo that extended up his entire arm. The knuckles of that hand were crusted with scabs, as if they had been skinned in a fight.

All the way to the boarding gate, Jim wondered what subculture the clerk swam in after he shed his uniform at the end of the work day and put on street clothes. He had a hunch the guy was nothing as mundane as a biker punk.

The plane took off to the south, with the merciless glare of the sun at the windows on Jim's side. Then it swung to the west and turned north over the ocean, and he could see the sun only as a reflection in the sea below, where its blazing image seemed to transform the water into a vast churning mass of magma erupting from beneath the planet's crust.

Jim realized he was clenching his teeth. He looked down at the armrests of his seat, where his hands were tightly hooked like the talons of an eagle to the rock of a precarious roost.

He tried to relax.

He was not afraid of flying. What he feared was Portland . . . and whatever form of death might be waiting there for him.

•2•

Holly Thorne was at a private elementary school on the west side of Portland to interview a teacher, Louise Tarvohl, who had sold a book of poetry to a major New York publisher; not an easy feat in an age when most people's knowledge of poetry was limited to the lyrics of pop songs and occasional rhyming television ads for dog food, underarm deodorant, or steel-belted radial tires. Only a few summer classes were under way. Another instructor assumed responsibility for Louise's kids, so she and Holly could talk.

They sat at a redwood picnic table on the playground, after Holly checked the bench to be sure there was no dirt on it that might stain her white cotton dress. A jungle gym was to their left, a swing set to their right. The day was pleasantly warm, and a breeze stirred an agreeable fragrance from some nearby Douglas firs.

'Smell the air!' Louise took a deep button-popping breath. 'You can sure tell we're on the edge of five thousand acres of parkland, huh? So little stain of humanity in the air.'

Holly had been given an advance copy of the book, *Soughing Cypress and Other Poems*, when Tom Corvey, the editor of the *Press*'s entertainment section, assigned her to the story. She had wanted to like it. She enjoyed seeing people succeed – perhaps because she had not achieved much in her own career as a journalist and needed to be reminded now and then that success was attainable. Unfortunately the poems were jejune, dismally sentimental celebrations of the natural world that read like something written by a Robert Frost *manqué*, then filtered through the sensibilities of a Hallmark editor in charge of developing saccharine cards for grandma's birthday.

Nevertheless Holly intended to write an uncritical piece. Over the years she had known far too many reporters who, because of envy or bitterness or a misguided sense of moral superiority, got a kick out of slanting and coloring a story to make their subjects look foolish. Except when dealing with exceptionally vile criminals and politicians, she had never been able to work up enough hatred to write that way – which was one reason her career spiral had spun her down through three major newspapers in three large cities to her current position in the more humble offices of the *Portland Press*. Biased journalism was often more colorful than balanced reporting, sold more papers, and was more widely commented upon and admired. But though she rapidly came to dislike Louise Tarvohl

9

even more than the woman's bad poetry, she could work up no enthusiasm for a hatchet job.

'Only in the wilderness am I alive, far from the sights and sounds of civilization, where I can hear the voices of nature in the trees, in the brush, in the lonely ponds, in the dirt.'

Voices in the dirt? Holly thought, and almost laughed.

She liked the way Louise looked: hardy, robust, vital, alive. The woman was thirty-five, Holly's senior by two years, although she appeared ten years older. The crow's feet around her eyes and mouth, her deep laugh lines, and her leathery sun-browned skin pegged her as an outdoors woman. Her sun-bleached hair was pulled back in a ponytail, and she wore jeans and a checkered blue shirt.

'There is a purity in forest mud,' Louise insisted, 'that can't be matched in the most thoroughly scrubbed and sterilized hospital surgery.' She tilted her face back for a moment to bask in the warm sunfall. 'The purity of the natural world cleanses your soul. From that renewed purity of soul comes the sublime vapor of great poetry.'

'Sublime vapor?' Holly said, as if she wanted to be sure that her tape recorder would correctly register every golden phrase.

'Sublime vapor,' Louise repeated, and smiled.

The inner Louise was the Louise that offended Holly. She had cultivated an otherworldly quality, like a spectral projection, more surface than substance. Her opinions and attitudes were insubstantial, based less on facts and insights than on whims – iron whims but whims nonetheless – and she expressed them in language that was flamboyant but imprecise, overblown but empty.

Holly was something of an environmentalist herself, and she was dismayed to discover that she and Louise fetched up on the same side of some issues. It was unnerving to have allies who struck you as goofy; it made your own opinions seem suspect.

Louise leaned forward on the picnic bench, folding her arms on the redwood table. 'The earth is a living thing. It could talk to us if we were worth talking to, could just open a mouth in any rock or plant or pond and talk as easily as I'm talking to you.'

'What an exciting concept,' Holly said.

'Human beings are nothing more than lice.'

'Lice?'

'Lice crawling over the living earth,' Louise said dreamily.

Holly said, 'I hadn't thought of it that way.'

'God is not only *in* each butterfly – God *is* each butterfly, each

10

bird, each rabbit, every wild thing. I would sacrifice a million human lives – ten million and more! – if it meant saving one innocent family of weasels, because God *is* each of those weasels.'

As if moved by the woman's rhetoric, as if she didn't think it was eco-fascism, Holly said, 'I give as much as I can every year to the Nature Conservancy, and I think of myself as an environmentalist, but I see that my consciousness hasn't been raised as far as yours.'

The poet did not hear the sarcasm and reached across the table to squeeze Holly's hand. 'Don't worry, dear. You'll get there. I sense an aura of great spiritual potentiality around you.'

'Help me to understand . . . God is butterflies and rabbits and every living thing, and God is rocks and dirt and water – but God isn't us?'

'No. Because of our one *unnatural* quality.'

'Which is?'

'Intelligence.'

Holly blinked in surprise. 'Intelligence is unnatural?'

'A high degree of intelligence, yes. It exists in no other creatures in the natural world. That's why nature shuns us, and why we subconsciously hate her and seek to obliterate her. High intelligence leads to the concept of progress. Progress leads to nuclear weapons, bio-engineering, chaos, and ultimately to annihilation.'

'God . . . or natural evolution didn't give us our intelligence?'

'It was an unanticipated mutation. We're mutants, that's all. Monsters.'

Holly said, 'Then the less intelligence a creature exhibits . . .'

'. . . the more natural it is,' Louise finished for her.

Holly nodded thoughtfully, as if seriously considering the bizarre proposition that a dumber world was a better world, but she was really thinking that she could not write this story after all. She found Louise Tarvohl so preposterous that she could not compose a favorable article and still hang on to her integrity. At the same time she had no heart for making a fool of the woman in print. Holly's problem was not her deep and abiding cynicism but her soft heart; no creature on earth was more certain to suffer frustration and dissatisfaction with life than a bitter cynic with a damp wad of compassion at her core.

She put down her pen, for she would be making no notes. All she wanted to do was get away from Louise, off the playground, back into the real world – even though the real world had always struck her as just slightly less screwy than this encounter. But the least she owed Tom Corvey was sixty to ninety minutes of taped interview,

11

which would provide another reporter with enough material to write the piece.

'Louise,' she said, 'in light of what you've told me, I think you're the most natural person I've ever met.'

Louise didn't get it. Perceiving a compliment instead of a slight, she beamed at Holly.

'Trees are sisters to us,' Louise said, eager to reveal another facet of her philosophy, evidently having forgotten that human beings were lice, not trees. 'Would you cut off the limbs of your sister, cruelly section her flesh, and build your house with pieces of her corpse?'

'No, I wouldn't,' Holly said sincerely. 'Besides, the city probably wouldn't approve a building permit for such an unconventional structure.'

Holly was safe: Louise had no sense of humor – therefore, no capacity to be offended by the wisecrack.

While the woman prattled on, Holly leaned into the picnic table, feigning interest, and did a fast-backward scan of her entire adult life. She decided that she had spent all of that precious time in the company of idiots, fools, and crooks, listening to their hare-brained or sociopathic plans and dreams, searching fruitlessly for nuggets of wisdom and interest in their boobish or psychotic stories.

Increasingly miserable, she began to brood about her personal life. She had made no effort to develop close women friends in Portland, perhaps because in her heart she felt that Portland was only one more stop on her peripatetic journalistic journey. Her experiences with men were, if anything, even more disheartening than her professional experiences with interviewees of both sexes. Though she still hoped to meet the right man, get married, have children, and enjoy a fulfilling domestic life, she wondered if anyone nice, sane, intelligent, and genuinely interesting would ever enter her life.

Probably not.

And if someone like that miraculously crossed her path one day, his pleasant demeanor would no doubt prove to be a mask, and under the mask would be a leering serial killer with a chainsaw fetish.

•3•

Outside the terminal at Portland International Airport, Jim Ironheart got into a taxi operated by something called the New Rose City Cab Company, which sounded like a corporate stepchild of the long-forgotten hippie era, born in the age of love beads and flower power. But the cabbie – Frazier Tooley, according to his displayed license – explained that Portland was called the City of Roses, which bloomed there in multitudes and were meant to be symbols of renewal and growth. 'The same way,' he said, 'that street beggars are symbols of decay and collapse in New York,' displaying a curiously charming smugness that Jim sensed was shared by many Portlanders.

Tooley, who looked like an Italian operatic tenor cast from the same mold as Luciano Pavarotti, was not sure he had understood Jim's instructions. 'You just want me to drive around for a while?'

'Yeah. I'd like to see some of the city before I check into the hotel. I've never been here before.'

The truth was, he didn't know at which hotel he should stay or whether he would be required to do the job soon, tonight, or maybe tomorrow. He hoped that he would learn what was expected of him if he just tried to relax and waited for enlightenment.

Tooley was happy to oblige – not with enlightenment but with a tour of Portland – because a large fare would tick up on the meter but also because he clearly enjoyed showing off his city. In fact it was exceptionally attractive. Historic brick structures and 19th-century cast-iron-front buildings were carefully preserved among modern glass highrises. Parks full of fountains and trees were so numerous that it sometimes seemed the city was in a forest, and roses were everywhere, not as many blooms as earlier in the summer but radiantly colorful.

After less than half an hour, Jim suddenly was overcome by the feeling that time was running out. He sat forward on the rear seat and heard himself say: 'Do you know the McAlbury School?'

'Sure,' Tooley said.

'What is it?'

'The way you asked, I thought you knew. Private elementary school over on the west side.'

Jim's heart was beating hard and fast. 'Take me there.'

Frowning at him in the rearview mirror, Tooley said, 'Something wrong?'

'I have to be there.'

Tooley braked at a red traffic light. He looked over his shoulder. 'What's wrong?'

'I just have to be there,' Jim said sharply, frustratedly.

'Sure, no sweat.'

Fear had rippled through Jim ever since he had spoken the words 'life line' to the woman in the supermarket more than four hours ago. Now those ripples swelled into dark waves that carried him toward McAlbury School. With an overwhelming sense of urgency that he could not explain, he said, 'I have to be there *in fifteen minutes*!'

'Why didn't you mention it earlier?'

He wanted to say, I didn't *know* earlier. Instead he said, 'Can you get me there in time?'

'It'll be tight.'

'I'll pay triple the meter.'

'Triple?'

'If you make it in time,' he said, withdrawing his wallet from his pocket. He extracted a hundred-dollar bill and thrust it at Tooley. 'Take this in advance.'

'It's that important?'

'It's life and death.'

Tooley gave him a look that said: What – are you nuts?

'The light just changed,' Jim told him. 'Let's move!'

Although Tooley's skeptical frown deepened, he faced front again, hung a left turn at the intersection, and tramped on the accelerator.

Jim kept glancing at his watch all the way, and they arrived at the school with only three minutes to spare. He tossed another bill at Tooley, paying even more than three times the meter, pulled open the door, and scrambled out with his suitcase.

Tooley leaned through his open window. 'You want me to wait?'

Slamming the door, Jim said, 'No. No, thanks. You can go.'

He turned away and heard the taxi drive off as he anxiously studied the front of McAlbury School. The building was actually a rambling white Colonial house with a deep front porch, on to which had been added two single-story wings to provide more classrooms. It was shaded by Douglas firs and huge old sycamores. With its lawn and playground, it occupied the entire length of that short block.

In the house part of the structure directly in front of him, kids were coming out of the double doors, on to the porch, and down the steps. Laughing and chattering, carrying books and large drawing tablets and bright lunchboxes decorated with cartoon characters, they approached him along the school walk, passed through the open gate in the spear-point iron fence, and turned either uphill or down, moving away from him in both directions.

Two minutes left. He didn't have to look at his watch. His heart was pounding two beats for every second, and he *knew* the time as surely as if he had been a clock.

Sunshine, filtered through the interstices of the arching trees, fell in delicate patterns across the scene and the people in it, as if everything had been draped over with an enormous piece of gossamer lacework stitched from golden thread. That netlike ornamental fabric of light seemed to shimmer in time to the rising and falling music of the children's shouts and laughter, and the moment should have been peaceful, idyllic.

But Death was coming.

Suddenly he knew that Death was coming for one of the children, not for any of the three teachers standing on the porch, just for one child. Not a big catastrophe, not an explosion or fire or a falling airplane that would wipe out a dozen of them. Just one, a small tragedy. But *which* one?

Jim refocused his attention from the scene to the players in it, studying the children as they approached him, seeking the mark of imminent death on one of their fresh young faces. But they all looked as if they would live forever.

'Which one?' he said aloud, speaking neither to himself nor to the children but to . . . Well, he supposed he was speaking to God. 'Which one?'

Some kids went uphill toward the crosswalks at that intersection, and others headed downhill toward the opposite end of the block. In both directions, women crossing-guards in bright orange safety vests, holding big red paddlelike 'stop' signs, had begun to shepherd their charges across the streets in small groups. No moving cars or trucks were in sight, so even without the crossing guards there seemed to be little threat from traffic.

One and a half minutes.

Jim scrutinized two yellow vans parked at the curb downhill from him. For the most part, McAlbury seemed to be a neighborhood school, where kids walked to and from their homes, but a few were boarding the vans. The two drivers stood by the doors, smiling and joking with the ebullient, energetic passengers. None of the kids boarding the vans seemed doomed, and the cheery yellow vehicles did not strike him as morgue wagons in bright dress.

But Death was nearer.

It was almost among them.

An ominous change had stolen over the scene, not in reality but in Jim's perception of it. He was now less aware of the golden lacework of light than he was of the shadows within that bright

15

filigree: small shadows the shape of leaves or bristling clusters of evergreen needles; larger shadows the shape of tree trunks or branches; geometric bars of shade from the iron rails of the spearpoint fence. Each blot of darkness seemed to be a potential doorway through which Death might arrive.

One minute.

Frantic, he hurried downhill several steps, among the children, drawing puzzled looks as he glanced at one then another of them, not sure what sort of sign he was searching for, the small suitcase banging against his leg.

Fifty seconds.

The shadows seemed to be growing, spreading, melting together all around Jim.

He stopped, turned, and peered uphill toward the end of the block, where the crossing guard was standing in the intersection, holding up her red stop sign, using her free hand to motion the kids across. Five of them were in the street. Another half dozen were approaching the corner and soon to cross.

One of the drivers at the nearby school vans said, 'Mister, is something wrong?'

Forty seconds.

Jim dropped the suitcase and ran uphill toward the intersection, still uncertain about what was going to happen and which child was at risk. He was pushed in that direction by the same invisible hand that had made him pack a suitcase and fly to Portland. Startled kids moved out of his way.

At the periphery of his vision, everything had become ink-black. He was aware only of what lay directly ahead of him. From one curb to the other, the intersection appeared to be a scene revealed by a spotlight on an otherwise night-dark stage.

Half a minute.

Two women looked up in surprise and failed to get out of his way fast enough. He tried to dodge them, but he brushed against a blonde in a summery white dress, almost knocking her down. He kept going because he could feel Death among them now, a cold presence.

He reached the intersection, stepped off the curb, and stopped. Four kids in the street. One was going to be a victim. But which of the four? And a victim of what?

Twenty seconds.

The crossing guard was staring at him.

All but one of the kids was nearing the curb, and Jim sensed that the sidewalks were safe territory. The street would be the killing ground.

He moved toward the dawdler, a little red-haired girl, who turned and blinked at him in surprise.

Fifteen seconds.

Not the girl. He looked into her jade-green eyes and knew she was safe. Just *knew* it somehow.

All the other kids had reached the sidewalk.

Fourteen seconds.

Jim spun around and looked back toward the far curb. Four more children had entered the street behind him.

Thirteen seconds.

The four new kids started to arc around him, giving him wary sidelong looks. He knew he appeared to be a little deranged, standing in the street, wide-eyed, gaping at them, his face distorted by fear.

Eleven seconds.

No cars in sight. But the brow of the hill was little more than a hundred yards above the intersection, and maybe some reckless fool was rocketing up the far side with the accelerator jammed to the floorboards. As soon as that image flashed through his mind, Jim knew it was a prophetic glimpse of the instrument Death would use: a drunk driver.

Eight seconds.

He wanted to shout, tell them to run, but maybe he would only panic them and cause the marked child to bolt straight *into* danger rather than away from it.

Seven seconds.

He heard the muffled growl of an engine, which instantly changed to a loud roar, then a piston-shattering scream. A pickup truck shot over the brow of the hill. It actually took flight for an instant, afternoon sun flashing off its windshield and coruscating across its chromework, as if it were a flaming chariot descending from the heavens on judgment day. With a shrill bark of rubber against blacktop, the front tires met the pavement again, and the rear of the truck slammed down with a jarring crash.

Five seconds.

The kids in the street scattered – except for a sandy-haired boy with violet eyes the shade of faded rose petals. He just stood there, holding a lunchbox covered with brightly colored cartoon figures, one tennis shoe untied, watching the truck bear down on him, unable to move, as if he sensed that it wasn't just a truck rushing to meet him but his destiny, inescapable. He was an eight- or nine-year-old boy with nowhere to go but to the grave.

Two seconds.

Leaping directly into the path of the oncoming pickup, Jim grabbed the kid. In what felt like a dream-slow swan dive off a high cliff, he carried the boy with him in a smooth arc to the pavement rolling toward the leaf-littered gutter, feeling nothing from his impact with the street, his nerves so numbed by terror and adrenaline that he might as well have been tumbling across a field of lush grass and soft loam.

The roar of the truck was the loudest thing he had ever heard, as if it were a thunder *within* him, and he felt something strike his left foot, hard as a hammer blow. In the same instant a terrible wrenching force seemed to wring his ankle as if it were a rag. A white-hot current of pain crackled up his leg, sizzling into his hip joint, exploding in that socket of bone like a Fourth of July bottle rocket bursting in a night sky.

*   *   *

Holly started after the man who had collided with her, angry and intending to tell him off. But before she reached the intersection, a gray and red pickup erupted over the brow of the hill, as if fired out of a giant slingshot. She halted at the curb.

The scream of the truck engine was a magic incantation that slowed the flow of time, stretching each second into what seemed to be a minute. From the curb, she saw the stranger sweep the boy out of the path of the pickup, executing the rescue with such singular agility and grace that he almost appeared to be performing mad, slow-motion ballet in the street. She saw the bumper of the truck strike his left foot, and watched in horror as his shoe was torn off and tossed high into the air, tumbling end over end. Peripherally, she was aware of the man and boy rolling toward the gutter, the truck swerving sharply to the right, the startled crossing guard dropping the paddle-like stop sign, the truck ricocheting off a parked car across the street, the man and boy coming to rest against the curb, the truck tipping on to its side and sliding downhill in cascades of yellow and blue sparks – but all the while her attention was focused primarily on that shoe tumbling up, up, into the air, silhouetted against the blue sky, hanging at the apex of its flight for what seemed like an hour, then tumbling slowly, slowly down again. She couldn't look away from it, was mesmerized by it,

18

because she had the macabre feeling that the foot was still in the shoe, torn off at the ankle, bristling with splinters of bone, trailing shorn ribbons of arteries and veins. Down it came, down, down, straight toward her, and she felt a scream swelling in the back of her throat.

Down . . . down . . .

The battered shoe – a Reebok – plopped into the gutter in front of her, and she lowered her eyes to it the way she always looked into the face of the monster in a nightmare, not wanting to see but unable to turn away, equally repelled by and attracted to the unthinkable. The shoe was empty. No severed foot. Not even any blood.

She swallowed the unreleased scream. She tasted vomit in the back of her throat, and swallowed that too.

As the pickup came to rest on its side more than half a block down the hill, Holly turned the other way and ran to the man and boy. She was the first to reach them as they started to sit up on the blacktop.

Except for a scraped palm and a small abrasion on his chin, the child appeared to be unhurt. He was not even crying.

She dropped to her knees in front of him. 'Are you OK, honey?'

Though dazed, the boy understood and nodded. 'Yeah. My hand hurts a little, that's all.'

The man in the white slacks and blue T-shirt was sitting up. He had rolled his sock halfway off his foot and was gingerly kneading his left ankle. Though the ankle was swollen and already enflamed, Holly was still surprised by the absence of blood.

The crossing guard, a couple of teachers, and other kids gathered around, and a babble of excited voices rose on all sides. The boy was helped up and drawn into a teacher's arms.

Wincing in pain as he continued to massage his ankle, the injured man raised his head and met Holly's gaze. His eyes were searingly blue and, for an instant, appeared as cold as if they were not human eyes at all but the visual receptors of a machine.

Then he smiled. In a blink, the initial impression of coldness was replaced by one of warmth. In fact Holly was overwhelmed by the clarity, morning-sky color, and beauty of his eyes; she felt as if she were peering through them into a gentle soul. She was a cynic who would equally distrust a nun and mafia boss on first encounter, so her instant attraction to this man was jolting. Though words were her first love and her trade, she was at a loss for them.

'Close call,' he said, and his smile elicited one from her.

19

•4•

Holly waited for Jim Ironheart in the school hallway, outside the boys' restroom. All of the children and teachers had at last gone home. The building was silent, except for the periodic muffled hum of the maintenance man's electric buffer as he polished the vinyl tiles up on the second floor. The air was laced with a faint perfume of chalk dust, craft paste, and pine-scented disinfectant wax.

Outside in the street, the police probably were still overseeing a couple of towing-company employees who were righting the overturned truck in order to haul it away. The driver had been drunk. At the moment he was in the hospital, where physicians were attending to his broken leg, lacerations, abrasions, and contusions.

Holly had gotten nearly everything she required to write the story: background on the boy – Billy Jenkins – who had nearly been killed, the facts of the event, the reactions of the eye-witnesses, a response from the police, and slurred expressions of regret mixed with self-pity from the inebriated driver of the truck. She lacked only one element, but it was the most important – information about Jim Ironheart, the hero of the whole affair. Newspaper readers would want to know everything about him. But at the moment all she could have told them was the guy's name and that he was from southern California.

His brown suitcase stood against the wall beside her, and she kept eyeing it. She had the urge to pop the latches and explore the contents of the bag, though at first she didn't know why. Then she realized it was unusual for a man to be carrying luggage through a residential neighborhood; a reporter was trained – if not genetically compelled – to be curious about anything out of the ordinary.

When Ironheart came out of the restroom, Holly was still staring at the suitcase. She twitched guiltily, as if caught pawing through the contents of the bag.

'How're you feeling?' she asked.

'Fine.' He was limping. 'But I told you – I'd rather not be interviewed.'

He had combed his thick brown hair and blotted the worst of the dirt off his white cotton pants. He was wearing both shoes again, although the left was torn in one spot and battered.

She said, 'I won't take much of your time.'

'Definitely,' he agreed, smiling.

'Oh, come on, be a good guy.'

20

'Sorry, but I'd make dull copy anyway.'

'You just saved a child's life!'

'Other than that, I'm boring.'

Something about him belied his claim to dullness, although at first Holly could not pinpoint the reason for his strong appeal. He was about thirty-five, an inch or two under six feet, lean but well muscled. Though he was attractive enough, he didn't have the looks that made her think of movie stars. His eyes were beautiful, yes, but she was never drawn to a man merely because of his looks and certainly not because of one exceptional feature.

He picked up his suitcase and began to limp along the corridor.

'You should see a doctor,' she said, falling in at his side.

'At worst, it's sprained.'

'It still should be treated.'

'Well, I'll buy an Ace bandage at the airport, or when I get back home.'

Maybe his manner was what she found so appealing. He spoke softly, smiled easily, rather like a Southern gentleman, though he had no accent. He also moved with unusual grace even when he was limping. She remembered how she had been reminded of ballet when, with the fluidity of a dancer, he had swept the little boy out of the path of the hurtling truck. Exceptional physical grace and an unforced gentility were appealing in a man. But neither of those qualities was what fascinated her. Something else. Something more elusive.

As they reached the front door, she said, 'If you're really intent on going home again, I can give you a ride to the airport.'

'Thank you. That's very kind, but I don't need a ride.'

She followed him on to the porch. 'It's a damned long walk.'

He stopped, and frowned. 'Oh. Yeah. Well . . . there's got to be a phone here. I'll call a cab.'

'Come on, you don't have to be afraid of me. I'm not a serial killer. I don't keep a chainsaw in my car.'

He stared at her a beat, then grinned disarmingly. 'Actually, you look more like the type who favors bludgeoning with a blunt instrument.'

'I'm a reporter. We use switchblades. But I haven't killed anyone this week.'

'Last week?'

'Two. But they were both door-to-door salesmen.'

'It's still homicide.'

'Justifiable, though.'

'OK, I accept your offer.'

Her blue Toyota was at the far curb, two back from the parked car into which the drunk driver had slammed. Downhill, the tow truck was just hauling away the totaled pickup, and the last of the policemen was getting into a patrol car. A few overlooked splinters of tempered glass from the truck's broken window still glimmered on the blacktop in the late-afternoon sunshine.

They rode for a block or so in silence.

Then Holly said, 'You have friends in Portland?'

'Yeah. From college.'

'That's who you were staying with?'

'Yeah.'

'They couldn't take you to the airport?'

'They could've if it was a morning flight, but this afternoon they were both at work.'

'Ah,' she said. She commented on clusters of brilliant yellow roses that hung from vines entwining a split-rail fence at a house they passed, and asked if he knew that Portland called itself the City of Roses, which he did. After another silence, she returned to the *real* conversation: 'Their phone wasn't working, huh?'

'Excuse me?'

'Your friends.' She shrugged. 'I just wondered why you didn't call a cab from their place.'

'I intended to walk.'

'To the airport?'

'My ankle was fine then.'

'It's still a long walk.'

'Oh, but I'm a fitness nut.'

'Very long walk – especially with a suitcase.'

'It's not that heavy. When I'm exercising, I usually walk with handweights to get an upper-body workout.'

'I'm a walker myself,' she said, braking for a red light. 'I used to run every morning, but my knees started hurting.'

'Mine too, so I switched to walking. Gives your heart the same workout if you keep up your pace.'

For a couple of miles, while she drove as slowly as she dared in order to extend the time she had with him, they chatted about physical fitness and fat-free foods. Eventually he said something that allowed her to ask, with complete naturalness, the names of his friends there in Portland.

'No,' he said.

'No what?'

22

'No, I'm not giving you their names. They're private people, nice people, I don't want them being pestered.'

'I've never been called a pest before,' she said.

'No offense, Miss Thorne, but I just wouldn't want them to have to be in the paper and everything, have their lives disrupted.'

'Lots of people *like* seeing their names in the newspaper.'

'Lots don't.'

'They might enjoy talking about their friend, the big hero.'

'Sorry,' he said affably, and smiled.

She was beginning to understand why she found him so appealing: his unshakable poise was irresistible. Having worked for two years in Los Angeles, Holly had known a lot of men who styled themselves as laid-back Californians; each portrayed himself as the epitome of self-possession, Mr Mellow – *rely on me, baby, and the world can never touch either of us; we are beyond the reach of fate* – but none actually possessed the cool nerves and unflappable temperament to which he pretended. A Bruce Willis wardrobe, perfect tan, and studied insouciance did not a Bruce Willis make. Self-confidence could be gained through experience, but real aplomb was something you were either born with or learned to imitate – and the imitation was never convincing to the observant eye. However, Jim Ironheart had been born with enough aplomb, if rationed equally to all the men in Rhode Island, to produce an entire state of cool, unflappable types. He faced hurtling trucks and a reporter's questions with the same degree of equanimity. Just being in his company was oddly relaxing and reassuring.

She said, 'That's an interesting name you have.'

'Jim?'

He was having fun with her.

'Ironheart,' she said. 'Sounds like an American Indian name.'

'Wouldn't mind having a little Chippewa or Apache blood, make me less dull, a little bit exotic, mysterious. But it's just the anglicized version of the family's original German name – Eisenherz.'

By the time they were on the East Portland Freeway, rapidly approaching the Killingsworth Street exit, Holly was dismayed at the prospect of dropping him at the airline terminal. As a reporter, she still had a lot of unanswered questions. More important, as a woman, she was more intrigued by him than she had been by any man in ages. She briefly considered taking a far more circuitous route to the airport; his lack of familiarity with the city might disguise her deception. Then she realized that the freeway signs were already announcing the upcoming exit to Portland International; even if he had not been reading them, he could not have failed to notice the steady air traffic in the deep blue eastern sky ahead of them.

She said, 'What do you do down there in California?'

'Enjoy life.'

'I meant – what do you do for a living?'

'What's your guess?' he asked.

'Well . . . one thing for sure: you're not a librarian.'

'Why do you say that?'

'You have a sense of mystery about you.'

'Can't a librarian be mysterious?'

'I've never known one who was.' Reluctantly she turned on to the airport exit ramp. 'Maybe you're a cop of some kind.'

'What gives you that idea?'

'Really good cops are unflappable, cool.'

'Gee, I think of myself as a warm sort of guy, open and easy. You think I'm cool?'

Traffic was moderately heavy on the airport approach road. She let it slow her even further.

'I mean,' she said, 'that you're very self-possessed.'

'How long have you been a reporter?'

'Twelve years.'

'All of it in Portland?'

'No. I've been here a year.'

'Where'd you work before?'

'Chicago . . . Los Angeles . . . Seattle.'

'You like journalism?'

Realizing that she had lost control of the conversation, Holly said, 'This isn't a game of twenty questions, you know.'

'Oh,' he said, clearly amused, 'that's exactly what I thought it was.'

She was frustrated by the impenetrable wall he had erected around himself, irritated by his stubbornness. She was not used to having her will thwarted. But he had no meanness in him, as far as she could see, and no great talent for deception; he was just determined to preserve his privacy. As a reporter who had ever-increasing doubts about a journalist's right to intrude in the lives of others, Holly sympathized with his reticence. When she glanced at him, she could only laugh softly. 'You're good.'

'So are you.'

As she stopped at the curb in front of the terminal, Holly said,

'No, if I were good, by now I'd at least have found out what the hell you do for a living.'

He had a charming smile. And those *eyes*. 'I didn't say you were as good as I am – just that you were good.' He got out and retrieved his suitcase from the back seat, then returned to the open front door. 'Look, I just happened to be in the right place at the right time. By sheer chance, I was able to save that boy. It wouldn't be fair to have my whole life turned upside-down by the media just because I did a good deed.'

'No, it wouldn't,' she agreed.

With a look of relief, he said, 'Thank you.'

'But I gotta say – your modesty's refreshing.'

He looked at her for a long beat, fixed her with his exceptional blue eyes. 'So are you, Miss Thorne.'

Then he closed the door, turned away, and entered the terminal.

Their last exchange played again in her mind:

Your modesty's refreshing.

So are you, Miss Thorne.

She stared at the terminal door through which he had disappeared, and he seemed too good to have been real, as if she had given a ride to a hitchhiking spirit. A thin haze filtered flecks of color from the late-afternoon sunlight, so the air had a vague golden cast of the kind that sometimes hung for an instant in the wake of a vanishing revenant in an old movie about ghosts.

A hard, hollow rapping noise startled her.

She snapped her head around and saw an airport security guard tapping with his knuckles on the hood of her car. When he had her attention, he pointed to a sign: LOADING ZONE.

Wondering how long she had sat there, mesmerized by thoughts of Jim Ironheart, Holly released the emergency brake and slipped the car in gear. She drove away from the terminal.

Your modesty's refreshing.

So are you, Miss Thorne.

All the way back into Portland, a sense of the uncanny lay upon her, a perception that someone preternaturally special had passed through her life. She was unsettled by the discovery that a man could so affect her, and she felt uncomfortably girlish, even foolish. At the same time, she enjoyed that pleasantly eerie mood and did not want it to fade.

So are you, Miss Thorne.

•5•

That evening, in her third-floor apartment overlooking Council Crest Park, as she was cooking a dinner of angel-hair pasta with pesto sauce, pine nuts, fresh garlic, and chopped tomatoes, Holly suddenly wondered how Jim Ironheart could have known that young Billy Jenkins was in danger even before the drunken driver in the pickup truck had appeared over the crest of the hill.

She stopped chopping in the middle of a tomato and looked out the kitchen window. Purple-red twilight was settling over the greensward below. Among the trees, the park lamps cast pools of warm amber light on the grass-flanked walkways.

When Ironheart had charged up the sidewalk in front of McAlbury School, colliding with her and nearly knocking her down, Holly started after him, intending to tell him off. By the time she reached the intersection, he was already in the street, turning right then left, looking a little agitated . . . wild. In fact he seemed so strange, the kids moved around him in a wide arc. She had registered his panicked expression and the kids' reaction to him a second or two *before* the truck had erupted over the crest like a daredevil's car flying off the top of a stunt ramp. Only then had Ironheart focused on Billy Jenkins, scooping the boy out of the path of the truck.

Perhaps he had heard the roar of the engine, realized something was approaching the intersection at reckless speed, and acted out of an instinctive perception of danger. Holly tried to remember if she had been aware of the racing engine as early as when Ironheart had collided with her, but she could not recall. Maybe she had heard it but had not been as alert to its meaning as he had. Or perhaps she hadn't heard it at all because she had been trying to shake off the indefatigable Louise Tarvohl, who had insisted on walking with her to her car; she had felt that she'd go stark raving mad if she were forced to listen to even another minute of the poet's chatter, and she had been distracted by the desperate need to escape.

Now, in her kitchen, she was conscious of only one sound: the vigorously boiling water in the big pot on the stove. She should turn the gas down, put in the pasta, set the timer . . . Instead she stood at the cutting board, tomato in one hand and knife in the other, staring out at the park but seeing the fateful intersection near the McAlbury School.

Even if Ironheart had heard the approaching engine from halfway down the block, how could he so quickly determine the direction from which the truck was approaching, that its driver was out of control, and that the children were consequently in danger? The crossing guard, initially much closer to the sound than Ironheart, had been taken by surprise, as had the kids themselves.

OK, well, some people had sharper senses than others – which was why composers of symphonies could hear more complex harmonies and rhythms in music than could the average concertgoer, why some baseball players could see a pop fly against a glary sky sooner than others, and why a master viniculturist could appreciate subtler qualities of a rare vintage than could a stoned-blind wino who was only concerned with the effect. Likewise, some people had far quicker reflexes than others, which was part of what made Wayne Gretzky worth millions a year to a professional ice-hockey team. She had seen that Ironheart had the lightning reflexes of an athlete. No doubt he was also blessed with especially keen hearing. Most people with a notable physical advantage also had other gifts: it was all a matter of good genes. That was the explanation. Simple enough. Nothing unusual. Nothing mysterious. Certainly nothing supernatural. Just good genes.

Outside in the park, the shadows grew deeper. Except at those places where lamplight was shed upon it, the pathway disappeared into gathering darkness. The trees seemed to crowd together.

Holly put down the knife and went to the stove. She lowered the gas flame under the big pot, and the vigorously bubbling water fell to a slow boil. She put the pasta in to cook.

Back at the cutting board, as she picked up the knife, she looked out the window again. Stars began to appear in the sky as the purple light of dusk faded to black and as the crimson smear on the horizon darkened to burgundy. Below, more of the park walkway lay in shadow than in lamplight.

Suddenly she was gripped by the peculiar conviction that Jim Ironheart was going to walk out of darkness into a pool of amber light on the pathway, that he was going to raise his head and look directly up at her window, that somehow he knew where she lived and had come back for her. It was a ridiculous notion. But a chill quivered along her spine, tightening each knotted vertebra.

* * *

Later, near midnight, when Holly sat on the edge of her bed and switched off the nightstand lamp, she glanced at her bedroom window, through which she also had a view of the park, and again a chill ran up her back. She started to lie down, hesitated, and got up instead. In panties and T-shirt, her usual sleeping attire, she moved through the dark room to the window, where she parted the sheers between the drapes.

He was not down there. She waited a minute, then another. He did not appear. Feeling foolish and confused, she returned to bed.

* * *

She woke in the dead hours of the night, shuddering. All she could remember of the dream were blue eyes, intensely blue, with a gaze that penetrated her as completely as a sharp knife slicing through soft butter.

She got up and went into the bathroom, guided only by the thin wash of moonglow that filtered through the sheers over the window. In the bathroom she did not turn on the light. After she peed, she washed her hands and stood for a while just looking at her dim, amorphous reflection in the silvery-black mirror. She washed her hands. She got a drink of cold water. She realized that she was delaying her return to the bedroom because she was afraid she would be drawn to the window again.

This is ridiculous, she told herself. What's gotten into you?

She re-entered the bedroom and found herself approaching the window instead of the bed. She parted the sheers.

He was not out there.

Holly felt as much disappointment as relief. As she stared into the night-swaddled reaches of Council Crest Park, an extended chill quivered through her again, and she realized that only half of it was generated by a nameless fear. A strange excitement coursed through her, as well, a pleasant anticipation of . . .

Of what?

She didn't know.

Jim Ironheart's effect on her was profound and lingering. She had never experienced anything like it. Although she struggled to understand what she was feeling, enlightenment eluded her. Mere sexual attraction was not the explanation. She was long past puberty, and neither the tidal pull of hormones nor the girlish desire for romance could affect her like this.

At last she returned to bed. She was certain that she would lie awake for the rest of the night, but to her surprise she soon drifted off again. As she trembled on the wire of consciousness, she heard herself mumble, '*those eyes*,' then fell into the yawning void.

* * *

In his own bed in Laguna Niguel, Jim woke just before dawn. His heart was pounding. Though the room was cool, he was bathed in sweat. He'd been having one of his frequent nightmares, but all he could recall of it was that something relentless, powerful, and vicious had been pursuing him . . .

His sense of onrushing death was so powerful that he had to turn on the lights to be certain that something inhuman and murderous was not actually in the room with him. He was alone.

'But not for long,' he said aloud.

He wondered what he meant by that.

20 AUGUST THROUGH 22 AUGUST

•1•

Jim Ironheart peered anxiously through the dirty windshield of the stolen Camaro. The sun was a white ball, and the light it shed was as white and bitter as powdered lime. Even with sunglasses, he had to squint. Rising off sun-scorched blacktop, currents of super-heated air formed into mirages of people and cars and lakes of water.

He was tired, and his eyes felt abraded. The heat illusions combined with occasional dust devils to hamper visibility. The endless vistas of the Mojave Desert made it difficult to maintain an accurate perception of speed; he didn't *feel* as if the car was streaking along at nearly a hundred miles an hour, but it was. In his condition, he should have been driving a lot slower.

But he was filled with a growing conviction that he was too late, that he was going to screw up. Someone was going to die because he had not been quick enough.

He glanced at the loaded shotgun angled in front of the other bucket seat, its butt on the floor, barrels pointed away from him. A full box of shells was on the seat.

Half sick with dread, he pressed the accelerator even closer to the floorboard. The needle on the speedometer dial shivered past the hundred mark.

He topped a long, gradual rise. Below lay a bowl-shaped valley twenty or thirty miles in diameter, so alkaline that it was mostly white, barren but for a few gray tumbleweed and a stubble of desert scrub. It might have been formed by an asteroid impact eons ago, its outlines considerably softened by the passage of millennia but otherwise still as primeval as any place on earth.

The valley was bisected by the black highway on which mirages of water glistened. Along the shoulders, heat phantoms shimmered and writhed languorously.

He saw the car first, a station wagon. It was pulled off to the right of the roadway, approximately a mile ahead, near a drainage culvert where no water flowed except during rare storms and flash floods.

His heart began to pound harder, and in spite of the rush of cool air coming out of the dashboard vents, he broke into a sweat. *This* was the place.

Then he spotted the motorhome, too, half a mile beyond the car, surfacing out of one of the deeper water mirages. It was lumbering away from him, toward the distant wall of the valley, where the highway sloped up between treeless, red-rock mountains.

Jim slowed as he approached the station wagon, not sure where his help was needed. His attention was drawn equally to the wagon and the motorhome.

As the speedometer needle fell back across the gauge, he waited for a clearer understanding of his purpose. It didn't come. Usually he was compelled to act, as if by an inner voice that spoke to him only on a subconscious level, or as if he were a machine responding to a pre-programmed course of action. Not this time. Nothing.

With growing desperation, he braked hard and fishtailed to a full stop next to the Chevy station wagon. He didn't bother to pull on to the shoulder. He glanced at the shotgun beside him, but he knew somehow that he did not need it. Yet.

He got out of the Camaro and hurried toward the station wagon. Luggage was piled in the rear cargo area. When he looked through the side window, he saw a man sprawled on the front seat. He pulled open the door – and flinched. So much blood.

The guy was dying but not dead. He had been shot twice in the chest. His head lay at an angle against the passenger-side door, reminding Jim of Christ's head tilted to one side as he hung upon the cross. His eyes cleared briefly as he struggled to focus on Jim.

In a voice as frantic as it was fragile, he said, 'Lisa . . . Susie . . . My wife, daughter . . .'

Then his tortured eyes slipped out of focus. A thin wheeze of breath escaped him, his head lolled to one side, and he was gone.

Sick, stricken by an almost disabling sense of responsibility for the stranger's death, Jim stepped back from the open door of the station wagon and stood for a moment on the black pavement under the searing white sun. If he had driven faster, harder, he might have been there a few minutes sooner, might have stopped what had happened.

A sound of anguish, low and primitive, rose from him. It was almost a whisper at first, swelling into a soft moan. But when he turned away from the dead man and looked down the highway toward the dwindling motorhome, his cry quickly became a shout of rage because suddenly he knew what had happened.

And he knew what he must do.

In the Camaro again, he filled the roomy pockets of his blue cotton slacks with shotgun shells. Already loaded, the short-barreled pump-action .12-gauge was within easy reach.

He checked the rearview mirror. On this Wednesday morning, the desert highway was empty. No help in sight. It was all up to him.

Far ahead, the motorhome vanished through shimmering thermal currents like undulant curtains of glass beads.

He threw the Camaro in gear. The tires spun in place for an instant, then skidded on the clutching sun-softened blacktop, issuing a scream that echoed eerily across the desert vastness. Jim wondered how the stranger and his family had screamed when he'd been shot pointblank in the chest. Abruptly the Camaro overcame all resistance and rocketed forward.

Tramping the accelerator to the floor, he squinted ahead to catch a glimpse of his quarry. In seconds the curtains of heat parted, and the big vehicle hove into view as if it were a sailing ship somehow making way on that dry sea.

The motorhome couldn't compete with the Camaro, and Jim was soon riding its bumper. It was an old thirty-foot Roadking that had seen a lot of miles. Its white aluminum siding was caked with dirt, dented and rust-spotted. The windows were covered with yellow curtains that had no doubt once been white. It looked like nothing more than the home of a couple of travel-loving retirees living on dwindling Social Security assets, unable to maintain it with the pride they had when it had been new.

Except for the motorcycle. A Harley was chained to a wrought-iron rack to the left of the roof-service ladder on the back of the motorhome. It wasn't the biggest bike made, but it was powerful – and not something that a pair of retirees typically tooled around on.

In spite of the cycle, nothing about the Roadking was suspicious. Yet in its wake Jim Ironheart was overcome by a sense of evil so strong that it might as well have been a black tide washing over him with all the power of the sea behind it. He gagged as if he could smell the corruption of those to whom the motorhome belonged.

At first he hesitated, afraid that any action he took might

jeopardize the woman and child who were evidently being held captive. But the riskiest thing he could do was delay. The longer the mother and daughter were in the hands of the people in the Roadking, the less chance they had of coming out of it alive.

He swung into the passing lane. He intended to get a couple of miles ahead of them and block the road with his car.

In the Roadking's rearview mirror, the driver must have seen Jim stop at the station wagon and get out to inspect it. Now he let the Camaro pull almost even before swinging the motorhome sharply left, bashing it against the side of the car.

Metal shrieked against metal, and the car shuddered.

The steering wheel spun in Jim's hands. He fought for control and kept it.

The Roadking pulled away, then swerved back and bashed him again, driving him off the blacktop and on to the unpaved shoulder. For a few hundred yards they rattled forward at high speed in those positions: the Roadking in the wrong lane, risking a head-on collision with any oncoming traffic that might be masked by the curtains of heat and sun glare; the Camaro casting up huge clouds of dust behind it, speeding precariously along the brink of the two-foot drop-off that separated the raised roadbed from the desert floor beyond.

Even a light touch of the brakes might pull the car a few inches to the left, causing it to drop and roll. He only dared to ease up on the accelerator and let his speed fall gradually.

The driver of the Roadking reacted, reducing his speed, too, hanging at Jim's side. Then the motorhome moved inexorably to the left, inch by inch, edging relentlessly on to the dirt shoulder.

Being much the smaller and less powerful of the two vehicles, the Camaro could not resist the pressure. It was pushed leftward in spite of Jim's efforts to hold it steady. The front tire found the brink first, and that corner of the car dropped. He bit the brakes; it didn't matter any more. Even as he jammed his foot down on the pedal, the rear wheel followed the front end into empty space. The Camaro tipped and rolled to the left.

Using a safety harness was a habit with him, so he was thrown sideways and forward, and his sunglasses flew off, but he didn't crack his face against the window post or shatter his breastbone against the steering wheel. Webs of cracks, like the work of a spider on Benzedrine, spread across the windshield. He squeezed his eyes shut, and gummy bits of tempered glass imploded over him. The car rolled again, then started to roll a third time but only made it halfway, coming to rest on its roof.

Hanging upside-down in the harness, he was unhurt but badly shaken. He choked on the clouds of white dust that poured in through the shattered windshield.

They'll be coming for me.

He fumbled frantically for the harness release, found it, and dropped the last few inches on to the ceiling of the overturned car. He was curled on top of the shotgun. He had been damn lucky the weapon hadn't discharged as it slammed around inside the tumbling Camaro.

Coming for me.

Disoriented, he needed a moment to find the door handle, which was over his head. He reached up, released it. At first the door would not open. Then it swung outward with a metallic popping and squeaking.

He crawled off the ceiling, out on to the floor of the desert, feeling as if he had become trapped in a surreal Daliesque world of weird perspectives. He reached back in for the shotgun.

Though the ash-fine dust was beginning to settle, he was still coughing it out of his lungs. Clenching his teeth, he tried to swallow each cough. He needed to be quiet if he were to survive.

Neither as quick nor as inconspicuous as the small desert lizards that scooted across his path, Jim stayed low and dashed to a nearby arroyo. When he arrived at the edge of that natural drainage channel, he discovered it was only about four feet deep. He slid over the lip, and his feet made a soft slapping sound as they hit the hard-packed bottom.

Crouching in that shallow declivity, he raised his head slowly to ground level and looked across the desert floor toward the overturned Camaro, around which the haze of alkaline dust had not yet entirely dissipated. On the highway, the Roadking finished reversing along the pavement and halted parallel to the wrecked car.

The door opened, and a man climbed out. Another man, having exited from the far side, hurried around the front of the motorhome to join his companion. Neither of them was the kindly-retiree-on-a-budget that one might have imagined behind the wheel of that aging caravan. They appeared to be in their early thirties and as hard as heat-tempered desert rock. One of them wore his dark hair pulled back and knotted into a redoubled ponytail – the passé style that kids now called a 'dork knob.' The other had short spiky hair on top, but his head was shaved on the sides – as if he thought he was in one of those old Mad Max movies. Both wore sleeveless T-shirts, jeans, and cowboy boots, and both carried handguns. They headed cautiously toward the Camaro, splitting up to approach it from opposite ends.

Jim drew down below the top of the arroyo, turned right – which was approximately west – and hurried in a crouch along the shallow channel. He glanced back to see if he was leaving a trail, but the silt, baked under months of fierce sun since the last rain, did not take footprints. After about fifty feet, the arroyo abruptly angled to the south, left. Sixty feet thereafter, it disappeared into a culvert that led under the highway.

Hope swept through him but did not still the tremors of fear that had shaken him continuously since he had found the dying man in the station wagon. He felt as if he was going to puke. But he had not eaten breakfast and had nothing to toss up. No matter what the nutritionists said, sometimes it paid to skip a meal.

Full of deep shade, the concrete culvert was comparatively cool. He was tempted to stop and hide there – and hope they would give up, go away.

He couldn't do that, of course. He wasn't a coward. But even if his conscience had allowed him to buy into a little cowardice this time, the mysterious force driving him would not permit him to cut and run. To some extent, he was a marionette on strings invisible, at the mercy of a puppeteer unseen, in a puppet-theater play with a plot he could not understand and a theme that eluded him.

A few tumbleweed had found their way into the culvert, and their brittle spines raked him as he shoved through the barrier they had formed. He came out on the other side of the highway, into another arm of the arroyo, and scrambled up the wall of that parched channel.

Lying belly-flat on the desert floor, he slithered to the edge of the elevated roadbed and eased up to look across the pavement, east toward the motorhome. Beyond the Roadking, he could see the Camaro like a dead roach on its back. The two men were standing near it, together now. Evidently, they had just checked the car and knew he was not in it.

They were talking animatedly, but they were too far away for Jim to hear what they were saying. A couple of words carried to him, but they were faded by distance and distorted by the furnace-dry air.

Sweat kept trickling into his eyes, blurring his vision. He blotted his face with his sleeve and squinted at the men again.

They were moving slowly away from the Camaro now, deeper into the desert. One of them was wary, swiveling his head from side to side, and the other studied the ground as they moved, no doubt searching for signs of Jim's passage. Just his luck, one of them would turn out to have been raised by Indian scouts, and they'd be all over him faster than an iguana on a sand beetle.

From the west came the sound of an engine, low at first but growing rapidly louder even as Jim turned his head to look in that direction. Out of a waterfall mirage came a Peterbilt. From Jim's low vantage point, the truck looked so huge that it didn't even seem like a truck but like some futuristic war machine that had traveled backward in time from the twenty-second century.

The driver of the Peterbilt would see the overturned Camaro. In the traditional Samaritan spirit that most truckers showed on the road, he would stop to offer assistance. His arrival would rattle the two killers, and while they were distracted, Jim would get the drop on them.

He had it all figured out – except it didn't work that way. The Peterbilt didn't slow as it approached, and Jim realized he was going to have to flag it down. But before he could even rise up, the big truck swept past with a dragon roar and a blast of hot wind, breaking the speed limit by a Guinness margin, as if it were a judgment wagon driven by a demon and loaded with souls that the devil wanted in hell *right now*.

Jim fought the urge to leap up and yell after it: Where's your traditional Samaritan spirit, you shithead?

Silence returned to the hot day.

On the far side of the road, the two killers looked after the Peterbilt for a moment, then continued their search for Jim.

Furious and scared, he eased back from the shoulder of the highway, flattened out again, and belly-crawled eastward toward the motorhome, dragging the shotgun with him. The elevated road-bed was between him and them; they could not possibly see him, yet he more than half expected them to sprint across the blacktop and pump half a dozen rounds into him.

When he dared look up again, he was directly opposite the parked Roadking, which blocked the two men from his view. If he couldn't see them, they couldn't see him. He scrambled to his feet and crossed the pavement to the passenger side of the motorhome.

The door on that flank was a third of the way from the front bumper to the rear, not opposite the driver's door. It was ajar.

He took hold of the handle. Then he realized that a third man might have stayed inside with the woman and girl. He couldn't risk going in there until he had dealt with the two outside, for he might be trapped between gunmen.

He moved to the front of the Roadking, and just as he reached the corner, he heard voices approaching. He froze, waiting for the guy with the weird haircut to come around the front bumper. But they stopped on the other side.

'—who gives a shit—'

'—but he mighta seen our license number—'

'—chances are, he's bad hurt—'

'—wasn't no blood in the car—'

Jim sank to one knee by the tire, looked under the vehicle. They were standing on the other side, near the driver's door.

'—we just take the next southbound—'

'—with cops on our tail—'

'—by the time he gets to any cops, we'll be in Arizona—'

'—you hope—'

'—I *know*—'

Rising, moving cautiously, Jim slipped around the front corner of the Roadking. He eased past the first pair of headlights and the engine hatch.

'—cut across Arizona into New Mexico—'

'—they got cops too—'

'—into Texas, put a few states between us, drive all night if we have to—'

Jim was grateful that the shoulder of the highway was dirt rather than loose gravel. He crept silently across it to the driver's-side headlights, staying low.

'—you know what piss-poor cooperation they got across state lines—'

'—he's out there somewhere, dammit—'

'—so're a million scorpions and rattlesnakes—'

Jim stepped around to their side of the motorhome, covering them with the shotgun. 'Don't move!'

For an instant they gaped at him the way *he* might have stared at a three-eyed Martian with a mouth in its forehead. They were only about eight feet away, close enough to spit on, which they looked like they deserved. At a distance they had appeared as dangerous as snakes with legs, and they still looked deadlier than anything that slithered in the desert.

They were holding their handguns, pointed at the ground. Jim thrust the shotgun at them and shouted, 'Drop 'em, dammit!'

Either they were the hardest of hard cases or they were nuts – probably both – because they didn't freeze at the sight of the shotgun. The guy with the redoubled ponytail flung himself to the ground and rolled. Simultaneously, the refugee from "Road Warrior" brought up his pistol, and Jim pumped a round into the guy's chest at pointblank range, blowing him backward and down and all the way to hell.

The survivor's feet vanished as he wriggled under the Roadking.

To avoid being shot in the foot and ankle, Jim grabbed the open door and jumped on to the step beside the driver's seat. Even as his feet left the ground, two shots boomed from under the motorhome, and one of them punctured the tire beside which he'd been standing.

Instead of retreating into the Roadking, he dropped back to the ground, fell flat, and shoved the shotgun under the vehicle, figuring to take his adversary by surprise. But the guy was already out from under on the other side. Jim could see only the black cowboy boots hurrying toward the rear of the motorhome. The guy turned the corner – and vanished.

The ladder. At the right rear corner. Next to the racked motorcycle.

The bastard was going on to the roof.

Jim hustled all the way under the Roadking before the killer could look over the edge of the roof, spot him, and fire down. It was no cooler beneath the vehicle, because the sun-scorched earthen shoulder radiated the heat it had been storing up since dawn.

Two cars roared by on the highway, one close after the other. He hadn't heard them coming, maybe because his heart was beating so hard that he felt as if he were inside a kettle drum. He cursed the motorists under his breath, then realized they couldn't be expected to stop when they saw a guy like Dork Knob prowling the top of the motorhome with a handgun.

He had a better chance of winning if he continued to do the unexpected, so he immediately crawled on his belly, fast as a marine under fire, to the rear of the Roadking. He twisted on to his back, eased his head out past the rear bumper, and peered up across the Harley, at the ascending rungs that appeared to dwindle into blazing white sun.

The ladder was empty. The killer was already on the roof. He might think that he had temporarily mystified his pursuer with his vanishing act, and in any case he wouldn't expect to be followed with utter recklessness.

Jim slid all the way into the open and went up the ladder. He gripped the hot side-rail with one hand, holding the compact shotgun with the other, trying to ascend as soundlessly as possible. His adversary was surprisingly quiet on the aluminum surface above, making barely enough noises of his own to cover an occasional pop and squeak from the aged rungs under Jim's feet.

At the top, Jim cautiously raised his head and squinted across the roof. The killer was two-thirds of the way toward the front of the Roadking, at the right side, looking down. He was moving along on hands and knees, which must have hurt; although the time-stained white paint reflected a lot of the sun, it had stored sufficient heat to sting even well-callused hands and to penetrate blue denim. But if the guy was in pain, he didn't show it; he was evidently as suicidally macho as his dead buddy had been.

Jim eased up another rung.

The killer actually lowered himself on to his belly, though the roof must have scorched instantly through his thin T-shirt. He was trying to maintain as low a profile as possible, waiting for Jim to appear below.

Jim eased up one more rung. The roof now met him at mid-torso. He turned sideways on the ladder and jammed one knee behind the outer upright, wedging himself in place so he would have both hands for the shotgun and so the recoil would not knock him backward to the ground.

If the guy on the roof didn't have a sixth sense, then he was just damned lucky. Jim had not made a sound, but the creep suddenly glanced back over his shoulder and spotted him.

Cursing, Jim swung the shotgun around.

The killer flung himself sideways, off the roof.

Without getting in a shot, Jim pulled his knee from behind the upright and jumped from the ladder. He hit the ground hard but kept his balance, stepped around the corner of the motorhome, and squeezed off one round.

But the creep was already bolting through the side door. At worst, he caught a few pellets in one leg. Probably not even that.

He was going after the woman and child.

Hostages.

Or maybe he just wanted to slaughter them before he was cut down himself. The past couple of decades had seen the rise of the vagabond sociopath, roaming the country, looking for easy prey, racking up long lists of victims, attaining sexual release as much from brutal murder as from rape.

In his mind, Jim heard the anguished voice of the dying man in the station wagon: *Lisa . . . Susie . . . my wife, daughter . . .*

40

With no time for caution, his anger having grown greater than his fear, he raced after the killer, through the door, into the Roadking, entering aft of the cockpit. His sun-dazzled eyes couldn't handle the comparative gloom of the motorhome's interior, but he was able to see the psychotic sonofabitch heading toward the rear of the motorhome, past the lounge area and into the galley.

A shadowy figure now, with just a dark oval for a face, the killer turned and fired. The slug tore a chunk out of a wall-hung storage cabinet to the left of Jim, showering him with splinters of Formica and smoking particle board.

He didn't know where the woman and child were. He was afraid of hitting them. A shotgun wasn't a precise weapon.

The killer fired again. The second bullet passed so close to Jim's face that it left a wake of stinging-hot wind, like a kiss of fire burning across his right cheek.

He pumped out one round, and the blast shook the tinny walls. The killer screamed and was flung hard against the kitchen sink. Jim fired again, reflexively, half-deafened by the double explosion. The guy was virtually lifted off his feet, hurled backward, slammed against the rear wall, beside a closed door that separated the main living area from the bedroom. Then he dropped.

Grabbing a couple of shells from his pants pocket, reloading the shotgun magazine, Jim moved deeper into the Roadking, past a tattered and sagging sofa.

He knew the man had to be dead, but he could not see well enough to be certain of anything. Though shafts of the Mojave sun shoved in like hot branding irons through the windshield and the open doors, the heavily draped side windows insured that the rear of the Roadking was filled with shadows, and there was a thin acrid haze of smoke from all the gunfire.

When he reached the end of the narrow chamber and looked down, he had no doubt that the man crumpled on the floor was dead. Bloody human garbage. Garbage alive, now garbage dead.

At the sight of the torn and battered corpse, a savage elation gripped him, a furious righteousness that was both thrilling and frightening. He wanted to be sickened by what he had done, even if the dead man had deserved to die, but although the carnage nauseated him, he was not morally repulsed. He had encountered purest evil in human form. Both these bastards deserved worse than he had been able to do to them, deserved long and slow deaths with great suffering, much terror. He felt like an avenging angel, come to judgment, filled with a holy rage. He knew he was teetering on the edge of a psychosis of his own, knew that only the insane were unreservedly certain of the virtue of even their most outrageous acts, but he could find no doubt within him. In fact his anger swelled as if he were God's avatar into whom flowed a direct current of the Almighty's apocalyptic wrath.

He turned to the closed door.

The bedroom lay beyond.

The mother and child had to be in there.

Lisa . . . Susie . . .

But who else?

Sociopathic killers usually operated alone, but sometimes they paired up as these two had done. Larger alliances, however, were rare. Charles Manson and his 'family,' of course. There were other examples. He couldn't rule anything out, not in a world where the trendiest professors of philosophy taught that ethics were always situational and that everyone's point of view was equally right and valuable, regardless of its logic or hate quotient. It was a world that bred monsters, and this beast might be hydraheaded.

He knew caution was called for, but the exhilarating righteous wrath that filled him also gave him a sense of invulnerability. He stepped to the bedroom door, kicked it open, and shouldered through, knowing he might be gut-shot, not giving a damn, shotgun in front of him, ready to kill and be killed.

The woman and child were alone. On the filthy bed. Bound at wrists and ankles with sturdy strapping tape. Tape across their mouths.

The woman, Lisa, was about thirty, slim, an unusually attractive blonde. But the daughter, Susie, was remarkably more beautiful than her mother, ethereally beautiful: about ten years old, with luminous green eyes, delicate features, and skin as flawless as the membraneous interior surface of an eggshell. The girl seemed, to Jim, to be an embodiment of innocence, goodness, and purity – an angel cast down into a cesspool. New power informed his rage at the sight of her bound and gagged in the bedroom's squalor.

Tears streamed down the child's face, and she choked on muffled sobs of terror behind the tape that sealed her lips. The mother was not crying, though grief and fear haunted her eyes. Her sense of responsibility to her daughter – and a visible rage not unlike Jim's – seemed to keep her from falling over the brink of hysteria.

He realized they were afraid of him. As far as they knew, he was in league with the men who had abducted them.

As he propped the shotgun against the built-in dresser, he said, 'It's all right. It's over now. I killed them. I killed them both.'

The mother stared at him wide-eyed, disbelieving.

He didn't blame her for doubting him. His voice sounded strange: full of fury, cracking on every third or fourth word, tremulous, going from a whisper to a hard bark to a whisper again.

He looked around for something with which to cut them free. A roll of the strapping tape and a pair of scissors lay on the dresser.

Grabbing the scissors, he noticed X-rated videotapes also stacked on the dresser. Suddenly he realized that the walls and ceiling of the small room were papered with obscene photographs torn from the pages of sex magazines, and with a jolt he saw it was filth with a twisted difference: child pornography. There were grown men in the photos, their faces always concealed, but there were no grown women, only young girls and boys, most of them as young as Susie, many of them younger, being brutalized in every way imaginable.

The men he had killed would have used the mother only briefly, would have raped and tortured and broken her only as an example to the child. Then they would have cut her throat or blown her brains out on some desolate dirt road out in the desert, leaving her body for the delectation of lizards and ants and vultures. It was the child they really wanted, and for whom they would have made the next few months or years a living hell.

His anger metastasized into something beyond mere rage, far beyond wrath. A terrible darkness rose inside of him like black crude oil gushing up from a wellhead.

He was furious that the child had seen those photographs, had been forced to lie in those stained and foul-smelling bedclothes with unspeakable obscenity on every side of her. He had the crazy urge to pick up the shotgun and empty a few more rounds into each of the dead men.

They had not touched her. Thank God for that. They hadn't had time to touch her.

But the room. Oh, Jesus, she had suffered an assault just by being in that room.

He was shaking.

He saw that the mother was shaking too.

After a moment he realized that her tremors were not of rage, like his, but of fear. Fear of *him*. She was terrified of him, more so now than when he had come into the room.

He was glad there was no mirror. He would not have wanted to see his own face. Right now there must be some kind of madness in it.

He had to get a grip on himself.

'It's all right,' he assured her again. 'I came to help you.'

Eager to free them, anxious to quiet their terror, he dropped to his knees beside the bed and cut the tape that was wound around the woman's ankles, tore it away. He snipped the tape around her wrists, as well, then left her to finish freeing herself.

When he cut the bindings from Susie's wrists, she hugged herself defensively. When he freed her ankles, she kicked at him and squirmed away across the gray and mottled sheets. He didn't reach for her, but backed off instead.

Lisa peeled the tape off her lips and pulled a rag out of her mouth, choking and gagging. She spoke in a raspy voice that was somehow simultaneously frantic and resigned: 'My husband, back at the car, my husband!'

Jim looked at her and said nothing, unable to put such bleak news into words in front of the child.

The woman saw the truth in his eyes, and for a moment her lovely face was wrenched into a mask of grief and agony. But for the sake of her daughter, she fought down the sob, swallowed it along with her anguish.

She said only, 'Oh, my God,' and each word reverberated with her loss.

'Can you carry Susie?'

Her mind was on her dead husband.

He said, 'Can you carry Susie?'

She blinked in confusion. 'How do you know her name?'

'Your husband told me.'

'But—'

'Before,' he said sharply, meaning *before he died*, not wanting to give false hope. 'Can you carry her out of here?'

'Yeah, I think so, maybe.'

He could have carried the girl himself, but he didn't believe that he should touch her. Though it was irrational and emotional, he felt that what those two men had done to her – and what they *would* have done to her, given a chance – was somehow the responsibility of all men, and that at least a small stain of guilt was his as well.

Right now, the only man in the world who should touch that child was her father. And he was dead.

44

Jim rose from his knees and edged away from the bed. He backed into a narrow closet door that sprang open as he stepped aside of it.

On the bed, the weeping girl squirmed away from her mother, so traumatized that she did not at first recognize the benign intention of even those familiar loving hands. Then abruptly she shattered the chains of terror and flew into her mother's arms. Lisa spoke softly and reassuringly to her daughter, stroked her hair, held her tight.

The air conditioning had been off ever since the killers had parked and gone to check the wrecked Camaro. The bedroom was growing hotter by the second, and it stank. He smelled stale beer, sweat, what might have been the lingering odor of dried blood rising from dark maroon stains on the carpet, and other foul odors that he dared not even try to identify.

'Come on, let's get out of here.'

Lisa did not appear to be a strong woman, but she lifted her daughter as effortlessly as she would have lifted a pillow. With the girl cradled in her arms, she moved toward the door.

'Don't let her look to the left when you go out,' he said. 'One of them's dead just beside the door. It isn't pretty.'

Lisa nodded once, with evident gratitude for the warning.

As he started to follow her through the doorway, he saw the contents of the narrow closet that had come open when he'd backed against it: shelves of homemade videotapes. On the spines were titles hand-printed on strips of white adhesive tape. Names. The titles were all names. CINDY. TIFFANY. JOEY. CISSY. TOMMY. KEVIN. Two were labeled SALLY. Three were labeled WENDY. More names. Maybe thirty in all. He knew what he was looking at, but he didn't want to believe it. Memories of savagery. Mementoes of perversion. Victims.

The bitter blackness welled higher in him.

He followed Lisa through the motorhome to the door, and out into the blazing desert sun.

•2•

Lisa stood in the white-gold sunshine on the shoulder of the highway, behind the motorhome. Her daughter stood at her side, clung to her. Light had an affinity for them: it slipped in scintillant currents through their flaxen hair, accented the color of

45

their eyes much the way a jeweler's display lamp enhanced the beauty of emeralds on velvet, and lent an almost mystical luminosity to their skin. Looking at them, it was difficult to believe that the light around them was not within them too, and that a darkness had entered their lives and filled them as completely as night filled the world in the wake of dusk.

Jim could barely endure their presence. Each time he glanced at them, he thought of the dead man in the station wagon, and sympathetic grief twisted through him, as painful as any physical illness he had ever known.

Using a key that he found on a ring with the motorhome ignition key, he unlocked the iron rack that held the Harley-Davidson. It was an FXRS-SP with a 1340cc. single-carburetor, two-valve, push-rod V-twin with a five-speed transmission that powered the rear wheel through a toothed belt instead of a greasy chain. He'd ridden fancier and more powerful machines. This one was standard, about as plain as a Harley could get. But all he wanted from the bike was speed and easy handling; and if it was in good repair, the SP would provide him with both.

Lisa spoke worriedly to him as he unracked the Harley and looked it over. 'Three of us can't ride out of here on that.'

'No,' he said. 'Just me.'

'Please don't leave us alone.'

'Someone'll stop for you before I go.'

A car approached. The three occupants gawked at them. The driver put on more speed.

'None of them stop,' she said miserably.

'Someone will. I'll wait until they do.'

She was silent a moment. Then: 'I don't want to get into a car with strangers.'

'We'll see who stops.'

She shook her head violently.

He said, 'I'll know if they're trustworthy.'

'I don't . . .' Her voice broke. She hesitated, regained control. 'I don't trust anyone.'

'There are good people in the world. In fact, most of them are good. Anyway, when they stop, I'll know if they're OK.'

'How? How in God's name can you know?'

'I'll know.' But he could not explain the *how* of it any more than he could explain how he had known that she and her daughter needed him out here in this sere and blistered wasteland.

He straddled the Harley and pressed the starter button. The

engine kicked in at once. He revved it a little, then shut it off.

The woman said, 'Who are you?'

'I can't tell you that.'

'But why not?'

'This one's too sensational. It'll make nationwide headlines.'

'I don't understand.'

'They'd splash my picture everywhere. I like my privacy.'

A small utility rack was bolted to the back of the Harley. Jim used his belt to strap the shotgun to it.

With a tremor of vulnerability in her voice that broke his heart, Lisa said, 'We owe you so much.'

He looked at her, then at Susie. The girl had one slender arm around her mother, clinging tightly. She was not listening to their conversation. Her eyes were out of focus, blank – and her mind seemed far away. Her free hand was at her mouth, and she was chewing on her knuckle; she had actually broken the skin and drawn her own blood.

He averted his eyes and stared down at the cycle again.

'You don't owe me anything,' he said.

'But you saved—'

'Not everyone,' he said quickly. 'Not everyone I *should* have.'

The distant growl of an approaching car drew their attention to the east. They watched a souped-up black Trans Am swim out of the water mirages. With a screech of brakes, it stopped in front of them. Red flames were painted on the fender back of the front wheel, and the rims of both the wheel wells were protected with fancy chrome trim. Fat twin chrome tailpipes glistened like liquid mercury in the fierce desert sun.

The driver got out. He was about thirty. His thick black hair was combed away from his face, full on the sides, a ducktail in back. He was wearing jeans and a white T-shirt with the sleeves rolled up to reveal tattoos on both biceps.

'Somethin' wrong here?' he asked across the car.

Jim stared at him for a beat, then said, 'These people need a ride to the nearest town.'

As the man came around the Trans Am, the passenger door opened, and a woman got out. She was a couple of years younger than her companion, dressed in baggy tan shorts, a white halter top, and a white bandana. Unruly dyed-blond hair sprayed out around that piece of headgear, framing a face so heavily made up that it looked like a testing ground for Max Factor. She wore too much clunky costume jewelry, as well: big dangling silver earrings;

three strands of glass beads in different shades of red; two bracelets on each wrist, a watch, and four rings. On the upper slope of her left breast was a blue and pink butterfly tattoo.

'You break down?' she asked.

Jim said, 'The motorhome has a flat.'

'I'm Frank,' the guy said. 'This is Verna.' He was chewing gum. 'I'll help you fix the tire.'

Jim shook his head. 'We can't use the motorhome anyway. There's a dead man in it.'

'Dead man?'

'And another one over there,' Jim said, gesturing beyond the Roadking.

Verna was wide-eyed.

Frank stopped chewing his gum for a beat, glanced at the shotgun on the Harley rack, then looked at Jim again. 'You kill them?'

'Yeah. Because they kidnapped this woman and her child.'

Frank studied him a moment, then glanced at Lisa. 'That true?' he asked her.

She nodded.

'Jesus jumpin' catfish,' Verna said.

Jim glanced at Susie. She was in another world, and she would need some professional help to reenter this one. He was certain she couldn't hear a thing they said.

Curiously, he felt as detached as the child looked. He was still sinking into that internal darkness, and before long it would swallow him completely. He told Frank: 'These guys I killed – they wasted the husband . . . the father. His body's in a station wagon a couple of miles west of here.'

'Oh, shit,' Frank said, 'that's a rough one.'

Verna drew against Frank's side and shuddered.

'I want you to take them to the nearest town, fast as you can. Get medical attention for them. Then contact the state police, get them out here.'

'Sure,' Frank said.

But Lisa said, 'Wait . . . no . . . I can't . . .' Jim went to her, and she whispered to him: 'They look like . . . I can't . . . I'm just afraid . . .'

Jim put a hand on her shoulder, stared directly into her eyes. 'Things aren't always what they appear to be. Frank and Verna are OK. You trust me?'

'Yes. Now. Of course.'

'Then believe me. You can trust them.'

'But how can you know?' she asked, her voice breaking.

'I *know*,' he said firmly.

She continued to meet his eyes for a few seconds, then nodded and said, 'All right.'

The rest was easy. As docile as if she had been drugged, Susie allowed herself to be lifted into the back seat. Her mother joined her there, cuddled her. When Frank was behind the wheel again and Verna at his side, Jim gratefully accepted a can of root beer from their ice chest. Then he closed Verna's door, leaned down to the open window, and thanked her and Frank.

'You're not waitin' here for the cops, are you?' Frank asked.

'No.'

'You're not in trouble, you know. You're the hero here.'

'I know. But I'm not waiting.'

Frank nodded. 'You got your reasons, I guess. You want us to say you was a bald guy with dark eyes, hitched a ride with a trucker going east?'

'No. Don't lie. Don't lie for me.'

'Whatever you want,' Frank said.

Verna said, 'Don't worry. We'll take good care of them.'

'I know you will,' Jim said.

He drank the root beer and watched the Trans Am until it had driven out of sight.

He climbed on the Harley, thumbed the starter button, used the long heavy shift to slide the gearwheel into place, rolled in a little throttle, released the clutch, and rode across the highway. He went off the shoulder, down the slight incline, on to the floor of the desert, and headed directly south into the immense and inhospitable Mojave.

For a while he rode at over seventy miles an hour, though he had no protection from the wind because the SP had no fairing. He was badly buffeted, and his eyes filled repeatedly with tears that he tried to blame entirely on the raw, hot air that assaulted him.

Strangely, he did not mind the heat. In fact he didn't even feel it. He was sweating, yet he felt cool.

He lost track of time. Perhaps an hour had passed when he realized that he had left the plains and was moving across barren hills the color of rust. He reduced his speed. His route was now filled with twists and turns between rocky outcroppings, but the SP was the machine for it. It had two inches more suspension travel fore and aft than did the regular FXRS, with compatible spring and shock rates, plus twin disc brakes on the front – which meant he could corner like a stunt rider when the terrain threw surprises at him.

After a while he was no longer cool. He was *cold*.

The sun seemed to be fading, though he knew it was still early afternoon. Darkness was closing on him from within.

Eventually he stopped in the shadow of a rock monolith about a quarter of a mile long and three hundred feet high. Weathered into eerie shapes by ages of wind and sun and by the rare but torrential rains that swept the Mojave, the formation thrust out of the desert floor like the ruins of an ancient temple now half-buried in sand.

He propped the Harley on its kickstand.

He sat down on the shaded earth.

After a moment he stretched out on his side. He drew up his knees. He folded his arms across his chest.

He had stopped not a moment too soon. The darkness filled him completely, and he fell away into an abyss of despair.

•3•

Later, in the last hour of daylight, he found himself on the Harley again, riding across gray and rose-colored flats where clumps of mesquite bristled. Dead, sun-blackened tumbleweed chased him in a breeze that smelled like powdered iron and salt.

He vaguely remembered breaking open a cactus and sucking the moisture out of the water-heavy pulp at the core of the plant, but he was dry again. Desperately thirsty.

As he came over a gentle rise and throttled down a little, he saw a small town about two miles ahead, buildings clustered along a highway. A scattering of trees looked supernaturally lush after the desolation – physical and spiritual – through which he had traveled for the past several hours. Half convinced that the town was only an apparition, he angled toward it nevertheless.

Suddenly, silhouetted against a sky that was growing purple and red with the onset of twilight, the spire of a church appeared, a cross at its pinnacle. Though he realized that he was to some extent delirious and that his delirium was at least partly related to serious dehydration, Jim turned at once toward the church. He felt as if he needed the solace of its interior spaces more than he needed water.

Half a mile from the town, he rode the Harley into an arroyo and left it there on its side. The soft sand walls of the channel gave way easily under his hands, and he quickly covered the bike.

He had assumed he could walk the last half mile with relative ease. But he was worse off than he had realized. His vision swam in and out of focus. His lips burned, his tongue stuck to the roof of his dry mouth, and his throat was sore – as if he were in the grip of a virulent fever. The muscles in his legs began to cramp and throb, and each foot seemed to be encased in a concrete boot.

He must have blacked out on his feet, because the next thing he knew, he was on the brick steps of the white clapboard church, with no recollection of the last few hundred yards of his journey. The words 'Our Lady of the Desert' were on a brass plaque beside the double doors.

He had been a Catholic once. In a part of his heart, he still was a Catholic. He had been many things – Methodist, Jew, Buddhist, Baptist, Moslem, Hindu, Taoist, more – and although he was no longer any of them in practice, he was still all of them in experience.

Though the door seemed to weigh more than the boulder that had covered the mouth of Christ's tomb, he managed to pull it open. He went inside.

The church was much cooler than the twilit Mojave, but not really cool. It smelled of myrrh and spikenard and the slightly sweetish odor of burning votive candles, causing memories of his Catholic days to flood back to him, making him feel at home.

At the doorway between narthex and nave, he dipped two fingers in the holy water font and crossed himself. He cupped his hands in the cool liquid, brought them to his mouth, and drank. The water tasted like blood. He looked into the white marble basin in horror, certain that it was brimming with gore, but he saw only water and the dim, shimmering reflection of his own face.

He realized that his parched and stinging lips were split. He licked them. The blood was his own.

Then he found himself on his knees at the front of the nave, leaning against the sanctuary railing, praying, and he did not know how he had gotten there. Must have blacked out again.

The last of the day had blown away as if it were a pale skin of dust, and a hot night wind pressed at the church windows. The only illumination was from a bulb in the narthex, the flickering flames of half a dozen votive candles in red glass containers, and a small spotlight shining down on the crucifix.

51

Jim saw that his own face was painted on the figure of Christ. He blinked his burning eyes and looked again. This time he saw the face of the dead man in the station wagon. The sacred countenance metamorphosed into the face of Jim's mother, his father, the child named Susie, Lisa – and then it was no face at all, just a black oval, as the killer's face had been a black oval when he had turned to shoot at Jim inside the shadow-filled Roadking.

Indeed, it wasn't Christ on the cross now, it *was* the killer. He opened his eyes, looked at Jim, and smiled. He jerked his feet free of the vertical support, a nail still bristling from one of them, a black nail hole in the other. He wrenched his hands free, too, a spike still piercing each palm, and he just *drifted* down to the floor, as if gravity had no claim on him except what he chose to allow it. He started across the altar platform toward the railing, toward Jim.

Jim's heart was racing, but he told himself that what he saw was only a delusion. The product of a fevered mind. Nothing more.

The killer reached him. Touched his face. The hand was as soft as rotting meat and as cold as a liquid gas.

Like a true believer in a tent revival, collapsing under the empowered hand of a faith healer, Jim shivered and fell away into darkness.

•4•

A white-walled room.

A narrow bed.

Spare and humble furnishings.

Night at the windows.

He drifted in and out of bad dreams. Each time that he regained consciousness, which was never for longer than a minute or two, he saw the same man hovering over him: about fifty, balding, slightly plump, with thick eyebrows and a squashed nose.

Sometimes the stranger gently worked an ointment into Jim's face, and sometimes he applied compresses soaked in ice-water. He lifted Jim's head off the pillows and encouraged him to drink cool water through a straw. Because the man's eyes were marked by concern and kindness, Jim did not protest.

Besides, he had neither the voice nor the energy to protest. His throat felt as if he had swallowed kerosene and then a match. He did not have the strength even to lift a hand an inch off the sheets.

'Just rest,' the stranger said. 'You're suffering heatstroke and a bad sunburn.'

Windburn. That's the worst of it, Jim thought, remembering the Harley SP, which had not been equipped with a Plexiglas fairing for weather protection.

*   *   *

Light at the windows. A new day.

His eyes were sore.

His face felt worse than ever. Swollen.

The stranger was wearing a clerical collar.

'Priest,' Jim said in a coarse and whispery voice that didn't sound like his own.

'I found you in the church, unconscious.'

'Our Lady of the Desert.'

Lifting Jim off the pillows again, he said, 'That's right. I'm Father Geary. Leo Geary.'

Jim was able to help himself a little this time. The water tasted sweet.

Father Geary said. 'What were you doing in the desert?'

'Wandering.'

'Why?'

Jim didn't answer.

'Where did you come from?'

Jim said nothing.

'What is your name?'

'Jim.'

'You're not carrying any ID.'

'Not this time, no.'

'What do you mean by that?'

Jim was silent.

The priest said, 'There was three thousand dollars in cash in your pockets.'

'Take what you need.'

The priest stared at him, then smiled. 'Better be careful what you offer, son. This is a poor church. We need all we can get.'

*   *   *

Later still, Jim woke again. The priest was not there. The house was silent. Once in a while a rafter creaked and a window rattled softly as desert wind stirred fitfully outside.

When the priest returned, Jim said, 'A question, Father.'
'What's that?'
His voice was still raspy, but he sounded a bit more like himself.
'If there's a God, why does He allow suffering?'
Alarmed, Father Geary said, 'Are you feeling worse?'
'No, no. Better. I don't mean my suffering. Just . . . why does He allow suffering in general?'
'To test us,' the priest said.
'Why do we have to be tested?'
'To determine if we're worthy.'
'Worthy of what?'
'Worthy of heaven, of course. Salvation. Eternal life.'
'Why didn't God *make* us worthy?'
'Yes, he made us perfect, without sin. But then we sinned, and fell from grace.'
'How could we sin if we were perfect?'
'Because we have free will.'
'I don't understand.'
Father Geary frowned. 'I'm not a nimble theologian. Just an ordinary priest. All I can tell you is that it's part of the divine mystery. We fell from grace, and now heaven must be earned.'
'I need to pee,' Jim said.
'All right.'
'Not the bedpan this time. I think I can make it to the bathroom with your help.'
'I think maybe you can, too. You're really coming around nicely, thank God.'
'Free will,' Jim said.
The priest frowned.

* * *

By late afternoon, nearly twenty-four hours after Jim stumbled into the church, his fever registered only three-tenths of a degree on the thermometer. His muscles were no longer spasming, his joints did not hurt any more, he was not dizzy, and his chest did not ache when he drew a deep breath. Pain still flared across his face periodically. When he spoke he did so without moving his facial muscles more than absolutely necessary, because the cracks in his lips and in the corners of his mouth reopened easily in spite of the prescription Cortizone cream that Father Geary applied every few hours.

He could sit up in bed of his own volition and move about the room with only minimal help. When his appetite returned, as well, Father Geary gave him chicken soup, then vanilla ice cream. He ate carefully, mindful of his split lips, trying to avoid tainting the food with the taste of his own blood.

'I'm still hungry,' Jim said when he finished.

'Let's see if you can keep that down first.'

'I'm fine. It was only sunstroke, dehydration.'

'Sunstroke can kill, son. You need more rest.'

When the priest relented a while later and brought him more ice cream, Jim spoke through half-clenched teeth and frozen lips: 'Why are some people killers? Not cops, I mean. Not soldiers. Not those who kill in self-defense. The other kind, the murderers. Why do they kill?'

Settling into a straight-backed rocker near the bed, the priest regarded him with one raised eyebrow. 'That's a peculiar question.'

'Is it? Maybe. Do you have an answer?'

'The simple one is – because there's evil in them.'

They sat in mutual silence for a minute or so. Jim ate ice cream, and the stocky priest rocked in his chair. Another twilight crept across the sky beyond the windows.

Finally Jim said, 'Murder, accidents, disease, old age . . . Why did God make us mortal in the first place? Why do we have to die?'

'Death's not the end. Or at least that's what I believe. Death is only our means of passage, only the train that conveys us to our reward.'

'Heaven, you mean.'

The priest hesitated. 'Or the other.'

Jim slept for a couple of hours. When he woke, he saw the priest standing at the foot of the bed, watching him intently.

'You were talking in your sleep.'

Jim sat up in bed. 'Was I? What'd I say?'

' "There is an enemy." '

'That's all I said?'

'Then you said, "It's coming. It'll kill us all." '

A shiver of dread passed through Jim, not because the words had any power of themselves, and not because he understood them, but because he sensed that on a subconscious level he knew all too well what he had meant.

He said, 'A dream, I guess. A bad dream. That's all.'

55

But shortly past three o'clock in the morning, during that second night in the rectory, he thrashed awake, sat straight up in bed, and heard the words escaping him again, *'It'll kill us all.'*

The room was lightless.

He fumbled for the lamp, switched it on.

He was alone.

He looked at the windows. Darkness beyond.

He had the bizarre but unshakable feeling that something hideous and merciless had been hovering near, something infinitely more savage and strange than anyone in recorded history had ever seen, dreamed, or imagined. Trembling, he got out of bed. He was wearing an ill-fitting pair of the priest's pajamas. For a moment he just stood there, not sure what to do.

Then he switched off the light and, barefoot, went to one window, then the other. He was on the second floor. The night was silent, deep, and peaceful. If something had been out there, it was gone now.

•5•

The following morning, he dressed in his own clothes, which Father Geary had laundered for him. He spent most of the day in the living room, in a big easy chair, his feet propped on a hassock, reading magazines and dozing, while the priest tended to parish business.

Jim's sunburnt and wind-abraded face was stiffening. Like a mask.

That evening, they prepared dinner together. At the kitchen sink, Father Geary cleaned lettuce, celery, and tomatoes for a salad. Jim set the table, opened a bottle of cheap chianti to let it breathe, then sliced canned mushrooms into a pot of spaghetti sauce on the stove.

They worked in a comfortable mutual silence, and Jim wondered about the curious relationship that had evolved between them. There had been a dreamlike quality to the past couple of days, as if he had not merely found refuge in a small desert town but in a place of peace outside the real world, a town in the Twilight Zone. The priest had stopped asking questions. In fact, it now seemed to Jim that Father Geary had never been half as probing or insistent as the circumstances warranted. And he suspected that the priest's Christian hospitality did not usually extend to the boarding of injured and suspicious strangers. Why he should receive special consideration at Geary's hands was a mystery to him, but he was grateful for it.

When he had sliced half the mushrooms in the can, he suddenly said, 'Life line.'

Father Geary turned from the sink, a stalk of celery in hand. 'Pardon me?'

A chill swept through Jim, and he almost dropped the knife into the sauce. He put it on the counter.

'Jim?'

Shivering, he turned to the priest and said, 'I've got to get to an airport.'

'An airport?'

'Right away, Father.'

The priest's plump face dimpled with perplexity, wrinkling his tanned forehead far past his long-vanished hairline. 'But there's no airport here.'

'How far to the nearest one?' Jim asked urgently.

'Well . . . two hours by car. All the way to Las Vegas.'

'You've got to drive me there.'

'What? Now?'

'Right now,' Jim said.

'But—'

'I have to get to Boston.'

'But you've been ill—'

'I'm better now.'

'Your face—'

'It hurts, and it looks like hell, but it's not fatal. Father, I *have* to get to Boston.'

'Why?'

He hesitated, then decided on a degree of revelation. 'If I don't get to Boston, someone there is going to be killed. Someone who shouldn't die.'

'Who? Who's going to die?'

Jim licked his peeling lips. 'I don't know.'

'You don't know?'

'But I will when I get there.'

Father Geary stared at him for a long time. At last he said, 'Jim, you're the strangest man I've ever known.'

Jim nodded. 'I'm the strangest man *I've* ever known.'

*   *   *

When they set out from the rectory in the priest's six-year-old Toyota, an hour of light remained in the long August day, although the sun was hidden behind clouds the color of fresh bruises.

They had been on the road only half an hour when lightning shattered the bleak sky and danced on jagged legs across the somber desert horizon. Flash after flash erupted, sharper and brighter in the pure Mojave air than Jim had ever seen lightning elsewhere. Ten minutes later, the sky grew darker and lower, and rain fell in silvery cataracts the equal of anything that Noah had witnessed while hurrying to complete his ark.

'Summer storms are rare here,' Father Geary said, switching on the windshield wipers.

'We can't let it delay us,' Jim said worriedly.

'I'll get you there,' the priest assured him.

'There can't be that many flights east from Vegas at night. They'd mostly leave during the day. I can't miss out and wait till morning. I've got to be in Boston *tomorrow*.'

The parched sand soaked up the deluge. But some areas were rocky or hard-packed from months of blistering sun, and in those places the water spilled off slopes, forming rivulets in every shallow declivity. Rivulets became streams, and streams grew swiftly into rivers, until every bridged arroyo they passed over was soon filled with roiling, churning torrents on which were borne clumps of uprooted desert bunch-grass, fragments of dead tumble-weed, driftwood, and dirty white foam.

Father Geary had two favorite cassette tapes, which he kept in the car: a collection of rock-'n'-roll golden oldies, and an Elton John best-of. He put on Elton. They moved through the storm-hammered day then through the rainswept night to the melodies of 'Funeral for a Friend,' 'Daniel,' and 'Benny and the Jets.'

The blacktop glimmered with quicksilver puddles. To Jim, it was eerie that the water mirages on the highway a few days ago had now become real.

He grew more tense by the minute. Boston called to him, but it was far away, and few things were darker or more treacherous than a blacktop highway through a storm-wracked desert at night. Unless, perhaps, the human heart.

The priest hunched over the wheel as he drove. He studied the highway intently while singing along softly with Elton.

After a while Jim said, 'Father, wasn't there a doctor in town?'

'Yes.'

'But you didn't call him.'

'I got the Cortizone prescription from him.'

'I saw the tube. It was a prescription for you, made out three months ago.'

'Well . . . I've seen sunstroke before. I knew I could treat you.'

'But you seemed awfully worried there at first.'

The priest was silent for a few miles. Then he said, 'I don't know who you are, where you come from, or why you really need to get to Boston. But I do know you're a man in trouble, maybe deep trouble, as deep as it ever gets. And I know . . . at least, I *think* I know that you're a good man at heart. Anyway, it seemed to me that a man in trouble would want to keep a low profile.'

'Thanks. I do.'

A couple of miles farther, the rain came down hard enough to overwhelm the windshield wipers and force Geary to reduce speed.

The priest said, 'You're the one who saved that woman and her little girl.'

Jim tensed but did not respond.

'You fit the description on TV,' the priest said.

They were silent for a few more miles.

Father Geary said, 'I'm not a sucker for miracles.'

Jim was baffled by that statement.

Father Geary switched off Elton John. The only sounds were the swish-hum of the tires on the wet pavement and the metronomic thump of the windshield wipers.

'I believe that the miracles of the Bible happened, yes, I accept all of that as real history,' the priest said, keeping his eyes on the road. 'But I'm reluctant to believe that some statue of the Holy Mother wept real tears in a church in Cincinnati or Peoria or Teaneck last week after the Wednesday-night bingo games, witnessed only by two teenagers and the parish cleaning lady. And I'm not ready to believe that a shadow resembling Jesus, cast on someone's garage wall by a yellow bug light, is a sign of impending apocalypse. God works in mysterious ways, but not with bug lights and garage walls.'

The priest fell silent again, and Jim waited, wondering where all this was leading.

'When I found you in the church, lying by the sanctuary railing,' Geary said in a voice that grew more haunted word by word, 'you were marked by the stigmata of Christ. There was a nail hole in each of your hands—'

Jim looked at his hands and saw no wounds.

'—and your forehead was scratched and prickled with what might have been punctures from a crown of thorns.'

His face was still such a mess from the punishment of sun and wind that it was no use searching in the rearview mirror for the minor injuries the priest had described.

Geary said, 'I was . . . frightened, I guess. But fascinated too.'

They came to a forty-foot-long concrete bridge at an arroyo where the runoff had overflowed the banks. A dark lake had formed and risen above the edge of the elevated roadbed. Geary bulled forward. Plumes of water, reflecting the car's lights, unfurled on both sides like great white wings.

'I'd never seen stigmata,' Geary continued when they were out of the flooded area, 'though I'd heard of the phenomenon. I pulled up your shirt . . . looked at your side . . . and found the enflamed scar of what might have been a spear wound.'

The events of recent months had been so filled with surprises and amazements that the threshold on Jim's sense of wonder had been raised repeatedly. But the priest's story leaped across it, got to him, and sent a chill of awe along his spine.

Geary's voice had fallen to little more than a whisper. 'By the time I got you back to the rectory and into bed, those signs were gone. But I knew I hadn't imagined them. I'd seen them, they'd been real, and I knew there was something special about you.'

The lightning had fizzled out long ago; the black sky was no longer adorned by bright, jagged necklaces of electricity. Now the rain began to abate, as well, and Father Geary was able to reduce the speed of the windshield wipers even as he increased that of the aging Toyota.

For a while neither of them seemed to know what to say. Finally the priest cleared his throat. 'Have you experienced this before – these stigmata?'

'No. Not that I'm aware of. But then, of course, I wasn't aware this time until you told me.'

'You didn't notice the marks on your hands before you passed out at the sanctuary railing?'

'No.'

'But this isn't the only unusual thing that's been happening to you lately.'

Jim's soft laugh was wrenched from him less by amusement than by a sense of dark irony. 'Definitely not the only unusual thing.'

'Do you want to tell me?'

Jim thought about it a while before replying. 'Yes, but I can't.'

'I'm a priest. I respect all confidences. Even the police have no power over me.'

'Oh, I trust you, Father. And I'm not particularly worried about the police.'

'Then?'

'If I tell you . . . the enemy will come,' Jim said, and frowned as he heard himself speaking those words. The statement seemed to have come *through* him rather than from him.

'What enemy?'

He stared out at the vast, lightless expanse of desert. 'I don't know.'

'The enemy you spoke of in your sleep last night?'

'Maybe.'

'You said it would kill us all.'

'And it will.' He went on, perhaps even more interested in what he said than the priest was, for he had no idea what words he would speak until he heard them. 'If it finds out about me, if it discovers that I'm saving lives, special lives, then it'll come to stop me.'

The priest glanced at him. 'Special lives? Exactly what do you mean by that?'

'I don't know.'

'If you tell me about yourself, I'll never repeat to another soul a word of what you say. So whatever this enemy is – how could it find out about you just because you confide in me?'

'I don't know.'

'You don't know.'

'That's right.'

The priest sighed in frustration.

'Father, I'm really not playing games or being purposefully obscure.' He shifted in his seat and adjusted the safety harness, trying to get more comfortable; however, his discomfort was less physical than spiritual, and not easily remedied. 'Have you heard the term "automatic writing"?'

Glowering at the road ahead, Geary said, 'Psychics and mediums talk about it. Superstitious claptrap. A spirit supposedly seizes control of the medium's hand, while he's in a trance, and writes out messages from Beyond.' He made a wordless sound of disgust. 'The same people who scoff at the idea of speaking with God – or even at the mere idea of God's existence – naively embrace any con-artist's claim to be a channeler for the spirits of the dead.'

'Well, nevertheless, what happens to me sometimes is that someone or something else seems to speak through me, an oral form of automatic writing. I know what I'm saying only because I listen to myself saying it.'

'You're not in a trance.'

'No.'

'You claim to be a medium, a psychic?'

'No. I'm sure I'm not.'

'You think the dead are speaking through you?'

'No. Not that.'

'Then who?'

'I don't know.'

'God?'

'Maybe.'

'But you don't know,' Geary said exasperatedly.

'I don't know.'

'You're not only the strangest man I've ever met, Jim. You're also the most frustrating.'

* * *

They arrived at McCarran International in Las Vegas at ten o'clock that night. Only a couple of taxis were on the approach road to the airport. The rain had stopped. The palm trees stirred in a mild breeze, and everything looked as if it had been scrubbed and polished.

Jim opened the door of the Toyota even as Father Geary braked in front of the terminal. He got out, turned, and leaned back in for a last word with the priest.

'Thank you, Father. You probably saved my life.'

'Nothing that dramatic.'

'I'd like to give Our Lady of the Desert some of the three thousand I'm carrying, but I might need it all. I just don't know what's going to happen in Boston, what I might have to spend it for.'

The priest shook his head. 'I don't expect anything.'

'When I get home again, I'll send some money. It'll be cash in an envelope, no return address, but it's honest money in spite of that. You can accept it in good conscience.'

'It's not necessary, Jim. It was enough just to meet you. Maybe you should know . . . you brought a sense of the mystical back into the life of a weary priest who had sometimes begun to doubt his calling – but who'll never doubt again.'

They regarded each other with a mutual affection that clearly surprised them both. Jim leaned into the car, Geary reached across the seat, and they shook hands. The priest had a firm, dry grip.

'Go with God,' Geary said.

'I hope so.'

24 AUGUST THROUGH 26 AUGUST

•1•

Sitting at her desk in the *Press* newsroom in the post-midnight hours of Friday morning, staring at her blank computer screen, Holly had sunk so low psychologically that she just wanted to go home, get into bed, and pull the covers over her head for a few days. She despised people who were always feeling sorry for themselves. She tried to shame herself out of her funk, but she began to pity herself for having descended to self-pity. Of course, it was impossible not to see the humor in that situation, but she was unable to manage a smile at her own expense; instead, she pitied herself for being such a silly and amusing figure.

She was glad that tomorrow morning's edition had been put to bed and that the newsroom was almost deserted, so none of her colleagues could see her in such a debased condition. The only other people in sight were Tommy Weeks - a lanky maintenance man who was emptying wastecans and sweeping up - and George Fintel.

George, who was on the city-government beat, was at his desk at the far end of the big room, slumped forward, head on his folded arms, asleep. Occasionally he snored loud enough for the sound to carry all the way to Holly. When the bars closed, George sometimes returned to the newsroom instead of to his apartment, just as an old dray horse, when left on slack reins, will haul its cart back along a familiar route to the place it thinks of as home. He would wake sometime during the night, realize where he was, and wearily weave off to bed at last. 'Politicians,' George often said, 'are the lowest form of life, having undergone devolution from that first slimy beast that crawled out of the primordial sea.' At fifty-seven, he was too burnt-out to start over, so he continued to spend his days writing about public officials whom he privately reviled, and in the process he had come to hate himself, as well, and to seek solace in a prodigious daily intake of vodka martinis.

If she'd had any tolerance for liquor, Holly would have worried about winding up like George Fintel. But one drink gave her a nice buzz, two made her tipsy, and three put her to sleep.

I hate my life, she thought.

'You self-pitying wretch,' she said aloud.

Well, I do. I hate it, everything's so hopeless.

'You nauseating despair junkie,' she said softly but with genuine disgust.

'You talking to me?' Tommy Weeks said, piloting a pushbroom along the aisle in front of her desk.

'No, Tommy. Talking to myself.'

'You? Gee, what've you got to be unhappy about?'

'My life.'

He stopped and leaned on his broom, crossing one long leg in front of the other. With his broad freckled face, jug ears, and mop of carroty hair, he looked sweet, innocent, kind. 'Things haven't turned out like you planned?'

Holly picked up a half-empty bag of M&Ms, tossed a few pieces of candy into her mouth, and leaned back in her chair. 'When I left the University of Missouri with a journalism degree, I was gonna shake up the world, break big stories, collect Pulitzers for door-stops – and now look at me. You know what I did this evening?'

'Whatever it was, I can tell you didn't enjoy it.'

'I was down at the Hilton for the annual banquet of the Greater Portland Lumber Products Association, interviewing manufac-turers of prefab pullmans, plyboard salesmen, and redwood-decking distributors. They gave out the Timber Trophy – that's what they call it – for the "lumber-products man of the year." I got to interview him too. Rushed back here to get it all written up in time for the morning edition. Hot stuff like that, you don't want to let the bastards at the *New York Times* scoop you on it.'

'I thought you were arts and leisure.'

'Got sick of it. Let me tell you, Tommy, the wrong poet can turn you off the arts for maybe a decade.'

She tossed more chocolate morsels into her mouth. She usually didn't eat candy because she was determined not to wind up with a weight problem like the one that had always plagued her mother, and she was gobbling M&Ms now just to make herself feel more miserable and worthless. She was in a bad downward spiral.

She said, 'TV and movies, they make journalism look so glamor-ous and exciting. It's all lies.'

'Me,' Tommy said, 'I haven't had the life I planned on either.

You think I figured to wind up head of maintenance for the *Press,*
just a glorified janitor?'

'I guess not,' she said, feeling small and self-centered for whining
at him when his lot in life was not as desirable as her own.

'Hell no. From the time I was a little kid, I *knew* I was gonna
grow up to drive one of those big damn old sanitation trucks, up
there in that high cab, pushin' the buttons to operate the hydraulic-
ram compactor.' His voice became wistful. 'Ridin' above the
world, all that powerful machinery at my command. It was my
dream, and I went for it, but I couldn't pass the city physical. Have
this kidney problem, see. Nothin' serious but enough for the city's
health insurers to disqualify me.'

He leaned on his broom, gazing off into the distance, smiling
faintly, probably visualizing himself ensconced in the kingly
driver's seat of a garbage truck.

Staring at him in disbelief, Holly decided that his broad face did
not, after all, look sweet and innocent and kind. She had misread
the meaning of its lines and planes. It was a *stupid* face.

She wanted to say, You idiot! I dreamed of winning Pulitzers,
and now I'm a hack writing industry puff pieces about the damn
Timber Trophy! *That* is tragedy. You think having to settle for
being a janitor instead of a garbage collector is in any way
comparable?

But she didn't say anything because she realized that they *were*
comparable. An unfulfilled dream, regardless of whether it was
lofty or humble, was still a tragedy to the dreamer who had given up
hope. Pulitzers never won and sanitation trucks never driven were
equally capable of inducing despair and insomnia. And that was the
most depressing thought she'd had yet.

Tommy's eyes swam into focus again. 'You gotta not dwell on it,
Miss Thorne. Life . . . it's like gettin' a blueberry muffin in a coffee
shop when what you ordered was the apricot-nut. There aren't any
apricots or nuts in it, and you can get tied up in knots just thinkin'
about what you're missin', when the smarter thing to do is realize
that blueberries have a nice taste too.'

Across the room, George Fintel farted in his sleep. It was a
window-rattler. If the *Press* had been a big newspaper, with
reporters hanging around who'd just returned from Beirut or some
war zone, they'd have all dived for cover.

My God, Holly thought, my life's nothing but a bad imitation of
a Damon Runyon story. Sleazy newsrooms after midnight. Half-
baked philosopher-janitors. Hard-drinking reporters who sleep at

their desks. But it was Runyon as revised by an absurdist writer in collaboration with a bleak existentialist.

'I feel better just having talked to you,' Holly lied. 'Thanks, Tommy.'

'Anytime, Miss Thorne.'

As Tommy set to work with his pushbroom again and moved on down the aisle, Holly tossed some more candy into her mouth and wondered if she would be able to pass the physical required of potential sanitation-truck drivers. On the positive side, the work would be different from journalism as she knew it – collecting garbage instead of dispensing it – and she would have the satisfaction of knowing that at least one person in Portland would desperately envy her.

She looked at the wall clock. One-thirty in the morning. She wasn't sleepy. She didn't want to go home and lie awake, staring at the ceiling, with nothing to do but indulge in more self-examination and self-pity. Well, actually, that *is* what she wanted, because she was in a wallowing mood, but she knew it wasn't a healthy thing to do. Unfortunately, she was without alternatives: weekday, wee-hour nightlife in Portland was a twenty-four-hour doughnut shop.

She was less than a day away from the start of her vacation, and she desperately needed it. She had made no plans. She was just going to relax, hang out, never once look at a newspaper. Maybe see some movies. Maybe read a few books. Maybe go to the Betty Ford Center to take the self-pity detox program.

She had reached that dangerous state in which she began to brood about her name. Holly Thorne. Cute. Real cute. What in God's name had possessed her parents to hang that one on her? Was it possible to imagine the Pulitzer committee giving that grand prize to a woman with a name more suitable to a cartoon character? Sometimes – always in the still heart of the night, of course – she was tempted to call her folks and demand to know whether this name thing had been just bad taste, a misfired joke, or conscious cruelty.

But her parents were salt-of-the-earth working-class people who had denied themselves many pleasures in order to give her a first-rate education, and they wanted nothing but the best for her. They would be devastated to hear that she loathed her name, when they no doubt thought it was clever and even sophisticated. She loved them fiercely, and she had to be in the deepest trenches of depression before she had the gall to blame them for her shortcomings.

Half afraid that she would pick up the phone and call them, she quickly turned to her computer again and accessed the current-edition file. The *Press*'s data-retrieval system made it possible for any reporter on staff to follow any story through editing, type-setting, and production. Now that tomorrow's edition had been formatted, locked down, and sent to press, she could actually call up an image of each page on her screen. Only the headlines were big enough to read, but any portion of the image could be enlarged to fill the screen. Sometimes she could cheer herself a little by reading a big story before the newspaper hit the street; it sparked in her at least a dim glimmer of the feeling of being an insider, which was one aspect of the job that attracted every dream-besotted young person to a vocation in journalism.

But as she scanned the headlines on the first few pages, looking for an interesting story to enlarge, her gloom deepened. A big fire in St. Louis, nine people dead. Presentiments of war in the Mid-East. An oil spill off Japan. A huge storm and flood in India, tens of thousands homeless. The federal government was raising taxes again. She had always known that the news industry flourished on gloom, disaster, scandal, mindless violence, and strife. But suddenly it seemed to be a singularly ghoulish business, and Holly realized that she no longer *wanted* to be an insider, among the first to know this dreadful stuff.

Then, just as she was about to close the file and switch off the computer, a headline arrested her: MYSTERIOUS STRANGER SAVES BOY. The events at McAlbury School were not quite twelve days in the past, and those four words had a special association for her. Curiosity triggered, she instructed the computer to enlarge the quadrant in which the story began.

The dateline was Boston, and the story was accompanied by a photograph. The picture was still blurry and dark, but the scale was now large enough to allow her to read the text, although not comfortably. She instructed the computer to further enlarge one of the already enlarged quadrants, pulling up the first column of the article so she could read it without strain.

The opening line made Holly sit up straighter in her chair: *A courageous bystander, who would say only that his name was Jim, saved the life of Nicholas O'Conner, 6, when a New England Power and Light Company vault exploded under a sidewalk in a Boston residential area Thursday evening.*

Softly, she said, 'What the hell . . . ?'

She tapped the keys, instructing the computer to shift the field of display rightward on the page to show her the multiply enhanced photo that accompanied the piece. She went to a bigger scale, then to a still bigger one, until the face filled the screen.

Jim Ironheart.

Briefly she sat in stunned disbelief, immobilized. Then she was stricken by a need to know more – not only an intellectual but a genuinely physical need that felt not unlike a sudden and intense pang of hunger.

She returned to the text of the story and read it through, then read it again. The O'Conner boy had been sitting on the sidewalk in front of his home, directly on the two-by-three-foot concrete lid that covered the entrance to the power company's vault, which was spacious enough for four men to work together within its subterranean confines. The kid had been playing with toy trucks. His parents had been within sight of him on the front porch of their house, when a stranger had sprinted along the street. 'He comes right at Nicky,' the boy's father was quoted, 'snatches him, so I felt sure he was a nutcase child molester going to steal my son.' Carrying the screaming child, the stranger leaped over a low picket fence, on to the O'Conners' lawn, just as a 17,000-volt line in the vault exploded behind him. The blast flipped the concrete lid high into the air, as if it were a penny, and a bright ball of fire roared up in its wake. Embarrassed by the effusive praise heaped on him by Nicky's grateful parents and by the neighbors who had witnessed his heroism, the stranger claimed that he had smelled burning insulation, heard a hissing coming from the vault, and knew what was about to happen because he had 'once worked for a power company.' Revealing only that his name was Jim, he insisted on leaving before the media arrived because, as he put it, 'I place a high value on my privacy.'

That hair's-breadth rescue had occurred at 7:40 Thursday evening in Boston – or 4:40 Portland time yesterday afternoon. Holly looked at the office wall clock. It was now 2:02 Friday morning. Nicky O'Conner had been plucked off that vault cover not quite nine and a half hours ago.

The trail was still fresh.

She had questions to ask the *Globe* reporter who had written the piece. But it was only a little after five in the morning in Boston. He wouldn't be at work yet.

She closed out the *Press*'s current-edition data file. On the computer screen, the standard menu replaced the enlarged newspaper text.

Through a modem she accessed the vast network of data services to which the *Press* subscribed. She instructed the Newsweb service to scan all the stories that had been carried by the wire services and published in the major US newspapers during the past three months, looking for instances in which the name 'Jim' had been used within ten words of either 'rescue' or the phrase 'saved the life.' She asked for a printout of every article, if there should be any, but asked to be spared multiples of the same incident.

While Newsweb was fulfilling her request, she snatched up the phone on her desk and called long-distance information for area-code 818, then 213, then 714, and 619, seeking a listing for Jim Ironheart in Los Angeles, Orange, Riverside, San Bernardino, and San Diego Counties. None of the operators was able to help her. If he actually lived in southern California, as he had told her he did, his phone was unlisted.

The laser printer that she shared with three other work stations was humming softly. The first of Newsweb's finds was sliding into the receiving tray.

She wanted to hurry to the cabinet on which the printer stood, grab the first printout, and read it at once; but she restrained herself, focusing her attention on the telephone instead, trying to think of another way to locate Jim Ironheart down there in the part of California that locals called 'the Southland.'

A few years ago, she simply could have accessed the California Department of Motor Vehicles computer and, for a small fee, received the street address of anyone holding a valid driver's license in the state. But after the actress Rebecca Schaeffer had been murdered by an obsessed fan who had tracked her down in that fashion, a new law had imposed restrictions on DMV records.

If she had been an accomplished computer hacker, steeped in their arcane knowledge, she no doubt could have finessed entrance to the DMV records in spite of their new safeguards, or perhaps she could have pried into credit-agency databanks to search for a file on Ironheart. She had known reporters who honed their computer skills for just that purpose, but she had always sought her sources and information in a strictly legitimate fashion, without deception.

Which is why you're writing about such thrilling stuff as the Timber Trophy, she thought sourly.

While she puzzled over a solution to the problem, she hurried to the vending room and got a cup of coffee from the coin-operated brewer. It tasted like yak bile. She drank it anyway, because she was going to need the caffeine before the night was through. She bought another cup and returned with it to the newsroom.

71

The laser printer was silent. She grabbed the pages from its tray and sat down at her desk.

Newsweb had turned up a thick stack of stories from the national press in which the name 'Jim' was used within ten words of 'rescue' or 'saved the life.' She counted them quickly. Twenty-nine.

The first was a human-interest piece from the *Chicago Sun-Times*, and Holly read the opening sentence aloud: 'Jim Foster, of Oak Park, has rescued over one hundred stranded cats from—'

She dropped that printout in her wastecan and looked at the next one. It was from the *Philadelphia Inquirer*: 'Jim Pilsbury, pitching for the Phillies, rescued his club from a humiliating defeat—'

Throwing that one aside, as well, she looked at the third. It was a movie review, so she didn't bother searching for the mention of Jim. The fourth was a reference to Jim Harrison, the novelist. The fifth was a story about a New Jersey politician who used the Heimlich maneuver to save the life of a Mafia boss in a barroom, where they were having a couple of beers together, when the *padrone* began to choke to death on a chunk of peppery-hot Slim Jim sausage.

She was beginning to worry that she would come up empty-handed by the bottom of the stack, but the sixth article, from the *Houston Chronicle*, opened her eyes wider than the vile coffee had done. WOMAN SAVED FROM VENGEFUL HUSBAND. On 14 July, after winning both financial and child-custody issues in a bitter divorce suit, Amanda Cutter had nearly been shot by her enraged husband, Cosmo, outside her home in the wealthy River Oaks district of the city. After Cosmo missed her with the first two shots, she had been saved by a man who 'appeared out of nowhere,' wrestled her maddened spouse to the ground, and disarmed him. Her savior had identified himself only as 'Jim,' and had walked off into the humid Houston afternoon before the police arrived. The thirty-year-old divorcée had clearly been smitten, for she described him as 'handsome, sort of muscular, like a superhero right out of a movie, with the dreamiest blue eyes.'

Holly could still picture Jim Ironheart's intensely blue eyes. She was not the kind of woman who would refer to them as 'dreamy,' although they were certainly the clearest and most arresting eyes she'd ever . . . Oh, hell, yes, they *were* dreamy. She was reluctant to admit to the adolescent reaction that he had inspired in her, but she was not any better at deceiving herself than she was at deceiving other people. She recalled an initial eerie impression of inhuman coldness, upon first meeting his gaze, but that passed and never returned from the moment he smiled.

The seventh article was about another modest Jim who had not hung around to accept thanks and praise – or media attention – after rescuing Carmen Diaz, 30, from a burning apartment house in Miami on the fifth of July. He had blue eyes.

Poring through the remaining twenty-two articles, Holly found two more about Ironheart, though only his first name was mentioned. On 21 June, Thaddeus Johnson, 12, had almost been pitched off the roof of an eight-story Harlem tenement by four members of a neighborhood youth gang who had not responded well to his disdainful rejection of an invitation to join their drug-peddling fraternity. He was rescued by a blue-eyed man who incapacitated the four thugs with a dazzling series of Tae Kwon Do kicks, chops, thrusts, and throws. 'He was like Batman without the funny clothes,' Thaddeus had told the *Daily News* reporter. Two weeks prior to that, on 7 June, another blue-eyed Jim 'just seemed to materialize' on the property of Louis Andretti, 28, of Corona, California, in time to warn the homeowner not to enter a crawlspace under his house to repair a plumbing leak. 'He told me a family of rattlers had settled in there,' Andretti told the reporter. Later, when agents from the county's Vector Control inspected the crawlspace from the perimeter, with the aid of a halogen lamp, they saw not just a nest but 'something out of a nightmare,' and eventually extracted forty-one snakes from beneath the structure. 'What I don't understand,' Andretti said, 'is how that guy knew the rattlers were there, when I *live* in the house and never had a clue.'

Now Holly had four linked incidents to add to the rescue of Nicky O'Conner in Boston and Billy Jenkins in Portland, all since the first of June. She typed in new instructions to Newsweb, asking for the same search to be made for the months of March, April, and May.

She needed more coffee, and when she got up to go to the vending room, she saw that George Fintel had evidently awakened and staggered home. She hadn't heard him leave. Tommy was gone, as well. She was alone.

She got another cup of coffee, and it didn't taste as bad as it had before. The brew hadn't improved; her sense of taste had just been temporarily damaged by the first two cups.

Eventually Newsweb located eleven stories in March through May that fit her parameters. After examining the printouts, Holly found only one of them of interest.

On 15 May, in Atlanta, Georgia, a blue-eyed Jim had entered a convenience store during an armed robbery. He shot and killed the perpetrator, Norman Rink, who had been about to kill two customers – Sam Newsome, 25, and his five-year-old daughter Emily. Flying high on a cocaine, Ice, and methamphetamine cocktail – Rink had already killed the clerk and two other customers merely for the fun of it. After wasting Rink and assuring himself that the Newsomes were unhurt, Jim had slipped away before the police arrived.

The store security camera had provided a blurry photograph of the heroic intruder. It was only the second photo Holly had found in all the articles. The image was poor. But she immediately recognized Jim Ironheart.

Some details of the incident unnerved her. If Ironheart had an amazing ability – psychic power, whatever – to foresee fatal moments in the lives of strangers and arrive in time to thwart fate, why hadn't he gotten to that convenience store a few minutes sooner, early enough to prevent the deaths of the clerk and other customers? Why had he saved the Newsomes and let the rest die?

She was further chilled by the description of his attack on Rink. He had pumped four rounds from a 12-gauge pistol-grip shotgun into the madman. Then, although Rink was indisputably dead, Jim reloaded and fired another four rounds. 'He was in such a rage,' Sam Newsome said, 'his face red, and he was sweating, you could see the arteries pounding in his temples, across his forehead. He was crying a little too, but the tears . . . they didn't make him seem any less angry.' When done, Jim had expressed regret for cutting Rink down so violently in front of little Emily. He'd explained that men like Rink, who killed innocent people, brought out 'a little madness of my own.' Newsome told the reporter, 'He saved our lives, yeah, but I gotta say the guy was *scary*, almost as scary as Rink.'

Realizing that Ironheart might not have revealed even his first name on some occasions, Holly instructed Newsweb to search the past six months for stories in which 'rescue' and 'saved the life' were within ten words of 'blue'. She had noticed that some witnesses were vague about his physical description, but that most remembered his singularly blue eyes.

She went to the john, got more coffee, then stood by the printer. As each find was transferred to hard copy, she snatched it up, scanned it, tossed it in the wastecan if it was of no interest or read it with excitement if it was about another nick-of-time rescue. Newsweb turned up four more cases that indisputably belonged in the Ironheart file, even though neither his first nor last name was used.

At her desk again, she instructed Newsweb to search the past six months for the name 'Ironheart' in the national media.

While she waited for a response, she put the pertinent printouts in order, then made a chronological list of the people whose lives Jim Ironheart had saved, incorporating the four new cases. She included their names, ages, the location of each incident, and the type of death from which each person had been spared.

She studied that compilation, noting some patterns with interest. But she put it aside when Newsweb completed its latest task.

As she rose from her chair to go to the laser printer, she froze, surprised to discover she was no longer alone in the newsroom. Three reporters and an editor were at their desks, all guys with reputations as early birds, including Hank Hawkins, editor of the business pages, who liked to be at work when the financial markets opened on the East Coast. She hadn't been aware of them coming in. Two of them were sharing a joke, laughing loudly, and Hawkins was talking on the phone, but Holly hadn't heard them until after she'd seen them. She looked at the clock: 6:10. Opalescent early-morning light played at the windows, though she had not realized that the tide of night had been receding. She glanced down at her desk and saw two more paper coffee cups than she remembered getting from the vending machine.

She realized that she was no longer wallowing in despair. She felt better than she had felt in days. Weeks. *Years.* She was a reporter again, for real.

She went to the laser printer, emptied the receiving tray, and returned with the pages to her desk. Ironhearts evidently were not newsmakers. There were only five stories involving people with that surname in the past six months.

Kevin Ironheart – Buffalo, New York. State senator. Announced his intention to run for governor.

Anna Denise Ironheart – Boca Raton, Florida. Found a live alligator in her family room.

Lori Ironheart – Los Angeles, California. Songwriter. Nominated for the Academy Award for best song of the year.

Valerie Ironheart – Cedar Rapids, Iowa. Gave birth to healthy quadruplets.

The last of the five was James Ironheart.

She looked at the heading. The story came from the Orange County *Register*, 10 April, and was one of scores of pieces on the same story that had been published statewide. Because of her instructions, the computer had printed out only this single instance, sparing her sheaves of similar articles on the same event.

She checked the dateline. Laguna Niguel. California. *Southern California*. The Southland.

The piece was not accompanied by a photograph, but the reporter's description of the man included a reference to blue eyes and thick brown hair. She was sure he was *her* James Ironheart.

She was not surprised to have found him. She had known that with determined effort she would locate him sooner or later. What surprised her was the subject of the piece in which his full name appeared at last. She expected it to be yet one more story about snatching someone out of death's grasp, and she was not prepared for the headline: LAGUNA NIGUEL MAN WINS SIX MILLION LOTTO JACKPOT.

·2·

Having followed the rescue of Nicholas O'Conner with his first untroubled night of sleep in the last four, Jim departed Boston on Friday afternoon, 24 August. Gaining three hours on the cross-country trip, he arrived at John Wayne Airport by 3:10 p.m. and was home half an hour later.

He went straight into his den and lifted the flap of carpet that revealed the safe built into the floor of the closet. He dialed the combination, opened the lid, and removed five thousand dollars, ten percent of the cash he kept there.

At his desk, he packed the hundred-dollar bills into a padded Jiffy envelope and stapled it shut. He typed a label to Father Leo Geary at Our Lady of the Desert, and affixed sufficient postage. He would mail it first thing in the morning.

He went into the family room and switched on the TV. He tried several movies on cable, but none held his interest. He watched the news for a while, but his mind wandered. After he heated a microwave pizza and popped open a beer, he settled down with a good book – which bored him. He paged through a stack of unread magazines, but none of the articles was intriguing.

Near twilight he went outside with another beer and sat on the patio. The palm fronds rustled in a light breeze. A sweet fragrance rose from the star jasmine along the property wall. Red, purple, and pink impatiens shone with almost Day-Glo radiance in the dwindling light; and as the sun finished setting, they faded as if they were hundreds of small lightbulbs on a rheostat. Night floated down like a great tossed cape of almost weightless black silk.

Although the scene was peaceful, he was restless. Day by day, week by week, since he had saved the lives of Sam Newsome and his daughter Emily on 15 May, Jim had found it increasingly difficult to involve himself in the ordinary routines and pleasures of life. He was unable to relax. He kept thinking of all the good he could do, all the lives he could save, the destinies he could alter, if only the call would come again: 'Life line.' Other endeavors seemed frivolous by comparison.

Having been the instrument of a higher power, he now found it difficult to settle for being anything less.

*   *   *

After spending the day collecting what information she could find on James Madison Ironheart, with only a two-hour nap to compensate for the night of sleep she had lost, Holly launched her long-anticipated vacation with a flight to Orange County. On arrival, she drove her rental car south from the airport to the Laguna Hills Motor Inn, where she had reserved a motel room.

Laguna Hills was inland, and not a resort area. But in Laguna Beach, Laguna Niguel, and other coastal towns during the summer, rooms had been booked far in advance. She didn't intend to swim or sunbathe anyway. Ordinarily, she was as enthusiastic a pursuer of skin cancer as anyone, but this had become a working vacation.

By the time she arrived at the motel, she felt as if her eyes were full of sand. When she carried her suitcase into her room, gravity played a cruel trick, pulling her down with five times the usual force.

The room was simple and clean, with enough air conditioning to recreate the environment of Alaska, in case it was ever occupied by an eskimo who got homesick.

From vending machines in the breezeway, she purchased a packet of peanut-butter-and-cheese crackers and a can of Diet Dr Pepper, and satisfied her hunger while sitting in bed. She was so tired that she felt numb. All of her senses were dulled by exhaustion, including her sense of taste. She might as well have been eating Styrofoam and washing it down with mule sweat.

As if the contact of head and pillow tripped a switch, she fell instantly asleep.

During the night, she began to dream. It was an odd dream, for it took place in absolute darkness, with no images, just sounds and smells and tactile sensations, perhaps the way people dreamed when they had been blind since birth. She was in a dank cool place that smelled vaguely of lime. At first she was not afraid, just confused,

77

carefully feeling her way along the walls of the chamber. They were constructed from blocks of stone with tight mortar joints. After a little exploration she realized there was actually just one wall, a single continuous sweep of stone, because the room was circular. The only sounds were those she made – and the background hiss and tick of rain drumming on a slate roof overhead.

In the dream, she moved away from the wall, across a solid wood floor, hands held out in front of her. Although she encountered nothing, her curiosity suddenly began to turn to fear. She stopped moving, stood perfectly still, certain that she had heard something sinister.

A subtle sound. Masked by the soft but insistent rattle of the rain. It came again. A squeak.

For an instant she thought of a rat, fat and sleek, but the sound was too protracted and of too odd a character to have been made by a rat. More of a creak than a squeak, but not the creak of a floor-board underfoot, either. It faded . . . came again a few seconds later . . . faded . . . came again . . . rhythmically.

When Holly realized that she was listening to the protest of an unoiled mechanism of some kind, she should have been relieved. Instead, standing in that tenebrous room, straining to imagine what machine it might be, she felt her heartbeat accelerate. The creaking grew only slightly louder, but it speeded up a lot; instead of one creak every five or six seconds, the sound came every three or four seconds, then every two or three, then once per second.

Suddenly a strange rhythmic *whoosh, whoosh, whoosh* struck up, as well, in syncopation with the creaking. It was the sound of a wide flat object cutting the air.

Whoosh.

It was close. Yet she felt no draft.

Whoosh.

She had the crazy idea that it was a blade.

Whoosh.

A large blade. Sharp. Cutting the air. Enormous.

Whoosh.

She sensed that something terrible was approaching, an entity so strange that even light – and the full sight of the thing – would not provide understanding. Although she was aware that she was dreaming, she knew she had to get out of that dark and stony place quickly – or die. A nightmare couldn't be escaped just by running from it, so she had to wake up, but she could not, she was too tired, unable to break the bonds of sleep. Then the lightless room seemed to be spinning, she had a sense of some great structure turning around and around (*creak, whoosh*), thrusting up into the rainy night (*creak, whoosh*) and turning (*creak, whoosh*), cutting the air (*creak, whoosh*), she was trying to scream (*creak, whoosh*), but she couldn't force a sound from herself (*whoosh, whoosh, whoosh*), couldn't awaken and couldn't scream for help. *WHOOSH!*

*   *   *

'No!'

Jim sat up in bed as he shouted the one-word denial. He was clammy and trembling violently.

He had fallen fast asleep with the lamp on, which he frequently did, usually not by accident but by design. For more than a year, his sleep had been troubled by nightmares with a variety of plots and a panoply of boogeymen, only some of which he could recall when he woke. The nameless, formless creature that he called 'the enemy,' and of which he had dreamed while recuperating at Our Lady of the Desert rectory, was the most frightening figure in his dreamscapes, though not the only monster.

This time, however, the focus of the terror had not been a person or creature. It was a *place*. The windmill.

He looked at the bedside clock. Three-forty-five in the morning.

In just his pajama bottoms, he got out of bed and padded into the kitchen.

The fluorescent light seared his eyes. Good. He wanted to evaporate what residue of sleep still clung to him.

The damn windmill.

He plugged in the coffeemaker and brewed a strong Colombian blend. He sipped half the first cup while standing at the counter, then refilled it and sat down at the breakfast table. He intended to empty the pot because he could not risk going back to bed and having that dream again.

Every nightmare detracted from the quality of rest that sleep provided, but the windmill dream actually took a real physical toll. Whenever he woke from it, his chest always ached, as though his heart had been bruised from hammering too hard against his breastbone. Sometimes the shakes took hours to fade away completely, and he often had headaches that, like now, arced across the top of his skull and throbbed with such power that it seemed as if an alien presence was trying to burst out of him. He knew that if he looked in a mirror, his face would be unnervingly pale and haggard, with blue-black circles around the eyes, like the face of a terminal cancer patient from whom disease had sucked the juice of life.

The windmill dream was not the most frequent of those that plagued him, and in fact it haunted his sleep only one or two nights a month. But it was by far the worst.

Curiously, nothing much happened in it. He was ten years old again, sitting on the dusty wooden floor of the smaller upper chamber, above the main room that held the ancient millstones, with only the flickering light of a fat yellow candle. Night pressed at the narrow windows, which were almost like castle embrasures in the limestone walls. Rain tapped against the glass. Suddenly, with a creak of unoiled and half-rusted machinery, the four great wooden sails of the mill began to turn outside, faster and faster, cutting like giant scythes through the damp air. The upright shaft, which came out of the ceiling and vanished through a bore in the center of the floor, also began to turn, briefly creating the illusion that the round floor itself was rotating in the manner of a carousel. One level below, the ancient millstones started to roll against each other, producing a soft rumble like distant thunder.

Just that. Nothing more. Yet it scared the hell out of him.

He took a long pull of his coffee.

Stranger still: in real life, the windmill had been a good place, never the scene of pain or terror. It had stood between a pond and a cornfield on his grandparents' farm. To a young boy born and raised in the city, the big mill had been an exotic and mysterious structure, a perfect place to play and fantasize, a refuge in a time of trouble. He could not understand why he was having nightmares about a place that held only good memories for him.

*　　*　　*

After the frightening dream passed without waking her, Holly Thorne slept peacefully for the rest of the night, as still as a stone on the floor of the sea.

•3•

Saturday morning, Holly ate breakfast in a booth at the motel coffeeshop. Most of the other customers were obviously vacationers: families dressed almost as if in uniforms of shorts or white slacks and brightly colored shirts. Some of the kids wore caps and

T-shirts that advertised Sea World or Disneyland or Knott's Berry Farm. Parents huddled over maps and brochures while they ate, planning routes that would take them to one of the tourist attractions that California offered in such plenitude. There were so many colorful Polo shirts or Polo-shirt knockoffs in the restaurant that a visitor from another planet might have assumed that Ralph Lauren was either the deity of a major religion or dictator of the world.

As she ate blueberry pancakes, Holly studied her list of people who had been spared from death by Jim Ironheart's timely intervention:

15 MAY
Sam (25) and Emily (5) Newsome – Atlanta, Georgia (murder)

7 JUNE
Louis Andretti (28) – Corona, California (snakebite)

21 JUNE
Thaddeus Johnson (12) – New York, New York (murder)

30 JUNE
Rachael Steinberg (23) – San Francisco, California (murder)

5 JULY
Carmen Diaz (30) – Miami, Florida (fire)

14 JULY
Amanda Cutter (30) – Houston, Texas (murder)

20 JULY
Steven Aimes (57) – Birmingham, Alabama (murder)

1 AUGUST
Laura Lenaskian (28) – Seattle, Washington (drowning)

8 AUGUST
Doogie Burkette (11) – Peoria, Illinois (drowning)

12 AUGUST
Billy Jenkins (8) – Portland, Oregon (traffic fatality)

20 AUGUST
Lisa (30) and Susan (10) Jawolski – Mojave Desert (murder)

23 AUGUST
Nicholas O'Conner (6) – Boston, Massachusetts (accident)

Certain patterns were obvious. Of the fourteen people saved, six were children. Seven others were between the ages of twenty-three and thirty. Only one was older – Steven Aimes, who was fifty-seven. Ironheart favored the young. And there was some evidence that his activities were increasing in frequency: one episode in May; three in June; three in July; and now five already in August with a full week of the month remaining.

Holly was particularly intrigued by the number of people on the list who would have been *murdered* without Ironheart's intervention. Far more people died each year in accidents than at the hands of others. Traffic fatalities alone were more numerous than murders. Yet Jim Ironheart intervened in a considerably greater number of homicides than accidents: eight of the fourteen people on the list had been spared from the malevolent intentions of murderers, over sixty percent.

Perhaps his premonitions more often related to murder than to other forms of death because human violence generated stronger psychic vibrations than accidents . . .

Holly stopped chewing and her hand froze halfway to her mouth with another forkful of blueberry pancake, as she realized just *how* strange this story was. She had been operating at a breathless pace, driven by reportorial ambition and curiosity. Her excitement, then her exhaustion, had prevented her from fully considering all of the implications and ramifications of Ironheart's activities. She put down her fork and stared at her plate, as if she could glean answers and explanations from the crumb patterns and smears in the same way that gypsies read tea leaves and palms.

What the hell *was* Jim Ironheart? A psychic?

She'd never had much interest in extra-sensory perception and strange mental powers. She knew there were people who claimed to be able to 'see' a murderer just by touching the clothes his victim wore, who sometimes helped police find the bodies of missing persons, who were paid well by the *National Enquirer* to foresee world events and forthcoming developments in the lives of celebrities, who said they could channel the voices of the dead to the living. But her interest in the supernatural was so minimal that she had never really formed an opinion of the validity of such claims. She didn't necessarily believe that all those people were frauds; the whole subject had bored her too much to bother thinking about it at all.

She supposed that her dogged rationality – and cynicism – could bend far enough to encompass the idea that now and then a psychic actually possessed real power, but she wasn't sure that 'psychic' was an adequate description of Jim Ironheart. This guy wasn't just going out on a limb in some cheap tabloid to predict that Steven Spielberg would make another hit picture next year (surprise!), or that Schwarzenegger would still speak English with an accent, or that Tom Cruise would dump his current girlfriend, or that Eddie Murphy would still be black for the foreseeable future. *This* guy knew the precise facts of each of those impending deaths – who, when, where, how – far enough in advance to derail fate. He wasn't bending spoons with the power of his mind, wasn't speaking in the gravelly voice of an ancient spirit named Rama-Lama-Dingdong, wasn't reading futures in entrails or wax drippings or Tarot cards. He was *saving lives*, for God's sake, altering destinies, having a profound impact not only on those he saved from death but on the lives of the friends and families who would have been left shattered and bereaved. And the reach of his power extended three thousand miles from Laguna Niguel to Boston!

In fact maybe his heroics were not confined to the borders of the continental United States. She had not researched the international media for the past six months. Perhaps he had saved lives in Italy, France, Germany, Japan, Sweden, or in Pago-Pago for all she knew.

The word 'psychic' definitely was inadequate. Holly couldn't even think of a suitable one-word description of his powers.

To her surprise, a sense of wonder had possessed her, like nothing she had felt since she was a kid. Now, an element of awe stole over her as well, and she shivered.

Who was this man? *What* was he?

Little more than thirty hours ago, when she had seen the story about young Nicholas O'Conner in Boston, Holly had known she was on to a big story. By the time she examined the material that Newsweb found for her, she felt it might be the biggest story of her career, regardless of how long she worked as a reporter. Now she had begun to suspect that it might grow into the biggest story of this decade.

'Everything OK?'

Holly said, 'Everything's weird,' before she realized that she had not asked the question of herself.

The waitress – Bernice, according to the name embroidered on her uniform blouse – was standing beside the table, looking concerned. Holly realized that she had been staring intently at her plate while she'd been thinking about Jim Ironheart, and she had not taken a bite in some time. Bernice had noticed and thought something was wrong.

'Weird?' Bernice said, frowning.

'Uh, yeah – it's weird that I should come into what looks like an ordinary coffeeshop and get the best blueberry pancakes I've ever eaten.'

Bernice hesitated, perhaps trying to decide if Holly was putting her on. 'You . . . you really like 'em?'

'Love them,' Holly said, forking up a mouthful and chewing the cold, sodden pancakes with enthusiasm.

'That's nice! You want anything else?'

'Just the check,' Holly said.

She continued to eat the pancakes after Bernice left, because she was hungry and they were there.

As she ate, Holly looked around the restaurant at the colorfully decked-out vacationers who were absorbed in discussions of amusements experienced and amusements yet to come, and the thrill of being an insider coursed through her for the first time in years. She knew something they did not. She was a reporter with a carefully husbanded secret. When fully researched, when written up in crystalline prose as direct and yet evocative as Hemingway's best journalism (well, she was going to *try* for that, anyway), the story would earn front-page, top-of-the-page exposure in every major newspaper in the country, in the world. And what made it so good, what made her tingle, was that her secret had nothing to do with a political scandal, toxic dumping, or the other myriad forms of terror and tragedy that fueled the engine of modern news media. Her story would be one of amazement and wonder, courage and hope, a story of tragedy avoided, lives spared, death thwarted.

Life is *so* good, she thought, unable to stop grinning at her fellow diners.

*   *   *

First thing after breakfast, with the aid of a book of street maps called the *Thomas Guide*, Holly located Jim Ironheart's house in Laguna Niguel. She had tracked down the address via computer from Portland, by checking the public records of real-estate trans-

actions in Orange County since the first of the year. She had
assumed that anyone winning six million dollars in a lottery might
spend some of it on a new house, and she had assumed correctly. He
hit the jackpot – presumably thanks to his clairvoyance – in early
January. On May third, he finalized the purchase of a house on
Bougainvillea Way. Since the records did not show that he had sold
any property, he apparently had been renting before his windfall.

She was somewhat surprised to find him living in such a modest
house. The neighborhood was new, just off Crown Valley Parkway,
and in the neat, well-landscaped, precision-planned tradition of
south Orange County. The streets were wide, gracefully curved,
lined with young palms and melaleucas, and the houses were all of
compatible Mediterranean styles with roofs in different shades of
red and sand and peach tiles. But even in such a desirable south-
county city as Laguna Niguel, where the per-square-foot cost of a
tract home could rival that of a Manhattan penthouse, Ironheart
could easily have afforded better than he had purchased: it looked
like a little more than two thousand square feet, the smallest model
in the neighborhood; creamy-white stucco; large-pane French
windows but no other apparent custom features; a lush green lawn,
but small, with azaleas and impatiens and a pair of willowy queen
palms that cast lacy shadows on the walls in the temperate morning
sun.

She drove by slowly, giving the house a thorough looking over.
No car stood in the driveway. The drapes were drawn at the windows. She had no way of knowing if Ironheart was home – short of
going up to his front door and ringing the bell. Eventually, she
would do just that. But not yet.

At the end of the block, she turned around and drove past the
house again. The place was attractive, pleasant, but so *ordinary*. It
was hard to believe that an exceptional man, with astonishing
secrets, lived behind those walls.

*   *   *

Viola Moreno's townhouse in Irvine was in one of those parklike
communities the Irvine Company had built in the sixties and seventies, where the plum-thorn hedges had entered woody maturity and
the red-gum eucalyptuses and Indian laurels towered high enough
to spread a wealth of shade on even the brightest and most cloudless
of summer days. It was furnished with an eye to comfort rather
than style: an overstuffed sofa, commodious armchairs and plump

footstools, everything in earth tones, with traditional landscape paintings meant to soothe rather than challenge the eye and mind. Stacks of magazines and shelves of books were everywhere at hand. Holly felt at home the moment she crossed the threshold.

Viola was as welcoming and easy to like as her home. She was about fifty, Mexican-American, with flawless skin the shade of lightly tarnished copper and eyes that were merry in spite of being as liquid-black as squid ink. Though she was on the short side and had broadened a little with age, it was easy to see that her looks would once have turned men's heads hard enough to crack vertebrae; she was still a lovely woman. She took Holly's hand at the door, then linked arms with her to lead her through the small house and out to the patio, as if they were old friends and had not just spoken for the first time on the phone the previous day.

On the patio, which overlooked a common greensward, a pitcher of icy lemonade and two glasses stood on a glass-topped table. The rattan chairs were padded with thick yellow cushions.

'I spend a lot of my summer out here,' Viola said as they settled into chairs. The day was not too hot, the air dry and clean. 'It's a beautiful little corner of the world, isn't it?'

The broad but shallow green vale separated this row of town-houses from the next, shaded by tall trees and decorated with a couple of circular beds of red and purple impatiens. Two squirrels scampered down a gentle slope and across a meandering walkway.

'Quite beautiful,' Holly agreed as Viola poured lemonade into their glasses.

'My husband and I bought it when the trees were just sticks and the Hydroseeded greenbelt was still patchy. But we could visualize what it would be like one day, and we were patient people, even when we were young.' She sighed. 'Sometimes I have bad moments, I get bitter about his dying so young and never having a chance to see what this all grew up into. But mostly I just enjoy it, knowing Joe is somewhere better than this world and that somehow he takes pleasure in my enjoyment.'

'I'm sorry,' Holly said, 'I didn't know you'd been widowed.'

'Of course you didn't, dear. How could you know? Anyway, it was a long time ago, back in 1969, when I was just thirty and he was thirty-two. My husband was a career Marine, proud of it, and so was I. So *am* I, still, though he died in Vietnam.'

Holly was startled to realize that many of the early victims of that conflict would now have been past middle-age. The wives they left behind had now lived far more years without them than with them.

How long until Vietnam seemed as ancient as the crusades of Richard the Lionheart or the Peloponnesian Wars?

'Such a waste,' Viola said with an edge to her voice. But the edge was gone an instant later when she said, 'So long ago . . .'

The life Holly had imagined for this woman – a calm and peaceful journey of small pleasures, warm and cozy, with perhaps more than its share of laughter – was clearly less than half the story. The firm and loving tone Viola used when she referred to Joe as 'my husband' made it clear that no amount of time elapsed could fade his memory in her mind, and that there had been no other man since him. Her life had been profoundly changed and constricted by his death. Although she was obviously an optimistic soul and outgoing by nature, there was a shadow of tragedy on her heart.

One basic lesson that every good journalist learned early in his career was that people were seldom only what they seemed to be – and never less complex than the mystery of life itself.

Viola sipped her lemonade. 'Too sweet. I always add too much sugar. Sorry.' She put her glass down. 'Now tell me about this brother you're searching for. You have me quite intrigued.'

'As I told you when I called from Portland, I was an adopted child. The people who took me in were wonderful parents, I have no less love for them than I would for my real parents, but . . . well . . .'

'Naturally, you have a desire to know your real parents.'

'It's as if . . . there's an emptiness in me, a dark place in my heart,' Holly said, trying not to trowel it on too thick.

She was not surprised by the ease with which she lied, but by how well she did it. Deception was a handy tool with which to elicit information from a source who might otherwise be reluctant to talk. Journalists as highly praised as Joe McGinness, Joseph Wambaugh, Bob Woodward, and Carl Bernstein had at one time or another argued the necessity of dishonesty in dealing with interviewees, all in the service of getting at the truth. But Holly had never been this skillful at it. At least she had the good grace to be dismayed and embarrassed by her lies – two feelings that she hid well from Viola Moreno.

'Though the adoption agency's records were barely adequate, I've learned that my real parents, my biological parents, died twenty-five years ago, when I was only eight.' Actually, it was Jim Ironheart's parents who had died twenty-five years ago, when he was ten, a fact she had turned up in stories about his lottery win. 'So I'll never have a chance to know them.'

'What a terrible thing. Now it's *my* turn to be sorry for *you,*' Viola said with a note of genuine sympathy in her soft voice.

Holly felt like a heel. By concocting this false personal tragedy, she seemed to be mocking Viola's very real loss. She went on anyway: 'But it's not as bleak as it might've been, because I've discovered I have a brother, as I told you on the phone.'

Leaning forward with her arms on the table, Viola was eager to hear the details and learn how she could help. 'And there's something I can do to help you find your brother?'

'Not exactly. You see, I've already found him.'

'How wonderful!'

'But . . . I'm afraid to approach him.'

'Afraid? But why?'

Holly looked out at the greensward and swallowed hard a couple of times, as if choking on emotion and struggling to maintain control of herself. She was good. Academy Award stuff. She loathed herself for it. When she spoke, she managed to get a subtle and convincing tremor in her voice: 'As far as I know, he's the only blood relative I have in the world, and my only link to the mother and father I'll never know. He's my brother, Mrs Moreno, and I love him. Even though I've never met him, I love him. But what if I approach him, open my heart to him . . . and he wishes I'd never shown up, doesn't like me or something?'

'Good heavens, of course he'll like you! Why wouldn't he like a nice young woman like you? Why wouldn't he be *delighted* to have someone as sweet as you for a sister?'

I'm going to rot in hell for this, Holly thought miserably.

She said, 'Well, it may sound silly to you, but I'm worried about it. I've never made good first impressions with people—'

'You've made an excellent one with me, dear.'

Grind my face under your heel, why don't you? Holly thought.

She said, 'I want to be careful. I want to know as much as possible about him before I knock on his door. I want to know what he likes, what he doesn't like, how he feels about . . . oh, about all sorts of things. God, Mrs Moreno, I don't want to blow this.'

Viola nodded. 'I assume you've come to me because I know your brother, probably had him years ago in one of my classes?'

'You do teach history at a junior high school here in Irvine—'

'That's right. I've worked there since before Joe died.'

'Well, my brother wasn't one of your students. He was an English instructor in the same school. I traced him there, and learned you'd taught in the room next to his for ten years, you knew him well.'

Viola's face brightened into a smile. 'You mean Jim Ironheart!'

'That's right. My brother.'

'This is lovely, wonderful, this is *perfect!*' Viola enthused.

The woman's reaction was so excessive that Holly blinked in surprise and didn't know quite what to say next.

'He's a good man,' Viola said with genuine affection. 'I'd have liked nothing better than to've had a son like him. He comes around now and then for dinner, not as often as he used to, and I cook for him, mother him. I can't tell you how much pleasure that gives me.' A wistful expression had settled on her, and she was silent a moment. 'Anyway . . . you couldn't have asked for a better brother, dear. He's one of the nicest people I've ever known, a dedicated teacher, so gentle and kind and patient.'

Holly thought of Norman Rink, the psychopath who had killed a clerk and two customers in that Atlanta convenience store last May, and who had been killed in turn by gentle, kind Jim Ironheart. Eight rounds from a shotgun at pointblank range. Four rounds fired into the corpse after Rink was obviously dead. Viola Moreno might know the man well, but she clearly had no concept of the rage that he could tap when he needed it.

'I've known good teachers in my time, but none as concerned about his students as Jim Ironheart was. He sincerely cared about them, as if they were his own kids.' She leaned back in her chair and shook her head, remembering. 'He gave so much to them, wanted so much to make their lives better, and all but the worst-case misfits responded to him. He had a rapport with his students that other teachers would sell their souls for, yet he didn't have to surrender a proper student-teacher relationship to get it. So many of them try to be pals with their students, you see, and that never really works.'

'Why did he quit teaching?'

Viola hesitated, smile fading. 'Partly, it was the lottery.'

'What lottery?'

'You don't know about that?'

Holly frowned and shook her head.

Viola said, 'He won six million dollars in January.'

'Holysmoke!'

'The first time he ever bought a ticket.'

Allowing her initial surprise to metamorphose into a look of worry, Holly said, 'Oh, God, now he's going to think I only came around because he's suddenly rich.'

'No, no,' Viola hastened to assure her. 'Jim would never think the worst of anyone.'

'I've done well myself,' Holly lied. 'I don't need his money, I wouldn't take it if he tried to give it to me. My adoptive parents are doctors, not wealthy but well-to-do, and I'm an attorney with a nice practice.'

OK, OK, you really *don't* want his money, Holly thought with self-disgust as caustic as acid, but you're still a mean little lying bitch with a frightening talent for invented detail, and you'll spend eternity standing hip-deep in dung, polishing Satan's boots.

Her mood changing, Viola pushed her chair back from the table, got up, and stepped to the edge of the patio. She plucked a weed from a large terracotta pot full of begonias, baby's breath, and copper-yellow marigolds. Absent-mindedly rolling the slender weed into a ball between the thumb and forefinger of her right hand, she stared thoughtfully out at the parklike grounds.

The woman was silent for a long time.

Holly worried that she had said something wrong, unwittingly revealing her duplicity. Second by second, she became more nervous, and she found herself wanting to blurt out an apology for all the lies she'd told.

Squirrels capered on the grass. A butterfly swooped under the patio cover, perched on the edge of the lemonade pitcher for a moment, then flew away.

Finally, with a tremor in her voice that was real this time, Holly said, 'Mrs Moreno? Is something wrong?'

Viola flicked the balled-up weed out on to the grass. 'I'm just having trouble deciding how to put this.'

'Put what?' Holly asked nervously.

Turning to her again, approaching the table, Viola said, 'You asked me why Jim . . . why your brother quit teaching. I said it was because he won the lottery, but that really isn't true. If he'd still loved teaching as much as he did a few years ago or even *one* year ago, he would've kept working even if he'd won a hundred million.'

Holly almost breathed a sigh of relief that her cover had not been penetrated. 'What soured him on it?'

'He lost a student.'

'Lost?'

'An eighth-grader named Larry Kakonis. A very bright boy with a good heart – but disturbed. From a troubled family. His father beat his mother, had been beating her as long as Larry could remember, and Larry felt as if he should be able to stop it, but he couldn't. He felt responsible, though he shouldn't have. That was the kind of kid he was, a real strong sense of responsibility.'

Viola picked up her glass of lemonade, returned to the edge of the patio, and stared out at the greensward again. She was silent once more.

Holly waited.

Eventually the woman said, 'The mother was a co-dependent type, a victim of the father but a collaborator in her own victimization. As troubled in her own way as the father. Larry couldn't reconcile his love for his mother and his respect for her with his growing understanding that, on some level, she liked and *needed* to be beaten.'

Suddenly Holly knew where this was going, and she did not want to hear the rest of it. However, she had no choice but to listen.

'Jim had worked so hard with the boy. I don't mean just on his English lessons, not just academically. Larry had opened up to him in a way he'd never been able to open up to anyone else, and Jim had been counseling him with the help of Dr Lansing, a psychologist who works part-time for the school district. Larry seemed to be coming around, struggling to understand his mother and himself – and to some extent succeeding. Then one night, 15 May of last year – over fifteen months ago, though it's hard to believe it's been that long – Larry Kakonis took a gun from his father's collection, loaded it, put the barrel in his mouth . . . and fired one bullet up into his brain.'

Holly flinched as if struck. In fact she *had* been struck, though the blows – two of them – were not physical. She was jolted, first, by the thought of a thirteen-year-old committing suicide when the best of life lay ahead of him. A small problem could seem like a large one at that age, and a genuinely serious problem could seem catastrophic and hopeless. Holly felt a pang of grief for Larry Kakonis, and an undirected anger because the kid had not been given time enough to learn that all horrors can be dealt with and that, on balance, life offered far more joy than despair. But she was equally rattled by the date on which the boy had killed himself: 15 May.

One year later, this past 15 May, Jim Ironheart had performed his first miraculous rescue. Sam and Emily Newsome. Atlanta, Georgia. Saved from murder at the hands of a sociopathic holdup man named Norman Rink.

Holly could sit still no longer. She got up and joined Viola at the edge of the patio. They watched the squirrels.

'Jim blamed himself,' Viola said.

'For Larry Kakonis? But he wasn't responsible.'

'He blamed himself anyway. That's how he is. But his reaction seemed excessive, even for Jim. After Larry's death, he lost interest in teaching. He stopped believing he could make a difference. He'd had so many successes, more than any teacher I've ever known, but that one failure was too much for him.'

Holly remembered the boldness with which Ironheart had scooped Billy Jenkins out of the path of the hurtling pickup truck. *That* certainly had not been a failure.

'He just sort of spiraled down into gloom,' Viola said. 'Couldn't pull himself out of it.'

The man Holly had met in Portland had not seemed depressive. Mysterious, yes, and self-contained. But he'd had a good sense of humor, and he'd been quick to smile.

Viola took a sip of her lemonade. 'Funny, it tastes too sour now.' She set the glass down on the concrete near her feet and wiped her damp hand on her slacks. She started to speak again, hesitated, but finally said. 'Then . . . he got a little strange.'

'Strange? In what way?'

'Withdrawn. Quiet. He started taking martial-arts training. Tae Kwon Do. Lots of people are interested in that sort of thing, I guess, but it seemed so out of character for Jim.'

It didn't seem out of character for the Jim Ironheart that Holly knew.

Viola said, 'It wasn't casual with him, either. Every day after school he went for a lesson at a place in Newport Beach. He became obsessive. I worried about him. So in January, when he won the lottery, I was happy. Six million dollars! That's such a good thing, such *big* luck, it seemed like it would have to turn his life around, bring him out of his depression.'

'But it didn't?'

'No. He didn't seem all that surprised or pleased by it. He quit teaching, moved out of his apartment into a house . . . and pulled back even further from his friends.' She turned to Holly and smiled. It was the first smile she had managed for a while. 'That's why I was so excited when you told me you were his sister, a sister he doesn't even know he has. Because maybe *you* can do for him what winning six million dollars couldn't do.'

Guilt over her deception suffused Holly again, bringing a hot blush to her face. She hoped Viola would mistake it for a blush of pleasure or excitement. 'It would be wonderful if I could.'

'You can, I'm sure. He's alone, or feels that he is. That's part of his problem. With a sister, he won't be alone any more. Go see him today, right now.'

Holly shook her head. 'Soon. But not yet. I need to . . . build my confidence. You won't tell him about me, will you?'

'Of course not, dear. You should have all the fun of telling him, and what a wonderful moment that'll be.'

Holly's smile felt like a pair of rigid plastic lips glued to her face, as false as part of a Halloween costume.

A few minutes later, at the front door, as Holly was leaving, Viola put a hand on her arm and said, 'I don't want to give you the wrong idea. It won't be *easy* lifting his spirits, getting him back on track. As long as I've known Jim, I've felt there's a sadness deep down in him, like a stain that won't come out, which isn't such a surprise, really, when you consider what happened to his parents – his being orphaned when he was only ten, all of that.'

Holly nodded. 'Thanks. You've been a real help.'

Viola impulsively hugged her, planted a kiss on her cheek, and said, 'I want to have both you and Jim to dinner as soon as possible. Homemade green-corn tamales, black beans, and jalapeno rice so hot it'll melt your dental fillings!'

Holly was simultaneously pleased and dismayed: pleased to have met this woman, who so quickly seemed to be a favorite aunt of long acquaintance; dismayed because she had met her and been accepted by her under false pretenses.

All the way back to her rental car, Holly fiercely berated herself under her breath. She was at no loss for ugly words and clever damning phrases. Twelve years in newsrooms, in the company of reporters, had acquainted her with enough obscene language to ensure her the trophy in a cursing contest with even the most foul-mouthed victim of Tourette's syndrome.

* * *

The Yellow Pages listed only one Tae Kwon Do school in Newport Beach. It was in a shopping center off Newport Boulevard, between a custom window-covering store and a bakery.

The place was called Dojo, the Japanese word for a martial-arts practice hall, which was like naming a restaurant 'Restaurant' or a dress shop 'Dress Shop.' Holly was surprised by the generic name, because Asian businessmen often brought a poetic sensibility to the titling of their enterprises.

Three people were standing on the sidewalk in front of Dojo's big window, eating eclairs and awash in the delicious aromas wafting from the adjacent bakery, watching a class of six students go through their routines with a squat but exceptionally limber Korean instructor in black pajamas. When the teacher threw a pupil to the mat inside, the plate-glass window vibrated.

Entering, Holly passed out of the chocolate-, cinnamon-, sugar-, yeast-scented air into an acidic environment of stale incense laced with a vague perspiration odor. Because of a story she'd written about a Portland teenager who won a medal in a national competition, she knew Tae Kwon Do was an aggressive Korean form of karate, using fierce punches, lightning-quick jabs, chops, blocks, chokeholds, and devastatingly powerful, leaping kicks. The teacher was pulling his blows, but there were still a lot of grunts, wheezes, guttural exclamations, and jarring thuds as students slammed to the mat.

In the far right corner of the room, a brunette sat on a stool behind a counter, doing paperwork. Every aspect and detail of her dress and grooming were advertisements for her sexuality. Her tight red T-shirt emphasized her ample chest and outlined nipples as large as cherries. With a tousled mane of chestnut hair given luster by artfully applied blonde highlights, eyes subtly but exotically shadowed, mouth too lushly painted with deep-coral lipstick, a just-right tan, disablingly long fingernails painted to match the lipstick, and enough silvery costume jewelry to stock a display case, she would have been the perfect advertisement if women had been a product for sale in every local market.

'Does this thudding and grunting go on all day?' Holly asked.

'Most of the day, yeah.'

'Doesn't it get to you?'

'Oh, yeah,' the brunette said with a lascivious wink, 'I know what you mean. They're like a bunch of bulls ramming at each other. I'm not here an hour every day till I'm so horny I can't stand it.'

That was not what Holly had meant. She was suggesting that the noise was headache-inducing, not arousing. But she winked back, girl-to-girl, and said, 'The boss in?'

'Eddie? He's doing a couple hundred flights of stairs,' the woman said cryptically. 'What d'you want?'

Holly explained that she was a reporter, working on a story that had a connection with Dojo.

The receptionist, if that's what she was, brightened at this news instead of glowering, as was often the case. Eddie, she said, was always looking to get publicity for the business. She rose from her stool and stepped to a door behind the counter, revealing that she was wearing high-heeled sandals and tight white shorts that clung to her butt as snugly as a coat of paint.

Holly was beginning to feel like a boy.

As the brunette had indicated, Eddie was delighted to hear that Dojo would be mentioned in a newspaper piece, even if tangentially, but he wanted her to interview him while he continued to do stairs. He was not an Asian, which perhaps explained the unimaginative generic name of his business. Tall, blond, shaggy-haired, blue-eyed, he was dressed only in muscles and a pair of black Spandex cyclist's shorts. He was on a StairMaster exercise machine, climbing briskly to nowhere.

'It's great,' he said, pumping his exquisitely developed legs. 'Six more flights, and I'll be at the top of the Washington monument.'

He was breathing hard but not as hard as Holly would have been breathing after running up six flights to her third-floor apartment in Portland.

She sat in a chair he had indicated, which put the StairMaster directly in front of her, giving her a full side view of him. His sun-bronzed skin glistened with sweat, which also darkened the hair at the nape of his thick neck. The Spandex embraced him as intimately as the white shorts had clung to the receptionist. It almost seemed as if he had known Holly was coming and had carefully arranged the StairMaster and her chair to display himself to his best advantage.

Although she was plunging into deception again, Holly did not feel as bad about lying to Eddie as she had felt when lying to Viola Moreno. For one thing, her cover story this time was somewhat less fanciful: that she was doing a multipart, in-depth piece about James Ironheart (the truth), focusing on the effect that winning a lottery had upon his life (a lie), all with his approval (a lie). A veracity percentage as high as thirty-three percent was enough to salve her guilt, which she supposed didn't say much for the quality of her conscience.

'Just so you spell Dojo right,' Eddie said. Looking back and down at his right leg, he added happily, 'Look at that calf, hard as rock.'

As if she hadn't been looking at it all along.

'The fat layer between my skin and the muscle underneath, it's hardly there, burned it all away.'

Another reason she didn't mind lying to Eddie was because he was a vain, self-involved jerk.

'Three more flights to the top of the monument,' he said. The rhythm of his speech was tied to the pattern of his breathing, the words rising and falling with each inhalation and exhalation.

'Just three? Then I'll wait.'

'No, no. Ask your questions. I won't stop at the top. I'm gonna see how much of the Empire State Building I can climb next.'

'Ironheart was a student of yours.'

'Yeah. Taught him myself.'

'He came to you long before he won the lottery.'

'Yeah. More than a year ago.'

'May of last year, I think.'

'Mighta been.'

'Did he tell you why he wanted to learn Tae Kwon Do?'

'Nope. But he had a passion.' He almost shouted his next words, as if he'd triumphantly completed a real climb: 'Top of the monument!' He increased his pace instead of slacking off.

'Did you think it was odd?'

'Why?'

'Him being a schoolteacher, I mean.'

'We get schoolteachers. We get all kinds. Everyone wants to kick ass.' He sucked in a very deep breath, blew it out, and said, 'In the Empire State now, going up.'

'Was Ironheart good?'

'Excellent! Coulda been a competitor.'

'Could've been? You mean he dropped out?'

Breathing a little harder than before, the words coming in a quicker though similar rhythm, he said: 'Hung in there seven or eight months. Every day. He was a real glutton for punishment. Pumping iron and doing aerobics *plus* martial arts. Ate his way through the pain. Man was getting tough enough to fuck a rock. Sorry. But he was. Then he quit. Two weeks after he won the bucks.'

'Ah, I see.'

'Don't get me wrong. Wasn't the money that made him quit.'

'Then what?'

'He said I'd given him what he needed, he didn't want any more.'

'What he needed?' she asked.

'Enough Tae Kwon Do for what he wanted to do.'

'Did he say what he wanted to do?'

'Nope. Kick someone's ass, I guess.'

Eddie was really pushing himself now, ramming his feet down on the StairMaster, pumping and pumping, so much sweat on his body

96

that he appeared to be coated in oil, droplets spraying off his hair when he shook his head, the muscles in his arms and across his broad back bulging almost as fiercely as those in his thighs and calves.

Sitting in the chair about eight feet from the man, Holly felt as if she were ringside at some sleazy strip club where the gender roles had been reversed. She got up.

Eddie was staring straight ahead at the wall. His face was creased by lines of strain, but he had a dreamy, faraway look in his eyes. Maybe, instead of the wall, he saw the endless stairwell in the Empire State Building.

'Anything else he ever told you that seemed . . . interesting, unusual?' she asked.

Eddie didn't answer. He was concentrating on the climb. The arteries in his neck had swelled and were throbbing as if evenly spaced, small, fat fish were schooling through his bloodstream.

As Holly reached the door, Eddie said, 'Three things.'

She turned to him again. 'Yeah?'

Without looking at her, his eyes still out of focus, not for an instant slackening his pace, speaking to her from the stairwell of that skyscraper in distant Manhattan, he said, 'Ironheart's the only guy I ever met who can obsess better than I can.'

Frowning, Holly thought about that. 'What else?'

'The only lessons he missed were two weeks in September. Went up north, Marin County somewhere, to take a course in aggressive driving.'

'What's that?'

'Mostly they teach chauffeurs for politicians, diplomats, rich businessmen how to handle a car like James Bond, escape terrorist traps, kidnappers, shit like that.'

'He talk about why he needed that kind of training?'

'Just said it sounded like fun.'

'That's two things.'

He shook his head. Sweat flew, spattered the surrounding carpet and furniture. Holly was just out of range. He still didn't look at her. 'Number three – after he figured he had enough Tae Kwon Do, the next thing he wanted was to learn guns.'

'Learn guns?'

'Asked me if I knew anyone could teach him marksmanship, all about weapons. Revolver, pistols, rifles, shotguns . . .'

'Who'd you send him to?'

He was panting now but still able to speak clearly between each gasping breath: 'Nobody. Guns aren't my thing. But you know what I think? I think he was one of these guys reads *Soldier of Fortune*. Gets caught up in the fantasy. Wants to be a mercenary. He sure was preparing for a war.'

'Didn't it worry you to be helping someone like that?'

'Not as long as he paid for his lessons.'

She opened the door, hesitated, watching him. 'You have a counter on that contraption?'

'Yeah.'

'What floor are you on?'

'Tenth,' Eddie said, the word distorted as he spoke it on a deep exhalation. The next time he breathed out, he also issued a whoop of pleasure along with his wind. 'Jesus, I have legs of stone, fuckin' granite, I think I could get a man in a scissor hold, crack him in half with my legs. You put that in your article, OK? I could crack a guy clean in half.'

Holly left, closing the door softly behind her.

In the main room, the martial-arts class was even more active than when she had entered. The current exercise involved a group attempt to gang up on their Korean instructor, but he was blocking and throwing and whirling and leaping like a dervish, dealing with them as fast as they came at him.

The brunette had removed her silvery jewelry. She had changed into Reeboks, looser shorts, a different T-shirt, and a bra. Now she was doing stretching exercises in front of the reception counter.

'One o'clock,' she explained to Holly. 'My lunch hour. I always run four or five miles instead of eating. Bye.' She jogged to the door, pushed through it into the warm August day, and sprinted out of sight along the front of the shopping center.

Holly went outside, too, and stood for a moment in the lovely sunshine, newly aware of how many of the shoppers, coming to and going from their cars, were in good physical shape. Having moved to the northwest almost a year and a half ago, she had forgotten how health-conscious many southern Californians were – and how aware of their appearance. Per capita, Orange County had a lot fewer jowls, love handles, spare tires, pot guts, and pear-shaped bottoms than Portland.

Looking good and feeling good were imperatives of the southern-California lifestyle. It was one of the things she loved about the place. It was also one of the things she hated about it.

She went next door to the bakery for lunch. From the display cases, she selected a chocolate éclair, a cream brulée tart with kiwi on top, a piece of white-chocolate macadamia-nut cheesecake with Oreo-crumb crust, a cinnamon wheel, and a slice of orange roulade. 'And a Diet Coke,' she told the clerk.

She carried her tray to a table near a window, where she could watch the passing parade of taut, tanned bodies in summer gear. The pastries were wonderful. She ate a little of this, now a little of that, savoring each bite, intending to polish off every crumb.

After a while she realized someone was watching her. Two tables away, a heavyset woman, about thirty-five, was staring with a mixture of disbelief and envy; she only had one miserable fruit tart, a bakery junkie's equivalent of a Nutrisystem multi-grain cracker.

Feeling both a need to explain herself and a certain sympathy, Holly said, 'I wish I wasn't doing this, but I can't help it. If I can't do anything else, then I always binge when I'm horny.'

The heavyset woman nodded. 'Me too.'

*　　*　　*

She drove to Ironheart's place on Bougainvillea Way. She knew enough about him now to risk approaching him, and that was what she intended to do. But instead of pulling into his driveway, she cruised slowly past the house again.

Instinct told her that the time was not right. The portrait of him that she had constructed only *seemed* to be complete. There was a hole in it somewhere. She sensed that it would be dangerous to proceed before that hole had been painted in.

She returned to the motel and spent the rest of the afternoon and early evening sitting by the window in her room, drinking Alka Seltzer, then Diet 7-UP, staring out at the jewel-blue pool in the middle of the lushly landscaped courtyard, and thinking. Thinking.

OK, she told herself, the story to date. Ironheart is a man with a sadness at his core, probably because of being orphaned when he was only ten. Let's say he's spent a lot of his life brooding about death, especially about the injustice of premature death. He dedicates his life to teaching and helping kids, maybe because no one was there for *him* when he was a boy and had to cope with the deaths of his mother and father. Then Larry Kakonis commits suicide. Ironheart is shattered, feels he should have been able to prevent it. The boy's death brings to the surface all of Ironheart's buried rage: rage at fate, destiny, the biological fragility of the human species – rage at God. In a state of severe mental distress bordering on outright imbalance, he decides to make himself over into Rambo and *do* something to fight back at fate, which is a weird response at best, absolutely nuts at worst. With weight lifting, aerobic endurance training, and Tae Kwon Do, he turns himself into a fighting machine. He learns to drive like a stuntman. He becomes knowledgeable in the use of all manner of guns. He's ready. Just one more thing. He teaches himself to be a clairvoyant, so he can win the lottery and be independently wealthy, making it possible to devote himself to his crusade – and so he can know just *when* a premature death is about to occur.

That was where it all fell apart. You could go to a place like Dojo to learn martial arts, but the Yellow Pages had no listing for schools of clairvoyance. Where the hell had he gotten his psychic power?

She considered the question from every imaginable angle. She wasn't trying to brainstorm an answer, only figure out an approach to researching possible explanations. But magic was magic. There was no way to research it.

She began to feel as though she was employed by a sleazy tabloid, not as a reporter but as a concocter of pieces about space aliens living under Cleveland, half-gorilla and half-human babies born to amoral female zookeepers, and inexplicable rains of frogs and chickens in Tajikistan. But, damn it, the hard facts were that Jim Ironheart had saved fourteen people from death, in every corner of the country, always at the penultimate moment, with miraculous foresight.

By eight o'clock, she had the urge to pound her head against the table, the wall, the concrete decking around the pool outside, against anything hard enough to crack her mental block and drive understanding into her. She decided that it was time to stop thinking, and go to dinner.

She ate in the motel coffeeshop again – just broiled chicken and a salad to atone for lunch at the bakery. She tried to be interested in the other customers, do a little people-watching. But she could not stop thinking about Ironheart and his sorcery.

He dominated her thoughts later, as well, when she was lying in bed, trying to sleep. Staring at the shadows on the ceiling, cast by the landscape lighting outside and the half-open Levolor blinds on the window, she was honest enough with herself to admit he fascinated her on other than professional levels. He was the most important story of her career, yes, true. And, yes, he was so mysterious that he would have intrigued anyone, reporter or not. But she was also drawn to him because she had been alone a long time, loneliness had carved an emptiness in her, and Jim Ironheart was the most appealing man she had met in ages.

Which was insane.

Because maybe *he* was insane.

She was not one of those women who chased after men who were all wrong for her, subconsciously seeking to be used, hurt, and abandoned. She was picky when it came to men. That was why she was alone, for God's sake. Few men measured up to her standards.

Sure. Picky, she thought sarcastically. That's why you've got this lech for a guy who has delusions of being Superman without the tights and cape. Get real, Thorne. Jesus.

Entertaining romantic fantasies about James Ironheart was shortsighted, irresponsible, futile, and just plain stupid.

But those *eyes*.

Holly fell asleep with an image of his face drifting in her mind, watching over her as if it were a portrait on a giant banner, rippling gently against a cerulean sky. His eyes were even bluer than that celestial backdrop.

In time she found herself in the dream of blindness again. The circular room. Wooden floor. Scent of damp limestone. Rain drumming on the roof. Rhythmic creaking. *Whoosh*. Something was coming for her, a part of the darkness that had somehow come alive, a monstrous presence that she could neither hear nor see but could feel. The Enemy. *Whoosh*. It was closing in relentlessly, hostile and savage, radiating cold the way a furnace radiated heat. *Whoosh*. She was grateful that she was blind, because she knew the thing's appearance was so alien, so terrifying, that just the sight of it would kill her. *Whoosh*. Something touched her. A moist, icy tendril. At the base of her neck. A pencil-thin tentacle. She cried out, and the tip of the probe bored into her neck, pierced the base of her skull—

Whoosh.

With a soft cry of terror, she woke. No disorientation. She knew immediately where she was: the motel, Laguna Hills.

Whoosh.

The sound of the dream was still with her. A great blade slicing through the air. But it was not a dream sound. It was real. And the room was as cold as the pitch-black place in the nightmare. As if weighted down by a heart swollen with terror, she tried to move, could not. She smelled damp limestone. From below her, as if there were vast rooms under the motel, came a soft rumbling sound of – she somehow knew – large stone wheels grinding against each other.

Whoosh.

Something unspeakable was still squirming along the back of her neck, writhing sinuously within her skull, a hideous parasite that had chosen her for a host, worming its way into her, going to lay its eggs in her brain. But she could not move.

Whoosh.

She could see nothing but bars of pale, pale light against part of the black ceiling, where the moonsoft glow of landscape lighting projected the image of the windowblind slats. She desperately wanted more light.

Whoosh.

She was making pathetic whimpers of terror, and she so thoroughly despised herself for her weakness that she was finally able to shatter her paralysis. Gasping, she sat up. Clawed at the back of her neck, trying to tear off the oily, frigid, wormlike probe. Nothing there. Nothing. Swung her legs over the edge of the bed. Fumbled for the lamp. Almost knocked it over. Found the switch. Light.

Whoosh.

She sprang off the bed. Felt the back of her head again. Her neck. Between her shoulderblades. Nothing. Nothing there. Yet she *felt* it.

Whoosh.

She was over the edge of hysteria and unable to return, making queer little animal sounds of fear and desperation. Out of the corner of her eye, she saw movement. Swung around. The wall behind the bed. Sweating. Glistening. The entire wall bulged toward her, as if it were a membrane against which a great and terrible mass was pressing insistently. It throbbed repulsively, like an enormous internal organ in the exposed and steaming guts of a prehistoric behemoth.

Whoosh.

She backed away from the wet, malignantly animated wall. Turned. Ran. Had to get out. Fast. The Enemy. It was coming. Had followed her. Out of the dream. The door. Locked. Deadbolt. Disengaged it. Hands shaking. The Enemy. Coming. Brass security chain. Rattled it free. Door. Jerked it open. Something was on the threshold, filling the doorway, bigger than she was, something beyond human experience, simultaneously insectile and arachnoid and reptilian, squirming and jittering, a tangled mass of spider legs and antennae and serpentine coils and roachlike mandibles and multifaceted eyes and rattlesnake fangs and claws, a thousand nightmares rolled into one, but she was *awake*. It burst through the door, seized her, pain exploding from her sides where its talons tore at her, and she screamed—

—a night breeze.

That was the only thing coming through the open door. A soft, summery night breeze.

Holly stood in the doorway, shuddering and gasping for breath, looking out in astonishment at the concrete promenade of the motel. Lacy queen palms, Australian tree ferns, and other greenery swayed sensuously under the caress of the tropical zephyr. The surface of the swimming pool rippled gently, creating countless ever-changing facets, refracting the pool-bottom lights, so it seemed as if there was not a body of water in the middle of the courtyard but a hole filled with a pirate's treasure of polished sapphires.

The creature that had attacked her was gone as if it had never existed. It had not scuttled away or scurried up some web; it had simply evaporated in an instant.

She no longer felt the icy, squirming tendril on the back of her neck or inside her skull.

A couple of other guests had come out of rooms farther along the promenade, evidently to investigate her scream.

Holly stepped back from the threshold. She did not want to attract their attention now.

She glanced over her shoulder. The wall behind the bed was only a wall again.

The clock built into the nightstand showed 5:08 a.m.

She eased the door shut, and suddenly she had to lean against it, because all the strength went out of her legs.

Instead of being relieved that the strange ordeal had ended, she was shattered. She hugged herself and shivered so hard, her teeth chattered. She began to cry softly, not from fear of the experience, concern for her current safety, or concern about her sanity, but from a profound sense of having been totally violated. Briefly but for too long, she had been helpless, victimized, enslaved by terror, controlled by an entity beyond her understanding. She'd been psychologically raped. Something needful had overpowered her, forced its way into her, denying her free will; though gone now, it had left traces of itself within her, a residue that stained her mind, her soul.

Just a dream, she told herself encouragingly.

But it had not been a dream when she sat up in bed and snapped on the lamp. The nightmare had followed her into the waking world.

Just a dream, don't make so much of it, get control of yourself, she thought, struggling to regain her equanimity. You dreamed you were in that lightless place, then you *dreamed* that you sat up in bed and turned on the light, then in your *dream* you saw the wall bulging and ran for the door. But you were only sleepwalking, you were still asleep when you pulled the door open, still asleep when you saw the boogeyman and screamed, which was when you finally woke up for real, screamed yourself awake.

She wanted to believe that explanation, but it was too pat to be credible. No nightmare she'd ever known had been that elaborate in its texture and detail. Besides, she never sleepwalked.

Something real had been reaching for her. Maybe not the insect-reptile-spider thing in the doorway. Maybe that was only an image in which another entity clad itself to frighten her. But something had been pushing through to this world from . . .

From where?

It didn't matter where. From out there. From beyond. And it almost got her.

No. That was ridiculous. Tabloid stuff. Even the *National Enquirer* didn't publish trash that trashy any more. I was MIND-RAPED BY A BEAST FROM BEYOND. Crap like that was three steps below CHER ADMITS BEING SPACE ALIEN, two steps below JESUS SPEAKS TO NUN FROM INSIDE A MICRO-WAVE, and even a full step below ELVIS HAD BRAIN TRANS-PLANTED, LIVES NOW AS ROSEANNE BARR.

The more foolish she felt for entertaining such thoughts, the calmer she became. Dealing with the experience was easier if she could believe that it was all a product of her overactive imagination, which had been unreasonably stimulated by the admittedly fantastic Ironheart case.

Finally she was able to stand on her own, without leaning on the door. She relocked the deadbolt, re-engaged the security chain.

As she stepped away from the door, she became aware of a hot, stinging pain in her left side. It wasn't serious, but it made her wince, and she realized that a similar but lesser pain sizzled in her right side as well.

She took hold of her T-shirt to lift it and look at herself – and discovered that the fabric was slashed. Three places on the left side. Two on the right. It was spotted with blood.

With renewed dread, Holly went into the bathroom and switched on the harsh fluorescent light. She stood in front of the mirror, hesitated, then pulled the torn T-shirt over her head.

A thin flow of blood seeped down her left flank from three shallow gashes. The first laceration was just under her breast, and the others were spaced at two-inch intervals. Two scratches blazed on her right side, though they were not as deep as those on the left and were not bleeding freely.

The claws.

*   *   *

Jim threw up in the toilet, flushed it, then rinsed his mouth twice with mint-flavored Listerine.

The face in the mirror was the most troubled he had ever seen. He had to look away from the reflection of his own eyes.

He leaned against the sink. For at least the thousandth time in the past year, he wondered what in God's name was happening to him.

In his sleep he had gone to the windmill again. Never before had the same nightmare troubled him two nights in a row. Usually, weeks passed between reoccurrences.

Worse, there had been an unsettling new element – more than just the rain on the narrow windows, the lambent flame of the candle and the dancing shadows it produced, the sound of the big sails turning outside, the low rumble of the millstones below, and an inexplicable pall of fear. This time he'd been aware of a malevolent presence, out of sight but drawing nearer by the second, so evil and alien that he could not even imagine its form or full intentions. He had expected it to burst out of the limestone wall, erupt through the plank floor, or explode in upon him from the heavy timbered door at the head of the mill stairs. He had been unable to decide which way to run. Finally he had yanked open the door – and awakened with a scream. If anything had been there, he could not remember what it had looked like.

Regardless of the appearance it might have had, Jim knew what to call it: the enemy. Except that now he thought of it with a capital T and a capital E. The Enemy. The amorphous beast that haunted many of his other nightmares had found its way into the windmill dream, where it had never terrorized him before.

Crazy as it seemed, he sensed that the creature was not merely a fantasy spawned by his subconscious while he slept. It was as real as he was himself. Sooner or later it would cross the barrier between the world of dreams and the waking world as easily as it had crossed the barrier between different nightmares.

•4•

Holly never considered going back to bed. She knew she would not sleep again for many hours, until she was so exhausted that she would be unable to keep her eyes open no matter how much strong black coffee she drank. Sleep had ceased to be a sanctuary. It was, instead, a source of danger, a highway to hell or somewhere worse, along which she might encounter an inhuman traveler.

That made her angry. Everyone needed and deserved the refuge of sleep.

As dawn came, she took a long shower, carefully but diligently scrubbing the shallow lacerations on her sides, although the soap and hot water stung the open flesh. She worried that she would develop an infection as strange as the briefly glimpsed monstrosity that had inflicted her wounds.

That sharpened her anger.

By nature, she was a good Girl Scout, always prepared for any eventuality. When traveling, she carried a few first-aid supplies in the same kit with her Lady Remington shaver: iodine, gauze pads, adhesive tape, Band-Aids, a small aerosol can of Bactine, and a tube of ointment that was useful for soothing minor burns. After toweling off from the shower, she sat naked on the edge of the bed, sprayed Bactine on her wounds, then daubed at them with iodine.

She had become a reporter, in part, because as a younger woman she had believed that journalism had the power to explain the world, to make sense of events that sometimes seemed chaotic and meaningless. More than a decade of newspaper employment had shaken her conviction that the human experience *could* be explained all or even most of the time. But she still kept a well-ordered desk, meticulously arranged files, and neat story notes. In her closets at home, her clothes were arranged according to season, then according to the occasion (formal, semi-formal, informal), then by color. If life insisted on being chaotic, and if journalism had failed her as a tool for bringing order to the world, at least she could depend on routine and habit to create a personal pocket universe of stability, however fragile, beyond which the disorder and tumult of life were kept at bay.

The iodine stung.

She was angrier. Seething.

The shower disturbed the clots that had coagulated in the deeper scratches on her left side. She was bleeding slightly again. She sat quietly on the edge of the bed for a while, holding a wad of Kleenex against the wounds, until the lacerations were no longer oozing.

By the time Holly had dressed in tan jeans and an emerald-green blouse, it was seven-thirty.

She already knew how she was going to start the day, and nothing could distract her from her plans. She had no appetite whatsoever for breakfast. When she stepped outside, she discovered that the morning was cloudless and unusually temperate even for Orange County, but the sublime weather had no mellowing influence on her and did not tempt her to pause even for a moment to relish the early sun on her face. She drove the rental car across the parking lot, out to the street, and headed toward Laguna Niguel. She was going to ring James Ironheart's doorbell and demand a lot of answers.

She wanted his full story, the explanation of how he could know when people were about to die and why he took such extreme risks to save total strangers. But she also wanted to know why last night's bad dream had become real, how and why her bedroom wall had begun to glisten and throb like flesh, and what manner of creature had popped out of her nightmare and seized her in talons formed of something more substantial than dreamstuff.

She was convinced that he would have the answers. Last night, for only the second time in her thirty-three years, she'd encountered the unknown, been sideswiped by the supernatural. The first time had been on 12 August, when Ironheart had miraculously saved Billy Jenkins from being mowed down by a truck in front of the McAlbury School – although she hadn't realized until later that he had stepped right out of the Twilight Zone. Though she was willing to cop to a lot of faults, stupidity was not one of them. Anyone but a fool could see that both collisions with the paranormal, Ironheart and the nightmare-made-real, were related.

She was more than merely angry. She was pissed.

As she cruised down Crown Valley Parkway, she realized that her anger sprang, in part, from the discovery that her big, career-making story was turning out not to be strictly about amazement and wonder and courage and hope and triumph, as she had anticipated. Like the vast majority of articles that had appeared on the front pages of newspapers since the invention of the printing press, this story had a dark side.

*   *   *

Jim had showered and dressed for church. He did not regularly attend Sunday Mass any more, or the services of any other of the religions to which he had been sporadically committed over the years. But having been in the control of a higher power since at least last May, when he had flown to Florida to save the lives of Sam and Emily Newsome, he was disposed to think about God more than usual. And since Father Geary had told him about the stigmata that had marked his body while he lay unconscious on the floor of Our Lady of the Desert, less than a week ago, he had felt the tidal pull of Catholicism for the first time in a couple of years. He didn't actually expect that the mystery of recent events would be cleared up by answers he would find in church – but he could hope.

As he plucked his car keys off the pegboard on the kitchen wall beside the door to the garage, he heard himself say, 'Life line.' Immediately, his plans for the day were changed. He froze, not sure what to do. Then the familiar feeling of being a marionette overcame him, and he hung the keys back on the pegboard.

He returned to the bedroom and stripped out of his loafers, gray slacks, dark-blue sportcoat, and white shirt. He dressed in chinos and a blousy Hawaiian shirt, which he wore over his pants in order to be as unhampered as possible by his clothing.

He needed to stay loose, flexible. He had no idea *why* looseness and flexibility were desirable for what lay ahead, but he felt the need just the same.

Sitting on the floor in front of the closet, he selected a pair of shoes – the most comfortable, broken-in pair of Rockports that he owned. He tied them securely but not too tightly. He stood up and tested the fit. Good.

He reached for the suitcase on the top shelf, then hesitated. He was not sure that he would require luggage. A few seconds later, he *knew* that he would be traveling light. He slid the closet door shut without taking down the bag.

No luggage usually meant that his destination would be within driving distance and that the round-trip, including the time needed to perform whatever work was expected of him, would take no more than twenty-four hours. But as he turned away from the closet, he surprised himself by saying, 'Airport.' Of course, there were a lot of places to which he could fly round-trip in a single day.

He picked his wallet off the dresser, waited to see if he felt compelled to put it down again, and finally slipped it into his hip pocket. Evidently he would need not only money but ID – or at least he would not risk exposure by carrying it.

As he walked to the kitchen again and took the car keys off the pegboard, fear played through him, although not as strongly as it had the last time he had left his house on a mission. That day he had been 'told' to steal a car so it could not be traced to him, and to drive into the Mojave Desert. This time he might encounter adversaries even more formidable than the two men in the Roadking, but he was not as worried as he'd been before. He knew he could die. Being the instrument of a higher power came with no guarantees of immortality; he was still only a man whose flesh could be torn, whose bones could be broken, and whose heart could be stopped instantly with a well-placed bullet. The amelioration of his fear was attributable solely to his somewhat mystical journey on the Harley, two days with Father Geary, the report of the stigmata that had appeared on him, and the resulting conviction that a divine hand was at work in all of this.

*　　*　　*

Holly was on Bougainvillea Way, a block from Ironheart's house, when a dark-green Ford backed out of his driveway. She did not know what kind of car he drove, but since he lived alone, she assumed the Ford had to be his.

She speeded up, half intending to swing around him, angle across his bow, force him to stop, and confront him right in the street. Then she slowed down again, figuring discretion was seldom a fatal error. She might as well see where he was going, what he was up to.

As she passed his house, the automatic garage door was rolling down. Just before it closed, she was able to see that no other car was in there. The man in the Ford had to be Ironheart.

Because she had never been assigned to stories about paranoid drug lords or bent politicians or corrupt businessmen, Holly was not expert at tailing a surveillance subject through traffic. The skills and techniques of clandestine operations were not necessary when you wrote exclusively about Timber Trophies, performance artists in radiation suits who juggled live mice on the steps of city hall and called it 'art,' and pie-eating contests. She was also mindful of the fact that Ironheart had taken a two-week course in aggressive driving at a special school in Marin County; if he knew how to handle a car well enough to shake off pursuing terrorists, he would leave her in the dust about thirty seconds after he realized she was following him.

She hung as far back as she dared. Fortunately, the Sunday-morning traffic was heavy enough to allow her to hide behind other cars. But it was light enough so she didn't have to worry that the lanes would suddenly clog up between her and Ironheart, cutting her off until he disappeared from sight.

He drove east on Crown Valley Parkway to Interstate 5, then north toward Los Angeles on 405.

By the time they had passed the clustered highrises around South Coast Plaza, the primary shopping and office center for the two million people in the Orange County metroplex, Holly's mood was better than it had been. She was proving to be adept at mobile surveillance, staying from two to six cars in back of Ironheart but always close enough to follow if he abruptly swung on to an exit ramp. Her anger was tempered by the pleasure she took in her skillful pursuit. Now and then she even found herself admiring the clarity of the blue sky and the profusely flowering pink and white oleanders that flanked the freeway in some places.

Passing Long Beach, however, she began to worry that she was going to spend the whole day on the road with him, only to discover that wherever he was going had nothing to do with the enigma that concerned her. Even a self-appointed superhero with clairvoyant powers might just spend a day taking in a theater matinee, doing nothing more dangerous than eating Szechwan Chinese with the chef's hottest mustard.

She began to wonder, as well, if he might become aware of her through his psychic powers. Sensing her a few cars back seemed a lot easier than foreseeing the approaching death of a small boy in Boston. On the other hand, maybe clairvoyance was an inconstant power, something he could not turn on and off at will, and maybe it only worked on the big things, zapping him with either visions of danger and destruction and death – or no visions at all. Which made sense in a way. It would probably drive you insane to have psychic visions that told you in advance whether you were going to enjoy a particular movie, have a good dinner, or get a bad case of gas and the bloats from that garlicky angel-hair pasta that you were enjoying so much. Nevertheless, she dropped back a little farther, putting one more car between them.

When Ironheart left the freeway at the exit for Los Angeles International Airport, Holly became excited. Perhaps he was only meeting someone on an incoming flight. But it was more likely that he was catching a plane out, embarking on one of his timely rescue missions, just as he had flown to Portland on 12 August, nearly two weeks ago. Holly was not prepared to travel; she didn't even have a change of clothes. However, she had cash and credit cards to handle expenses, and she could buy a fresh blouse anywhere. The prospect of tailing him all the way to the scene of the action tantalized her. Ultimately, when she wrote about him, she would be able to do so with more authority if she had been an eye-witness at *two* of his rescues.

She almost lost her nerve when he swung off the airport service loop into a parking garage, because there was no longer a convenient car between them to mask her presence. But the alternative was to drive on, park in another garage, and lose him. She hung back only as far as she dared and took a ticket from the dispenser seconds after he did.

Ironheart found an empty slot halfway along a row on the third level, and Holly pulled in ten spaces past him. She slumped down in her seat a little and remained in her car, giving him a headstart so there was less chance of him glancing back and seeing her.

She almost waited too long. When she got out of her car, she was barely in time to glimpse him as he turned right and disappeared around a wall at the bottom of the ramp.

She hurried after him. The soft, flat *slap-slap* of her footsteps echoed hollowly off the low concrete ceiling. At the base of the ramp, when she turned the corner, she saw him enter the stairwell. By the time she passed through that door after him, she heard him descend the final flight and open the door below.

Thanks to his colorful Hawaiian shirt, she was able to stay well behind him, mingling with other travelers, as he crossed the service road and entered the United Airlines terminal. She hoped they weren't going to Hawaii. Researching a story without the financial backing of the newspaper was expensive enough. If Ironheart was going to save someone's life today, she hoped he would do it in San Diego instead of Honolulu.

In the terminal, she hung back behind a group of tall Swedes using them for cover, while Ironheart stood for a while at a bank of monitors, studying the schedule of upcoming departures. Judging by the frown on his face, he didn't see the flight he wanted. Or maybe he simply didn't yet *know* which flight he wanted. Perhaps his premonitions did not come to him full-blown; he might have to work at them, nurse them along, and he might not know exactly where he was going or whose life he would be saving until he got there.

After a few minutes, he turned from the monitors and strode along the concourse to the ticket counter. Holly continued to stay.

well back of him, watching from a distance, until she realized that she would not know his destination unless she was close enough to hear him give it to the clerk. Reluctantly she closed the gap.

She could wait until he had bought the ticket, of course, follow him to see which gate he waited at, then book herself on the same flight. But what if the plane took off while she was dashing through the endless hallways of the terminal? She could also try to cajole the clerk into telling her what flight Ironheart had taken by claiming to have picked up a credit card he'd dropped. But the airline might offer to return it to him; or if they found her story suspicious, they might even call security guards.

In the line at the ticket counter, she dared to close within one person of Ironheart. The only traveler between them was a burly, big-bellied man who looked like an NFL linebacker gone to seed; he had mildly offensive body odor, but he provided considerable cover, for which she was grateful.

The short line moved quickly. When Ironheart stepped up to the counter, Holly eased out around the fat man and strained forward to hear whatever destination was mentioned.

The public-address system inconveniently brought forth a woman's soft, sensuous, yet zombie-like voice, announcing the discovery of a lost child. At the same time, a noisy group of New Yorkers went past, complaining about the perceived phoniness of California's have-a-nice-day service ethic, apparently homesick for hostility. Ironheart's words were drowned out.

Holly inched nearer to him.

The fat man frowned down at her, evidently suspecting her of attempted line-jumping. She smiled at him in such a way as to assure him that she had no evil intentions and that she knew he was large enough to squash her like a bug.

If Ironheart glanced back now, he would look directly into her face. She held her breath, heard the clerk say, '. . . O'Hare Airport in Chicago, leaving in twenty minutes . . .' and slipped back behind the fat man, who looked over his shoulder to frown down at her again.

She wondered why they had come to LAX for a flight to Chicago. She was pretty sure there were plenty of connections to O'Hare from John Wayne in Orange County. Well . . . though Chicago was farther than San Diego, it was preferable to – and cheaper than – Hawaii.

Ironheart paid for his ticket and hurried off in search of his gate without glancing in Holly's direction.

Some psychic, she thought.

She was pleased with herself.

112

When she reached the counter, she presented a credit card and asked for a seat on the same flight to Chicago. For a moment she had the terrible feeling that the clerk would say the plane was fully booked. But there were seats left, and she got her ticket.

The departure lounge at the gate was nearly empty. Boarding of the flight had virtually been completed. Ironheart was nowhere in sight.

On the way along the tunnel-like boarding gate to the door of the aircraft, she began to worry that he would see her when she had to walk down the aisle to her seat. She could pretend not to notice him, or pretend not to recognize him if he approached her. But she doubted that he would believe her presence on his flight was sheer coincidence. An hour and a half ago, she'd been in a rush to confront him. Now she wanted nothing more than to *avoid* confrontation. If he saw her, he would abort his trip; she might never get another chance to be present at one of his last-minute rescues.

The plane was a wide-body DC-10 with two aisles. Each row of nine seats was divided into three sections: two by the window on the port side, five down the center, two by the window on the starboard side. Holly was assigned to row twenty-three, seat H, which was on the starboard flank, one seat removed from the window. As she headed down the aisle, she scanned the faces of her fellow passengers, hoping she wouldn't lock eyes with Jim Ironheart. In fact, she would rather not see him at all during the flight, and worry about catching sight of him again at O'Hare. The DC-10 was an immense aircraft. Though a number of seats were empty, more than two hundred and fifty people were on board. She and Ironheart might very well fly around the world together without bumping into each other; getting through the few hours to Chicago should be a cinch.

Then she saw him. He was sitting in the five-wide middle section of row sixteen, the port-aisle seat, on the other side of the plane. He was paging through an issue of the airline's magazine, and she prayed that he would not look up until she was past him. Though she had to step aside for a flight attendant escorting a small boy who was flying alone, her prayer was answered. Ironheart's head remained bowed over the publication until she was past him. She reached 23-H and sat down, sighing with relief. Even if he went to the restroom, or just got up to stretch his legs, he would probably never have any reason to come around to the starboard aisle. Perfect.

She glanced at the man in the window seat beside her. He was in his early thirties, tanned, fit, and intense. He was wearing a dark-blue business suit, white shirt, and tie even on a Sunday flight. His brow was as furrowed as his suit was well-pressed, and he was working on a laptop computer. He was wearing headphones, listening to music or pretending to, in order to discourage conversation, and he gave her a cool smile calculated to do the same.

That was fine with her. Like a lot of reporters, she was not garrulous by nature. Her job required her to be a good listener, not necessarily a good talker. She was content to pass the trip with the airline's magazine and her own Byzantine thoughts.

*   *   *

Two hours into the flight, Jim still had no idea where he was expected to go when he got off the plane at O'Hare. He was not concerned about it, however, because he had learned to be patient. The revelation always came, sooner or later.

Nothing in the airline's magazine was of interest to him, and the in-flight movie sounded as if it were about as much fun as a vacation in a Soviet prison. The two seats to the right of him were empty, so he was not required to make nice conversation with a stranger. He tilted his seat slightly, folded his hands on his stomach, closed his eyes, and passed the time – between the flight attendants' inquiries about his appetite and comfort – by brooding about the windmill dream, puzzling out what significance it had, if any.

That was what he *tried* to brood about, anyway. But for some curious reason, his mind wandered to Holly Thorne, the reporter.

Hell, now he was being disingenuous, because he knew perfectly well why she had been drifting in and out of his thoughts ever since he had met her. She was a treat for the eyes. She was intelligent, too; one look at her, and you knew about a million gears were spinning in her head, all meshing perfectly, well-oiled, quiet and productive.

And she had a sense of humor. He would give anything to share his days and his long, dream-troubled nights with a woman like that. Laughter was usually a function of sharing – an observation, a joke, a moment. You didn't laugh a lot when you were always alone; and if you did, that probably meant you should make arrangements for a long stay in a resort with padded walls.

He had never been smooth with women, so he had often been without them. And he had to admit, even before this recent strangeness had begun, he was sometimes difficult to live with. Not depressive exactly but too aware that death was life's companion.

Too inclined to brood about the coming darkness. Too slow to seize the moment and succumb to pleasure. If . . .

He opened his eyes and sat up straighter in his seat, because suddenly he received the revelation that he had been expecting. Or part of it, at least. He still did not know what was going to happen in Chicago, but he knew the names of the people whose lives he was expected to save: Christine and Casey Dubrovek.

To his surprise, he realized they were on this plane with him – which led him to suspect that the trouble might come in the terminal at O'Hare, or at least soon after touchdown. Otherwise he would not have crossed their path so early. Usually, he encountered the people he saved only minutes before their lives were thrown into jeopardy.

Compelled by those forces that had been guiding him periodically since last May, he got up, headed to the front of the plane, crossed over to the starboard side, and started down that aisle. He had no idea what he was doing until he stopped at row twenty-two and looked down at the mother and child in seats H and J. The woman was in her late twenties; she had a sweet face, not beautiful but gentle and pretty. The child was five or six years old.

The woman looked up at him curiously, and Jim heard himself say, 'Mrs Dubrovek?'

She blinked in surprise. 'I'm sorry . . . do I know you?'

'No, but Ed told me you were taking this flight and asked me to look you up.' When he spoke that name, he knew Ed was her husband, though he had no idea where that knowledge had come from. He squatted down beside her seat and gave his best smile. 'I'm Steve Harkman. Ed's in sales, I'm in advertising, so we drive each other nuts in about a dozen meetings a week.'

Christine Dubrovek's madonna face brightened. 'Oh, yes, he's spoken about you. You only joined the company, what, a month ago?'

'Six weeks now,' Jim said, flowing with it, confident the right answers would pour out of him even if he didn't know what in the hell they were. 'And this must be Casey.'

The little girl was in the seat by the window. She raised her head, shifting her attention from a pop-up storybook. 'I'm gonna be six tomorrow, it's my birthday, and we're gonna visit grandpop and grandma. They're real old, but they're nice.'

He laughed and said, 'I'll bet they're sure proud to have a granddaughter cute as you.'

*   *   *

When Holly saw him coming along the starboard aisle, she was so startled that she almost popped out of her seat. At first she thought he was looking straight at her. She had the urge to start blurting out a confession – 'yes, all right, I've been following you, checking up on you, invading your privacy with a vengeance' – even before he reached her. She knew precious few other reporters who would have felt guilty about probing into his life, but she couldn't seem to eliminate that streak of decency that had interfered with her career advancement ever since she'd gotten her journalism degree. It almost wrecked everything for her again – until she realized he was looking not at her but at the brunette immediately in front of her. Holly swallowed hard, and slid down a few inches in her seat instead of leaping up in a frenzy of confession. She picked up the airline's magazine, which she'd previously discarded; slowly, deliberately she opened it to cover her face, afraid that too quick a move would draw his attention before she had concealed herself behind those glossy pages.

The magazine blocked her view of him, but she could hear every word he was saying and most of the woman's responses. She listened to him identify himself as Steve Harkman, a company ad executive, and wondered what his charade was all about.

She dared to tilt her head far enough to peek around the magazine with one eye. Ironheart was hunkered down in the aisle beside the woman's seat, so close that Holly could have spit on him, although she was no more practiced at target-spitting than she was at clandestine surveillance.

She realized her hands were trembling, making the magazine rattle softly. She untilted her head, stared at the pages in front of her, and concentrated on being calm.

*   *   *

'How on earth did you recognize me?' Christine Dubrovek asked.

'Well, Ed doesn't *quite* paper his office with pictures of you two,' Jim said.

'Oh, that's right,' she said.

'Listen, Mrs Dubrovek—'

'Call me Christine.'

'Thank you. Christine . . . I've got an ulterior motive for coming over here and pestering you like this. According to Ed, you've got a knack for matchmaking.'

That must have been the right thing to say. Already aglow, her sweet face brightened further. 'Well, I do like getting people together if I think they're right for each other, and I've got to admit I've had more than a little success at it.'

'You make matches, Mommy?' Casey Dubrovek asked.

Uncannily in synch with the workings of her six-year-old's mind, Christine said, 'Not the cigarette kind, honey.'

'Oh. Good,' Casey said, then returned to her pop-up storybook.

'The thing is,' Jim said, 'I'm new in Los Angeles, been there only eight weeks, and I'm your classic, original lonely guy. I don't like singles' bars, don't want to buy a gym membership just to meet women, and figure anybody I'd connect with through a computer service has to be as desperate and messed up as I am.'

She laughed. 'You don't look desperate or messed up to me.'

'Excuse me, sir,' a stewardess said with friendly firmness, touching Jim's shoulder, 'but I can't allow you to block the aisle.'

'Oh, sure, yeah,' he said, standing up. 'Just give me a minute.' Then to Christine: 'Listen, this is embarrassing, but I'd really like to talk to you, tell you about myself, what I'm looking for in a woman, and see if maybe you know someone . . .'

'Sure, I'd love that,' Christine said with such enthusiasm that she was surely the reincarnation of either some hillbilly woman who had been a much sought-after troth-finder or a successful *schatchen* from Brooklyn.

'Hey, you know, the two seats next to mine are empty,' he said. 'Maybe you could sit with me the rest of the way . . .'

He expected her to be reluctant to give up window seats, and an inexplicable twist of anxiety knotted his stomach while he waited for her response.

But she hesitated for only a second or two. 'Yes, why not.'

The stewardess, still hovering near them, nodded her approval.

To Jim, Christine said, 'I thought Casey would like the scenery from way up here, but she doesn't seem to care much. Besides, we're almost at the back of the wing, and it blocks a lot of our view.'

Jim did not understand the reason for the wave of relief that swept through him when he secured her agreement to move, but a lot of things mystified him these days. 'Good, great. Thank you, Christine.'

As he stepped back to let Christine Dubrovek get up, he noticed the passenger in the seat behind her. The poor woman was evidently terrified of flying. She was holding a copy of *Vis à Vis* in front of her face, trying to take her mind off her fears with a little reading, but her hands were shaking so badly that the magazine rattled continuously.

'Where are you sitting?' Christine asked.

'The other aisle, row sixteen. Come on, I'll show you.'

He lifted her single piece of carry-on luggage while she and Casey gathered up a few other small items, then he led them to the front of the plane and around to the port aisle. Casey entered row sixteen, and her mother followed.

Before Jim settled down himself, something impelled him to look back across the wide-bodied plane to the aerophobic woman whom they had left behind in row twenty-three. She had lowered the magazine. She was watching him. He knew her.

Holly Thorne.

He was stunned.

Christine Dubrovek said, 'Steve?'

Across the plane, the reporter realized that Jim had seen her. She was wide-eyed, frozen. Like a deer caught in car headlights.

'Steve?'

He looked down at Christine and said, 'Uh, excuse me a minute, Christine. Just a minute. I'll be right back. Wait here. OK? Wait right here.'

He went forward and across to the starboard aisle again.

His heart was hammering. His throat was tight with fear. But he didn't know why. He was not afraid of Holly Thorne. He knew at once that her presence was no coincidence, that she had tumbled to his secret and had been following him. But right now he didn't care. Discovery, being unmasked – that was not what frightened him. He had no idea what *was* cranking up his anxiety, but it was escalating to a level at which adrenalin would soon start to squirt out his ears.

As he made his way down the aisle toward the reporter, she started to get up. Then a look of resignation slid across her face, and she sat down again. She was as easy to look at as he remembered, though the skin around her eyes was slightly dark, as if from lack of sleep.

When he arrived at row twenty-three, he said, 'Come on.' He reached for her hand.

She did not give it to him.

'We've got to talk,' he said.

'We can talk here.'

'No, we can't.'

The stewardess who had warned him about blocking the aisle was approaching again.

When Holly would not take his hand, he gripped her by the arm and urged her to get up, hoping she would not force him to yank her out of the seat. The stewardess probably already thought he was some pervert Svengali who was herding up the best-looking women on the flight to surround himself with a harem over there on the port side. Happily, the reporter rose without further protest.

He led her back through the plane to a restroom. It was not occupied, so he pushed her inside. He glanced back, expecting to see the stewardess watching him, but she was attending to another passenger. He followed Holly into the tiny cubicle and pulled the door shut.

She squeezed into the corner, trying to stay as far away from him as possible, but they were still virtually nose to nose.

'I'm not afraid of you,' she said.

'Good. There's no reason to be.'

Vibrations were conducted well by the burnished-steel walls of the lavatory. The deep drone of the engines was somewhat louder there than in the main cabin.

She said, 'What do you want?'

'You've got to do exactly what I tell you.'

She frowned. 'Listen, I—'

'*Exactly* what I tell you, and no arguments, there's no time for arguments,' he said sharply, wondering what the hell he was talking about.

'I know all about your—'

'I don't care what you know. That's not important now.'

She frowned. 'You're shaking like a leaf.'

He was not only shaking but sweating. The lavatory was cool enough, but he could feel beads of sweat forming across his forehead. A thin trickle coursed down his right temple and past the corner of his eye.

Speaking rapidly, he said, 'I want you to come forward in the plane, sit farther front near me, there're a couple of empty seats in that area.'

'But I—'

'You can't stay where you are, back there in row twenty-three, no way.'

She was not a docile woman. She knew her own mind, and she was not used to being told what to do. 'That's my seat. Twenty-three H. You can't strongarm me—'

119

Impatiently, he said, 'If you sit there, you're going to die.'

She looked no more surprised than he felt – which was plenty damn surprised. 'Die? What do you mean?'

'I don't know.' But then unwanted knowledge came to him. 'Oh, Jesus. Oh, my God. We're going down.'

'What?'

'The plane.' Now his heart was racing faster than the turbine blades in the great engines that were keeping them aloft. 'Down. All the way down.'

He saw her incomprehension give way to a dreadful understanding. 'Crash?'

'Yes.'

'When?'

'I don't know. Soon. Beyond row twenty, almost nobody's going to survive.' He did not know what he was going to say until he said it, and as he listened to his own words he was horrified by them. 'There'll be a better survival rate in the first nine rows, but not good, not good at all. You've got to move into my section.'

The aircraft shuddered.

Holly stiffened and looked around fearfully, as if she expected the lavatory walls to crumple in on them.

'Turbulence,' he said. 'Just turbulence. We've got . . . a few minutes yet.'

Evidently she had learned enough about him to have faith in his prediction. She did not express any doubt. 'I don't want to die.'

With an increasing sense of urgency, Jim gripped her by the shoulders. 'That's why you've got to come forward, sit near me. Nobody's going to be killed in rows ten through twenty. There'll be injuries, a few of them serious, but nobody's going to die in that section, and a lot of them are going to walk out of it unhurt. Now, for God's sake, come on.'

He reached for the door handle.

'Wait. You've got to tell the pilot.'

He shook his head. 'It wouldn't help.'

'But maybe there's something he can do, stop it from happening.'

'He wouldn't believe me, and even if he did . . . I don't know what to tell him. We're going down, yeah, but I don't know why. Maybe a mid-air collision, maybe structural failure, maybe there's a bomb aboard – it could be anything.'

'But you're a psychic, you must be able to see more details if you try.'

'If you believe I'm a psychic, you know less about me than you think you do.'

'You've got to try.'

'Oh, lady, I'd try, I'd try like a sonofabitch if it would do any good. But it won't.'

Terror and curiosity fought for control of her face. 'If you're not a psychic – what are you?'

'A tool.'

'Tool?'

'Someone or something uses me.'

The DC-10 shuddered again. They froze, but the aircraft did not take a sudden plunge. It went on as before, its three big engines droning. Just more turbulence.

She grabbed him. 'You can't let all those people die!'

A rope of guilt constricted his chest and knotted his stomach at the implication that the deaths of the others aboard would somehow be his fault.

He said, 'I'm here to save the woman and the girl, no one else.'

'That's horrible.'

Opening the lavatory door, he said, 'I don't like it any more than you do, but that's the way it is.'

She did not let go of his arm but jerked at it angrily. Her green eyes were haunted, probably with her own visions of battered bodies strewn across the earth among smoking chunks of wreckage. She repeated herself, whispering fiercely this time: 'You can't let all those people die.'

Impatiently, he said, 'Either come with me, or die with the rest of them.'

He stepped out of the lavatory, and she followed him, but he did not know whether she was going to accompany him back to his section. He hoped to God she would. He really could not be held responsible for all the other people who would perish, because they would have died even if he had not come aboard; that was their fate, and he had not been sent to alter *their* destinies. He could not save the whole world, and he had to rely on the wisdom of whatever higher power was guiding him. But he most definitely would be responsible for Holly Thorne's death, because she would never have taken the flight if, unwittingly, he had not led her on to it.

As he moved forward along the port aisle, he glanced to his left at the portholes and clear blue sky beyond. He had a too vivid sense of the yawning void under his feet, and his stomach flopped.

When he reached his seat in row sixteen, he dared to look back.

Relief flooded through him at the sight of Holly trailing close.

He pointed to a pair of empty seats immediately behind his and Christine's.

Holly shook her head. 'Only if you'll sit down with me. We have to talk.'

He glanced down at Christine, then at Holly. He was acutely aware of time slipping away like water swirling down a drain. The awful moment of impact was drawing closer. He wanted to pick the reporter up, stuff her into the seat, engage her seatbelt, and lock her in place. But seatbelts didn't have locks.

Unable to conceal his extreme frustration, he spoke to her through gritted teeth. 'My place is with them,' he said, meaning with Christine and Casey Dubrovek.

He had spoken quietly, as had Holly, but other passengers were beginning to look at them.

Christine frowned up at him, craned her neck to look back at Holly, and said, 'Is something wrong, Steve?'

'No. Everything's fine,' he lied.

He glanced at the portholes again. Blue sky. Vast. Empty. How many miles to the earth below?

'You don't look well,' Christine said.

He realized that his face was still sheathed in a greasy film of sweat. 'Just a little warm. Uh, look, I ran into an old friend. Gimme five minutes?'

Christine smiled. 'Sure, sure. I'm still going over a mental list of the most-eligible.'

For a moment he had no idea what the hell she was talking about. Then he remembered that he had asked her to play matchmaker for him. 'Good,' he said. 'Great. I'll be right back, we'll talk.'

He ushered Holly into row seventeen. He took the aisle seat next to her.

On the other side of Holly was a grandmotherly tub of a woman in a flower-print dress, with blue-tinted gray hair in a mass of tight curls. She was sound asleep, snoring softly. A pair of gold-framed eyeglasses, suspended around her neck on a bead chain, rested on her matronly bosom, rising and falling with her steady breathing.

Leaning close to him, keeping her voice so low it could not even carry across the narrow aisle, but speaking with the conviction of an impassioned political orator, Holly said, 'You can't let all those people die.'

'We've been through this,' he said restively, matching her nearly inaudible pitch.

'It's your responsibility—'

'I'm just one man!'

'But one very special man.'

'I'm not God,' he said plaintively.

'Talk to the pilot.'

'Jesus, you're relentless.'

'Warn the pilot,' she whispered.

'He won't believe me.'

'Then warn the passengers.'

'There aren't enough empty seats in this section for all of them to move here.'

She was furious with him, quiet but so intense that he could not look away from her or dismiss what she was saying. She put a hand on his arm, gripping him so tightly that it hurt. 'Damn it, maybe they could do *something* to save themselves.'

'I'd only cause a panic.'

'If you can save more, but you let them die, it's murder,' she whispered insistently, anger flashing in her eyes.

That accusation hit him hard and had something of the effect of a hammer blow to the chest. For a moment he could not draw his breath. When he could speak, his voice broke repeatedly: 'I hate death, people dying, I *hate* it. I want to save people, stop all the suffering, be on the side of life, but I can only do what I can do.'

'Murder,' she repeated.

What she was doing to him was outrageous. He could not carry the load of responsibility she wanted to pile on his shoulders. If he could save the Dubroveks, he would be working two miracles, mother and child spared from the early graves that had been their destinies. But Holly Thorne, in her ignorance about his abilities, was not satisfied with two miracles; she wanted three, four, five, ten, a hundred. He felt as if an enormous weight was bearing down on him, the weight of the whole damned airplane, crushing him into the ground. It was not right of her to put the blame on him; it wasn't fair. If she wanted to blame someone, she should cast her accusations at God, who worked in such mysterious ways that He had ordained the necessity of the plane crash in the first place.

'Murder.' She dug her fingers into his arm even harder.

He could feel anger radiating from her like the heat of the sun reflected off a metal surface. Reflected. Suddenly, he realized that image was too apt to be anything less than Freudian. Her anger over his unwillingness to save everyone on the plane was no greater than his own anger over his inability to do so; her rage was a reflection of his own.

'Murder,' she repeated, evidently aware of the profound effect that accusation had on him.

He looked into her beautiful eyes, and he wanted to hit her, punch her in the face, smash her with all of his strength, knock her unconscious, so she wouldn't put his own thoughts into words. She was too perceptive. He hated her for being *right*.

Instead of hitting her, he got up.

'Where are you going?' she demanded.

'To talk to a flight attendant.'

'About what?'

'You win, OK? You win.'

Making his way toward the back of the plane, Jim looked at the people he passed, chilled by the knowledge that many of them would be dead soon. As his desperation intensified, so did his imagination, and he saw skulls beneath their skin, the glowing images of bones shining through their flesh, for they were the living dead. He was nauseous with fear, not for himself but for them.

The plane bucked and shimmied as if it had driven over a port-hole in the sky. He grabbed at the back of a seat to steady himself. But this was not the big one.

The flight attendants were gathered farther back in the plane, in their work area, preparing to serve the lunch trays that had just come up from the galley. They were a mixed group, men and women, a couple in their twenties and the others as old as fifty-something.

Jim approached the oldest of them. According to the tag she wore, her name was Evelyn.

'I've got to talk to the pilot,' he said, keeping his voice low, although the nearest passengers were well forward of them.

If Evelyn was surprised by his request, she didn't show it. She smiled just as she had been trained to smile. 'I'm sorry, sir, but that isn't possible. Whatever the problem is, I'm sure I can help—'

'Listen, I was in the lavatory, and I heard something, a *wrong* sound,' he lied, 'not the right kind of engine noise.'

Her smile became a little wider but less sincere, and she went into her reassure-the-nervous-traveller mode. 'Well, you see, during flight it's perfectly normal for the pitch of the engines to change as the pilot alters airspeed and—'

'I know that.' He tried to sound like a reasonable man to whom she ought to listen. 'I've flown a lot. This was different.' He lied again: 'I know aircraft engines, I work for McDonnell Douglas. We designed and built the DC-10. I *know* this plane, and what I heard in the lav was *wrong*.'

Her smile faltered, most likely not because she was starting to take his warning seriously but merely because she considered him to be a more inventive aerophobe than most who panicked in mid-flight.

The other flight attendants had paused in their lunch-service preparations and were staring at him, no doubt wondering if he was going to be a problem.

Evelyn said carefully, 'Well, really, everything's functioning well. Aside from some turbulence—'

'It's the tail engine,' he said. That was not another lie. He was receiving a revelation, and he was letting the unknown source of that revelation speak through him. 'The fan assembly is starting to break apart. If the blades tear loose, that's one thing, the pieces can be contained, but if the entire fan-blade assembly shatters, God knows what could happen.'

Because of the specificity of his fear, he did not sound like a typical aerophobic passenger, and all of the flight attendants were staring at him with, if not respect, at least a wary thoughtfulness.

'Everything's fine,' Evelyn said, per training. 'But even if we lost an engine, we can fly on two.'

Jim was excited that the higher power guiding him had evidently decided to give him what he needed to convince these people. Maybe something *could* be done to save everyone on the flight.

Striving to remain calm and impressive, he heard himself saying, 'That engine has forty thousand pounds of thrust, it's a real monster, and if it blows up, it's like a bomb going off. The compressors can back-vent, and those thirty-eight titanium blades, the fan assembly, even pieces of the rotor can explode outward like shrapnel, punching holes in the tail, screwing up the rudders and elevators . . . The whole tail of the plane could disintegrate.'

One of the flight attendants said, 'Maybe somebody should just mention this to Captain Delbaugh.'

Evelyn did not instantly object.

'I know these engines,' Jim said. 'I can explain it to him. You don't have to take me on the flight deck, just let me speak to him on the intercom.'

Evelyn said, 'McDonnell Douglas?'

'Yeah. I've been an engineer there for twelve years,' he lied.

She was now full of doubt about the wisdom of the standard

response she had learned in training. She was almost won over.

With hope blossoming, Jim said, 'Your captain's got to shut down engine number two. If he shuts it down and goes the rest of the way on one and three, we'll make it, all of us, we'll make it alive.'

Evelyn looked at the other flight attendants, and a couple of them nodded. 'I guess it wouldn't hurt if . . .'

'Come on,' Jim said urgently. 'We might not have much time.'

He followed Evelyn out of the attendants' work area and into the starboard aisle in the economy-class section, heading forward.

The plane was rocked by an explosion.

Evelyn was thrown hard to the deck. Jim pitched forward, too, grabbed at a seat to avoid falling atop the woman, overcompensated and fell to one side instead, against a passenger, then to the floor, as the plane started to shimmy. He heard lunch trays still crashing to the deck behind him, people crying out in surprise and alarm, and one thin short scream. As he tried to scramble to his feet, the aircraft nosed down, and they started to lose altitude.

*　　*　　*

Holly moved forward from row seventeen, sat beside Christine Dubrovek, introduced herself as a friend of Steve Harkman's, and was nearly thrown out of her seat when a sickening shockwave pumped through the aircraft. It was followed a fraction of a second later by a solid *thump*, as if they had been struck by something.

'Mommy!' Casey had been belted in her seat, even though the seatbelt signs were not on. She was not thrown forward, but the storybooks on her lap clattered to the deck. Her eyes were huge with fear.

The plane started to lose altitude.

'Mommy?'

'It's OK,' Christine said, obviously struggling to conceal her own fear from her daughter. 'Just turbulence, an air pocket.'

They were dropping fast.

'You're gonna be OK,' Holly told them, leaning past Christine to make sure the little girl heard her reassurances. 'Both of you are going to be OK if you just stay here, don't move, stay right in these seats.'

Knifing down . . . a thousand feet . . . two thousand . . .

Holly frantically belted herself in her seat.

. . . three thousand . . . four thousand . . .

An initial wave of horror and panic gripped the passengers. But that was followed quickly by a breathless silence, as they all clung to the arms of their seats and waited to see if the damaged aircraft was going to pull up in time – or tip downward at an even more severe angle.

To Holly's surprise, the nose slowly came up. The plane leveled off again.

A communal sigh of relief and a smattering of applause swept through the cabin.

She turned and grinned at Christine and Casey. 'We're going to be all right. We're all going to make it.'

The captain came on the loudspeaker and explained that they had lost one of their engines. They could still fly just fine on the remaining two, he assured them, though he suggested they might need to divert to a suitable airfield closer than O'Hare, only to be safe. He sounded calm and confident, and he thanked the passengers for their patience, implying that the worst they would suffer was inconvenience.

A moment later Jim Ironheart appeared in the aisle, and squatted beside Holly. A spot of blood glimmered at the corner of his mouth; he had evidently been tossed around a little.

She was so exhilarated, she wanted to kiss him, but she just said, 'You did it, you changed it, you made a difference somehow.'

He looked grim. 'No.' He leaned close to her, put his face almost against hers, so they could talk in whispers as before, though she thought Christine Dubrovek must be hearing some of it. He said, 'It's too late.'

Holly felt as if he had punched her in the stomach. 'But we leveled off.'

'Pieces of the exploding engine tore holes in the tail. Severed most of the hydraulic lines. Punctured the others. Soon they won't be able to steer the airplane.'

Her fear had melted. Now it came back like ice crystals forming and linking together across the gray surface of a winter pond.

They were going down.

She said, 'You know *exactly* what happened, you should be with the captain, not here.'

'It's over. I was too late.'

'No. Never—'

'Nothing I can do now.'

'But—'

A flight attendant appeared, looking shaken but sounding calm. 'Sir, please return to your seat.'

'All right, I will,' Jim said. He took Holly's hand first, and squeezed it. 'Don't be afraid.' He looked past her at Christine, then at Casey. 'You'll be all right.'

He moved back to row seventeen, the seat immediately behind Holly. She was loath to lose sight of him. He helped her confidence just by being within view.

*　　*　　*

For twenty-six years, Captain Sleighton Delbaugh had earned his living in the cockpits of commercial airliners, the last eighteen as a pilot. He had encountered and successfully dealt with a daunting variety of problems, a few of them serious enough to be called crises, and he had benefitted from United's rigorous program of continuous instruction and periodic recertification. He felt he was prepared for anything that could happen in a modern aircraft, but he found it difficult to believe what *had* happened to Flight 246.

After engine number two failed, the bird went into an unplanned descent, and the controls stiffened. They managed to correct its altitude, however, and dramatically slow its descent. But losing eleven thousand feet of altitude was the least of their problems.

'We're turning right,' Bob Anilov said. He was Delbaugh's first officer, forty-three, and an excellent pilot. 'Still turning right. It's locking up, Slay.'

'We've got partial hydraulic failure,' said Chris Lodden, their flight engineer. He was the youngest of the three and a favorite of virtually every female flight attendant who met him, partly because he was good looking in a fresh-faced farmboy way, but largely because he was a little shy, which made him a novelty among the cocksure men on most flight crews. Chris was seated behind Anilov and in charge of monitoring the mechanical systems.

'It's going harder right,' Anilov said.

Already Delbaugh was pulling the yoke full aft, left wheel. 'Damn.'

Anilov said, 'No response.'

'It's worse than a partial loss,' Chris Lodden said, tapping and adjusting his instruments as if he was having trouble believing what they were telling him. 'How can this be right?'

The DC-10 had three hydraulic systems, well-designed backup. They couldn't have lost everything. But they had.

Pete Yankowski – a balding, red-mustached flight instructor from the company's training facility in Denver – was riding with the crew on his way to visit his brother in Chicago. As an

OMC – observing member of crew – he was in the fold-down jumpseat immediately behind Delbaugh, virtually peering over the captain's shoulder. He said, 'I'll go have a look at the tail, assess the damage.'

As Yankowski left, Lodden said, 'The only control we've got is engine thrust.'

Captain Delbaugh had already begun to use it, cutting the power to the engine on the right, increasing it to the other – the port – engine in order to pull them to the left and out of their unwanted turn. When they began to swing too far to the left, he would have to increase the power to the starboard engine again and bring them around that way a little.

With the flight engineer's assistance, Delbaugh determined that the outboard and inboard elevators on the tail were gone, dead, useless. The inboard ailerons on the wings were dead. The outboard ailerons were dead. Same for the flaps and spoilers.

The DC-10 had a wingspan of over one hundred and fifty-five feet. Its fuselage was a hundred and seventy feet long. It was more than just an airplane. It was literally a ship that sailed the sky, the very definition of a 'jumbo jet,' and virtually the only way they now had to steer it was with the two General Electric/Pratt & Whitney engines. Which was only a little better than a driver trying to steer a runaway automobile by leaning to one side and then to the other, desperately struggling to influence its course with his shifting weight.

* * *

A few minutes had passed since the tail engine exploded, and they were still aloft.

Holly believed in a god, not due to any life-altering spiritual experience, but largely because the alternative to belief was simply too grim. Although she had been raised a Methodist and for a while toyed with the idea of conversion to Catholicism, she had never made up her mind what sort of god she preferred, whether one of the gray-suited Protestant varieties or the more passionate Catholic divinity or something else altogether. In her daily life she did not turn to heaven for help with her problems, and she only said grace before meals when she was visiting her parents in Philadelphia. She would have felt like a hypocrite if she had fallen into prayer now, but she nevertheless hoped that God was in a merciful mood and watching over the DC-10, whatever His or Her gender might be and regardless of His or Her preference in worshipers.

Christine was reading one of the pop-up storybooks with Casey, adding her own amusing commentary to the adventures of the animal characters, trying to distract her daughter from the memory of the muffled explosion and subsequent plunge. The intensity of her focus on the child was a giveaway of her true inner feelings: she was scared, and she knew that the worst had not yet passed.

Minute by minute, Holly slipped deeper into a state of denial, unwilling to accept what Jim Ironheart had told her. It was not her own survival, or his, or that of the Dubroveks that she doubted. He had proven himself to be singularly successful when he entered combat with fate; and she was reasonably confident that their lives were secure in the forward section of the economy-class seats, as he had promised. What she wanted to deny, *had* to deny, was that so many others on the flight were going to die. It was intolerable to think that the old and young, men and women, innocent and guilty, moral and immoral, the kind and the mean-spirited were going to die in the same event, compacted together against some rocky escarpment or on a field of wildflowers set afire by burning jet fuel, with no favor given to those who had led their lives with dignity and respect for others.

*　　*　　*

Over Iowa, Flight 246 passed out of Minneapolis Center, the air-traffic-control jurisdiction after Denver Center, and now responded only to Chicago Center. Unable to regain hydraulics, Captain Delbaugh requested and received permission from United's dispatcher and from Chicago to divert from O'Hare to the nearest major airport, which was Dubuque, Iowa. He relinquished control of the plane to Anilov, so he and Chris Lodden would be able to concentrate on finding a way through their crisis.

As a first step, Delbaugh radioed System Aircraft Maintenance (SAM) at San Francisco International Airport. SAM was United's central maintenance base, an enormous state-of-the-art complex with a staff of over ten thousand.

'We have a situation here,' Delbaugh told them calmly. 'Complete hydraulic failure. We can stay up a while, but we can't maneuver.'

At SAM, in addition to United's own employees, experts were also on duty twenty-four hours a day from suppliers of every model of aircraft currently in operation by the airline – including a man

130

from General Electric, where the CF-6 engines had been built, and another from McDonnell Douglas, which had designed and manufactured the DC-10. Manuals, books, and a massive amount of computer-accessible data about each airplane type was available to staff at SAM, in addition to an exhaustively detailed maintenance history of every craft in the United fleet. They could tell Delbaugh and Lodden about every mechanical problem their particular plane had experienced during its lifetime, exactly what had been done to it during its most recently scheduled maintenance, and even when upholstery damage had been repaired – virtually everything except how much loose change had fallen into its seats from passengers' pockets and been left behind during the past twelve months.

Delbaugh also hoped they could tell him how the hell he was supposed to fly an aircraft as large as an apartment building without the aid of elevators, rudders, ailerons, and other equipment that allowed him to maneuver. Even the best flight training programs were structured under the assumption that a pilot would retain *some* degree of control in a catastrophic incident, thanks to redundant systems provided by the designers. Initially, the people at SAM had trouble accepting that he had lost all hydraulics, assuming he meant he'd had a fractional loss. He finally had to snap at them to make them understand, which he deeply regretted not only because he wanted to uphold the tradition of quiet professionalism that pilots before him had established in dire circumstances, but also because he was seriously spooked by the sound of his own angry voice and thereafter found it more difficult to deceive himself that he actually felt as calm as he was pretending to be.

Pete Yankowski, the flight instructor from Denver, returned from his trip to the rear of the plane and reported that through a window he had spotted an eighteen-inch hole in the horizontal part of the tail. 'There's probably more damage I couldn't see. Figure shrapnel ripped up the rear section behind the aft bulkhead, where all the hydraulic systems pass through. At least we didn't depressurize.'

Dismayed at the rippling sensation that quivered through his bowels, achingly aware that two hundred and fifty-three passengers and ten other crew members were depending on him to bring them home alive, Delbaugh conveyed Yankowski's information to SAM. Then he asked for assistance in determining how to fly the severely disabled aircraft. He was not surprised when, after an urgent consultation, the experts in San Francisco could come up with no recommendations. He was asking them to do the impossible, tell him how to remain the master of this behemoth with no substantial controls other than the throttles – the same unfair request that God was making of him.

He stayed in touch with United's dispatcher office, as well, which tracked the progress of all the company's hardware in the air. In addition, both channels – the dispatcher and SAM – were patched in to United's headquarters near O'Hare International in Chicago. A lot of interested and anxious people were tied to Delbaugh by radio, but they were all as much at a loss for good suggestions as were the experts in San Francisco.

To Yankowski, Delbaugh said, 'Ask Evelyn to find that guy from McDonnell Douglas she told us about. Get him up here quick.'

As Pete left the flight deck again, and as Anilov struggled with his control wheel in a determined if vain attempt to get at least some response from the craft, Delbaugh told the shift manager at SAM that a McDonnell Douglas engineer was aboard. 'He warned us something was wrong with the tail engine just before it exploded. He could tell from the sound of it, I guess, so we'll get him in here, see if he can help.'

At SAM, the General Electric expert on CF-6 turbofan engines came back at him: 'What do you mean, he could tell by the sound? How could he tell by the sound? What did it sound like?'

'I don't know,' Delbaugh replied. 'We didn't notice any unusual noises or unexpected changes in pitch, and neither did the flight attendants.'

The voice in Delbaugh's headset crackled in response: 'That doesn't make sense.'

McDonnell Douglas's DC-10 specialist at SAM sounded equally baffled: 'What's this guy's name?'

'We'll find out. All we know right now is his first name,' Sleighton Delbaugh said. 'It's Jim.'

* * *

As the captain announced to the passengers that they would be landing in Dubuque as a result of mechanical problems, Jim watched Evelyn approach him along the port aisle, weaving because the plane was no longer as steady as it had been. He wished she would not ask him what he knew she had to ask.

'. . . and it might be a little rough,' the captain concluded.

As the pilots reduced power to one engine and increased it to the other, the wings wobbled, and the plane wallowed like a boat in a swelling sea. Each time it happened, they recovered quickly, but between those desperate course corrections, when they were unlucky enough to hit air turbulence, the DC-10 did not ride through it as confidently as it had done all the way out from LAX.

'Captain Delbaugh would like you to come forward if you could,' Evelyn said when she reached him, soft-voiced and smiling as if delivering an invitation to a pleasant little luncheon of tea and finger sandwiches.

He wanted to refuse. He was not entirely sure that Christine and Casey – or Holly, for that matter – would live through the crash and its immediate aftermath without him at their side. He knew that on impact a ten-row chunk of the fuselage aft of first-class would crack loose from the rest of the plane, and that less damage would be done to it than to the forward and rear sections. Before he had intervened in the fate of Flight 246, all of the passengers in those favored seats had been destined to come out of the crash with comparatively minor injuries or no injuries at all. He was sure that all of those marked for life were still going to live, but he was not certain that merely moving the Dubroveks into the middle of the safety zone was sufficient to alter their fate and ensure their survival. Perhaps, after impact, he would have to be there to get them through the fire and out of the wreckage – which he could not do if he was with the flight crew.

Besides, he had no idea whether the crew was going to survive. If he was with them in the cockpit on impact . . .

He went with Evelyn anyway. He had no choice – at least not since Holly Thorne had insisted that he might be able to do more than save one woman and one child, might thwart fate on a large scale instead of a small one. He remembered too clearly the dying man in the station wagon out on the Mojave Desert and the three murdered innocents in the Atlanta convenience store last May, people who could have been spared along with others if he had been allowed to arrive in time to save them.

As he went by row sixteen, he checked out the Dubroveks, who were huddled over a storybook, then he met Holly's eyes. Her anxiety was palpable.

Following Evelyn forward, Jim was aware of the passengers looking at him speculatively. He was one of their own, elevated to special status by their predicament, which they were beginning to suspect was worse than they were being told. They were clearly

133

wondering what special knowledge he possessed that made his presence in the cockpit desirable. If only they knew.

The plane was wallowing again.

Jim picked up a trick from Evelyn. She did not just weave where the tilting deck forced her to go, but attempted to anticipate its movement and lean in the opposite direction, shifting her point of gravity to maintain her balance.

A couple of the passengers were discreetly puking into airsickness bags. Many others, though able to control their nausea, were gray-faced.

When Jim entered the cramped, instrument-packed cockpit, he was appalled by what he saw. The flight engineer was paging through a manual, a look of quiet desperation on his face. The two pilots – Delbaugh and First Officer Anilov, according to the flight attendant who had not entered with Jim – were struggling with the controls, trying to wrench the right-tending jumbo jet back on to course. To free them to concentrate on that task, a red-haired balding man was on his knees between the two pilots, operating the throttles at the captain's direction, using the thrust of the remaining two engines to provide what steering they had.

Anilov said, 'We're losing altitude again.'

'Not serious,' Delbaugh said. Aware that someone had entered, Delbaugh glanced back at Jim. In the captain's position, Jim would have been sweating like a race-lathered horse, but Delbaugh's face glistened with only a fine sheen of perspiration, as if someone had sprayed him with a plant mister. His voice was steady: 'You're Jim?'

'Yeah,' Jim said.

Delbaugh looked forward again. 'We're coming around,' he said to Anilov, and the co-pilot nodded. Delbaugh ordered a throttle change, and the man on the floor complied. Then, speaking to Jim without looking at him, the captain said, 'You knew it was going to happen.'

'Yeah.'

'So what else can you tell me?'

Bracing himself against a bulkhead as the plane shuddered and wallowed again, Jim said, 'Total hydraulic failure.'

'I mean, something I don't know,' Delbaugh replied with cool sarcasm. It justifiably could have been an angry snarl, but he was admirably in command of himself. Then he spoke to approach control, obtaining new instructions.

Listening, Jim realized that the Dubuque tower was going to

bring in Flight 246 by way of a series of 360-degree turns, in an attempt to line it up with one of the runways. The pilots could not easily guide the plane into a straight approach, as they would usually do, because they had no real control. The disabled craft's maddening tendency to turn endlessly to the right was now to be incorporated into a breathtakingly conceived plan that would let it find its way into the barn like a stubborn bull determined to resist the herder and follow its own route home. If the radius of each turn was carefully calculated and matched to an equally precise rate of descent, they might eventually be able to bring 246 head-on to a runway and all the way in.

Impact in five minutes.

Jim twitched in shock and almost spoke those four words aloud when they came to him.

Instead, when the captain finished talking to the tower, Jim said, 'Is your landing gear operable?'

'We got it down and locked,' Delbaugh confirmed.

'Then we might make it.'

'We *will* make it,' Delbaugh said. 'Unless there's another surprise waiting for us.'

'There is,' Jim said.

The captain glanced worriedly at him again. 'What?'

Impact in four minutes.

'For one thing, there'll be a sudden windshear as you're going in, oblique to you, so it won't drive you into the ground. But the reflected updraft from it will give you a couple of bad moments. It'll be like you're flying over a washboard.'

'What're you talking about?' Anilov demanded.

'When you're making your final approach, a few hundred feet from the end of the runway, you'll still be at an angle,' Jim said, once more allowing some omniscient higher power to speak through him, 'but you'll have to go for it anyway, no other choice.'

'How can you know that?' the flight engineer demanded.

Ignoring the question, Jim went on, and the words came in a rush: 'The plane'll suddenly drop to the right, the wing'll hit the ground, and you'll cartwheel down the runway, end over end, off it, into a field. The whole damn plane'll come apart and burn.'

The red-haired man in civilian clothes, operating the throttles, looked back at Jim in disbelief. 'What crock of shit is this, who the hell do you think you are?'

'He knew about engine number two before it blew up,' Delbaugh said coolly.

Aware that they were entering the second of the trio of planned 360-degree turns and that time was swiftly running out, Jim said, 'None of you in the cockpit will die, but you'll lose a hundred and forty-seven passengers, plus four flight attendants.'

'Oh my God,' Delbaugh said softly.

'He can't *know* this,' Anilov objected.

Impact in three minutes.

Delbaugh gave additional instructions to the red-haired man, who manipulated the throttles. One engine grew louder, the other softer, and the big craft began its second turn, shedding some altitude as it went.

Jim said, 'But there's a warning, just before the plane tips to the right.'

'What?' Delbaugh said, still unable to look at him, straining to get what response he could from the wheel.

'You won't recognize what it means, it's a strange sound, like nothing you've heard before, because it's a structural failure in the wing coupling, where it's fixed to the fuselage. A sharp twang, like a giant steel-guitar string. When you hear it, if you increase power to the port engine immediately, compensating to the left, you'll keep her from cartwheeling.'

Anilov had lost his patience. 'This is nuts. Slay, I can't *think* with this guy here.'

Jim knew Anilov was right. Both System Aircraft Maintenance in San Francisco and the dispatcher had been silent for a while, hesitant to interfere with the crew's concentration. If he stayed there, even without saying another word, he might unintentionally distract them at a crucial moment. Besides, he sensed that there was nothing more of value that he would be given to tell them.

He left the flight deck and moved as quickly as possible toward row sixteen.

Impact in two minutes.

*   *   *

Holly kept watching for Jim Ironheart, hoping he would rejoin them. She wanted him nearby when the worst happened. She had not forgotten the bizarre dream from last night, the monstrous creature that had seemed to come out of her nightmare and into her motel room; neither had she forgotten how many people he had killed in his quest to protect the lives of the innocent, nor how savagely he slaughtered Norman Rink in that Atlanta convenience store. But the dark side of him was outweighed by the light. Though an aura of danger surrounded him, she also felt curiously safe in his company, as if within the protective nimbus of a guardian angel.

Through the public-address system, one of the flight attendants was instructing them on emergency procedures. Other attendants were positioned throughout the plane, making sure everyone was following directions.

The DC-10 was wallowing and shimmying again. Worse, although without a wooden timber anywhere in its structure, it was creaking like a sailing ship on a storm-tossed sea. The sky was blue beyond the portholes, but evidently the air was more than blustery; it was raging, tumultuous.

None of the passengers had any illusions now. They knew they were going in for a landing under the worst conditions, and that it would be rough. Maybe fatal. Throughout the enormous plane, people were surprisingly quiet, as if they were in a cathedral during a solemn service. Perhaps, in their minds' eyes, they were experiencing their own funerals.

Jim appeared out of the first-class section and approached along the port aisle. Holly was immensely relieved to see him. He paused only to smile encouragingly at the Dubroveks, and to put his hand on Holly's shoulder and give her a gentle squeeze of reassurance. Then he settled into the seat behind her.

The plane hit a patch of turbulence worse than anything before. She was half convinced that they were no longer flying but sledding across corrugated steel.

Christine took Holly's hand and held it briefly, as if they were old friends – which, in a curious way, they were, thanks to the imminence of death, which had a bonding effect on people.

'Good luck, Holly.'

'You too,' Holly said.

Beyond her mother, little Casey looked so small.

Even the flight attendants were seated now, and in the position they had instructed the passengers to take. Finally Holly followed their example and assumed the posture that contributed to the best chance of survival in a crash: belted securely in the seat, bent forward, head tucked between her knees, gripping her ankles with her hands.

The plane came out of the shattered air, slipping down glass-smooth for a moment. But before Holly had time to feel any relief, the whole sky seemed to be shaking as though gremlins were standing at the four corners and snapping it like a blanket.

Overhead storage compartments popped open. Traincases, valises, jackets, and personal items flew out and rained down on the seats. Something struck the center of Holly's bowed back, bouncing off her. It was not heavy, hardly hurt at all, but she suddenly worried that a traincase, laden with some woman's makeup and jars of face cream, would drop at precisely the right angle to crack her spine.

* * *

Captain Sleighton Delbaugh called out instructions to Yankowski, who continued to kneel between the pilots, operating the throttles while they were preoccupied with maintaining what little control they had left. He was braced, but a hard landing was not going to be kind to him.

They were coming out of the third and final 360-degree turn. The runway was ahead of them, but not straight-on, just as Jim – damn, he'd never gotten the guy's last name – had predicted.

Also as the stranger had foreseen, they were descending through exceptional turbulence, bucking and shuddering as if they were in a big old bus with a couple of bent axles, thundering down a steep and rugged mountain road. Delbaugh had never seen anything like it; even if the plane had been intact, he'd have been concerned about landing in those treacherous crosswinds and powerful rising thermals.

But he could not pull up and go on, hoping for better conditions at another airport or on another pass at this one. They had kept the jumbo jet in the air for thirty-three minutes since the tail-engine explosion. That was a feat of which they could be proud, but skill and cleverness and intelligence and nerve were not enough to carry them much farther. Minute by minute, and now second by second, keeping the stricken DC-10 in the air was increasingly like trying to fly a massive rock.

They were about two thousand meters from the end of the runway and closing fast.

Delbaugh thought of his wife and seventeen-year-old son at home in Westlake Village, north of Los Angeles, and he thought of his other son, Tom, who was already on his way to Willamette to get ready for his junior year. He longed to touch their faces and hold them close.

He was not afraid for himself. Well, not much. His relatively mild concern for his own safety was not a result of the stranger's prediction that the flight crew would survive, because he didn't know if the guy's premonitions were always correct. In part, it was just that he didn't have *time* to be concerned about himself.

Fifteen hundred meters.

Mainly, he was worried about his passengers and crew, who trusted him with their lives. If any part of the crash was his fault, due to a lack of resolve or nerve or quickness, all the good he had done and tried to do in his life would not compensate for this one catastrophic failure. Perhaps that attitude proved that he was, as some friends suggested, too hard on himself, but he knew that many pilots worked under no less heavy a sense of responsibility.

He remembered what the stranger had said: '. . . *you'll lose a hundred and forty-seven passengers . . .*'

His hands throbbed with pain as he kept a tight grip on the yoke, which vibrated violently.

'. . . *plus four flight attendants . . .*'

Twelve hundred meters.

'She wants to come right,' Delbaugh said.

'Hold her!' Anilov said, for at this low altitude and on an approach, it was all in Delbaugh's hands.

One hundred and fifty-one dead, all those families bereaved, countless other lives altered by a single tragedy.

Eleven hundred meters.

But how the hell could that guy know how many would die? Not possible. Was he trying to say he was clairvoyant or what? It was all a crock, as Yankowski had said. Yeah, but he knew about the engine before it exploded, he knew about the washboard turbulence, and only an idiot would discount all of that.

A thousand meters.

'Here we go,' Delbaugh heard himself say.

*   *   *

Bent forward in his seat, head between his knees, gripping his ankles, Jim Ironheart thought of the punchline to an old joke: kiss your ass goodbye.

He prayed that by his own actions he had not disrupted the river of fate to such an extent that he would wash away not only himself and the Dubroveks but other people on Flight 246 who had never been meant to die in the crash. Because of what he had told the pilot, he had potentially altered the future, and now what happened might be worse, not better, than what had been *meant* to happen.

The higher power working through him had seemed, ultimately, to approve of his attempt to save more lives than just those of Christine and Casey. On the other hand, the nature and identity of that power was so enigmatic that only a fool would presume to understand its motives or intentions.

The plane shivered and shook. The scream of the engines seemed to grow ever more shrill.

He stared at the deck beneath his feet, expecting it to burst open in his face.

More than anything, he was afraid for Holly Thorne. Her presence on the flight was a profound deviation from the script that fate had originally written. He was eaten by a fear that he might save the lives of more people on the plane than he'd at first intended – but that Holly would be broken in half by the impact.

* * *

As the DC-10 quaked and rattled its way toward the earth, Holly squeezed herself into as tight a package as she could, and closed her eyes. In her private darkness, faces swam through her mind: her mom and dad, which was to be expected; Lenny Callaway, the first boy she had ever loved, which was not expected, because she had not seen him since they were both sixteen; Mrs Rooney, a high-school teacher who had taken a special interest in her; Lori Clugar, her best friend all through high school and half of college, before life had carried them to different corners of the country and out of touch; and more than a dozen others, all of whom she had loved and still loved. No one person could have occupied her thoughts for more than a fraction of a second, yet the nearness of death seemed to distort time, so she felt as if she were lingering with each beloved face. What flashed before her was not her life, but the special people in it – though in a way that was the same thing.

Even above the creak-rumble-shriek of the jet, and in spite of her focus on the faces in her mind, she heard Christine Dubrovek speak to her daughter in the last moments of their shaky descent: 'I love you, Casey.'

Holly began to cry.

* * *

Three hundred meters.

Delbaugh had the nose up.

140

Everything looked good. As good as it *could* look under the circumstances.

They were at a slight angle to the runway, but he might be able to realign the aircraft once they were on the ground. If he couldn't bring it around to any useful degree, they would roll three thousand or maybe even four thousand feet before their angle of approach carried them off the edge of the pavement and into a field where it appeared that a crop of some kind had been harvested recently. That was not a desirable termination point, but at least by then a lot of their momentum would have been lost; the plane might still break up, depending on the nature of the bare earth under its wheels, but there was little chance that it would disintegrate catastrophically.

Two hundred meters.

Turbulence gone.

Floating. Like a feather.

'All right,' Anilov said, just as Delbaugh said, 'Easy, easy,' and they both meant the same thing: it looked good, they were going to make it.

One hundred meters.

Nose still up.

Perfect, perfect.

Touchdown and—

TWANG!

—the tires barked on the blacktop simultaneously with the queer sound. Delbaugh remembered the stranger's warning, so he said, 'Power number one!' and pulled hard to the left. Yankowski remembered as well, though he had said it was all a crock, and he responded to Delbaugh's throttle command even as it was being given. The right wing dipped, just as they had been told it would, but their quick action pulled the plane left, and the right wing came back up. There was a danger of overcompensation, so Delbaugh issued a new throttle command while still trying to hold the craft to the left. They were rolling along, rolling along, the plane shaking, and he gave the order to reverse engines because they couldn't, for God's sake, continue to accelerate, they were in mortal danger as long as they were moving at high speed, rolling, rolling, moving inexorably at an angle on the runway, rolling and slowing now, but rolling. And the right wing was tipping down again, accompanied by hellish popping and metallic tearing noises as age-fatigued steel – trouble in the joining of wing and fuselage, Jim had said – succumbed to the stress of their wildly erratic flight and

141

once-in-a-century crosswinds. Rolling, rolling, but Delbaugh couldn't do a damn thing about a structural failure, couldn't get out there and reweld the joints or hold the damn rivets in place. Rolling, rolling, their momentum dropping, but the right wing still going down, none of his countermeasures working any longer, the wing down, and down, oh God, the wing—

*   *   *

Holly felt the plane tipping farther to the right than before. She held her breath – or thought she did, but at the same time she heard herself gasping frantically.

The creaks and squeals of tortured metal, which had been echoing eerily through the fuselage for a couple of minutes, suddenly grew much louder. The aircraft tipped farther to the right. A sound like a cannonshot boomed through the passenger compartment, and the plane bounced up, came down hard. The landing gear collapsed.

They were sliding along the runway, rocking and jolting, then the plane began to turn as it slid, making Holly's heart clutch up and her stomach knot. It was the biggest carnival ride in the world, except it wasn't any fun at all; her seatbelt was like a blade against her midriff, cutting her in half, and if there had been a carny ticket-taker, she knew he would have had the ghastly face of a rotting corpse and a rictus for a smile.

The noise was intolerable, though the passengers' screaming was not the worst of it. For the most part their voices were drowned out by the scream of the aircraft itself as its belly dissolved against the pavement and other pieces of it were torn loose. Maybe dinosaurs, sinking into Mesozoic pits of tar, had equalled the volume of that dying cry, but nothing on the face of the earth since that era had protested its demise at such a piercing pitch and thunderous volume. It wasn't purely a machine sound; it was metallic but somehow alive, and it was so eerie and chilling that it might have been the combined, tortured cries of all the denizens of hell, hundreds of millions of despairing souls wailing at once. She was sure her eardrums would burst.

Disregarding the instructions she had been given, she raised her head and looked quickly around. Cascades of white, yellow, and turquoise sparks foamed past the portholes, as if the airplane was passing through an extravagant fireworks display. Six or seven rows ahead, the fuselage cracked open like an eggshell rapped against the edge of a ceramic bowl.

She had seen enough, too much. She tucked her head between her knees again.

She heard herself chanting at the deck in front of her, but she was caught in such a whirlpool of horror that the only way she could discover what she was saying was to strain to hear herself above the cacophony of the crash: 'Don't, don't, don't, don't, don't, don't . . .'

Maybe she passed out for a few seconds, or maybe her senses shut down briefly due to extreme overload, but in a wink everything was still. The air was filled with acrid odors that her recovering senses could not identify. The ordeal was over, but she could not recall the plane coming to rest.

She was alive.

Intense joy swept through her. She raised her head, sat up, ready to whoop with the uncontainable thrill of survival – and saw the fire.

*   *   *

The DC-10 had not cartwheeled. The warning to Captain Delbaugh had paid off.

But as Jim had feared, the chaotic aftermath of the crash held as many dangers as the impact itself.

Along the entire starboard side of the plane, where jet fuel had spilled, orange flames churned at the windows. It appeared as if he was voyaging aboard a submarine in a sea of fire on an alien world. Some of the windows had shattered on impact, and flames were spouting through those apertures, as well as through the ragged tear in the fuselage that now separated economy class from the forward section of the airliner.

Even as Jim uncoupled his seatbelt and got shakily to his feet, he saw seats catching afire on the starboard side. Passengers over there were crouching or dropping down on their hands and knees to scramble under the spreading flames.

He stepped into the aisle, grabbed Holly, and hugged her as she struggled to her feet. He looked past her at the Dubroveks. Mother and child were uninjured, though Casey was crying.

Holding Holly by the hand, searching for the quickest way out, Jim turned toward the back of the aircraft and for a moment could not understand what he was seeing. Like a voracious blob out of an old horror movie, an amorphous mass churned toward them from the hideously gouged and crumpled rear of the DC-10, black and billowy, devouring everything over which it rolled. Smoke. He hadn't instantly realized it was smoke because it was so thick that it appeared to have the substance of a wall of oil or mud.

Death by suffocation, or worse, lay behind them. They would have to go forward in spite of the fire ahead. Flames licked around the torn edge of the fuselage on the starboard side, reaching well into the cabin, fanning across more than half the diameter of the sliced-open aircraft. But they should be able to exit toward the port side, where no fire was yet visible.

'Quick,' he said, turning to Christine and Casey as they came out of row sixteen. 'Forward, fast as you can, go, go!'

However, other passengers from the first six rows of the economy section were in the aisle ahead of them. Everyone was trying to get out fast. A valiant young flight attendant was doing what she could to help, but progress was not easy. The aisle was littered with carry-on luggage, purses, paperback books, and other items that had fallen out of the overhead storage compartments, and within a few shuffling steps, Jim's feet had become entangled in debris.

The churning smoke reached them from behind, enfolded them, so pungent that his eyes teared at once. He not only choked on the first whiff of fumes but gagged with revulsion, and he did not want to think about what might be burning behind him in addition to upholstery, foam seat cushions, carpet, and other elements of the aircraft's interior decor.

As the thick oily cloud poured past him and engulfed the forward section, the passengers ahead began to vanish. They appeared to be stepping through the folds of a black velvet curtain.

Before visibility dropped to a couple of inches, Jim let go of Holly and touched Christine's shoulder. 'Let me take her,' he said, and scooped Casey into his arms.

A paper bag from an LAX giftshop was in the aisle at his feet. It had burst open as people tramped across it. He saw a white T-shirt – I LOVE LA – with pink and peach and pale-green palm trees.

He snatched up the shirt and pushed it into Casey's small hands. Coughing, as was everyone around him, he said, 'Hold it over your face, honey, breathe through it!'

Then he was blind. The foul cloud around him was so dark that he could not even see the child he was carrying. Indeed, he could not actually perceive the churning currents of the cloud itself. The blackness was deeper than what he saw when he closed his eyes, for behind his lids, pinpoint bursts of color formed ghostly patterns that lit his inner world.

They were maybe twenty feet from the open end of the crash-severed fuselage. He was not in danger of getting lost, for the aisle was the only route he could follow.

He tried not to breathe. He could hold his breath for a minute, anyway, which ought to be long enough. The only problem was that he had already inhaled some of the bitter smoke, and it was caustic, burning his throat as if he had swallowed acid. His lungs heaved and his esophagus spasmed, forcing him to cough, and every cough ended in an involuntary though thankfully shallow inhalation.

Probably less than fifteen feet to go.

He wanted to scream at the people in front of him: *move, damn you, move!* He knew they were stumbling forward as fast as they could, every bit as eager to get out as he was, but he wanted to shout at them anyway, felt a shriek of rage building in him, and he realized he was teetering on the brink of hysteria.

He stepped on several small, cylindrical objects, floundering like a man walking on marbles. But he kept his balance.

Casey was wracked by violent coughs. He could not hear her, but holding her against his chest, he could feel each twitch and flex and contraction of her small body as she struggled desperately to draw half-filtered breaths through the I LOVE LA shirt.

Less than a minute had passed since he had started forward, maybe only thirty seconds since he had scooped up the girl. But it seemed like a long journey down an endless tunnel.

Although fear and fury had thrown his mind into a turmoil, he was thinking clearly enough to remember reading somewhere that smoke rose in a burning room and hung near the ceiling. If they didn't reach safety within a few seconds, he would have to drop to the deck and crawl in the hope that he would escape the toxic gases and find at least marginally cleaner air down there.

Sudden heat coalesced around him.

He imagined himself stepping into a furnace, his skin peeling off in an instant, flesh blistering and smoking. His heart already thudded like a wild thing throwing itself against the bars of a cage, but it began to beat harder, faster.

Certain that they had to be within a few steps of the hole in the fuselage that he had glimpsed earlier, Jim opened his eyes, which stung and watered copiously. Perfect blackness had given way to a charcoal-gray swirl of fumes through which throbbed blood-red pulses of light. The pulses were flames shrouded by smoke and seen only as reflections bouncing off millions of swirling particles of ash.

At any moment the fire could burst upon him from out of the smoke and sear him to the bone.

He was not going to make it.

No breathable air.

Fire seeking him on all sides.

He was going to ignite. Burn like a living tallow candle. In a vision sparked by terror rather than by a higher power, he saw himself dropping to his knees in defeat. The child in his arms. Fusing with her in a steel-melting inferno . . .

A sudden wind pulled at him. The smoke was sucked away toward his left.

He saw daylight, cool and gray and easily differentiated from the deadly glow of burning jet fuel.

Propelled by a gruesome image of himself and the child fried by a flash fire on the very brink of safety, he threw himself toward the grayness and fell out of the airliner. No portable stairs were waiting, of course, no emergency chute, just bare earth. Fortunately a crop had recently been harvested, and the stubble had been plowed under for mulch. The newly tilled earth was hard enough to knock the wind out of him but far too soft to break his bones.

He clung fiercely to Casey, gasping for breath. He rolled on to his knees, got up, still holding her in his arms, and staggered out of the corona of heat that radiated from the blazing plane.

Some of the survivors were running away, as if they thought the DC-10 had been loaded with dynamite and was going to blow half the state of Iowa to smithereens any second now. Others were wandering aimlessly in shock. Still others were lying on the ground: some too stunned to go another inch; some injured; and perhaps some of them were dead.

Grateful for the clean air, coughing out sour fumes from his soiled lungs, Jim looked for Christine Dubrovek among the people in the field. He turned this way and that, calling her name, but he couldn't see her. He began to think that she had perished in the airplane, that he might not have been treading over only passengers' possessions in the port aisle but also over a couple of the passengers themselves.

Perhaps sensing what Jim was thinking, Casey let the palm-tree-decorated T-shirt fall from her grasp. Clinging to him, coughing out the last of the smoke, she began to ask for her mother in a fearful tone of voice that indicated she expected the worst.

A burgeoning sense of triumph had taken hold of him. But now a new fear rattled in him like ice cubes in a tall glass. Suddenly the warm August sun over the Iowa field and the waves of heat pouring off the DC-10 did not touch him, and he felt as though he was standing on an arctic plain.

'Steve?'

At first he did not react to the name.

'Steve?'

Then he remembered that he had been Steve Harkman to her – which she and her husband and the *real* Steve Harkman would probably puzzle about for the rest of their lives – and he turned toward the voice. Christine was there, stumbling through the freshly tilled earth, her face and clothes stained from the oily smoke, shoeless, arms out to receive her little girl.

Jim gave the child to her.

Mother and daughter hugged each other fiercely.

Weeping, looking across Casey's shoulder at Jim, Christine said, 'Thank you, thank you for getting her out of there, my God, Steve, I can't ever thank you enough.'

He did not want thanks. All he wanted was Holly Thorne, alive and uninjured.

'Have you seen Holly?' he asked worriedly.

'Yes. She heard a child crying for help, she thought maybe it was Casey.' Christine was shaking and frantic, as if she was not in the least convinced their ordeal was over, as if she thought the earth might crack open and hot lava spew out, beginning a new chapter of the nightmare. 'How did we get separated? We were behind one another, then we were outside, and in the turmoil, somehow you and Casey just weren't there.'

'Holly,' he said impatiently. 'Where'd she go?'

'She wanted to go back inside for Casey, but then she realized the cry was coming from the forward section.' Christine held up a purse and chattered on: 'She carried her purse out of there without realizing she did it, so she gave it to me and went back, she knew it couldn't be Casey, but she went anyway.'

Christine pointed, and for the first time Jim saw that the front of the DC-10, all the way back through the first-class section, had completely torn free from the portion in which they had been riding. It was two hundred feet farther along the field. Though it was burning less vigorously than the larger mid-section, it was considerably more mangled than the rest of the craft, including the badly battered rear quarter.

He was appalled to hear that Holly had re-entered *any* part of the smouldering wreckage. The cockpit and forward section rested in that Iowa field like a monolith in an alien graveyard on a faraway world, wildly out of place here, and therefore infinitely strange, huge and looming, thoroughly ominous.

He ran toward it, calling Holly's name.

*   *   *

Though she knew it was the very plane in which she had departed Los Angeles a few hours ago, Holly could barely believe that the forward section of the DC-10 had actually once been part of a whole and functioning aircraft. It seemed more like a deeply disturbed sculptor's interpretation of a DC-10, welded together from parts of real airliners but also from junk of every description, from pie pans and cake tins and garbage cans and old lengths of pipe, from auto fenders and scrap wire and aluminum siding and pieces of a wrought-iron fence. Rivets had popped; glass had dissolved; seats had torn loose and piled up like broken and unwanted armchairs in the corner of an auction barn; metal had bent and twisted, and in places it had shattered as completely as crystal met by a hammer. Interior fuselage panels had peeled back, and heavy structural beams had burst inward. The floor had erupted upward in places, either from the impact or from an explosion below. Everywhere jagged, gnarled metal objects bristled in profusion, and it looked like nothing so much as a junkyard for old machines just after a tornado had passed through.

Trying to track down what sounded like the cries of a frightened child, Holly could not always proceed erect. She had to crouch and squirm through pinched spaces, pushing things aside when she could, going over or around or under whenever an obstacle proved to be immovable. The neat rows and aisles of the plane had been pulled and hammered into a maze.

She was shaken when she spotted yellow and red flickers of flame along the perimeter of the deck and in the starboard front corner by the bulkhead that separated the passenger cabin from the cockpit. But the fire was fitful, unlike the blistering conflagration that she had fled moments ago. It might abruptly flare up, of course, consuming everything in its path, although currently it seemed unable to find sufficiently combustible material or oxygen to do more than barely sustain itself.

Smoke curled around her in sinuous tendrils, but it was more annoying than threatening. Breathable air was in good supply, and she didn't even cough much.

More than anything, the corpses were what unnerved her. Though the crash apparently had been somewhat less severe than it would have been without Jim Ironheart's intervention, not everyone had survived, and a number of fatalities had occurred in the first-class section. She saw a man pinned to his seat by a foot-long, inch-diameter steel tube that had pierced his throat; his sightless eyes were wide open in a final expression of surprise. A woman, nearly decapitated, was on her side, still belted into her seat, which had torn free of the deck plates to which it had been bolted. Where other seats had broken free and slammed together, she saw injured passengers and cadavers heaped on one another, and the only way to tell the quick from the dead was to listen closely to determine which of them was groaning.

She blanked out the horror. She was aware of the blood, but she looked through it rather than at it. She averted her eyes from the most grievous wounds, refused to dwell on the nightmare images of the shattered passengers whom she kept confronting. Human bodies became abstract forms to her, as if they were not real but only blocks of shape and color put down on canvas by a cubist imitating Picasso. If she allowed herself to think about what she was seeing, she would either have to retrace the route she had taken and get out, or curl into a fetal ball and weep.

She encountered a dozen people who needed to be extracted from the wreckage and given immediate medical treatment, but they were all either too large or too tightly wedged in the rubble for her to be of any assistance. Besides, she was drawn forward by the haunting cries of the child, driven by that instinctive understanding that children were always to be saved first: one of the major clauses of nature's genetically programmed triage policy.

Sirens rose in the distance. She had never paused to think that professional rescuers would be on their way. It didn't matter. She couldn't go back and wait for them to handle this. What if reaching the child a minute or two sooner made all the difference between death and survival?

As Holly inched forward, now and then glimpsing anemic but worrisome flames through gaps in the web of destruction, she heard Jim Ironheart behind her, calling her name at the opening where the forward part of the plane had been amputated from the rest of it. In the chaos after falling from the mid-section of the DC-10, they had apparently emerged from the smoke at different places, heading in opposite directions, for she had not been able to find him even though he should have been right behind her. She had been pretty sure that he and Casey had survived, if only because he obviously had a talent for survival; but it was good to hear his voice.

'In here!' she shouted, although the tangle of devastation prevented her from seeing him.

'What're you doing?'

'Looking for a child,' she called back. 'I hear him, I'm getting closer, but I can't see him yet.'

'Get out of there!' He shouted above the increasingly loud wail of approaching emergency vehicles. 'Paramedics are on the way, they're trained for this.'

'Come on,' she said, pushing forward. 'There're other people in here who need help *now*!'

Holly was nearing the front of the first-class section, where the steel ribs of the fuselage had broken inward but not in such profusion as in the area behind her. Detached seats, carry-on luggage, and other detritus had flown forward on impact, however, piling up deeper there than anywhere else. More people had wound up in that pile, too, both dead and alive.

When she shoved a broken and empty seat out of her way and paused to get her breath, she heard Jim clawing into the wreckage behind her.

Lying on her side, she squirmed through a narrow passage and into a pocket of open space, coming face to face with the boy whose cries she had been following. He was about five years old, with enormous dark eyes. He blinked at her in amazement and swallowed a sob, as if he had never really expected anyone to reach him.

He was under an inverted bank of five seats, in a peaked space formed by the seats themselves, as if in a tent. He was lying on his belly, looking out, and it seemed as if he ought to be able to slither into the open easily enough.

'Something's got my foot,' he said. He was still afraid, but manageably so. He had cast off the greater part of his terror the moment he had seen her. Whether you were five years old or fifty, the worst thing always was being alone. 'Got my foot, won't let go.'

Coughing, she said, 'I'll get you out, honey. You'll be OK.'

Holly looked up and saw another row of seats piled atop the lower bank. Both were wedged in by a mass of twisted steel pressing down from the caved-in ceiling, and she wondered if the forward section had rolled once before coming to rest right-side up.

With her fingertips she wiped the tears off his cheeks. 'What's your name, honey?'

'Norwood. Kids call me Norby. It don't hurt. My foot, I mean.'
She was glad to hear that.

But then, as she studied the wreckage around him and tried to figure out what to do, he said, 'I can't feel it.'

'Feel what, Norby?'

'My foot. It's funny, like something's holding it, 'cause I can't get loose, but then I can't *feel* my foot – you know? – like it maybe isn't there.'

Her stomach twisted at the image his words conjured in her mind. Maybe it wasn't that bad. Maybe his foot was only pinched between two surfaces, just numb, but she had to think fast and move fast because he might be losing blood at an alarming rate.

The space in which he lay was too cramped for her to squeeze in past him, find his foot, and disentangle it. Instead, she rolled on to her back, bent her legs, and braced the soles of her shoes against the seats that peaked over him.

'OK, honey, I'm going to straighten my legs, try to shove this up a little, just a couple inches. When it starts lifting, try to pull your foot out of there.'

As a snake of thin gray smoke slipped from the dark space behind Norby and coiled in front of his face, he wheezed and said, 'There's d-d-dead people in here with me.'

'That's OK, baby,' she said, tensing her legs, flexing them a little to test the weight she was trying to lever off him. 'You won't be there for long, not for long.'

'My seat, then an empty seat, then dead people,' Norby said shakily.

She wondered how long the trauma of this experience would shape his nightmares and bend the course of his life.

'Here goes,' she said.

She pressed upward with both feet. The pile of seats and junk and bodies was heavy enough, but the half-collapsed section of the ceiling, pushing down on everything else, did not seem to have any give in it. Holly strained harder until the steel deck, covered with only a thin carpet, pressed painfully into her back. She let out an involuntary sob of agony. Then she strained even harder, harder, angry that she could not move it, *furious*, and—

—it moved.

Only a fraction of an inch.

But it moved.

Holly put even more into it, found reserves she did not know she possessed, forced her feet upward until the pain throbbing in her legs was markedly worse than that in her back. The intruding tangle of ceiling plates and struts creaked and bent back an inch, two inches; the seats shoved up just that far.

'It's still got me,' the boy said.

More smoke was oozing out of the lightless space around him. It was not pale-gray but darker than before, sootier, oilier, and with a new foul stench. She hoped to God the desultory flames had not, at last, ignited the upholstery and foam padding that formed the cocoon from which the boy was struggling to emerge.

The muscles in her legs were quivering. The pain in her back had seeped all the way through to her chest; each heartbeat was an aching thud, each inhalation was a torment.

She did not think she could hold the weight any longer, let alone lift it higher. But abruptly it jolted up another inch, then slightly more.

Norby issued a cry of pain and excitement. He wriggled forward. 'I got away, it let go of me.'

Relaxing her legs and easing the load back into place, Holly realized that the boy had thought what she, too, might have thought if she'd been a five-year-old in that hellish position: that his ankle had been clenched in the cold and iron-strong hand of one of the dead people in there with him.

She slid aside, giving Norby room to pull himself out of the hollow under the seats. He joined her in the pocket of empty space amidst the rubble and snuggled against her for comforting.

From farther back in the plane, Jim shouted: 'Holly!'

'I found him!'

'I've got a woman here, I'm getting her out.'

'Great!' she shouted.

Outside, the pitch of the sirens spiraled lower and finally down into silence as the rescue teams arrived.

Although more blackish smoke was drifting out of the dark space from which Norby had escaped, Holly took the time to examine his foot. It flopped to one side, sickeningly loose, like the foot of an old rag doll. It was broken at the ankle. She tore his sneaker off his rapidly swelling foot. Blood darkened his white sock, but when she looked at the flesh beneath, she discovered that it was only abraded and scored by a few shallow cuts. He was not going to bleed to death, but soon he was going to become aware of the excruciating pain of the broken ankle.

'Let's go, let's get out,' she said.

She intended to take him back the way she had come, but when she glanced to her left, she saw another crack in the fuselage. This one was immediately aft of the cockpit bulkhead, only a few feet away. It extended up the entire curve of the wall but did not continue on to the ceiling. A section of interior paneling, the insulation beneath it, structural beamwork, and exterior plating had either blown inward among the other debris or been wrenched out into the field. The resultant hole was not large, but it was plenty big enough for her to squeeze through with the boy.

As they balanced on the rim of the ravaged hull, a rescue worker appeared in the plowed field about twelve feet below them. He held his arms out for the boy.

Norby jumped. The man caught him, moved back.

Holly jumped, landed on her feet.

'You his mother?' the man asked.

'No. I just heard him crying, went in after him. He's got a broken ankle there.'

'I was with my Uncle Frank,' Norby said.

'OK,' the rescue worker said, trying to strike a cheerful note, 'then let's find Uncle Frank.'

Norby said flatly, 'Uncle Frank's dead.'

The man looked at Holly, as if she might know what to say.

Holly was mute and shaken, filled with despair that a boy of five should have to experience such an ordeal. She wanted to hold him, rock him in her arms, and tell him that everything would be right with the world.

But nothing is right with the world, she thought, because Death is part of it. Adam disobeyed and ate the apple, gobbled up the fruit of knowledge, so God decided to let him know all sorts of things, both light and dark. Adam's children learned to hunt, to farm, to thwart the winter and cook their food with fire, make tools, build shelters. And God, wanting to give them a *well-rounded* education, let them learn, oh, maybe a million ways to suffer and die. He encouraged them to learn language, reading and writing, biology, chemistry, physics, the secrets of the genetic code. And He taught them the exquisite horrors of brain tumors, muscular dystrophy, bubonic plague, cancer run amok in their bodies – and not least of all airplane crashes. You wanted knowledge, God was happy to oblige, He was an enthusiastic teacher, a *demon* for knowledge, piling it on in such weight and exotic detail that sometimes you felt you were going to be crushed under it.

By the time the rescue worker turned away and carried Norby across the field toward a white ambulance parked on the edge of the runway, Holly had gone from despair to anger. It was a useless rage, for there was no one but God against whom she could direct it, and the expression of it could change nothing. God would not free the human race from the curse of death just because Holly Thorne thought it was a gross injustice.

She realized that she was in the grip of a fury not unlike that which seemed to motivate Jim Ironheart. She remembered what he had said during their whispered conversation in row seventeen, when she had tried to bully him into saving not just the Dubroveks but everyone aboard Flight 246: '*I hate death, people dying, I* hate *it!*' Some of the people he saved had quoted him making similar remarks, and Holly remembered what Viola Moreno had said about the deep and quiet sadness in him that perhaps grew out of being orphaned at the age of ten. He quit teaching, walked away from his career, because Larry Kakonis's suicide had made all his effort and concern seem pointless. That reaction at first appeared extreme to Holly, but now she understood it perfectly. She felt the same urge to cast aside a mundane life and do something more meaningful, to crack the rule of fate, to wrench the very fabric of the universe into a shape other than that which God seemed to prefer for it.

For a fragile moment, standing in that Iowa field with the wind blowing the stink of death to her, watching the rescue worker walk away with the little boy who had almost died, Holly felt closer to Jim Ironheart than she had ever been to another human being.

She went looking for him.

The scene around the broken DC-10 had become more chaotic than it had been immediately after the crash. Fire trucks had driven onto the plowed field. Streams of rich white foam arced over the broken plane, frosted the fuselage in whipped-cream-like gobs, and damped the flames on the surrounding fuel-soaked earth. Smoke still churned out of the mid-section, plumed from every rent and shattered window; shifting to the whims of the wind, a black canopy spread over them and cast eerie, constantly changing shadows as it filtered the afternoon sunshine, raising in her mind the image of a grim kaleidoscope in which all the pieces of glass were either black or gray. Rescue workers and paramedics swarmed over the wreckage, searching for survivors, and their numbers were so unequal to the awesome task that some of the more fortunate passengers pitched in to help. Other passengers – some so untouched by the experience that they appeared freshly showered and dressed, others filthy and disheveled – stood alone or in small groups, waiting for the minibuses that would take them to the Dubuque terminal, chattering nervously or stunned into silence. The only things threading the crash scene together and providing it with some coherence were the static-filled voices crackling on shortwave radios and walkie-talkies.

Though Holly was searching for Jim Ironheart, she found instead a young woman in a yellow shirtwaist dress. The stranger was in her early twenties, slender, auburn-haired, with a porcelain face; and though uninjured she badly needed help. She was standing back from the still-smoking rear section of the airliner, shouting a name over and over again: 'Kenny! Kenny! Kenny!' She had shouted it so often that her voice was hoarse.

Holly put a hand on the woman's shoulder and said, 'Who is he?'

The stranger's eyes were the precise blue of wisteria – and glazed. 'Have you seen Kenny?'

'Who is he, dear?'

'My husband.'

'What does he look like?'

Dazed, she said, 'We were on our honeymoon.'

'I'll help you look for him.'

'No.'

'Come on, kid, it'll be all right.'

'I don't want to look for him,' the woman said, allowing Holly to turn her away from the plane and lead her toward the ambulances. 'I don't want to see him. Not the way he'll be. All dead. All broken up and burned and dead.'

They walked together through the soft, tilled earth, where a new crop would be planted in late winter and sprout up green and tender in the spring, by which time all signs of death would have been eradicated and nature's illusion of life everlasting restored.

•5•

Something was happening to Holly. A fundamental change was taking place in her. She didn't understand what it was yet, didn't know what it would mean or how different a person she would be when it was complete, but she was aware of profound movement in the bedrock of her heart, her mind.

Because her inner world was in such turmoil, she had no spare energy to cope with the outer world, so she placidly followed the standard post-crash program with her fellow passengers.

She was impressed by the web of emotional, psychological, and practical support provided to survivors of Flight 246. Dubuque's medical and civil-defense community – which obviously had planned for such an emergency – responded swiftly and effectively. In addition psychologists, counsellors, ministers, priests, and a rabbi were available to the uninjured passengers within minutes of their arrival at the terminal. A large VIP lounge – with mahogany tables and comfortable chairs upholstered in nubby blue fabric – had been set aside for their use, ten or twelve telephone lines sequestered from normal airport operations, and nurses provided to monitor them for signs of delayed shock.

United's employees were especially solicitous, assisting with local overnight accommodation and new travel arrangements, as quickly as possible reuniting the uninjured with friends or relatives who had been transported to various hospitals, and compassionately conveying word of loved ones' deaths. Their horror and grief seemed as deep as that of the passengers, and they were shaken and remorseful that such a thing could happen with one of their planes. Holly saw a young woman in a United jacket turn suddenly and leave the room in tears, and all the others, men and women alike, were pale and shaky. She found herself wanting to console *them*, put an arm around them and tell them that even the best-built and best-maintained machines were doomed to fail sooner or later because human knowledge was imperfect and darkness was loose in the world.

Courage, dignity, and compassion were so universally in evidence under such trying circumstances that Holly was dismayed by the full-scale arrival of the media. She knew that dignity, at least, would be an early victim of their assault. To be fair, they were only doing their job, the problems and pressures of which she knew too well. But the percentage of reporters who could perform their work properly was no greater than the percentage of plumbers who were competent or the percentage of carpenters who could miter a doorframe perfectly every time. The difference was that unfeeling, inept, or downright hostile reporters could cause their subjects considerable embarrassment and, in some cases, malign the innocent and permanently damage reputations, which was a lot worse than a backed-up drain or mismatched pieces of wood molding.

The whole spectrum of TV, radio, and print journalists swarmed into the airport and soon penetrated even those areas where their presence was officially restricted. Some were respectful of the survivors' emotional and mental condition, but most of them badgered the United employees about 'responsibility' and 'moral obligation,' or hounded the survivors to reveal their innermost fears and relive the recent horror for the delectation of news consumers. Though Holly knew the drill and was expert at fending them off, she was asked the same question half a dozen times by four different reporters within fifteen minutes: How did you feel? How did you feel when you heard it might be a crash landing? How did you *feel* when you thought you were going to die? How did you feel when you saw that some of those around you *had* died?

Finally, cornered near a large observation window that looked out on arriving and departing flights, she blew up at an eager and expensively coiffured CNN reporter named Anlock, who simply could not understand that she was unflattered by his attentions. 'Ask me what I saw, or ask me what I think,' she told him. 'Ask me who, what, where, why, and how, but for God's sake don't ask me how I feel, because if you're a human being you've got to *know* how I feel. If you have any empathy at all for the human condition, you've got to know.'

Anlock and his cameraman tried to back off, move on to other prey. She was aware that most of the people in the crowded room had turned to see what the commotion was about, but she didn't care. She was not going to let Anlock off that easily. She stayed with him:

'You don't want facts, you just want drama, you want blood and thunder, you want people to bare their souls to you, then you edit what they say, change it, misreport it, get it all wrong most of the time, and that's a kind of rape, damn it.'

She realized that she was in the grip of the same rage she had experienced at the crash site, and that she was not half as angry at Anlock as she was at God, futile as that might be. The reporter was just a more convenient target than the Almighty, who could stay hidden in some shadowy corner of His heaven. She'd thought her anger had subsided; she was disconcerted to find that same black fury welling high within her again.

She was over the top, out of control, and she didn't care – until she realized CNN was on the air live. A predatory glint in Anlock's eyes and a twist of irony in his expression alerted her that he was not entirely dismayed by her outburst. She was giving him good color, first-rate drama, and he could not resist using it even if he was the object of her abuse. Later, of course, he would magnanimously excuse her behavior to viewers, insincerely sympathizing with the emotional trauma she had endured, thus coming off as a fearless reporter *and* compassionate guy.

Furious with herself for playing his game when she should have known that only the reporter ever wins, Holly turned from the camera. Even as she walked away, she heard Anlock saying, '. . . quite understandable, of course, given what the poor woman has just been through . . .'

She wanted to go back and smash him in the face. And wouldn't *that* please him!

What's wrong with you, Thorne? she demanded of herself. You never lose it. Not like this. You never lose it, but now you're definitely, absolutely losing it.

Trying to ignore the reporters and suppress her sudden interest in self-analysis, she went looking for Jim Ironheart again but still had no luck locating him. He was not among the latest group arriving from the crash site. None of the United employees could find his name on the passenger roster, which did not exactly surprise Holly.

She figured he was still in the field, assisting the search-and-rescue team in whatever way he could. She was eager to speak with him, but she would have to be patient.

Although some of the reporters were wary of her after the way she verbally assaulted Anlock, she knew how to manipulate her own kind. Sipping from a Styrofoam cup of bitter black coffee – as if she needed caffeine to improve her edge – she drifted around the room and into the hall outside, pumping them without revealing that she was one of them, and she was able to obtain bits of interesting information. Among other things, she discovered that two hundred survivors were already accounted for, and that the death toll was unlikely to exceed fifty, a miraculously low number of fatalities, considering the breakup of the plane and the subsequent fire. She should have been exhilarated by that good news, for it meant Jim's intervention had permitted the captain to save many more lives than fate had intended; but instead of rejoicing, she brooded about those who, in spite of everything, had been lost.

She also learned that members of the flight crew, all of whom survived, were hoping to find a passenger who had been a great help to them, a man described as 'Jim Something, sort-of-a-Kevin-Costner-lookalike with very blue eyes.' Because the first federal officials to arrive on the scene were also eager to talk to Jim Something, the media began looking for him as well.

Gradually Holly realized that Jim would not be putting in an appearance. He would fade, just as he always did after one of his exploits, moving quickly beyond the reach of reporters and officialdom of all stripes. Jim was the only name for him that they would ever have.

Holly was the first person, at the site of one of his rescues, to whom he had given his full name. She frowned, wondering why he had chosen to reveal more to her than to anyone else.

Outside the door of the nearest women's restroom, she encountered Christine Dubrovek, who returned her purse and asked about Steve Harkman, never realizing that he was the mysterious Jim after whom everyone else was inquiring.

'He had to be in Chicago this evening, no matter what, so he's already rented a car and left,' Holly lied.

'I wanted to thank him again,' Christine said. 'But I guess I'll have to wait until we're both back in Los Angeles. He works in the same company as my husband, you know.'

Casey, close at her mother's side, had scrubbed the soot off her face and combed her hair. She was eating a chocolate bar, but she did not appear to be enjoying it.

As soon as she could, Holly excused herself and returned to the emergency-assistance center that United had established in a corner of the VIP lounge. She tried to arrange for a flight that, regardless of the number of connections, would return her to Los Angeles that night. But Dubuque was not exactly the hub of the universe, and all seats to anywhere in southern California were already booked. The best she could do was a flight to Denver in the morning, followed by a noon flight from Denver to LAX.

United arranged overnight lodging for her, and at six o'clock, Holly found herself alone in a clean but cheerless room at the Best Western Midway Motor Lodge. Maybe it was not really so cheerless; in her current state of mind, she would not have been capable of appreciating a suite at the Ritz.

She called her parents in Philadelphia to let them know she was safe, in case they had seen her on CNN or spotted her name among a list of Flight 246 survivors in tomorrow's newspaper. They were happily unaware of her close call, but they insisted on whipping up a prime case of retrospective fright. She found herself consoling them, instead of the other way around, which was touching because it confirmed how much they loved her. 'I don't care how important this story is you're working on,' her mother said, 'you can take a bus the rest of the way, and a bus home.'

Knowing she was loved did not improve Holly's mood.

Though her hair was a tangled mess and she smelled of smoke, she walked to a nearby shopping center, where she used her Visa card to purchase a change of clothes: socks, underwear, blue jeans, a white blouse, and a lightweight denim jacket. She bought new Reeboks, too, because she could not shake the suspicion that the discolorations on her old pair were bloodstains.

In her room again, she took the longest shower of her life, lathering and re-lathering herself until one entire complimentary motel-size bar of soap had been reduced to a crumbling sliver. She still did not feel clean, but she finally turned the water off when she realized that she was trying to scrub away something that was inside of her.

She ordered a sandwich, salad, and fruit from room service. When it came, she could not eat it.

She sat for a while, just staring at the wall.

She dared not turn on the television. She didn't want to risk catching a news report about the crash of Flight 246.

If she could have called Jim Ironheart, she would have done so at once. She would have called him every ten minutes, hour after hour, until he arrived home and answered. But she already knew that his number was not listed.

Eventually she went down to the cocktail lounge, sat at the bar, and ordered a beer – a dangerous move for someone with her pathetic tolerance for alcohol. Without food to accompany it, one bottle of Becks would probably knock her unconscious for the rest of the night.

A traveling salesman from Omaha tried to strike up a conversation with her. He was in his mid-forties, not unattractive, and seemed nice enough, but she didn't want to lead him on. She told him, as nicely as she could, that she was not looking to get picked up.

'Me neither,' he said, and smiled. 'All I want is someone to talk to.'

She believed him, and her instincts proved reliable. They sat at the bar together for a couple of hours, chatting about movies and television shows, comedians and singers, weather and food, never touching on politics, plane crashes, or the cares of the world. To her surprise, she drank three beers and felt nothing but a light buzz.

'Howie,' she said quite seriously when she left him, 'I'll be grateful to you for the rest of my life.'

She returned to her room alone, undressed, slid under the sheets, and felt sleep stealing over her even as she put her head on the pillow. Pulling the covers around her to ward off the chill of the air conditioner, she spoke in a voice slurred more by exhaustion than by beer: 'Snuggle down in my cocoon, be a butterfly soon.' Wondering where *that* had come from and what she meant by it, she fell asleep.

Whoosh, whoosh, whoosh, whoosh, whoosh . . .

Though she was in the stone-walled room again, the dream was different in many ways from what it had been previously. For one thing, she was not blind. A fat yellow candle stood in a blue dish, and its dancing orange flame revealed stone walls, windows as narrow as embrasures, a wooden floor, a turning shaft that came through the ceiling above and disappeared through a hole into the room below, and a heavy door of iron-bound timbers. Somehow she knew that she was in the upper chamber of an old windmill, that the sound – *whoosh, whoosh, whoosh* – was produced by the mill's giant sails cutting the turbulent night wind, and that beyond the door lay curved limestone steps that led down to the milling room. Though she was standing when the dream began, circumstances changed with a ripple, and she was suddenly sitting, though not in an ordinary chair. She was in an airline seat, belted in place, and when she turned her head to the left, she saw Jim Ironheart seated beside her. 'This old mill won't make it to Chicago,' he said solemnly. And it seemed quite logical that they were flying in that stone structure, lifted by its four giant wood-slat sails the way an airliner was kept aloft by its jets or propellers. 'We'll survive, though – won't we?' she asked. Before her eyes, Jim faded and was replaced by a ten-year-old boy. She marvelled at this magic. Then she decided that the boy's thick brown hair and electric-blue eyes meant he was Jim from another time. According to the liberal rules of dreams, that made his transformation less magical and, in fact, altogether logical. The boy said, 'We'll survive if *it* doesn't come.' And she said, 'What is *it*?' And he said, 'The Enemy.' Around them the mill seemed to respond to his last two words, flexing and contracting, pulsing like flesh, just as her motel-room wall in Laguna Hills had bulged with malevolent life last night. She thought she glimpsed a monstrous face and form taking its substance from the very limestone. 'We'll die here,' the boy said, 'we'll all die here,' and he seemed almost to welcome the creature that was trying to come out of the wall. *WHOOSH!*

Holly came awake with a start, as she had at some point during each of the past three nights. But this time no element of the dream followed her into the real world, and she was not terrified as she had been before. Afraid, yes. But it was a low-grade fear, more akin to disquiet than to hysteria.

More important, she rose from the dream with a buoyant sense of liberation. Instantly awake, she sat up in bed, leaned back against the headboard, and folded her arms across her bare breasts. She was shivering neither with fear nor because of a chill, but with excitement.

Earlier in the night, tongue lubricated by beer, she had spoken a truth as she had slipped off the precipice of sleep: '*Snuggle down in my cocoon, be a butterfly soon.*' Now she knew what she had meant, and she understood the changes that she had been going through ever since she had tumbled to Ironheart's secret, changes that she had only begun to realize were underway when she had been in the VIP lounge at the airport after the crash.

She was never going back to the *Portland Press*.

She was never going to work on a newspaper again.

She was finished as a reporter.

That was why she had over-reacted to Anlock, the CNN reporter at the airport. Loathing him, she was nevertheless eaten by guilt on a subconscious level because he was chasing a major story that she was ignoring even though she was a *part* of it. If she was a reporter, she should have been interviewing her fellow survivors and rushing to write it up for the *Press*. No such desire touched her, however, not even for a fleeting moment, so she took the raw cloth of her subconscious self-disgust and tailored a suit of rage with enormous shoulders and wide, wide lapels; then she dressed herself in it and strutted and seethed for the CNN camera, all in a frantic attempt to deny that she didn't care about journalism any more and that she was going to walk away from a career and a commitment that she had once thought would last all her life.

Now she got out of bed and paced, too excited to sit still.

She was finished as a reporter.

Finished.

She was free. As a working-class kid from a powerless family, she had been obsessed by a lifelong need to feel important, included, a real insider. As a bright child who grew into a brighter woman, she had been puzzled by the apparent disorderliness of life, and she had been compelled to explain it as best she could with the inadequate tools of journalism. Ironically, the dual quest for acceptance and explanations – which had driven her to work and study seventy- and eighty-hour weeks for as long as she could remember – had left her rootless, with no significant lover, no children, no real friends, and no more answers to the difficult questions of life than those with which she had started. Now she was suddenly free of those needs and obsessions, no longer concerned about belonging to any elite club or explaining human behavior.

She had thought she hated journalism. She didn't. What she hated was her failure at it; and she had failed because journalism had never been the right thing for her.

To understand herself and break the bonds of habit, all she had needed was to meet a man who could work miracles, and survive a devastating airline tragedy.

'Such a *flexible* woman, Thorne,' she said aloud, mocking herself. 'So insightful.'

Why, good heavens, if meeting Jim Ironheart and walking away from a plane crash hadn't made her see the light, then surely she'd have figured it out just as soon as Jiminy Cricket rang her doorbell and sang a cleverly rhymed lesson-teaching song about the differences between wise and stupid choices in life.

She laughed. She pulled a blanket off the bed, wound it around her nude body, sat in one of the two armchairs, drew her legs up under her, and laughed as she had not laughed since she had been a giddy teenager.

No, that was where the problem began: she had *never* been giddy. She had been a serious-minded teenager, already hooked on current events, worried about World War Three because they told her she was likely to die in a nuclear holocaust before she graduated from high school; worried about overpopulation because they told her that famine would claim one and a half billion lives by 1990, cutting the world population in half, decimating even the United States; worried because manmade pollution was causing the planet to cool down drastically, insuring another ice age that would destroy civilization *within her own lifetime!!!!*, which was front-page news in the late seventies, before the Greenhouse Effect and worries about planetary warming. She had spent her adolescence and early adulthood worrying too much and enjoying too little. Without joy, she had lost perspective and had allowed every news sensation – some based on genuine problems, some entirely fraudulent – to consume her.

Now she laughed like a kid. Until they hit puberty and a tide of hormones washed them into a new existence, kids knew that life was scary, yeah, dark and strange, but they also knew that it was silly, that it was meant to be fun, that it was an adventurous journey down a long road of time to an unknown destination in a far and wondrous place.

Holly Thorne, who suddenly liked her name, knew where she was going and why.

She knew what she hoped to get from Jim Ironheart – and it was not a good story, journalistic accolades, a Pulitzer. What she wanted from him was better than that, more rewarding and enduring, and she was eager to confront him with her request.

The funny thing was, if he agreed and gave her what she wanted, she might be buying into more than excitement, joy, and a meaningful existence. She knew there was danger in it, as well. If she got what she asked from him, she might be dead a year from now, a month from now – or next week. But for the moment, at least, she focused on the prospect of joy and was not deterred by the possibility of early death and endless darkness.

Part Two

THE WINDMILL

Nowhere can a secret keep
always secret, dark and deep,
half so well as in the past,
buried deep to last, to last.

Keep it in your own dark heart,
otherwise the rumors start.

After many years have buried
secrets over which you worried,
no confidant can then betray
all the words you didn't say.

Only you can then exhume
secrets safe within the tomb
of memory, of memory,
within the tomb of memory.

   – The Book of Counted Sorrows

In the real world
as in dreams,
nothing is quite
what it seems.

   – The Book of Counted Sorrows

AUGUST 27 INTO AUGUST 29

·1·

Holly changed planes in Denver, gained two time zones traveling west, and arrived at Los Angeles International at eleven o'clock Monday morning. Unencumbered by luggage, she retrieved her rental car from the parking garage, drove south along the coast to Laguna Niguel, and reached Jim Ironheart's house by twelve-thirty.

She parked in front of his garage, followed the tile-trimmed walkway directly to his front door, and rang the bell. He did not answer. She rang it again. He still did not answer. She rang it repeatedly, until a reddish impression of the button marked the pad of her right thumb.

Stepping back, she studied the first- and second-floor windows. Plantation shutters were closed over all of them. She could see the wide slats through the glass.

'I know you're in there,' she said quietly.

She returned to her car, put the windows down, and sat behind the steering wheel, waiting for him to come out. Sooner or later he would need food, or laundry detergent, or medical attention, or toilet paper, *something*, and then she would have him.

Unfortunately, the weather was not conducive to a long stake-out. The past few days had been warm but mild. Now the August heat had returned like a bad dragon in a storybook: scorching the land with its fiery breath. The palm trees drooped and the flowers began to wilt in the blistering sun. Behind all of the elaborate watering systems that maintained the lush landscaping, the dispossessed desert waited to reassert itself.

Baking as swiftly and evenly as a muffin in a convection oven, Holly finally put up the windows, started the car, and switched on the air-conditioner. The cold draft was heavenly, but before long the car began to overheat; the needle rose swiftly toward the red section of the arc on the temperature gauge.

At one-fifteen, just three-quarters of an hour after she had arrived, Holly threw the car in reverse, backed out of the driveway, and returned to the Laguna Hills Motor Inn. She changed into tan shorts and a canary-yellow Calypso blouse that left her belly bare. She put on her new running shoes, but without socks this time. At a nearby Sav-On drugstore, she bought a vinyl-strap folding lounge chair, beach towel, tube of tanning cream, picnic cooler, bag of ice, six-pack of diet soda, and a Travis McGee paperback by John D. MacDonald. She already had sunglasses.

She was back at Ironheart's house on Bougainvillea Way before two-thirty. She tried the doorbell again. He refused to answer.

Somehow she knew he was in there. Maybe *she* was a little psychic.

She carried the ice chest, folding lounger, and other items around the side of the house to the lawn in back. She set up the chair on the grass, just beyond the redwood-covered patio. In a few minutes, she was comfy.

In the MacDonald novel, Travis McGee was sweltering down there in Fort Lauderdale, where they were having a heatwave so intense it even took the bounce out of the beach bunnies. Holly had read the book before; she chose to re-read it now because she had remembered that the plot unfolded against a background of tropical heat and humidity. Steamy Florida, rendered in MacDonald's vivid prose, made the dry air of Laguna Niguel seem less torrid by comparison, even though it had to be well over ninety degrees.

After about half an hour, she glanced at the house and saw Jim Ironheart standing at the big kitchen window. He was watching her.

She waved.

He did not wave back at her.

He walked away from the window but did not come outside.

Opening a diet soda, returning to the novel, she relished the feel of the sun on her bare legs. She was not worried about a burn. She already had a little tan. Besides, though blond and fair-skinned, she had a tanning gene that insured against a burn as long as she didn't indulge in marathon sunbathing.

After a while, when she got up to readjust the lounger so she could lie on her stomach, she saw Jim Ironheart standing on the patio, just outside the sliding glass door of his family room. He was in rumpled slacks and a wrinkled T-shirt, unshaven. His hair was lank and oily. He didn't look well.

He was about fifteen feet away, so his voice carried easily to her: 'What do you think you're doing?'

'Bronzing up a little.'

'Please leave, Miss Thorne.'

'I need to talk to you.'

'We have nothing to talk about.'

'Hah!'

He went back inside and slid the door shut. She heard the latch click.

After lying on her stomach for almost an hour, dozing instead of reading, she decided she'd had enough sun. Besides, at three-thirty in the afternoon, the best tanning rays were past.

She moved the lounger, cooler, and the rest of her paraphernalia on to the shaded patio. She opened a second diet soda and picked up the MacDonald novel again.

At four o'clock she heard the family-room door sliding open again. His footsteps approached and stopped behind her. He stood there for a while, evidently looking down at her. Neither of them spoke, and she pretended to keep reading.

His continued silence was eerie. She began to think about his dark side – the eight shotgun rounds he had pumped into Norman Rink in Atlanta, for one thing – and she grew increasingly nervous until she decided that he was *trying* to spook her.

When Holly picked up her can of soda from the top of the cooler, took a sip, sighed with pleasure at the taste, and put the can down again all without letting her hand tremble even once, Ironheart at last came around the lounge chair and stood where she could see him. He was still slovenly and unshaven. Dark circles ringed his eyes. He had an unhealthy pallor.

'What do you want from me?' he asked.

'That'll take a while to explain.'

'I don't have a while.'

'How long do you have?'

'One minute,' he said.

She hesitated, then shook her head. 'Can't do it in a minute. I'll just wait here till you've got more time.'

He stared at her intimidatingly.

She found her place in the novel.

He said, 'I could call the police, have you put off my property.'

'Why don't you do that?' she said.

He stood there a few seconds longer, impatient and uncertain, then re-entered the house. Slid the door shut. Locked it.

'Don't take forever,' Holly muttered. 'In about another hour, I'm gonna have to use your bathroom.'

Around her, two hummingbirds drew nectar from the flowers, the shadows lengthened, and exploding bubbles made hollow ticking sounds inside her open can of soda.

Down in Florida, there were also hummingbirds and cool shadows, icy bottles of Dos Equis instead of diet cola, and Travis McGee was getting into deeper trouble by the paragraph.

Her stomach began to grumble. She had eaten breakfast at the airport in Dubuque, surprised that her appetite had not been suppressed forever by the macabre images burned into her mind at the crash scene. She had missed lunch, thanks to the stakeout; now she was famished. Life goes on.

Fifteen minutes ahead of Holly's bathroom deadline, Ironheart returned. He had showered and shaved. He was dressed in a blue boatneck shirt, white cotton slacks, and white canvas Topsiders.

She was flattered by his desire to make a better appearance.

'OK,' he said, 'what do you want?'

'I need to use your facilities first.'

A long-suffering look lengthened his face. 'OK, OK, but then we talk, get it over with, and you go.'

She followed him into the family room, which was adjacent to an open breakfast area, which was adjacent to an open kitchen. The mismatched furniture appeared to have been purchased on the cheap at a warehouse clearance sale immediately after he had graduated from college and taken his first teaching job. It was clean but well worn. Hundreds of paperback books filled free-standing cases. But there was no artwork of any kind on the walls, and no decor pieces such as vases or bowls or sculptures or potted plants lent warmth to the room.

He showed her the powder room off the main entrance foyer. No wallpaper, white paint. No designer soaps shaped like rosebuds, just a bar of Ivory. No colorful or embroidered handtowels, just a roll of Bounty standing on the counter.

As she closed the door, she looked back at him and said, 'Maybe we could talk over an early supper. I'm starved.'

When she finished in the bathroom, she peeked in his living room. It was decorated – to use the word as loosely as the language police would allow – in a style best described as Early Garage Sale, though it was even more Spartan than the family room. His house was surprisingly modest for a man who had won six million in the state lottery, but his furniture made the house seem Rockefellerian by comparison.

170

She went out to the kitchen and found him waiting at the round breakfast table.

'I thought you'd be cooking something,' she said, pulling out a chair and sitting opposite him.

He was not amused. 'What do you want?'

'Let me start by telling you what I *don't* want,' she said. 'I don't want to write about you, I've given up reporting, I've had it with journalism. Now, you believe that or not, but it's true. The good work you're doing can only be hampered if you're being hounded by media types, and lives will be lost that you might otherwise save. I see that now.'

'Good.'

'And I don't want to blackmail you. Anyway, judging by the unconscionably lavish style in which you live, I doubt you've got more than eighteen bucks left.'

He did not smile. He just stared at her with those gas-flame-blue eyes.

She said, 'I don't want to inhibit your work or compromise it in any way. I don't want to venerate you as the Second Coming, marry you, bear your children, or extract from you the meaning of life. Anyway, only Elvis Presley knows the meaning of life, and he's in a state of suspended animation in an alien vault in a cave on Mars.'

His face remained as immobile as stone. He was *tough*.

'What I want,' Holly said, 'is to satisfy my curiosity, learn how you do what you do, and why you do it.' She hesitated. She took a deep breath. Here came the big one: 'And I want to be part of it all.'

'What do you mean?'

She spoke fast, running sentences together, afraid he would interrupt her before she got it all out, and never give her another chance to explain herself. 'I want to work with you, help you, contribute to your mission, or whatever you call it, however you think of it, I want to save people, at least help *you* save them.'

'There's nothing you could do.'

'There must be something,' she insisted.

'You'd only be in the way.'

'Listen, I'm intelligent—'

'So what?'

'—well educated—'

'So am I.'

'—gutsy—'

'But I don't need you.'

'—competent, efficient—'

171

'Sorry.'

'Damn it!' she said, more frustrated than angry. 'Let me be your secretary, even if you don't need one. Let me be your girl Friday, your good right hand – at least your *friend*.'

He seemed unmoved by her plea. He stared at her for so long that she became uncomfortable, but she would not look away from him. She sensed that he used his singularly penetrating gaze as an instrument of control and intimidation, but she was not easily manipulated. She was determined not to let him shape this encounter before it had begun.

At last he said, 'So you want to be my Lois Lane.'

For a moment she had no idea what he was talking about. Then she remembered: Metropolis, the *Daily Planet*, Jimmy Olsen, Perry White, Lois Lane, Clark Kent, Superman.

Holly knew he was trying to irritate her. Making her angry was another way of manipulating her; if she became abrasive, he would have an excuse to turn her away. She was determined to remain calm and reasonably congenial in order to keep the door open between them.

But she could not sit still and control her temper at the same time. She needed to work off some of the energy of anger that was overcharging her batteries. She pushed her chair back, got up, and paced as she responded to him: 'No, that's exactly what I *don't* want to be. I don't want to be your chronicler, intrepid girl reporter. I'm sick of journalism.' Succinctly, she told him why. 'I don't want to be your swooning admirer, either, or that well-meaning but bumbling gal who gets herself in trouble all the time and has to rely on you to save her from the evil clutches of Lex Luthor. Something amazing is happening here, and I want to be part of it. It's also dangerous, yeah, but I still want to be a part of it, because what you're doing is so . . . so meaningful. I want to contribute any way I can, do something more worthwhile with my life than I've done so far.'

'Do-gooders are usually so full of themselves, so unconsciously arrogant, they do more damage than good,' he said.

'I'm not a do-gooder. That's not how I see myself. I'm not at all interested in being praised for my generosity and self-sacrifice. I don't need to feel morally superior. Just *useful*.'

'The world is full of do-gooders,' he said, refusing to relent. 'If I needed an assistant, which I don't, why would I choose you over all the *other* do-gooders out there?'

He was an impossible man. She wanted to smack him.

Instead she kept moving back and forth as she said, 'Yesterday, when I crawled back into the plane for that little boy, for Norby, I just . . . well, I amazed myself. I didn't know I had anything like that in me. I wasn't brave, I was scared to death the whole time, but I got him out of there, and I never felt better about myself.'

'You like the way people look at you when they know you're a hero,' he said flatly.

She shook her head. 'No, that's not it. Aside from one rescue worker, no one *knew* I'd pulled Norby out of there. I liked the way *I* looked at me after I'd done it, that's all.'

'So you're hooked on risk, heroism, you're a courage junkie.'

Now she wanted to smack him twice. In the face. *Crack, crack.* Hard enough to set his eyes spinning. It would make her feel so good.

She restrained herself. 'OK, fine, if that's the way you want to see it, then I'm a courage junkie.'

He did not apologize. He just stared at her.

She said, 'But that's better than inhaling a pound of cocaine up my nose every day, don't you think?'

He did not respond.

Getting desperate but trying not to show it, Holly said, 'When it was all over yesterday, after I handed Norby to that rescue worker, you know what I felt? More than anything else? Not elation at saving him – that too, but not mainly that. And not pride or the thrill of defeating death myself. Mostly I felt *rage*. It surprised me, even scared me. I was so furious that a little boy almost died, that his uncle had died beside him, that he'd been trapped under those seats with corpses, that all of his innocence had been blown away and that he couldn't ever again just enjoy life the way a kid ought to be able to, I wanted to punch somebody, wanted to make somebody apologize to him for what he'd been through. But fate isn't a sleazeball in a cheap suit, you can't put the arm on fate and make it say it's sorry, all you can do is stew in your anger.'

Her voice was not rising, but it was increasingly intense. She paced faster, more agitatedly. She was getting passionate instead of angry, which was even more certain to reveal the degree of her desperation. But she couldn't stop herself:

'Just stew in anger. Unless you're Jim Ironheart. *You* can do something about it, make a difference in a way nobody ever made a difference before. And now that I know about you, I can't just get on with my life, can't just shrug my shoulders and walk away, because you've given me a chance to find a strength in myself I didn't know I had, you've given me hope when I didn't even realize I was longing for it, you've shown me a way to satisfy a need that, until yesterday, I didn't even know I had, a need to fight back, to spit in Death's face. Damn it, you can't just close the door now and leave me standing out in the cold!'

He stared at her.

Congratulations, Thorne, she told herself scornfully. You were a monument to composure and restraint, a towering example of self-control.

He just stared at her.

She had met his cool demeanor with heat, had answered his highly effective silences with an even greater cascade of words. One chance, that was all she'd had, and she'd blown it.

Miserable, suddenly drained of energy instead of overflowing with it, she sat down again. She propped her elbows on the table and put her face in her hands, not sure if she was going to cry or scream. She didn't do either. She just sighed wearily.

'Want a beer?' he asked.

'God, yes.'

*   *   *

Like a brush of flame, the westering sun slanted through the tilted plantation shutters on the breakfast-nook window, slathering bands of copper-gold fire on the ceiling. Holly slumped in her chair, and Jim leaned forward in his. She stared at him while he stared at his half-finished bottle of Corona.

'Like I told you on the plane, I'm not a psychic,' he insisted. 'I can't foresee things just because I want to. I don't have visions. It's a higher power working through me.'

'You want to define that a little?'

He shrugged. 'God.'

'God's talking to you?'

'Not talking. I don't hear voices, His or anybody else's. Now and then I'm compelled to be in a certain place at a certain time . . .'

As best he could, he tried to explain how he had ended up at the McAlbury School in Portland and at the sites of the other miraculous rescues he had performed. He also told her about Father Geary finding him on the floor of the church, by the sanctuary railing, with the stigmata of Christ marking his brow, hands, and side.

It was off-the-wall stuff, a weird brand of mysticism that might have been concocted by an heretical Catholic and peyote-inspired

Indian medicine man in association with a no-nonsense Clint-Eastwood-style cop. Holly was fascinated. But she said, 'I can't honestly tell you I see God's big hand in this.'

'I do,' he said quietly, making it clear that his conviction was solid and in no need of her approval.

Nevertheless she said, 'Sometimes you've had to be pretty damned violent, like with those guys who kidnapped Susie and her mother in the desert.'

'They got what they deserved,' he said flatly. 'There's too much darkness in some people, corruption that could never be cleaned out in five lifetimes of rehabilitation. Evil is real, it walks the earth. Sometimes the devil works by persuasion. Sometimes he just sets loose these sociopaths who don't have a gene for empathy or one for compassion.'

'I'm not saying you didn't *have* to be violent in some of these situations. Far as I can see, you had no choice. I just meant – it's hard to see God encouraging his messenger to pick up a shotgun.'

He drank some beer. 'You ever read the Bible?'

'Sure.'

'Says in there that God wiped out the evil people in Sodom and Gomorrah with volcanoes, earthquakes, rains of fire. Flooded the whole world once, didn't He? Made the Red Sea wash over the Pharaoh's soldiers, drowned them all. I don't think He's going to be skittish about a little old shotgun.'

'I guess I was thinking about the God of the New Testament. Maybe you heard about Him – understanding, compassionate, merciful.'

He fixed her with those eyes again, which could be so appealing that they made her knees weak or so cold they made her shiver. A moment ago they had been warm; now they were icy. If she'd had any doubt, she knew from his frigid response that he had not yet decided to welcome her into his life. 'I've met up with some people who're such walking scum, it'd be an insult to animals to call them animals. If I thought God always dealt mercifully with their kind, I wouldn't want anything to do with God.'

*   *   *

Holly stood at the kitchen sink, cleaning mushrooms and slicing tomatoes, while Jim separated egg whites from yolks to make a pair of comparatively low-calorie omelettes.

'All the time, people are dying conveniently, right in your own

175

backyard. But often you go clear across the country to save them.'

'Once to France,' he said, confirming her suspicion that he had ventured out of the country on his missions. 'Once to Germany, twice to Japan, once to England.'

'Why doesn't this higher power give you only local work?'

'I don't know.'

'Have you ever wondered what's so special about the people you save? I mean – why them and not others?'

'Yeah. I've wondered about it. I see stories on the news every week about innocent people being murdered or dying in accidents right here in southern California, and I wonder why He didn't choose to save them instead of some boy in Boston. I just figure the boy in Boston – the devil was conspiring to take him before his time, and God used me to prevent that.'

'So many of them are young.'

'I've noticed that.'

'But you don't know why?'

'Not a clue.'

*   *   *

The kitchen was redolent of cooking eggs, onions, mushrooms, and green peppers. Jim made one big omelette in a single pan, planning to cut it in half when it was done.

While Holly monitored the progress of the whole-wheat bread in the toaster, she said, 'Why would God want you to save Susie and her mother out there in the desert – but not the girl's father?'

'I don't know.'

'The father wasn't a bad man, was he?'

'No. Didn't seem to be.'

'So why not save them all?'

'If He wants me to know, He'll tell me.'

Jim's certainty about being in God's good grace and under His guidance, and his easy acceptance that God *wanted* some people to die and not others, made Holly uneasy.

On the other hand, how could he react to his extraordinary experience in any other way? No point in arguing with God.

She recalled an old saying, a real chestnut that had become a cliché in the hands of the pop psych crowd: God grant me the courage to change those things I can't accept, to accept those things I can't change, and the wisdom to know the difference. Cliché or not, that was an eminently sane attitude.

When the two pieces of bread popped up, she plucked them from the toaster. As she toasted two more, she said, 'If God wanted to save Nicholas O'Conner from being fried when that power-company vault went up, why didn't He just prevent it from exploding in the first place?'

'I don't know.'

'Doesn't it seem odd to you that God has to use you, run you clear across the country, throw you at the O'Conner boy an instant before that 17,000-volt line blows up? Why couldn't He just . . . oh, I don't know . . . just spit on the cable or something, fix it up with a little divine saliva before it went blooey? Or instead of sending you all the way to Atlanta to kill Norman Rink in that convenience store, why didn't God just tweak Norman's brain a little, give him a timely stroke?'

Jim artfully tilted the pan to turn over the omelette. 'Why did He make mice to torment people and cats to kill the mice? Why did He create aphids that kill plants, then ladybugs to eat the aphids? And why didn't He give us eyes in the back of our head – when He gave us so many reasons to need them there?'

She finished lightly buttering the first two slices of toast. 'I see what you're saying. God works in mysterious ways.'

'Very.'

*   *   *

They ate at the breakfast table. In addition to toast, they had sliced tomatoes and cold bottles of Corona with the omelettes.

The purple cloth of twilight slid across the world outside, and the undraped form of night began to reveal itself.

Holly said, 'You aren't entirely a puppet in these situations.'

'Yes, I am.'

'You have some power to determine the outcome.'

'None.'

'Well, God sent you on Flight 246 to save just the Dubroveks.'

'That's right.'

'But then you took matters into your own hands and saved more than just Christine and Casey. How many were supposed to die?'

'A hundred and fifty-one.'

'And how many actually died?'

'Forty-seven.'

'OK, so you saved a hundred and two more lives than He sent you to save.'

'A hundred and three, counting yours – but only because He allowed me to do it, helped me to do it.'

'What – you're saying God wanted you to save just the Dubroveks, but then He changed His mind?'

'I guess so.'

'God isn't sure what He wants?'

'I don't know.'

'God is sometimes confused?'

'I don't know.'

'God is a waffler?'

'Holly, I just don't know.'

'Good omelette.'

'Thank you.'

'I have trouble understanding why God would ever change His mind about anything. After all, He's infallible, right? So He can't have made the wrong decision the first time.'

'I don't concern myself with questions like that. I just don't think about it.'

'Obviously,' she said.

He glared at her, and she felt the full effect of his eyes in their arctic mode. Then focusing on his food and beer, he refused to respond to Holly's next few conversational gambits.

She realized that she was no closer to winning his trust than she had been when he had reluctantly invited her in from the patio. He was still judging her, and on points she was probably losing. What she needed was a solid knockout punch, and she thought she knew what it was, but she didn't want to use it until the right moment.

When Jim finished eating, he looked up from his empty plate and said, 'OK, I've listened to your pitch, I've fed you, and now I want you to go.'

'No, you don't.'

He blinked. 'Miss Thorne—'

'You called me Holly before.'

'Miss Thorne, please don't make me *throw* you out.'

'You don't want me to go,' Holly said, striving to sound more confident than she felt. 'At all the scenes of these rescues, you've given only your first name. No one's learned anything more about you. Except me. You told me you lived in southern California. You told me your last name was Ironheart.'

'I never said you were a bad reporter. You're good at prying information—'

'I didn't pry. You gave it. And if it wasn't something you wanted to give, a grizzly bear with an engineering degree and crowbar couldn't pry it out of you. I want another beer.'

'I asked you to go.'

'Don't stir yourself. I know where you keep the suds.'

She got up, stepped to the refrigerator, and withdrew another bottle of Corona. She was walking on the wild side now, at least for her, but a third beer gave her an excuse – even if a flimsy one – to stay and argue with him. She had downed three bottles last night, at the motel cocktail lounge in Dubuque. But then she had still been saturated with adrenaline, as super-alert and edgy as a Siamese cat on benzedrine, which cancelled out the alcohol as fast as it entered her bloodstream. Even so, she had hit the bed as hard as a lumber-jack who'd downed a dozen boilermakers. If she passed out on Ironheart, she'd no doubt wake up in her car, out in the street, and she would never get inside his house again. She opened the beer and returned to the table with it.

'You *wanted* me to find you,' she said as she sat down.

He regarded her with all the warmth of a dead penguin frozen to an ice floe. 'I did, huh?'

'Absolutely. That's why you told me your last name and where I could find you.'

He said nothing.

'And you remember your last words to me at the airport in Portland?'

'No.'

'It was the best come-on line any guy's ever dropped on me.'

He waited.

She made him wait a little longer while she took a sip of beer straight from the bottle. 'Just before you closed the car door and went into the terminal, you said, "So are you, Miss Thorne." '

'Doesn't sound like much of a come-on line to me.'

'It was romantic as hell.'

' "So are you, Miss Thorne." And what had you just said to me. "You're an asshole, Mr Ironheart"?'

'Ho, ho, ho,' she said. 'Try to spoil it, go ahead, but you can't. I'd told you that your modesty was refreshing, and you said, "So are you, Miss Thorne." My heart just now went pitty-pat-pitty-pat again, remembering it. Oh, you knew just what you were doing, you smoothie. Told me your name, told me where you lived, gave me a lot of those eyes, those damned eyes, played coy, then hit me with "So are you, Miss Thorne," and walked away like Bogart.'

'I don't think you should have any more of that beer.'

'Yeah? Well, I think I'll sit here all night, drinking one of 'em after another.'

He sighed. 'In that case, I'd better have another one myself.'

He got another beer and sat down again.

Holly figured she was making progress.

Or maybe he was setting her up. Maybe getting cozy over Corona was a trick of some kind. He was clever, all right. Maybe he was going to try to drink her under the table. Well, he'd lose *that* one, because she'd be under the table long before him!

'You wanted me to find you,' she told him.

He said nothing.

'You know why you wanted me to find you?'

He said nothing.

'You wanted me to find you because you really did think I was refreshing, and you're the loneliest, sorriest guy between here and Hardrock, Missouri.'

He said nothing. He was good at that. He was the best guy in the world at saying nothing at just the right time.

She said, 'You make me want to smack you.'

He said nothing.

Whatever confidence the Corona had given her suddenly began to drain away. She sensed that she was losing again. For a couple of rounds, there, she had definitely been winning on points, but now she was being beaten back by his silence.

'Why are all these boxing metaphors running through my head?' she asked him. 'I hate boxing.'

He slugged down some of his Corona and, with a nod, indicated her bottle, from which she had drunk only a third. 'You really insist on finishing that?'

'Hell, yes.' She was aware that the brewski was beginning to affect her, perhaps dangerously, but she was still plenty sober enough to recognize that the moment had come for her knockout punch. 'If you don't tell me about that place, I'm going to sit here and drink myself into a fat, slovenly, alcoholic old crone. I'm going to die here at the age of eighty-two, with a liver the size of Vermont.'

'Place?' He looked baffled. 'What place?'

Now. She chose a soft but clear whisper in which to deliver the punch: 'The windmill.'

He didn't exactly fall to the canvas, and no cartoon stars swarmed around his head, but Holly could see that he had been rocked.

'You've been to the windmill?' he asked.

'No. You mean it's a real place?'

'If you don't know that much, then how could you know about it at all?'

'Dreams. Windmill dreams. Each of the last three nights.'

He paled. The overhead light was not on. They were sitting in shadows, illuminated only by the secondhand glow of the range-hood and sink lights in the kitchen and by a table lamp in the adjacent family room, but Holly saw him go pale under his tan. His face seemed to hover before her in the gloom like the face-shaped wing configuration of a big snow-white moth.

The extraordinary vividness and unusual nature of the nightmare – and the fact that the effects of the dream had continued after she had awakened in her motel room – had encouraged her to believe that it was somehow connected with Jim Ironheart. Two encounters with the paranormal in such close succession *had* to be linked. But she was relieved, all the same, when his stunned reaction confirmed her suspicion.

'Limestone walls,' she said. 'Wooden floor. A heavy wooden door, banded in iron, that opens on some limestone steps. A yellow candle in a blue dish.'

'I've dreamed about it for years,' he said softly. 'Once or twice a month. Never more often than that. Until the last three nights. But how can we be having the same dream?'

'Where's the real windmill?'

'On my grandparents' farm. North of Santa Barbara. In the Santa Ynez Valley.'

'Did something terrible happen to you there, or what?'

He shook his head. 'No. Not at all. I loved that place. It was . . . a sanctuary.'

'Then why did you go pale when I mentioned it?'

'Did I?'

'Picture an albino cat chasing a mouse around a corner and running into a Doberman. That pale.'

'Well, when I dream of the mill, it's always frightening—'

'Don't I know it. But if it was a good place in your life, a sanctuary like you say, then why does it feature in nightmares?'

'I don't know.'

'Here we go again.'

'I really don't,' he insisted. 'Why did *you* dream about it, if you've never even been there?'

She drank more beer, which did not clarify her thinking. 'Maybe because you're projecting your dream at me. As a way to sort of make a connection between us, draw me to you.'

'Why would I want to draw you to me?'

'Thanks a lot.'

'Anyway, like I told you before, I'm no psychic, I don't have abilities like that. I'm just an instrument.'

'Then it's this higher power of yours,' she said. 'It's sending me the same dream because it wants us to connect.'

He wiped one hand down his face. 'This is too much for me right now. I'm so damned tired.'

'Me too. But it's only nine-thirty, and we've still got a lot to talk about.'

'I only slept about an hour last night,' he said.

He really did look exhausted. A shave and a shower had made him presentable, but the bruise-dark rings around his eyes were getting darker; and he had not regained color in his face after turning pale at the mention of her windmill dreams.

He said, 'We can pick this up in the morning.'

She frowned. 'No way. I'll come back in the morning, and you won't let me in.'

'I'll let you in.'

'That's what you say now.'

'If you're having that dream, then you're part of this whether I like it or not.'

His tone of voice had gone from cool to cold again, and it was clear that what he meant by 'whether I like it or not' was really 'even though I don't like it.'

He was a loner, evidently always had been. Viola Moreno, who had great affection for him, claimed he was well liked by his students and colleagues. She'd spoken of a fundamental sadness in him, however, that separated him from other people, and since quitting his teaching position, he had seen little of Viola or his other friends from that life. Though intrigued by the news that he and Holly were sharing a dream, though he had called her 'refreshing,' though he was to some degree attracted to her, he obviously resented her intrusion into his solitude.

Holly said, 'No good. You'll be gone when I get here in the morning, I won't know where you went, maybe you'll never come back.'

He had no energy for resistance. 'Then stay the night.'

'You have a spare bedroom?'

'Yeah. But there's no spare bed. You can sleep on the family-room couch, I guess, but it's damned old and not too comfortable.'

She carried her half-empty beer into the adjacent family room, and tested the sagging, brown sofa. 'It'll be good enough.'

'Whatever you want.' He seemed indifferent, but she sensed that his indifference was a pretense.

'You have any spare pajamas?'

'Jesus.'

'Well, I'm sorry, but I didn't bring any.'

'Mine'll be too big for you.'

'Just makes them more comfortable. I'd like to shower too. I'm sticky from tanning lotion and being in the sun all afternoon.'

With the put-upon air of a man who had found his least favorite relative standing on his doorstep unannounced, he took her upstairs, showed her the guest bath, and got a pair of pajamas and a set of towels for her.

'Try to be quiet,' he said. 'I plan to be sound asleep in five minutes.'

* * *

Luxuriating in the fall of hot water and clouds of steam, Holly was pleased that the shower did not take the edge off her beer buzz. Though she had slept better last night than Ironheart claimed to have done, she had not gotten a solid eight hours in the past few days, and she was looking forward to a Corona-induced sleep even on the worn and lumpy sofa.

At the same time, she was uneasy about the continued fuzziness of her mind. She needed to keep her wits about her. After all, she was in the house of an undeniably strange man who was largely a cipher to her, a walking mystery. She understood little of what was in his heart, which pumped secrets and shadows in greater quantity than blood. For all his coolness toward her, he seemed basically a good man with benign intentions, and it was difficult to believe that he was a threat to her. On the other hand, it was not unusual to see a news story about a berserk mass murderer who – after brutally slaying his friends, family, and co-workers – was described by his astonished neighbors as 'a really nice guy.' For all she knew, in spite of his claim to be the avatar of God, by day Jim Ironheart heroically risked his own life to save the lives of strangers – and, by night, tortured kittens with maniacal glee.

Nevertheless, after she dried off on the clean-smelling, fluffy bath towel, she took another long swallow of her Corona. She decided that a full night of deep and dreamless sleep was worth the risk of being butchered in her bed.

She put on his pajamas, rolled up the cuffs of the pants and the sleeves.

Carrying her bottle of Corona, which still contained a swallow or two, she quietly opened the bathroom door and stepped into the second-floor hallway. The house was eerily silent.

Heading toward the stairs, she passed the open door of the master bedroom and glanced inside. Extension-arm brass reading lamps were mounted on the wall on both sides of the bed, and one of them cast a narrow wedge of amber light on the rumpled sheets. Jim was lying on his back in bed, his arms folded on the two pillows under his head, and he seemed to be awake.

She hesitated, then stepped into the open doorway. 'Thanks,' she said, speaking softly in case he was asleep, 'I feel a lot better.'

'Good for you.'

Holly entered the room and moved close enough to the bed to see his blue eyes shining in the backsplash of the lamp. The covers were pulled up past his navel, but he was not wearing pajama tops. His chest and arms were lean but well muscled.

She said, 'Thought you'd be asleep by now.'

'Want to be, need to be, but I can't shut my mind off.'

Looking down at him, she said, 'Viola Moreno says there's a deep sadness in you.'

'Been busy, haven't you?'

She took a small swallow of Corona. One left. She sat down on the edge of the bed. 'Do your grandparents still have the farm with the windmill?'

'They're dead.'

'I'm sorry.'

'Grandma died five years ago, Grandpa eight months later – as if he really didn't want to go on without her. They had good, full lives. But I miss them.'

'You have anybody?'

'Two cousins in Akron,' he said.

'You stay in touch?'

'Haven't seen them in twenty years.'

She drank the last of the Corona. She put the empty bottle on the nightstand.

For a few minutes neither of them spoke. The silence was not awkward. Indeed, it was comfortable.

She got up and went around to the other side of the bed. She pulled back the covers, stretched out beside him, and put her head on the other two pillows.

Apparently, he was not surprised. Neither was she.

After a while, they held hands, lying side by side, staring at the ceiling.

She said, 'Must've been hard, losing your parents when you were just ten.'

'Real bad.'

'What happened to them?'

He hesitated. 'A traffic accident.'

'And you went to live with your grandparents?'

'Yeah. The first year was the hardest. I was . . . in bad shape. I spent a lot of time in the windmill. It was my special place, where I went to play . . . to be alone.'

'I wish we'd been kids together,' she said.

'Why?'

She thought of Norby, the boy she had pulled from the sarcophagus under the DC-10's overturned seats. 'So I could've known you before your parents died, what you were like then, untouched.'

Another stretch of time passed in silence.

When he spoke, his voice was so low that Holly could barely hear it above the thumping of her own heart: 'Viola has a sadness in her too. She looks like the happiest lady in the world, but she lost her husband in Vietnam, never got over it. Father Geary, the priest I told you about, he looks like every devout parish rector from every old sentimental Catholic movie ever made in the thirties and forties, but when I met him he was weary and unsure of his calling. And you . . . well, you're pretty and amusing, and you have an air of efficiency about you, but I'd never have guessed that you could be as relentless as you are. You give the impression of a woman who moves easy through life, interested in life and in her work, but never moving against a current, always with it, easy. Yet you're really like a bulldog when you get your teeth in something.'

Staring at the dapple of light and shadow on the ceiling, holding his strong hand, Holly considered his statement for a while. Finally she said, 'What's your point?'

'People are always more . . . complex than you figure.'

'Is that just an observation . . . or a warning?'

He seemed surprised by her question. 'Warning?'

'Maybe you're warning me that you're not what you seem to be.'

After another long pause, he said, 'Maybe.'

She matched his silence. Then she said, 'I guess I don't care.'

He turned toward her. She moved against him with a shyness that she had not felt in many years. His first kiss was gentle, and more intoxicating than three bottles or three cases of Corona.

Holly realized she'd been deceiving herself. She had needed the beer not to soothe her nerves, not to insure an uninterrupted night of sleep, but to give her the courage to seduce him – or to be seduced. She had sensed that he was abysmally lonely, and she had told him so. Now she understood that her loneliness had exceeded his, and that only the smallest part of her desolation of spirit had resulted from her disenchantment with journalism; most of it was simply the result of being alone, for the most part, all of her adult life.

Two pajama bottoms and one top seemed to dissolve between them like clothes sometimes evaporate in erotic dreams. She moved her hands over him with increasing excitement, marvelling that the sense of touch could convey such intricacies of shape and texture, or give rise to such exquisite longings.

She'd had a ridiculously romantic idea of what it would be like to make love to him, a dreamy-eyed girl's fantasy of unmatched passion, of sweet tenderness and pure hot sex in perfect balance, every muscle in both of them flexing and contracting in sublime harmony or, at times, in breathless counterpoint, each invasive stroke a testament to mutual surrender, two becoming one, the outer world of reason overwhelmed by the inner world of feeling, no wrong word spoken, no sigh mistimed, bodies moving and meshing in precisely the same mysterious rhythms by which the great invisible tidal forces of the universe ebbed and flowed, elevating the act above mere biology and making of it a mystical experience. Her expectations proved, of course, to be ridiculous. In reality, it was more tender, more fierce, and far better than her fantasy.

*   *   *

They fell asleep like spoons in a drawer, her belly against his back, her loins against his warm bottom. Hours later, in those reaches of the night that were usually – but no longer – the loneliest of all, they woke to the same quiet alarm of renewed desire. He turned to her, she welcomed him, and this time they moved together with an even greater urgency, as if the first time had not taken the edge off their need but had sharpened it the way one dose of heroin only increases the addict's desire for the next.

At first, looking up into Jim's beautiful eyes, Holly felt as if she were gazing into the pure fire of his soul. Then he gripped her by the

186

sides, half lifting her off the mattress as he eased deep into her, and she felt the scratches burning in her flanks and remembered the claws of the thing that had stepped magically out of a dream. For an instant, with pain flashing in her shallow wounds, her perception shifted, and she had the queer feeling that it was a cold blue fire into which she gazed, burning without heat. But that was only a reaction to the stinging scratches and the pain-engendered memory of the nightmare. When he slid his hands off her sides and under her, lifting, she rose to meet him, and he was all warmth now, not the faintest chill about him. Together they generated enough heat to sear away that brief image of a soul on ice.

* * *

The frost-pale glow of the unseen moon backlit banks of coaly clouds that churned across the night sky.

Unlike in other recent dreams, Holly was standing outside on a graveled path that led between a pond and a cornfield toward the door in the base of the old windmill. The limestone structure rose above her at a severe angle, recognizably a mill but nonetheless an alien place, unearthly.

The huge sails, ragged with scores of broken or missing vanes, were silhouetted against the foreboding sky and angled like a tilted cross. Although a blustery wind sent moon-silvered ripples across the ink-dark pond and rattled the nearby cornstalks, the sails were still. The mill obviously had been inoperable for many years, and the mechanisms were most likely too rusted to allow the sails to turn.

A spectral muddy-yellow light flickered at the narrow windows of the upper room. Beyond the glass, strange shadows moved across the interior limestone walls of that high chamber.

She didn't want to get any closer to the building, had never been more frightened of a place in her life, but she was unable to halt herself. She was drawn forward as if she were in the spellbound thrall of some powerful sorcerer.

In the pond to her left, something was wrong with the moon-cast reflection of the windmill, and she turned to look at it. The pattern of light and shade on the water was reversed from what it should have been. The mill shadow was not a dark geometric form imposed on the water over the filigree of moonlight; instead, the image of the mill was brighter than the surface of the pond around it, as if the mill were luminous, the brightest object in the night, when in fact its stones rose in an ebony and forbidding pile. Where the high windows were filled with lambent light in the real mill, black rectangles floated in the impossible reflection, like the empty eye holes in a fleshless skull.

Creak . . . creak . . . creak . . .

She looked up.

The massive sails were trembling in the wind and beginning to move. They forced the corroded gears that drove the windshaft and, in turn, the grinding stones in the millroom at its base.

Wanting only to wake up or, failing that, to flee back along the gravel path over which she had come, Holly drifted inexorably forward. The giant sails began to turn clockwise, gaining speed, producing less creaking as the gears unfroze. It seemed to her that they were like the fingers of a monstrous hand, and the jagged end of every broken vane was a claw.

She reached the door.

She did not want to go inside. She knew that within lay a hell of some kind, as bad as the pits of torture described by any fire-and-brimstone preacher who had ever thundered a sermon in old Salem. If she went in there, she would never come out alive.

The sails swooped down at her, passing just a couple of feet over her head, the splintered wood reaching for her: *Whoosh, whoosh, whoosh, whoosh.*

In the grip of a trance even more commanding than her terror, she opened the door. She stepped across the threshold. With the malevolent animation that objects possessed only in dreams, the door pulled out of her hand, slammed shut behind her.

Ahead lay the lightless lower room of the mill, in which the worn stone wheels ground against each other.

To her left, barely visible in the gloom, stairs led up. Ululant squeals and haunting cries echoed from above, like the night concert performed by the wildlife in a jungle, except none of these voices was quite that of a panther or monkey or bird or hyena. Electronic sounds were part of the mix, and what seemed to be the brittle shrieks of insects passed through a stereo amplifier. Underlying the cacophony was a monotonous, throbbing, three-note bass refrain that reverberated in the stone walls of the stairwell and, before she had climbed halfway to the second floor, in Holly's bones as well.

She passed a narrow window on her left. An extended series of lightning bolts crackled across the vault of the night, and at the foot of the mill, like a trick mirror in a funhouse, the dark pond turned transparent. Its depths were revealed, as though the lightning came from under the water, and Holly saw an infinitely strange shape resting on the bottom. She squinted, trying to get a better look at the object, but the lightning sputtered out.

The merest glimpse of the thing, however, sent a cold wind through the hollows of her bones.

She waited, hoping for more lightning, but the night remained as opaque as tar, and black rain suddenly spattered against the window. Because she was halfway to the second floor of the mill, more muddy-orange and yellow light flickered around her than had reached her at the foot of the stairs. The window glass, backed by utter darkness now and painted with sufficient luminescence to serve as a dim mirror, presented her reflection.

But the face she possessed in this dream was not her own. It belonged to a woman twenty years older than Holly, to whom she bore no resemblance.

She'd never before had a dream in which she occupied the body of another person. But now she understood why she had been unable to turn back from the mill when she'd been outside, and why she was unable to stop herself from climbing to the high room even though, on one level, she knew she was dreaming. Her lack of control was not the usual helplessness that transformed dreams into nightmares, but the result of sharing the body of a stranger.

The woman turned from the window and continued upward toward the unearthly shrieks, cries, and whispers that echoed down to her with the fluctuant light. Around her the limestone walls pounded with the tripartite bass beat, as if the mill were alive and had a massive three-chambered heart.

Stop, turn back, you're going to die up there, Holly shouted, but the woman could not hear her. Holly was only an observer in her own dream, not an active participant, unable to influence events.

Step by step. Higher.

The iron-bound timber door stood open.

She crossed the threshhold. Into the high room.

The first thing she saw was the boy. He was standing in the middle of the room, terrified. His small hands, curled in fists, were at his sides. A three-inch-diameter decorative candle stood in a blue dish at his feet. A hardcover book lay beside the dish, and she glimpsed the word 'mill' on the colorful dustjacket.

Turning to look at her, his beautiful blue eyes darkened by terror, the boy said, 'I'm scared, help me, the walls, the *walls!*'

She realized that the single candle was not producing all of the peculiar glow suffusing the room. Other light glimmered in the walls, as if they were not made of solid limestone but of semi-transparent and magically radiant quartz in shades of amber. At once she saw that something was alive *within* the stone, something luminous which could move through solid matter as easily as a swimmer could move through water.

The wall swelled and throbbed.

'It's coming,' the boy said with evident fear but also with what might have been a perverse excitement, 'and nobody can stop it!'

Suddenly it was born out of the wall. The curve of mortared blocks split like the spongy membrane of an insect's egg. And taking shape from a core of foul muck where limestone should have been—

'No!'

Choking on a scream, Holly woke.

She sat up in bed, something touched her, and she wrenched away from it. Because the room was awash in morning light, she saw that it was only Jim.

A dream. Just a dream.

As had happened two nights ago in the Laguna Hills Motor Inn, however, the creature of the dream was trying to force its way into the waking world. It was not coming through a wall this time. The ceiling. Directly over the bed. The white-painted drywall was no longer white or dry, but mottled amber and brown, semi-transparent and luminous as the stone in the dream had been, oozing a noxious mucus, bulging as some shadowy entity struggled to be born into the bedroom.

The dream-thing's thunderous three-part heartbeat – *lub-dub-DUB, lub-dub-DUB* – shuddered through the house.

Jim rolled off the bed and on to his feet. He had slipped into his pajama bottoms again during the night, just as Holly had slipped into the roomy top which hung halfway to her knees. She scrambled to his side. They stared up in horror at the pulsing birth sac which the ceiling had become, and at the shadowy writhing form struggling to breach that containing membrane.

Most frightening of all – this apparition was in daylight. The plantation shutters had not been completely closed over the windows, and slats of morning sunshine banded the room. When something from Beyond found you in the dead hours of the night, you half expected it. But sunshine was supposed to banish all monsters.

Jim put a hand against Holly's back, pushed her toward the open door to the hallway. 'Go, get out!'

She took only two steps in that direction before the door slammed shut of its own accord. As if an exceptionally powerful poltergeist were at work, a mahogany highboy, as old and well used as everything in the house, erupted away from the wall beside her, almost knocking her down. It flew across the bedroom, slammed into the door. A dresser and a chair followed that tall chest of drawers, effectively barricading the only exit.

The windows in the far wall presented an avenue of escape, but they would have to crouch to slip under the increasingly distended central portion of the ceiling. Having accepted the illogic of the waking nightmare, Holly was now loath to press past that greasy and obscenely throbbing pouch, for fear that it would split open as she moved under it, and that the creature within would seize her.

Jim pulled her back with him into the adjoining bathroom. He kicked the door shut.

Holly swung around, searching. The only window was set high and was too small to provide a way out.

The bathroom walls were untainted by the organic transformation that had overcome the bedroom, but they still shook with the triple bass thud of the inhuman heartbeat.

'What the hell is that?' he demanded.

'The Enemy,' she said at once, surprised that he didn't know. 'The Enemy, from the dream.'

Above them, starting from the partition that the bath shared with the bedroom, the white ceiling began to discolor as if abruptly saturated with red blood, brown bile. The sheen of semigloss paint on drywall metamorphosed into a biological surface and began to throb in time with the thunderous heartbeat.

Jim pulled her into a corner by the vanity, and she huddled helplessly against him. Beyond the pregnant droop of the lowering ceiling, she saw repulsive movement like the frenzied squirming of a million maggots.

The thudding heartbeat increased in volume, booming around them.

She heard a wet, tearing sound. None of this could be happening, yet it was, and that sound made it more real than the things she was seeing with her own eyes, because it was such a filthy sound and so hideously intimate, too *real* for a delusion or a dream.

The door crashed open, and the ceiling burst overhead, showering them with debris.

But with that implosion, the power of the lingering nightmare was exhausted, and reality finally, fully reasserted itself. Nothing monstrous surged through the open door; only the sun-filled bedroom lay beyond. Although the ceiling had looked entirely organic when it had burst in upon them, no trace of its transformed state remained; it was only a ceiling again. The rain of debris included chunks of wallboard, flaked and powdered drywall paste, splinters of wood, and wads of fluffy fiberglass insulation – but nothing alive.

The hole itself was astonishing enough to Holly.

Two nights ago, in the motel, though the wall had bulged and rippled as if alive, it had returned to its true composition without a crack. No evidence of the dream creature's intrusion had been left behind except the scratches in her sides, which a psychologist might have said were self-inflicted. When the dust settled, everything might have been just a fantastically detailed delusion.

But the mess in which they were now standing was no delusion. The pall of white dust in the air was real.

In a state of shock, Jim took her hand and led her out of the bathroom. The bedroom ceiling had not crashed down. It was as it had been last night: smooth, white. But the furniture was piled up against the door as if washed there by a flood.

Madness favored darkness, but light was the kingdom of reason. If the waking world provided no sanctuary from nightmares, if daylight offered no sanctuary from unreason, then there was no sanctuary anywhere, anytime, for anyone.

·2·

The attic light, a single sixty-watt bulb dangling from a beam, did not illuminate every corner of that cramped and dusty space. Jim probed into the many recesses with a flashlight, edged around heating ducts, peered behind each of the two fireplace chimneys, searching for . . . whatever had torn apart the bathroom ceiling. He had no idea what he expected to find. Besides the flashlight, he carried a loaded revolver. The thing that destroyed the ceiling had not descended into the bathroom, so it had to be in the attic above. However, because he lived with a minimum of possessions, Jim had nothing to store up there under the roof, which left few possible hiding places. He was soon satisfied that those high reaches of his house were untenanted except by spiders and by a small colony of wasps that had constructed a nest in a junction of rafters.

Nothing could have escaped those confines, either. Aside from the trapdoor by which he had entered, the only exits from the attic were the ventilation cut-outs in opposing eaves. Each was about two feet long and twelve inches high, covered with tightly fitted screens that could be removed only with a screwdriver. Both screens were secure.

Part of that space had plank flooring, but in some places nothing but insulation lay between the exposed floor studs, which were also the ceiling studs of the rooms below. Duck-walking on those parallel supports, Jim cautiously approached the rupture above the master bathroom. He peered down at the debris-strewn floor where he and Holly had been standing.

What in the hell had happened?

At last conceding that he would find no answers up there, he returned to the open access and climbed down into the second-floor linen closet. He folded up the accordion ladder into the closet ceiling, which neatly closed off the attic entrance.

Holly was waiting for him in the hallway. 'Well?'

'Nothing,' he said.

'I knew there wouldn't be.'

'What happened here?'

'It's like in the dream.'

'What dream?' he demanded.

'You said you've had the windmill dreams too.'

'I do.'

'Then you know about the heartbeat in the walls.'

'No.'

'And the way the walls change.'

'No, none of that, for Christ's sake! In my dream, I'm in the high room of the windmill, there's a candle, rain at the windows.'

She remembered how surprised he had been at the sight of the bedroom ceiling distended and strange above them.

He said, 'In the dream, I have a sense that something's coming, something frightening and terrible—'

'The Enemy,' she said.

'Yes! Whatever that might be. But it never comes, not in *my* dreams. I always wake up before it comes.'

He stalked down the hall and into the master bedroom, and she followed him. Standing beside the battered furniture that he had shoved away from the door, he stared up in consternation at the undamaged ceiling.

'I saw it,' he said, as if she had called him a liar.

'I know you did,' she said. 'I saw it too.'

He turned to her, looking more desperate than she had seen him even aboard the doomed DC-10. 'Tell me about your dreams, I want to hear all of them, every detail.'

'Later, I'll tell you everything. First let's shower and get dressed. I want out of this place.'

'Yeah, OK, me too.'

'I guess you realize where we've got to go.'

He hesitated.

She answered for him, 'The windmill.'

He nodded.

They showered together in the guest bathroom, only to save time – and because both of them were too edgy to be alone at the moment. She supposed that, in a different mood, she would have found the experience pleasantly erotic. But it was surprisingly platonic, considering the fierce passion of the night just passed.

He touched her only when they had stepped out of the shower and were hurriedly toweling dry. He leaned close, kissed the corner of her mouth, and said, 'What have I gotten you into, Holly Thorne?'

*　　*　　*

Later, while Jim hurriedly packed a suitcase, Holly wandered only as far as the upstairs study, which was next to his bedroom. There he had most likely done his lesson plans and graded papers when he'd been a teacher. But now not even one red pencil lay atop the desk; nothing but dust covered the Formica.

Like the rest of the house, his study was humble. The cheap desk had probably been purchased at a cut-rate office-supplies ware-house. The other furniture included just two lamps, an armchair on a wheel-and-swivel base, two free-standing bookcases overflowing with worn volumes, and a worktable as bare as the long-unused desk.

All of the two hundred or more books were about religion: fat histories of Islam, Judaism, Buddhism, Zen Buddhism, Christian-ity, Hinduism, Taoism, Shintoism, and others; the collected essays of St Thomas Aquinas, Martin Luther; *Scientists and Their Gods*; the Bible in several versions – Douay, King James, American Revised; the Koran; the Torah, including the Old Testament and the Talmud; the Tripitaka of Buddhism, the Agama of Hinduism, the Zend-Avesta of Zoroastrianism, and the Veda of Brahmanism.

In spite of the curious completeness of that part of his personal library, the most interesting thing in the room was the gallery of photographs that occupied two walls. Of the thirty-some 8 × 10 prints, a few were in color but most were black and white. The same three people featured in all of them: a strikingly lovely brunette, a good-looking man with bold features and thinning hair, and a child who could be no one but Jim Ironheart. Those eyes. One photograph showed Jim with the couple – obviously his parents – when he was only an infant swaddled in a blanket, but in the others he was not much younger than four and never older than about ten.

When he'd been ten, of course, his parents had died.

Some photos showed young Jim with his dad, some with his mom, and Holly assumed the missing parent had always been the one with the camera. A handful included all three Ironhearts. Over the years, the mother only grew more striking; the father's hair continued to thin, but he appeared to be happier as time passed; and Jim, taking a lesson from his mother, became steadily better looking.

Often the backdrop of the picture was a famous landmark or the sign for one. Jim and both parents in front of Radio City Music Hall when he'd been about six. Jim and his father on the boardwalk at Atlantic City when Jim was four or five. Jim and his mother at a sign for Grand Canyon National Park, with a panoramic vista behind them. All three Ironhearts in front of Sleeping Beauty's Castle in the heart of Disneyland, when Jim was only seven or eight. Beal Street in Memphis. The sun-splashed Fountainebleu Hotel in Miami Beach. An observation deck overlooking the faces of Mount Rushmore. Buckingham Palace in London. The Eiffel Tower. The Tropicana Hotel, Las Vegas. Niagara Falls. They seemed to have been everywhere.

In every case, no matter who was holding the camera or where they were, those in the shot looked genuinely happy. Not one face in one print was frozen in an insincere smile, or caught with one of those snap-the-damn-picture expressions of impatience that could be found in abundance in most family photo albums. Often, they were laughing instead of merely smiling, and in several instances they were caught in the middle of horseplay of one kind or another. All three were touchers, too, not simply standing side by side or in brittle poses. They were usually shown with their arms around one another, sometimes hugging, occasionally kissing one another on the cheek or casually expressing affection in some fashion.

The boy in the photographs revealed no hint of the sometimes moody adult he would become, and Holly could see that the untimely death of his parents had changed him profoundly. The carefree, grinning boy in the photographs had been lost forever.

One black-and-white particularly arrested her. It showed Mr Ironheart sitting on a straight-backed chair. Jim, maybe seven years old, was on his father's lap. They were in tuxedos. Mrs Ironheart stood behind her husband, her hand on his shoulder, wearing a slinky sequined cocktail dress that emphasized her wonderful figure. They faced the camera directly. Unlike the other shots, this one was carefully posed, with nothing but a piece of artfully draped cloth as a backdrop, obviously set up by a professional photographer.

'They were wonderful,' Jim said from the doorway. She had not heard him approaching. 'No kid ever had better folks than them.'

'You traveled a lot.'

'Yeah. They were always going somewhere. They loved to show me new places, teach me things firsthand. They would've made wonderful schoolteachers, let me tell you.'

'What work did they do?'

'My dad was an accountant at Warner Brothers.'

'The movie studio?'

'Yeah.' Jim smiled. 'We lived in L.A. Mom – she wanted to be an actress, but she never got a lot of jobs. So mostly she was a hostess at a restaurant on Melrose Avenue, not far from the Paramount lot.'

'You were happy, weren't you?'

'Always.'

She pointed to the photo in which the three of them were dressed with glittery formality. 'Special occasion?'

'Times just the two of them should have celebrated, like wedding anniversaries, they insisted on including me. They always made me feel special, wanted, loved. I was seven years old when that photo was taken, and I remember them making big plans that night. They were going to be married a hundred years, they said, and be happier each year than the one before, have lots more children, own a big house, see every corner of the world before they died together in their sleep. But just three years later they were . . . gone.'

'I'm sorry, Jim.'

He shrugged. 'It's a long time ago. Twenty-five years.' He looked at his wristwatch. 'Come on, let's go. It'll take us four hours to reach the farm, and it's already nine o'clock.'

*   *   *

At the Laguna Hills Motor Inn, Holly quickly changed into jeans and a blue-checkered blouse, then packed the rest of her belongings. Jim put her suitcase in the trunk of his car.

While she returned her room key and paid her bill at the front desk in the motel office, she was aware of him watching her from behind the wheel of his Ford. She would have been disappointed, of course, if he had not liked to watch her. But every time she looked through the plate-glass window at him, he was so motionless, so cool and expressionless behind his heavily tinted sunglasses, that his undivided attention was disconcerting.

She wondered if she was doing the right thing by going with him to the Santa Ynez Valley. When she walked out of the office and got in the car with him, he would be the only person in the world who knew where she was. All of her notes about him were in her suitcase; they could disappear with her. Then she would be just a woman, alone, who had vanished while on vacation.

As the clerk finished filling out the credit-card form, Holly considered phoning her parents in Philadelphia to let them know where she was going and with whom. But she would only alarm them and be on the phone half an hour trying to reassure them that she was going to be just fine.

Besides, she had already decided that the darkness in Jim was less important than the light, and she had made a commitment to him. If he occasionally made her uneasy . . . well, that was part of what had drawn her to him in the first place. A sense of danger sharpened the edge of his appeal. At heart, he was a good man.

It was foolish to worry about her safety after she had already made love to him. For a woman, in a way that could never be true for a man, the first night of sexual surrender involved one of the moments of greatest vulnerability in a relationship. Assuming, of course, that she had surrendered not solely because of physical need but because she loved him. And Holly loved him.

'I'm in love with him,' she said aloud, surprised because she had convinced herself that his appeal was largely the result of his exceptional male grace, animal magnetism, and mystery.

The clerk, ten years younger than Holly and therefore more inclined to think that love was everywhere and inevitable, grinned at her. 'It's great, isn't it?'

Signing the charge slip, Holly said, 'Do you believe in love at first sight?'

197

'Why not?'

'Well, it's not first sight, really. I've known the guy since August twelfth, which is . . . sixteen days.'

'And you're not married yet?' the clerk joked.

When Holly went out to the Ford and got in beside Jim, she said, 'When we get where we're going, you won't carve me up with a chainsaw and bury me under the windmill, will you?'

Apparently he understood her sense of vulnerability and took no offense, for he said with mock solemnity, 'Oh, no. It's full-up under the mill. I'll have to bury pieces of you all over the farm.'

She laughed. She was an idiot for fearing him.

He leaned over and kissed her. It was a lovely, lingering kiss.

When they parted, he said, 'I'm taking as big a risk as you are.'

'Let me assure you, I've never hacked anyone to bits with an ax.'

'I mean it. I haven't been lucky in love.'

'Me neither.'

'This time will be different for both of us.'

He gave her another kiss, shorter and sweeter than the first one, then started the car and backed out of the parking space.

In a determined attempt to keep the dying cynic in her alive, Holly reminded herself that he had not actually said he loved her. His commitment had been carefully and indirectly phrased. He might be no more reliable than other men she had trusted over the years.

On the other hand, she had not actually said that she loved him, either. Her commitment had been no more effusively stated than his. Perhaps because she still felt the need to protect herself to some extent, she had found it easier to reveal her heart to the motel clerk than to Jim.

*   *   *

Washing down blueberry muffins with black coffee, for which they had stopped at a convenience store, they traveled north on the San Diego Freeway. The Tuesday-morning rush hour had passed, but at some places traffic still clogged all lanes and moved like a snail herd being driven toward a gourmet restaurant.

Comfortably ensconced in the passenger seat, Holly told Jim about her four nightmares, as promised. She started with the initial dream of blindness on Friday night, concluding with last night's spookshow, which had been the most bizarre and fearful of all.

He was clearly fascinated that she had dreamed about the mill without even knowing of its existence. And on Sunday night, after surviving the crash of Flight 246, she had dreamed of him at the mill *as a ten-year-old boy,* when she could not yet have known either that the mill was a familiar place to him or that he had spent a lot of time there when he was ten.

But the majority of his questions related to her most recent nightmare. Keeping his eyes on the traffic ahead, he said, 'Who was the woman in the dream if she wasn't you?'

'I don't know,' Holly said, finishing the final bite of the last muffin. 'I had no sense of her identity.'

'Can you describe her?'

'I only saw her reflection in that window, so I can't tell you much, I'm afraid.' She drank the last of the coffee from her big Styrofoam cup, and thought a moment. It was easier to visualize the scenes of that dream than it should have been, for dreams were usually quick to fade from memory. Images from that one returned to her quite vividly, however, as if she had not dreamed them but experienced them in real life. 'She had a broad clear face, more handsome in a womanly way than pretty. Wide-set eyes, full mouth. A beauty mark high on her right cheek, I don't think it could've been a spot on the glass, just a little round dot. Curly hair. Do you recognize her?'

'No,' he replied. 'Can't say that I do. Tell me what you saw at the bottom of the pond when the lightning flashed.'

'I'm not sure what it was.'

'Describe it as best you can.'

She pondered for a moment, then shook her head. 'I can't. The woman's face was fairly easy to recall because when I saw it in the dream I knew what it was, a face, a human face. But whatever was lying at the bottom of the pond . . . that was strange, like nothing I'd ever seen before. I didn't know what I was looking at, and I had such a brief glimpse of it and . . . well, now it's just gone. Is there really something peculiar under that pond?'

'Not that I know of,' he said. 'Could it've been a sunken boat, a rowboat, anything like that?'

'No,' she said. 'Nothing at all like that. Much bigger. Did a boat sink in the pond once?'

'I never heard of it, if one did. It's a deceptive-looking bit of water though. You expect a millpond to be shallow, but this one is deep, forty or fifty feet toward the center. It never dries out, and it doesn't shrink during dry years, either, because it's formed over an artesian well, not just an aquifer.'

'What's the difference?'

'An aquifer is what you drill into when you're sinking a well, it's sort of a reservoir or stream of underground water. Artesian wells are rarer. You don't drill into one to find water, 'cause the water is already coming to the surface under pressure. You'd have the devil's own time trying to *stop* the stuff from percolating up.'

The snarl of traffic began to loosen, but Jim did not take full advantage of opportunities to change lanes and swing around slower-moving vehicles. He was more interested in her answers than in making better time.

He said, 'And in the dream when you got to the top of the stairs – or when this woman got to the top of the stairs – you saw a ten-year-old boy standing there, and somehow you knew he was me.'

'Yes.'

'I don't look much like I looked when I was ten, so how'd you recognize me?'

'Mostly it was your eyes,' Holly said. 'They haven't changed much in all these years. They're unmistakable.'

'Lots of people have blue eyes.'

'Are you serious? Honey, your blue eyes are to other blue eyes what Sinatra's voice is to Donald Duck's.'

'You're prejudiced. What did you see in the wall?'

She described it again.

'Alive in the stone? This just gets stranger and stranger.'

'I haven't been bored in days,' she agreed.

Beyond the junction with Interstate 10, traffic on the San Diego Freeway became even lighter, and finally Jim began to put some of his driving skills to use. He handled the car the way a first-rate jockey handled a thoroughbred horse, finessing from it that extra degree of performance that won races. The Ford was only a stock model with no modification, but it responded to him as if it wanted to be a Porsche.

After a while Holly began to ask questions of her own. 'How come you're a millionaire but you live relatively cheap?'

'Bought a house, moved out of my apartment. Quit my job.'

'Yeah, but a modest house. And your furniture's falling apart.'

'I needed the privacy of my own house to meditate and rest between . . . assignments. But I didn't need fancy furniture.'

Following a few minutes of mutual silence, she said, 'Did I catch your eye the way you caught mine, right off the bat, up in Portland?'

He smiled but didn't look away from the highway. ' "So are you, Miss Thorne." '

'So you admit it!' Holly said, pleased. 'It *was* a come-on line.'

They made excellent time from the west side of Los Angeles all the way to Ventura, but then Jim began to slack off again. Mile by mile, he drove with less aggression.

Initially Holly thought he was lulled by the view. Past Ventura, Route 101 hugged beautiful stretches of coastline. They passed Pitas Point, then Rincon Point, and the beaches of Carpinteria. The blue sea rose, the blue sky fell, the golden land wedged itself between them, and the only visible turbulence in the serene summer day was the white-capped surf, which slipped to the shore in low combers and broke with a light, foamy spray.

But there was a turbulence in Jim Ironheart, too, and Holly only became aware of his new edginess when she realized that he was not paying any attention to the scenery. He had slowed down not to enjoy the view but, she suspected, to delay their arrival at the farm.

By the time they left the superhighway, turned inland at Santa Barbara, crossed the city, and headed into the Santa Ynez Mountains, Jim's mood was undeniably darker. His responses to her conversational sallies grew shorter, more distracted.

State Route 154 led out of the mountains into an appealing land of low hills and fields painted gold by dry summer grass, clusters of California live oaks, and horse ranches with neat white fencing. This was not the farming-intense, agribusiness atmosphere of the San Joaquin and certain other valleys; there were serious vineyards here and there, but the occasional farms appeared to be, as often as not, gentlemen's operations maintained as getaways for rich men in Los Angeles, more concerned with cultivating a picturesque alternate lifestyle than with real crops.

'We'll need to stop in New Svenborg to get a few things before we head out to the farm,' Jim said.

'What things?'

'I don't know. But when we stop . . . I'll know what we need.'

Lake Cachuma came and went to the east. They passed the road to Solvang on the west, then skirted Santa Ynez itself. Before Los Olivos, they headed east on another state route, and finally into New Svenborg, the closest town to Ironheart Farm.

In the early nineteen hundreds, groups of Danish-Americans from the Midwest had settled in the Santa Ynez Valley, many of them with the intention of establishing communities that would preserve Danish folk arts and customs and, in general, the ways of Danish life. The most successful of these settlements was Solvang, about which Holly had once written a story; it had become a major tourist attraction because of its quaint Danish architecture, shops, and restaurants.

New Svenborg, with a population of fewer than two thousand, was not as elaborately, thoroughly, authentically, *insistently* Danish as Solvang. Depressing desert-style stucco buildings with white-rock roofs, weathered clapboard buildings with unpainted front porches that reminded Holly of parts of rural Texas, Craftsman bungalows, and white Victorian houses with lots of gingerbread and wide front porches stood beside structures that were distinctly Danish with half-timbered walls and thatched roofs and leaded-glass windows. Half a dozen windmills dotted the town, their vanes silhouetted against the August sky. All in all, it was one of those singular California mixes that sometimes resulted in delightful and unexpected harmonies; but in New Svenborg, the mix did not work, and the mood was discordancy.

'I spent the end of my childhood and my entire adolescence here,' Jim said as he drove slowly down the quiet, shadowy main street.

She figured that his moodiness could be attributed as much to New Svenborg as to his tragic family history.

To an extent, that was unfair. The streets were lined with big trees, the charming streetlamps appeared to have been imported from the Old Country, and most of the sidewalks were gracefully curved and time-hoved ribbons of well-worn brick. About twenty percent of the town came straight from the nostalgic Midwest of a Bradbury novel, but the rest of it still belonged in a David Lynch film.

'Let's take a little tour of the old place,' he said.

'We should be getting to the farm.'

'It's only a mile north of town, just a few minutes away.'

That was all the more reason to get there, as far as Holly was concerned. She was tired of being on the road.

But she sensed that for some reason he wanted to show her the town – and not merely to delay their arrival at Ironheart Farm. Holly acquiesced. In fact she listened with interest to what he had to tell her. She had learned that he found it difficult to talk about himself and that he sometimes made personal revelations in an indirect or even casual manner.

He drove past Handahl's Pharmacy on the east end of Main Street, where locals went to get a prescription filled, unless they preferred to drive twenty miles to Solvang. Handahl's was also one of only two restaurants in town, with (according to Jim) 'the best soda fountain this side of 1955.' It was also the post office and only newsstand. With its multiply peaked roof, verdigris-copper cupola, and beveled-glass windows, it was an appealing enterprise.

Without shutting the engine off, Jim parked across the street from the library on Copenhagen Lane, which was quartered in one of the smaller Victorian houses with considerably less gingerbread than most. The building was freshly painted, with well-tended shrubbery, and both the United States and California flags fluttered softly on a tall brass pole along the front walkway. It looked like a small and sorry library nonetheless.

'A town this size, it's amazing to find a library at all,' Jim said. 'And thank God for it. I rode my bike to the library so often . . . if you added up all the miles, I probably pedaled halfway around the world. After my folks died, books were my friends, counselors, psychiatrists. Books kept me sane. Mrs Glynn, the librarian, was a great lady, she knew just how to talk to a shy, mixed-up kid without talking *down* to him. She was my guide to the most exotic regions of the world and distant times – all without leaving her aisles of books.'

Holly had never heard him speak so lovingly or half so lyrically of anything before. The Svenborg library and Mrs Glynn had clearly been lasting and favorable influences on his life.

'Why don't we go in and say hello to her?' Holly suggested.

Jim frowned. 'Oh, I'm sure she's not the librarian any more, most likely not even alive. That was twenty-five years ago when I started coming here, seventeen years ago when I left town to go to college. Never saw her after that.'

'How old was she?'

He hesitated. 'Quite old,' he said, and put an end to the talk of a nostalgic visit by slipping the Ford into gear and driving away from there.

They cruised by Tivoli Gardens, a small park at the corner of Main and Copenhagen, which fell laughably short of its namesake. No fountains, no musicians, no dancing, no games, no beer gardens. There were just some roses, a few beds of late-summer flowers, patchy grass, two park benches, and a well-maintained windmill in the far corner.

'Why aren't the sails moving?' she asked. 'There's some wind.'

'None of the mills actually pump water or grind grain any more,' he explained. 'And since they're largely decorative, no sense in having to live with the noise they make. Brakes were put on the mechanisms long ago.' As they turned the corner at the end of the park, he added: 'They made a movie here once.'

'Who did?'

'One of the studios.'

'Hollywood studio?'

'I forget which.'

'What was it called?'

'Don't remember.'

'Who starred in it?'

'Nobody famous.'

Holly made a mental note about the movie, suspecting that it was more important to Jim and to the town than he had said. Something in the offhand way he'd mentioned it, and his terse responses to her subsequent questions, alerted her to an unspoken subtext.

Last of all, at the southeast corner of Svenborg, he drove slowly past Zacca's Garage, a large corrugated-steel Quonset hut perched on a cement-block foundation, in front of which stood two dusty cars. Though the building had been painted several times during its history, no brush had touched it in many years. Its numerous coats of paint were worn in a random patchwork and marked by liberal encrustations of rust, which created an unintended camouflage finish. The cracked blacktop in front of the place was pitted with potholes that had been filled with loose gravel, and the surrounding lot bristled with dry grass and weeds.

'I went to school with Ned Zacca,' Jim said. 'His dad, Vernon, had the garage then. It was never a business to make a man rich, but it looked better than it does now.'

The big airplane-hangar-style roll-aside doors were open, and the interior was clotted with shadows. The rear bumper of an old Chevy gleamed dully in the gloom. Although the garage was seedy, nothing about it suggested danger. Yet the queerest chill came over Holly as she peered through the hangar doors into the murky depths of the place.

'Ned was one mean sonofabitch, the school bully,' Jim said. 'He could sure make a kid's life hell when he wanted to. I lived in fear of him.'

'Too bad you didn't know Tae Kwon Do then, you could've kicked his ass.'

He did not smile, just stared past her at the garage. His expression was odd and unsettling. 'Yeah. Too bad.'

When she glanced at the building again, she saw a man in jeans and a T-shirt step out of the deepest darkness into gray half-light, moving slowly past the back of the Chevy, wiping his hands on a rag. He was just beyond the infall of sunshine, so she could not see what he looked like. In a few steps he rounded the car, fading into the gloom again, hardly more material than a specter glimpsed in a moonlit graveyard.

Somehow, she knew the ghostly presence in the Quonset was Ned Zacca. Curiously, though he had been a menacing figure to Jim, not to her, Holly felt her stomach twist and her palms turn damp.

Then Jim touched the accelerator, and they were past the garage, heading back into town.

'What did Zacca do to you exactly?'

'Anything he could think of. He was a regular little sadist. He's been in prison a couple of times since those days. But I figured he was back.'

'Figured? How?'

He shrugged. 'I just sensed it. Besides, he's one of those guys who never gets caught at the big stuff. Devil's luck. He might do a fall every great once in a while, but always for something smalltime. He's dumb but he's clever.'

'Why'd you want to go there?'

'Memories.'

'Most people, when they want a little nostalgia, they're only interested in good memories.'

Jim did not reply to that. Even before they arrived in Svenborg, he had settled into himself like a turtle gradually withdrawing into its shell. Now he was almost back into that brooding, distant mood in which she had found him yesterday afternoon.

The brief tour had given her not a comfortable feeling of small-town security and friendliness, but a sense of being cut off at the back end of nowhere. She was still in California, the most populous state in the union, not much farther than sixty miles from the city of Santa Barbara. Svenborg had almost two thousand people of its own, which made it bigger than a lot of gas-and-graze stops along the interstate highways. The sense of isolation was more psychological than real, but it hovered over her.

Jim stopped at The Central, a prospering operation that included a service station selling generic gasoline, a small sporting-goods outlet peddling supplies to fishermen and campers, and a well-stocked convenience store with groceries, beer, and wine. Holly filled the Ford's tank at the self-service pump, then joined Jim in the sporting-goods shop.

The store was cluttered with merchandise, which overflowed the shelves, hung from the ceiling, and was stacked on the linoleum floor. Wall-eyed fishing lures dangled on a rack near the door. The air smelled of rubber boots.

At the check-out counter, Jim already had piled up a pair of high-quality summerweight sleeping bags with air-mattress liners, a

Coleman lantern with a can of fuel, a sizable Thermos ice chest, two big flashlights, packages of batteries for the flashes, and a few other items. At the cash register, farther along the counter from Jim, a bearded man in spectacles as thick as bottle glass was ringing up the sale, and Jim was waiting with an open wallet.

'I thought we were going to the mill,' Holly said.

'We are,' Jim said. 'But unless you want to sleep on a wooden floor without benefit of *any* conveniences, we need this stuff.'

'I didn't realize we were staying overnight.'

'Neither did I. Until I walked in here and heard myself asking for these things.'

'Couldn't we stay at a motel?'

'Nearest one's clear over to Santa Ynez.'

'It's a pretty drive,' she said, much preferring the commute to spending a night in the mill.

Her reluctance arose only in part from the fact that the old mill promised to be uncomfortable. The place was, after all, the focus of both their nightmares. Besides, since arriving in Svenborg, she had felt vaguely . . . threatened.

'But something's going to happen,' he said. 'I don't know what. Just . . . something. At the mill. I feel it. We're going to . . . get some answers. But it might take a little time. We've got to be ready to wait, be patient.'

Though Holly was the one who had suggested going to the mill, she suddenly didn't *want* answers. In a dim premonition of her own, she perceived an undefined but oncoming tragedy, blood, death, and darkness.

Jim, on the other hand, seemed to shed the lead weight of his previous apprehension and take on a new buoyancy. 'It's good – what we're doing, where we're going. I *sense* that, Holly. You know what I mean? I'm being told we made the right move in coming here, that there's something frightening ahead of us, yes, something that's going to shock the hell out of us, maybe very real danger, but there's also something that's going to lift us up.' His eyes were shining and he was excited. She had never seen him like this, not even when they had been making love. In whatever obscure way it touched him, this higher power of his was in contact with him now. She could see his quiet rapture. 'I feel a . . . a strange sort of jubilation coming, a wonderful discovery, revelations . . .'

The bespectacled clerk had stepped away from the cash register to show them the total on the tape. Grinning, he said, 'Newlyweds?'

At the convenience store next door, they bought ice for the chest,

206

then orange juice, diet soda, bread, mustard, bologna-olive loaf, and pre-packaged cheese slices.

'Olive loaf,' Holly said wonderingly. 'I haven't eaten this stuff since I was maybe fourteen and I learned I had arteries.'

'And how about these,' he said, snatching a box of chocolate-covered doughnuts off a shelf, adding it to the market basket that he was carrying. 'Bologna sandwiches, chocolate doughnuts . . . and potato chips, of course. Wouldn't be a picnic without chips. The crinkled kind, OK? Some cheese twists too. Chips and cheese twists, they go together.'

Holly had never seen him like this: almost boyish, with no apparent weight on his shoulders. He might have been setting out on a camping trip with friends, a little adventure.

She wondered if her own apprehension was justified. Jim was, after all, the one whose presentiments had proven to be accurate. Maybe they *were* going to discover something wonderful at the mill, unravel the mystery behind the last-minute rescues he had performed, maybe even encounter this higher power to which he referred. Perhaps The Enemy, in spite of its ability to reach out of a dream into the real world, was not as formidable as it seemed.

At the cash register, after the clerk finished bagging their purchases and was making change, Jim said, 'Wait a minute, one more thing,' and hurried to the rear of the store. When he returned, he was carrying two lined yellow tablets and one black, fine-point felt-tip pen. To Holly, he said, 'We'll be needing these tonight.'

When they had loaded the car and pulled out of the parking lot at The Central, heading for the Ironheart farm, Holly indicated the pen and tablets, which she was holding in a separate bag. 'What'll we be needing these for?'

'I haven't the slightest idea. I just suddenly knew we have to have them.'

'That's just like God,' she said, 'always being mysterious and obscure.'

After a silence, he said, 'I'm not so sure any more that it's God talking to me.'

'Oh? What changed your mind?'

'Well, the issues you raised last evening, for one thing. If God didn't want little Nick O'Conner to die up there in Boston, why didn't He just stop that vault from exploding? Why chase me clear across the country and 'throw' me at the boy, as you put it? And why would He up and change His mind about the people on the airliner, let more of them live, just because I decided they should?

They were all questions I'd asked myself, but you weren't willing to settle for the easy answers that satisfied me.' He looked away from the street for a moment as they reached the edge of town, smiled at her, and repeated one of the questions she had asked him yesterday when she had been needling him: 'Is God a waffler?'

'I would've expected . . .'

'What?'

'Well, you were so sure you could see a divine hand in this, it must be a bit of a letdown to consider less exalted possibilities. I'd expect you to be a little bummed out.'

He shook his head. 'I'm not. You know, I always had trouble accepting that it was God working through me, it seemed like such a crazy idea, but I lived with it just because there wasn't any better explanation. There still *isn't* a better explanation, I guess, but another possibility has occurred to me, and it's something so strange and wonderful in its way that I don't mind losing God from the team.'

'What other possibility?'

'I don't want to talk about it just yet,' he said as sunlight and tree shadows dappled the dusty windshield and played across his face. 'I want to think it through, be sure it makes sense, before I lay it out for you, 'cause I know now you're a hard judge to convince.'

He seemed happy. Really happy. Holly had liked him pretty much since she had first seen him, regardless of his moodiness. She had perceived a hopefulness beneath his glower, a tenderness beneath his gruffness, a better man beneath the exterior of a lesser one, but in his current buoyant mood, she found him easier than ever to like.

She playfully pinched his cheek.

'What?' he said.

'You're cute.'

As they drove out of Svenborg, it occurred to Holly that the distribution pattern of the houses and other buildings was more like a pioneer settlement than like a modern community. In most towns, buildings were concentrated more densely in the center, with larger lots and increasing open space toward the perimeter, until finally the last structures gave way to rural precincts. But when they came to the city limits of Svenborg, the delineation between town and country was almost ruler-straight and unmistakable. Houses stopped and brushland began, with only an intervening firebreak, and Holly could not help but think of pioneers in the Old West constructing their outposts with a wary eye toward the threats that might arise out of the lawless badlands all around them.

Inside its boundaries, the town seemed ominous and full of dark secrets. Seen from the outside – and Holly turned to stare back at it as the road rose toward the brow of a gentle hill – it looked not threatening but threatened, as if its residents knew, in their bones, that something frightful in the golden land around them was waiting to claim them all.

Perhaps fire was all they feared. Like much of California, the land was parched where human endeavor had not brought water to it.

Nestled between the Santa Ynez Mountains to the west and the San Rafael Mountains to the east, the valley was so broad and deep that it contained more geographical variety than some entire states back East – though at this time of year, untouched by rain since early spring, most of it was brown and crisp. They traveled across rounded golden hills, brown meadows. The better vantage points on their two-mile route revealed vistas of higher hills overgrown with chaparral, valleys within the valley where groves of California live oaks flourished, and small green vineyards encircled by vast sere fields.

'It's beautiful,' Holly said, taking in the pale hills, shining-gold meadows, and oily chaparral. Even the oaks, whose clusters indicated areas with a comparatively high water table, were not lush but a half-parched silver-green. 'Beautiful, but a tinderbox. How would they cope with a fire out here?'

Even as she posed that question, they came around a bend in the road and saw a stretch of blackened land to the right of the two-lane county road. Brush and grass had been reduced to veins of gray-white ash in coal-black soot. The fire had taken place within the past couple of days, for it was still recent enough to lend a burnt odor to the August air.

'That one didn't get far,' he said. 'Looks like ten acres burned at most. They're quick around here, they jump at the first sign of smoke. There's a good volunteer group in town, plus a Department of Forestry station in the valley, lookout posts. If you live here, you don't forget the threat – you just realize after a while that it can be dealt with.'

Jim sounded confident enough, and he had lived there for seven or eight years, so Holly tried to suppress her pyrophobia. Nevertheless, even after they had passed the charred land and could no longer smell the scorched brush, Holly had an image in her mind of the huge valley at night, aflame from end to end, vortexes of red-orange-white fire whirling like tornadoes and consuming everything that lay between the ramparts of the two mountain ranges.

'Ironheart Farm,' he said, startling her.

As Jim slowed the Ford, Holly looked to the left of the blacktop county route.

A farmhouse stood a hundred feet back from the road, behind a withered lawn. It was of no particular architectural style, just a plain but cozy-looking two-story farmhouse with white aluminum siding, a red-shingle roof, and a commodious front porch. It might have been lifted off its foundation anywhere in the Midwest and plunked down on new footings here, for there were thousands like it in those cornbelt states.

Maybe a hundred yards to the left of the house, a red barn rose to a tarnished horse-and-carriage weather vane at the pinnacle of its peaked roof. It was not huge, only half again as large as the unimposing house.

Behind the house and barn, visible between them, was the pond, and the structure at its far side was the most arresting sight on the farm. The windmill.

•3•

Jim stopped in the driveway turnaround between house and barn, and got out of the Ford. He *had* to get out because the sight of the old place hit him harder than he had expected, simultaneously bringing a chill to the pit of his stomach and a flush of heat to his face. In spite of the cool draft from the dashboard vents, the air in the car seemed warm and stale, too low in oxygen content to sustain him. He stood in the fresh summer air, drawing deep breaths, and tried not to lose control of himself.

The blank-windowed house held little power over him. When he looked at it, he felt only a sweet melancholy that might, given time, deepen into a more disturbing sadness or even despair. But he could stare at it, draw his breath normally, and turn away from it without being seized by a powerful urge to look at it again.

The barn exerted no emotional pull on him whatsoever, but the windmill was another story. When he turned his gaze on that cone of limestone beyond the wide pond, he felt as though he were being transformed into stone himself, as had been the luckless victims of the mythological serpent-haired Medusa when they had seen her snake-ringed face.

He'd read about Medusa years ago. In one of Mrs Glynn's books. That was in the days when he wished with all his heart that he, too, could see the snake-haired woman and be transformed into unfeeling rock . . .

'Jim?' Holly said from the other side of the car. 'You OK?'

With its high-ceilinged rooms – highest on the first floor – the two-story mill was actually four stories in height. But to Jim, at that moment, it looked far taller, as imposing as a twenty-story tower. Its once-pale stones had been darkened by a century of grime. Climbing ivy roots, nurtured by the pond that abutted one flank of the mill, twined up the rough stone face, finding easy purchase in deep-mortared joints. With no one to perform needed mainte-nance, the plant had covered half the structure, and had grown entirely over a narrow first-floor window near the timbered door. The wooden sails looked rotten. Each of those four arms was about thirty feet in length, making a sixty-foot spread across adjoining spans, and each was five feet wide with three rows of vanes. Since he had last seen the mill, more vanes had cracked or fallen away altogether. The time-frozen sails were stopped not in a cruciform but in an X, two arms reaching toward the pond and two toward the heavens. Even in hot bright daylight, the windmill struck Jim as menacing and seemed like a monstrous, ragged-armed scarecrow clawing at the sky with skeletal hands.

'Jim?' Holly said, touching his arm.

He jumped as if he had not known who she was. In fact, for an instant, as he looked down at her, he saw not only Holly but a long-dead face, the face of . .

But the moment of disorientation passed. She was only Holly now, her identity no longer entwined with that of another woman as it had been in her dream last night.

'You OK?' she asked again.

'Yeah, sure, just . . . memories.'

Jim was grateful when Holly directed his attention from the mill to the farmhouse. She said, 'Were you happy with your grand-parents?'

'Lena and Henry Ironheart. Wonderful people. They took me in. They suffered so much for me.'

'Suffered?' she said.

He realized that it was too strong a word, and he wondered why he had used it. 'Sacrificed, I mean. In lots of ways, little things, but they added up.'

'Taking on the support of a ten-year-old boy isn't something anyone does lightly,' Holly said. 'But unless you demanded caviar and champagne, I wouldn't think you'd have been much of a hardship to them.'

'After what happened to my folks, I was . . . withdrawn, in bad shape, uncommunicative. They put in a lot of time with me, a lot of love, trying to bring me back . . . from the edge.'

'Who lives here these days?'

'Nobody.'

'But didn't you say your grandparents died five years ago?'

'The place wasn't sold. No buyers.'

'Who owns it now?'

'I do. I inherited it.'

She surveyed the property with evident bewilderment. 'But it's lovely here. If the lawn was being watered and kept green, the weeds cut down, it would be charming. Why would it be so hard to sell?'

'Well, for one thing, it's a damned quiet life out here, and even most of the back-to-nature types who dream of living on a farm really mean a farm close to a choice of movie theaters, bookstores, good restaurants, and dependable European-car mechanics.'

She laughed at that. 'Baby, there's an amusing little cynic lurking in you.'

'Besides, it's hard scrabble all the way, trying to earn a living on a place like this. It's just a little old hundred-acre farm, not big enough to make it with milk cows or a beef herd – or any one crop. My grandpa and grandma kept chickens, sold the eggs. And thanks to the mild weather, they could get two crops. Strawberries came into fruit in February and all the way into May. That was the money crop – berries. Then came corn, tomatoes – *real* tomatoes, not the plastic ones they sell in the markets.'

He saw that Holly was still enamored of the place. She stood with her hands on her hips, looking around as if she might buy it herself.

She said, 'But aren't there people who work at other things, not farmers, who would just like to live here for the peace and quiet?'

'This isn't a real affluent area, not like Newport Beach, Beverly Hills. Locals around here don't have extra money just to spend on lifestyle. The best hope of selling a property like this is to find some rich movie producer or recording executive in L.A. who wants to buy it for the land, tear it down, and put up a showplace, so he can say he has a getaway in the Santa Ynez Valley, which is the trendy thing to have these days.'

As they talked, he grew increasingly uneasy. It was three o'clock. Plenty of daylight left. But suddenly he dreaded nightfall.

Holly kicked at some wiry weeds that had pushed up through one of the many cracks in the blacktop driveway. 'It needs a little cleanup, but everything looks pretty good. Five years since they died? But the house and barn are in decent shape, like they were painted only a year or two ago.'

'They were.'

'Keep the place marketable, huh?'

'Sure. Why not?'

The high mountains to the west would eat the sun sooner than the ocean swallowed it down in Laguna Niguel. Twilight would come earlier here than there, although it would be prolonged. Jim found himself studying the lengthening purple shadows with the fearfulness of a man in a vampire movie hastening toward shelter before the coffin lids banged open.

What's wrong with me? he wondered.

Holly said, 'You think you'd ever want to live here yourself?'

'Never!' he said so sharply and explosively that he startled not only Holly but himself. As if overcome by a dark magnetic attraction, he looked at the windmill again. A shudder swept through him.

He was aware that she was staring at him.

'Jim,' she said softly, 'what happened to you here? What in the name of God happened twenty-five years ago in that mill?'

'I don't know,' he said shakily. He wiped one hand down his face. His hand felt warm, his face cold. 'I can't remember anything special, anything odd. It was where I played. It was . . . cool and quiet . . . a nice place. Nothing happened there. Nothing.'

'Something,' she insisted. 'Something happened.'

*   *   *

Holly had not been close to him long enough to know if he was frequently on an emotional roller coaster as he had been since they had left Orange County, or if his recent rapid swings in mood were abnormal. In The Central, buying food for a picnic, he'd soared out of the gloom that had settled over him when they crossed the Santa Ynez Mountains, and he'd been almost jubilant. Then the sight of the farm was like a plunge into cold water for him, and the windmill was the equivalent of a drop into an ice chasm.

He seemed as troubled as he was gifted, and she wished that she could do something to ease his mind. She wondered if urging him to come to the farm had been wise. Even a failed career in journalism had taught her to leap into the middle of unfolding events, seize the moment and run with it. But perhaps this situation demanded greater caution, restraint, thought, and planning.

They got back into the Ford and drove between the house and barn, around the big pond. The graveled path, which she remembered from last night's dream, had been made wide enough for horses and wagons in another era. It easily accommodated the Ford, allowing them to park at the base of the windmill.

When she stepped from the car again, she was beside a cornfield. Only a few parched wild stalks thrust up from that abandoned plot of earth beyond the split-rail fence. She walked around the back of the car, across the gravel, and joined Jim where he stood on the bank of the pond.

Mottled blue-green-gray, the water resembled a slab of slate two hundred feet in diameter. It was almost as still as a piece of slate, as well. Dragonflies and other insects, alighting briefly on the surface, caused occasional dimples. Languid currents, far too subtle to produce ripples, made the water shimmer almost imperceptibly near the shore, where green weeds and a few clusters of white-plumed pampas grass thrived.

'Still can't remember quite what you saw in that dream?' Jim asked.

'No. It probably doesn't matter anyway. Not everything in a dream is significant.'

In a low voice, almost as if speaking to himself, he said, 'It was significant.'

Without turbulence to stir up sediment, the water was not muddy, but neither was it clear. Holly figured she could see only a few feet below the surface. If it actually was fifty or sixty feet deep at the center, as Jim had said, that left a lot of volume in which something could remain hidden.

'Let's have a look in the mill,' she said.

Jim got one of the new flashlights from the car and put batteries in it. 'Even in daylight, it can be kind of dark in there.'

The door was in an antechamber appended to the base of the conical main structure of the mill, much like the entrance to an Eskimo igloo. Although unlocked, the door was warped, and the hinges were rusted. For a moment it resisted Jim, then swung inward with a screech and a brittle splintering sound.

The short, arched antechamber opened on to the main room of the mill, which was approximately forty feet in diameter. Four windows, evenly spaced around the circumference, filtered sunlight through filthy panes, leeching the summer-yellow cheer from it and imparting a wintry gray tint that did little to alleviate the gloom. Jim's big flashlight revealed dust- and cobweb-shrouded machinery that could not have appeared more exotic to Holly if it had been the turbine room of a nuclear submarine. It was the cumbersome low technology of another century – massive wooden gears, cogs, shafts, grinding stones, pulleys, old rotting lengths of rope – so oversized and complicated that it all seemed like the work not merely of human beings from another age but of a different and less evolved species altogether.

Because he had grown up around mills, even though they had not been in use since before his birth, Jim knew the names of everything. Pointing with the flashlight beam, he tried to explain how the mill had functioned, talking about the spurwheel and the quant, the mace and the rynd, the runner stone and the bed stone. 'Ordinarily you couldn't look up through the mechanisms quite like this. But, see, the floor of the spurwheel loft is rotted out, not much of it left, and the bridge floor gave way when those huge stones broke loose and fell.'

Though he had regarded the mill with fear when they had stood outside, his mood had begun to change after they entered it. To Holly's surprise, as Jim tried to explain the millworks to her, he began to exhibit some of that boyish enthusiasm that she had first seen when they had been grocery shopping at The Central in Svenborg. He was pleased by his knowledge, and he wanted to show it off a little, the way a bookish kid was always happy to demonstrate what he had learned at the library while others his age were out playing baseball.

He turned to the limestone stairs on their left and climbed without hesitation, running one hand lightly along the curved wall as he went. There was a half-smile on his face as he looked around, as if only the good memories were flooding in on him now.

Puzzled by his extremely mercurial mood, trying to imagine how the mill could frighten and delight him simultaneously, Holly somewhat reluctantly followed him up toward what he had called 'the high room.' She had no good memories to associate with the mill, only the fearful images of her nightmares, and those returned to her as she ascended behind Jim. Thanks to her dream, the narrow twist of stairs was familiar to her, though she was climbing it for the first time – which was an uncanny feeling, far more eerie than mere *déjà vu*.

Halfway up the stairs, she stopped at the window that overlooked

215

the pond. The glass was frosted with dust. She used her hand to wipe one pane, and squinted at the water below. For an instant she thought she saw something strange beneath the placid surface – then realized she was seeing only the reflection of a cloud drifting across the sky.

'What is it?' Jim asked with boyish eagerness. He had stopped a few steps above her.

'Nothing. A shadow.'

They continued all the way to the upper chamber, which proved to be an unremarkable room, about twelve or fourteen feet in diameter, less than fifteen feet high at its apex. The curved limestone wall wrapped around to meet itself, and curved up to form the ceiling, so it seemed as if they were standing inside the domed nose cone of a rocket. The stone was not semi-transparent as it had been in her dream, and no strange amber lights played within it. An arcane mechanism was offset in the dome, through which the motion of the wind-turned sails outside was translated into horizontal movement to crank a vertical wood shaft. The thick shaft disappeared through a hole in the center of the floor.

Remembering how they had stood downstairs and looked up through the buckled and broken decks within the multi-level millworks, Holly gingerly tested the wood floor. No rot was visible. The planks and the joists under them seemed sturdy.

'Lots of dust,' Jim said, as their feet stirred up little clouds with each step.

'And spiders,' Holly noted.

Wrinkling her face in disgust, she peered up at the husks of sucked-dry insects dangling in the elaborate webs that had been spun around the long-stilled mechanism overhead. She didn't fear spiders, but she didn't like them either.

'We need to do some cleaning before we set up camp,' he said.

'Should've bought a broom and a few other things while we were in town.'

'There're cleaning materials at the house. I'll bring them here while you start unloading the car.'

'The house!' Holly was exhilarated by a lovely inspiration. 'When we set out for the mill, I didn't realize this property was still yours, no one living here. We can put the sleeping bags in the house, stay there, and visit this room as often as we need to.'

'Nice thought,' Jim said, 'but it's not that easy. Something's going to happen here, Holly, something that'll give us answers or put us on the road to finding them. I feel it. I know it . . . well, just the way I know these things. But we can't pick the time for the revelation. It doesn't work that way. We can't ask God – or whatever is behind this – to punch a time clock and deliver revelations only between regular business hours. We have to stay here and be patient.'

She sighed. 'OK, yeah, if you—'

Bells interrupted her.

It was a sweet silvery ringing, neither heavy nor clangorous, lasting only two or three seconds, pleasingly musical. It was so light and gay, in fact, that it should have seemed a frivolous sound against the backdrop of that ponderous stone structure. It was not in the least frivolous, however, because inexplicably it triggered in Holly serious associations – thoughts of sin and penitence and redemption.

The trilling faded even as she turned in search of the source. But before she could ask Jim what it had been, it came again.

This time, Holly understood why she associated the sound with issues of spirituality. It was the precise tone of the bells that an altar boy rang during Mass. The sweet ringing brought back to her the smell of spikenard and myrrh from her college days when she had toyed with the idea of converting to Catholicism.

The bells faded again.

She turned to Jim and saw him grinning.

'What is it?' she asked.

'I forgot all about this,' he said wonderingly. 'How could I have forgotten all about this?'

The bells tinkled again, silvery and pure.

'Forgot what?' she asked. 'What're those bells?'

'Not bells,' he said as they faded. He hesitated, and as the sound returned a fourth time, he finally said, 'The ringing is in the stone.'

'Ringing stone?' she said in bewilderment.

As the bells sounded twice again, she circled the room, cocking her head this way and that, until it seemed to her that the music did, indeed, originate from the limestone wall, pealing out not from any single location but equally from every block of that curved surface, no louder at one point than another.

She told herself that stone could not ring, certainly not in such a dulcet voice. A windmill was an unusual structure and could have tricky acoustics. From a high-school-class trip to Washington, she remembered a tourguide showing them a spot in the Capitol's rotunda from which even a whispered conversation was picked up and, by a quirk of architecture, transmitted across the huge dome to

217

the far side of that great space, where eavesdroppers could hear it with perfect clarity. Perhaps something similar was at work here. If bells were rung or other sounds made at a particular place in a far corner of the first floor of the mill, a peculiarity of acoustics might transmit it in equal volume along all the walls on every floor. That explanation was more logical than the concept of magical, ringing stone – until she tried to imagine who would be secretly ringing the bell, and why.

She put one hand against the wall.

The limestone was cool. She detected faint vibrations in it.

The bell fell silent.

The vibrations in the wall subsided.

They waited.

When it was clear that the ringing would not resume, Holly said, 'When did you hear it before?'

'When I was ten.'

'And what happened after the ringing, what did it signify?'

'I don't know.'

'But you said you just remembered it.'

His eyes were shining with excitement. 'Yeah. I remember the ringing. But not what caused it or what followed it. Though I think . . . it's a good sign, Holly.' A note of rapture entered his voice. 'It means something very fine is going to happen, something . . . wonderful.'

Holly was frustrated. In spite of the mystical aspect of Jim's life-saving missions – and in spite of her own paranormal experiences with dreams and the creatures in them – she had come to the farm with the hope of finding logical answers to all that had transpired. She had no idea what those answers could be. But she'd had an unspoken faith in the scientific method. Rigorous investigative procedures combined with careful thought, the use of deductive and inductive reasoning as needed, would lead to solutions. But now it seemed that logic was out the window. She was perturbed by Jim's taste for mysticism, though she had to admit that he had embraced illogic from the start, with all his talk of God, and had taken no pains to conceal it.

She said, 'But, Jim, how could you have forgotten anything as weird as ringing stones or any of the rest of whatever happened to you here?'

'I don't think I just forgot. I think I was *made* to forget.'

'By whom?'

'By whomever or whatever just made the stone ring again, by

whatever's behind all these recent events.' He moved toward the open door. 'Come on, let's get this place cleaned up, move in. We want to be ready for whatever's going to happen next.'

She followed him to the head of the steps but stopped there and watched him descend two at a time, with the air of a kid excited by the prospect of adventure. All of his misgivings about the mill and his fear of The Enemy seemed to have evaporated like a few beads of water on a red-hot griddle. His emotional rollercoaster was cresting the highest point on the track thus far.

Sensing something above her head, Holly looked up. A large web had been spun above the door, across the curve where the wall became the ceiling. A fat spider, its body as big around as her thumbnail and its spindly legs almost as long as her little finger, greasy as a dollop of wax and dark as a drop of blood, was feeding greedily on the pale quivering body of a snared moth.

•4•

With a broom, dustpan, bucket of water, mop, and a few rags, they made the small upper chamber habitable in short order. Jim even brought some Windex and paper towels from the store of cleaning supplies at the house, so they could scrub the grime off the windows, letting in a lot more light. Holly chased down and killed not only the spider above the door but seven others, checking darker corners with one of the flashlights until she was sure she had found them all.

Of course the mill below them was surely crawling with countless other spiders. She decided not to think about that.

By six o'clock, the day was waning but the room was bright enough without the Coleman lantern. They were sitting Indian fashion on their inflatable-mattress sleeping bags, with the big cooler between them. Using the closed lid as a table, they made thick sandwiches, opened the potato chips and cheese twists, and popped the tops off cans of root beer. Though she had missed lunch, Holly had not thought about food until they'd begun to prepare it. Now she was hungrier than she would have expected under the circumstances. Everything was delicious, better than gourmet fare. Olive loaf and cheese on white bread, with mustard, recalled for her the appetites of childhood, the intense flavors and forgotten innocent sensuality of youth.

They did not talk much as they ate. Silences did not make either of them feel awkward, and they were taking such primal pleasure from the meal that no conversation, regardless of how witty, could have improved the moment. But that was only part of the reason for their mutual reticence. Holly, at least, was also unable to think *what* to say under these bizarre circumstances, sitting in the high room of a crumbling old mill, waiting for an encounter with something supernatural. No small talk of any kind felt adequate to the moment, and a serious discussion of just about anything would seem ludicrous.

'I feel sort of foolish,' she said eventually.

'Me too,' he admitted. 'Just a little.'

At seven o'clock, when she was opening the box of chocolate-covered doughnuts, she suddenly realized the mill had no lavatory. 'What about a bathroom?'

He picked up his ring of keys from the floor and handed them to her. 'Go on over to the house. The plumbing works. There's a half-bath right off the kitchen.'

She realized the room was filling with shadows, and when she glanced at the window, she saw that twilight had arrived. Putting the doughnuts aside, she said, 'I want to zip over there and get back before dark.'

'Go ahead.' Jim raised one hand as if pledging allegiance to the flag. 'I swear on all that I hold sacred, I'll leave you at least one doughnut.'

'Half the box better be there when I get back,' she said, 'or I'll kick your butt all the way into Svenborg to buy more.'

'You take your doughnuts seriously.'

'Damn right.'

He smiled. 'I like that in a woman.'

Taking a flashlight to negotiate the mill below, she rose and went to the door. 'Better start up the Coleman.'

'Sure thing. When you get back, it'll be a right cozy little campsite.'

Descending the narrow stairs, Holly began to worry about being separated from Jim, and step by step her anxiety increased. She was not afraid of being alone. What bothered her was leaving him by himself. Which was ridiculous. He was a grown man and far more capable of effective self-defense than was the average person.

The lower floor of the mill was much darker than when she had first seen it. Curtained with cobwebs, the dirty windows admitted almost none of the weak light of dusk.

As she crossed toward the arched opening to the antechamber, she was overcome by a creepy sense of being watched. She knew they were alone in the mill, and she chided herself for being such a ninny. But by the time she reached the archway, her apprehension had swelled until she could not resist the urge to turn and shine the flashlight into the chamber behind her. Shadows were draped across the old machinery as copiously as black crepe in an amusement-park haunted house; they slid aside when the flashlight beam touched them, fell softly back into place as the beam moved on. Each corner, undraped, revealed no spy. Someone could be sheltering behind one part of the millworks or another, and she considered prowling through the ruins in search of an intruder.

But abruptly she felt foolish, too easily spooked. Wondering what had happened to the intrepid reporter she had once been, Holly left the mill.

The sun was beyond the mountains. The sky was purple and that deep iridescent blue seen in old Maxfield Parrish paintings. A few toads were croaking from their shadowy niches along the banks of the pond.

All the way around the water, past the barn, to the back door of the house, Holly continued to feel watched. However, though it was possible that someone might be lurking in the mill, it was not too likely that a virtual platoon of spies had taken up positions in the barn, the surrounding fields, and the distant hills, intent on observing her every move.

'Idiot,' she said self-mockingly as she used one of Jim's keys to open the back door.

Though she had the flashlight, she tried the wall switch unthinkingly. She was surprised to discover that the electrical service was still connected.

She was more surprised, however, by what the light revealed: a fully furnished kitchen. A breakfast table and four chairs stood by the window. Copper pots and pans dangled from a ceiling fixture, and twin racks of knives and other utensils hung on the wall near the cooktop. A toaster, toaster oven, and blender stood on the counters. A shopping list of about fifteen items was affixed to the refrigerator with a magnet in the shape of a can of Budweiser.

Hadn't Jim gotten rid of his grandparents' belongings when they had died five years ago?

Holly ran a finger along one of the counters, drawing a line through the thin coat of dust. But it was, at most, a three-month accumulation, not five years' worth of dirt.

After she used the bathroom adjacent to the kitchen, she

wandered along the hallway, through the dining room and living room, where a full complement of furniture also stood under a light shroud of dust. Some of the paintings hung aslant. Crocheted antimacassars protected the backs and arms of the chairs and sofas. Long unwound, the tall grandfather clock was not ticking. In the living room, the magazine rack beside the La-Z-Boy recliner was crammed full of publications, and inside a mahogany display case, bibelots gleamed dully beneath their own skin of dust.

Her first thought was that Jim had left the house furnished in order to be able to rent it out while searching for a buyer. But on one wall of the living room were framed 8×10 photographs that would not have been left to the mercy of a tenant: Jim's father as a young man of about twenty-one; Jim's father and mother in their wedding finery; Jim at the age of five or six, with both parents.

The fourth and final picture was a two-shot, head and shoulders, of a pleasant-looking couple in their early fifties. The man was on the burly side, with bold square features, yet recognizably an Ironheart; the woman was more handsome, in a female way, than pretty, and elements of her face could also be seen in Jim and his father. Holly had no doubt that they were Jim's paternal grandparents, Lena and Henry Ironheart.

Lena Ironheart was the woman in whose body Holly had ridden like a spirit during last night's dream. Broad, clear face. Wide-set eyes. Full mouth. Curly hair. A natural beauty spot, just a little round dot of skin discoloration, marked the high curve of her right cheek.

Though Holly had described this woman accurately to Jim, he had not recognized her. Maybe he didn't think of her eyes as being wide-set or her mouth as being full. Maybe her hair had been curly only during part of her life, due to the attentions of a beautician. But the beauty spot had to have clicked a switch in his memory, even five years after his grandmother's death.

The sense of being watched had not entirely left Holly even after she had entered the house. Now, as she stared at Lena Ironheart's face in the photograph, the feeling of being under observation grew so acute that she abruptly wheeled around and looked back across the living room.

She was alone.

She stepped quickly to the archway and through it into the front hall. Deserted.

A dark mahogany staircase led up to the second floor. The dust on the newel post and banister was undisturbed: no palm marks, no fingerprints.

Looking up the first flight, she said, 'Hello?' Her voice sounded queerly flat in the empty house.

No one responded to her.

Hesitantly, she started to climb the stairs.

'Who's there?' she called.

Only silence answered her.

Frowning, she stopped on the third step. She glanced down into the front hall, then up toward the landing again.

The silence was too deep, unnatural. Even a deserted house had some noise in it, occasional creaks and ticks and pops from old wood swelling or contracting, a rattle from a loose windowpane tapped by a finger of wind. But the Ironheart house was so hushed, Holly might have thought that she'd gone deaf, except that she could hear the sounds she made herself.

She climbed two more steps. Stopped again.

She *still* felt she was under observation. It was as if the old house itself watched her with malevolent interest, alive and sentient, possessed of a thousand eyes hidden in the wood moldings and in the pattern of the wallpaper.

Dust motes drifted in the rays of the landing light above.

Twilight pressed its purple face to the windows.

Standing just four steps below the landing, partly under the second flight that led into the unseen upstairs hallway, she became convinced that something was waiting for her on the second floor. It was not necessarily The Enemy up there, not even anything alive and hostile – but something horrible, the discovery of which would shatter her.

Her heart was hammering. When she swallowed, she found a lump in her throat. She drew breath with a startling, ragged sound.

The feeling of being watched and of trembling on the brink of a monstrous revelation became so overpowering that she turned and hurried down the steps. She did not flee pell-mell out of the house; she retraced her path and turned off all the lights as she went; but she did not dally, either.

Outside, the sky was purple-black where it met the mountains in the east, purplish-red where it touched the mountains in the west, and sapphire-blue between. The golden fields and hills had changed to pale gray fading to charcoal, as if a fire had swept them while she was in the house.

As she crossed the yard and moved past the barn, the conviction that she was under observation only grew more intense. She glanced apprehensively at the open black square of the hay loft, the windows

223

on either side of the big red double doors. It was a gut-clenching sensation of such primitive power that it transcended mere instinct. She felt as if she were a guinea pig in a laboratory experiment, with wires hooked into her brain, while scientists sent pulses of current directly into the raw cerebral tissues that controlled the fear reflex and generated paranoid delusions. She had never experienced anything like it, knew that she was teetering on the thin edge of panic, and struggled to get a grip on herself.

By the time she reached the graveled drive that curved around the pond, she was running. She held the extinguished flashlight like a club, prepared to swing it hard at anything that darted toward her.

The bells rang. Even above her frantic breathing, she heard the pure, silvery trilling of clappers rapidly striking the inner curves of perfectly tuned bells.

For an instant she was amazed that the phenomenon was audible outside the windmill and at a distance, as the building was halfway around the pond from her. Then something flickered in her peripheral vision even before the first spell of ringing ended, and she looked away from the mill, toward the water.

Pulses of blood-red light, originating at the center of the pond, spread outward toward the banks in tight concentric circles, like the measured ripples that radiated from the point at which a dropped stone struck deep water. That sight brought Holly to a stumbling halt; she almost went to her knees as gravel rolled under her feet.

When the bells fell silent, the crimson light in the pond was immediately snuffed out. The water was much darker now than when she had first seen it in mid-afternoon. It no longer had all the somber hues of slate, but was as black as a polished slab of obsidian.

The bells rang again, and the crimson light pulsed from the heart of the pond, radiating outward. She could see that each new bright blossom was not born on the surface of the water but in its depths, dim at first but swiftly rising, almost bursting like an overheated incandescent bulb when it neared the surface, casting waves of light toward the shore.

The ringing ceased.

The water darkened.

The toads along the shoreline were not croaking any more. The ever-murmuring world of nature had fallen as silent as the interior of the Ironheart farmhouse. No coyote howl, no insect cry, no owl hoot, no bat shriek or flap of wing, no rustling in the grass.

The bells sounded again, and the light returned, but this time it was not as red as gore, more of an orange-red, though it was brighter than before. At the water's edge, the feathery white panicles of the pampas grass caught the curious radiance and glowed like plumes of iridescent gas.

Something was rising from the bottom of the pond.

As the throbbing luminescence faded with the next cessation of the bells, Holly stood in the grip of awe and fear, knowing she should run but unable to move.

Ringing.

Light. Muddy-orange this time. No red tint at all. Brighter than ever.

Holly broke the chains of fear and sprinted toward the windmill.

On all sides, the palpitant light enlivened the dreary dusk. Shadows leapt rhythmically like Apaches dancing around a war fire. Beyond the fence, dead cornstalks bristled as repulsively as the spiny legs and plated torsos of praying mantises. The windmill appeared to be in the process of changing magically from stone to copper or even to gold.

The ringing stopped and the light went out as she reached the open door of the mill.

She raced across the threshold, then skidded to a stop in the darkness, on the brink of the lower chamber. No light at all came through the windows now. The blackness was tarry, cloying. As she fumbled for the switch on the flashlight, she found it hard to draw breath, as if the darkness itself had begun flowing into her lungs, suffocating her.

The flashlight came on just as the bells began to ring again. She slashed the beam across the room and back, to be sure nothing was there in the gloom, reaching for her. Then she found the stairs to her left and hurried toward the high room.

When she reached the window at the halfway point, she put her face to the pane of glass that she had wiped clean with her hand earlier in the day. In the pond below, the rippling bull's-eye of light was brighter still, now amber instead of orange.

Calling for Jim, Holly ran up the remaining stairs.

As she went, lines of Edgar Allan Poe's poetry, studied an age ago in junior high school and thought forgotten, rang crazily through her mind:

> *Keeping time, time, time,*
> *In a sort of Runic rhyme,*
> *To the tintinnabulation that so musically wells*

From the bells, bells, bells, bells
Bells, bells, bells—

She burst into the high room, where Jim stood in the soft winter-white glow of the Coleman gas lantern. He was smiling, turning in a circle and looking expectantly at the walls around him.

As the bells died away, she said, 'Jim, come look, come quick, something's in the lake.'

She dashed to the nearest window, but it was just far enough around the wall from the pond to prevent her seeing the water. The other two windows were even more out of line with the desired view, so she did not even try them.

'The ringing in the stone,' Jim said dreamily.

Holly returned to the head of the stairs as the bells began to ring again. She paused and looked back just long enough to be sure that Jim was following her, for he seemed in something of a daze.

Hurrying down the stairs, she heard more lines of Poe's poem reverberating in her mind:

Hear the loud alarum bells—
Brazen bells!
What a tale of terror, now, their turbulency tells!

She had never been the kind of woman to whom sprang lines of verse appropriate to the moment. She couldn't recall quoting a line of poetry or even reading any – other than Louise Tarvohl's treacle! – since college.

When she reached the window, she scrubbed frantically at another pane with the palm of her hand, to give them a better view of the spectacle below. She saw that the light was blood-red again and dimmer, as if whatever had been rising through the water was now sinking again.

Oh, the bells, bells, bells!
What a tale their terror tells

It seemed crazy to be mentally reciting poetry in the midst of these wondrous and frightening events, but she had never been under such stress before. Maybe this was the way the mind worked – giddily dredging up long-forgotten knowledge – when you were about to meet a higher power. Because that's just what she felt was about to happen, an encounter with a higher power, perhaps God but most likely not. She didn't really think God lived in a pond, although any minister or priest would probably tell her that God lived everywhere, in all things. God was like the eight-hundred-pound gorilla who could live anywhere he wanted.

Just as Jim reached her, the ringing stopped, and the crimson light in the pond quickly faded. He squeezed in beside her and put his face to the glass.

They waited.

Two seconds ticked by. Two more.

'No,' she said. 'Damn it, I wanted you to see.'

But the ringing did not resume, and the pond remained dark out there in the steadily dimming twilight. Night would be upon them within a few minutes.

'What was it?' Jim asked, leaning back from the window.

'Like something in a Spielberg film,' she said excitedly, 'rising up out of the water, from deep under the pond, light throbbing in time with the bells. I think that's where the ringing originates, from the thing in the pond, and somehow it's transmitted through the walls of the mill.'

'Spielberg film?' He looked puzzled.

She tried to explain: 'Wonderful and terrifying, awesome and strange, scary and damned exciting all at once.'

'You mean like in *Close Encounters*? Are you talking a starship or something?'

'Yes. No. I'm not sure. I don't know. Maybe something weirder than that.'

'Weirder than a starship?'

Her wonder, and even her fear, subsided in favor of frustration. She was not accustomed to finding herself at a complete loss for words to describe things that she had felt or seen. But with this man and the incomparable experiences in which he became entangled, even her sophisticated vocabulary and talent for supple phrase-making failed her miserably.

'Shit, yes!' she said at last. 'Weirder than a starship. At least weirder than the way they show them in the movies.'

'Come on,' he said, ascending the stairs again, 'let's get back up there.' When she lingered at the window, he returned to her and took her hand. 'It isn't over yet. I think it's just beginning. And the place for us to be is the upper room. I *know* it's the place. Come on, Holly.'

•5•

They sat on the inflatable-mattress sleeping bags again.

The lantern cast a pearly-silver glow, whitewashing the yellow-beige blocks of limestone. In the baglike wicks inside the glass chimney of the lamp, the gas burned with a faint hiss, so it seemed as if whispering voices were rising through the floorboards of that high room.

Jim was poised at the apex of his emotional rollercoaster, full of childlike delight and anticipation, and this time Holly was right there with him. The light in the pond had terrified her, but it had also touched her in other ways, sparking deep psychological responses on a primitive sub-subconscious level, igniting fuses of wonder and hope which were fizzing, burning unquenchably toward some much-desired explosion of faith, emotional catharsis.

She had accepted that Jim was not the only troubled person in the room. His heart might contain more turmoil than hers, but she was as empty, in her own way, as he was in his. When they'd met in Portland, she had been a burnt-out cynic, going through the motions of a life, not even trying to identify and fill the empty spaces in her heart. She had not experienced the tragedy and grief that he had known, but now she realized that leading a life equally devoid of tragedy *and* joy could breed despair. Passing days and weeks and years in the pursuit of goals that had not really mattered to her, driven by a purpose she had not truly embraced, with no one to whom she was profoundly committed, she had been eaten by a dry-rot of the soul. She and Jim were the two pieces of a yin-yang puzzle, each shaped to fill the hollowness in the other, healing each other merely by their contact. They fit together astonishingly well, and the match seemed inevitable; but the puzzle might never have been solved if the halves of it had not been brought together in the same place at the same time.

Now she waited with nervous excitement for contact with the power that had led Jim to her. She was ready for God or for something quite different but equally benign. She could not believe that what she had seen in the pond was The Enemy. That creature was apart from this, connected somehow but different. Even if Jim had not told her that something fine and good was coming, she eventually would have sensed, on her own, that the light in the water and the ringing in the stone heralded not blood and death but rapture.

They spoke tersely at first, afraid that voluble conversation

228

would inhibit that higher power from initiating the next stage of contact.

'How long has the pond been here?' she asked.

'A long time.'

'Before the Ironhearts?'

'Yeah.'

'Before the farm itself?'

'I'm sure it was.'

'Possibly forever?'

'Possibly.'

'Any local legends about it?'

'What do you mean?'

'Ghost stories, Loch Ness, that kind of stuff.'

'No. Not that I've ever heard.'

They were silent. Waiting.

Finally Holly said, 'What's your theory?'

'Huh?'

'Earlier today you said you had a theory, something strange and wonderful, but you didn't want to talk about it till you'd thought it through.'

'Oh, right. Now maybe it's more than a theory. When you said you'd seen something under the pond in your dream . . . well, I don't know why, but I started thinking about an encounter . . .'

'Encounter?'

'Yeah. Like what you said. Something . . . alien.'

'Not of this world,' Holly said, remembering the sound of the bells and the light in the pond.

'They're out there in the universe somewhere,' he said with quiet enthusiasm. 'It's too big for them not to be out there. And someday they'll be coming. Someone will encounter them. So why not me, why not you?'

'But it must've been there under the pond when you were ten.'

'Maybe.'

'Why would it be there all this time?'

'I don't know. Maybe it's been there a lot longer. Hundreds of years. Thousands.'

'But why a starship at the bottom of a pond?'

'Maybe it's an observation station, a place where they monitor human civilization, like an outpost we might set up in Antarctica to study things there.'

Holly realized they sounded like kids sitting under the stars on a summer night, drawn like all kids to the contemplation of the unknown and to fantasies of exotic adventure. On one level she found their musings absurd, even laughable, and she was unable to believe that recent events could have such a neat yet fanciful explanation. But on another level, where she was still a child and always would be, she desperately wanted the fantasy to be made real.

Twenty minutes passed without a new development, and gradually Holly began to settle down from the heights of excitement and nervous agitation to which the lights in the pond had catapulted her. Still filled with wonder but no longer mentally numbed by it, she remembered what had happened to her just prior to the appearance of the radiant presence in the millpond: the overwhelming, preternatural, almost panic-inducing awareness of being watched. She was about to mention it to Jim when she recalled the *other* strange things she had found at the farmhouse.

'It's completely furnished,' she said. 'You never cleaned the house out after your grandfather died.'

'I left it furnished in case I was able to rent it while waiting for a buyer.'

Those were virtually the same words she had used, standing in the house, to explain the curious situation to herself. 'But you left all their personal belongings there too.'

He did not look at her but at the walls, waiting for some sign of a superhuman presence. 'I'd have taken that stuff away if I'd ever found a renter.'

'You've left it there for almost five years?'

He shrugged.

She said, 'It's been cleaned more or less regularly since then, though not recently.'

'A renter might always show up.'

'It's sort of creepy, Jim.'

Finally he looked at her. 'How so?'

'It's like a mausoleum.'

His blue eyes were utterly unreadable, but Holly had the feeling she was annoying him, perhaps because this mundane talk of renters and house cleaning and real estate was pulling him away from the more pleasurable contemplation of alien encounters.

He sighed and said, 'Yeah, it is creepy, a little.'

'Then why . . . ?'

He slowly twisted the lantern control, reducing the flow of gas to the wicks. The hard white light softened to a moon-pale glow, and the shadows eased closer. 'To tell you the truth, I couldn't bear to pack up my granddad's things. Together, we'd sorted through grandma's belongings only eight months earlier, when she'd died, and that had been hard enough. When he . . . passed away so soon after her, it was too much for me. For so long, they'd been all I had. Then suddenly I didn't even have them.'

A tortured expression darkened the blue of his eyes.

As a flood of sympathy washed through Holly, she reached across the ice chest and took his hand.

He said, 'I procrastinated, kept procrastinating, and the longer I delayed sorting through his things, the harder it became *ever* to do it.' He sighed again. 'If I'd have found a renter or a buyer, that would have forced me to put things in order, no matter how unpleasant the job. But this old farm is about as marketable as a truckload of sand in the middle of the Mojave.'

Closing the house upon the death of his grandfather, touching nothing in it for four years and four months, except to clean it once in a while – that was eccentric. Holly couldn't see it any other way. At the same time, however, it was an eccentricity that touched her, moved her. As she had sensed from the start, he was a gentle man beneath his rage, beneath his steely superhero identity, and she liked the soft-hearted part of him too.

'We'll do it together,' Holly said. 'When we've figured out what the hell is happening to us, wherever and however we go on from here, there'll be time for us to sort through your grandfather's things. It won't be so difficult if we do it together.'

He smiled at her and squeezed her hand.

She remembered something else. 'Jim, you recall the description I gave you of the woman in my dream last night, the woman who came up the mill stairs?'

'Sort of.'

'You said you didn't recognize her.'

'So?'

'But there's a photo of her in the house.'

'There is?'

'In the living room, that photograph of a couple in their early fifties – are they your grandparents, Lena and Henry?'

'Yeah. That's right.'

'Lena was the woman in my dream.'

He frowned. 'Isn't that odd . . ?'

'Well, maybe. But what's odder is, you didn't recognize her.'

'I guess your description wasn't that good.'

'But didn't you hear me say she had a beauty mark—'

His eyes narrowed, and his hand tightened around hers. 'Quick, the tablets.'

Confused, she said, 'What?'

'Something's about to happen, I feel it, and we need the tablets we bought at The Center.'

He let go of her hand, and she withdrew the two yellow, lined tablets and felt-tip pen from the plastic bag at her side. He took them from her, hesitated, looking around at the walls and at the shadows above them, as if waiting to be told what to do next.

The bells rang.

*   *   *

That musical tintinnabulation sent a thrill through Jim. He knew that he was on the verge of discovering the meaning not merely of the events of the past year but of the last two and a half decades. And not just that, either. More. Much more. The ringing heralded the revelation of even greater understanding, transcendental truths, an explanation of the fundamental meaning of his entire life, past and future, origins and destiny, and of the meaning of existence itself. Grandiose as such a notion might be, he sensed that the secrets of creation would be revealed to him before he left the windmill, and that he would reach the state of enlightenment he had sought – and failed to find – in a score of religions.

As the second spell of ringing began, Holly started to get up.

Jim figured she intended to descend to the window on the stairs and look into the pond. He said, 'No, wait. It's going to happen *here* this time.'

She hesitated, then sat down.

As the ringing stopped again, Jim felt compelled to push the ice-chest out of the way and put one of the yellow, lined tablets on the floor between him and Holly. He was not sure what he was expected to do with the other tablet and the pen, but after a brief moment of indecision, he held on to them.

When the melodic ringing began a third time, it was accompanied by an impossible pulse of light within the limestone walls. The red glow seemed to well up from inside the stone at a point directly in front of them, then suddenly raced around the room, encircling them with a throbbing band of luminescence.

Even as the strange flare whipped around them, Holly issued a wordless sound of fear, and Jim remembered what she had told him of her dream last night. The woman – whether it had been his

232

grandmother or not – had climbed the stairs into the high room, had seen an amber emanation within the walls, as if the mill was made of colored glass, and had witnessed something unimaginably hostile being born out of those mortared blocks.

'It's OK.' He was eager to reassure her. 'This isn't The Enemy. It's something else. There's no danger here. This is a different light.'

He was only sharing with her the reassurances that were flooding into him from a higher power. He hoped to God that he was correct, that no threat was imminent, for he remembered too well the hideous biological transformation of his own bedroom ceiling in Laguna Niguel little more than twelve hours ago. Light had pulsed within the oily, insectile birth sac that had blistered out of ordinary drywall, and the shadowy form within, writhing and twitching, had been nothing he would ever want to see more directly.

During two more bursts of melodic ringing, the color of the light changed to amber. But otherwise it in no way resembled the menacing radiance in his bedroom ceiling, which had been a different shade of amber altogether – the vile yellow of putrescent matter or of rich dark pus – and which had throbbed in sympathy with an ominous tripartite heartbeat that was not audible now.

Holly looked scared nonetheless.

He wished he could pull her close, put his arm around her. But he needed to give his undivided attention to the higher power that was striving to reach him.

The ringing stopped, but the light did not fade. It quivered, shimmered, dimmed and brightened. It moved through the otherwise dark wall in scores of separate amoeba-like forms that constantly flowed together and separated into new shapes; it was like a one-dimensional representation of the kaleidoscopic display in one of those old Lava Lamps. The ever-changing patterns evolved on all sides of them, from the base of the wall to the apex of the domed ceiling.

'I feel like we're in a bathysphere, all glass, suspended far, far down in the ocean,' Holly said. 'And great schools of luminescent fish are diving and soaring and swirling past us on all sides, through the deep black water.'

He loved her for putting the experience into better words than he could summon, words that would not let him forget the images they described, even if he lived a hundred years.

Unquestionably, the ghostly luminosity lay within the stone, not merely on the surface of it. He could see *into* that now-translucent

233

substance, as if it had been alchemized into a dark but well-clarified quartz. The amber radiance brightened the room more than did the lantern, which he had turned low. His trembling hands looked golden, as did Holly's face.

But pockets of darkness remained, and the constantly moving light enlivened the shadows as well.

'What now?' Holly asked softly.

Jim noticed that something had happened to the yellow tablet on the floor between them. 'Look.'

Words had appeared on the top third of the first page. They looked as if they had been formed by a finger dipped in ink:

I AM WITH YOU.

•6•

Holly had been distracted – to say the least! – by the lightshow, but she did not think that Jim could have leaned to the tablet and printed the words with the felt-tip pen or any other instrument without drawing her attention. Yet she found it hard to believe that some disembodied presence had conveyed the message.

'I think we're being encouraged to ask questions,' Jim said.

'Then ask it what it is,' she said at once.

He wrote a question on the second tablet, which he was holding, and showed it to her:

Who are you?

As they watched, the answer appeared on the first tablet, which lay between and slightly in front of them at such an angle that they could both read it. The words were not burnt on to the paper and were not formed by ink that dripped magically from the air. Instead, the irregular, wavery letters appeared as dim gray shapes and grew darker as they seemed to float up out of the paper, as though a page of the tablet were not one-five-hundredth of an inch thick but a pool of liquid many feet deep. She recognized immediately that this was similar to the effect she had seen earlier when the balls of light had risen to the center of the pond before bursting and casting concentric rings of illumination outward through the water; this was, as well, how the light had first welled up in the limestone walls before the blocks had become thoroughly translucent.

THE FRIEND.

Who are you? The Friend.

234

It seemed to be an odd self-description. Not 'your friend' or 'a friend' but *The* Friend.

For an alien intelligence, if indeed that's all it was, the name had curious spiritual implications, connotations of divinity. Men had given God many names – Jehovah, Allah, Brahma, Zeus, Aesir – but even more titles. God was The Almighty, The Eternal Being, The Infinite, The Father, The Savior, The Creator, The Light. The Friend seemed to fit right into that list.

Jim quickly wrote another question and showed it to Holly: *Where do you come from?*

ANOTHER WORLD.

Which could mean anything from heaven to Mars.

Do you mean another planet?

YES.

'My God,' Holly said, awed in spite of herself.

So much for the great hereafter.

She looked up from the tablet and met Jim's eyes. They seemed to shine brighter than ever, although the chrome-yellow light had imparted to them an exceptional green tint.

Restless with excitement, she rose onto her knees, then eased back again, sitting on her calves. The top tablet page was filled with the entity's responses. Holly equivocated only briefly, then tore it off and set it aside, so they could see the second page. She glanced back and forth between Jim's questions and the rapidly appearing answers.

From another solar system?

YES.

From another galaxy?

YES.

Is it your vessel we've seen in the pond?

YES.

How long have you been here?

10,000 YEARS.

As she stared at that figure, it seemed to Holly that this moment was more like a dream than some of the actual dreams she'd been having lately. After so much mystery, there were answers – but they seemed to be coming too easily. She did not know what she had expected, but she had not imagined that the murkiness in which they had been operating would clear as quickly as if a drop of a magical universal detergent had been dropped into it.

'Ask her why she's here,' Holly said, tearing off the second sheet and putting it with the first.

Jim was surprised. *'She?'*

'Why not?'

He brightened. 'Why not?' he agreed.

He turned to a new page in his own tablet and wrote her question: *Why are you here?*

Floating up through the paper to the surface: TO OBSERVE, TO STUDY, TO HELP MANKIND.

'You know what this is like?' Holly said.

'What's it like?'

'An episode of *Outer Limits*.'

'The old TV show?'

'Yeah.'

'Wasn't that before your time?'

'It's on cable.'

'But what do you mean it's like an episode of *Outer Limits*?'

She frowned at TO OBSERVE, TO STUDY, TO HELP MANKIND and said, 'Don't you think it's a little . . . trite?'

'Trite?' He was irritated. 'No, I don't. Because I haven't any idea what alien contact *should* be like. I haven't had a whole lot of experience with it, certainly not enough to have expectations or be jaded.'

'I'm sorry. I don't know . . . it's just . . . OK, let's see where this leads.'

She had to admit that she was no less awed than she had been when the light had first appeared in the walls. Her heart continued to thud hard and fast, and she was still unable to draw a really deep breath. She still felt that they were in the presence of something superhuman, maybe even a higher power by one definition or another, and she was humbled by it. Considering what she had seen in the pond, the pulsing luminescence even now swimming through the wall, and the words that kept shimmering into view on the tablet, she would have been hopelessly stupid if she had *not* been awed.

Undeniably, however, her sense of wonder was dulled by the feeling that this entity was structuring the encounter like an old movie or TV script. With a sarcastic note in his voice, Jim had said that he had too little experience with alien contact to have developed any expectations that could be disappointed. But that was not true. Having grown up in the sixties and seventies, he had been as media-saturated as she had been. They'd been exposed to the same TV shows and movies, magazines and books; science fiction had been a major influence in popular culture all their lives. He had acquired plenty of detailed expectations about what alien contact would be like – and the entity in the wall was playing to all of them. Holly's only conscious expectation had been that a *real* close encounter of the third kind would be like nothing the novelists and screen-writers imagined in all their wildest flights of fantasy, because when referring to life from another world, alien *meant* alien, different, beyond easy comparison or comprehension.

'OK,' she said, 'maybe familiarity is the point. I mean, maybe it's using our modern myths as a convenient way to present itself to us, a way to make itself comprehensible to us. Because it's probably so radically different from us that we could never understand its true nature or appearance.'

'Exactly,' Jim said. He wrote another question: *What is the light we see in the walls?*

THE LIGHT IS ME.

Holly didn't wait for Jim to write the next question. She addressed the entity directly: 'How can you move through a wall?'

Because the alien seemed such a stickler about form, she was somewhat surprised when it did not insist on hewing to the written question-reply format. It answered her at once: I CAN BECOME PART OF ANYTHING, MOVE WITHIN IT, TAKE SHAPE FROM IT WHENEVER I CHOOSE.

'Sounds a little like bragging,' she said.

'I can't believe you can be sarcastic at a time like this,' Jim said impatiently.

'I'm not being sarcastic,' she explained. 'I'm just trying to understand.'

He looked doubtful.

To the alien presence, she said, 'You understand the problems I'm having with this, don't you?'

On the tablet: YES.

She ripped away that page, revealing a fresh one. Increasingly restless and nervous, but not entirely sure why, Holly got to her feet and turned in a circle, looking at the play of light in the walls as she formulated her next question. 'Why is your approach marked by the sound of bells?'

No answer appeared on the tablet.

She repeated the question.

The tablet remained blank.

Holly said, 'Trade secret, I guess.'

She felt a bead of cold sweat trickle out of her right armpit and down her side, under her blouse. A childlike wonder still worked in her, but fear was on the rise again. Something was wrong. Something more than the clichéd nature of the story the entity was giving them. She couldn't quite put her finger on what spooked her.

On his own tablet, Jim quickly wrote another question, and Holly leaned down to read it: *Did you appear to me in this room when I was ten years old?*

YES. OFTEN.

Did you make me forget it?

YES.

'Don't bother writing your questions,' Holly said. 'Just ask them like I do.'

Jim was clearly startled by her suggestion, and she was surprised that he had persisted with his pen and tablet even after seeing that the questions she asked aloud were answered. He seemed reluctant to put aside the felt-tip and the paper, but at last he did. 'Why did you make me forget?'

Even standing, Holly could easily read the bold words that appeared on the yellow tablet:

YOU WERE NOT READY TO REMEMBER.

'Unnecessarily cryptic,' she muttered. 'You're right. It must be male.'

Jim tore off the used page, put it with the others, and paused, chewing his lip, evidently not sure what to ask next. Finally he said, 'Are you male or female?'

I AM MALE.

'More likely,' Holly said, 'it's neither. It's *alien*, after all, and it's as likely to reproduce by parthenogenesis.'

I AM MALE, it repeated.

Jim remained seated, legs folded, an undiminished look of wonder on his face, more boylike now than ever.

Holly did not understand why her anxiety level was soaring while Jim continued to bounce up and down – well, virtually – with enthusiasm and delight.

He said, 'What do you look like?'

WHATEVER I CHOOSE TO LOOK LIKE.

'Could you appear to us as a man or woman?' Jim asked.

YES.

'As a dog?'

YES.

'As a cat?'

YES.

'As a beetle?'

238

YES.

Without the security of his pen and tablet, Jim seemed to have been reduced to inane questions. Holly half expected him to ask the entity what its favorite color was, whether it preferred Coke or Pepsi, and if it liked Barry Manilow music.

But he said, 'How old are you?'

I AM A CHILD.

'A child?' Jim responded. 'But you told us you've been on our world for ten thousand years.'

I AM STILL A CHILD.

Jim said, 'Then is your species very long-lived?'

WE ARE IMMORTAL.

'Wow.'

'It's lying,' Holly told him.

Appalled by her effrontery, he said, 'Jesus, Holly!'

'Well, it is.'

And *that* was the source of her renewed fear – the fact that it was not being straight with them, was playing games, deceiving. She had a sense that it regarded them with enormous contempt. In which case, she probably should have shut up, been meekly adoring before its power, and tried not to anger it.

Instead she said, 'If it were really immortal, it wouldn't think of itself as a child. It *couldn't* think that way about itself. Infancy, childhood, adolescence, adulthood – those are age categories a species concerns itself with if it has a finite lifespan. If you're immortal, you might be born innocent, ignorant, uneducated, but you aren't born young because you're never really going to get old.'

'Aren't you splitting hairs?' Jim asked almost petulantly.

'I don't think so. It's lying to us.'

'Maybe its use of the word "child" was just another way it was trying to make its alien nature more understandable.'

YES.

'Bullshit,' Holly said.

'Damn it, Holly!'

As Jim removed another page from the tablet, detaching it neatly along its edge, Holly moved to the wall and studied the patterns of light churning through it. Seen close up, they were quite beautiful and strange, not like a smooth-flowing phosphorescent fluid or fiery streams of lava, but like scintillant swarms of fireflies, millions of spangled points not unlike her analogy of luminous, schooling fish.

Holly half expected the wall in front of her to bulge suddenly. Split open. Give birth to a monstrous form.

She wanted to step back. Instead she moved closer. Her nose was only an inch from the transmuted stone. Viewed this intimately, the surge and flux and whirl of the millions of bright cells was dizzying. There was no heat from it, but she imagined she could feel the flicker of light and shadow across her face.

'Why is your approach marked by the sound of bells?' she asked.

After a few seconds, Jim spoke from behind her: 'No answer.'

The question seemed innocent enough, and one that they should logically be expected to ask. The entity's unwillingness to answer alerted her that the ringing must be somehow vitally important. Understanding the bells might be the first step toward learning something real and true about this creature.

'Why is your approach marked by the sound of bells?'

Jim reported: 'No answer. I don't think you should ask that question again, Holly. It obviously doesn't want to answer, and there's nothing to be gained by aggravating it. This isn't The Enemy, this is—'

'Yeah, I know. It's The Friend.'

She remained at the wall and felt herself to be face-to-face with an alien presence, though it had nothing that corresponded to a face. It was focused on her now. It was right *there*.

Again she said, 'Why is your approach marked by the sound of bells?'

Instinctively she knew that her innocent question and her not-so-innocent repetition of it had put her in great danger. Her heart was thudding so loud that she wondered if Jim could hear it. She figured The Friend, with all its powers, could not only hear her hammering heart but see it jumping like a panicked rabbit within the cage of her chest. It knew she was afraid, all right. Hell, it might even be able to read her mind. She had to show it that she would not allow fear to deter her.

She put one hand on the light-filled stone. If those luminous clouds were not merely a projection of the creature's consciousness, not just an illusion or representation for their benefit, if the thing was, as it claimed, actually alive in the wall, then the stone was now its flesh. Her hand was upon its body.

Faint vibrations passed across the wall in distinctive, whirling vortexes. That was all she felt. No heat. The fire within the stone was evidently cold.

'Why is your approach marked by the sound of bells?'

'Holly, don't,' Jim said. Worry tainted his voice for the first time. Perhaps he, too, had begun to sense that The Friend was not entirely a friend.

But she was driven by a suspicion that willpower mattered in this confrontation, and that a demonstration of unflinching will would set a new tone in their relationship with The Friend. She could not have explained why she felt so strongly about it. Just instinct – not a woman's but an ex-reporter's.

'Why is your approach marked by the sound of bells?'

She thought she detected a slight change in the vibrations that tingled across her palm, but she might have imagined it, for they were barely perceptible in the first place. Through her mind flickered an image of the stone cracking open in a jagged mouth and biting off her hand, blood spurting, white bone bristling from the ragged stump of her wrist.

Though she was shaking uncontrollably, she did not step back or lift her hand off the wall.

She wondered if The Friend had sent her that horrifying image.

'Why is your approach marked by the sound of bells?'

'Holly, for Christ's sake—' Jim broke off, then said, 'Wait, an answer's coming.'

Willpower *did* matter. But for God's sake, why? Why should an all-powerful alien force from another galaxy be intimidated by her unwavering resolution?

Jim reported the response: 'It says . . . "For drama?" '

'For drama?' she repeated.

'Yeah. F-O-R, then D-R-A-M-A, then a question mark.'

To the thing in the wall, she said, 'Are you telling me the bells are just a bit of theater to dramatize your apparitions?'

After a few seconds, Jim said, 'No answer.'

'And why the question mark?' she asked The Friend. 'Don't you know what the bells mean yourself, where the sound comes from, what makes it, why? Are you only guessing when you say "for drama"? How can you not know what it is if it always accompanies you?'

'Nothing,' Jim told her.

She stared into the wall. The churning, schooling cells of light were increasingly disorienting her, but she did not close her eyes.

'A new message,' Jim said. ' "I am going." '

'Chicken,' Holly said softly into the amorphous face of the thing in the wall. But she was sheathed in cold sweat now.

The amber light began to darken, turn orange.

Stepping away from the wall at last, Holly swayed and almost fell. She moved back to her bedroll and dropped to her knees.

New words appeared on the tablet: I WILL BE BACK.

'When?' Jim asked.
WHEN THE TIDE IS MINE.
'What tide?'
THERE IS A TIDE IN THE VESSEL, AN EBB AND FLOW, DARKNESS AND LIGHT. I RISE WITH THE LIGHT TIDE, BUT HE RISES WITH THE DARK.
'He?' Holly asked.
THE ENEMY.
The light in the walls was red-orange now, dimmer, but still ceaselessly changing patterns around them.
Jim said, 'Two of you share the starship?'
YES. TWO FORCES. TWO ENTITIES.
It's lying, Holly thought. This, like all the rest of its story, is just like the bells: good theater.
WAIT FOR MY RETURN.
'We'll wait,' Jim said.
DO NOT SLEEP.
'Why can't we sleep?' Holly asked, playing along.
YOU MIGHT DREAM.
The page was full. Jim ripped it off and stacked it with the others.
The light in the walls was blood-red now, steadily fading.
DREAMS ARE DOORWAYS.
'What are you telling us?'
The same three words again: DREAMS ARE DOORWAYS.
'It's a warning,' Jim said.
DREAMS ARE DOORWAYS.
No, Holly thought, it's a threat.

•7•

The windmill was just a windmill again. Stones and timbers. Mortar and nails. Dust sifting, wood rotting, iron rusting, spiders spinning in secret lairs.

Holly sat directly in front of Jim, in pow-wow position, their knees touching. She held both his hands, partly because she drew strength from his touch, and partly because she wanted to reassure him and take the sting out of what she was about to say.

'Listen, babe, you're the most interesting man I've ever known, the sexiest, for sure, and I think, at heart, the kindest. But you do a lousy interview. For the most part, your questions aren't well thought-out, you don't get at the meat of an issue, you follow up on irrelevancies but generally fail to follow up on the really important answers. And you're a naive enough reporter to think that the subject is always being straight with you, when they're almost never straight with an interviewer, so you don't *probe* the way you should.'

He did not seem offended. He smiled and said, 'I didn't think of myself as a reporter doing an interview.'

'Well, kiddo, that's exactly what the situation was. The Friend, as he calls himself, has information, and we need information to know where we stand, to do our job.'

'I thought of it more as . . . I don't know . . . as an epiphany. When God came to Moses with the Ten Commandments, I figure He just told Moses what they were, and if Moses had other questions he didn't feel he had to grill the Big Guy.'

'This wasn't God in the walls.'

'I know that. I'm past that idea now. But it was an alien intelligence so superior to us that it almost might as well *be* God.'

'We don't know that,' she said patiently.

'Sure we do. When you consider the high degree of intelligence and the millennia needed to build a civilization capable of traveling across galaxies – good heavens, we're only monkeys by comparison!'

'There, you see, that's what I'm talking about. How do you know it's from another galaxy? Because you believe what it told you. How do you know there's a spaceship under the pond? Because you believe what it told you.'

Jim was getting impatient now. 'Why would it lie to us, what would it have to gain from lies?'

'I don't know. But we can't be sure that it isn't manipulating us. And when it comes back, like it promised, I want to be ready for it. I want to spend the next hour or two or three – however long we've got – making a list of questions, so we can put it through a carefully planned inquisition. We've got to have a strategy for squeezing *real* information from it, facts not fantasies, and our questions have to support that strategy.' When he frowned, she hastened on before he could interrupt. 'OK, all right, maybe it's incapable of lying, maybe it's noble and pure, maybe everything it's told us is the gospel truth. But listen, Jim, this is not an epiphany. The Friend set the rules by influencing you to buy the tablets and pen. It established the question-and-answer format. If it didn't want us to make the best of that format, it would've just told you to shut up and would've blabbered at you from a burning bush!'

He stared at her. He chewed his lip thoughtfully.

He shifted his gaze to the walls where the creature of light had swum in the stone.

Pressing her point, Holly said, 'You never even asked it why it wants you to save people's lives, or why some people and not others.'

He looked at her again, obviously surprised to realize that he had not pursued the answer to the most important question of all. In the lactescent glow of the softly hissing gas lantern, his eyes were blue again, not green as the amber light had temporarily made them. And troubled.

'OK,' he said. 'You're right. I guess I was just swept away by it all. I mean, Holly, whatever the hell it is – it's astounding.'

'It's astounding,' she acknowledged.

'We'll do what you want, make up a list of carefully thought-out questions. And when it comes back, you should be the one to ask all of them, 'cause you'll be better at ad-libbing other questions if it says anything that needs follow-up.'

'I agree,' she said, relieved that he had suggested it without being pressured.

She was better schooled at interviewing than he was, but she was also more trustworthy in this particular situation than Jim could ever be. The Friend had a long past relationship with him and had, admittedly, already messed with his memory by making him forget about the encounters they'd had twenty-five years ago. Holly had to assume that Jim was co-opted, to one degree or another corrupted, though he could not realize it. The Friend had been *in his mind*, perhaps on scores or hundreds of occasions, when he had been at a formative age, and when he had been particularly vulnerable due to the loss of his parents, therefore even more susceptible to manipulation and control than most ten-year-old boys. On a subconscious level, Jim Ironheart might be programmed to protect The Friend's secrets rather than help to reveal them.

Holly knew she was walking a thread-thin line between judicious precaution and paranoia, might even be treading more on the side of the latter than the former. Under the circumstances, a little paranoia was a prescription for survival.

When Jim said he was going outside to relieve himself, however, she much preferred to be with him than alone in the high room. She followed him downstairs and stood by the Ford with her back to him while he peed against the split-rail fence beside the cornfield.

She stared out at the deep black pond.

She listened to the toads, which were singing again. So were the cicadas. The events of the day had rattled her. Now even the sounds of nature seemed malevolent.

She wondered if they had come up against something too strange and too powerful to be dealt with by just a failed reporter and an ex-schoolteacher. She wondered if they ought to leave the farm right away. She wondered if they would be allowed to leave.

Since the departure of The Friend, Holly's fear had not abated. If anything, it had increased. She felt as if they were living under a thousand-ton weight that was magically suspended by a single human hair, but the magic was weakening and the hair was stretched as taut and brittle as a filament of glass.

*   *   *

By midnight, they had eaten six chocolate doughnuts and composed seven pages of questions for The Friend. Sugar was an energizer and a consolation in times of trouble, but it was no help to already-frayed nerves. Holly's anxiety had a sharp refined-sugar edge to it now, like a well-stropped razor.

Pacing with the tablet in her hand, Holly said, 'And we're not going to let it get away with written answers this time. That just slows down the give and take between interviewer and interviewee. We're going to insist that it talk to us.'

Jim was lying on his back, his hands folded behind his head. 'It can't talk.'

'How do you know that?'

'Well, I'm assuming it can't, or otherwise it would've talked right from the start.'

'Don't assume anything,' she said. 'If it can mix its molecules with the wall, swim through stone – through *anything*, if it's to be believed – and if it can assume any form it wishes, then it can sure as hell form a mouth and vocal cords and talk like any self-respecting higher power.'

'I guess you're right,' he said uneasily.

'It already said that it could appear to us as a man or woman if it wanted, didn't it?'

'Well, yeah.'

'I'm not even asking for a flashy materialization. Just a voice, a disembodied voice, a little sound with the old lightshow.'

Listening to herself as she talked, Holly realized that she was using her edginess to pump herself, to establish an aggressive tone

245

that would serve her well when The Friend returned. It was an old trick she had learned when she had interviewed people whom she found imposing or intimidating.

Jim sat up. 'OK, it could talk if it wanted to, but maybe it doesn't want to.'

'We already decided we can't let it set all the rules, Jim.'

'But I don't understand why we have to antagonize it.'

'I'm not antagonizing it.'

'I think we should be at least a little respectful.'

'Oh, I respect the hell out of it.'

'You don't seem to.'

'I'm convinced it could squash us like bugs if it wanted to, and that gives me tremendous respect for it.'

'That's not the kind of respect I mean.'

'That's the only kind of respect it's earned from me so far,' she said, pacing around him now instead of back and forth. 'When it stops trying to manipulate me, stops trying to scare the crap out of me, starts giving me answers that ring true, then maybe I'll respect it for other reasons.'

'You're getting a little spooky,' he said.

'*Me?*'

'You're so hostile.'

'I am not.'

He was frowning at her. 'Looks like blind hostility to me.'

'It's adversarial journalism. It's the modern reporter's tone and theme. You don't question your subject and later explain him to readers, you *attack* him. You have an agenda, a version of the truth you want to report regardless of the full truth, and you fulfill it. I never approved of it, never indulged in it, which is why I was always losing out on stories and promotions to other reporters. Now, here, tonight, I'm all for the attack part. The big difference is, I *do* care about getting to the truth, not shaping it, and I just want to twist and yank some real facts out of this alien of ours.'

'Maybe he won't show up.'

'He said he would.'

Jim shook his head. 'But why should he if you're going to be like this?'

'You're saying he might be *afraid* of me? What kind of higher power is that?'

The bells rang, and she jumped in alarm.

Jim got to his feet. 'Just take it easy.'

The bells fell silent, rang again, fell silent. When they rang a third

246

time, a sullen red light appeared at one point in the wall. It grew more intense, assumed a brighter shade, then suddenly burst across the domed room like a blazing fireworks display, after which the bells stopped ringing and the multitude of sparks coalesced into the pulsing, constantly moving amoeba-like forms that they had seen before.

'Very dramatic,' Holly said. As the light swiftly progressed from red through orange to amber, she seized the initiative. 'We would like you to dispense with the cumbersome way you answered our questions previously and simply speak to us directly.'

The Friend did not reply.

'Will you speak to us directly?'

No response.

Consulting the tablet that she held in one hand, she read the first question. 'Are you the higher power that has been sending Jim on life-saving missions?'

She waited.

Silence.

She tried again.

Silence.

Stubbornly, she repeated the question.

The Friend did not speak, but Jim said, 'Holly, look at this.'

She turned and saw him examining the other tablet. He held it toward her, flipping through the first ten or twelve pages. The eerie and inconstant light from the stone was bright enough to show her that the pages were filled with The Friend's familiar printing.

Taking the tablet from him, she looked at the first line on the top page: YES. I AM THAT POWER.

Jim said, 'He's already answered every one of the questions we've prepared.'

Holly threw the tablet across the room. It hit the far window without breaking the glass, and clattered to the floor.

'Holly, you can't—'

She cut him off with a sharp look.

The light moved through the transmuted limestone with greater agitation than before.

To The Friend, Holly said, 'God gave Moses the Ten Commandments on tablets of stone, yeah, but He also had the courtesy to talk to him. If God can humble Himself to speak directly with human beings, then so can you.'

She did not look to see how Jim was reacting to her adversarial tack. All she cared about was that he did not interrupt her.

When The Friend remained silent, she repeated the first question on her list. 'Are you the higher power that has been sending Jim on life-saving missions?'

'*Yes. I am that power.*' The voice was a soft, mellifluous baritone. Like the ringing of the bells, it seemed to come from all sides of them. The Friend did not materialize out of the wall in human form, did not sculpt a face from the limestone, but merely produced its voice out of thin air.

She asked the second question on her list. 'How can you know these people are about to die?'

'*I am an entity that lives in all aspects of time.*'

'What do you mean by that?'

'*Past, present, and future.*'

'You can foresee the future?'

'*I* live *in the future as well as in the past and present.*'

The light was coruscating through the walls with less agitation now, as if the alien presence had accepted her conditions and was mellow again.

Jim moved to her side. He put a hand on her arm and squeezed gently, as if to say 'good work.'

She decided not to ask for any more clarification on the issue of its ability to see the future, for fear they would be off on a tangent and never get back on track before the creature next announced that it was departing. She returned to the prepared questions. 'Why do you want these particular people saved?'

'*To help mankind,*' it said sonorously. There might have been a note of pomposity in it, too, but that was hard to tell because the voice was so evenly modulated, almost machine-like.

'But when so many people are dying every day – and *most* of them are innocents – why have you singled out these particular people to be rescued?'

'*They are special people.*'

'In what way are they special?'

'*If allowed to live, each of them will make a major contribution to the betterment of mankind.*'

Jim said, 'I'll be damned.'

Holly had not been expecting that answer. It had the virtue of being fresh. But she was not sure she believed it. For one thing, she was bothered that The Friend's voice was increasingly familiar to her. She was sure she had heard it before, and in a context that undermined its credibility now, in spite of its deep and authoritative tone. 'Are you saying you not only see the future as it will be but as it *might* have been?'

'*Yes.*'

'Aren't we back to your being God now?'

'*No. I do not see as clearly as God. But I see.*'

In his boyish best humor again, Jim smiled at the kaleidoscopic patterns of light, obviously excited and pleased by all that he was hearing.

Holly turned away from the wall, crossed the room, squatted beside her suitcase, and opened it.

Jim loomed over her. 'What're you doing?'

'Looking for this,' she said, producing the notebook in which she had chronicled the discoveries she'd made while researching him. She got up, opened the notebook, and paged to the list of people whose lives he had saved prior to Flight 246. Addressing the entity throbbing through the limestone, she said, 'May fifteenth. Atlanta, Georgia. Sam Newsome and his five-year-old daughter Emily. What are they going to contribute to humanity that makes them more important than all the other people who died that day?'

No answer was forthcoming.

'Well?' she demanded.

'*Emily will become a great scientist and discover a cure for a major disease.*' Definitely a note of pomposity this time.

'What disease?'

'*Why do you not believe me, Miss Thorne?*' The Friend spoke as formally as an English butler on duty, yet in that response, Holly felt she heard the subtle pouting tone of a child under the dignified, reserved surface.

She said, 'Tell me what disease, and maybe I'll believe you.'

'*Cancer.*'

'Which cancer? There are many types of cancer.'

'*All cancers.*'

She referred to her notebook again. 'June seventh. Corona, California. Louis Andretti.'

'*He will father a child who will grow up to become a great diplomat.*'

Better than dying of multiple rattlesnake bites, she thought.

She said, 'June twenty-first. New York City. Thaddeus—'

'*He will become a great artist whose work will give millions of people hope.*'

'He seemed like a nice kid,' Jim said happily, buying into the whole thing. 'I liked him.'

Ignoring him, Holly said, 'June thirtieth. San Francisco—'

'Rachael Steinberg will give birth to a child who will become a great spiritual leader.'

That voice was bugging her. She knew she had heard it before. But where?

'July fifth—'

'Miami, Florida. Carmen Diaz. She will give birth to a child who will become President of the United States.'

Holly fanned herself with the notebook and said, 'Why not president of the world?'

'July fourteenth. Houston, Texas. Amanda Cutter. She will give birth to a child who will be a great peacemaker.'

'Why not the Second Coming?' Holly asked.

Jim had moved away from her. He was leaning against the wall between two windows, the display of light quietly exploding around him. 'What's the matter with you?' he asked.

'It's all too much,' she said.

'What is?'

'OK, it says it wants you to save special people.'

'To help mankind.'

'Sure, sure,' Holly said to the wall.

To Jim she said, 'But these people are all just too special, don't you think? Maybe it's me, but it all seems overblown, it's gotten trite again. Nobody's growing up to be just a damned good doctor, or a businessman who creates a new industry and maybe ten thousand jobs, or an honest and courageous cop, or a terrific nurse. No, they're great diplomats, great scientists, great politicians, great peacemakers. Great, great, great!'

'Is this adversarial journalism?'

'Damn right.'

He pushed away from the wall, used both hands to smooth his thick hair back from his forehead, and cocked his head at her. 'I see your point, why it's starting to sound like another episode of *Outer Limits* to you, but let's think about this. It's a crazy, extravagant situation. A being from another world, with powers that seem godlike to us, decides to use me to better the chances of the human race. Isn't it logical that he'd send me out to save special, *really* special people instead of your theoretical business tycoon?'

'Oh, it's logical,' she said. 'It just doesn't ring true to me, and I've got a fairly well-developed nose for deception.'

'Is that why you were a great success as a reporter?'

She might have laughed at the image of an alien, vastly superior to human beings, stooping to engage in a bickering match. But the impatience and poutiness she'd thought she detected as an undercurrent in some of its previous answers were now unmistakable, and the concept of a hyper-sensitive, resentful creature with godlike power was too unnerving to be funny at the moment.

'How's that for a higher power?' she asked Jim. 'Any second now, he's going to call me a bitch.'

The Friend said nothing.

Consulting her notebook again, she said, 'July twentieth. Steven Aimes. Birmingham, Alabama.'

Schools of light swam through the walls. The patterns were less graceful and less sensuous than before; if the lightshow had been the visual equivalent of one of Brahms's most pacific symphonies, it was now more like the discordant wailing of bad progressive jazz.

'What about Steven Aimes?' she demanded, scared but remembering how an exertion of will had been met with respect before.

'I am going now.'

'That was a short tide,' she said.

The amber light began to darken.

'The tides in the vessel are not regular or of equal duration. But I will return.'

'What about Steven Aimes? He was fifty-seven, still capable of siring a great something-or-other, though maybe a little long in the tooth. Why did you save Steve?'

The voice grew somewhat deeper, slipping from baritone toward bass, and it hardened. *'It would not be wise for you to attempt to leave.'*

She had been waiting for that. As soon as she heard the words, she knew she had been tensed in expectation of them.

Jim, however, was stunned. He turned, looking around at the dark-amber forms swirling and melding and splitting apart again, as if trying to figure out the biological geography of the thing, so he could look it in the eyes. 'What do you mean by that? We'll leave any time we want.'

'You must wait for my return. You will die if you attempt to leave.'

'Don't you want to help mankind any more?' Holly asked sharply.

'Do not sleep.'

Jim moved to Holly's side. Whatever estrangement she had caused between her and Jim, by taking an aggressive stance with

The Friend, was apparently behind them. He put an arm around her protectively.

'You dare not sleep.'

The limestone was mottled with a deep red glow.

'Dreams are doorways.'

The bloody light went out.

The lantern provided the only illumination. And in the deeper darkness that followed The Friend's departure, the quiet hiss of the burning gas was the only sound.

•8•

Holly stood at the head of the stairs, shining a flashlight into the gloom below. Jim supposed she was trying to make up her mind whether they really would be prevented from leaving the mill – and if so, how violently.

Watching her from where he sat on his sleeping bag, he could not understand why it was all turning sour.

He had come to the windmill because the bizarre and frightening events in his bedroom in Laguna Niguel, over eighteen hours ago, had made it impossible to continue ignoring the dark side to the mystery in which he had become enwrapped. Prior to that, he had been willing to drift along, doing what he was compelled to do, pulling people out of the fire at the last minute, a bemused but game superhero who had to rely on airplanes when he wanted to fly and who had to do his own laundry. But the increasing intrusion of The Enemy – whatever the hell it was – its undeniable evil and fierce hostility, no longer allowed Jim the luxury of ignorance. The Enemy was struggling to break through from some other place, another dimension perhaps, and it seemed to be getting closer on each attempt. Learning the truth about the higher power behind his activities had not been at the top of his agenda, because he had felt that enlightenment would be granted to him in time, but learning about The Enemy had come to seem urgently necessary for his survival – and Holly's.

Nevertheless, he had traveled to the farm with the expectation that he would encounter good as well as evil, experience joy as well as fear. Whatever he learned by plunging into the unknown should at least leave him with a greater understanding of his sacred life-saving mission and the supernatural forces behind it. But now he was more confused than before he'd come. Some developments *had* filled him with the wonder and joy for which he longed: the ringing in the stone, for one; and the beautiful, almost divine, light that was the essence of The Friend. He had been moved to rapture by the revelation that he was not merely saving lives but saving people so special that their survival would improve the fate of the entire human race. But that spiritual bliss had been snatched away from him by the growing realization that The Friend was either not telling them the whole truth or, worst case, was not telling them anything true at all. The childish petulance of the creature was unnerving in the extreme, and now Jim was not sure that *anything* he had done since saving the Newsomes last May was in the service of good rather than evil.

Yet his fear was still tempered by hope. Though a splinter of despair had lodged in his heart and begun to fester, that spiritual infection was held in check by the core of optimism, however fragile, that had always been at the center of him.

Holly switched off the flashlight, returned from the open door, and sat down on her mattress. 'I don't know, maybe it was an empty threat, but there's no way of telling till we try to leave.'

'You want to?'

She shook her head. 'What's the point in getting off the farm anyway? From everything we know, it can reach out to us anywhere we go. Right? I mean it reached you in Laguna Niguel, sent you on these missions, reached you out there in Nevada and sent you on to Boston to rescue Nicholas O'Conner.'

'I've felt it with me, at times, no matter where I've gone. In Houston, in Florida, in France, in England – it guided me, let me know what was coming, so I could do the job it wanted done.'

Holly looked exhausted. She was drawn and paler than the eerie glow of the gas lantern could account for, and her eyes were shadowed with rings of weariness. She closed her eyes for a moment and pinched the bridge of her nose with thumb and forefinger, a strained look on her face, as if she was trying to suppress a headache.

With all his heart, Jim regretted that she had been drawn into this. But like his fear and despair, his regret was impure, tempered by the deep pleasure he took in her very presence. Though it was a selfish attitude, he was glad that she was with him, no matter where this strange night led them. He was no longer alone.

Still pinching the bridge of her nose, the lines in her forehead carved deep by her scowl, Holly said, 'This creature isn't restricted to the area near the pond, or just to psychic contact across great distances. It can manifest itself anywhere, judging by the scratches it left in my sides and the way it entered the ceiling of your bedroom this morning.'

'Well, now wait,' he said, 'we know The Enemy can materialize over considerable distance, yes, but we don't know that The Friend has that ability. It was The Enemy that came out of your dream and The Enemy that tried to reach us this morning.'

Holly opened her eyes and lowered her hand from her face. Her expression was bleak. 'I think they're one and the same.'

'What?'

'The Enemy and The Friend. I don't believe two entities are living under the pond, in that starship, if there *is* a starship, which I guess there is. I think there's only a single entity. The Friend and The Enemy are nothing more than different aspects of it.'

Holly's implication was clear, but it was too frightening for Jim to accept immediately. He said, 'You can't be serious? You might as well be saying . . . it's insane.'

'That *is* what I'm saying. It's suffering the alien equivalent of a split personality. It's acting out both personalities, but isn't consciously aware of what it's doing.' Jim's almost desperate need to believe in The Friend as a separate and purely benign creature must have been evident in his face, for Holly took his right hand, held it in both hers, and hurried on before he could interrupt: 'The childish petulance, the grandiosity of its claim to be reshaping the entire destiny of our species, the flamboyance of its apparitions, its sudden fluctuations between an attitude of syrupy goodwill and sullen anger, the way it lies so damned transparently yet deludes itself into believing it's clever, its secretiveness about some issues when there is no apparent reason to be secretive – all of that makes sense if you figure we're dealing with an unbalanced mind.'

He looked for flaws in her reasoning, and found one. 'But you can't believe an insane person, an insane alien individual, could pilot an unimaginably complex spacecraft across light years, through countless dangers, while completely out of its mind.'

'It doesn't have to be like that. Maybe the insanity set in *after* it got here. Or maybe it didn't have to pilot the ship, maybe the ship is essentially automatic, an entirely robotic mechanism. Or maybe there were others of its kind aboard who piloted it, and maybe they're all dead now. Jim, it's never mentioned a crew, only The Enemy. And assuming you buy its extra-terrestrial origins, does it really ring true that only two individuals would set out on an intergalactic exploration? Maybe it killed the others.'

Everything she was theorizing could be true, but then *anything* she theorized could be true. They were dealing with the Unknown, capital U, and the possibilities in an infinite universe were infinite in number. He remembered reading somewhere – even many scientists believed that anything the human imagination conceived, regardless of how fanciful, could conceivably exist somewhere in the universe, because the infinite nature of creation meant that it was no less fluid, no less fertile than any man's or woman's dreams.

Jim expressed that thought to Holly, then said, 'But what bothers me is that you're doing now what you rejected earlier. You're trying hard to explain it in human terms, when it may be too alien for us to understand at all. How can you assume that an alien species can even suffer insanity the way we can, or that it's capable of multiple personalities? These are all strictly human concepts.'

She nodded. 'You're right, of course. But at the moment, this theory's the only one that makes sense to me. Until something happens to disprove it, I've got to operate on the assumption that we're not dealing with a rational being.'

With his free hand, he reached out and increased the gas flow to the wicks in the Coleman lantern, providing more light. 'Jesus, I've got a bad case of the creeps,' he said, shivering.

'Join the club.'

'If it is schizo, and if it slips into the identity of The Enemy and can't get back out . . . what might it do to us?'

'I don't even want to think about that,' Holly said. 'If it's as intellectually superior to us as it seems to be, if it's from a long-lived race with experience and knowledge that makes the whole of the human experience seem like a short story compared to the Great Books of the Western World, then it sure as hell knows some tortures and cruelties that would make Hitler and Stalin and Pol Pot look like Sunday-school teachers.'

He thought about that for a moment, even though he tried not to. The chocolate doughnuts he had eaten lay in an undigested, burning wad in his stomach.

Holly said, 'When it comes back—'

'For God's sake,' he interrupted, 'no more adversarial tactics!'

'I screwed up,' she admitted. 'But the adversarial approach was the correct one. I just carried it too far. I pushed too hard. When it comes back, I'll modify my technique.'

He supposed he had more fully accepted her insanity theory than he was willing to acknowledge. He was now in a cold sweat about what The Friend might do if their behavior tipped it into its other, darker identity. 'Why don't we jettison confrontation altogether, play along with it, stroke its ego, keep it as happy as we—'

'That's no good. You can't control madness by indulging it. That only creates more and deeper madness. I suspect any nurse in a mental institution would tell you the best way to deal with a potentially violent paranoid is to be nice, respectful, but *firm*.'

He withdrew his hand from hers because his palms were clammy. He blotted them on his shirt.

The mill seemed unnaturally silent, as if it were in a vacuum where sound could not travel, sealed in an immense bell jar, on display in a museum in a land of giants. At another time Jim might have found the silence disturbing, but now he embraced it because it probably meant The Friend was sleeping or at least preoccupied with concerns other than them.

'It *wants* to do good,' he said. 'It might be insane, and it might be violent and even evil in its second identity, a regular Dr Jekyll and Mr Hyde. But like Dr Jekyll it really wants to do good. At least we've got that going for us.'

She thought about it a moment. 'OK, I'll give you that one. And when it comes back, I'll try to pry some truth out of it.'

'What scares me most – is there really anything we can learn from it that could help us? Even if it tells us the whole truth about everything, if it's insane it's going to turn to irrational violence sooner or later.'

She nodded. 'But we gotta try.'

They settled into an uneasy silence.

When he looked at his watch, Jim saw that it was ten minutes past one in the morning. He was not sleepy. He didn't have to worry about drifting off and dreaming and thereby opening a doorway, but he was physically drained. Though he had not done anything but sit in a car and drive, then sit or stand in the high room waiting for revelations, his muscles ached as if he had put in ten hours of heavy manual labor. His face felt slack with weariness, and his eyes were hot and grainy. Extreme stress could be every bit as debilitating as strenuous physical activity.

He found himself wishing The Friend would never return, wishing not in an idle way but with the whole-hearted commitment of a young boy wishing that an upcoming visit to the dentist would not transpire. He put every fiber of his being into the wish, as if convinced, the way a kid sometimes could be, that wishes really did now and then come true.

He remembered a quote from Chazal, which he had used when

teaching a literature unit on the supernatural fiction of Poe and Hawthorne: *Extreme terror gives us back the gestures of our childhood*. If he ever went back into the classroom, he would be able to teach that unit a hell of a lot better, thanks to what had happened to him in the old windmill.

At 1:25 The Friend disproved the value of wishing by putting in a sudden appearance. This time no bells heralded its approach. Red light blossomed in the wall, like a burst of crimson paint in clear water.

Holly scrambled to her feet.

So did Jim. He could no longer sit relaxed in the presence of this mysterious being, because he was now more than half-convinced that at any moment it might strike at them with merciless brutality.

The light separated into many swarms, surged all the way around the room, then began to change from red to amber.

The Friend spoke without waiting for a question: *'August first. Seattle, Washington. Laura Lenaskian, saved from drowning. She will give birth to a child who will become a great composer and whose music will give solace to many people in times of trouble. August eighth. Peoria, Illinois. Doogie Burkette. He will grow up to be a paramedic in Chicago, where he will do much good and save many lives. August twelfth. Portland, Oregon. Billy Jenkins. He will grow up to be a brilliant medical technologist whose inventions will revolutionize medical care—'*

Jim met Holly's eyes and did not even have to wonder what she was thinking: the same thing he was thinking. The Friend was in its testy, I'll-show-you mode, and it was providing details which it expected would lend credibility to its extravagant claim to be altering human destiny. But it was impossible to know if what it said was true – or merely fantasies that it had worked up to support its story. The important thing, perhaps, was that it seemed to care deeply that they believe it. Jim had no idea why his or Holly's opinion should matter at all to a being as intellectually superior to them as they were to a fieldmouse, but the fact that it *did* evidently matter seemed to be to their advantage.

'—Twentieth August. The Mojave Desert, Nevada. Lisa and Susan Jawolski. Lisa will provide her daughter with the love, affection, and counseling that will make it possible for the girl eventually to overcome the severe psychological trauma of her father's murder and grow up to be the greatest woman statesman in the entire history of the world, a force for enlightenment and compassionate government policies. August twenty-third. Boston, Massachusetts.

Nicholas O'Conner, saved from an electrical-vault explosion. He will grow up to become a priest who will dedicate his life to caring for the poor in the slums of India—'

The Friend's attempt to answer Holly's criticism and present a less grandiose version of its work was childishly transparent. The Burkette boy was not going to save the world, just be a damned good paramedic, and Nicholas O'Conner was going to be a humble man leading a self-effacing existence among the needy – but the rest of them were still great or brilliant or staggeringly talented in one way or another. The entity now recognized the need for credibility in its tale of grandeur, but it could not bring itself significantly to water down its professed accomplishments.

And something else was bothering Jim: that voice. The longer he listened to it, the more he became convinced that he had heard it before, not in this room twenty-five years ago, not within its current context at all. The voice had to be appropriated, of course, because in its natural condition the alien almost certainly did not possess anything similar to human vocal cords; its biology would be inhuman. The voice it was imitating, as if it were an impersonator performing in a cosmic cocktail lounge, was that of a person Jim had once known. He could not quite identify it.

'—*Twenty-sixth August. Dubuque, Iowa. Christine and Casey Dubrovek. Christine will give birth to another child who will grow up to be the greatest geneticist of the next century. Casey will become an exceptional schoolteacher who will tremendously influence the lives of her students, and who will never fail one of them to the extent that a suicide results.'*

Jim felt as if he had been hit in the chest with a hammer. That insulting accusation, directed at him and referring to Larry Kakonis, shook his remaining faith in The Friend's basic desire to do good.

Holly said, 'Shit, that was low.'

The entity's pettiness sickened Jim, because he wanted so badly to believe in its stated purpose and goodness.

The scintillant amber light swooped and swirled through the walls, as if The Friend was delighted by the effect of the blow it had struck.

Despair welled so high in Jim that for a moment he even dared to consider that the entity under the pond was not good at all but purely evil. Maybe the people he had saved since May fifteenth were not destined to elevate the human condition but debase it. Maybe Nicholas O'Conner was really going to grow up to be a serial killer.

Maybe Billy Jenkins was going to be a bomber pilot who went rogue and found a way to override all the safeguards in the system in order to drop a few nuclear weapons on a major metropolitan area; and maybe instead of being the greatest woman statesman in the history of the world, Susie Jawolski was going to be a radical activist who planted bombs in corporate boardrooms and machine-gunned those with whom she disagreed.

But as he swayed precariously on the rim of that black chasm, Jim saw in memory the face of young Susie Jawolski, which had seemed to be the essence of innocence. He could not believe that she would be anything less than a positive force in the lives of her family and neighbors. He *had* done good works; therefore The Friend had done good works, whether or not it was insane, and even though it had the capacity to be cruel.

Holly addressed the entity within the wall: 'We have more questions.'

'Ask them, ask them.'

Holly glanced at her tablet, and Jim hoped she would remember to be less aggressive. He sensed that The Friend was more unstable than at any previous point during the night.

She said, 'Why did you choose Jim to be your instrument?'

'He was convenient.'

'You mean because he lived on the farm?'

'Yes.'

'Have you ever worked through anyone else the way you've been working through Jim?'

'No.'

'Not in all these ten thousand years?'

'Is this a trick question? Do you think you can trick me? Do you still not believe me when I tell you the truth?'

Holly looked at Jim, and he shook his head, meaning that this was no time to be argumentative, that discretion was not only the better part of valor but their best hope of survival.

Then he wondered if this entity could read his mind as well as intrude into it and implant directives. Probably not. If it could do that, it would flare into anger now, incensed that they still thought it insane and were patronizing it.

'I'm sorry,' Holly said. 'It wasn't a trick question, not at all. We just want to know about you. We're fascinated by you. If we ask questions that you find offensive, please understand that we do so unintentionally, out of ignorance.'

The Friend did not reply.

The light pulsed more slowly through the limestone, and though Jim knew the danger of interpreting alien actions in human terms, he felt that the changed patterns and tempo of the radiance indicated The Friend was in a contemplative mood. It was chewing over what Holly had just said, deciding whether or not she was sincere.

Finally the voice came again, more mellow than it had been in a while: *'Ask your questions.'*

Consulting her tablet again, Holly said, 'Will you ever release Jim from this work?'

'Does he want to be released?'

Holly looked at Jim inquiringly.

Considering what he had been through in the past few months, Jim was a bit surprised by his answer: 'Not if I'm actually doing good.'

'You are. How can you doubt it? But regardless of whether you believe my intentions to be good or evil, I would never release you.'

The ominous tone of that last statement mitigated the relief Jim felt at the reassurance that he had not saved the lives of future murderers and thieves.

Holly said, 'Why have you—'

The Friend interrupted. *'There is one other reason that I chose Jim Ironheart for this work.'*

'What's that?' Jim asked.

'You needed it.'

'I did?'

'Purpose.'

Jim understood. His fear of The Friend was as great as ever, but he was moved by the implication that it had wanted to salvage him. By giving meaning to his broken and empty life, it had redeemed him just as surely as it had saved Billy Jenkins, Susie Jawolski, and all the others, though they had been rescued from more immediate deaths than the death of the soul that had threatened Jim. The Friend's statement seemed to reveal a capacity for pity. And Jim knew he'd deserved pity after the suicide of Larry Kakonis, when he had spiraled into an unreasonable depression. This compassion, even if it was another lie, affected Jim more strongly than he would have expected, and a shimmer of tears came to his eyes.

Holly said, 'Why have you waited ten thousand years to decide to use someone like Jim to shape human destinies?'

'I had to study the situation first, collect data, analyze it, and then decide if my intervention was wise.'

'It took ten thousand years to make that decision? Why? That's longer than recorded history.'

No reply.

She tried the question again.

At last The Friend said, *'I am going now.'* Then, as if it did not want them to interpret its recent display of compassion as a sign of weakness, it added: *'If you attempt to leave, you will die.'*

'When will you be back?' Holly asked.

'Do not sleep.'

'We're going to have to sleep sooner or later,' Holly said as the amber light turned red and the room seemed to be washed in blood.

'Do not sleep.'

'It's two in the morning,' she said.

'Dreams are doorways.'

Holly flared up: 'We can't stay awake forever, damn it!'

The light in the limestone was snuffed out.

The Friend was gone.

* * *

Somewhere people laughed. Somewhere music played and dancers danced, and somewhere lovers strained toward ecstasy.

But in the high room of the mill, designed for storage and now stacked to the ceiling with an anticipation of violence, the mood was decidedly grim.

Holly loathed being so helpless. Throughout her life she had been a woman of action, even if the actions she took were usually destructive rather than constructive. When a job turned out to be less satisfying than she had hoped, she never hesitated to resign, move on. When a relationship soured or just proved uninteresting, she was always quick to terminate it. If she had often retreated from problems – from the responsibilities of being a conscientious journalist when she had seen that journalism was as corrupt as anything else, from the prospect of love, from putting down roots and committing to one place – well, at least retreat was a form of action. Now she was denied even that.

The Friend had that one good effect on her. It was not going to let her retreat from *this* problem.

For a while she and Jim discussed the latest visitation and went over the remaining questions on her list, to which they made changes and additions. The most recent portion of her ongoing interview with The Friend had resulted in some interesting and potentially useful information. It was only *potentially* useful, however, because they both still felt that nothing The Friend said could be relied upon to be true.

By 3:15 in the morning, they were too weary to stand and too bottom-sore to continue sitting. They pulled their sleeping bags together and stretched out side by side, on their backs, staring at the domed ceiling.

To help guard against sleep, they left the gas lantern at its brightest setting. As they waited for The Friend to return, they kept talking, not about anything of importance, small talk of every kind, anything to keep their minds occupied. It was difficult to doze off in the middle of a conversation; and if one did slip away, the other would know it by the lack of a response. They also held hands, her right in his left – the logic being that even during a brief pause in the conversation, if one of them started to take a nap, the other would be warned by the sudden relaxation of the sleeper's grip.

Holly did not expect to have difficulty staying awake. In her university days she had pulled all-nighters before exams or when papers were due, and had stayed awake for thirty-six hours without much of a struggle. During her early years as a reporter, when she'd still believed that journalism mattered to her, she had labored away all night on a story, poring over research or listening yet again to interview tapes or sweating over the wording of a paragraph. She had missed nights of sleep in recent years, as well, if only because she was occasionally plagued by insomnia. She was a night owl by nature anyway. Piece of cake.

But though she had not yet been awake twenty-four hours since bolting out of bed in Laguna Niguel yesterday morning, she felt the sandman sliding up against her, whispering his subliminal message of sleep, sleep, sleep. The past few days had been a blur of activity and personal change, both of which could be expected to take a toll on her resources. And some nights she had gotten too little rest, only in part because of the dreams. *Dreams are doorways.* Sleep was dangerous, she had to stay awake. Damn it, she shouldn't need sleep this badly yet, no matter how much stress she had been under lately. She struggled to keep up her end of the conversation with Jim, even though at times she realized that she was not sure what they were talking about and did not fully understand the words that came out of her own mouth. *Dreams are doorways.* It was almost as if she had been drugged, or as if The Friend, after warning them against sleep, was secretly exerting pressure on a narcoleptic button in her brain. *Dreams are doorways.* She fought against the descending oblivion, but she found that she did not possess the strength or will to sit up . . . or to open her eyes. Her eyes were closed. She had not realized that her eyes were closed. *Dreams are doorways*. Panic could not arouse her. She continued to drift deeper under the sandman's spell even as she heard her heart pound harder and faster. She felt her hand loosening its grip on Jim's hand, and she knew he would respond to that warning, would keep her awake, but she felt *his* grip loosening on her hand, and she realized they were succumbing to the sandman simultaneously.

She drifted in darkness.

She felt that she was being watched.

It was both a reassuring and a frightening feeling.

Something was going to happen. She sensed it.

For a while, however, nothing happened. Except darkness.

Then she became aware that she had a mission to perform.

But that couldn't be right. Jim was the one who was sent on missions, not her.

A mission. *Her* mission. She would be sent on a mission of her own. It was vitally important. Her life depended on how well she performed. Jim's life depended on it as well. The whole world's continued existence depended on it.

But the darkness remained.

She just drifted. It felt nice.

She slept and slept.

At some point during the night, she dreamed. As nightmares went, this one was a lulu, all the stops pulled out, but it was nothing like her recent dreams of the mill and The Enemy. It was worse than those because it was painted in excruciating detail and because throughout the experience she was in the grip of anguish and terror so intense that nothing in her experience prepared her for it, not even the crash of Flight 246.

Lying on a tile floor, under a table. On her side. Peering out at floor level. Directly ahead is a chair, tubular metal and orange plastic, under the chair a scattering of golden french fries and a cheeseburger, the meat having slid halfway out of the bun on a skid of ketchup-greased lettuce. Then a woman, an old lady, also lying on the floor, head turned toward Holly. Looking through the tubular legs of the chair, across the fries and disarranged burger, the lady stares at her, a look of surprise, stares and stares, never blinking, and then Holly sees that the lady's eye nearer the floor isn't there anymore, an empty hole, blood leaking out. Oh, lady. Oh, lady, I'm sorry, I'm so sorry. Holly hears a terrible sound, *chuda-chuda-chuda-chuda-chuda-chuda-chuda*, doesn't recognize it, hears people screaming, a lot of people, *chuda-chuda-chuda-chuda*, still screaming but not as much as before, glass shattering, wood breaking, a man shouting like a bear, roaring, very angry and roaring, *chuda-chuda-chuda-chuda-chuda-chuda-chuda-chuda*. She knows now that it's gunfire, the heavy rhythmic pounding of an automatic weapon, and she wants to get out of there. So she turns in the opposite direction from which she's been facing because she doesn't want to – can't, just can't! – crawl by the old lady whose eye has been shot out. But behind her is a little girl, about eight, lying on the floor in a pink dress with black patent-leather shoes and white socks, a little girl with white-blond hair, a little girl with, a little girl with, a little girl with patent-leather shoes, a little girl with, a little girl with, a little girl with white socks, a little girl with, a little girl with with with with *with half her face shot off!* A red smile. Broken white teeth in a red, lopsided smile. Sobbing, screaming, and still more *chuda-chuda-chuda-chuda*, it's never going to stop, it's going to go on forever, that terrible sound, *chuda-chuda-chuda*. Then Holly's moving, scrambling on her hands and knees, away from both the old lady and the little girl with half a face. Unavoidably her hands slap-skip-skid-slide through warm french fries, a hot fish sandwich, a puddle of mustard, as she moves, moves, staying under the tables, between the chairs, then she puts her hand down on the icy slush of a spilled Coke, and when she sees the image of Dixie Duck on the large paper cup from which the soda has spilled, she knows where she is, she's in a Dixie Duck Burger Palace, one of her favorite places in the world. Nobody's screaming now, maybe they realize that a Dixie Duck is not a place you should scream, but somebody is sobbing and groaning, and somebody else is saying please-please-please-please over and over again. Holly starts to crawl out from under another table, and she sees a man in a costume standing a few feet from her, turned half away from her, and she thinks maybe this is all just a trick, trick-or-treat, a Halloween performance. But it isn't Halloween. Yet the man is in a *costume*, he's wearing combat boots like G. I. Joe and camouflage pants and black T-shirt and a beret, like the Green Berets wear, only this one is black, and it must be a costume because he isn't really a soldier, can't be a soldier with that big sloppy belly overhanging his pants, and he hasn't shaved in maybe a week, soldiers have to shave, so he's only wearing soldier stuff. This girl is kneeling on the floor in front of him, one of the teenagers who works at Dixie Duck, the pretty one with the red hair, she winked at Holly when she took her order, now she's kneeling in front of the guy in the soldier costume, with her head bowed like she's praying, except what she's saying is please-please-please-please. The guy is shouting at her about the CIA and mind control and secret spy networks operated out of the Dixie Duck storeroom. Then the guy stops shouting and he looks at the red-haired girl a while, just looks down at her, and then he says look-at-me, and she says please-please-don't, and he says look-at-me again, so she raises her head and looks at him, and he says what-do-you-think-I-am-stupid? The girl is so scared, she is just so scared, and she says no-please-I-don't-know-anything-about-this, and he says like-shit-you-don't, and he lowers the big gun, he puts the big gun right there in her face, just maybe an inch or two from her face. She says oh-my-god-oh-my-god, and he says you're-one-of-the-rat-people, and Holly is sure the guy will now throw the gun aside and laugh and everyone playing dead people will get up and laugh, too, and the manager will come out and take bows for the Halloween performance, except it isn't Halloween. Then the guy pulls the trigger, *chuda-chuda-chuda-chuda-chuda*, and the red-haired girl dissolves. Holly reels around and heads back the way she came, moving so fast, trying to get away from him before he sees her, because he's crazy, that's what he is, he's a crazyman. Holly is splashing through the same spilled food and drinks that she splashed through before, past the little girl in the pink dress and right through the girl's blood, praying the crazyman can't hear her scuttling away from him. *CHUDA-CHUDA-CHUDA-CHUDA-CHUDA-CHUDA!* But he must be shooting the other direction, because no bullets are smashing into anything around her, so she keeps going, right across a dead man with his insides coming out, hearing sirens now, sirens wailing outside, the cops'll get this crazyman. Then she hears a crash behind her, a table being overturned, and it sounds so close, she looks back, she sees him, the crazyman, he's coming straight toward her, pushing tables out of his way, kicking aside chairs, he sees her. She clambers over another dead woman and then she's in a corner, on top of a dead man who's slumped in the corner, she's in the lap of the dead man, in the arms of the dead man, and no way to get out of there because the crazyman is coming. The crazyman looks so scary, so bad and scary, that she can't watch him coming, doesn't want to see the gun in her face the way the red-haired girl saw it, so she turns her head away, turns her face to the dead man—

She woke from the dream as she had never awakened from another, not screaming, not even with an unvoiced cry caught in her throat, but gagging. She was curled into a tight ball, hugging herself, dry-heaving, choking not on anything she had eaten but on sheer throat-clogging repulsion.

Jim was turned away from her, lying on his side. His knees were drawn up slightly in a modified fetal position. He was still sound asleep.

When she could get her breath, she sat up. She was not merely shaking, she was rattling. She was convinced she could hear her bones clattering against one another.

She was glad that she had not eaten anything after the doughnuts last evening. They had passed through her stomach hours ago. If she had eaten anything else, she'd be wearing it now.

She hunched forward and put her face in her hands. She sat like that until the rattling quieted to a shudder and the shudder faded to spasms of shivering.

When she raised her face from her hands, the first thing she noticed was daylight at the narrow windows of the high room. It was opalescent gray-pink, a weak glow rather than a sunny-blue glare, but daylight nonetheless. Seeing it, she realized that she had not been convinced she would ever see daylight again.

She looked at her wristwatch. 6:10. Dawn must have broken only a short while ago. She could have been asleep only two to two-and-a-half hours. It had been worse than no sleep at all; she did not feel in the least rested.

The dream. She suspected that The Friend had used its telepathic power to push her down into sleep against her will. And because of the unusually intense nature of the nightmare, she was convinced it had sent her that gruesome reel of mindfilm.

But why?

Jim murmured and stirred, then grew still again, breathing deeply but quietly. His dream must not be the same one she'd had; if it was, he would be writhing and crying out like a man on the rack.

She sat for a while, considering the dream, wondering if she had been shown a prophetic vision. Was The Friend warning her that she was going to wind up in a Dixie Duck Burger Palace scrambling for her life through food and blood, stalked by a raving maniac with an automatic carbine? She had never even heard of Dixie Duck, and she couldn't imagine a more ludicrous place to die.

She was living in a society where the streets were crawling with casualties of the drug wars, some of them so brain-blasted that they might well pick up a gun and go looking for the rat people who were working with the CIA, running spy networks out of burger restaurants. She had worked on newspapers all her adult life. She had seen stories no less tragic, no more strange.

After about fifteen minutes, she couldn't bear to think about the nightmare any more, not for a while. Instead of getting a handle on it through analysis, she became more confused and distressed the longer she dwelt on it. In memory, the images of slaughter did not fade, as was usually the case with a dream, but became more vivid. She didn't need to puzzle it out right now.

Jim was sleeping, and she considered waking him. But he needed his rest as much as she did. There was no sign of The Enemy making use of a dream doorway, no change in the limestone walls or the oak-plank floor, so she let Jim sleep.

As she had looked around the room, studying the walls, she had noticed the yellow tablet lying on the floor under the far window. She had pitched it aside last evening when The Friend had resisted vocalizing its answers and had tried, instead, to present her with responses to all her written questions at once, before she was able to read them aloud. She'd never had a chance to ask it all of the questions on her list, and now she wondered what might be on that answer-tablet.

She eased off her bedding as quietly as possible, rose, and walked carefully across the room. She tested the floorboards as she went to make sure they weren't going to squeak when she put her full weight on them.

As she stooped to pick up the tablet, she heard a sound that froze her. Like a heartbeat with an extra thump in it.

She looked around at the walls, up at the dome. The light from the high-burning lantern and the windows was sufficient to be certain that the limestone was only limestone, the wood only wood.

Lub-dub-DUB, lub-dub-DUB . . .

It was faint, as if someone was tapping the rhythm out on a drum far away, outside the mill, somewhere up in the dry brown hills.

But she knew what it was. No drum. It was the tripartite beat that always preceded the materialization of The Enemy. Just as the bells had, until its final visit, preceded the arrival of The Friend.

As she listened, it faded away.

She strained to hear it.

Gone.

Relieved but still trembling, she picked up the tablet. The pages were rumpled, and they made some noise falling into place.

Jim's steady breathing continued to echo softly around the room, with no change of rhythm or pitch.

Holly read the answers on the first page, then the second. She saw that they were the same responses The Friend had vocalized – although without the spur-of-the-moment questions that she had not written down on the question-tablet. She skimmed down the third and fourth pages, on which it had listed the people Jim had saved – Carmen Diaz, Amanda Cutter, Steven Aimes, Laura Lanaskian – explaining what great things each of them was destined to achieve.

Lub-dub-DUB, lub-dub-DUB, lub-dub-DUB . . .

She snapped her head up.

The sound was still distant, no louder than before.

Jim groaned in his sleep.

Holly took a step away from the window, intending to wake him, but the dreaded sound faded away again. Evidently The Enemy was in the neighborhood, but it had not found a doorway in Jim's dream. He *had* to get his sleep, he couldn't function without it. She decided to let him alone.

Easing back to the window again, Holly held the answer-tablet up to the light. She turned to the fifth page – and felt the flesh on the nape of her neck go as cold and nubbly as frozen turkey skin.

Peeling the pages back with great delicacy, so as not to rustle them more than absolutely necessary, she checked the sixth page, the seventh, the eighth. They were all the same. Messages were printed on them in the wavery hand that The Friend had used when pulling its little words-rising-as-if-through-water trick. But they were not answers to her questions. They were two alternating statements, unpunctuated, each repeated three times per page:

> HE LOVES YOU HOLLY
> HE WILL KILL YOU HOLLY
> HE LOVES YOU HOLLY
> HE WILL KILL YOU HOLLY
> HE LOVES YOU HOLLY
> HE WILL KILL YOU HOLLY

Staring at those obsessively repeated statements, she knew that 'he' could be no one but Jim. She focused only on the five hateful words, trying to understand.

And suddenly she thought that she did. The Friend was warning her that in its madness it would act against her, perhaps because it hated her for bringing Jim to the mill, for making him seek answers, and for being a distraction from his mission. If The Friend, which was the sane half of the alien consciousness, could reach into Jim's mind and compel him to undertake life-saving missions, was it possible that The Enemy, the dark half, could reach into his mind and compel him to kill? Instead of the insane personality materializing in monstrous form as it had done for an instant at the motel Friday night and as it attempted to do in Jim's bedroom yesterday, might it choose to use Jim against her, take command of him to a greater extent than The Friend had ever done, and turn him into a killing machine? That might perversely delight the mad-child aspect of the entity.

She shook herself as if casting off a pestering wasp.

No. It was impossible. All right, Jim could kill in the defense of innocent people. But he was incapable of killing someone innocent. No alien consciousness, no matter how powerful, could override his true nature. In his heart he was good and kind and caring. His love for her could not be subverted by this alien force, no matter how strong it was.

But how did she know that? She was engaging in wishful thinking. For all she knew, The Enemy's powers of mental control were so awesome that it could reach into her brain right now and tell her to drown herself in the pond, and she would do as told.

She remembered Norman Rink. The Atlanta convenience store. Jim had pumped eight rounds from a shotgun into the guy, blasting at him again and again, long after he was dead.

Lub-dub-DUB, lub-dub-DUB . . .

Still far away.

Jim groaned softly.

She moved away from the window again, intent on waking him, and almost called out his name, before she realized that The Enemy might be in him already. *Dreams are doorways.* She didn't have a clue as to what The Friend meant by that, or if it was anything more than stage dressing like the bells. But maybe what it had meant was that The Enemy could enter the dreamer's dream and thus the dreamer's mind. Maybe this time The Enemy did not intend to materialize from the wall but from Jim, in the person of Jim, in total control of Jim, just for a murderous little lark.

Lub-dub-DUB, Lub-dub-DUB, lub-dub-DUB . . .

A little louder, a little closer?

Holly felt that she was losing her mind. Paranoid, schizoid, flat-out crazy. No better than The Friend and his other half. She was frantically trying to understand a totally alien consciousness, and the more she pondered the possibilities, the stranger and more varied the possibilities became. In an infinite universe, anything can happen, any nightmare can be made flesh. In an infinite universe, life was therefore essentially the same as a dream. Contemplation of *that*, under the stress of a life-or-death situation, was guaranteed to drive you bugshit.

Lub-dub-DUB, lub-dub-DUB . . .

She could not move.

She could only wait.

The tripartite beat faded again.

Letting her breath out in a rush, she backed up against the wall beside the window, less afraid of the limestone now than she was of Jim Ironheart. She wondered if it was all right to wake him when the three-note heartbeat was not audible. Maybe The Enemy was only in his dream – and therefore in him – when that triple thud could be heard.

Afraid to act and afraid not to act, she glanced down at the tablet in her hand. Some of the pages had fallen shut, and she was no longer looking at the HE LOVES YOU HOLLY/HE WILL KILL YOU HOLLY litany. Before her eyes, instead, was the list of people who had been saved by Jim, along with The Friend's grandiose explanations of their importance.

She saw 'Steven Aimes' and realized at once that he was the only one on the list whose fate The Friend had not vocalized during one or another of their conversations last night. She remembered him because he was the only older person on the list, fifty-seven. She read the words under his name, and the chill that had touched her nape earlier was nothing compared to the spike of ice that drove through it now and pierced her spine.

Steven Aimes had not been saved because he would father a child who would be a great diplomat or a great artist or a great healer. He had not been saved because he would make an enduring contribution to the welfare of mankind. The reason for his salvation was expressed in just eleven words, the most horrifying eleven words that Holly had ever read or hoped to read: BECAUSE HE LOOKS LIKE MY FATHER WHOM I FAILED TO SAVE. Not 'like *Jim's* father' which The Friend would have said. Not 'whom *he* failed to save,' as the alien would surely have put it. MY FATHER. I FAILED. MY. I.

The infinite universe just kept expanding, and now an entirely new possibility presented itself to her, revealed in the telling words about Steven Aimes. No starship rested under the pond. No alien had been in hiding on the farm for ten thousand years, ten years, or ten days. The Friend and The Enemy were real enough: they were thirds, not halves, of the same personality, three in one entity, an entity with enormous and wonderful and terrifying powers, an entity both godlike and yet as human as Holly was. Jim Ironheart. Who had been shattered by tragedy when he was ten years old. Who had painstakingly put himself together again with the help of a complex fantasy about star-travelling gods. Who was as insane and dangerous as he was sane and loving.

She did not understand where he had gotten the power that he so obviously possessed, or why he was not aware whatsoever that the power was within him rather than coming from some imaginary alien presence. The realization that he was everything, that the end and beginning of this mystery lay solely in him and not beneath the pond, raised more questions than it answered. She didn't understand how such a thing could be true, but she knew it was, at last, the truth. Later, if she survived, she might have the time to seek a better understanding.

Lub-dub-DUB, lub-dub-DUB . . .

Closer but not close.

Holly held her breath, waiting for the sound to get louder.

Lub-dub-DUB, lub-dub-DUB . . .

Jim shifted in his sleep. He snorted softly and smacked his lips, just like any ordinary dreamer.

But he was three personalities in one, and at least two of them possessed incredible power, and at least one of them was deadly. And it was coming.

Lub-dub-DUB . . .

Holly pressed back against the limestone. Her heart was pounding so hard that it seemed to have hammered her throat half shut; she had trouble swallowing.

The tripartite beat faded.

Silence.

She moved along the curved wall. Easy little steps. Sideways. Toward the timbered, ironbound door. She eased away from the wall just far enough to reach out and snare her purse by its straps.

The closer she got to the head of the stairs, the more certain she became that the door was going to slam shut before she reached it, that Jim was going to sit up and turn to her. His blue eyes would not be beautiful but cold, as she had twice glimpsed them, filled with rage but cold.

She reached the door, eased through it backward on to the first step, not wanting to take her eyes off Jim. But if she tried to back down those narrow stairs without a handrail, she would fall, break an arm or leg. So she turned away from the high room and hurried toward the bottom as quickly as she dared, as quietly as she could.

Though the velvety-gray morning light outlined the windows, the lower chamber was treacherously dark. She had no flashlight, only the extra edge of an adrenaline rush. Unable to remember if any rubble was stacked along the wall that might set up a clatter when she knocked it over, she moved slowly along that limestone curve, her back to it, edging sideways again. The antechamber archway was somewhere ahead on her right. When she looked to her left, she could barely see the foot of the stairs down which she had just descended.

Feeling the wall ahead of her with her right hand, she discovered the corner. She stepped through the archway and into the antechamber. Though that space had been blind-dark last night, it was dimly lit now by the pale post-dawn glow that lay beyond the open outside door.

The morning was overcast. Pleasantly cool for August.

The pond was still and gray.

Morning insects issued a thin, almost inaudible background buzz, like faint static on a radio with the volume turned nearly off.

She hurried to the Ford and stealthily opened the door.

Another panic hit her as she thought of the keys. Then she felt them in a pocket of her jeans, where she had slipped them last night after using the bathroom at the farmhouse. One key for the farmhouse, one key for his house in Laguna Niguel, two keys for the car, all on a simple brass-bead chain.

She threw the purse and tablet into the back seat and got behind the wheel, but didn't close the door for fear the sound would wake him. She was not home free yet. He might burst out of the windmill, The Enemy in charge of him, leap across the short expanse of gravel, and drag her from the car.

Her hands shook as she fumbled with the keys. She had trouble inserting the right one in the ignition. But then she got it in, twisted it, put her foot on the accelerator, and almost sobbed with relief when the engine turned over with a roar.

She yanked the door shut, threw the Ford in reverse, and backed along the gravel path that circled the pond. The wheels spun up a hail of gravel, which rattled against the back of the car as she reversed into it.

When she reached the area between the barn and the house, where she could turn around and head out of the driveway front-first, she jammed on the brakes instead. She stared at the windmill, which was now on the far side of the water.

She had nowhere to run. Wherever she went, he would find her. He could see the future, at least to some extent, if not as vividly or in as much detail as The Friend had claimed. He could transform drywall into a monstrous living organism, change limestone into a transparent substance filled with whirling light, project a beast of hideous design into her dreams and into the doorway of her motel, track her, find her, trap her. He had drawn her into his mad fantasy and most likely still wanted her to play out her role in it. The Friend in Jim – and Jim himself – might let her go. But the third personality – the murderous part of him, The Enemy – would want her blood. Maybe she would be fortunate, and maybe the two benign thirds of him would prevent the other third from taking control and coming after her. But she doubted it. Besides, she could not spend the rest of her life waiting for a wall to bulge outward unexpectedly, form into a mouth, and bite her hand off.

And there was one other problem.

She could not abandon him. He needed her.

Part Three

THE ENEMY

From childhood's hour
I have not been
As others were—
I have not seen
As others saw.

   – Alone, *Edgar Allan Poe*

Vibrations in a wire.
Ice crystals
in a beating heart.
Cold fire.

A mind's frigidity:
frozen steel,
dark rage, morbidity.
Cold fire.

Defense against
a cruel life
death and strife:
Cold fire.

   – The Book of Counted Sorrows

THE REST OF AUGUST 29

•1•

Holly sat in the Ford, staring at the old windmill, scared and exhilarated. The exhilaration surprised her. Maybe she felt upbeat because for the first time in her life she had found something to which she was willing to commit herself. Not a casual commitment, either. Not an until-I-get-bored commitment. She was willing to put her life on the line for this, for Jim and what he could become if he could be healed, for what they could become together.

Even if he had told her she could go, and even if she had felt that his release of her was sincere, she would not have abandoned him. He was her salvation. And she was his.

The mill stood sentinel against the ashen sky. Jim had not appeared at the door. Perhaps he had not yet awakened.

There were still many mysteries within this mystery, but so much was painfully obvious now. He sometimes failed to save people – like Susie Jawolski's father – because he was not really operating on behalf of an infallible god or a prescient alien; he was acting on his own phenomenal but imperfect visions; he was just a man, special but only a man, and even the best of men had limits. He evidently felt that he had failed his parents somehow. Their deaths weighed heavily on his conscience, and he was trying to redeem himself by saving the lives of others: HE LOOKED LIKE MY FATHER, WHOM I FAILED TO SAVE.

It was now obvious, as well, why The Enemy broke through only when Jim was asleep: he was terrified of that dark aspect of himself, that embodiment of his rage, and he strenuously repressed it when he was awake. At his place in Laguna, The Enemy had materialized in the bedroom while Jim was sleeping and actually had been sustained for a while after Jim had awakened, but when it had crashed through the bathroom ceiling, it had simply evaporated like the lingering dream it was. *Dreams*

277

are doorways, The Friend had warned, which had been a warning from Jim himself. Dreams were doorways, yes, but not for evil, mind-invading alien monsters; dreams were doorways to the subconscious, and what came out of them was all too human.

She had other pieces of the puzzle too. She just didn't know how they fitted together.

Holly was angry with herself for not having asked the correct questions on Monday, when Jim had finally opened his patio door and let her into his life. He'd insisted that he was only an instrument, that he had no powers of his own. She'd bought it too quickly. She should have probed harder, asked tougher questions. She was as guilty of amateurish interviewing technique as Jim had been when The Friend had first appeared to them.

She had been annoyed by his willingness to accept what The Friend said at face value. Now she understood that he had created The Friend for the same reason that other victims of multiple-personality syndrome generated splinter personalities: to cope in a world that confused and frightened them. Alone and afraid at the age of ten, he had taken refuge in fantasy. He created The Friend, a magical being, as a source of solace and hope. When Holly pressed The Friend to explain itself logically, Jim resisted her because her probing threatened a fantasy which he desperately needed to sustain himself.

For similar reasons of her own, she had not questioned him as toughly as she should have on Monday evening. *He* was *her* sustaining dream. He had come into her life like a heroic figure in a dream, saving Billy Jenkins with dreamlike grace and panache. Until she had seen him, she had not realized how much she needed someone like him. And instead of probing deeply into him as any good reporter would have done, she had let him be what he wanted to pretend to be, for she had been reluctant to lose him.

Now their only hope was to press hard for the whole truth. He could not be healed until they understood why this particular and bizarre fantasy of his had evolved and how in the name of God he had developed the superhuman powers to support it.

She sat with her hands on the steering wheel, prepared to act but with no idea what to do. There seemed to be no one to whom she could turn for help. She needed answers that were to be found only in the past or in Jim's subconscious mind, two terrains that at the moment were equally inaccessible.

Then, hit by a thunderbolt of insight, she realized Jim already had given her a set of keys to unlock his remaining mysteries.

When they had driven into New Svenborg, he had taken her on a tour of the town which, at the time, seemed like a tactic to delay their arrival at the farm. But she realized now that the tour had contained the most important revelations he had made to her. Each nostalgic landmark was a key to the past and to the remaining mysteries that, once unlocked, would make it possible for her to help him.

He wanted help. A part of him understood that he was sick, trapped in a schizophrenic fantasy, and he wanted out. She just hoped that he would suppress The Enemy until they had time to learn what they needed to know. That darkest splinter of his mind did not want her to succeed; her success would be its death, and to save itself, it would destroy her if it got the chance.

If she and Jim were to have a life together, or any life at all, their future lay in the past, and the past lay in New Svenborg.

She swung the wheel hard right, began to turn around to head out of the driveway to the county road – then stopped. She looked at the windmill again.

Jim had to be part of his own cure. She could not track down the truth and *make* him believe it. He had to see it himself.

She loved him.

She was afraid of him.

She couldn't do anything about the love; that was just part of her now, like blood or bone or sinew. But almost any fear could be overcome by confronting the cause of it.

Wondering at her own courage, she drove back along the graveled path to the foot of the windmill. She pumped three long blasts from the horn, then three more, waited a few seconds and hit it again, again.

Jim appeared in the doorway. He came out into the gray morning light, squinting at her.

Holly opened her door and stepped out of the car. 'You awake?'

'Do I look like I'm sleepwalking?' he asked as he approached her. 'What's going on?'

'I want to be damn sure you're awake, *fully* awake.'

He stopped a few feet away. 'Why don't we open the hood, I'll put my head under it, then you can let out maybe a two-minute blast, just to be sure. Holly, what's going on?'

'We have to talk. Get in.'

Frowning, he went around to the passenger's side and got into the Ford with her.

279

When he settled into the passenger's seat, he said, 'This isn't going to be pleasant, is it?'

'No. Not especially.'

In front of them, the sails of the windmill stuttered. They began to turn slowly, with much clattering and creaking, shedding chunks and splinters of rotten vanes.

'Stop it,' she said to Jim, afraid that the turning sails were only a prelude to a manifestation of The Enemy. 'I know you don't want to hear what I have to say, but don't try to distract me, don't try to stop me.'

He did not respond. He stared with fascination at the mill, as if he had not heard her.

The speed of the sails increased.

'Jim, damn it!'

At last he looked at her, genuinely baffled by the anger underlying her fear. 'What?'

Around, around, around-around-around, aroundaround-around. It turned like a haunted Ferris wheel in a carnival of the damned.

'Shit!' she said, her fear accelerating with the pace of the windmill sails. She put the car in reverse, looked over her shoulder, and backed at high speed around the pond.

'Where are we going?' he asked.

'Not far.'

Since the windmill lay at the center of Jim's delusion, Holly thought it was a good idea to put it out of sight while they talked. She swung the car around, drove to the end of the driveway, and parked facing out toward the county road.

She cranked down her window, and he followed suit.

Switching off the engine, she turned more directly toward him. In spite of everything she now knew – or suspected – about him, she wanted to touch his face, smooth his hair, hold him. He elicited a mothering urge from her of which she hadn't even known she'd been capable – just as he engendered in her an erotic response and passion that were beyond anything she had experienced before.

Yeah, she thought, and evidently he engenders in you a suicidal tendency. Jesus, Thorne, the guy as much as said he'll kill you!

But he also had said he loved her.

Why wasn't *anything* easy?

She said, 'Before I get into it . . . I want you to understand that I love you, Jim.' It was the dumbest line in the world. It sounded so insincere. Words were inadequate to describe the real thing, partly because the feeling ran deeper than she had ever imagined it would, and partly because it was not a single emotion but was mixed up with other things like anxiety and hope. She said it again anyway: 'I really do love you.'

He reached for her hand, smiling at her with obvious pleasure. 'You're wonderful, Holly.'

Which was not exactly I-love-you-too-Holly, but that was OK. She didn't harbor romance-novel expectations. It was not going to be that simple. Being in love with Jim Ironheart was like being in love simultaneously with the tortured Max de Winter from *Rebecca*, Superman, and Jack Nicholson in any role he'd ever played. Though it wasn't easy, it wasn't dull either.

'The thing is, when I was paying my motel bill yesterday morning and you were sitting in the car watching me, I realized you hadn't said you loved me. I was going off with you, putting myself in your hands, and you hadn't said the words. But then I realized I hadn't said them either, I was playing it just as cool, holding back and protecting myself. Well, I'm not holding back any more, I'm walking out on that highwire with no net below – and largely because you told me you loved me last night. So you better have meant it.'

A quizzical expression overtook him.

She said, 'I know you don't remember saying it, but you did. You have problems with the L word. Maybe because you lost your folks when you were so young, you're afraid to get close to anyone for fear of losing them too. Instant analysis. Holly Freud. Anyway, you did tell me you loved me, and I'll prove it in a little while, but right now, before I get into this mess, I want you to know I never imagined I could feel about anyone the way I feel about you. So if whatever I say to you in the next few minutes is hard to take, even *impossible* to take, just know where it comes from, only from love, from nothing else.'

He stared at her. 'Yeah, all right. But Holly, this—'

'You'll get your turn.' She leaned across the seat, kissed him, then pulled back. 'Right now, you've got to listen.'

She told him everything she had theorized, why she had crept out of the mill while he'd been asleep – and why she had returned. He listened with growing disbelief, and she repeatedly cut off his protests by lightly squeezing his hand, putting a hand to his lips, or giving him a quick kiss. The answer-tablet, which she produced from the back seat, stunned him and rendered his objections less vehement. BECAUSE HE LOOKS LIKE MY FATHER WHOM I FAILED TO SAVE. His hands shook as he held the tablet and stared at that incredible line. He turned back to the other surprising messages, repeated page after page – HE LOVES YOU HOLLY/HE WILL KILL YOU HOLLY – and the tremors in his hands became even more severe.

'I would never harm you,' he said shakily, staring down at the tablet. 'Never.'

'I know you'd never want to.'

Dr Jekyll had never wanted to be the murderous Mr Hyde.

'But you think I sent you this, not The Friend.'

'I know you did, Jim. It feels right.'

'So if The Friend sent it but the The Friend is me, a part of me, then you believe it really says "I love you Holly." '

'Yes,' she said softly.

He looked up from the tablet, met her eyes. 'If you believe the I-love-you part, why don't you believe the I-will-kill-you part?'

'Well, that's the thing. I do believe a small, dark part of you wants to kill me, yes.'

He flinched as if she had struck him.

She said, 'The Enemy wants me dead, it wants me dead real bad, because I've made you face up to what's behind these recent events, brought you back here, forced you to confront the source of your fantasy.'

He started to shake his head in denial.

But she went on: 'Which is what you *wanted* me to do. It's why you drew me to you in the first place.'

'No. I didn't—'

'Yes, you did.' Pushing him toward enlightenment was extremely dangerous. But that was her only hope of saving him. 'Jim, if you can just understand what's happened, accept the existence of two other personalities, even the possibility of their existence, maybe that'll be the beginning of the end of The Friend and The Enemy.'

Still shaking his head, he said, 'The Enemy won't go peacefully,' and immediately blinked in surprise at the words he had spoken and the implication that they conveyed.

'Damn,' Holly said, and a thrill coursed through her, not merely because he had just confirmed her entire theory, whether he could admit it or not, but because the five words he had spoken were proof that he wanted out of the Byzantine fantasy in which he had taken refuge.

He was as pale as a man who had just been told that a cancer was growing in him. In fact a malignancy *did* reside within him, but it was mental rather than physical.

A breeze wafted through the open car windows, and it seemed to wash new hope into Holly.

That buoyant feeling was short-lived, however, because new words suddenly appeared on the tablet in Jim's hands: YOU DIE.

'This isn't me,' he told her earnestly, in spite of the subtle admission he had made a moment ago. 'Holly, this can't be me.'

On the tablet, more words appeared: I AM COMING. YOU DIE.

Holly felt as if the world had become a carnival funhouse, full of ghouls and ghosts. Every turn, any moment, without warning, something might spring at her from out of a shadow – or from broad daylight, for that matter. But unlike a carnival monster, this one would inflict real pain, draw blood, kill her if it could.

In hopes that The Enemy, like The Friend, would respond well to firmness, Holly grabbed the tablet from Jim's hand and threw it out the window. 'To hell with that. I won't read that crap. Listen to me, Jim. If I'm right, The Enemy is the embodiment of your rage over the deaths of your parents. Your fury was so great, at ten, it terrified you, so you pushed it outside yourself, into this other identity. But you're a unique victim of multiple-personality syndrome because your power allows you to create physical existences for your other identities.'

Though acceptance had a toehold in him, he was still struggling to deny the truth. 'What're we saying here? That I'm insane, that I'm some sort of socially functional lunatic, for Christ's sake?'

'Not insane,' she said quickly. 'Let's say disturbed, troubled. You're locked in a psychological box that you built for yourself, and you want out, but you can't find the key to the lock.'

He shook his head. Fine beads of sweat had broken out along his hairline, and he was into whiter shades of pale. 'No, that's putting too good a face on it. If what you think is true, then I'm all the way off the deep end, Holly, I should be in some damned rubber room, pumped full of Thorazine.'

She took both of his hands again, held them tight. 'No. Stop that. You can find your way out of this, you can do it, you can make yourself whole again, I know you can.'

'How can you know? Jesus, Holly, I—'

'Because you're not an ordinary man, you're special,' she said sharply. 'You have this power, this incredible force inside you, and you can do such good with it if you want. The power is something you can draw on that ordinary people don't have, it can be a *healing* power. Don't you see? If you can cause ringing bells and alien heartbeats and voices to come out of thin air, if you can turn walls into flesh, project images into my dreams, see into the future to save lives, then you can make yourself whole and right again.'

Determined disbelief lined his face. 'How could any man have the power you're talking about?'

'I don't know, but you've got it.'

'It has to come from a higher being. For God's sake, I'm not Superman.'

Holly pounded a fist against the horn ring and said, 'You're telepathic, telekinetic, tele-fucking-everything! All right, you can't fly, you don't have X-ray vision, you can't bend steel with your bare hands, and you can't race faster than a speeding bullet. But you're as close to Superman as any man's likely to get. In fact in some ways you've got him beat because you can see into the future. Maybe you see only bits and pieces of it, and only random visions when you aren't trying for them, but you *can* see the future.'

He was shaken by her conviction. 'So where'd I get all this magic?'

'I don't know.'

'That's where it falls apart.'

'It doesn't fall apart just because I don't know,' she said frustratedly. 'Yellow doesn't stop being yellow just because I don't know anything about why the eye sees different colors. You *have* the power. You *are* the power, not God or some alien under the millpond.'

He pulled his hands from hers and looked out the windshield toward the county road and the dry fields beyond. He seemed afraid to face up to the tremendous power he possessed – maybe because it carried with it responsibilities that he was not sure he could shoulder.

She sensed that he was also shamed by the prospect of his own mental illness, and unable to meet her eyes any longer. He was so stoical, so strong, so proud of his strength that he could not accept this suggested weakness in himself. He had built a life that placed a high value on self-control and self-reliance, that made a singular virtue out of self-imposed solitude, in the manner of a monk who needed no one but himself and God. Now she was telling him that his decision to become an iron man and a loner was not a well-considered choice, that it was a desperate attempt to deal with emotional turmoil that had threatened to destroy him, and that his need for self-control had carried him over the line of rational behavior.

She thought of the words on the tablet: I AM COMING. YOU DIE.

She switched on the engine.

He said, 'Where are we going?'

As she put the car in gear, pulled out on to the county road, and turned right toward New Svenborg, she did not answer him. Instead, 'Was there anything special about you as a boy?'

'No,' he said a little too quickly, too sharply.

'Never any indication that you were gifted or—'

'No, hell, nothing like that.'

Jim's sudden nervous agitation, betrayed by his restless movement and his trembling hands, convinced Holly that she had touched on a truth. He *had* been special in some way, a gifted child. Now that she had reminded him of it, he saw in that early gift the seeds of the powers that had grown in him. But he didn't want to face it. Denial was his shield.

'What have you just remembered?'

'Nothing.'

'Come on, Jim.'

'Nothing, really.'

She didn't know where to go with that line of questioning, so she could only say, 'It's true. You're gifted. No aliens, only you.'

Because of whatever he had just remembered and was not willing to share with her, his adamancy had begun to dissolve. 'I don't know.'

'It's true.'

'Maybe.'

'It's true. Remember last night when The Friend told us it was a child by the standards of its species? Well, that's because it *is* a child, a perpetual child, forever the age at which you created it – ten years old. Which explains its childlike behavior, its need to brag, its poutiness. Jim, The Friend didn't behave like a ten-thousand-year-old alien child, it just behaved like a ten-year-old human being.'

He closed his eyes and leaned back, as if it was exhausting to consider what she was telling him. But his inner tension remained at a peak, revealed by his hands, which were fisted in his lap.

'Where are we going, Holly?'

'For a little ride.' As they passed through the golden fields and

285

hills, she kept up a gentle attack: 'That's why the manifestation of The Enemy is like a combination of every movie monster that ever frightened a ten-year-old boy. The thing I caught a glimpse of in my motel-room doorway wasn't a *real* creature, I see that now. It didn't have a biological structure that made sense, it wasn't even alien. It was too familiar, a ten-year-old boy's hodgepodge of boogeymen.'

He did not respond.

She glanced at him. 'Jim?'

His eyes were still closed.

Her heart began to pound. 'Jim!'

At the note of alarm in her voice, he sat up straighter and opened his eyes. 'What?'

'For God's sake, don't close your eyes that long. You might've been asleep, and I wouldn't have realized it until—'

'You think I can sleep with *this* on my mind?'

'I don't know. I don't want to take the chance. Keep your eyes open, OK? You obviously suppress The Enemy when you're awake, it only comes through all the way when you're asleep.'

In the windshield glass, like a computer readout in a fighter-plane cockpit, words began to appear from left to right, in letters about one inch high: DEAD DEAD DEAD DEAD DEAD DEAD.

Scared but unwilling to show it, she said, 'To hell with that,' and switched on the windshield wipers, as if the threat was dirt that could be scrubbed away. But the words remained, and Jim stared at them with evident dread.

As they passed a small ranch, the scent of new-mown hay entered with the wind through the windows.

'Where are we going?' he asked again.

'Exploring.'

'Exploring what?'

'The past.'

Distressed, he said, 'I haven't bought this scenario yet. I can't. How the hell can I? And how can we ever prove it's true or isn't?'

'We go to town,' she said. 'We take that tour again, the one you took me on yesterday. Svenborg – port of mystery and romance. What a dump. But it's got *something*. You wanted me to see those places, your subconscious was telling me answers can be found in Svenborg. So let's go find them together.'

New words appeared under the first six: DEAD DEAD DEAD DEAD DEAD DEAD.

Holly knew that time was running out. The Enemy wanted through, wanted to gut her, dismember her, leave her in a steaming heap of her own entrails before she had a chance to convince Jim of her theory – and it did not want to wait until Jim was asleep. She was not certain that he could repress that dark aspect of himself as she pushed him closer to a confrontation with the truth. His self-control might crack, and his benign personalities might sink under the rising dark force.

'Holly, if I had this bizarre multiple personality, wouldn't I be cured as soon as you explained it to me, wouldn't the scales immediately fall off my eyes?'

'No. You have to *believe* it before you can hope to deal with it. Believing that you suffer an abnormal mental condition is the first step toward an understanding of it, and understanding is only the first painful step toward a cure.'

'Don't talk at me like a psychiatrist, you're no psychiatrist.'

He was taking refuge in anger, in that arctic glare, trying to intimidate her as he had tried on previous occasions when he'd not wanted her to get any closer. Hadn't worked then, wouldn't work now. Sometimes men could be so dense.

She said, 'I interviewed a psychiatrist once.'

'Oh, terrific, that makes you a qualified therapist.'

'Maybe it does. The psychiatrist I interviewed was crazy as a loon himself, so what does a university degree matter?'

He took a deep breath and let it out with a shudder. 'OK, suppose you're right and somehow we do turn up undeniable proof that *I'm* crazy as loon—'

'You aren't crazy, you're—'

'Yeah, yeah, I'm disturbed, troubled, in a psychological box. Call it whatever you want. If we find proof somehow – and I can't imagine how – then what happens to me? Maybe I just smile and say, "Oh, yes, of course, I made it all up, I was living in a delusion, I'm ever so much better now, let's have lunch." But I don't think so. I think what happens is . . . I blow apart, into a million pieces.'

'I can't promise you that the truth, if we find it, will be any sort of salvation, because so far I think you've found your salvation in fantasy not in truth. But we can't go on like this because The Enemy resents me, and sooner or later it'll kill me. You warned me yourself.'

He looked at the words on the windshield, and said nothing. He was running out of arguments, if not resistance.

The words quickly faded, then vanished.

Maybe that was a good sign, an indication of his subconscious accommodation to her theory. Or maybe The Enemy had decided that she could not be intimidated with threats – and was struggling to burst through and savage her.

She said, 'When it's killed me, you'll realize it *is* part of you. And if you love me, like you told me you did through The Friend last night, then what's that going to do to you? Isn't that going to destroy the Jim I love? Isn't that going to leave you with just one personality – the dark one, The Enemy? I think it's a damned good bet. So we're talking your survival here as well as mine. If you want to have a future, then let's dig to the bottom of this.'

'Maybe we dig and dig – but there is no bottom. Then what?'

'Then we dig a little deeper.'

*   *   *

As they were entering town, making the abrupt transition from dead-brown land to tightly grouped pioneer settlement, Holly suddenly said aloud: 'Robert Vaughn.'

Jim twitched with surprise, not because she had said something mystifying but because that name made an immediate connection for him.

'My God,' he said, 'that was the voice.'

'The voice of The Friend,' she said, glancing at him. 'So you realized it was familiar, too.'

Robert Vaughn, the wonderful actor, had been the hero of television's *The Man from U.N.C.L.E.* and exquisitely oily villain of countless films. He possessed one of those voices with such a rich timbre and range that it could be as threatening, or as fatherly and reassuring, as he chose to make it.

'Robert Vaughn,' Holly said. 'But why? Why not Orson Welles or Paul Newman or Sean Connery or Fred Flintstone? It's too quirky a choice not to be meaningful.'

'I don't know,' Jim said thoughtfully, but he had the unnerving feeling he *should* know. The explanation was within his grasp.

Holly said, 'Do you still think it's an alien? Wouldn't an alien just manufacture a nondescript voice? Why would it imitate any one particular actor?'

'I saw Robert Vaughn once,' Jim said, surprised by a dim memory stirring within him. 'I mean, not on TV or in the movies, but for real, up close. A long time ago.'

'Where, when?'

'I can't . . . it won't . . . won't come to me.'

Jim felt as if he were standing on a narrow spine of land between two precipices, with safety to neither side. On the one hand was the life he had been living, filled with torment and despair that he had tried to deny but that had overwhelmed him at times, as when he had taken his spiritual journey on the Harley into the Mojave desert, looking for a way out even if the way was death. On the other hand lay an uncertain future that Holly was trying to paint in for him, a future that she insisted was one of hope but which looked to him like chaos and madness. And the narrow spine on which he stood was crumbling by the minute.

He remembered an exchange they'd had as they lay side by side in his bed two nights ago, before they had made love for the first time. He'd said, *People are always more . . . complex than you figure.*

Is that just an observation . . . or a warning?

Warning?

Maybe you're warning me that you're not what you seem to be.

After a long pause, he had said, *Maybe.*

And after her own long pause, she had said, *I guess I don't care.*

He was sure, now, that he had been warning her. A small voice within told him that she was right in her analysis, that the entities at the mill had only been different aspects of him. But if he was a victim of multiple-personality syndrome, he did not believe that his condition could be casually described as a mere mental disturbance or a troubled state of mind, as she had tried to portray it. Madness was the only word that did it justice.

They entered Main Street. The town looked strangely dark and threatening – perhaps because it held the truth that would force him to step off his narrow mental perch into one world of chaos or another.

He remembered reading somewhere that only mad people were dead-certain of their sanity. He was dead-certain of nothing, but he took no comfort from that. Madness was, he suspected, the very essence of uncertainty, a frantic but fruitless search for answers, for solid ground. Sanity was that place of certainty above the whirling chaos.

Holly pulled to the curb in front of Handahl's Pharmacy at the east end of Main Street. 'Let's start here.'

'Why?'

'Because it's the first stop we made when you were pointing out places that had meant something to you as a kid.'

He stepped out of the Ford under the canopy of a Wilson

289

Magnolia, one of several interspersed with other trees along both sides of the street. That landscaping softened the hard edges but contributed to the unnatural look and discordant feeling of the town.

When Holly pushed open the front door of the Danish-style building, its glass panes glimmered like jewels along their beveled edges, and a bell tinkled overhead. They went inside together.

Jim's heart was hammering. Not because the pharmacy seemed likely to be a place where anything significant had happened to him in his childhood, but because he sensed it was the first stone on a path to the truth.

The cafe and soda fountain were to the left, and through the archway Jim saw a few people at breakfast. Immediately inside the door was the small newsstand, where morning papers were stacked high, mostly the Santa Barbara daily; there were also magazines, and to one side a revolving wire rack filled with paperback books.

'I used to buy paperbacks here,' he said. 'I loved books even back then, couldn't get enough of them.'

The pharmacy was through another archway to the right. It resembled any modern American pharmacy in that it stocked more cosmetics, beauty aids, and hair-care products than patent medicines. Otherwise, it was pleasantly quaint: wood shelves instead of metal or fiberboard; polished-granite counters; an appealing aroma composed of Bayberry candles, nickle candy, cigar-tobacco effluviums filtering from the humidified case behind the cash register, faint traces of ethyl alcohol, and sundry pharmaceuticals.

Though the hour was early, the pharmacist was on duty, serving as his own checkout clerk. It was Corbett Handahl himself, a heavy wide-shouldered man with a white mustache and white hair, wearing a crisp blue shirt under his starched white lab jacket.

He looked up and said, 'Jim Ironheart, bless my soul. How long's it been – at least three, four years?'

They shook hands.

'Four years and four months,' Jim said. He almost added, *since grandpa died,* but checked himself without quite knowing why.

Spritzing the granite prescription-service counter with Windex, Corbett wiped it with paper towels. He smiled at Holly. 'And *whoever* you are, I am eternally grateful to you for bringing beauty into this gray morning.'

Corbett was the perfect smalltown pharmacist: just jovial

enough to seem like ordinary folks in spite of being placed in the town's upper social class by virtue of his occupation, enough of a tease to be something of a local character, but with an unmistakable air of competence and probity that made you feel the medicines he compounded would always be safe. Townfolk stopped in just to say hello, not only when they needed something, and his genuine interest in people served his commerce. He had been working at the pharmacy for thirty-three years and had been the owner since his father's death twenty-seven years ago.

Handahl was the least threatening of men, yet Jim suddenly felt threatened by him. He wanted to get out of the pharmacy before . . .

Before what?

Before Handahl said the wrong thing, revealed too much.

But what could he reveal?

'I'm Jim's fiancée,' Holly said, somewhat to Jim's surprise.

'Congratulations, Jim,' Handahl said, 'You're a lucky man. Young lady, I just hope you know, the family changed its name from Ironhead, which was more descriptive. Stubborn group.' He winked and laughed.

Holly said, 'Jim's taking me around town, showing me favorite places. Sentimental journey, I suppose you'd call it.'

Frowning at Jim, Handahl said, 'Didn't think you ever liked this town well enough to feel sentimental about it.'

Jim shrugged. 'Attitudes change.'

'Glad to hear it.' Handahl turned to Holly again. 'He started coming in here soon after he moved in with his grandfolks, every Tuesday and Friday when new books and magazines arrived from the distributor in Santa Barbara.' He had put aside the Windex. He was arranging counter displays of chewing gum, breath mints, disposable lighters, and pocket combs. 'Jim was a real reader then. You still a real reader?'

'Still am,' Jim said with growing uneasiness, terrified of what Handahl might say next. Yet for the life of him, he did not know what the man could say that would matter so much.

'Your tastes were kinda narrow, I remember.' To Holly: 'Used to spend his allowance buying most every science fiction or spook-'em paperback that came in the door. 'Course, in those days, a two-dollar-a-week allowance went pretty far, if you remember that a book was about forty-five or fifty cents.'

Claustrophobia settled over Jim, thick as a heavy shroud. The pharmacy began to seem frighteningly small, crowded with merchandise, and he wanted to get out of there.

291

It's coming, he thought, with a sudden quickening of anxiety. It's coming.

Handahl said, 'I suppose maybe he got his interest in weird fiction from his mom and dad.'

Frowning, Holly said, 'How's that?'

'I didn't know Jamie, Jim's dad, all that well, but I was only one year behind him at county high school. No offense, Jim, but your dad had some exotic interests – though the way the world's changed, they probably wouldn't seem as exotic now as back in the early fifties.'

'Exotic interests?' Holly prodded.

Jim looked around the pharmacy, wondering where it would come from, which route of escape might be blocked and which might remain open. He was swinging between tentative acceptance of Holly's theory and rejection of it, and right now, he was sure she had to be wrong. It wasn't a force inside him. It was entirely a separate being, just as The Friend was. It was an evil alien, just as The Friend was good, and it could go anywhere, come out of anything, at any second, and it *was* coming, he knew it was coming, it wanted to kill them all.

'Well,' Handahl said, 'when he was a kid, Jamie used to come in here – it was my dad's store then – and buy those old pulp magazines with robots, monsters, and scantily-clad women on the covers. He used to talk a lot about how we'd put men on the moon someday, and everyone thought he was a little strange for that, but I guess he was right after all. Didn't surprise me when I heard he'd given up being an accountant, found a showbiz wife, and was making his living doing a mentalist act.'

'Mentalist act?' Holly said, glancing at Jim. 'I thought your dad was an accountant, your mom was an actress.'

'They were,' he said thinly. 'That's what they were – before they put together the act.'

He had almost forgotten about the act, which surprised him. How could he have forgotten the act? He had all the photographs from the tours, so many of them on his walls; he looked at them every day, yet he'd pretty much forgotten that they had been taken during travels between performances.

It was coming very fast now.

Close. It was very close.

He wanted to warn Holly. He couldn't speak.

Something seemed to have stolen his tongue, locked his jaws.

It was coming.

It didn't want him to warn her. It wanted to take her by surprise.

Arranging the last of the counter displays, Handahl said, 'It was a tragedy, what happened to them, all right. Jim, when you first came to town to stay with your grandfolks, you were so withdrawn, nobody could get two words out of you.'

Holly was watching Jim rather than Handahl. She seemed to sense that he was in grave distress.

'Second year, after Lena died,' Handahl said, 'Jim pretty much clammed up altogether, totally mute, like he was never going to talk another word as long as he lived. You remember that, Jim?'

In astonishment, Holly turned to Jim and said, 'Your grandmother died the second year you were here, when you were only eleven?'

I told her five years ago, Jim thought. Why did I tell her five years ago when the truth is twenty-four?

It was coming.

He sensed it.

Coming.

The Enemy.

He said, 'Excuse me, gotta get some fresh air.' He hurried outside and stood by the car, gasping for breath.

Looking back, he discovered that Holly had not followed him. He could see her through the pharmacy window, talking to Handahl.

It was coming.

Holly, don't talk to him, Jim thought. Don't listen to him, get out of there.

It was coming.

Leaning against the car, he thought: the only reason I fear Corbett Handahl is because he knows more about my life in Svenborg than I remember myself.

Lub-dub-DUB.

It was here.

*   *   *

Handahl stared curiously after Jim.

Holly said, 'I think he's never gotten over what happened to his parents . . . or to Lena.'

Handahl nodded. 'Who could get over a horrible thing like that? He was such a nice little kid, it broke your heart.' Before Holly could ask anything more about Lena, Handahl said, 'Are you two moving into the farmhouse?'

'No. Just staying for a couple of days.'

'None of my business, really, but it's a shame that land isn't being farmed.'

'Well, Jim's not a farmer himself,' she said, 'and with nobody willing to buy the place—'

'Nobody willing to buy it? Why, young lady, they'd stand twenty deep to buy it if Jim would put it on the market.'

She blinked at him.

He went on: 'You have a real good artesian well on that property, which means you always have water in a county that's usually short of it.' He leaned against the granite counter and folded his arms across his chest. 'The way it works – when that big old pond is full up, the weight of all that water puts pressure on the natural wellhead and slows the inflow of new water. But you start pumping it out of there to irrigate crops, and the flow picks up, and the pond is pretty much always full, like the magic pitcher in that old fairytale.' He tilted his head and squinted at her. 'Jim tell you he couldn't sell it?'

'Well, I assumed—'

'Tell you what,' Handahl said, 'maybe that man of yours *is* more sentimental than I'd thought. Maybe he doesn't want to sell the farm because it has too many memories for him.'

'Maybe,' she said. 'But there're bad as well as good memories out there.'

'You're right about that.'

'Like his grandmother dying,' she nudged, trying to get him back on that subject. 'That was—'

A rattling sound interrupted her. She turned and saw bottles of shampoo, hairspray, vitamins, and cold medicines jiggling on their shelves.

'Earthquake,' Handahl said, looking up worriedly at the ceiling, as if he thought it might tumble in on them.

The containers rattled more violently than ever, and Holly knew they were disturbed by something worse than an earthquake. She was being warned not to ask Handahl any more questions.

Lub-dub-DUB, lub-dub-DUB.

The cozy world of the quaint pharmacy started coming apart. The bottles exploded off the shelves, straight at her. She swung away, drew her arms over her head. The containers hammered her, flew past her and pelted Handahl. The humidor, which stood behind the counter, was vibrating. Instinctively Holly dropped to the floor. Even as she went down, the glass door of that case blew outward. Glass shrapnel cut the air where she had been standing.

She scrambled toward the exit as glittering shards rained to the floor. Behind her the heavy cash register crashed off the granite counter, missing her by inches, barely sparing her a broken spine. Before the walls could begin to blister and pulse and bring forth an alien form, she reached the door, fled through the newsstand, and went into the street, leaving Handahl in what he no doubt assumed was earthquake rubble.

The tripartite beat was throbbing up from the brick walkway beneath her feet.

She found Jim leaning against the car, shuddering and whey-faced, with the expression of a man standing on a precipice, peering into a gulf – longing to jump. He did not respond to her when she said his name. He seemed on the verge of surrendering to the dark force that he'd held within – and nurtured – all these years and that now wanted its freedom.

She jerked him away from the car, put her arms around him, held him tight, tighter, repeating his name, expecting the sidewalk to erupt in geysers of brick, expecting to be seized by serrated pincers, tentacles, or cold damp hands of inhuman design. But the triple-thud heartbeat faded, and after a while Jim raised his arms and put them around her.

The Enemy had passed.

But it was only a temporary reprieve.

* * *

Svenborg Memorial Park was adjacent to Tivoli Gardens. The cemetery was separated from the park by a spear-point wrought-iron fence and a mix of trees – mostly white cedars and spreading California Peppers.

Jim drove slowly along the service road that looped through the graveyard. 'Here.' He pulled to the side and stopped.

When he got out of the Ford, he felt almost as claustrophobic as he had in the pharmacy, even though he was standing in the open air. The slate-dark sky seemed to press down toward the gray granite monuments, while those rectangles and squares and spires strained up like the knobs of ancient time-stained bones half buried in the earth. In that dreary light, the grass looked gray-green. The trees were gray-green, too, and seemed to loom precariously, as if about to topple on him.

Going around the car to Holly's side, he pointed north. 'There.'

She took his hand. He was grateful to her for that.

Together they walked to his grandparents' gravesite. It was on a slight rise in the generally flat cemetery. A single rectangular granite marker served both plots.

Jim's heart was beating hard, and he had difficulty swallowing.

Her name was chiseled into the righthand side of the monument. LENA LOUISE IRONHEART.

Reluctantly he looked at the dates of her birth and death. She had been fifty-three when she died. And she had been dead twenty-four years.

This must be what it felt like to have been brainwashed, to have had one's memory painted over, false memories air-brushed into the blanks. His past seemed like a fogbound landscape revealed only by the eerie and inconstant luminescent face of a cloud-shrouded moon. He suddenly could not see back through the years with the same clarity he had enjoyed an hour ago, and he could not trust the reality of what he still did see; clear recollections might prove to be nothing more than tricks of fog and shadow when he was forced to confront them closely.

Disoriented and afraid, he held fast to Holly's hand.

'Why did you lie to me about this, why did you say five years?' she asked gently.

'I didn't lie. At least . . . I didn't realize I was lying.' He stared at the granite as if its polished surface was a window into the past, and he struggled to remember. 'I can recall waking up one morning and knowing that my grandmother was dead. Five years ago. I was living in the apartment then, down in Irvine.' He listened to his own voice as if it belonged to someone else, and the haunted tone of it gave him a chill. 'I dressed . . . drove north . . . bought flowers in town . . . then came here . . .'

After a while, when he did not continue, Holly said, 'Do you remember a funeral that day?'

'No.'

'Other mourners?'

'No.'

'Other flowers on the grave?'

'No. All I remember is . . . kneeling at the headstone with the flowers I'd brought for her . . . crying . . . I cried for a long time, couldn't stop crying.'

Passing him on the way to other graves, people had looked at him with sympathy, then with embarrassment as they had realized the extent of his emotional collapse, then with uneasiness as they had seen a grief in him so wild that it made him seem unbalanced.

He could even now remember how wild he had felt that day, glaring back at those who stared at him, wanting nothing more than to claw his way down into the earth and pull it over him as if it were a blanket, taking rest in the same hole as his grandmother. But he could not remember *why* he had felt that way or why he was beginning to feel that way again.

He looked at the date of her death once more – 25 September – and he was too frightened now to cry.

'What is it? Tell me,' Holly urged.

'That's when I came with the flowers, the only other time I've ever come, the day I remember as the day she died. September twenty-fifth . . . but five years ago, not twenty-four. It was the nineteenth anniversary of her death . . . but at the time it seemed to me, and always has, that she'd only just then died.'

They were both silent.

Two large blackbirds wheeled across the somber sky, shrieking, and disappeared over the treetops.

Finally Holly said, 'Could it be, you denied her death, refused to accept it when it really happened, twenty-four years ago? Maybe you were only able to accept it nineteen years later . . . the day you came here with the flowers. That's why you remember her dying so much more recently than she did. You date her death from the day you finally accepted it.'

He knew at once that she had hit upon the truth, but the answer did not make him feel better. 'But, Holly, my God, that *is* madness.'

'No,' she said calmly. 'It's self-defense, part of the same defenses you erected to hide so much of that year when you were ten.' She paused, took a deep breath, and said, 'Jim, how did your grandma die?'

'She . . .' He was surprised to realize that he could not recall the cause of Lena Ironheart's death. One more fog-filled blank. 'I don't know.'

'I think she died in the mill.'

He looked away from the tombstone, at Holly. He tensed with alarm, although he did not know why. 'In the windmill? How? What happened? How can you know?'

'The dream I told you about. Climbing the mill stairs, looking through the window at the pond below, and seeing another woman's face reflected in the glass, your grandmother's face.'

'It was only a dream.'

Holly shook her head. 'No, I think it was a memory, your

297

memory, which you projected from your sleep into mine.'

His heart fluttered with panic for reasons he could not quite discern. 'How can it have been my memory if I don't have it now?'

'You have it.'

He frowned. 'No. Nothing like that.'

'It's locked down in your subconscious, where you can access it only when you're dreaming, but it's there all right.'

If she had told him that the entire cemetery was mounted on a carousel, and that they were slowly spinning around under the bleak gun-metal sky, he would have accepted what she said more easily than he could accept the memory toward which she was leading him. He felt as if he were spinning through light and darkness, light and darkness, fear and rage . . .

With great effort, he said, 'But in your dream . . . I was in the high room when grandma got there.'

'Yes.'

'And if she died there . . .'

'You witnessed her death.'

He shook his head adamantly. 'No. My God, I'd remember that, don't you think?'

'No. I think that's why you needed nineteen years even to admit to yourself that she died. I think you saw her die, and it was such a shock that it threw you into long-term amnesia, which you overlaid with fantasies, always more fantasies.'

A breeze stirred, and something crackled around his feet. He was sure it was the bony hands of his grandmother clawing out of the earth to seize him, but when he looked down he saw only withered leaves rattling against one another as they blew across the grass.

With each heartbeat now like a fist slamming into a punching bag, Jim turned away from the grave, eager to get back to the car.

Holly put a hand on his arm. 'Wait.'

He tore loose of her, almost shoved her away. He glared at her and said, 'I want to get out of here.'

Undeterred, she grabbed and halted him again. 'Jim, where is your grandfather? Where is he buried?'

Jim pointed to the plot beside his grandmother's. 'He's there, of course, with her.'

Then he saw the left half of the granite monument. He had been so intently focused on the right half, on the impossible date of his grandmother's death, that he had not noticed what was missing from the left side. His grandfather's name was there, as it should be, engraved at the same time that Lena's had been: HENRY JAMES IRONHEART. And the date of his birth. But that was all. The date of his death had never been chiseled into the stone.

The iron sky was pressing lower.

The trees seemed to be leaning closer, arching over him.

Holly said, 'Didn't you say he died eight months after Lena?'

His mouth was dry. He could hardly work up enough spit to speak, and the words came out in dry whispers like susurrant bursts of sand blown against desert stone. 'What the hell do you want from me? I told you . . . eight months . . . May twenty-fourth of the next year . . .'

'How did he die?'

'I . . . I don't . . . I don't remember.'

'Illness?'

Shut up, shut up!

'I don't know.'

'An accident?'

'I . . . just . . . I think . . . I think it was a stroke.'

Large parts of the past were mists within a mist. He realized now that he rarely thought about the past. He lived totally in the present. He had never realized there were huge holes in his memories simply because there were so many things he had never before *tried* to remember.

'Weren't you your grandfather's nearest relative?' Holly asked.

'Yes.'

'Didn't you attend to the details of his funeral?'

He hesitated, frowning. 'I think . . . yes . . .'

'Then did you just forget to have the date of his death added to the headstone?'

He stared at the blank spot in the granite, frantically searching an equally blank spot in his memory, unable to answer her. He felt sick. He wanted to curl up and close his eyes and sleep and never wake up, let something else wake up in his place . . .

She said, 'Or did you bury him somewhere else?'

Across the ashes of the burnt-out sky, the shrieking blackbirds swooped again, slashing calligraphic messages with their wings, their meaning no more decipherable than the elusive memories darting through the deeper grayness of Jim's mind.

* * *

Holly drove them around the corner to Tivoli Gardens.

When they had left the pharmacy, Jim had wanted to drive to the cemetery, worried about what he would find there but at the same time eager to confront his misremembered past and wrench his recollections into line with the truth. The experience at the gravesite had shaken him, however, and now he was no longer in a rush to find out what additional surprises awaited him. He was content to let Holly drive, and she suspected that he would be happier if she just drove out of town, turned south, and never spoke to him of New Svenborg again.

The park was too small to have a service road. They left the car at the street and walked in.

Holly decided that Tivoli Gardens was even less inviting close up than it had been when glimpsed from a moving car yesterday. The dreary impression it made could not be blamed solely on the overcast sky. The grass was half parched from weeks of summer sun, which could be quite intense in any central California valley. Leggy runners had sprouted unchecked from the rose bushes; the few remaining blooms were faded and dropping petals in the thorny sprawl. The other flowers looked wilted, and the two benches needed painting.

Only the windmill was well maintained. It was a bigger, more imposing mill than the one at the farm, twenty feet higher, with an encircling deck about a third of the way up.

'Why are we here?' she asked.

'Don't ask me. You're the one who wanted to come.'

'Don't be thick, babe,' she said.

She knew that pushing him was like kicking a package of unstable dynamite, but she had no choice. He was going to blow anyway, sooner or later. Her only hope of survival was to force him to acknowledge that he was The Enemy before that personality seized control of him permanently. She sensed that she was running out of time.

She said, 'You're the one who put it on the itinerary yesterday. You said they'd made a movie here once.' She was jolted by what she had just said. 'Wait a sec – is *this* where you saw Robert Vaughn? Was he in the movie they made here?'

With a bewildered expression that slowly gave way to a frown, Jim turned in place, surveying the small park. At last he headed toward the windmill, and she followed him.

Two historical-marker lecterns flanked the flagstone path in front of the mill door. They were all-weather stone stands. The reading material on the slanted tops was protected behind sheets of Plexiglas in watertight frames. The lectern on the left, to which they stepped first, provided background information about the use of windmills for grain milling, water pumping, and electricity production in the Santa Ynez Valley from the 1800s until well into the twentieth century, followed by a history of the preserved mill in front of them, which was called, rather aptly, the New Svenborg Mill.

That material was as dull as dirt, and Holly turned to the second lectern only because she still had some of the doggedness and appetite for facts that had made her a passable journalist. Her interest was instantly piqued by the title at the top of the second plaque – 'The Black Windmill: Book and Movie.'

'Jim, look at this.'

He joined her by the second marker.

There was a photograph of the jacket of a young-adult novel – *The Black Windmill* by Arthur J. Willott, and the illustration on it was obviously based on the New Svenborg Mill. Holly read the lectern text with growing astonishment. Willott, a resident of the Santa Ynez Valley – Solvang, not Svenborg – had been a successful author of novels for young adults, turning out fifty-two titles before his death in 1982, at the age of eighty. His most popular and enduring book, by far, had been a fantasy adventure about a haunted old mill and a boy who discovered that the ghosts were actually aliens from another world and that under the mill-pond was a spaceship which had been there for ten thousand years.

'No,' Jim said softly but with some anger, 'no, this makes no sense, this can't be right.'

Holly recalled a moment from the dream in which she had been in Lena Ironheart's body, climbing the mill stairs. When she had reached the top, she had found ten-year-old Jim standing with his hands fisted at his sides, and he had turned to her and said, 'I'm scared, help me, the walls, the *walls!*' At his feet had been a yellow candle in a blue dish. Until now she'd forgotten that beside the dish lay a hardcover book in a colorful dustjacket. It was the same dustjacket reproduced on the lectern: *The Black Windmill*.

'No,' Jim said again, and he turned away from the plaque. He stared around worriedly at the breeze-ruffled trees.

Holly read on and discovered that twenty-five years ago, the very year that ten-year-old Jim Ironheart had come to town, *The Black Windmill* had been made into a motion picture. The New

Svenborg Mill had served as the primary location. The motion-picture company had created a shallow but convincing millpond around it, then paid to restore the land after filming and to establish the current pocket park.

Still turning slowly around, frowning at the trees and shrubs, at the gloom beneath them that the overcast day could not dispel, Jim said, 'Something's coming.'

Holly could see nothing coming, and she believed that he was just trying to distract her from the plaque. He did not want to accept the implications of the information on it, so he was trying to make her turn away from it with him.

The movie must have been a dog, because Holly had never heard of it. It appeared to have been the kind of production that was big news nowhere but in New Svenborg and, even there, only because it was based on a book by a valley resident. On the historical marker, the last paragraph of copy listed, among other details of the production, the names of the five most important members of the cast. No big box-office draws had appeared in the flick. Of the first four names, she recognized only M. Emmet Walsh, who was a personal favorite of hers. The fifth cast member was a young and then-unknown Robert Vaughan.

She looked up at the looming mill.

'What is happening here?' she said aloud. She lifted her gaze to the dismal sky, then lowered it to the photo of the dustjacket for Willott's book. 'What the *hell* is happening here?'

In a voice quaking with fear but also with an eerie note of desire, Jim said, 'It's coming!'

She looked where he was staring, and saw a disturbance in the earth at the far end of the small park, as if something was burrowing toward them, pushing up a yard-wide hump of dirt and sod to mark its tunnel, moving fast, straight at them.

She whirled on Jim, grabbed him. 'Stop it!'

'It's coming,' he said, wide-eyed.

'Jim, it's you, it's only you.'

'No . . . not me . . . The Enemy.' He sounded half in a trance.

Holly glanced back and saw the thing passing under the concrete walkway, which cracked and heaved up in its wake.

'Jim, damn it!'

He was staring at the approaching killer with horror but also with, she thought, a sort of longing.

One of the park benches was knocked over as the earth bulged then sank under it.

The Enemy was only forty feet from them, coming fast.

She grabbed Jim by the shirt, shook him, tried to make him look at her. 'I saw this movie when I was a kid. What was it called, huh? Wasn't it *Invaders from Mars*, something like that, where the aliens open doors in the sand and suck you down?'

She glanced back. It was thirty feet from them.

'Is that what's going to kill us, Jim? Something that opens a door in the sand, sucks us down, something from a movie to give ten-year-old boys nightmares?'

Twenty feet away.

Jim was sweating, shuddering. He seemed to be beyond hearing anything Holly said.

She shouted in his face anyway: 'Are you going to kill me *and* yourself, suicide like Larry Kakonis, just stop being strong and put an end to it, let one of your own nightmares pull you into the ground?'

Ten feet.

Eight.

'Jim!'

Six.

Four.

Hearing a monstrous grinding of jaws in the ground under them, she raised her foot, rammed the heel of her shoe down across the front of his shin, as hard as she could, to make him feel it through his sock. Jim cried out in pain as the ground shifted under them, and Holly looked down in horror at the rupturing earth. But the burrowing stopped simultaneously with his sharp cry. The ground didn't open. Nothing erupted from it or sucked them down.

Shaking, Holly stepped back from the ripped sod and cracked earth on which she had been standing.

Jim looked at her, aghast. 'It wasn't me. It can't have been.'

*   *   *

Back in the car, Jim slumped in his seat.

Holly folded her arms on the steering wheel, put her forehead on her arms.

He looked out the side window at the park. The giant mole trail was still there. The sidewalk was cracked and tumbled. The bench lay on its side.

He just couldn't believe that the thing beneath the park had

303

been only a figment of his imagination, empowered only by his mind. He had been in control of himself all his life, living a Spartan existence of books and work, with no vices or indulgences. (Except a frighteningly convenient forgetfulness, he thought sourly.) Nothing about Holly's theory was harder for him to accept than that a wild and savage part of him, beyond his conscious control, was the only real danger that they faced.

He was beyond ordinary fear now. He was no longer perspiring or shivering. He was in the grip of a primal terror that left him rigid and Dry-Ice dry.

'It wasn't me,' he repeated.

'Yes, it was.' Considering that she believed he'd almost killed her, Holly was surprisingly gentle with him. She did not raise her voice; it was softened by a note of great tenderness.

He said, 'You're still on this split-personality kick.'

'Yes.'

'So it was my dark side.'

'Yes.'

'Embodied in a giant worm or something,' he said, trying to hone a sharp edge on his sarcasm, failing. 'But you said The Enemy only broke through when I was sleeping, and I wasn't sleeping, so even if I *am* The Enemy, how could I have been that thing in the park?'

'New rules. Subconsciously, you're getting desperate. You're not able to control that personality as easily as before. The closer you're forced to the truth, the more aggressive The Enemy's going to become in order to defend itself.'

'If it was me, why wasn't there an alien heartbeat like before?'

'That's always just been a dramatic effect, like the bells ringing before The Friend put in an appearance.' She raised her head from her arms and looked at him. 'You dropped it because there wasn't time for it. I was reading that plaque, and you wanted to stop me as fast as you could. You needed a distraction. Let me tell you, babe, it was a lulu.'

He looked out the window again, toward the windmill and the lectern that held the information about *The Black Windmill*.

Holly put a hand on his shoulder. 'You were in a black despair after your parents died. You needed to escape. Evidently a writer named Arthur Willott provided you with a fantasy that fit your needs perfectly. To one extent or another, you've been living in it ever since.'

Though he could not admit it to her, he had to admit to himself that he *was* groping toward understanding, that he was on the brink of seeing his past from a new perspective that would make all of the mysterious lines and angles fall into a new and comprehensible shape. If selective amnesia, carefully constructed false memories, and even multiple personalities were not indications of madness but only the hooks he had used to hold on to sanity – as Holly insisted – then what would happen to him if he let go of those hooks? If he dug up the truth about his past, faced the things he had refused to face when he had turned to fantasy as a child, would the truth drive him mad *this* time? What was he hiding from?

'Listen,' she said, 'the important thing is that you shut it down before it reached us, before it did any harm.'

'My shin hurts like hell,' he said, wincing.

'Good,' she said brightly.

She started the engine.

'Where are we going now?' he asked.

'Where else? The library.'

*   *   *

Holly parked on Copenhagen Lane in front of the small Victorian house that served as the New Svenborg Library.

She was pleased that her hands were not shaking, that her voice was level and calm, and that she had been able to drive from Tivoli Gardens without weaving all over the road. After the incident in the park, she was amazed that her pants were still clean. She had been reduced to raw terror – a pure, intense emotion untainted by any other. Diluted now, it was still with her, and she knew it would remain with her until they were out of these spooky old woods – or dead. But she was determined not to reveal the depth of her fear to Jim, because he had to be worse off than she was. After all, it was *his* life that was turning out to be a collage of flimsy lies. He needed to lean on her.

As she and Jim went up the front walk to the porch (Jim limping), Holly noticed he was studying the lawn around him, as if he thought something might start burrowing toward them.

Better not, she thought, or you'll have *two* bleeding shins.

But as she went through the front door, she wondered if a jolt of pain would work a second time.

In the paneled foyer, a sign announced NONFICTION SECOND FLOOR. An arrow pointed to a staircase on her right.

The foyer funneled into a first-floor hallway off which lay two large rooms. Both were filled with bookshelves. The chamber on the left also contained reading tables with chairs and a large oak desk.

The woman at the desk was a good advertisement for country living: flawless complexion, lustrous chestnut hair, clear hazel eyes. She looked thirty-five but was probably twelve years older.

The nameplate in front of her said 'Eloise Glynn.'

Yesterday, when Holly had wanted to come into the library to see if the much-admired Mrs Glynn was there, Jim had insisted that she would be retired, that she had been 'quite old' twenty-five years ago, when in fact she obviously had been fresh out of college and starting her first job.

By comparison with previous discoveries, this was only a minor surprise. Jim hadn't wanted Holly to come into the library yesterday, so he'd simply lied. And from the look on his face now, it was clear that Eloise Glynn's youth was no surprise to him either; he had known, yesterday, that he was not telling the truth, though perhaps he had not understood *why* he was lying.

The librarian did not recognize Jim. Either he had been one of those kids who left little impression or, more likely, he had been telling the truth when he'd said he had not been to the library since he'd left for college eighteen years ago.

Eloise Glynn had the bouncy manner and attitude of a girls' sports coach that Holly remembered from high school. 'Willott?' she said in answer to Holly's question. 'Oh, yes, we've got a truckload of Willott.' She bounced up from her chair. 'I can show you right where he's at.' She came around her desk, stepping briskly, and led Holly and Jim across the hall to the other large room. 'He was local, as I'm sure you know. Died a decade ago, but two-thirds of his books are still in print.' She stopped in front of the young-adult section and made a sweeping gesture with one hand to indicate two three-foot shelves of Willott titles. 'He was a productive man, Artie Willott, so busy that beavers hung their heads in shame when he walked by.'

She grinned at Holly, and it was infectious. Holly grinned back at her. 'We're looking for *The Black Windmill.*'

'That's one of his most popular titles, never met a kid didn't love it.' Mrs Glynn plucked the book off the shelf almost without looking to see where it was, handed it to Holly. 'This for your kid?'

'Actually for me. I read about it on the plaque over in Tivoli Gardens.'

'I've read the book,' Jim said. 'But she's curious.'

With Jim, Holly returned to the main room and sat at the table farthest from the desk. With the book between them, they read the first two chapters.

She kept touching him – his hand, shoulder, knee – gentling him. Somehow she had to hold him together long enough for him to learn the truth and be healed by it, and the only glue she could think of was love. She had convinced herself that each small expression of love – each touch, smile, affectionate look or word – was a bonding agent that prevented him from shattering completely.

The novel was well and engagingly written. But what it revealed about Jim Ironheart's life was so astonishing that Holly began to skim and spot read, whispering passages to him, urgently seeking the next startling revelation.

The lead character was named Jim, not Ironheart but Jamison. Jim Jamison lived on a farm that had a pond and an old windmill. The mill was supposedly haunted, but after witnessing a number of spooky incidents, Jim discovered that an alien presence, not a spirit, was quartered in a spacecraft under the pond and was manifesting itself in the mill. It revealed itself to Jim as a soft light that glowed within the mill walls. Communication between Jim and the alien was achieved with the use of two lined, yellow tablets – one for Jim's questions, and one for the alien's answers, which appeared as if by magic. According to the extra-terrestrial, it was a being of pure energy and was on earth 'TO OBSERVE, TO STUDY, TO HELP MANKIND.' It referred to itself as THE FRIEND.

Marking her place with a finger, Holly flipped through the rest of the book to see if The Friend continued to use the awkward tablets for communication all the way to the end. It did. In the story on which Jim Ironheart had based his fantasy, the alien never vocalized.

'Which is why you doubted that *your* alien could vocalize and why you resisted my suggestion that we refuse to play along with the tablet system.'

Jim was beyond denial now. He stared at the book with wonder.

His response gave Holly hope for him. In the cemetery, he had been in such distress, his eyes so cold and bleak, that she had begun to doubt if, indeed, he could turn his phenomenal power inward to heal himself. And in the park, for one terrible moment, she had thought that his fragile shell of sanity would crack and spill the yolk of madness. But he had held together, and now his curiosity seemed to be overcoming his fear.

Mrs Glynn had gone off to work in the stacks. No other patrons had come in to browse.

Holly returned to the story, skim-reading. At the midpoint of the tale, just after Jim Jamison and the alien had their second encounter, the ET explained that it was an entity that lived 'IN ALL ASPECTS OF TIME,' could perceive the future, and wanted to save the life of a man who was fated to die.

'I'll be damned,' Jim said softly.

Without warning, a vision burst in Holly's mind with such force and brilliance that the library vanished for a moment and her inner world became the only reality: she saw herself naked and nailed to a wall in an obscene parody of a crucifix, blood streaming from her hands and feet (a voice whispering: *die, die, die*), and she opened her mouth to scream but, instead of sound, swarms of cockroaches poured out between her lips, and she realized she was already dead (*die, die, die*), her putrid innards crawling with pests and vermin—

The hateful phantasm flickered off the screen of her mind as suddenly as it had appeared, and she snapped back into the library with a jolt.

'Holly?' Jim was looking at her worriedly.

A part of him had sent the vision to her, no question about that. But the Jim she was looking at now was not the Jim who had done it. The dark child within him, The Enemy, hate-filled and murderous, was striking at her with a new weapon.

She said, 'It's OK. It's all right.'

But she didn't feel all right. The vision had left her nauseous and somewhat disoriented.

She had to struggle to refocus on *The Black Windmill:*

The man Jim Jamison had to save, The Friend explained, was a candidate for the United States Presidency, soon to pass through Jim's hometown, where he was going to be assassinated. The alien wanted him to live, instead, because 'HE IS GOING TO BE A GREAT STATESMAN AND PEACEMAKER WHO WILL SAVE THE WORLD FROM A GREAT WAR.' Because it had to keep its presence on earth a secret, The Friend wanted to work through Jim Jamison to thwart the assassins: 'YOU WILL THROW HIM A LIFE LINE, JIM.'

The novel did not include an evil alien. The Enemy had been entirely Jim Ironheart's embellishment, an embodiment of his own rage and self-hatred, which he had needed to separate from himself and control.

With a crackle of inner static, another vision burst across her mind-screen, so intense that it blotted out the real world: she was in a coffin, dead but somehow still in possession of all her senses; she could feel worms churning in her (*die, die, die, die*), could smell the vile stench of her own decaying body, could see her rotted face reflected on the inside of the coffin lid as if it was lit and mirrored. She raised skeletal fists and beat on the lid, heard the blows reverberating into the yards of compacted earth above her—

The library again.

'Holly, for God's sake, what's happening?'

'Nothing.'

'Holly?'

'Nothing,' she said, sensing that it would be a mistake to admit that The Enemy was rattling her.

She finished skimming *The Black Windmill*.

At the end of the novel, when Jim Jamison had saved the future president, The Friend had subsided into quiescence under the pond, instructing Jim to forget that their encounter had ever taken place, and to remember only that he had saved the politician on his own initiative. If a repressed memory of the alien ever surfaced in Jim's mind, he was told that he would 'REMEMBER ME ONLY AS A DREAM, AN ENTITY IN A DREAM YOU ONCE HAD.' When the alien light faded out of the wall for the last time, the messages on the tablet vanished, leaving no trace of the contact.

Holly closed the book.

She and Jim sat for a while, staring at the dustjacket.

Around her, thousands of times and places, people and worlds, from Mars to Egypt to Yoknapatawpha County, were closed up in the bindings of books like the shine trapped under the tarnished veneer of a brass lamp. She could almost feel them waiting to dazzle with the first turn of a page, come alive with brilliant colors and pungent odors and delicious aromas, with laughter and sobbing and cries and whispers. Books were packaged dreams.

'Dreams are doorways,' she told Jim, 'and the story in any novel is a kind of dream. Through Arthur Willott's dream of alien contact and adventure, you found a doorway out of your despair, and escape from a crushing sense of having failed your mother and father.'

He had been unrelievedly pale since she had shown him the tablet with The Friend's answers. HE LOVES YOU HOLLY/HE

WILL KILL YOU HOLLY. Now some color had returned to his face. His eyes were still ghost-ridden, and worry clung to him like shadows to the night, but he seemed to be feeling his way toward an accommodation with all the lies that were his life.

Which was what frightened The Enemy in him. And made it desperate.

Mrs Glynn had returned from the stacks. She was working at her desk.

Lowering her voice even further, Holly said to Jim, 'But why would you hold yourself to blame for the traffic accident that killed them? And how could any kid that age have such a tremendously heavy sense of responsibility?'

He shook his head. 'I don't know.'

Remembering what Corbett Handahl had told her, Holly put a hand on Jim's knee and said, 'Think, honey. Did the accident happen when they were on the road with this mentalist act of theirs?'

He hesitated, frowned. 'Yes . . . on the road.'

'You traveled with them, didn't you?'

He nodded.

Recalling the photograph of his mother in a glittery gown, Jim and his father in tuxedos, Holly said, 'You were part of the act.'

Some of his memories apparently were rising like the rings of light had risen in the pond. The play of emotions in his face could not have been faked; he was genuinely astonished to be moving out of a life of darkness.

Holly felt her own excitement growing with his. She said, 'What did you do in the act?'

'It was . . . a form of stage magic. My mom would take objects from people in the audience. My dad would work with me, and we would . . . I would hold the objects and pretend to have psychic impressions, tell the people things about themselves that I couldn't know.'

'Pretend?' she asked.

He blinked. 'Maybe not. It's so strange . . . how little I remember even when I try.'

'It wasn't a trick. You could really do it. That's why your folks put together the act in the first place. You *were* a gifted child.'

He ran his fingers down the Bro-Dart-protected jacket of *The Black Windmill*. 'But . . .'

'But?'

'There's so much I still don't understand . . .'

310

'Oh, me too, kiddo. But we're getting closer, and I have to believe that's a good thing.'

A shadow, cast from within, stole across his face again.

Not wanting to see him slip back into a darker mood, Holly said, 'Come on.' She picked up the book and took it to the librarian's desk. Jim followed her.

The energetic Mrs Glynn was drawing on posterboard with a rainbow of colored pencils and magic markers. The colorful images were of well-rendered boys and girls dressed as spacemen, spelunkers, sailors, acrobats, and jungle explorers. She had penciled in but not yet colored the message: THIS IS A LIBRARY. KIDS AND ADVENTURERS WELCOME. ALL OTHERS STAY OUT!

'Nice,' Holly said sincerely, indicating the poster. 'You really put yourself into this job.'

'Keeps me out of barrooms,' Mrs Glynn said, with a grin that made it clear why any kid would like her.

Holly said, 'My fiancé here has spoken so highly of you. Maybe you don't remember him after twenty-five years.'

Mrs Glynn looked speculatively at Jim.

He said, 'I'm Jim Ironheart, Mrs Glynn.'

'Of course I remember you! You were the most special little boy.' She got up, leaned across the desk, and insisted on getting a hug from Jim. Releasing him, turning to Holly, she said, 'So you're going to be marrying my Jimmy. That's wonderful! A lot of kids have passed through here since I've been running the place, even for a town this small, and I can't pretend I'd remember all of them. But Jimmy was special. He was a very special boy.'

Holly heard, again, how Jim had had an insatiable appetite for fantasy fiction, how he'd been so terribly quiet his first year in town, and how he'd been totally mute during his second year, after the sudden death of his grandmother.

Holly seized that opening: 'You know, Mrs Glynn, one of the reasons Jim brought me back here was to see if we might like to live in the farmhouse, at least for a while—'

'It's a nicer town than it looks,' Mrs Glynn said. 'You'd be happy here, I'll guarantee it. In fact, let me issue you a couple of library cards!' She sat down and pulled open a desk drawer.

As the librarian withdrew two cards from the drawer and picked up a pen, Holly said, 'Well, the thing is . . . there're as many bad memories for him as good, and Lena's death is one of the worst.'

'And the thing is,' Jim picked up, 'I was only ten when she

311

died – well, almost eleven – and I guess maybe I made myself forget some of what happened. I'm not too clear on how she died, the details, and I was wondering if you remember . . .'

Holly decided that he might make a decent interviewer after all.

Mrs Glynn said, 'I can't say I recall the details of it. And I guess nobody'll ever know what on earth she was doing out in that old mill in the middle of the night. Henry, your grandpa, said she sometimes went there just to get away from things. It was peaceful and cool, a place she could do a little knitting and sort of meditate. And, of course, in those days it wasn't quite the ruin it's become. Still . . . it seemed odd she'd be out there knitting at two o'clock in the morning.'

As the librarian recounted what she could recall of Lena's death, confirming that Holly's dream had really been Jim's memory, Holly was touched by both dread and nausea. What Eloise Glynn did not seem to know, what perhaps no one knew, was that Lena had not been in that mill alone.

Jim had been there too.

And only Jim had come out of it alive.

Holly glanced at him and saw that he had lost all color in his face again. He was not merely pale now. He was as gray as the sky outside.

Mrs Glynn asked Holly for her driver's license, to complete the library card, and even though Holly didn't want the card, she produced the license.

The librarian said, 'Jim, I think what got you through all that pain and loss, more than anything, was books. You pulled way into yourself, read *all* the time, and I think you used fantasy as sort of a painkiller.' She handed Holly the license and library card, and said to her: 'Jim was an awfully bright boy. He could get totally *into* a book, it became real for him.'

Yeah, Holly thought, did it ever.

'When he first came to town and I heard he'd never been to a real school before, been educated by his parents, I thought that was just terrible, even if they did have to travel all the time with that nightclub act of theirs—'

Holly recalled the gallery of photographs on Jim's study walls in Laguna Niguel: Miami, Atlantic City, New York, London, Chicago, Las Vegas . . .

'—but they'd actually done a pretty fine job. At least they'd turned him into a booklover, and that served him well later.' She turned to Jim. 'I suppose you haven't asked your grandpa about

Lena's death because you figure it might upset him to talk about it. But I think he's not as fragile as you imagine, and he'd know more about it than anyone, of course.' Mrs Glynn addressed Holly again: 'Is something wrong, dear?'

Holly realized she was standing with the blue library card in her hand, statue-still, like one of those waiting-to-be-reanimated people in the worlds within the books upon the shelves within these rooms. For a moment she could not respond to the woman's question.

Jim looked too stunned to pick up the ball this time. His grandfather was alive somewhere. But where?

'No,' Holly said, 'nothing's wrong. I just realized how late it's getting—'

A shatter of static, a vision: her severed head screaming, her severed hands crawling like spiders across a floor, her decapitated body writhing and twisting in agony; she was dismembered but not dead, impossibly alive, in a thrall of horror beyond endurance—

Holly cleared her throat, blinked at Mrs Glynn, who was staring at her curiously. 'Uh, yeah, quite late. And we're supposed to go see Henry before lunch. It's already ten. I've never met him.' She was babbling now, couldn't stop. 'I'm really looking forward to it.'

Unless he really *did* die over four years ago, like Jim had told her, in which case she wasn't looking forward to it at all. But Mrs Glynn did not appear to be a spiritualist who would blithely suggest conjuring up the dead for a little chat.

'He's a nice man,' Eloise Glynn said. 'I know he must've hated having to move off the farm after his stroke, but he can be thankful it didn't leave him worse than he is. My mother, God rest her soul, had a stroke, left her unable to walk, talk, blind in one eye, and so confused she couldn't always recognize her own children. At least poor Henry has his wits about him, as I understand it. He can talk, and I hear he's the leader of the wheelchair pack over there at Fair Haven.'

'Yes,' Jim said, sounding as wooden as a talking post, 'that's what I hear.'

'Fair Haven's such a nice place,' Mrs Glynn said, 'it's good of you to keep him there, Jim. It's not a snakepit like so many nursing homes these days.'

* * *

The Yellow Pages at a public phone booth provided an address for Fair Haven on the edge of Solvang. Holly drove south and west across the valley.

313

'I remember he had a stroke,' Jim said. 'I was in the hospital with him, came up from Orange County, he was in the intensive-care unit. I hadn't . . . hadn't seen him in thirteen years or more.'

Holly was surprised by that, and her look generated a hot wave of shame that withered Jim. 'You hadn't seen your own grandfather in thirteen years?'

'There was a reason . . .'

'What?'

He stared at the road ahead for a while, then let out a guttural sound of frustration and disgust. 'I don't know. There was a reason, but I can't remember it. Anyway, I came back when he had his stroke, when he was dying in the hospital. And I remember him dead, damn it.'

'Clearly remember it?'

'Yes.'

She said, 'You remember the sight of him dead in the hospital bed, all his monitor lines flat?'

He frowned. 'No.'

'Remember a doctor telling you he'd passed away?'

'No.'

'Remember making arrangements for his burial?'

'No.'

'Then what's so clear about this memory of him being dead?'

Jim brooded about that a while as she whipped the Ford around the curving roads, between gentle hills on which scattered houses stood, past white-fenced horse pastures green as pictures of Kentucky. This part of the valley was lusher than the area around New Svenborg. But the sky had become a more somber gray, with a hint of blue-black in the clouds – bruised.

At last he said, 'It isn't clear at all, now that I look close at it. Just a muddy impression . . . not a real memory.'

'Are you paying to keep Henry at Fair Haven?'

'No.'

'Did you inherit his property?'

'How could I inherit if he's alive?'

'A conservatorship then?'

He was about to deny that, as well, when he suddenly remembered a hearing room, a judge. The testimony of a doctor. His granddad's counsel, appearing on the old man's behalf to testify that Henry was of sound mind and wanted his grandson to manage his property.

314

'Good heavens, yes,' Jim said, shocked that he was capable not only of forgetting events from the distant past but from as recently as four years ago. As Holly swung around a slow-moving farm truck and accelerated along a straight stretch of road, Jim told her what he had just remembered, dim as the recollection was. 'How can I do this, live this way? How can I totally rewrite my past when it suits me?'

'Self-defense,' she said, as she had said before. She swung in front of the truck. 'I'd bet that you remember a tremendous amount of precise detail about your work as a teacher, about your students over the years, colleagues you've taught with—'

It was true. As she spoke, he could flash back, at will, through his years in the classroom, which seemed so vivid that those thousands of days might have occurred concurrently only yesterday.

'—because that life held no threat for you, it was filled with purpose and peace. The only things you forget, push relentlessly down into the deepest wells of memory, are those things having to do with the deaths of your parents, the death of Lena Ironheart, and your years in New Svenborg. Henry Ironheart is part of that, so you continue to wipe him from your mind.'

The sky was contusive.

He saw blackbirds wheeling across the clouds, more of them now than he had seen in the cemetery. Four, six, eight. They seemed to be paralleling the car, following it to Solvang.

Strangely, he recalled the dream with which he had awakened on the morning that he had gone to Portland, saved Billy Jenkins, and met Holly. In the nightmare, a flock of large blackbirds shrieked around him in a turbulent flapping of wings and tore at him with hooked beaks as precision-honed as surgical instruments.

'The worst is yet to come,' he said.

'What do you mean?'

'I don't know.'

'You mean what we learn at Fair Haven?'

Above, the blackbirds swam through the high, cold currents.

Without having a clue as to what he meant, Jim said, 'Something very dark is coming.'

•2•

Fair Haven was housed in a large, U-shaped, single-story building outside the town limits of Solvang, with no trace of Danish influence in its architecture. It was strictly off-the-rack design, functional and

315

no prettier than it had to be: cream-tinted stucco, concrete-tile roof, boxy, flat-walled, without detail. But it was freshly painted and in good repair; the hedges were neatly trimmed, the lawn recently mown, and the sidewalks swept clean.

Holly liked the place. She almost wished she lived there, was maybe eighty, watching some TV every day, playing some checkers, with no worry bigger than trying to figure out where she had put her false teeth when she'd taken them out last night.

Inside, the hallways were wide and airy, with yellow vinyl-tile floors. Unlike in many nursing homes, the air was neither tainted with the stench of incontinent patients left unclean by inattentive staff nor with a heavy aerosol deodorant meant to eliminate or mask that stench. The rooms she and Jim passed looked attractive, with big windows opening to valley views or a garden courtyard. Some of the patients lay in their beds or slumped in their wheelchairs with vacant or mournful expressions on their faces, but they were the unfortunate victims of major strokes or late-stage Alzheimer's disease, locked away in memories or torment, largely unconnected to the world around them. Everyone else appeared happy; and patients' laughter actually could be heard, a rarity in such places.

According to the supervisor on duty at the nurses' station, Henry Ironheart had been a resident of Fair Haven for over four years.

Mrs Danforth, the administrator into whose office they were shown, was new since Henry Ironheart had been checked in. She had the slightly plump, well-groomed, and inoffensively self-satisfied look of a minister's wife in a prosperous parish. Though she could not understand why they needed her to verify something that Jim knew already, she checked her records and showed them that, indeed, Henry Ironheart's monthly bill was always promptly paid by James Ironheart, of Laguna Niguel, by check.

'I'm glad you've come to visit at last, and I hope you'll have a pleasant time,' Mrs Danforth said, with genteel reproach meant to make him feel guilty for not visiting his grandfather more often while at the same time not directly offending him.

After they left Mrs Danforth, they stood in a corner of the main hallway, out of the bustle of nurses and wheelchair-bound patients.

'I can't just walk in on him,' Jim said adamantly. 'Not after all this time. I feel . . . my stomach's clutched up, cramped. Holly, I'm afraid of him.'

'Why?'

'I'm not sure.' Desperation, bordering on panic, made his eyes so disquieting that she did not want to look into them.

'When you were little, did he ever harm you?'

'I don't think so.' He strained to see back through the clouds of memory, then shook his head. 'I don't know.'

Largely because she was afraid to leave Jim alone, Holly tried to convince him that it would be better for them to meet the old man together.

But he insisted she go first. 'Ask him most of what we need to know, so when I come into it, we won't have to stay much longer if we don't want to . . . in case it goes bad, gets awkward, unpleasant. Prepare him for seeing me, Holly. Please.'

Because he appeared ready to bolt if she did not play things his way, Holly finally agreed. But watching Jim walk into the courtyard to wait there, she already regretted letting him move out of her sight. If he started to lose control again, if The Enemy began to break through, nobody would be with him to encourage him to resist the onslaught.

A friendly nurse helped Holly find Henry Ironheart when he proved not to be in his room. She pointed him out at a card table in the cheery recreation center, at the other end of which a half-dozen residents were watching a game show on television.

Henry was playing poker with his cronies. Four of them were at a table designed to accommodate wheelchairs, and none wore the standard nursing-home attire of pajamas or sweatsuits. Besides Henry, there were two fragile-looking elderly men – one in slacks and a red Polo shirt; the other in slacks, white shirt, and bow tie – and a birdlike woman with snow-white hair, who was in a bright pink pantsuit. They were halfway through a hotly contested hand, with a substantial pile of blue plastic chips in the pot, and Holly waited to one side, reluctant to interrupt them. Then one by one, exhibiting a flair for drama, they revealed their cards, and with a whoop of delight the woman – Thelma, her name was – raked in her winnings, theatrically gloating as the men good-naturedly questioned her honesty.

Finally intruding into their banter, Holly introduced herself to Henry Ironheart, though without identifying herself as Jim's fiancée. 'I'd like to have a few minutes to talk with you about something if I could.'

'Jesus, Henry,' the man in the Polo shirt said, 'she's less than half your age!'

317

'He always was an old pervert,' said the guy in the bow tie.

'Oh, get a life, Stewart,' Thelma said, speaking to Mr Bow Tie. 'Henry's a gentleman, and he's never been anything else.'

'Jesus, Henry, you're gonna be married for sure before you get out of this room today!'

'Which *you* certainly won't be, George,' Thelma continued. 'And as far as I'm concerned' – she winked – 'if it's Henry, marriage doesn't have to be part of it.'

They all roared at that, and Holly said, 'I can see I'm going to be aced out of this one.'

George said, 'Thelma gets what she's after more often than not.'

Noticing that Stewart had gathered the cards up and was shuffling the deck, Holly said, 'I don't mean to interrupt your game.'

'Oh, don't worry yourself,' Henry said. His words were slightly slurred as a result of his stroke, but he was quite intelligible. 'We'll just take a bathroom break.'

'At our age,' George said, 'if we didn't coordinate our bathroom breaks, there'd never be more than two of us at the card table at any one time!'

The others wheeled away, and Holly pulled up a chair to sit near Henry Ironheart.

He was not the vital-looking, square-faced man she had seen in the photograph on the living-room wall of the farmhouse last evening, and without help Holly might not have recognized him. His stroke had left his right side weak, though not paralyzed, and a lot of the time he held that arm curled against his chest, the way an injured animal might favor a paw. He had lost a lot of weight and was no longer a burly man. His face was not gaunt but nearly so, though his skin had good color; the facial muscles on the right side were unnaturally relaxed, allowing his features to droop a little.

His appearance, combined with the slur that thickened every word he spoke, might have sent Holly into a depression over the inevitable direction of every human life – if not for his eyes, which revealed an unbowed soul. And his conversation, though slowed somewhat by his impediment, was that of a bright and humorous man who would not give the fates the satisfaction of his despair; his treacherous body was to be cursed, if at all, in private.

'I'm a friend of Jim's,' she told him.

He made a lopsided O of his mouth, which she decided was an

318

expression of surprise. At first he did not seem to know what to say, but then he asked, 'How is Jim?'

Deciding to opt for the truth, she said, 'Not so good, Henry. He's a very troubled man.'

He looked away from her, at the pile of poker chips on the table. 'Yes,' he said softly.

Holly had half expected him to be a child-abusing monster who had been at least in part responsible for Jim's withdrawal from reality. He seemed anything but that.

'Henry, I wanted to meet you, talk to you, because Jim and I are more than friends. I love him, and he's said that he loves me, and it's my hope that we're going to be together a long, long time.'

To her surprise, tears brimmed up and slipped from Henry's eyes, forming bright beads in the soft folds of his aged face.

She said, 'I'm sorry, have I upset you?'

'No, no, good lord, no,' he said, wiping at his eyes with his left hand. 'Excuse me for being an old fool.'

'I can tell you're anything but that.'

'It's just, I never thought . . . Well, I figured Jim was going to spend his life alone.'

'Why did you think that?'

'Well . . .'

He seemed distressed at having to say anything negative about his grandson, completely dispelling her lingering expectations that he would be a tyrant of some kind.

Holly helped him. 'He does have a way of keeping people at arm's length. Is that what you mean?'

Nodding, he said, 'Even me. I've loved him with all my heart, all these years, and I know he loves me in his way, though he's always had real trouble showing it, and he could *never* say it.' As Holly was about to ask him a question, he suddenly shook his head violently and wrenched his distorted face into an expression of anguish so severe that for an instant she thought he was having another stroke. 'It's not all him. God knows, it's not.' The slur in his voice thickened when he grew more emotional. 'I've got to face it – part of the distance between us is me, my fault, the blame I put on him that I never should've.'

'Blame?'

'For Lena.'

A shadow of fear passed across her heart and induced a quiver of angina-like pain.

She glanced at the window that looked out on a corner of the courtyard. It was not the corner to which Jim had gone. She wondered where he was, how he was . . . *who* he was.

'For Lena? I don't understand,' she said, though she was afraid that she did.

'It seems unforgivable to me now, what I did, what I allowed myself to think.' He paused, looking not at her but through her now, toward a distant time and place. 'But he was just so strange in those days, not the child he had been. Before you can even hope to understand what I did, you have to know that, after Atlanta, he was so very strange, all locked up inside.'

Immediately Holly thought of Sam and Emily Newsome, whose lives Jim had saved in an Atlanta convenience store – and Norman Rink, into whom he had pumped eight rounds from a shotgun in a blind rage. But Henry obviously was not talking about a recent event in Atlanta; he was referring to some previous incident, much further in the past.

'You don't know about Atlanta?' he asked, reacting to her evident mystification.

A queer sound chittered through the room, alarming Holly. For an instant she could not identify the noise, then realized it was several birds shrieking the way they did when protecting their nests. No birds were in the room, and she supposed their cries were echoing down the fireplace chimney from the roof. Just birds. Their chatter faded.

She turned to Henry Ironheart again. 'Atlanta? No, I guess I don't know about that.'

'I didn't think you did. I'd be surprised if he talked about it, even to you, even if he loves you. He just doesn't talk about it.'

'What happened in Atlanta?'

'It was a place called the Dixie Duck—'

'Oh, my God,' she whispered. She had *been* there in the dream.

'Then you do know some of it,' he said. His eyes were pools of sorrow.

She felt her face crumple in grief, not for Jim's parents, whom she had never known, and not even for Henry who presumably had loved them, but for Jim. 'Oh, my God.' And then she couldn't say any more because her words backed up behind her own tears.

Henry reached out to her with one liver-spotted hand, and she took it, held it, waiting until she could speak again.

At the other end of the room, bells were ringing, horns blaring, on the TV gameshow.

No traffic accident had killed Jim's parents. That story was his way of avoiding a recounting of the terrible truth.

She had known. She had known, and refused to know.

Her latest dream had not been a warning prophecy but another memory that Jim had projected into her mind as they had both slept. She had not been herself in the dream. She had been Jim. Just as she had been Lena in a dream two nights ago. If a mirror had given her a look at her face, she would have seen Jim's countenance instead of her own, as she had seen Lena's in the windmill window. The horror of the blood-drenched restaurant returned to her now in vivid images that she could not block from memory, and she shuddered violently.

She looked toward the window, the courtyard, frightened for him.

'They were performing for a week at a club in Atlanta,' Henry said. 'They went out for lunch to Jimmy's favorite place, which he remembered from the last time they'd played Atlanta.'

Voice trembling, Holly said, 'Who was the gunman?'

'Just a nut. That's what made it so hard. No meaning to it. Just a crazy man.'

'How many people died?'

'A lot.'

'How many, Henry?'

'Twenty-four.'

She thought of young Jim Ironheart in that holocaust, scrambling for his life through the shattered bodies of the other customers, the room filled with cries of pain and terror, reeking with the stench of blood and vomit, bile and urine from the slaughtered corpses. She heard the heavy sound of the automatic weapon again, *chuda-chuda-chuda-chuda-chuda-chuda*, and the please-please-please-please of the terrified young waitress. Even as a dream, it had been almost beyond endurance, all the random horror of existence and all the cruelty of humankind boiled down to one devastating experience, a savage ordeal from which full psychological recovery, even for an adult, would take a lifetime of struggle. For a ten-year-old boy, recovery might seem impossible, reality intolerable, denial necessary, and fantasy the only tool with which to hold on to a shred of sanity.

'Jimmy was the only survivor,' Henry said. 'If the police had gotten there a few seconds later, Jimmy wouldn't have made it either. They shot the man down.' Henry's grip tightened slightly on Holly's hand. 'They found Jim in a corner, in Jamie's lap, in his daddy's lap, his daddy's arms, all covered with . . . with his daddy's blood.'

Holly remembered the end of the dream—

—the crazyman is coming straight at her, knocking tables and chairs aside, so she scrambles away and into a corner, on top of a dead body, and the crazyman is coming closer, closer, raising his gun, she can't bear to look at him the way the waitress looked at him and then died, so she turns her face to the corpse—

—and she remembered awakening with a jolt, gagging in revulsion.

If she'd had time to look into the face of the corpse, she would have seen Jim's father.

The avian shriek shrilled through the recreation room again. It was louder this time. A couple of the ambulatory residents went to the fireplace to see if any birds were caught behind the damper in the chimney.

'In his daddy's blood,' Henry repeated softly. It was clear that, even after all these years, the consideration of that moment was intolerably painful to him.

The boy had not only been in his dead father's arms but surely had known that his mother lay dead among the ruins, and that he was orphaned, alone.

*   *   *

Jim sat on a redwood bench in the Fair Haven courtyard. He was alone.

For a day late in August, when the seasonal drought should have been at its peak, the sky was unusually heavy with unshed moisture, yet it looked like an inverted bowl of ashes. Mixes of late-summer flowers, cascading from planting beds on to the wide concrete walkways, were missing half their color without the enhancement of sunshine. The trees shivered as if chilled by the mild August breeze.

Something was coming. Something bad was coming.

He clung to Holly's theory, told himself that nothing would come unless he caused it to appear. He only had to control himself, and they would all survive.

But he still felt it coming.

Something.

He heard the screaky cries of birds.

*   *   *

The birds had fallen silent.

After a while Holly let go of Henry Ironheart's hand, took some Kleenex from her purse, blew her nose, and blotted her eyes. When she could speak, she said, 'He blames himself for what happened to his mom and dad.'

'I know. He always did. He'd never talk about it, but there were ways it showed, how he blamed himself, how he thought he should have saved them.'

'But why? He was only ten years old, a small boy. He couldn't have done anything about a grown man with a submachine gun. For God's sake, how could he feel responsible?'

For the moment, the brightness had gone out of Henry's eyes. His poor lopsided face, already pulled down to the right, was pulled down farther by an inexpressible sadness.

At last he said, 'I talked to him about it lots of times, took him on my lap and held him and talked about it, like Lena did, too, but he was so much locked in himself, wouldn't open up, wouldn't say why he blamed himself – hated himself.'

Holly looked at her watch.

She had left Jim alone too long.

But she could not interrupt Henry Ironheart in the middle of the revelations that she had come to hear.

'I've thought about it all these long years,' Henry continued, 'and maybe I figured it out a little. But by the time I started to understand, Jim was grown up, and we'd stopped talking about Atlanta so many years ago. To be completely honest, we'd stopped talking about everything by then.'

'So what is it you figured out?'

Henry put his weak right hand in his strong left and stared down at the gnarled lumps that his knuckles made within his time-thinned skin. From the old man's attitude, Holly sensed that he was not sure he should reveal what he needed and wanted to reveal.

'I love him, Henry.'

He looked up and met her eyes.

She said, 'Earlier you said I'd come here to learn about Atlanta because Jim wouldn't talk about it, and in a way you were right. I came to find out a number of things, because he's frozen me out of some areas of his life. He really loves me, Henry, I've no doubt of that, but he's clenched up like a fist, he can't let loose of certain

323

things. If I'm going to marry him, if it's going to come to that, then I've got to know all about him – or we'll never have a chance to be happy. You can't build a life together on mysteries.'

'Of course, you're right.'

'Tell me why Jim blames himself. It's killing him, Henry. If I have any hope of helping him, I've got to know what you know.'

He sighed and made up his mind. 'What I've got to say will sound like superstitious nonsense, but it isn't. I'll make it simple and short, 'cause it sounds even screwier if I dress it up at all. My wife, Lena, had a power. Presentiment, you'd call it, I guess. Not that she could see the future, tell you who would win a horserace or where you'd be a year from now or anything like that. But sometimes . . . well, you might invite her to a picnic Sunday a week, and without thinking, she'd say it was going to rain like-for-Noah come Sunday a week. And by God it would. Or some neighbor would be pregnant, and Lena would start referring to the baby as either a "he" or a "she", when there was no way for her to know which it would be – and she was always right.'

Holly sensed some of the last pieces of the puzzle falling into place. When Henry gave her a maybe-you-think-I'm-an-old-fool look, she took his bad hand and held it reassuringly.

After studying her a moment, he said, 'You've seen something special Jim did, haven't you, something like magic?'

'Yes.'

'So you maybe know where this is going.'

'Maybe.'

The unseen birds began to screech again. The residents at the television set turned the sound off and looked around, trying to identify the source of the squealing.

Holly looked toward the courtyard window. No birds there. But she knew why their cries made the hair stand up on the back of her neck: they were somehow connected with Jim. She remembered the way he had looked up at them in the graveyard and how he had studied them in the sky during the drive to Solvang.

'Jamie, our son, was like his mother,' Henry said, as if he did not even hear the birds. 'He just sometimes *knew* things. Fact is, he was a little more gifted than Lena. And after Jamie had been married to Cara for a while, when she got pregnant, Lena just one day up and said, "The baby's going to be special, he's going to be a real mage." '

'Mage?'

'Country talk for someone with a power, with something special about him the way Lena had something special and Jamie too. Only she meant *real* special. So Jim was born, and by the time he was four . . . well, he was doing things. Like once he touched my pocket comb, which I'd bought at the local barber shop here, and he started talking about things that were in the shop, though he'd never been in there in his life 'cause he lived with Jamie and Cara down in Los Angeles.'

He paused and took a few deep breaths. The slur in his voice had begun to thicken. His right eyelid drooped. Talking seemed to tire him as if it were a physical labor.

A male nurse with a flashlight was at the fireplace. He was squinting up into the flue, past the cracks around the damper, trying to see if any birds were trapped up in there.

The shrieking was now overlaid by the frenzied flapping of wings.

'Jimmy would touch an item and *know* where it'd been, bits and pieces about who owned it. Not everything about them, mind you. He just knew whatever he knew, that was it. Maybe he'd touch a personal item of yours and know the names of your parents, what you did for a living. Then he'd touch a personal item from someone else and only know where they'd gone to school, names of their children. Always different things, he couldn't control it. But he always came up with *something* when he tried.'

The nurse, trailed by three patients offering advice, had moved away from the fireplace and was frowning up at the air-conditioning vents. The quarrelsome sound of birds still echoed through the room.

'Let's go out to the courtyard,' Holly said, getting up.

'Wait,' Henry said with some distress, 'let me finish this, let me tell you.'

Jim, for God's sake, Holly thought, hold on another minute, just another minute or two.

Reluctantly she sat down.

Henry said, 'Jim's specialness was a family secret, like Lena's and Jamie's. We didn't want the world to know, come snooping around, call us freaks and God knows what. But Cara, she always wanted so bad to be in show business. Jamie worked down there at Warner Brothers, which was where he'd met her, and he wanted what Cara wanted. They decided they could form an act with Jimmy, call him the boy-wonder mentalist, but nobody would ever suspect he really had a power. They played it as a trick, lots of winking at the audience, daring them to figure out just how it was all done – when all the time it was *real*. They made a good living at it too, and it was good for them as a family, kept them together every day. They'd been so close before the act, but they were closer than ever after they went on the road. No parents ever loved their child more than they loved Jim – or ever got more love given back to them. They were so close . . . it was impossible to think of them ever being apart.'

*　*　*

Blackbirds streaked across the bleak sky.

Sitting on the redwood bench, Jim stared up at them.

They almost vanished into the eastern clouds, then turned sharply and came back.

For a while they kited overhead.

Those dark, jagged forms against the sere sky composed an image that might have come from some poem by Edgar Allan Poe. As a kid he'd had a passion for Poe and had memorized all of the more macabre pieces of his poetry. Morbidity had its fascination.

*　*　*

The bird shrieks suddenly stopped. The resulting quiet was a blessing, but Holly was, oddly, more frightened by the cessation of the cries than she had been by the eerie sound of them.

'And the power grew,' Henry Ironheart said softly, thickly. He shifted in his wheelchair, and his right side resisted settling into a new position. For the first time he showed some frustration at the limitations of his stroke-altered body. 'By the time Jim was six, you could put a penny on the table, and he could move it just by *wanting* it to move, slide it back and forth, make it stand on end. By the time he was eight, he could pitch it in the air, float it there. By the time he was ten, he could do the same with a quarter, a phonograph record, a cake tin. It was the most amazing thing you ever saw.'

You should see what he can do at thirty-five, Holly thought.

'They never used any of that in their act,' Henry said, 'they just stuck to the mentalism, taking personal items from members of the audience, so Jim could tell them things about themselves that just, you know, astonished them. Jamie and Cara figured to include some of his levitations eventually, but they just hadn't figured out how to do it yet without giving the truth away. Then they went to the Dixie Duck down in Atlanta . . . and that was the end of everything.'

Not the end of everything. It was the end of one thing, the dark beginning of another.

She realized why the absence of the birds' screams was more disturbing than the sound itself. The cries had been like the hiss of a sparking fuse as it burned down toward an explosive charge. As long as she could hear the sound, the explosion was still preventable.

'And *that's* why I figure Jim thought he should've been able to save them,' Henry said. 'Because he could do those little things with his mind, float and move things, he thought he should've been able maybe to jam the bullets in that crazy man's gun, freeze the trigger, lock the safety in place, something, something . . .'

'Could he have done that?'

'Yeah, maybe. But he was just a scared little boy. To do those things with pennies and records and cake tins, he had to concentrate. No time to concentrate when the bullets started flying that day.'

Holly remembered the murderous sound: *chuda-chuda-chuda-chuda* . . .

'So when we brought him back from Atlanta, he would hardly talk, just a word or two now and then. Wouldn't meet your eyes. Something died in him when Jamie and Cara died, and we could never bring it back again, no matter how much we loved him and how hard we tried. His power died too. Or seemed to. He never did one of his tricks again, and after a lot of years it was sometimes hard to believe he'd ever done those strange things when he was little.'

In spite of his good spirits, Henry Ironheart had looked every one of his eighty years. Now he appeared to be far older, ancient.

He said, 'Jimmy was so strange after Atlanta, so unreachable and full of rage . . . sometimes it was possible to love him and still be a little afraid of him. Later, God forgive me, I suspected him of . . .'

'I know,' Holly said.

His slack features tightened, and he looked sharply at her.

'Your wife,' she said. 'Lena. The way she died.'

More thickly than usual, he said, 'You know so much.'

'Too much,' she said. 'Which is funny. Because all my life I've known too little.'

327

Henry looked down at his culpable hands again. 'How could I believe that a boy of ten, even a disturbed boy, could've shoved her down the mill stairs when he loved her so much? Too many years later, I saw that I'd been so damned cruel to him, so unfeeling, so damned stupid. By then, he wouldn't give me the chance to apologize for what I'd done . . . what I'd thought. After he left for college, he never came back. Not once in more than thirteen years, until I had my stroke.'

He came back once, Holly thought, nineteen years after Lena's death, to face up to it and put flowers on her grave.

Henry said, 'If there was some way I could explain to him, if he'd just give me one chance . . .'

'He's here now,' Holly said, getting up again.

The weight of fear that pulled on the old man's face made him appear even more gaunt than he had been. 'Here?'

'He's come to give you that chance,' was all that Holly could say. 'Do you want me to take you to him?'

* * *

The blackbirds were flocking. Eight of them had gathered now in the sky above, circling.

> *Once upon a midnight dreary, while I pondered, weak and*
>   *weary*
> *Over many a quaint and curious volume of forgotten lore—*
> *While I nodded, nearly napping, suddenly there came a*
>   *tapping,*
> *As of some one gently rapping, rapping at my chamber door.*

To the real birds above, Jim whispered, ' "Quoth the Raven, *Nevermore.*" '

He heard a soft rhythmic creaking, as of a wheel going around and around, and footsteps. When he looked up, he saw Holly pushing his wheelchair-bound grandfather along the walkway toward the bench.

Eighteen years had passed since he had gone away to college, and he had seen Henry only once before in all this time. Initially, there had been a few telephone calls, but soon Jim stopped making those and, eventually, stopped accepting them as well. When letters came, he threw them away unopened. He remembered all of that now – and he was beginning to remember why.

He began to rise. His legs would not support him. He remained on the bench.

* * *

Holly parked the wheelchair facing Jim, then sat beside him. 'How you doing?'

Nodding dumbly, he glanced up at the birds circling against the ashen clouds, rather than face his grandfather.

The old man could not look at Jim, either. He studied the beds of flowers intently, as if he had been in a great rush to get outside and have a look at those blooms and nothing else.

Holly knew this was not going to be easy. She was sympathetic toward each of the men and wanted to do her best to bring them together at last.

First, she had to burn away the tangled weeds of one last lie that Jim had told her and that, consciously if not subconsciously he had successfully told himself. 'There was no traffic accident, honey,' she said, putting a hand on his knee. 'That isn't how it happened.'

Jim lowered his eyes from the blackbirds and regarded her with nervous expectation. She could see that he longed to know the truth and dreaded hearing it.

'It happened in a restaurant—'

Jim slowly shook his head in denial.

'—down in Atlanta, Georgia—'

He was still shaking his head, but his eyes were widening.

'—you were with them—'

He stopped denying, and a terrible expression stained his face.

'—it was called the Dixie Duck,' she said.

When the memory exploded back to him with pile-driver force, he hunched forward on the bench as if he might vomit, but he did not. He curled his hands into fists on his knees, and his face tightened into a clench of pain, and he made small inarticulate sounds that were beyond grief and horror.

She put an arm around his bent shoulders.

Henry Ironheart looked at her and said, 'Oh, my God,' as he began to realize the extremity of denial to which his grandson had been driven. 'Oh, my God.' As Jim's strangled gasps of pain changed into quiet sobs, Henry Ironheart looked at the flowers again, then at his aged hands, then at his feet on the tilted braces of the wheelchair, everywhere he could think to look to avoid Jim and Holly, but at last he met Holly's eyes again. 'He had therapy,' he said, trying hard to expiate his guilt. 'We knew he might need therapy. We took him to a psychiatrist in Santa Barbara. Took him there several times. We did what we could. But the psychiatrist – Hemphill, his name was – he said Jim was all right, he said there was no reason to bring him any more, just after six visits, he said Jim was all right.'

Holly said, 'What do they ever know? What could Hemphill have done when he didn't really know the boy, didn't love him?'

Henry Ironheart flinched as if she had struck him, though she had not meant her comment to be a condemnation of him.

'No,' she said quickly, hoping he would believe her, 'what I meant was, there's no mystery why I've gotten farther than Hemphill ever could. It's just because I love him. It's the only thing that ever leads to healing.' Stroking Jim's hair, she said, 'You couldn't have saved them, baby. You didn't have the power then, not like you have it now. You were lucky to get out alive. Believe me, honey, listen and believe me.'

For a moment they sat unspeaking, all of them in pain.

Holly noticed more blackbirds had gathered in the sky. Maybe a dozen of them now. She didn't know how Jim was drawing them there – or why – but she knew that he was, and regarded them with growing dread.

She put a hand over one of Jim's hands, encouraging him to relax it. Though he slowly stopped crying, he kept his fist as tight as a fist of sculpted stone.

To Henry, she said, 'Now. This is your chance. Explain why you turned away from him, why you did . . . whatever you did to him.'

Clearing his throat, wiping nervously at his mouth with his weak right hand, Henry spoke at first without looking at either of them. 'Well . . . you have to know . . . how it was. A few months after he came back from Atlanta, there was this film company in town, shooting a movie—'

'The Black Windmill,' Holly said.

'Yeah. He was reading all the time . . .' Henry stopped, closed his eyes as if to gather strength. When he opened them, he stared at Jim's bowed head and seemed prepared to meet his eyes if he looked up. 'You were reading all the time, going through the library shelf by shelf, and because of the film you read the Willott book. For a while it became . . . hell, I don't know . . . I guess maybe you'd have to say it was an obsession with you, Jim. It was the only thing that brought you out of your shell, talking about that book, so we encouraged you to go watch them shoot the picture. Remember? After a while, you started telling us an alien was in our pond and windmill, just like in the book and movie. At first we thought you were just play-acting.'

He paused.

The silence lengthened.

About twenty birds in the sky above.

Circling. Silent.

To Henry, Holly said, 'Then it began to worry you.'

Henry wiped one shaky hand down his deeply lined face, not so much as if he was trying to scrub away his weariness but as if he was trying to slough off the years and bring that lost time closer. 'You spent more and more hours in the mill, Jim. Sometimes you'd be out there all day. And evenings too. Sometimes we'd get up in the middle of the night to use the john, and we'd see a light out there in the mill, two or three or four o'clock in the morning. And you wouldn't be in your room.'

Henry paused more often. He wasn't tired. He just didn't want to dig into this part of the long-buried past.

'If it was the middle of the night, we'd go out there to the mill and bring you in, either me or Lena. And you'd be telling us about The Friend in the mill. You started spooking us, we didn't know what to do . . . so I guess . . . we didn't do anything. Anyway, that night . . . the night she died . . . a storm was coming up—'

Holly recalled the dream:

. . . a fresh wind blows as she hurries along the gravel path . . .

'—and Lena didn't wake me. She went out there by herself and up to the high room—'

. . . she climbs the limestone stairs . . .

'—pretty good thunderstorm, but I used to be able to sleep through anything—'

. . . the heavens flash as she passes the stairwell window, and through the glass she sees an object in the pond below . . .

'—I guess, Jim, you were just doing what we always found you doing out there at night, reading that book by candlelight—'

. . . inhuman sounds from above quicken her heart, and she climbs to the high room, afraid, but also curious and concerned for Jim . . .

'—a crash of thunder finally woke me—'

. . . she reaches the top of the stairs and sees him standing, hands fisted at his sides, a yellow candle in a blue dish on the floor, a book beside the candle . . .

331

'—I realized Lena was gone, looked out the bedroom window, and saw that dim light in the mill—'

. . . the boy turns to her and cries out, *I'm scared, help me, the walls, the walls!* . . .

'—and I couldn't believe my eyes because the sails of the mill were turning, and even in those days the sails hadn't turned in ten or fifteen years, been frozen up—'

. . . she sees an amber light within the walls, the sour shades of pus and bile; the limestone bulges, and she realizes something is impossibly *alive* in the stone . . .

'—but they were spinning like airplane propellors, so I pulled on my pants, and hurried downstairs—'

. . . with fear but also with perverse excitement, the boy says, *It's coming, and nobody can stop it!* . . .

'—I grabbed a flashlight and ran out into the rain—'

. . . the curve of mortared blocks splits like the spongy membrane of an insect's egg; taking shape from a core of foul muck, where limestone should have been, is the embodiment of the boy's black rage at the world and its injustice, his self-hatred made flesh, his own death-wish given a vicious and brutal form so solid that it is an entity itself, quite separate from him . . .

'—I reached the mill, couldn't believe how those old sails were spinning, whoosh, whoosh, whoosh!—'

Holly's dream had ended there, but her imagination too easily supplied a version of what might have happened thereafter. Horrified at the materialization of The Enemy, stunned that the boy's wild tales of aliens in the mill were true, Lena had stumbled backward and fallen down the winding stone stairs, unable to arrest her fall because there was no handrail at which to grab. Somewhere along the way she broke her neck.

'—went inside the mill . . . found her at the bottom of the stairs all busted up, neck twisted . . . dead.'

Henry paused for the first time in a while and swallowed hard. He had not looked at Holly once throughout his account of that stormy night, only at Jim's bowed head. With less of a slur in his voice, as if it were vitally important to him to tell the rest of it as clearly as he could, he said:

'I went up the steps and found you in the high room, Jimmy. Do you remember that? Sitting by the candle, holding the book in your hands so tight it couldn't be taken from you till hours later. You wouldn't speak.' The old man's voice quavered now. 'God forgive me, but all I could think about was Lena being dead, my dear Lena gone, and you being such a strange child all year, and still strange even at that moment, with your book, refusing to talk to me. I guess . . . I guess I went a little mad right then, for a while. I thought you might've pushed her, Jimmy. I thought you might've been in one of your . . . upsets . . . and maybe you pushed her.'

As if it had become too much for him to address himself to his grandson any longer, Henry shifted his gaze to Holly. 'That year after Atlanta, he'd been a strange boy . . . almost like a boy we didn't know. He was quiet, like I said, but there was rage in him, too, a fury like no child should ever have. It sometimes scared us. The only time he ever showed it was in his sleep . . . dreaming . . . we'd hear him screeching, and we'd go down the hall to his room . . . and he'd be kicking and punching at the mattress, the pillows, clawing at the sheets, furious, taking it all out on something in his dreams, and we'd have to wake him.'

Henry paused and looked away from Holly, down at his bent right hand, which lay half useless in his lap.

Jim's fist, under Holly's hand, remained vise-tight.

'You never struck out at Lena or me, Jimmy, you were a good boy, never gave us that kind of trouble. But in the mill that night, I grabbed you and shook you, Jimmy, tried to make you admit how you'd pushed her down the stairs. There was no excuse for what I did, how I behaved . . . except I was grief-crazy over Jamie and Cara, and now over Lena, everyone dying around me, and there was only you, and you were so strange, so strange and locked up in yourself that you scared me, so I turned on you when I should have been taking you in my arms. Turned on you that night . . . and didn't realize what I'd done until a lot of years later . . . too late.'

The birds were in a tighter circle now. Directly overhead.

'Don't,' she said softly to Jim. 'Please don't.'

Until Jim responded, Holly could not know if these revelations were for better or worse. If he had blamed himself for his grandma's death merely because Henry had instilled the guilt in him, then he would get past this. If he blamed himself because Lena had come into the high room, had seen The Enemy materializing from the wall, and had stumbled backward down the stairs in terror, he might still overcome the past. But if The Enemy had torn itself free of the wall and *pushed* her . . .

'I treated you like a murderer for the next six years, until you went away to college,' Henry said. 'When you were gone . . . well,

333

in time, I started to think about it with a clearer head, and I knew what I'd done. You'd had nowhere to turn for comfort. Your mum and dad were gone, your grandma. You went into town to get books, but you couldn't join in with other kids because that little Zacca bastard, Ned Zacca, he was twice your size and wouldn't ever let you alone. You had no peace except in books. I tried to call you, but you wouldn't take the calls. I wrote but I think you never read the letters.'

Jim sat unmoving.

Henry Ironheart shifted his attention to Holly. 'He came back at last when I had my stroke. He sat beside me when I was in intensive care. I couldn't speak right, couldn't say what I tried to say, the wrong words kept coming out, making no sense—'

'Aphasia,' Holly said. 'A result of the stroke.'

Henry nodded. 'Once, hooked up to all those machines, I tried to tell him what I'd known for almost thirteen years – that he wasn't a killer and that I'd been cruel to him.' New tears flooded his eyes. 'But when it came out, it wasn't right at all, not what I meant, and he misunderstood it, thought I'd *called* him a murderer and was afraid of him. He left, and now's the first I've seen him since. More than four years.'

Jim sat with his head bowed.

Hands fisted.

What had he remembered of that night in the mill, the part that no one but him could know?

Holly got up from the bench, unable to endure the wait for Jim's reaction. She stood there, with no idea where to go. At last she sat down again. She put her hand over his fist, as before.

She looked up.

More birds. Maybe thirty of them now.

'I'm afraid,' Jim said, but that was all.

'After that night,' Henry said, 'he never went into the mill again, never mentioned The Friend or the Willott book. And at first I thought it was good he turned away from that obsession . . . he seemed less strange. But later I've wondered . . . maybe he lost the one comfort he had.'

'I'm afraid to remember,' Jim said.

She knew what he meant: only one last long-hidden memory waited to be revealed. Whether his grandmother had died by accident. Or whether The Enemy had killed her. Whether *he*, as The Enemy, had killed her.

Unable to stare at Jim's bowed head a moment longer, unable

to bear Henry Ironheart's wretched look of guilt and fragile hope, Holly glanced up at the birds again – and saw them coming. More than thirty of them now, dark knives slicing down through the somber sky, still high up but coming straight toward the courtyard.

'Jim, no!'

Henry looked up.

Jim lifted his face, too, but not to see what was coming. He *knew* what was coming. He raised his face as if to offer his eyes to their sharp beaks and frenzied claws.

Holly leaped to her feet, making herself a more prominent target than he was. 'Jim, face it, remember it, for Christ's sake!'

She could hear the shrieks of the swiftly descending birds.

'Even if The Enemy did it,' she said, pulling Jim's upturned face to her breast, shielding him, 'you can get past that somehow, you can go on.'

Henry Ironheart cried out in shock, and the birds burst over Holly, flapping and squirming against her, swooping away, then more of them fluttering and scraping, trying to get past her and at Jim's face, at his eyes.

They didn't tear at her with either their beaks or talons, but she did not know how long they would spare her. They were The Enemy, after all, manifesting itself in a whole new way, and The Enemy hated her as much as it hated Jim.

The birds swirled out of the courtyard, back into the sky, gone like so many leaves in a violent updraft.

Henry Ironheart was frightened but unhurt. 'Move away,' she told him.

'No,' he said. He reached helplessly for Jim, who would not reach for him.

When Holly dared look up, she knew that the birds were not finished. They had only soared to the fringe of the bearded gray clouds, where another score of them had collected. Fifty or sixty now, churning and dark, hungry and quick.

She was aware of people at the windows and sliding glass doors that opened on to the courtyard. Two nurses came through the same slider that she had used when wheeling Henry out to meet Jim.

'Stay back!' she shouted at them, not sure how much danger they might be in.

Jim's rage, while directed at himself and perhaps at God for the very fact of death's existence, might nevertheless spill over and spend itself on the innocent. Her shouted warning must have frightened the nurses, for they retreated and stood in the doorway.

She raised her eyes again. The larger flock was coming.

'Jim,' she said urgently, holding his face in both hands, peering into his beautiful blue eyes, icy now with a cold fire of self-hatred, 'only one more step, only one more thing to remember.' Though their eyes were only a few inches apart, she did not believe that he saw her; he seemed to be looking through her as he had earlier in Tivoli Gardens when the burrowing creature had been racing at them.

The descending flock squealed demonically.

'Jim, damn you, what happened to Lena might not be *worth* suicide!'

The rustle-roar of wings filled the day. She pulled Jim's face against her body, and as before he did not struggle when she shielded him, which gave her hope. She bent her head and closed her eyes as tightly as she could.

They came: silken feathers; smooth cold beaks ticking, prying, searching; claws scrabbling gently, then not so gently, but still not drawing blood; swarming around her almost as if they were hungry rats, swirling, darting, fluttering, squirming along her back and legs, between her thighs, up along her torso, trying to get between his face and her bosom, where they could tear and gouge; batting against her head; and always the shrieking, as shrill as the cries of madwomen in a psychopathic fury, screaming in her ears, wordless demands for blood, blood, blood and then she felt a sharp pain in her arm as one of the flock ripped open her sleeve and pinched skin with it.

'No!'

They rose and departed again. Holly did not realize they were gone, because her own beating heart and fluttering breath continued to sound like thunderous wings to her. Then she raised her head, opened her eyes, and saw they were spiraling back into the leaden sky to join a storm cloud of other birds, a mass of dark bodies and wings, perhaps two hundred of them high overhead.

She glanced at Henry Ironheart. The birds had drawn blood from one of his hands. Having huddled back into his chair during the attack, he now leaned forward again, reached out with one hand, and called Jim's name pleadingly.

Holly looked down into Jim's eyes as he sat on the bench in front of her, and still he was not there. He was in the mill, most likely, on the night of the storm, looking at his grandmother just one second before the fall, frozen at that moment in time, unable to advance the memory-film one more frame.

The birds were coming.

They were still far away, just under the cloud cover, but there were so many of them now that the thunder of their wings carried a greater distance. Their shrieks were like the voices of the damned.

'Jim, you can take the path that Larry Kakonis took, you can kill yourself. I can't stop you. But if The Enemy doesn't want me any more, if it wants only you, don't think I'm spared. If you die, Jim, I'm dead too, as good as dead, I'll do what Larry Kakonis did, I'll kill myself, and I'll rot in hell with you if I can't have you anywhere else!'

The Enemy of countless parts fell upon her as she pulled Jim's face against her a third time. She didn't hide her own face or close her eyes as before, but stood in that maelstrom of wings and beaks and talons. She looked back into scores of small, glistening, pure-black eyes that circled her unblinking, each as wet and deep as the night reflected on the face of the sea, each as merciless and cruel as the universe itself and as anything in the heart of humankind. She knew that, staring into those eyes, she was staring into a part of Jim, his most secret and darkest part, which she could not reach otherwise, and she said his name. She did not shout, did not scream, did not beg or plead, did not vent her anger or fear, but said his name softly, again and again, with all the tenderness that she felt for him, with all the love she had. They battered against her so hard that pinions snapped, opened their hooked beaks and shrieked in her face, plucked threateningly at her clothes and hair, tugging but not ripping, giving her one last chance to flee. They tried to intimidate her with their eyes, the cold and uncaring eyes of beasts of prey, but she was not intimidated, she just kept repeating his name, then the promise that she loved him, over and over until—

—they were gone.

They didn't whirl up into the sky, as before. They vanished. One moment the air was filled with them and their fierce cries – but the next moment they were gone as if they had never been.

Holly held Jim against her for a moment, then let him go. He still looked through her more than at her and seemed to be in a trance.

'Jim,' Henry Ironheart said beseechingly, still reaching out toward his grandson.

After a hesitation, Jim slid off the bench, on to his knees in front of the old man. He took the withered hand and kissed it.

Without looking up at either Holly or Henry, Jim said, 'Grandma saw The Enemy coming out of the wall. First time it happened, first time I saw it too.' His voice sounded faraway, as if a part of him were still back in the past, reliving that dreaded moment, grateful that there had not been as much reason to dread it as he had thought. 'She saw it, and it frightened her, and she stumbled back into the stairs, tripped, fell . . .' He pressed his grandfather's hand to his cheek and said, 'I didn't kill her.'

'I know you didn't, Jim,' Henry Ironheart said. 'My God, I know you didn't.'

The old man looked up at Holly with a thousand questions about birds and enemies and things in walls. But she knew he would have to wait for answers until another day, as she had waited – as Jim had waited too.

•3•

During the drive over the mountains and down into Santa Barbara, Jim slumped in his seat, eyes closed. He seemed to have fallen into a deep sleep. She supposed he needed sleep as desperately as any man could need it, for he'd enjoyed almost no real rest in twenty-five years.

She was no longer afraid to let him sleep. She was certain that The Enemy was gone, with The Friend, and that only one personality inhabited his body now. Dreams were no longer doorways.

For the time being, she did not want to return to the mill, even though they had left some gear there. She'd had enough of Svenborg, too, and all it represented in Jim's life. She wanted to hole up in a new place, where neither of them had been, where new beginnings might be forged with no taint of the past.

As she drove through that parched land under the ashen sky, she put the pieces together and studied the resulting picture:

. . . an enormously gifted boy, far more gifted than even he knows, lives through the slaughter in the Dixie Duck, but comes out of the holocaust with a shattered soul. In his desperation to feel good about himself again, he borrows Arthur Willott's fantasy, using his special power to create The Friend, an embodiment of his most noble aspirations, and The Friend tells him he has a mission in life.

But the boy is so full of despair and rage that The Friend alone is not enough to heal him. He needs a third personality, something into which he can shove all his negative feelings, all the darkness in himself that frightens him. So he creates The Enemy, embellishing Willott's story structure. Alone in the windmill, he has exhilarating conversations with The Friend – and works out his rage through the materialization of The Enemy.

Until, one night, Lena Ironheart walks in at the wrong moment. Frightened, she falls backward . . .

In shock because of what The Enemy has done, merely by its presence, Jim forces himself to forget the fantasy, both The Friend and The Enemy, just as Jim Jamison forgot his alien encounter after saving the life of the future President of the United States. For twenty-five years, he struggles to keep a lid firmly on those fragmented personalities, suppressing both his very best and his very worst qualities, leading a relatively quiet and colorless life because he dares not tap his stronger feelings.

He finds purpose in teaching, which to some extent redeems him – until Larry Kakonis commits suicide. Without purpose any more, feeling that he has failed Kakonis as he failed his parents and, even more profoundly, his grandmother, he subconsciously longs to live out Jim Jamison's courageous and redeeming adventure, which means freeing The Friend.

But when he frees The Friend, he frees The Enemy as well. And after all these years of being bottled inside him, his rage has only intensified, become blacker and more bitter, utterly inhuman in its intensity. The Enemy is something even more evil now than it was twenty-five years ago, a creature of singularly murderous appearance and temperament . . .

So Jim was like any victim of multiple-personality syndrome. Except for one thing. One little thing. He created nonhuman entities to embody aspects of himself, not other human identities – and had the power to give them flesh of their own. He hadn't been like Sally Field playing Sybil, sixteen people in one body. He had been three beings in three bodies, and one of them had been a killer.

Holly turned on the car heater. Though it must have been seventy degrees outside, she was chilled. The heat from the dashboard vents did nothing to warm her.

*　　*　　*

The clock behind the registration desk showed 1:11 p.m. when Holly checked them into a quality motor lodge in Santa Barbara. While she filled out the form and provided her credit card to the clerk, Jim continued to sleep in the Ford.

When she returned with their key, she was able to rouse him enough to get him out of the car and into their room. He was in a stupor and went directly to the bed, where he curled up and once more fell instantly into a deep sleep.

She got diet sodas, ice, and candy bars from the vending-machine center near the pool.

In the room again, she closed the drapes. She switched on one lamp and arranged a towel over the shade to soften the light.

She pulled a chair near the bed and sat down. She drank diet soda and ate candy while she watched him sleep.

The worst was over. The fantasy had been burned away, and he had plunged completely into cold reality.

But she did not know what the aftermath would bring. She had never known him without his delusions, and she didn't know what he would be like when he had none. She didn't know if he would be a more optimistic man – or a darker one. She didn't know if he would still have the same degree of superhuman powers that he'd had before. He had summoned those powers from within himself only because he had needed them to sustain his fantasy and cling to his precarious sanity; perhaps, now, he would be only as gifted as he had been before his parents had died – able to levitate a pie pan, flip a coin with his mind, nothing more. Worst of all, she didn't know if he would still love her.

By dinner time he was still asleep.

She went out and got more candy bars. Another binge. She *would* end up as plump as her mother if she didn't get control of herself.

He was still asleep at ten o'clock. Eleven. Midnight.

She considered waking him. But she realized that he was in a chrysalis, waiting to be born from his old life into a new one. A caterpillar needed time to turn itself into a butterfly. That was her hope, anyway.

Sometime between midnight and one o'clock in the morning, Holly fell asleep in her chair. She did not dream.

He woke her.

She looked up into his beautiful eyes, which were not cold in the dim light of the towel-draped lamp, but which were still mysterious.

340

He was leaning over her chair, shaking her gently. 'Holly, come on. We've got to go.'

Instantly casting off sleep, she sat up. 'Go where?'

'Scranton, Pennsylvania.'

'Why?'

Grabbing up one of her uneaten candy bars, peeling off the wrapper, biting into it, he said, 'Tomorrow afternoon, three-thirty, a reckless school bus driver is going to try to beat a train at a crossing. Twenty-six kids are going to die if we're not there first.'

Rising from her chair, she said, 'You know all that, the whole thing, not just a part of it?'

'Of course,' he said around a mouthful of candy bar. He grinned. 'I know these things, Holly. I'm psychic, for God's sake.'

She grinned right back at him.

'We're going to be something, Holly,' he said enthusiastically. 'Superman? Why the hell did he waste so much time holding down a job on a newspaper when he could've been doing good?'

In a voice that cracked with relief and with love for him, Holly said, 'I always wondered about that.'

Jim gave her a chocolaty kiss. 'The world hasn't seen anything like us, kid. Of course, you're going to have to learn martial arts, how to handle a gun, a few other things. But you're gonna be good at it, I know you are.'

She threw her arms around him and hugged him fiercely, with unadulterated joy.

Purpose.

THE FACE
OF FEAR

For Barbara Norville

Part One

FRIDAY
12:01 A.M.–8:00 P.M.

•1•

Wary, not actually expecting trouble but prepared for it, he parked his car across the street from the four-story brownstone apartment house. When he switched off the engine, he heard a siren wail in the street behind him.

They're coming for me, he thought. Somehow they've found out I'm the one.

He smiled. He wouldn't let them put the handcuffs on him. He wouldn't go easily. That wasn't his style.

Frank Bollinger was not easily frightened. In fact, he couldn't remember *ever* having been frightened. He knew how to take care of himself. He had reached six feet when he was thirteen years old, and he hadn't quit growing until he was six-four. He had a thick neck, broad shoulders and the biceps of a young weightlifter. At thirty-seven he was in virtually the same good condition, at least outwardly, as he had been when he was twenty seven – or even seventeen. Curiously enough, he never exercised. He had neither the time nor the temperament for endless series of push-ups and sit-ups and running in place. His size and his hard-packed muscles were nature's gifts, simply a matter of genetics. Although he had a voracious appetite and never dieted, he was not girdled with rings of extra weight in the hips and stomach, as were most men his age. His doctor had explained to him that, because he suffered constantly from extreme nervous tension and because he refused to take the drugs that would bring his condition under control, he would most likely die young of hypertension. Strain, anxiety, nervous tension – these were what kept the weight off him, said the doctor. Wound tight, roaring inside like a perpetually accelerating engine, he burned away the fat, regardless of how much he ate.

But Bollinger found that he could agree with only half of that diagnosis. Nervous: no. Tension: yes. He was never nervous; that word had no meaning for him. However, he was always tense. He *strove* for tension, worked at building it, for he thought of it as a survival factor. He was always watchful. Always aware. Always tense. Always ready. Ready for anything. That was why there was nothing that he feared: nothing on earth could surprise him.

As the siren grew louder, he glanced at the rear-view mirror. A bit more than a block away, a revolving red light pulsed in the night.

He took the .38 revolver out of his shoulder holster. He put one hand on the door and waited for the right moment to throw it open.

The squad car bore down on him – then swept past. It turned the corner two blocks away.

They weren't on his trail after all.

He felt slightly disappointed.

He put the gun away and studied the street. Six mercury vapor street lamps – two at each end of the block and two in the middle – drenched the pavement and the automobiles and the buildings in an eerie purple-white light. The street was lined with three- and four-story town houses, some of them brownstones and some brick, most of them in good repair. There didn't seem to be anyone at any of the lighted windows. That was good; he did not want to be seen. A few trees struggled for life at the edges of the sidewalks, the scrawny plane trees and maples and birches that were all that New York City could boast beyond the boundaries of its public parks, all of them stunted trees, skeletal, their branches like charred bones reaching for the midnight sky. A gentle but chilly January wind pushed scraps of paper along the gutters; and when the wind gusted, the branches of the trees rattled like children's sticks on a rail fence. The other parked cars looked like animals huddling against the cold air; they were empty. Both sidewalks were deserted for the length of the block.

He got out of the car, quickly crossed the street and went up the front steps of the apartment house.

The foyer was clean and brightly lighted. The complex mosaic floor – a garland of faded roses on a beige background – was highly polished, and there were no pieces of tile missing from it. The inner foyer door was locked and could only be opened by key or with a lock-release button in one of the apartments.

There were three apartments on the top floor, three on the second floor and two on the ground level. Apartment 1A belonged to Mr and Mrs Harold Nagly, the owners of the building, who were on their annual pilgrimage to Miami Beach. The small apartment at the rear of the first floor was occupied by Edna Mowry, and he supposed that right now Edna would be having a midnight snack or a well-deserved martini to help her relax after a long night's work.

He had come to see Edna. He knew she would be home. He had followed her for six nights now, and he knew that she lived by strict routine, much too strict for such a young and attractive woman. She always arrived home from work at twelve, seldom more than five minutes later.

Pretty little Edna, he thought. You've got such long and lovely legs.

He smiled.

He pressed the call button for Mr and Mrs Yardley on the third floor.

A man's voice echoed tinnily from the speaker at the top of the mailbox. 'Who is it?'

'Is this the Hutchinson apartment?' Bollinger asked, knowing full well that it was not.

'You pressed the wrong button, mister. The Hutchinsons are on the second floor. Their mailbox is next to ours.'

'Sorry,' Bollinger said as Yardley broke the connection.

He rang the Hutchinson apartment.

The Hutchinsons, apparently expecting visitors and less cautious than the Yardleys, buzzed him through the inner door without asking who he was.

The downstairs hall was pleasantly warm. The brown tile floor and tan walls were spotless. Halfway along the corridor, a marble bench stood on the left, and a large beveled mirror hung above it. Both apartment doors, dark wood with brassy fixtures, were on the right.

He stopped in front of the second door and flexed his gloved fingers. He pulled his wallet from an inside coat pocket and took a knife from an overcoat pocket. When he touched the button on the burnished handle, the spring-hinged blade popped into sight; it was seven inches long, thin and nearly as sharp as a razor.

The gleaming blade transfixed Bollinger and caused bright images to flicker behind his eyes.

He was an admirer of William Blake's poetry; indeed, he fancied himself an intimate spiritual student of Blake's. It was not surprising, then, that a passage from Blake's work should come to him at that moment, flowing through his mind like blood running down the troughs in an autopsy table.

> *Then the inhabitants of those cities*
> *Felt their nerves change into marrow,*
> *And the hardening bones began*

In swift diseases and torments,
In shootings and throbbings and grindings
Through all the coasts; till, weakened,
The senses inward rushed, shrinking
Beneath the dark net of infection.

I'll change their bones to marrow, sure as hell, Bollinger thought. I'll have the inhabitants of *this* city hiding behind their doors at night. Except that I'm not the infection; I'm the cure. I'm the cure for all that's wrong with this world.

He rang the bell. After a moment he heard her on the other side of the door, and he rang the bell again.

'Who is it?' she asked. She had a pleasant, almost musical voice, marked now with a thin note of apprehension.

'Miss Mowry?' he asked.

'Yes?'

'Police.'

She didn't reply.

'Miss Mowry? Are you there?'

'What's it about?'

'Some trouble where you work.'

'I never cause trouble.'

'I didn't say that. The trouble doesn't involve you. At least not directly. But you might have seen something important. You might have been a witness.'

'To what?'

'That will take a while to explain.'

'I couldn't have been a witness. Not me. I wear blinders in that place.'

'Miss Mowry,' he said sternly, 'if I must get a warrant in order to question you, I will.'

'How do I know you're really the police?'

'New York,' Bollinger said with mock exasperation. 'Isn't it just wonderful? Everyone suspects everyone else.'

'They have to.'

He sighed. 'Perhaps. Look, Miss Mowry, do you have a security chain on the door?'

'Of course.'

'Of course. Well, leave the chain on and open up. I'll show you my identification.'

Hesitantly, she slid back a bolt lock. The chain lock allowed the door to open an inch and no farther.

He held up his wallet. 'Detective Bollinger,' he said. The knife was in his left hand, pointed at the floor, pressed flat against his overcoat.

She squinted through the narrow crack. She peered for a moment at the badge that was pinned to the inside of his wallet, then carefully studied the photo-identification card in the plastic window below the badge.

When she stopped squinting at the ID and looked up at him, he saw that her eyes were not blue, as he had thought – having seen her no closer than when she was on stage and he was in the shadowed audience – but a deep shade of green. They were truly the most attractive eyes he had ever seen. 'Satisfied?' he asked.

Her thick dark hair had fallen across one eye. She pushed it away from her face. Her fingers were long and perfectly formed, the nails painted blood red. When she was on stage, bathed in that intense spotlight, her nails appeared to be black. She said, 'What's this trouble you mentioned?'

'I have quite a number of questions to ask you, Miss Mowry. Must we discuss this through a crack in the door for the next twenty minutes?'

Frowning, she said, 'I suppose not. Wait there just a minute while I put on a robe.'

'I can wait. Patience is the key to content.'

She looked at him curiously.

'Mohammed,' he said.

'A cop who quotes Mohammed?'

'Why not?'

'Are you – of that religion?'

'No.' He was amused at the way she phrased the question. 'It's just that I've acquired a considerable amount of knowledge for the sole purpose of shocking those people who think all policemen are hopelessly ignorant.'

She winced. 'Sorry.' Then she smiled. He had not seen her smile before, not once in the entire week since he had first seen her. She had stood in that spotlight, moving with the music, shedding her clothes, bumping, grinding, caressing her own bare breasts, observing her audience with the cold eyes and almost lipless expression of a snake. Her smile was dazzling.

'Get your robe, Miss Mowry.'

She closed the door.

Bollinger watched the foyer door at the end of the hall, hoping no one would come in or go out while he was standing there, exposed.

He put away his wallet.

He kept the knife in his left hand.

In less than a minute she returned. She removed the security chain, opened the door and said, 'Come in.'

He stepped past her, inside.

She closed the door and put the bolt lock in place and turned to him and said, 'Whatever trouble –'

Moving quickly for such a large man he slammed her against the door, brought up the knife, shifted it from his left hand to his right hand, and lightly pricked her throat with the point of the blade.

Her green eyes were very wide. She'd had the breath knocked out of her and could not scream.

'No noise,' Bollinger said fiercely. 'If you try to call for help, I'll push this pig sticker straight into your lovely throat. I'll ram it right out the back of your neck. Do you understand?'

She stared at him.

'*Do you understand?*'

'Yes,' she said thinly.

'Are you going to cooperate?'

She said nothing. Her gaze traveled down from his eyes, over his proud nose and full lips and strong jawline, down to his fist and to the handle of the knife.

'If you aren't going to cooperate,' he said quietly, 'I can skewer you right here. I'll pin you to the damn door.' He was breathing hard.

A tremor passed through her.

He grinned.

Still trembling, she said, 'What do you want?'

'Not much. Not very much at all. Just a little loving.'

She closed her eyes. 'Are you – him?'

A slender, all but invisible thread of blood trickled from beneath the needlelike point of the knife, slid along her throat to the neck of her bright red robe. Watching the minuscule flow of blood as if he were a scientist observing an extremely rare bacterium through a microscope, pleased by it, nearly mesmerized by it, he said, 'Him? Who is "him"? I don't know what you're talking about.'

'You know,' she said weakly.

'I'm afraid not.'

'Are you *him*?' She bit her lip. 'The one who – who's cut up all those other women?'

Looking up from her throat, he said, 'I see. I see how it is. Of course. You mean the one they call the Butcher. You think I'm the Butcher.'

'Are you?'

352

'I've been reading a great deal about him in the *Daily News*. He slits their throats, doesn't he? From one ear to the other. Isn't that right?' He was teasing her and enjoying himself immensely. 'Sometimes he even disembowels them. Doesn't he? Correct me if I'm wrong. But that's what he does sometimes, isn't it?'

She said nothing.

'I believe I read in the *News* that he sliced the ears off one of them. When the police found her, her ears were on the nightstand beside her bed.'

She shuddered more violently than ever.

'Poor little Edna. You think I'm the Butcher. No wonder you're so frightened.' He patted her shoulder, smoothed her dark hair as if he were quieting an animal. 'I'd be scared too if I were in your shoes right now. But I'm not. I'm not in your shoes and I'm not this guy they call the Butcher. You can relax.'

She opened her eyes and searched his, trying to tell whether he spoke the truth.

'What kind of man do you think I am, Edna?' he asked, pretending to have been hurt by her suspicion. 'I don't want to harm you. I will if I must. I will cause you a great deal of harm if you don't cooperate with me. But if you're docile, if you're good to me, I'll be good to you. I'll make you very happy, and I'll leave you just like I found you. Flawless. You are flawless, you know. Perfectly beautiful. And your breath smells like strawberries. Isn't that nice? That's such a wonderful way for us to begin, such a nice touch, that scent of strawberries on your breath. Were you eating when I knocked?'

'You're crazy,' she said softly.

'Now, Edna, let's have cooperation. Were you eating strawberries?'

Tears began to form in the corners of her eyes.

He pressed a bit harder with the knife.

She whimpered.

'Well?' he said.

'Wine.'

'What?'

'It was wine.'

'Strawberry wine?'

'Yes.'

'Is there any left?'

'Yes.'

'I'd like to have some.'

'I'll get it for you.'

'I'll get it myself,' he said. 'But first I've got to take you into the bedroom and tie you up. Now, now. Don't be scared. If I didn't tie you up, sooner or later you'd try to escape. If you tried to escape, I'd have to kill you. So, you see, I'm going to tie you up for your own good, so that you won't make it necessary for me to hurt you.'

Still holding the knife at her throat, he kissed her. Her lips were cold and stiff.

'Please don't,' she said.

'Relax and enjoy yourself, Edna.' He untied the sash at her waist. The robe fell open. Under it, she was naked. He gently squeezed her breasts. 'If you cooperate you'll come out of this just fine. And you'll have a lot of fun. I'm not going to kill you unless you force me to it. I'm no butcher, Edna. Me . . . I'm nothing but your ordinary, everyday rapist.'

·2·

Graham Harris sensed that there was trouble coming. He shifted in his chair but could not get comfortable. He glanced at the three television cameras and suddenly felt as if he were surrounded by intelligent and hostile robots. He almost laughed at that bizarre image; the tension made him slightly giddy.

'Nervous?' Anthony Prine asked.

'A little.'

'No need to be.'

'Maybe not while the commercials are running, but –'

'Not when we're back on the air again, either,' Prine said. 'You've handled yourself well so far.' Although he was as American as Harris, Prine managed to look like the stereotypical British gentleman: sophisticated, rather jaded yet just a bit stuffy, completely relaxed, a model of self-confidence. He was sitting in a high-backed leather armchair, an exact copy of the chair in which Graham had suddenly found himself so uncomfortable. 'You're a most interesting guest, Mr Harris.'

'Thank you. You're interesting yourself. I don't see how you can keep your wits about you. I mean, doing this much *live* television, five nights a week –'

'But the fact that it's live is what makes it so exciting,' Prine said. 'Being on the air *live*, risking all, taking a chance of making a fool of yourself – that keeps the juices flowing. That's why I hesitate to accept one of these offers to syndicate the show or to go network with it. They'd want it on tape, all neatly edited down from two hours to ninety minutes. And that wouldn't be the same.'

The program director, a heavyset man in a white turtleneck sweater and houndstooth-check slacks, said, 'Twenty seconds, Tony.'

'Relax,' Prine told Harris. 'You'll be off in fifteen more minutes.'

Harris nodded. Prine seemed friendly – yet he could not shake the

355

feeling that the night was going to go sour for him, and soon.

Anthony Prine was the host of *Manhattan at Midnight*, an informal two-hour-long interview program that originated from a local New York City station. *Manhattan at Midnight* provided the same sort of entertainment to be found on all other talk shows – actors and actresses plugging their latest movies, authors plugging their latest books, musicians plugging their latest records, politicians plugging their latest campaigns (as yet unannounced campaigns and thus unfettered by the equal-time provisions of the election laws) – except that it presented a greater number of mind readers and psychics and UFO 'experts' than did most talk shows. Prine was a *Believer*. He was also damned good at his job, so good there were rumors that ABC wanted to pick him up for a nationwide audience. He was not so witty as Johnny Carson or so homey as Mike Douglas, but no one asked better or more probing questions than he did. Most of the time he was serene, in lazy command of his show; and when things were going well, he looked somewhat like a slimmed-down Santa Claus: completely white hair, a round face and merry blue eyes. He appeared to be incapable of rudeness. However, there were occasions – no more often than once a night, sometimes only once a week – when he would lash out at a guest, prove him a liar or in some other way thoroughly embarrass and humiliate him with a series of wickedly pointed questions. The attack never lasted more than three or four minutes, but it was as brutal and as relentless as it was surprising.

Manhattan at Midnight commanded a large and faithful audience primarily because of this element of surprise that magnified the ferocity of Prine's interrogations. If he had subjected every guest to this abuse, he would have been a bore; but his calculated style made him as fascinating as a cobra. Those millions of people who spend most of their leisure hours in front of a television set apparently enjoyed secondhand violence more than they did any other form of entertainment. They watched the police shows to see people beaten, robbed and murdered; they watched Prine for those unexpected moments when he bludgeoned a guest with words that were nearly as devastating as clubs.

He had started twenty-five years earlier as a nightclub comic and impressionist, doing old jokes and mimicking famous voices in cheap lounges. He had come a long way.

The director signaled Prine. A red light shone on one camera.

Addressing his unseen audience, Prine said, 'I'm talking with

Mr Graham Harris, a resident of Manhattan who calls himself a "clairvoyant," a seer of visions. Is that the proper definition of the term, Mr Harris?'

'It'll do,' Graham said. 'Although when you put it that way, it sounds a bit religious. Which it isn't. I don't attribute my extrasensory perception to God – nor to any other supernatural force.'

'As you said earlier, you're convinced that the clairvoyance is a result of a head injury you received in a rather serious accident. Subsequent to that, you began to have these visions. If that's God's work, His methods are even more roundabout than we might have thought.'

Graham smiled. 'Precisely.'

'Now, anyone who reads the newspapers knows that you've been asked to assist the police in uncovering a clue to the identity of this man they call the Butcher. But what about your last case, the murder of the Havelock sisters in Boston? That was very interesting too. Tell us about that.'

Graham shifted uneasily in his chair. He still sensed trouble coming, but he couldn't imagine what it might be or how he might avoid it. 'The Havelock sisters . . .'

Nineteen-year-old Paula and twenty-two-year-old Paige Havelock had lived together in a cozy Boston apartment near the university where Paula was an undergraduate student and where Paige was working for her master's degree in sociology. On the morning of last November second, Michael Shute had stopped by the apartment to take Paige to lunch. The date had been made by telephone the previous evening. Shute and the elder Havelock sister were lovers, and he had a key to the apartment. When no one responded to the bell, he decided to let himself in and wait for them. Inside, however, he discovered that they *were* at home. Paula and Paige had been awakened in the night by one or more intruders who had stripped them naked; pajamas and robes were strewn on the floor. The women had been tied with a heavy cord, sexually molested and finally shot to death in their own living room.

Because the proper authorities were unable to come up with a single major lead in the case, the parents of the dead girls got in touch with Graham on the tenth of November and asked for his assistance. He arrived in Boston two days later. Although the police were skeptical of his talents – a number of them were downright hostile toward him – they were anxious to placate the

Havelocks, who had some political influence in the city. He was taken to the sealed apartment and permitted to examine the scene of the crime. But he got absolutely nothing from that: no emanations, no psychic visions – just a chill that slithered down his spine and coiled in his stomach. Later, under the suspicious gaze of a police property officer, he was allowed to handle the pillow that the killer had used to muffle the gunshots – and then the pajamas and the robes that had been found next to the bodies. As he caressed the blood-stiffened fabric, his paranormal talent abruptly blossomed; his mind was inundated with clairvoyant images like a series of choppy, frothing waves breaking on a beach.

Anthony Prine interrupted Graham. 'Wait a minute. I think we need some elaboration on this point. We need to make it much clearer. Do you mean that the simple act of touching the blood-stained pajamas caused your clairvoyant visions?'

'No. It didn't cause them. It *freed* them. The pajamas were like a key that unlocked the clairvoyant part of my mind. That's a quality common to nearly all murder weapons and to the last garments worn by the victims.'

'Why do you think that is?'

'I don't know,' Graham said.

'You've never thought about it?'

'I've thought about it endlessly,' Graham said. 'But I've never reached any conclusions.'

Although Prine's voice held not even the slightest note of hostility, Graham was almost certain that the man was searching for an opening to launch one of his famous attacks.

For a moment he thought *that* might be the oncoming trouble which he had known about, in a somewhat psychic fashion, for the past quarter of an hour. Then he suddenly understood, through the powers of his sixth sense, that the trouble would happen to someone else, beyond the walls of this studio.

'When you touched the pajamas,' Prine said, 'did you see the murders as if they were actually taking place in front of you at that very moment?'

'Not exactly. I saw it all take place – well, *behind* my eyes.'

'What do you mean by that? Are your visions sort of like daydreams?'

'In a way. But much more vivid than daydreams. Full of color and sound and texture.'

'Did you see the Havelocks' killer in this vision?'

'Yes. Quite clearly.'

'Did you also intuit his name?'

'No,' Graham said. 'But I was able to give the police a thorough description of him. He was in his early thirties, not shorter than five-ten or taller than six feet. Slightly heavy. Receding hairline. Blue eyes. A thin nose, generally sharp features. A small strawberry birthmark on his chin . . . As it turned out, that was a perfect description of the building superintendent.'

'And you'd never seen him?'

'My first glimpse of him was in that vision.'

'You'd never seen a photograph of him?'

'No.'

'Had he been a suspect before you gave the police this description?' Prine asked.

'Yes. But the murders took place in the early morning hours of his day off. He swore that he had gone to his sister's house to spend the night, hours before the Havelock girls were killed; and his sister supported his story. Since she lived over eighty miles away, he seemed out of the running.'

'Was his sister lying?'

'Yes.'

'How did you prove it?'

While handling the dead girls' clothing, Graham sensed that the killer had gone to his sister's house a full two hours after the murder had taken place – not early the previous evening as she insisted. He also sensed that the weapon – a Smith & Wesson Terrier .32 – was hidden in the sister's house, in the bottom drawer of a china closet.

He accompanied a Boston city detective and two state troopers to the sister's place. Arriving unannounced and uninvited, they told her they wanted to question her on some new evidence in the case. Ten seconds after he stepped into her house, while the woman was still surprised at the sight of them, Graham asked her why she had said that her brother had come to stay on the evening of November first when in fact he actually had not arrived until well after dawn on November second. Before she could answer that, before she could get her wits about her, he asked her why she was hiding the murder weapon in the bottom drawer of her china closet. Shocked by his knowledge, she withstood only half a dozen questions from the detective before she finally admitted the truth.

'Amazing,' Prine said. 'And you had never seen the inside of her house before you had that vision?'

'I'd never even seen the outside of it,' Graham said.

'Why would she protect her brother when she knew he was guilty of such a horrible crime?'

'I don't know. I can see things that have happened – and very occasionally, things that soon will happen – in places where I've never been. But I can't read minds. I can't explain human motivations.'

The program director signaled Prine: five minutes until they broke for the commercials.

Leaning toward Harris, Prine said, 'Who asked you to help catch this man they're calling the Butcher? Parents of one of the murdered women?'

'No. One of the detectives assigned to the case isn't as skeptical as most policemen. He believes that I can do what I say I can do. He wants to give me a chance.'

'Have you gone to the scenes of the nine murders?'

'I've seen five of them.'

'And handled the clothes of the victims?'

'Some of them.'

Prine slid forward on his chair, leaning conspiratorially toward Harris. 'What can you tell us about the Butcher?'

'Not much,' Graham Harris said, and he frowned, because that bothered him. He was having more trouble than usual on this case. 'He's a big man. Good-looking. Young. Very sure of himself and sure of the –'

'How much are you being paid?' Prine asked.

Confused by the question, Graham said, 'For what?'

'For helping the police,' Prine said.

'I'm not being paid anything.'

'You're just doing it for the good of society, then?'

'I'm doing it because I *have* to. I'm compelled –'

'How much did the Havelocks pay you?'

He realized that Prine had been leaning toward him not conspiratorially but hungrily, like a beast preparing to pounce on its prey. His hunch had been correct: that son of a bitch had chosen him for the nightly trouncing. But *why*?

'Mr Harris?'

Graham had temporarily forgotten the cameras (and the audience beyond), but now he was uncomfortably aware of them again. 'The Havelocks didn't pay me anything.'

'You're certain of that?'

'Of course I'm certain.'

'You *are* sometimes paid for your services, aren't you?'

'No. I earn my living by –'

'Sixteen months ago a young boy was brutally murdered in the Midwest. We'll skip the name of the town to spare the family publicity. His mother asked for your assistance in uncovering the killer. I spoke with her yesterday. She says that she paid you slightly more than one thousand dollars – and then you failed to find the killer.'

What the hell is he trying to prove? Graham wondered. He knows I'm far from poor. He knows I don't need to run halfway across the country to hustle a few hundred dollars. 'First of all, I *did* tell them who killed the child and where they could look for the evidence that would make their case. But both the police and this woman refused to follow up on the lead that I gave them.'

'Why would they refuse?'

'Because the man I fingered for the murder is the son of a wealthy family in that town. He's also a respected clergyman in his own right, and the stepfather of the dead boy.'

Prine's expression was proof enough that the woman had not told him this part of it. Nevertheless, he pressed the attack. That was uncharacteristic of him. Ordinarily, he was vicious with a guest only when he *knew* that he had evidence enough to ruin him. He was not entirely an admirable man; however, he usually didn't make mistakes. 'But she did pay you the thousand dollars?'

'That was for my expenses. Airline fares, car rentals, meals and lodging while I was working on the case.'

Smiling as if he had made his point, Prine said, 'Do they usually pay your expenses?'

'Naturally. I can't be expected to travel all about, spending thousands of my own money for –'

'Did the Havelocks pay you?'

'My expenses.'

'But didn't you just tell us a minute ago that the Havelocks didn't pay you anything?'

Exasperated, Graham said, 'They didn't *pay* me. They just reimbursed me for –'

'Mr Harris, forgive me if I seem to be accusing you of something you haven't done. But it occurs to me that a man with your reputation for performing psychic miracles could easily take many thousands of dollars a year from the gullible. If he was unscrupulous, that is.'

'Look here –'

'When you're on one of these investigations, do you ever pad your expenses?' Prine asked.

Graham was stunned. He slid forward on his chair, leaned toward Prine. 'That's outrageous!' He realized that Prine had settled back and crossed his legs the instant that he got a strong reaction. That was a clever maneuver that made Graham's response seem exaggerated. He suddenly felt as if *he* were the predator. He supposed that his justifiable indignation looked like the desperate and weak self-defense of a guilty man. 'You know I don't need the money. I'm not a millionaire, but I'm well fixed. My father was a successful publisher. I received a substantial trust fund. Furthermore, I've got a moderately successful business of my own.'

'I know you publish two expensive magazines about mountain climbing,' Prine said. 'But they *do* have small circulations. As for the trust fund . . . I hadn't heard about that.'

He's lying, Graham thought. He prepares meticulously for these shows. When I walked into this studio, he knew almost as much about me as I know about myself. So why is he lying? What will he gain by slandering me? What in hell is happening here?

The woman has green eyes, clear and beautiful green eyes, but there is terror in them now, and she stares up at the blade, the shining blade, and she sucks in her breath to scream, and the blade starts its downward arc . . .

The images passed as suddenly as they had come, leaving him badly shaken. He knew that some clairvoyants – including the two most famous, Peter Hurkos and his fellow Dutchman Gerard Croiset – could receive, interpret and catalogue their psychic perceptions while holding an uninterrupted conversation. Only rarely could Graham manage that. Usually he was distracted by the visions. Occasionally, when they had to do with a particularly violent murder, he was so overwhelmed by them that he blanked out reality altogether. The visions were more than an intellectual experience; they affected him emotionally and spiritually as well. For a moment, seeing the green-eyed woman behind his eyes, he had not been *fully* aware of the world around him: the television audience, the studio, the cameras, Prine. He was trembling.

'Mr Harris?' Prine said.

He looked up from his hands.

'I asked you a question,' Prine said.

'I'm sorry. I didn't hear it.'

As the blood explodes from her throat and her scream dies unborn, he pulls the blade free and raises it high and brings it down, down again, with all of his strength, down between her bare breasts, and he neither scowls nor grins, and he does not laugh maniacally, but goes about the killing in a workmanlike manner, as if this is his profession, as if this is just a job, as if this is no different from a man selling cars for a living or washing windows, merely a task to be finished, stab and rip and tear and bring the blood welling up in pools . . . and then stand up and go home and sleep contentedly, satisfied with a job well done . . .

Graham was shaking uncontrollably. His face was greasy with perspiration, yet he felt as if he were sitting in a cool draft. His own power scared him. Ever since the accident in which he had nearly died, he had been frightened of many things; but these inexplicable visions were the ultimate fear.

'Mr Harris?' Prine said. 'Are you feeling all right?'

The second wave of impressions had lasted only three or four seconds, although it had seemed much longer than that. During that time he was totally unaware of the studio and the cameras.

'He's doing it again,' Graham said softly. 'Right now, this minute.'

Frowning, Prine said, 'Who? Doing what?'

'Killing.'

'You're talking about – the Butcher?'

Graham nodded and licked his lips. His throat was so dry that it hurt him a bit to speak. There was an unpleasant metallic taste in his mouth.

Prine was excited. He faced one of the cameras and said, 'Remember, New York, you heard it and saw it here first.' He turned back to Graham and said, 'Who is he killing?' He was suddenly charged with ghoulish anticipation.

'A woman. Green eyes. Pretty.'

'What's her name?'

Perspiration trickled into the corners of Graham's eyes and stung them. He wiped his forehead with the back of his hand – and wondered how foolish he looked to the hundreds of thousands who were watching.

'Can you tell me her name?' Prine asked.

Edna . . . pretty little Edna . . . poor little Edna . . . .

'Edna,' Graham said.

'Last name?'

'I don't . . . can't see it.'

'Try. You must try.'

'Maybe . . . dancer.'

'Edna Dancer?'

'I don't . . . maybe not . . . maybe the dancer part isn't right . . . maybe just . . . just the Edna . . .'

'Reach for it,' Prine said. 'Try harder. Can't you force it out?'

'No use.'

'*His* name?'

'Daryl . . . no . . . Dwight.'

'Like Dwight Eisenhower?'

'I'm not certain that's actually his first name . . . or even first or last . . . but people have called him that . . . Dwight . . . yes . . . and he's answered to it.'

'Incredible,' Prine said, apparently having forgotten that he had been in the process of destroying his guest's reputation. 'Do you see his other name, first or last?'

'No. But I sense . . . the police already know him . . . somehow . . . and they . . . they know him well.'

'You mean that he's already a suspect?' Prine asked.

The cameras seemed to move in closer.

Graham wished they would go away. He wished Prine would go away. He should never have come here tonight. Most of all, he wished his clairvoyant powers would go away, vanish back into that lockbox, deep within his mind, from which they had been sprung by the accident.

'I don't know,' Graham said. 'I suppose . . . he must be a suspect. But whatever the situation . . . they know him. They –' He shuddered.

'What is it?' Prine asked.

'Edna . . .'

'Yes?'

'She's dead now.'

Graham felt as if he were going to be sick.

'*Where* did it happen?' Prine asked.

Graham sank back in his armchair, struggling to keep control of himself. He felt almost as if he were Edna, as if the knife had been plunged into him.

'Where was she murdered?' Prine asked again.

'In her apartment.'

364

'What's the address?'

'I don't know.'

'But if the police could get there in time –'

'I've lost it,' Graham said. 'It's gone. I'm sorry. It's all gone for now.'

He felt cold and hollow inside.

•3•

Shortly before two o'clock in the morning, after a conference on the set with the director, Anthony Prine left the studio and went down the hall to his suite, which served him as office, dressing room and home away from home. Inside, he walked straight to the bar, put two ice cubes in a glass and reached for the bottle of bourbon.

His manager and business partner, Paul Stevenson, was sitting on the couch. He wore expensive, well-tailored clothes. Prine was a smart dresser, and he appreciated that quality in other men. The problem was that Stevenson always destroyed the effect of his outfit with one bizarre accessory. Tonight he was wearing a Savile Row suit – a hard-finished gray worsted with a midnight-blue Thai silk lining – a hand-sewn light blue shirt, maroon tie, black alligator shoes. And bright pink socks – with green clocks on the sides. Like cockroaches on a wedding cake.

For two reasons, Stevenson was a perfect business partner: he had money, and he did what he was told to do. Prine had great respect for the dollar. And he did not believe that anyone lived who had the experience, the intelligence or the right to tell *him* what to do.

'Were there any calls for me on the private line?' Prine asked.

'No calls.'

'You're certain?'

'Of course.'

'You were here all the time?'

'Watching the show on that set,' Stevenson said.

'I was expecting a call.'

'I'm sorry. There wasn't one.'

Prine scowled.

'Terrific show,' Stevenson said.

'Just the first thirty minutes. Following Harris, the other

367

guests looked duller than they were. Did we get viewer calls?'

'Over a hundred, all favorable. Do you believe he really saw the killing take place?'

'You heard the details he gave. The color of her eyes. Her name. He convinced me.'

'Until the next victim's found, you don't know that his details were accurate.'

'They were accurate,' Prine said. He finished his bourbon and refilled his glass. He could drink a great deal of whiskey without becoming drunk. Likewise, when he ate he gorged himself, yet he had never been overweight. He was constantly on the prowl for pretty young women, and when he paid for sex he usually went to bed with two call girls. He was not simply a middle-aged man desperately trying to prove his youth. He *needed* those fuels – whiskey, food and women – in large doses. For most of his life he had been fighting ennui, a deep and abiding boredom with the way the world was. Pacing energetically, sipping his bourbon, he said, 'A green-eyed woman named Edna . . . He's right about that. We'll be reading it in the papers tomorrow.'

'You can't *know* –'

'If you'd been sitting there beside him, Paul, you'd have no doubts about it.'

'But wasn't it odd that he had his "vision" just when you about had him nailed?'

'Nailed for what?' Prine asked.

'Well . . . for taking money. For –'

'If he's ever been paid more than his expenses for that kind of work, I've no proof of it,' Prine said.

Perplexed, Stevenson said, 'Then why did you go after him?'

'I wanted to break him. Reduce him to a babbling, defenseless fool.' Prine smiled.

'But if he wasn't guilty –'

'He's guilty of other things.'

'Like what?'

'You'll know eventually.'

Stevenson sighed. 'You enjoy humiliating them right there on television.'

'Of course.'

'Why?'

'Why not?'

'Is it the sense of power?'

'Not at all,' Prine said. 'I enjoy exposing them as fools because they *are* fools. Most men are fools. Politicians, clergymen, poets, philosophers, businessmen, generals and admirals. Gradually, I'm exposing the leaders in every profession. I'm going to show the ignorant masses that their leaders are as dull-witted as they are.' He swallowed some bourbon. When he spoke again, his voice was hard. 'Maybe someday all those fools will go at one another's throats and leave the world to the few of us who can appreciate it.'

'What are you saying?'

'I spoke English, didn't I?'

'You sound so – bitter.'

'I've got a right to.'

'You? After your success?'

'Aren't you drinking, Paul?'

'No. Tony, I don't understand –'

'I think you should have a drink.'

Stevenson knew when he was expected to change the subject. 'I really don't want a drink.'

'Have you ever gotten blind drunk?'

'No. I'm not much of a drinker.'

'Ever gone to bed with two girls at once?'

'What's that got to do with anything?'

'You don't reach out for life like you should,' Prine said. 'You don't *experience*. You don't get loose enough often enough. That's the only thing wrong with you, Paul – other than your socks.'

Stevenson looked at his feet. 'What's wrong with my socks?'

Prine went to the windows. He didn't look at the bright city beyond but stared instead at his reflection in the glass. He grinned at himself. He felt marvelous. Better than he had felt in weeks, and all thanks to Harris. The clairvoyant had brought some excitement and danger into his life, new purpose and interest. Although Graham Harris didn't know it as yet, he was the most important target of Prine's career. We'll destroy him, Prine thought happily; wipe him out, finish him off for good. He turned to Stevenson. 'Are you certain about the phone? I *must* have gotten a call.'

'No. Nothing.'

'Maybe you stepped out of here for a minute.'

'Tony, *I'm* not a fool. Give me some credit. I was here all the time, and the private line never rang.'

Prine finished his second bourbon. It burned his throat. A

welcome and pleasant heat rose in him. 'Why don't you have a drink with me?'

Stevenson stood and stretched. 'No. I've really got to go.'

Prine went to the bar.

'You're drinking those awfully fast, Tony.'

'Celebrating,' Prine said as he added ice and bourbon to his glass.

'Celebrating what?'

'The downfall of another fool.'

•4•

Connie Davis was waiting for Graham when he came home to the townhouse they shared in Greenwich Village. She took his coat and hung it in the closet.

She was pretty. Thirty-four years old. Slender. Brunette. Gray eyes. Proud nose. Wide mouth. Sexy.

She owned a prosperous hole-in-the-wall antique shop on Tenth Street. In business she was every bit as tough as she was pretty.

For the past eighteen months she and Graham had lived together. Their relationship was the closest thing to genuine romance that either of them had ever known.

However, it was more than a romance. She was his doctor and nurse as well as his lover. Since the accident five years ago, he had been losing faith in himself. His self-respect faded year by year. She was here to help him, to heal him. She was not certain that he understood this, but she saw it as the most important task of her life.

'Where have you been?' she asked. 'It's two-thirty.'

'I had to think. I went walking. You saw the program?'

'We'll talk about it. But first you need to get warm.'

'Do I ever. It must be twenty below out there.'

'Go into the study and sit down. Relax,' she said. 'I've got a fire going. I'll bring you a drink.'

'Brandy?'

'What else on a night like this?'

'You're nearly perfect.'

'*Nearly?*'

'Mustn't give you a swelled head.'

'I'm too perfect to be immodest.'

He laughed.

She turned from him and went to the bar at the far end of the living room.

With a sixth sense of her own, she knew that he stared after her for a moment before he left the room. Good. Just as planned. He was *meant* to watch. She was wearing a clinging white sweater and tight blue jeans that accentuated her waistline and her bottom. If he hadn't stared after her, she would have been disappointed. After what he had been through tonight, he needed more than a seat in front of the fireplace and a snifter of brandy. He needed her. Touching. Kissing. Making love. And she was willing – more than willing, delighted – to provide it.

She was not merely plunging into her Earth Mother role again. Unquestionably, she *did* have a tendency to overwhelm her men, to be so excessively affectionate and understanding and dependable that she smothered their self-reliance. However, this affair was different from all the others. She wanted to depend on Graham as much as he depended on her. This time she wanted to receive as much as she gave. He was the first man to whom she had ever responded in quite that fashion. She wanted to make love to him in order to soothe him, but she wanted to soothe herself as well. She had always had strong, healthy sexual drives, but Graham had put a new and sharper edge on her desire.

She carried the glasses of Remy Martin into the den. She sat beside him on the sofa.

After a moment of silence, still staring at the fire, he said, 'Why the interrogation? What was he after?'

'Prine?'

'Who else?'

'You've seen his show often enough. You know what he's like.'

'But he usually has a reason for his attacks. And he's always got proof of what he says.'

'Well, at least you shut him up with your visions of the tenth murder.'

'They were real,' he said.

'I know they were.'

'It was so vivid . . . as if I were right there.'

'Was it bad? Bloody?'

'One of the worst. I saw him . . . ram the knife into her throat and then twist it.' He quickly sipped his brandy.

She leaned against him, kissed him on the cheek.

'I can't figure this Butcher,' he said worriedly. 'I've never had so much trouble getting an image of a killer.'

'You sensed his name.'

'Maybe. Dwight . . . I'm not entirely sure.'

'You've given the police a fairly good description of him.'

'But I can't pick up much more about him,' he said. 'When the visions come and I try to force an image of this man, this Butcher, to the center of them, all I get are waves of . . . evil. Not illness, not an impression of a sick mind. Just overwhelming evil. I don't know how to explain this – but the Butcher isn't a lunatic. At least not in the classical sense. He doesn't kill in a maniacal frenzy.'

'He's chopped up nine innocent women,' Connie said. '*Ten* if you count the one they haven't found yet. He cuts off their ears and fingers sometimes. Sometimes he disembowels them. And you say he isn't *crazy*?'

'He's not a lunatic, not by any definition we have of the word. I'd stake my life on it.'

'Maybe you don't sense mental illness because he doesn't know he's sick. Amnesia –'

'No. No amnesia. No schizophrenia. He's very aware of his murders. He's no Dr Jekyll and Mr Hyde. I'll bet he'd pass any psychiatric examination you'd care to give him, and with flying colors. This isn't easy to explain. But I have the feeling that if he *is* a lunatic, he's a whole new breed. No one's ever encountered anything like him before. I think – dammit, I *know* – he's not even angry or particularly excited when he kills these women. He's just – methodical.'

'You're giving me the shivers.'

'You? I feel as if I've been inside his head. I've got a *chronic* case of shivers.'

A coal popped in the fireplace.

She took hold of his free hand. 'Let's not talk about Prine or the killings.'

'After tonight, how can I not talk about them?'

'You looked wonderful on television,' she said, working him away from the subject.

'Oh, yeah. Wonderful. Sweating, pale, shaking –'

'Not during the visions. Before them. You're a natural for television. Even for movies. Leading-man type.'

Graham Harris was handsome. Thick reddish-blond hair. Blue eyes, heavily crinkled at the corners. Leathery skin with sharply carved lines from all the years he had spent in an outdoor life. Five-ten; not tall, but lean and hard. He was thirty-eight, yet he still had a trace of boyish vulnerability about him.

'Leading-man type?' he said. He smiled at her. 'Maybe you're right. I'll give up the publishing business and all this messy psychic stuff. I'll go into the movies.'

'The next Robert Redford.'

'Robert Redford? I was thinking maybe the next Boris Karloff.'

'Redford,' Connie insisted.

'Come to think of it, Karloff was a rather elegant-looking man out of makeup. Perhaps I'll try for being the next Wallace Beery.'

'If you're Wallace Beery, then I'm Marie Dressler.'

'Hi, Marie.'

'Do you really have an inferiority complex, or do you cultivate it as part of your charm?'

He grinned, then sipped the brandy. 'Remember that Tugboat Annie movie with Beery and Dressler? Do you think Annie ever went to bed with her husband?'

'Sure!'

'They were always fighting. He lied to her every chance he got – and most of the time he was drunk.'

'But in their own way they *loved* each other,' Connie said. 'They couldn't have been married to anyone else.'

'I wonder what it was like for them. He was such a weak man, and she was such a strong woman.'

'Remember, though, he was always strong when the chips were down: right near the end of the picture, for example.'

'Some good in all of us, huh?'

'He could have been strong from the start. He just didn't respect himself enough.'

Graham stared at the fire. He turned the brandy snifter around and around in his hand.

'What about William Powell and Myrna Loy?' she asked.

'The Thin Man movies.'

'Both of them were strong,' she said. 'That's who we could be. Nick and Nora Charles.'

'I always liked their dog. Asta. Now *that* was a good part.'

'How do you think Nick and Nora made love?' she asked.

'Passionately.'

'But with a lot of fun.'

'Little jokes.'

'That's it.' She took the brandy glass out of his hand and put it on the hearth with her own snifter. She kissed him lightly, teasing his lips with her tongue. 'I bet we could play Nick and Nora.'

'I don't know. It's such a strain making love and being witty at the same time.'

374

She sat in his lap. She put her arms around his neck and kissed him more fully this time and drew back and smiled when he slid a hand beneath her sweater.

'Nora?' he said.

'Yes, Nicky?'

'Where's Asta?'

'I put him to bed.'

'We wouldn't want him interrupting.'

'He's asleep.'

'Might traumatize the little fella if he saw –'

'I made sure he'd be asleep.'

'Oh?'

'I drugged his Alpo.'

'Such a smart girl.'

'And now *we* belong in bed.'

'Such a *very* smart girl.'

'With a lovely body,' she said.

'Yes, you're ravishing.'

'Am I?'

'Oh, yes.'

'Ravish me, then.'

'With pleasure.'

'I would hope so.'

·5·

An hour later he was asleep, but Connie was not. She lay on her side, studying his face in the soft glow of the bedside lamp.

His experience and attitudes were stamped on his features. His toughness shone through clearly, yet there was the boyish quality too. Kindness. Intelligence. Humor. Sensitivity. He was a deep-down *good* man. But the fear shone through as well, the fear of falling, and all of the ugly things that had grown from it.

During his twenties and early thirties, Graham had been one of the best mountain climbers in the world. He lived for the vertical trek, for the risk and the triumph. Nothing else in his life mattered half so much as that. He had been an active climber from the age of thirteen, year by year setting higher and more difficult goals for himself. At twenty-six he was organizing parties to scale the most taxing peaks in Europe, Asia and South America. When he was thirty he led an expedition up the South Col route of Everest, climbed the West Ridge to traverse the mountain, and returned down the South Col. At thirty-one he tackled the Eiger Direct with an Alpine-style single push up the hideously sheer face without using fixed ropes. Accomplishments such as these, his good looks, his wit, and his reputation as a Casanova (exaggerated by both his friends and the press) made him the most colorful and popular figure in mountaineering at that time.

Five years ago, with only a few challenging climbs remaining, he put together a team to assault the most dangerous wall of rock known to man, the Southwest Face of Everest, a route that had never been taken to the top. Two-thirds of the way through the climb, he fell, breaking sixteen bones and suffering internal injuries. He was given first aid in Nepal, then flown to Europe with a doctor and two friends at his side in what everyone assumed would conclude as a death watch. Instead of adding one more outstanding achievement to his record, he spent seven months in a

377

private Swiss clinic. However, the ordeal was not at an end when he left the hospital. This Goliath had not been beaten, and had left this David with a warning: Graham limped.

The doctors told him he could still scale easy cliffs and ridges as a weekend sport if he wished. With sufficient practice he might even learn to compensate for his partially game left leg and move on to more ambitious climbs. Not Eiger. Not Everest, by any route. But there were hundreds of lesser palisades that should interest him.

At first he was convinced that he would be back on Everest within a year. Three times he tried to climb, and three times he was reduced to panic in the first hundred feet of the ascent. Forced to retreat from even the simplest climbs, he quickly saw that Everest or anything remotely like it would most likely scare him to death.

Over the years, that fear had undergone a metamorphosis, had grown and spread like a fungus. His fear of climbing had become a generalized fear that affected every aspect of his life. He was convinced that his inheritance would be lost in bad investments, and he began following the stock market with a nervous interest that made him the bane of his broker. He started his three low-circulation, high-priced mountain-climbing magazines as a hedge against a collapse of the market; and although they were quite profitable, he periodically predicted their demise. He began to see the dread specter of cancer in every cold, case of flu, headache and bout with acid indigestion. His clairvoyance frightened him, and he attempted to deal with it only because he could not run from it. At times the fear intruded between him and Connie in the most intimate moments, leaving him impotent.

Recently he had sunk into a depression far deeper than any that had come before it, and for several days he had seemed unable and unwilling to claw his way out of it. Two weeks ago he had witnessed a mugging, heard the victim's cries for help – and walked away. Five years ago he would have waded into the fight without hesitation. He came home and told Connie about the mugging, belittled himself, called himself names and argued with her when she tried to defend him. She was afraid that he had come to loathe himself, and she knew that for a man like Graham such an attitude would lead inevitably to some form of madness.

She knew that she was not particularly qualified to put him back together again. Because of her strong will, because of her competitive and fiercely self-sufficient nature, she felt that she had done more harm than good to her previous lovers. She had never thought of herself as a women's liberationist and certainly not as a ball breaker; she simply had been, from the age of consent, sharper and tougher and more self-reliant than most men of her acquaintance. In the past her lovers had been emotionally and intellectually weaker than she. Few men seemed able to accept a woman as anything but an inferior. She had nearly destroyed the man she lived with before Graham, merely by assuming her equality and – in his mind, at least – invalidating the male role he needed to sustain himself.

With Graham's ego in a fragile state, she had to modify her basic personality to an extent she would have thought impossible. It was worth the strain, because she saw the man he had been prior to the accident. She wanted to break his shell of fear and let out the old Graham Harris. What he had once been was what she had hoped for so long to find: a man who was her equal and who would not feel threatened by a woman who was his match. However, while trying to bring that Graham back to life, she had to be cautious and patient, for *this* Graham could be shattered so very easily.

A gust of wind rattled the window.

Although she was warm under the covers, she shivered.

The telephone rang.

Startled, she rolled away from Graham.

The phone was strident. Like the cry of a halidon, it echoed eerily in the room.

She snatched up the receiver to stop the ringing before it woke him. 'Hello?' she said softly.

'Mr Harris, please.'

'Who's calling?'

'Ira Preduski.'

'I'm sorry, but I –'

'Detective Preduski.'

'It's four in the morning,' she said.

'I apologize. Really. I'm sorry. Sincerely. If I've wakened you . . . terrible of me. But, you see, he wanted me to call him immediately if we had any – major developments in the Butcher case.'

'Just a minute.' She looked at Graham.

He was awake, watching her.

She said, 'Preduski.'

He took the receiver. 'Harris speaking.'

A minute later, when he was finished, she hung up for him. 'They found number ten?'

'Yeah.'

'What's her name?' Connie asked.

'Edna. Edna Mowry.'

·6·

The bedclothes were sodden with blood. The carpet at the right of the bed was marred by a dark stain like a Rorschach blot. Dried blood spotted the wall behind the brass headboard.

Three police lab technicians were working in the room under the direction of the coroner. Two of them were on their hands and knees beside the bed. One man was dusting the nightstand for fingerprints, although he must have known that he would not find any. This was the work of the Butcher, and the Butcher always wore gloves. The coroner was plotting the trajectory of the blood on the wall in order to establish whether the killer was left-handed or right-handed.

'Where's the body?' Graham asked.

'I'm sorry, but they took it to the morgue ten minutes ago,' Detective Preduski said, as if he felt responsible for some inexcusable breach of manners. Graham wondered if Preduski's entire life was an apologia. The detective was quick to take the blame for everything – and to find fault with himself even when he behaved impeccably. He was a nondescript man with a pale complexion and watery brown eyes. In spite of his appearance and his apparent inferiority complex, he was a highly respected member of the Manhattan homicide detail. More than one of the detective's associates had made it clear to Graham that he was working with the best, that Ira Preduski was the top man in the department. 'I held the ambulance as long as I could. You took so much time to get here. Of course I woke you in the dead of night. I shouldn't have done that. And then you probably had to call a cab and wait around for it. I'm so sorry. Now I've probably ruined everything for you. I should have tried to keep the body here just a bit longer. I *knew* you'd want to see it where it was found.'

'That doesn't matter,' Graham said. 'In a sense, I've already had a firsthand look at her.'

381

'Of course you have,' Preduski said. 'I saw you on the Prine show earlier.'

'Her eyes were green, weren't they?'

'Just as you said.'

'She was found nude?'

'Yes.'

'Stabbed many times?'

'Yes.'

'With a particularly brutal wound in the throat?'

'That's right.'

'He mutilated her, didn't he?'

'Yes.'

'How?'

'Awful thing,' Preduski said. 'I wish I didn't have to tell you. Nobody should have to hear it.' Preduski seemed about to wring his hands. 'He cut a plug of flesh out of her stomach. It's almost like a cork, with her navel in the center of it. Terrible.'

Graham closed his eyes and shuddered. 'This . . . cork . . .' He was beginning to perspire. He felt ill. He wasn't receiving a vision, just a strong sense of what had happened, a hunch that was difficult to ignore. 'He put this cork . . . in her right hand and closed her fingers around it. That's where you found it.'

'Yes.'

The coroner turned away from the blood-spattered wall and stared curiously at Graham.

Don't look at me that way, Graham thought. I don't *want* to know these things.

He would have been delighted if his clairvoyance had allowed him to predict sharp rises in the stock market rather than isolated pockets of maniacal violence. He would have preferred to see the names of winning horses in races not yet run rather than the names of victims in murders he'd never seen committed.

If he could have wished away his powers, he would have done that long ago. But because that was impossible, he felt as if he had a responsibility to develop and interpret his psychic talent. He believed, perhaps irrationally, that by doing so he was compensating, at least in part, for the cowardice that had overwhelmed him these past five years.

'What do you make of the message he left us?' Preduski asked.

On the wall beside the vanity bench there were lines of poetry printed in blood.

> *Rintah roars and shakes his fires*
> *in the burden'd air;*
> *Hungry clouds swag on the deep*

'Have any idea what it means?' Preduski asked.

'I'm afraid not.'

'Recognize the poet?'

'No.'

'Neither do I.' Preduski shook his head sorrowfully. 'I'm not very well educated. I only had one year of college. Couldn't afford it. I read a lot but there's so *much* to read. If I were educated, maybe I'd know whose poetry that is. I should know. If the Butcher takes the time to write it down, it's something important to him. It's a lead. What kind of detective am I if I can't follow up a lead as plain as that?' He shook his head again, clearly disgusted with himself. 'Not a good one. Not a very good one.'

'Maybe it's his own poetry,' Graham said.

'The Butcher's?'

'Maybe.'

'A murderous poet? T.S. Eliot with a homicidal urge?'

Graham shrugged.

'No,' Preduski said. 'A man usually commits this sort of crime because it's the only way he can express the rage inside him. Slaughter releases pressures that have built in him. But a poet can express his feelings with words. No. If it were doggerel, perhaps it could be the Butcher's own verse. But this is too smooth, too sensitive, too good. Anyway, it rings a bell. Way back in this thick head of mine, it rings a bell.' Preduski studied the bloody message for a moment, then turned and went to the bedroom door. It was standing open; he closed it. 'Then there's this one.'

On the back of the door, five words were printed in the dead woman's blood.

> *a rope over an abyss*

'Has he ever left anything like this before?' Graham asked.

'No. I would have told you if he had. But it's not unusual in this sort of crime. Certain types of psychopaths like to communicate with whoever finds the corpse. Jack the Ripper wrote notes to the police. The Manson family used blood to scrawl one-word messages on the walls. ''A rope over an abyss.'' What is he trying to tell us?'

'Is it from the same poem as the other?'

'I haven't the faintest idea.' Preduski sighed, thrust his hands into his pockets. He looked dejected. 'I'm beginning to wonder if I'm *ever* going to catch him.'

The living room of Edna Mowry's apartment was small but not mean. Indirect lighting bathed everything in a relaxing amber glow. Gold velvet drapes. Textured light tan burlap-pattern wallpaper. Plush brown carpet. A beige velour sofa and two matching armchairs. A heavy glass coffee table with brass legs. Chrome and glass shelves full of books and statuary. Limited editions of prints by some fine contemporary artists. It was tasteful, cozy and expensive.

At Preduski's request, Graham settled down in one of the armchairs.

Sarah Piper was sitting on one end of the sofa. She looked as expensive as the room. She was wearing a knitted pantsuit – dark blue with Kelly green piping – gold earrings and an elegant watch as thin as a half dollar. She was no older than twenty-five, a strikingly lovely, well-built blonde, marked by experience.

Earlier she had been crying. Her eyes were puffy and red. She was in control of herself now.

'We've been through this before,' she said.

Preduski was beside her on the couch. 'I know,' he said. 'And I'm sorry. Truly sorry. It's terribly late, too late for this. But there *is* something to be gained by asking the same questions two and even three times. You think you've told me all the pertinent facts. But it's possible you overlooked something. God knows, *I'm* forever overlooking things. This questioning may seem redundant to you, but it's the way I work. I have to go over things again and again to make sure I've done them right. I'm not proud of it. That's just the way I am. Some other detective might get everything he needs the first time he speaks to you. Not me, I'm afraid. It was your misfortune that the call came in while I was on duty. Bear with me. I'll be able to let you go home before much longer. I promise.'

The woman glanced at Graham and cocked her head as if to say, *Is this guy for real?*

Graham smiled.

'How long had you known – the deceased?' Preduski asked.

She said, 'About a year.'

'How well did you know her?'

'She was my best friend.'

'Do you think that in her eyes you were *her* best friend?'

'Sure. I was her only friend.'

Preduski raised his eyebrows. 'People didn't like her?'

'Of course they liked her,' Sarah Piper said. 'What wasn't to like? She just didn't make friends easily. She was a quiet girl. She kept mostly to herself.'

'Where did you meet her?'

'At work.'

'Where is work?'

'You know that. The Rhinestone Palace.'

'And what did she do there?'

'You know that too.'

Nodding, patting her knee in a strictly fatherly manner, the detective said, 'That's correct. I know it. But, you see, Mr Harris doesn't know it. I neglected to fill him in. My fault. I'm sorry. Would you tell him?'

She turned to Graham. 'Edna was a stripper. Just like me.'

'I know the Rhinestone Palace,' Graham said.

'You've been there?' Preduski asked.

'No. But I know it's fairly high class, not like most strip-tease clubs.'

For a moment Preduski's watery brown eyes seemed less out of focus than usual. He stared intently at Graham. 'Edna Mowry was a stripper. How about that?'

He knew precisely what the detective was thinking. On the Prine show he had said that the victim's name might be Edna Dancer. He had not been right – but he had not been altogether wrong either; for although her name was Mowry, *she earned her living as a dancer.*

According to Sarah Piper, Edna had reported for work at five o'clock the previous evening. She performed a ten-minute act twice every hour for the next seven hours, peeling out of a variety of costumes until she was entirely nude. Between acts, dressed in a black cocktail dress, sans bra, she mixed with the customers – mostly men, alone and in groups – hustling drinks in a cautious, demure and stylish way that skipped successfully along the edge of the state's B-girl laws. She had finished her last performance at twenty minutes of twelve and left the Rhinestone Palace no more than five minutes after that.

'You think she came straight home?' Preduski asked.

'She always did,' Sarah said. 'She never wanted to go out and have fun. The Rhinestone Palace was all the night life she could stomach. Who could blame her?'

Her voice wavered, as if she might begin to cry again.

385

Preduski took her hand and squeezed it reassuringly. She let him hold it, and that appeared to give him an innocent pleasure. 'Did you dance last evening?'

'Yeah. Till midnight.'

'When did you come here?'

'A quarter of three.'

'Why would you be visiting at that hour?'

'Edna liked to sit and read all night. She never went to bed until eight or nine in the morning. I told her I'd stop around for breakfast and gossip. I often did.'

'You've probably already told me . . .' Preduski made a face: embarrassment, apology, frustration. 'I'm sorry. This mind of mine – like a sieve. Did you tell me why you didn't come here at midnight, when you got off work?'

'I had a date,' she said.

Graham could tell from her expression and from the tone of her voice that the 'date' had been a paying customer. That saddened him a bit. He liked her already. He couldn't help but like her. He was receiving low-key waves, threshold psychic vibrations from her; they were very positive, mellow and warm vibrations. She was a damned nice person. He *knew*. And he wanted only pleasant things to happen to her.

'Did Edna have a date tonight?' Preduski asked.

'No. I told you. She came right home.'

'Maybe her boyfriend was waiting for her.'

'She was between boyfriends.'

'Maybe an old boyfriend stopped in to talk.'

'No. When Edna dropped a guy, he *stayed* dropped.'

Preduski sighed, pinched the bridge of his nose, shook his head sadly. 'I hate to have to ask this . . . You were her best friend. But what I'm going to say – please understand I don't mean to put her down. Life is tough. We all have to do things we'd rather not do. I'm not proud of every day of my life. God knows. Don't judge. That's my motto. There's only one crime I can't rationalize away. Murder. I really hate to ask this . . . Well, was she . . . do you think she ever . . .'

'Was she a prostitute?' Sarah asked for him.

'Oh, I wouldn't put it that way! That's such an awful . . . I really meant . . .'

'Don't worry,' she said. She smiled sweetly. 'I'm not offended.'

Graham was amused to see her squeeze the detective's hand. Now *she* was comforting *Preduski*.

'I do some light hooking myself,' Sarah said. 'Not much. Once a week, maybe. I've got to like the guy, and he's got to have two hundred bucks to spare. It's all the same as stripping to me, really. But it wouldn't have been something Edna could do. She was surprisingly straight.'

'I shouldn't have asked. It was none of my business,' said Preduski. 'But it occurred to me that in her line of work there would be a lot of temptation for a girl who needed money.'

'She made eight hundred a week stripping and hustling drinks,' Sarah said. 'She only spent money on her books and apartment. She was socking it in the bank. She didn't need more.'

Preduski was somber. 'But you see why I had to ask? If she opened the door to the killer, he must have been someone she knew, however briefly. That's what puzzles me most about this whole case. How does the Butcher get them to open the door?'

Graham had never thought about that. The dead women were all young, but they were from varied backgrounds. One was a housewife. One was a lawyer. Two were schoolteachers. Three secretaries, one model, one sales clerk . . . How *did* the Butcher get so many different women to open their doors to him late at night?

The kitchen table was littered with the remains of a hastily prepared and hastily eaten meal. Bits of bread. The dried edge of a slice of bologna. Smears of mustard and mayonnaise. Two apple cores. A can of cling peaches empty of everything except an inch of packing syrup. A drumstick gnawed to the bone. Half a doughnut. Three crushed beer cans. The Butcher had been ravenous and sloppy.

'Ten murders,' Preduski said, 'and he always goes to the kitchen for a snack afterward.'

Stifled by the psychic atmosphere of the kitchen, by the incredibly strong, lingering presence of the killer which was nearly as heavy here as it had been in the dead woman's bedroom, Graham could only nod. The mess on the table, in contrast with the otherwise tidy kitchen, disturbed him deeply. The peach can and the beer can were covered with reddish-brown stains; the killer had eaten while wearing his bloody gloves.

Preduski shuffled forlornly to the window by the sink. He stared at the neighboring apartment house. 'I've talked to a few psychiatrists about these feasts he has when he's done the dirty work. As I understand it, there are two basic ways a psychopath will act when he's finished with his victim. Number one, there's Mr Meek. The killing is everything for him, his whole reason for living, the only color and desire in his life. When he's done killing, there's nothing, he's nothing. He goes home and watches television. Sleeps a lot. He sinks into a deep pit of boredom until the pressures build up and he kills again. Number two, there's the man who gets psyched up by the murder. His real excitement comes not during the killing but after it. He'll go straight from the scene of the crime to a bar and drink everyone under the table. His adrenalin is up. His heartbeat is up. He eats like a lumberjack and sometimes picks up whores by the six-pack. Apparently, our man is number two. Except . . .'

'Except what?' Graham asked.

Turning away from the window, Preduski said, 'Seven times he's eaten a big meal in the dead women's own homes. But the other three times, he's taken the food out of the refrigerator and faked a big meal.'

'Faked it? What do you mean?'

'The fifth murder, the Liedstrom woman,' Preduski said. He closed his eyes and grimaced as if he could still see her body and blood. 'We were aware of his style by then. We checked the kitchen right away. There was an empty pear can on the table, an empty cottage cheese container, the remains of an apple and several other items. But there wasn't a mess. The first four times, he'd been sloppy – like he was tonight. But in the Liedstrom kitchen, he hadn't left a lot of crumbs. No smears of butter or mustard or mayonnaise or ketchup. No bloodstains on the beer cans.'

He opened his eyes and walked to the table. 'We'd found well-gnawed apple cores in two of the first four kitchens.' He pointed at an apple core on the table in front of him. 'Like that one. The lab had even studied the teeth marks on them. But in the Liedstrom kitchen he peeled the apple and removed the center with a corer. The skins and the core were piled neatly on one corner of his dinner plate. That was a change from what we'd seen previously, and it got me thinking. Why had he eaten like a Neanderthal the first four times – and like a gentleman the fifth? I had the forensic boys open the plumbing under the sink and take out the garbage disposal unit. They ran tests on it and found that each of the eight kinds of food on the table had been put through the disposal within the past few hours. In short, the Butcher hadn't taken a bite of anything in the Liedstrom kitchen. He got the food from the refrigerator and tossed it down the drain. Then he set the table so it would *look* as if he'd had a big meal. He did the same thing at the scene of murders seven and eight.'

That sort of behavior struck Graham as particularly eerie. The air in the room seemed suddenly more moist and oppressive than before. 'You said his eating after a murder was part of a psychotic compulsion.'

'Yes.'

'If for some reason he didn't feel that compulsion at the Liedstrom house, why would he bother to fake it?'

'I don't know,' Preduski said. He wiped one slender hand across his face as if he were trying to pull off his weariness. 'It's too much for me. It really is. Much too much. If he's crazy, why isn't he crazy in the same way all of the time?'

Graham hesitated. Then: 'I don't think any court-appointed psychiatrist would find him insane.'

'Say again?'

'In fact, I think even the best psychiatrist, if not informed of the murders, would find this man saner and more reasonable than he would most of us.'

Preduski blinked his watery eyes in surprise. 'Well, hell. He carves up ten women and leaves them for garbage, and you don't think he's crazy?'

'That's the same reaction I got from a lady friend when I told her.'

'I don't wonder.'

'But I'll stick by it. Maybe he *is* crazy. But not in any traditional, recognizable way. He's something altogether new.'

'You sense this?'

'Yes.'

'Psychically?'

'Yes.'

'Can you be more specific?'

'Sorry.'

'Sense anything else?'

'Just what you heard on the Prine show.'

'Nothing new since you came here?'

'Nothing.'

'If he's not insane *at all*, then there's a reason behind the killings,' Preduski said thoughtfully. 'Somehow they're connected. Is that what you're saying?'

'I'm not sure *what* I mean.'

'I don't see how they could be connected.'

'Neither do I.'

'I've been looking for a connection, really looking. I was hoping you could pick up something here. From the bloody bedclothes. Or from this mess on the table.'

'I'm blank,' Harris said. 'That's why I'm positive that either he is sane, or he is insane in some whole new fashion. Usually, when I study or touch an item intimately connected with the murder, I can pick up on the emotion, the mania, the passion behind the crime. It's like leaping into a river of violent thoughts, sensations, images . . . This time all I get is a feeling of cool, implacable, evil *logic*. I've never had so much trouble drawing a lead on this kind of killer.'

'Me either,' Preduski said. 'I never claimed to be Sherlock Holmes. I'm no genius. I work slow. Always have. And I've been lucky. God knows. It's luck more than skill that's kept my arrest record high. But this time I'm having no luck at all. None at all. Maybe it's time for me to be put out to pasture.'

On his way out of the apartment, having left Ira Preduski in the kitchen to ponder the remnants of the Butcher's macabre meal, Graham passed through the living room and saw Sarah Piper. The detective had not yet dismissed her. She was sitting on the sofa, her feet propped on the coffee table. She was smoking a cigarette and staring at the ceiling, smoke spiraling like dreams from her head; her back was to Graham.

The instant he saw her, a brilliant image flashed behind his eyes, intense, breathtaking: *Sarah Piper with blood all over her*.

He stopped. Shaking. Waiting for more.

Nothing.

He strained. Tried to pluck more pictures from the ether.

Nothing. Just her face. And the blood. Gone now as quickly as it had come to him.

She became aware of him. She turned around and said, 'Hi.'

He licked his lips, forced a smile.

'You predicted this?' she asked, waving one hand toward the dead woman's bedroom.

'I'm afraid so.'

'That's spooky.'

'I want to say . . .'

'Yes?'

'It was nice meeting you.'

She smiled too.

'I wish it could have been under other circumstances,' he said, stalling, wondering how to tell her about the brief vision, wondering whether he should tell her at all.

'Maybe we will,' she said.

'What?'

'Meet under other circumstances.'

'Miss Piper . . . be careful.'

'I'm always careful.'

'For the next few days . . . be especially careful.'

'After what I've seen tonight,' she said, no longer smiling, 'you can bet on it.'

·7·

Frank Bollinger's apartment near the Metropolitan Museum of Art was small and Spartan. The bedroom walls were cocoa brown, the wooden floor polished and bare. The only furniture in the room was a queen-size bed, one nightstand and a portable television set. He had built shelves into the closets to hold his clothes. The living room had white walls and the same shining wood floor. The only furniture was a black leather couch, a wicker chair with black cushions, a mirrored coffee table, and shelves full of books. The kitchen held the usual appliances and a small table with two straight-backed chairs. The windows were covered with venetian blinds, no drapes. The apartment was more like a monk's cell than a home, and that was how he liked it.

At nine o'clock Friday morning he got out of bed, showered, plugged in the telephone, and brewed a pot of coffee.

He had come directly to his apartment from Edna Mowry's place and had spent the early morning hours drinking Scotch and reading Blake's poetry. Halfway through the bottle, still not drunk but so happy, very happy, he went to bed and fell asleep reciting lines from *The Four Zoas*. When he awoke five hours later, he felt new and fresh and pure, as if he had been reborn.

He was pouring his first cup of coffee when the telephone rang.

'Hello?'

'Dwight?'

'Yeah.'

'This is Billy.'

'Of course.'

Dwight was his middle name – Franklin Dwight Bollinger – and had been the name of his maternal grandfather, who had died when Frank was less than a year old. Until he met and came to know Billy, until he trusted Billy, his grandmother had been the only one who ever used his middle name. Shortly after his fourth birthday, his father abandoned the family, and his mother discovered that a four-year-old interfered with the hectic social life of a divorcee. Except for a few scattered and agonizing months with his mother – who managed to provide occasional bursts of affection only when her conscience began to bother her – he had spent his childhood with his grandmother. She not only wanted him, she cherished him. She treated him as if he were the focus not just of her own life but of the very rotation of the earth.

'Franklin is such an ordinary name,' his grandmother used to say. 'But *Dwight* . . . well, now, that's *special*. It was your grandfather's name, and he was a wonderful man, not at all like other people, one of a kind. You're going to grow up to be just like him, set apart, set above, more important than others. Let everyone call you Frank. To me you'll always be Dwight.' His grandmother had died ten years ago. For nine and a half years no one had called him Dwight; then, six months ago, he'd met Billy. Billy understood what it was like to be one of the new breed, to have been born superior to most men. Billy was superior too, and had a right to call him Dwight. He liked hearing the name again after all this time. It was a key to his psyche, a pleasure button that lifted his spirits each time it was pushed, a reminder that he was destined for a dizzyingly high station in life.

'I tried calling you several times last night,' Billy said.

'I unplugged the phone so I could drink some Scotch and sleep in peace.'

'Have you seen the papers this morning?'

'I just got up.'

'You haven't heard anything about Harris?'

'Who?'

'Graham Harris. The psychic.'

'Oh. No. Nothing. What's to hear?'

'Get the papers, Dwight. And then we'd better have lunch. You are off work today, aren't you?'

'I'm always off Thursdays and Fridays. But what's wrong?'

'The *Daily News* will tell you what's wrong. Be sure to get a copy. We'll have lunch at The Leopard at eleven-thirty.'

Frowning, Bollinger said, 'Look –'

'Eleven-thirty, Dwight.'

Billy hung up.

The day was dreary and cold. Thick dark clouds scudded southward; they were so low they seemed to skim the tops of the highest buildings.

Three blocks from the restaurant, Bollinger left his taxi and bought the *Daily News* at a kiosk. In his bulky coat and sweaters and gloves and scarves and wool toboggan cap, the vendor looked like a mummy.

The lower half of the front page held a publicity photograph of Edna Mowry provided by the Rhinestone Palace. She was smiling, quite lovely. The upper half of the page featured bold black headlines:

BUTCHER KILLS NUMBER 10
PSYCHIC PREDICTS MURDER

At the corner he turned to the second page and tried to read the story while waiting for the traffic light to change. The wind stung his eyes and made them water. It rattled the paper in his hands and made it impossible for him to read.

He crossed the street and stepped into the sheltered entranceway of an office building. His teeth still chattering from the cold, but free of the wind, he read about Graham Harris and *Manhattan at Midnight*.

His name is Dwight, Harris had said.

The police already know him, Harris had said.

Christ! How could the son of a bitch possibly know so much? Psychic powers? That was a lot of bullshit. There weren't such things. Were there?

Worried now, Bollinger walked to the corner, threw the newspaper into a litter basket, hunched his shoulders against the wind, and hurried toward the restaurant.

The Leopard, on Fiftieth Street near Second Avenue, was a charming restaurant with only a handful of tables and excellent food. The dining area was no larger than an average living room. A hideous display of artificial flowers filled the center of the room, but that was the only really outrageous element in a generally bland decor.

Billy was sitting at a choice table by the window. In an hour The Leopard would be full of diners and noisy conversation. This early, fifteen minutes or more before the executive lunch crowd could slip away from conference rooms and desks, Billy was the only customer. Bollinger sat opposite him. They shook hands and ordered drinks.

'Nasty weather,' Billy said. His Southern accent was heavy.

'Yes.'

They stared at each other over the bud vase and single rose that stood in the center of the table.

'Nasty news,' Billy said at last.

'Yes.'

'What do you think?'

'This Harris is incredible,' Bollinger said.

'Dwight . . . Nobody but me knows you by that name. He hasn't given them much of a clue.'

'My middle name's on all my records – on my employee file at the department.'

Unfolding a linen napkin, Billy said, 'They've got no reason to believe the killer's a policeman.'

'Harris told them they already knew the Butcher.'

'They'll just suppose that he's someone they've already questioned.'

Frowning, Bollinger said, 'If he gives them one more bit of detail, one more clue, I'm blown.'

'I thought you didn't believe in psychics.'

'I was wrong. You were right.'

'Apology accepted,' Billy said, smiling thinly.

'This Harris – can we reason with him?'

'No.'

'He wouldn't understand?'

'He's not one of us.'

The waiter came with their drinks.

When they were alone again, Bollinger said, 'I've never seen this Harris. What does he look like?'

'I'll describe him to you later. Right now . . . do you mind telling me what you're going to do?'

Bollinger didn't have to think about that. Without hesitation he said, 'Kill him.'

'Ah,' Billy said softly.

'Objections?'

'Absolutely none.'

'Good.' Bollinger swallowed half of his drink. 'Because I'd do it even if you had objections.'

The captain came to the table and asked if they would like to hear the menu.

'Give us five minutes,' Billy said. When the captain had gone, he said, 'When you've killed Harris, will you leave him like the Butcher would?'

'Why not?'

'Well, the others have been women.'

'This will confuse and upset them even more.' Bollinger said.

'When will you do it?'

'Tonight.'

Billy said, 'I don't think he lives alone.'

'With his mother?' Bollinger asked sourly.

'No. I believe he lives with a woman.'

'Young?'

'I would imagine so.'

'Pretty?'

'He *does* seem to be a man of good taste.'

'Well, that's just fine,' Bollinger said.

'I thought you'd see it that way.'

'A double-header,' Bollinger said. 'That just adds to the fun.' He grinned.

·8·

'Detective Preduski is on the line, Mr Harris.'

'I'll talk to him. Put him through. Hello?'

'Sorry to bother you, Graham. Can we be less formal than we've been? May I call you Graham?'

'Sure.'

'Please call me Ira.'

'I'd be honored.'

'You're very kind. I hope I didn't interrupt something.'

'No.'

'I know you're a busy man. Would you rather I called you back later? Or would you like to call me back at your convenience?'

'You didn't interrupt. What is it you want?'

'You know that writing we found on the walls of the Mowry apartment?'

'Too clearly.'

'Well, I've been trying to track down the source for the past few hours, and –'

'You're still on duty at two in the afternoon?'

'No, no. I'm at home.'

'Don't you ever sleep?'

'I wish I could. I haven't been able to sleep more than four or five hours a day for the past twenty years. I'm probably ruining my health. I *know* I am. But I've got this twisted brain. My head's full of garbage, thousands of useless facts, and I can't stop thinking about them. I keep picking at the damndest things. Like the writing on the walls at the Mowry apartment. I couldn't sleep for thinking about it.'

'And you've come up with something?'

'Well, I told you last night the poetry rang a bell. "Rintah roars and shakes his fires in the burden'd air; Hungry clouds swag on the deep." As soon as I saw it I said to myself, "Ira, that's from

399

something William Blake wrote.'' You see, when I was in college for that one year, my major was literature. I had to write a paper on Blake. Twenty-five years ago. You see what I mean about garbage in my head? I remember the most useless things. Anyway this morning I bought the Erdman edition of Blake's poetry and prose. Sure enough, I found those lines in ''The Argument,'' part of *The Marriage of Heaven and Hell*. Do you know Blake?'

'I'm afraid not.'

'He was a mystic and a psychic.'

'Clairvoyant?'

'No. But with a psychic bent. He thought men had the power to be gods. For an important part of his career he was a poet of chaos and cataclysm – and yet he was fundamentally a table-pounding optimist. Now, do you remember the line the Butcher printed on the bedroom door?'

'Yes. ''A rope over an abyss.'' '

'Do you have any idea what that's from?'

'None.'

'Neither did I. My head is full of garbage. There's no room for anything important. And I'm not a well-educated man. Not well educated at all. So I called a friend of mine, a professor in the Department of English at Columbia. He didn't recognize the line either, but he passed it around to a few of his colleagues. One of them thought he knew it. He got a concordance of the major philosophers and located the full quotation. ''Man is rope stretched between the animal and the Superman – a rope over an abyss.'' '

'Who said it?'

'Hitler's favorite philosopher.'

'Nietzsche.'

'You know his work?'

'In passing.'

'He believed men could be gods – or at least that certain men could be gods if their society allowed them to grow and exercise their powers. He believed mankind was evolving toward godhood. You see, there's a superficial resemblance between Blake and Nietzsche. That's why the Butcher might quote both of them. But there's a problem, Graham.'

'What's that?'

'Blake was an optimist all the way. Nietzsche was a raving pessimist. Blake thought mankind had a bright future. Nietzsche thought mankind *should* have a bright future, but he believed that it would destroy itself before the Supermen ever evolved from it.

Blake apparently liked women. Nietzsche despised them. In fact, he thought women constituted one of the greatest obstacles standing between man and his climb to godhood. You see what I'm getting at?'

'You're saying that if the Butcher subscribes to both Blake and Nietzsche's philosophies, then he's a schizophrenic.'

'Yet you say he's not even crazy.'

'Wait a minute.'

'Last night –'

'All I said was that if he's a maniac, he's a *new kind* of maniac. I said he wasn't crazy in any traditional sense.'

'Which rules out schizophrenia?'

'I guess it does, Ira.'

'But I think it's a good bet . . . maybe I'm wrong . . . God knows . . . but maybe he looks at himself as one of Nietzsche's Supermen. A psychiatrist would call that delusions of grandeur. And delusions of grandeur characterize schizophrenia and paranoia. Do you *still* think the Butcher could pass any psychiatric test we could give him?'

'Yes.'

'You sense this psychically.'

'That's right.'

'Have you ever sensed something and been wrong?'

'Not seriously wrong. No worse than thinking Edna Mowry's name was Edna Dancer.'

'Of course. I know your reputation. I know you're good. I didn't mean to imply anything. You understand? But still – now where do I stand?'

'I don't know.'

'Graham . . . if you were to sit down with a book of Blake's poems, if you were to spend an hour or so reading them, would that maybe put you in tune with the Butcher? Would it spark something – if not a vision, at least a hunch?'

'It might.'

'Would you do me a favor then?'

'Name it.'

'If I send a messenger right over with an edition of Blake's work, will you sit down with it for an hour and see what happens?'

'You can send it over today if you want, but I won't get to it until tomorrow.'

'Maybe just *half* an hour.'

'Not even that. I've got to finish working on one of my magazines

401

and get it off to the printer tomorrow morning. I'm already three days late with the issue. I'll be working most of tonight. But tomorrow afternoon or evening, I'll make time for Blake.'

'Thank you. I appreciate it. I really do. I'm counting on you. You're my only hope. This Butcher is too much for me, too sharp for me. I'm getting nowhere. Absolutely nowhere. If we don't get a solid lead soon, I don't know what's going to happen.'

·9·

Paul Stevenson was wearing a hand-sewn blue shirt, a blue-and-black-striped silk tie, an expensive black suit, black socks, and light brown shoes with white stitching. When he came into Anthony Prine's office at two o'clock Friday afternoon, unaware that Prine winced when he saw the shoes, he was upset. Because he was incapable of shouting and screaming at Prine, he pouted. 'Tony, why are you keeping secrets from me?'

Prine was stretched out on the couch, his head propped on a bolster pillow. He was reading *The New York Times*. 'Secrets?'

'I just found out that at your direction the company has hired a private detective agency to snoop on Graham Harris.'

'They're not snooping. All I've asked them to do is establish Harris's whereabouts at certain hours on certain days.'

'You asked the detectives not to approach Harris or his girl friend directly. That's snooping. And you asked them for a forty-eight-hour rush job, which triples the cost. If you want to know where he was, why don't you ask him yourself?'

'I think he'd lie to me.'

'Why should he lie? What certain hours? What certain dates?'

Prine put down the paper, sat up, stood up, stretched. 'I want to know where he was when each of those ten women was killed.'

Perplexed, blinking somewhat stupidly, Stevenson said, 'Why?'

'If on all ten occasions he was alone – working alone, seeing a movie alone, walking alone – then maybe he could have killed them.'

'*Harris*? You think Harris is the Butcher?'

'Maybe.'

'You hire detectives on a maybe?'

'I told you, I've distrusted that man from the start. And if I'm right about this, what a scoop we'll have!'

'But Harris isn't a killer. He *catches* killers.'

403

Prine went to the bar. 'If a doctor treats fifty patients for influenza one week and fifty more the next, would it surprise you if he got influenza himself during the third week?'

'I'm not sure I get your point.'

Prine filled his glass with bourbon. 'For years Harris has been tuning in to murder with the deepest levels of his mind, exposing himself to trauma as few of us ever do. He has been literally delving into the minds of wife killers, child killers, mass murderers. . . . He's probably seen more blood and violence than most career cops. Isn't it conceivable that a man, unstable to begin with, could crack from all the violent input? Isn't it conceivable that he could become the kind of maniac he's worked so hard to catch?'

'Unstable?' Stevenson frowned. 'Graham Harris is as stable as you or me.'

'How well do you know him?'

'I saw him on the show.'

'There's a bit more you should know.' Prine caught sight of himself in the mirror behind the bar cabinet; he smoothed his lustrous white hair with one hand.

'For example?'

'I'll indulge myself in amateur psychoanalysis – amateur but probably accurate. First of all, Graham Harris was born into border line poverty and –'

'Hold on. His old man was Evan Harris, the publisher.'

'His stepfather. His real father died when Graham was a year old. His mother was a cocktail waitress. She had trouble keeping a roof over their heads because she had to pay off her husband's medical bills. For years they lived day to day, on the edge of disaster. That would leave marks on a child.'

'How did she meet Evan Harris?' Stevenson asked.

'I don't know. But after they were married, Graham took his stepfather's name. He spent the latter part of his childhood in a mansion. After he got his university degree, he had enough time and money to become one of the world's leading climbers. Old man Harris encouraged him. In some circles, Graham was famous, a star. Do you realize how many beautiful women are drawn to the sport of climbing?'

Stevenson shrugged.

'Not as participants,' Prine said. 'As companions to the participants, as bedmates. More women than you'd think. I guess it's the nearness of death that attracts them. For more than a decade, Graham was adored, made over. Then he took a bad fall. When he recovered, he was terrified of climbing.' Prine was listening to his own voice, fascinated by the theory he had developed. 'Do you understand, Paul? He was born a nobody, lived the first six years of his life as a nobody – then overnight he became a somebody when his mother married Evan Harris. Now is it any wonder that he's afraid of being a nobody again?'

Stevenson went to the bar and poured himself some bourbon. 'It's not likely he'll be a nobody again. He *did* inherit his step-father's money.'

'Money isn't the same as fame. Once he'd been a celebrity, even within the tight circle of climbing enthusiasts, maybe he developed a habit for it. Maybe he became a fame junkie. It can happen to the best. I've seen it.'

'So have I.'

'If that's what he is . . . well, maybe he's decided that being infamous is as good as being famous. As the Butcher, he's grabbing headlines; he's infamous, even if only under a *nom de guerre*.'

'But he was with you in the studio last night when the Mowry girl was murdered.'

'Maybe not.'

'What? He predicted her death.'

'Did he? Or did he simply tell us who he had selected for his next victim?'

Stevenson stared at him as if he were mad.

Laughing, Prine said, 'Of course Harris was in the studio with me but perhaps not when the murder took place. I used a source in the police department and got a copy of the coroner's report. According to the pathologist Edna Mowry was murdered sometime between eleven-thirty Thursday night and one-thirty Friday morning. Now, Graham Harris left the studio at twelve-thirty Friday morning. He had an hour to get to Edna Mowry.'

Stevenson swallowed some bourbon. 'Jesus, Tony, if you're right, if you break a story like this, ABC will give you a late-night talk show and let you do it your way, *live*!'

'They might.'

Stevenson finished his bourbon. 'But you don't have any proof. It's just a theory. And a pretty far-out theory at that. You can't convict a man because he was born to poor parents. Hell, your childhood was worse than his, and you're not a killer.'

'At the moment I've got no proof,' Prine said. But if it can't be found, it can be manufactured, he thought.

·10·

Sarah Piper spent the early part of Friday afternoon packing for a five-day trip to Las Vegas. Ernie Nolan, a men's clothing manufacturer who had been on her special list of customers for three years, went to Vegas every six months and took her with him. He paid her fifteen hundred dollars for her time in bed and gave her five hundred as a gambling stake. Even if Ernie had been a beast, which he was not, it would have been a good vacation for her.

Beginning today, she was on a week's leave from the Rhinestone Palace, and she was glad that she hadn't tried to squeeze in one more night's work before catching the flight to Vegas tomorrow morning. She'd had only two hours' sleep after returning from Edna's place, and those two hours had been plagued by nightmares. She would need to rest well tonight if she was going to be at the top of her form for Ernie.

As she packed, she wondered if there was something missing from her. Heart? Normal emotions? She had cried last night, had been deeply affected by Edna's death. But already her spirits were high again. She was excited, pleased to be getting away from New York. Introspection didn't give rise to any guilt. She had seen too much of the world – too much violence, desperation, selfishness and grubbiness – to chastise herself for being unable to sustain her grief. That was the way people were built: forgetfulness was the hub of the wheel, the core of the mind, the thing that kept you sane. Maybe that was not pleasant to contemplate, but it was true.

At three o'clock, as she was locking the third suitcase, a man called. He wanted to set up a date for that evening. She didn't know him, but he claimed to have gotten her name from one of her regular clients. Although he sounded quite nice – a genuine Southern gentleman with a mellow accent – she had to turn him down.

'If you've got something else going,' he said, 'I can make it worth your while to drop him for tonight.'

407

'There's no one else. But I'm going to Vegas in the morning, and I need my rest.'

'What's your usual rate?' he asked.

'Two hundred. But –'

'I'll give you three hundred.'

She hesitated.

'Four hundred.'

'I'll give you the names of a couple of girls –'

'I want to spend the evening with *you*. I hear you're the loveliest woman in Manhattan.'

She laughed. 'You'd be in for a big disappointment.'

'I've made up my mind. When I've made up my mind, nothing on God's earth can change it. Five hundred dollars.'

'That's too much. If you –'

'Young lady, five hundred is peanuts. I've made millions in the oil business. Five hundred – and I won't tie you up all evening. I'll be there around six o'clock. We'll relax together – then go out to dinner. You'll be home by ten, plenty of time to rest up for Vegas.'

'You don't give up easily, do you?'

'That's my trademark. I'm blessed with perseverance. Down home they call it pure mule-headed stubbornness.'

Smiling, she said, 'All right. You win. Five hundred. But you promise we'll be back by ten?'

'Word of honor,' he said.

'You haven't told me your name.'

'Plover,' he said. 'Billy James Plover.'

'Do I call you Billy James?'

'Just Billy.'

'Who recommended me?'

'I'd rather not use his name on the phone.'

'Okay. Six o'clock it is.'

'Don't you forget.'

'I'm looking forward to it,' she said.

'So am I,' Billy said.

·11·

Although Connie Davis had slept late and hadn't opened the antique shop until after lunch, and although she'd had only one customer, it was a good day for business. She had sold six perfectly matched seventeenth-century Spanish chairs. Each piece was of dark oak with bowed legs and claw feet. The arms ended in snarling demon heads, elaborately carved gargoyles the size of oranges. The woman who purchased the chairs had a fourteen-room apartment overlooking Fifth Avenue and Central Park; she wanted them for the room in which she sometimes held séances.

Later, when she was alone in the shop, Connie went to her alcove office at the rear of the main room. She opened a can of fresh coffee, prepared the percolator.

At the front of the room the big windows rattled noisily. Connie looked up from the percolator to see who had come in. No one was there. The windows were trembling from the sudden violence of the winter weather; the wind had picked up and was gusting fiercely.

She sat down at a neatly kept Sheraton desk from the late 1780s and dialed the number of Graham's private office phone, bypassing his secretary. When he answered she said, 'Hello, Nick.'

'Hi, Nora.'

'If you've made any headway with your work, let me take you to dinner tonight. I just sold the Spanish chairs, and I feel a need to celebrate.'

'Can't do, I'm afraid. I'm going to have to work most of the night to finish here.'

'Can't the staff work a bit of overtime?' she asked.

'They've done their job. But you know how I am. I have to double-check and triple-check everything.'

'I'll come help.'

'There's nothing you can help with.'

'Then I'll sit in the corner and read.'

'Really, Connie, you'd be bored. You go home and relax. I'll show up sometime around one or two in the morning.'

'Nothing doing. I won't get in your way, and I'll be perfectly comfortable reading in an office chair. Nora needs her Nick tonight. I'll bring supper.'

'Well . . . okay. Who am I kidding? I knew you'd come.'

'A large pizza and a bottle of wine. How's that?'

'Sounds good.'

'When?' she asked.

'I've been dozing over my typewriter. If I'm to get this work done tonight, I'd better take a nap. As soon as the staff clears out for the day, I'll lie down. Why don't you bring the pizza at seven-thirty?'

'Count on it.'

'We'll have company at eight-thirty.'

'Who?'

'A police detective. He wants to discuss some new evidence in the Butcher case.'

'Preduski?' she asked.

'No. One of Preduski's lieutenants. A guy named Bollinger. He called a few minutes ago and wanted to come to the house this evening. I told him that you and I would be working here until late.'

'Well, at least he's coming after we eat,' she said. 'Talking about the Butcher *before* dinner would spoil my appetite.'

'See you at seven-thirty.'

'Sleep tight, Nicky.'

When the percolator shut off, she poured steaming coffee into a mug, added cream, went to the front of the store and sat in a chair near one of the mullioned show windows. She could look over and between the antiques for a many-paned view of a windswept section of Tenth Street.

A few people hurried past, dressed in heavy coats, their hands in their pockets, heads tucked down.

Scattered snowflakes followed the air currents down between the buildings and ricocheted along the pavement.

She sipped her coffee and almost purred as the warmth spread through her.

She thought about Graham and felt warmer still. Nothing could chill her when Graham was on her mind. Not wind. Not snow. Not the Butcher. She felt safe with Graham – even with just the thought of him. Safe and protected. She knew that, in spite of the fear that had grown in him since his fall, he would lay down his life for her if that was ever required of him. Just as she would give her life to save his. It wasn't likely that either of them would be presented with such a dramatic choice; but she was convinced that Graham would find his courage gradually in the weeks and months ahead, would find it without the help of a crisis.

Suddenly the wind exploded against the window, howled and moaned and pasted snow, like specks of froth and spittle, to the cold glass.

·12·

The room was long and narrow with a brown tile floor, beige walls, a high ceiling and fluorescent lights. Two metal desks stood just inside the door; they held typewriters, letter trays, vases full of artificial flowers, and the detritus of a day's work. The two well-dressed matronly women behind the desks were cheerful in spite of the drab institutional atmosphere. There were five cafeteria tables lined up, short end to short end, so that whoever sat at them would always be sideways to the desks. The ten metal chairs were all on the same side of the table row. Except for the relationship of the tables to the desks, it might have been a schoolroom, a study hall monitored by two teachers.

Frank Bollinger identified himself as Ben Frank and said he was an employee of a major New York City firm of architects. He asked for the complete file on the Bowerton Building, took off his coat and sat at the first table.

The two women, as efficient as they appeared to be, quickly brought him the Bowerton material from an adjacent storage room: original blueprints, amendments to the blueprints, cost estimates, applications for dozens of different building permits, final cost sheets, remodeling plans, photographs, letters . . . Every form – and everything else required by law – that was related to the Bowerton highrise and that had passed officially through a city bureau or department was in that file. It was a formidable mound of paper, even though each piece was carefully labeled and both categorically and sequentially arranged.

The forty-two-story Bowerton Building, facing a busy block of Lexington Avenue, had been completed in 1929 and stood essentially unchanged. It was one of Manhattan's art deco masterpieces, even more effectively designed than the justly acclaimed art deco Chanin Building which was only a few blocks away. More than a year ago a group of concerned citizens had launched a campaign to have the building declared a landmark in order to keep its most spectacular art deco features from being wiped away during sporadic flurries of 'modernization.' But the most important fact, so far as Bollinger was concerned, was that Graham Harris had his offices on the fortieth floor of the Bowerton Building.

For an hour and ten minutes, Bollinger studied the paper image of the structure. Main entrances. Service entrances. One-way emergency exits. The placement and operation of the bank of sixteen elevators. The placement of the two stairwells. A minimal electronic security system, primarily a closed-circuit television guard station, had been installed in 1969; and he went over and over the paper on that until he was certain that he had overlooked no detail of it.

At four forty-five he stood up, yawned and stretched. Smiling, humming softly, he put on his overcoat.

Two blocks from City Hall he stepped into a telephone booth and called Billy. 'I've checked it out.'

'Bowerton?'

'Yeah.'

'What do you think?' Billy asked anxiously.

'It can be done.'

'My God. You're sure?'

'As sure as I can be until I start it.'

'Maybe I should be more help. I could –'

'No,' Bollinger said. 'If anything goes wrong, I can flash my badge and say I showed up to investigate a complaint. Then I can slip quietly away. But if we were both there, how could we explain our way out of it?'

'I suppose you're right.'

'We'll stick to thc original plan.'

'All right.'

'You be in that alleyway at ten o'clock.'

Billy said, 'What if you get there and discover it won't work? I don't want to be waiting –'

'If I have to give it up,' Bollinger said, 'I'll call you well before ten. But if you don't get the call, *be in that alley*.'

'Of course. What else? But I won't wait past ten-thirty. I *can't* wait longer than that.'

'That'll be long enough.'

Billy sighed happily. 'Are we going to stand this city on its ear?'

'Nobody will sleep tomorrow night.'

'Have you decided what lines you'll write on the wall?'

Bollinger waited until a city bus rumbled past the booth. His choice of quotations was clever; and he wanted Billy to appreciate them. 'Yeah. I've got a long one from Nietzsche. "I want to teach men the sense of their existence, which is Superman, the lightning out of the dark cloud man." '

'Oh, that's excellent,' Billy said. 'I couldn't have chosen better myself.'

'Thank you.'

'And Blake?'

'Just a fragment from the alternate seventh night of *The Four Zoas*. "Hearts laid open to the light . . ." '

Billy laughed.

'I knew you'd like it.'

'I suppose you *do* intend to lay their hearts open?'

'Naturally,' Bollinger said. 'Their hearts and everything else, from throat to crotch.'

·13·

Promptly at six o'clock, the doorbell rang.

Sarah Piper answered it. Her professional smile slipped when she saw who was standing in the hall. 'What are *you* doing here?' she asked, surprised.

'May I come in?'

'Well . . .'

'You look beautiful tonight. Absolutely stunning.'

She was wearing a tight burnt-orange pantsuit, flimsy, with a low neckline that revealed too much of her creamy breasts. Self-consciously she put one hand over her cleavage. 'I'm sorry, but I can't ask you in. I'm expecting someone.'

'You're expecting me,' he said. 'Billy James Plover.'

'What? That's not your name.'

'It surely is. It's the name I was born with. I changed it years ago, of course.'

'Why didn't you give me your real name on the phone?'

'I've got to protect my reputation.'

Still confused, she stepped back to let him pass. She closed the door and locked it. Aware that she was being rude but unable to control herself, she stared openly at him. She couldn't think what to say.

'You seem shocked, Sarah.'

'Yeah,' she said. 'I guess I am. It's just that you don't seem like the sort of man who would come to a woman – to someone like me.'

He had been smiling from the moment she'd opened the door. Now his face broke into a broad grin. 'What's wrong with someone like you? You're gorgeous.'

This is crazy, she thought.

She said, 'Your voice.'

'The Southern accent?'

'Yeah.'

417

'That's also part of my youth, just like the name. Would you prefer I dropped it?'

'Yeah. Your talking like that – it's not right. It's creepy.' She hugged herself.

'Creepy? I thought you'd be amused. And when I'm Billy . . . I don't know . . . I kind of have fun with it . . . kind of feel like someone altogether new.' He stared hard at her and said, 'Something's wrong. We're off on the wrong foot. Or maybe worse than that. Is it worse than that? If you don't want to go to bed with me, say so. I'll understand. Maybe something about me repels you. I haven't always been successful with women. I've lost out many times. God knows. So just tell me. I'll leave. No hard feelings.'

She put on her professional smile again and shook her head. Her thick blond hair bounced prettily. 'I'm sorry. There's no need for you to go. I was just surprised, that's all.'

'You're sure?'

'Positive.'

He looked at the living room beyond the foyer arch, reached down to finger the antique umbrella stand beside the door. 'You have a nice place.'

'Thank you.' She opened the foyer closet, plucked a hanger from the clothes rod. 'Let me take your coat.'

He took it off, handed it to her.

As she put the coat in the closet, she said, 'Your gloves too. I'll put them in a coat pocket.'

'I'll keep my gloves,' he said.

When she turned back to him, he was standing between her and the front door, and he was holding a wicked switchblade knife in his right hand.

She said, 'Put that away.'

'What did you say?'

'*Put that away!*'

He laughed.

'I mean it,' she said.

'You're the coolest bitch I've ever met.'

'Put that knife in your pocket. Put it away and then get out of here.'

Waving the knife at her, he said, 'When they realize I'm going to slit them open, they say some silly things. But I don't believe any of them ever *seriously* thought she could talk me out of it. Until you. So very cool.'

She twisted away from him. She ran out of the foyer, into the living room. Her heart was pounding; she was shaking badly; but she was determined not to be incapacitated by fear. She kept a gun in the top drawer of her nightstand. If she could get into the bedroom, close and lock the door between them, she could hold him off long enough to put her hands on the pistol.

Within a few steps he caught her by the shoulder.

She tried to jerk free.

He was stronger than he looked. His fingers were like talons. He swung her around and shoved her backward.

Off balance, she collided with the coffee table, fell over it. She struck her hip on one of the heavy wooden legs; pain like an incandescent bulb flashed along her thigh.

He stood over her, still holding the knife, still grinning.

'Bastard,' she said.

'There are two ways you can die, Sarah. You can try to run and resist, forcing me to kill you now – painfully and slowly. Or you can cooperate, come into the bedroom, let me give you some fun. Then I promise you'll die quickly and painlessly.'

Don't panic, she told herself. You're Sarah Piper, and you came out of nothing, and you made something of yourself, and you have been knocked down dozens of times before, knocked down figuratively and literally, and you've always gotten up, and you'll get up this time, and you'll survive, you will, dammit, you will.

'Okay,' she said. She stood up.

'Good girl.' He held the knife out at his side. He unbuttoned the bodice of her pantsuit and slipped his free hand under the thin material. 'Nice,' he said.

She closed her eyes as he moved nearer.

'I'll make it fun for you,' he said.

She drove her knee into his crotch.

Although the blow didn't land squarely, he staggered backward.

She grabbed a table lamp and threw it. Without waiting to see if it hit him, she ran into the bedroom and shut the door.

Before she could lock it, he slammed against the far side and pushed the door open two or three inches.

She tried to force it shut again so that she could throw the lock, but he was stronger than she. She knew she couldn't hold out against him for more than a minute or two. Therefore, when he was pressing the hardest and would expect it the least, she let go of the door altogether and ran to the nightstand.

Surprised, he stumbled into the room and nearly fell.

She pulled open the nightstand drawer and picked up the gun.

He knocked it out of her hand. It clattered against the wall and dropped to the floor, out of reach.

Why didn't you scream? she asked herself. Why didn't you yell for help while you could hold the door shut? It's unlikely anyone would hear you in soundly built apartments like these, but at least it was worth a try when you had a chance.

But she knew why she didn't cry out. She was Sarah Piper. She had never called for help in her life. She had always solved her own problems, had always fought her own battles. She was tough and proud of it. She did not scream.

She was terrified, trembling, sick with fear, but she knew that she had to die the same way she had lived. If she broke now, whimpered and mewled when there wasn't any chance of salvation, she would be making a lie of her life. If her life was to have meant anything, anything at all, she would have to die as she had lived: resolute, proud, tough.

She spat in his face.

•14•

'Homicide.'
   'I want to speak to a detective.'
   'What's his name?'
   'Any detective. I don't care.'
   'Is this an emergency?'
   'Yes.'
   'Where are you calling from?'
   'Never mind. I want a detective.'
   'I'm required to take your address, telephone number, name –'
   'Stuff it! Let me talk to a detective or I'll hang up.'

'Detective Martin speaking.'
   'I just killed a woman.'
   'Where are you calling from?'
   'Her apartment.'
   'What's the address?'
   'She was very beautiful.'
   'What's the address?'
   'A lovely girl.'
   'What was her name?'
   'Sarah.'
   'Do you know her last name?'
   'Piper.'
   'Will you spell that?'
   'P-i-p-e-r.'
   'Sarah Piper.'
   'That's right.'
   'What's your name?'
   'The Butcher.'
   'What's your real name?'
    'I'm not going to tell you.'

'Yes, you are. That's why you called.'

'No. I called to tell you I'm going to kill some more people before the night's out.'

'Who?'

'One of them is the woman I love.'

'What's her name?'

'I wish I didn't have to kill her.'

'Then don't. You –'

'But I think she suspects.'

'Why don't we –'

'Nietzsche was right.'

'Who?'

'Nietzsche.'

'Who's he?'

'A philosopher.'

'Oh.'

'He was right about women.'

'What did he say about women?'

'They just get in our way. They hold us back from perfection. All those energies we put into courting them and screwing them – wasted! All that wasted sex energy could be put to other use, to thought and study. If we didn't waste our energies on women, we would evolve into what we were meant to be.'

'And what were we meant to be?'

'Are you trying to trace this call?'

'No, no.'

'Yes. Of course you are.'

'No, really we aren't.'

'I'll be gone from here in a minute. I just wanted to tell you that tomorrow you'll know who I am, who the Butcher is. But you won't catch me. I'm the lightning out of the dark cloud man.'

'Let's try to –'

'Good-bye, Detective Martin.'

·15·

At seven o'clock Friday evening, a fine dry snow began to fall in Manhattan, not merely flurries but a full-scale storm. The snow sifted out of the black sky and made pale, shifting patterns on the dark streets.

In his living room, Frank Bollinger watched the millions of tiny flakes streaming past the window. The snow pleased him no end. With the weekend ahead, and now especially with the change of weather, it was doubtful that anyone other than Harris and his woman would be working late in the Bowerton Building. He felt that his chances of getting to them and pulling off the plan without a hitch had improved considerably. The snow was an accomplice.

At seven-twenty, he took his overcoat from the hall closet, slipped into it and buttoned up.

The pistol was already in the right coat pocket. He wasn't using his police revolver, because bullets from that could be traced too easily. This was a Walther PPK, a compact .38 that had been banned from importation into the United States since 1969. (A slightly larger pistol, the Walther PPK/S, was now manufactured for marketing in the United States; it was less easily concealed than the original model). There was a silencer on the piece, not homemade junk but a precision-machined silencer made by Walther for use by various elite European police agencies. Even with the silencer screwed in place, the gun fit easily out of sight in the deep overcoat pocket. Bollinger had taken the weapon off a dead man, a suspect in a narcotics and prostitution investigation. The moment he saw it he knew that he must have it, and he failed to report finding it as he should have done. That was nearly a year ago; he'd had no occasion to use it until tonight.

In his left coat pocket, Bollinger was carrying a box of fifty bullets. He didn't think he'd need more than were already in the pistol's magazine, but he intended to be prepared for any eventuality.

423

He left the apartment and took the stairs two at a time, eager for the hunt to begin.

Outside, the grainy, wind-driven snow was like bits of ground glass. The night howled spectrally between the buildings and rattled the branches of the trees.

Graham Harris's office, the largest of the five rooms in the Harris Publications suite on the fortieth floor of the Bowerton Building, didn't look like a place where business was transacted. It was paneled in dark wood – real and solid wood, not veneer – and had a textured beige acoustical ceiling. The forest-green ceiling-to-floor drapes matched the plush carpet. The desk had once been a Steinway piano; the guts had been ripped out, the lid lowered and cut to fit the frame. Behind the desk rose bookshelves filled with volumes about skiing and climbing. The light came from four floor-lamps with old-fashioned ceramic sconces and glass chimneys that hid the electric bulbs. There were also two brass reading lamps on the desk. A small conference table and four armchairs occupied the space in front of the windows. A richly carved seventeenth-century British coatrack stood by the door to the corridor, and an antique bar of cut glass, beveled mirrors and inlaid woods stood by the door to the reception lounge. On the walls were photographs of climbing teams in action, and there was one oil painting, a mountain snowscape. The room might have been a study in the home of a retired professor, where books were read and pipes were smoked and where a spaniel lay curled at the feet of its master.

Connie opened the foil-lined box on the conference table. Steam rose from the pizza; a spicy aroma filled the office.

The wine was chilled. In the pizzeria, she had made them keep the bottle in their refrigerator until the pie was ready to go.

Famished, they ate and drank in silence for a few minutes.

Finally she said, 'Did you take a nap?'

'Did I ever.'

'How long?'

'Two hours.'

'Sleep well?'

'Like the dead.'

'You don't look it.'

'Dead?'

'You don't look like you'd slept.'

'Maybe I dreamed it.'

'You've got dark rings under your eyes.'

'My Rudolph Valentino look.'

'You should go home to bed.'

'And have the printer down my throat tomorrow?'

'They're *quarterly* magazines. A few days one way or the other won't matter.'

'You're talking to a perfectionist.'

'Don't I know it.'

'A perfectionist who loves you.'

She blew him a kiss.

Frank Bollinger parked his car on a side street and walked the last three blocks to the Bowerton Building.

A skin of snow, no more than a quarter inch but growing deeper, sheathed the sidewalks and street. Except for a few taxicabs that spun past too fast for the road conditions, there was not much traffic on Lexington Avenue.

The main entrance to the Bowerton Building was set back twenty feet from the sidewalk. There were four revolving glass doors, three of them locked at this hour. Beyond the doors the large lobby, rich with marble and brasswork and copper trim, was overflowing with warm amber light.

Bollinger patted the pistol in his pocket and went inside.

Overhead, a closed-circuit television camera was suspended from a brace. It was focused on the only unlocked door.

Bollinger stamped his feet to knock the snow from his shoes and to give the camera time to study him. The man in the control room wouldn't find him suspicious if he faced the camera without concern.

A uniformed security guard was sitting on a stool behind a lectern near the first bank of elevators.

Bollinger walked over to him, stepped out of the camera's range.

'Evening,' the guard said.

As he walked, he took his wallet from an inside pocket and flashed the gold badge. 'Police.' His voice echoed eerily off the marble walls and the high ceiling.

'Something wrong?' the guard asked.

'Anybody working late tonight?'

'Just four.'

'All in the same office?'

'No. What's up?'

Bollinger pointed to the open registry on the lectern. 'I'd like all four names.'

'Let's see here . . . Harris, Davis, Ott and MacDonald.'

'Where would I find Ott?'

'Sixteenth floor.'

'What's the name of the office?'

'Cragmont Imports.'

The guard's face was round and white. He had a weak mouth and a tiny Oliver Hardy mustache. When he tried for an expression of curiosity, the mustache nearly disappeared up his nostrils.

'What floor for MacDonald?' Bollinger asked.

'Same. Sixteenth.'

'He's working with Ott?'

'That's right.'

'Just those four?'

'Just those four.'

'Maybe someone else is working late, and you don't know it.'

'Impossible. After five-thirty, anyone going upstairs has to sign in with me. At six o'clock we go through every floor to see who's working late, and then they check out with us when they leave. The building management has set down strict fire-prevention rules. This is part of them.' He patted the registry. 'If there's ever a fire, we'll know exactly who's in the building and where we can find them.'

'What about maintenance crews?'

'What about them?'

'Janitors. Cleaning women. Any working now?'

'Not on Friday night.'

'You're sure?'

'Sure I'm sure.' He was visibly upset by the interrogation and beginning to wonder if he should cooperate. 'They come in all day tomorrow.'

'Building engineer?'

'Schiller. He's night engineer.'

'Where is Schiller?'

'Downstairs.'

'Where downstairs?'

'Checking one of the heat pumps, I think.'

'Is he alone?'

'Yeah.'

'How many other security guards?'

'Are you going to tell me what's up?'

'For God's sake, this is an emergency!' Bollinger said. 'How many security guards besides you?'

'Just two. What emergency?'

'There's been a bomb threat.'

The guard's lips trembled. The mustache seemed about to fall off. 'You're kidding.'

'I wish I were.'

The guard slid off his stool, stepped from behind the lectern.

At the same time Bollinger took the Walther from his pocket.

The guard blanched. 'What's that?'

'A gun. Don't go for yours.'

'Look, this bomb threat . . . *I* didn't call it in.'

Bollinger laughed.

'It's true.'

'I'm sure it is.'

'Hey . . . that gun has a silencer on it.'

'Yeah.'

'But policemen don't –'

Bollinger shot him twice in the chest.

The impact of the bullets threw the guard into the sheet marble. For an instant he stood very straight, as if he were waiting for someone to measure his height and mark it on the wall. Then he collapsed.

Part Two

FRIDAY
8:00–8:30 P.M.

·16·

Bollinger turned immediately from the dead man and looked at the revolving doors. Nobody was there, no one on the sidewalk beyond, no one who might have seen the killing.

Moving quickly but calmly, he tucked the pistol into his pocket and grabbed the body by the arms. He dragged it into the waiting area between the first two banks of elevators. Now, anyone coming to the doors would see only an empty lobby.

The dead man stared at him. The mustache seemed to have been painted on his lip.

Bollinger turned out the guard's pockets. He found quarters, dimes, a crumpled five-dollar bill, and a key ring with seven keys.

He returned to the main part of the lobby.

He wanted to go straight to the door, but he knew that was not a good idea. That would put him in camera range. If the men monitoring the closed-circuit system saw him locking the door, they would be curious. They'd come to investigate, and he would lose the advantage of surprise.

Keeping in mind the details of the plans he had studied at City Hall that afternoon, he walked quietly to the rear of the lobby and stepped into a short corridor on the left. Four rooms led off the hall. The second on the right was the guards' room, and the door was open.

Wondering if the squeaking of his wet shoes sounded as loud to the guards as it did to him, he edged up to the open door.

Inside, two men were talking laconically about their jobs, complaining, but only half-heartedly.

Bollinger took the pistol from his coat pocket. He walked through the doorway.

The men were sitting at a small table in front of three television screens. They weren't watching the monitors. They were playing two-handed pinochle.

431

The older of the two was in his fifties. Heavy. Gray-haired. He had a prizefighter's lumpy face. The name 'Neely' was stitched on his left shirt pocket. He was slow. He looked up at Bollinger, failed to react as he should have to the gun, and said without fear, 'What's this?'

The other guard was in his thirties. Trim. Ascetic face. Pale hands. As he turned to see what had caught Neely's attention, Bollinger saw 'Faulkner' stitched on his shirt.

He shot Faulkner first.

Reaching with both hands for his ruined throat, too late to stop the life from gushing out of him, Faulkner toppled backward in his chair.

'Hey!' Fat Neely was finally on his feet. His holster was snapped shut. He grappled with it.

Bollinger shot him twice.

Neely did an ungraceful pirouette, fell on the table, collapsed it, and went to the floor in a flutter of pinochle cards.

Bollinger checked their pulses.

They were dead.

When he left the room, he closed the door.

At the front of the big lobby, he locked the last revolving door and put the keys into his pocket.

He went to the lectern, sat on the stool. He took the box of bullets from his left coat pocket and replenished the pistol's magazine.

He looked at his watch. 8:10. He was right on schedule.

•17•

'That was good pizza,' Graham said.

'Good wine, too. Have another glass.'

'I've had enough.'

'Just a little one.'

'No. I've got to work.'

'Dammit.'

'You knew that when you came.'

'I was trying to get you drunk.'

'On one bottle of wine?'

'And then seduce you.'

'Tomorrow night,' he said.

'I'll be blind with desire by then.'

'Doesn't matter. Love is a Braille experience.'

She winced.

He got up, came around the table, kissed her cheek. 'Did you bring a book to read?'

'A Nero Wolfe mystery.'

'Then read.'

'Can I look at you from time to time?'

'What's to look at?'

'Why do *men* buy *Playboy* magazine?' she asked.

'I won't be working in the nude.'

'You don't have to be.'

'Pretty dull.'

'You're even sexy with your clothes on.'

'Okay,' he said, smiling. 'Look but don't talk.'

'Can I drool?'

'Drool if you must.'

He was pleased with the flattery, and she was delighted by his reaction. She felt that she was gradually chipping away at his inferiority complex, peeling it layer by layer.

·18·

The building engineer for the night shift was a stocky, fair-skinned blond in his late forties. He was wearing gray slacks and a gray-white-blue checkered shirt. He was smoking a pipe.

When Bollinger came down the steps from the lobby corridor, the gun in his right hand, the engineer said, 'Who the hell are you?' He spoke with a slight German accent.

'*Sie sind Herr Schiller, nicht wahr?*' Bollinger asked. His grandfather and grandmother had been German-Americans; he had learned the language when he was young and had never forgotten it.

Surprised to hear German spoken, worried about the gun but confused by Bollinger's smile, Schiller said. '*Ja, ich bin's.*'

'*Es freut mich sehr Sie kennenzulernen.*'

Schiller took the pipe from his mouth. He licked his lips nervously. '*Die Pistole?*'

'*Fur den Mord,*' Bollinger said. He squeezed off two shots.

Upstairs, on the lobby floor, Bollinger opened the door directly across the hall from the guards' room. He switched on the lights.

The narrow room was lined with telephone and power company equipment. The ceiling and walls were unfinished concrete. Two bright red fire extinguishers were hung where they could be reached quickly.

He went to the far side of the room, to a pair of yard-square metal cabinets that were fixed to the wall. The lid of each cabinet bore the insignia of the telephone company. Although the destruction of the contents would render useless all other routing boxes, switchboards and backup systems, neither of the cabinets was locked. Each housed twenty-six small levers, circuit breakers in a fuse box. They were all inclined toward the 'on' mark. Bollinger switched them off, one by one.

He moved to a box labeled 'Fire Emergency,' forced it open, and tinkered with the wires inside.

That done, he went to the guards' room across the hall. He stepped around the bodies and picked up one of the two telephones that stood in front of the closed-circuit television screens.

No dial tone.

He jiggled the cut-off spikes.

Still no dial tone.

He hung up, picked up the other phone: another dead line.

Whistling softly, Bollinger entered the first elevator.

There were two keyholes in the control panel. The top one opened the panel for repairs. The one at the bottom shut down the lift mechanism.

He tried the keys that he had taken from the dead guard. The third one fit the bottom lock.

He pushed the button for the fifth floor. The number didn't light; the doors didn't close; the elevator didn't move.

Whistling louder than before, he proceeded to shut down fourteen of the remaining fifteen elevators. He would use the last one to go to the sixteenth floor, where Ott and MacDonald were working, and later to the fortieth floor, where Harris and his woman were waiting.

·19·

Although Graham hadn't spoken, Connie knew that something was wrong. He was breathing heavily. She looked up from her book and saw that he had stopped working and was staring at empty air, his mouth slightly open, his eyes sort of glazed. 'What's the matter?'

'Nothing.'

'You're pale.'

'Just a headache.'

'You're shaking.'

He said nothing.

She got up, put down her book, went to him. She sat on the corner of his desk. 'Graham?'

'It's okay. I'm fine now.'

'No, you aren't.'

'I'm fine.'

'There for a minute you weren't.'

'For a minute I wasn't,' he agreed.

She took his hand; it was icy. 'A vision?'

'Yeah,' Graham said.

'Of what?'

'Me. Getting shot.'

'That's not the least bit funny.'

'I'm not joking.'

'You've never had a *personal* vision before. You've always said the clairvoyance works only when other people are involved.'

'Not this time.'

'Maybe you're wrong.'

'I doubt it. I felt as if I had been hit between the shoulders with a sledgehammer. The wind was knocked out of me. I saw myself falling.' His blue eyes grew wide. 'There was blood. A great deal of blood.'

437

She felt sick in her soul, in her heart. He had never been wrong, and now he was predicting he would be shot.

He squeezed her hand tightly, as if he were trying to press strength from her into him.

'Do you mean shot – and killed?'

'I don't know,' he said. 'Maybe killed or maybe just wounded. Shot in the back. That much is clear.'

'Who did it – will do it?'

'The Butcher, I think.'

'You saw him?'

'No. Just a strong impression.'

'Where did it happen?'

'Someplace I know well.'

'Here?'

'Maybe . . .'

'At home?'

'Maybe.'

A fierce gust of wind boomed along the side of the highrise. The office windows vibrated behind the drapes.

'When will it happen?' she asked.

'Soon.'

'Tonight?'

'I can't be sure.'

'Tomorrow?'

'Possibly.'

'Sunday?

'Not as late as that.'

'What are we going to do?'

·20·

The lift stopped at the sixteenth floor.

Bollinger used the key to shut off the elevator before he stepped out of it. The cab would remain where it was, doors open, until he needed it again.

For the most part, the sixteenth floor was shrouded in darkness. An overhead fluorescent tube brightened the elevator alcove, but the only light in the corridor came from two dim red emergency exit bulbs, one at each end of the building.

Bollinger had anticipated the darkness. He took a pencil flashlight from an inside coat pocket, flicked it on.

Ten small businesses maintained offices on the sixteenth floor, six to the right and four to the left of the elevators. He went to the right. Two suites down the hall he found a door that bore the words CRAGMONT IMPORTS.

He turned off the flashlight and put it away.

He took out the Walther PPK.

Christ, he thought, it's going so smoothly. So easily. As soon as he finished at Cragmont Imports, he could go after the primary targets. Harris first. Then the woman. If she was good-looking . . . well, he was so far ahead of schedule now that he had an hour to spare. An hour for the woman if she rated it. He was ready for a woman, full of energy and appetite and excitement. A woman, a table filled with good food, and a lot of fine whiskey. But mostly a woman. In an hour he could use her up, really use her up.

He tried the door to Cragmont Imports. It wasn't locked.

He walked into the reception lounge. The room was gloomy. The only light came from an adjacent office where the door was standing halfway open.

He went to the shaft of light, stood in it, listened to the men talking in the inner office. At last he pushed open the door and went inside.

They were sitting at a conference table that was piled high with papers and bound folders. They weren't wearing their suit jackets or their ties, and their shirt sleeves were rolled up; one was wearing a blue shirt, the other a white shirt. They saw the pistol at once, but they needed several seconds to adjust before they could raise their eyes to look at his face.

'This place smells like perfume,' Bollinger said.

They stared at him.

'Is one of you wearing perfume?'

'No,' said blue shirt. 'Perfume's one of the things we import.'

'Is one of you MacDonald?'

They looked at the gun, at each other, then at the gun again.

'MacDonald?' Bollinger asked.

The one in the blue shirt said, 'He's MacDonald.'

The one in the white shirt said, '*He's* MacDonald.'

'That's a lie,' said the one in the blue shirt.

'No, *he's* lying,' said the other.

'I don't know what you want with MacDonald,' said the one in the blue shirt. 'Just leave me out of it. Do what you have to do to him and go away.'

'Christ almighty!' said the one in the white shirt. 'I'm *not* MacDonald! You want *him*, that son of a bitch there, not me!'

Bollinger laughed. 'It doesn't matter. I'm also here to get Mr Ott.'

'*Me?*' said the one in the blue shirt. 'Who in the hell would want *me* killed?'

·21·

Connie said, 'You'll have to call Preduski.'

'Why?'

'To get police protection.'

'It's no use.'

'He believes in your visions.'

'I know he does.'

'He'll give you protection.'

'Of course,' Graham said. 'But that's not what I meant.'

'Explain.'

'Connie, I've seen myself shot in the back. It's going to happen. Things I see *always* happen. Nobody can do anything to stop this.'

'There's no such thing as predestination. The future can be changed.'

'Can it?'

'You know it can.'

A haunted look filled his bright blue eyes. 'I doubt that very much.'

'You can't be sure.'

'But I am sure.'

This attitude of his, this willingness to ascribe all of his failings to predestination, worried and upset her more than anything else about him. It was an especially pernicious form of cowardice. He was rejecting all responsibility for his own life.

'Call Preduski,' she said.

He lowered his eyes and stared at her hand but didn't seem to see how tightly he was gripping it.

She said, 'If this man comes to the *house* to kill you, I'll probably be there too. Do you think he's going to shoot you, then just walk away and let *me* live?'

Shocked, as she had known he would be, by the thought of her under the Butcher's knife, he said, 'My God.'

441

'Call Preduski.'

'All right.' He let go of her hand. He picked up the receiver, listened for a moment, played with the dial, jiggled the buttons.

'What's wrong?'

Frowning, he said, 'No dial tone.' He hung up, waited a few seconds, picked up the receiver again. 'Still nothing.'

She slid off the desk. 'Let's try your secretary's phone.'

They went out to the reception room.

That phone was dead too.

'Funny,' he said.

Her heartbeat quickening, she said, 'Is he going to come after you tonight?'

'I told you, I don't know for sure.'

'Is he in the building right now?'

'You think he cut the telephone line.'

She nodded.

'That's pretty farfetched,' he said. 'It's just a breakdown in service.'

She went to the door, opened it, stepped into the hall. He came behind her, favoring his injured leg.

Darkness lay on most of the corridor. Dim red emergency lights shone at each end of the hall, above the doors to the staircases. Fifty feet away a pool of wan blue light marked the elevator alcove.

Except for the sound of their breathing, the fortieth floor was silent.

'I'm not a clairvoyant,' she said, 'but I don't like the way it feels. I sense it, Graham. Something's wrong.'

'In a building like this, the telephone lines are in the walls. Outside of the building they're underground. All the lines are underground in this city. How would he get to them?'

'I don't know. But maybe *he* knows.'

'He'd be taking such a risk,' Graham said.

'He's taken risks before. Ten times before.'

'But not like this. We're not alone. The security guards are in the building.'

'They're forty stories below.'

'A long way,' he agreed. 'Let's get out of here.'

'We're probably being silly.'

'Probably.'

'We're probably safe where we are.'

'Probably.'

'I'll grab our coats.'

'Forget the coats.' He took hold of her hand. 'Come on. Let's get to those elevators.'

Bollinger needed eight shots to finish off MacDonald and Ott. They kept ducking behind the furniture.

By the time he had killed them, the Walther PPK was no longer firing silently. No silencer could function at peak efficiency for more than a dozen shots; the baffles and wadding were compacted by the bullets, and sound escaped. The last three shots were like the sharp barks of a medium-sized guard dog. But that didn't matter. The noise wouldn't carry to the street or up to the fortieth floor.

In the outer office of Cragmont Imports, he switched on a light. He sat on a couch, reloaded the Walther's magazine, unscrewed the silencer and put it into his pocket. He didn't want to risk fouling the barrel with loose steel fibers from the silencer; besides, there was no one left in the building to hear shots when he killed Harris and the woman. And a shot fired on the fortieth floor would not penetrate walls and windows and travel all the way down to Lexington Avenue.

He looked at his watch. 8:25.

He turned off the light, left Cragmont Imports, and went down the hall to the elevator.

Eight elevators served the fortieth floor, but none of them was working.

Connie pushed the call button on the last lift. When nothing happened, she said, 'The telephone, and now this.'

In the spare yet harsh fluorescent light, Graham's laugh lines looked deeper and sharper than usual; his face resembled that of a kabuki actor painted to represent extreme anxiety. 'We're trapped.'

'It could be just an ordinary breakdown of some sort,' she said. 'Mechanical failure. They might be making repairs right now.'

'The telephones?'

'Coincidence. Maybe there's nothing sinister about it.'

Suddenly the numerals above the elevator doors in front of them began to light up, one after the other: 16 . . . 17 . . . 18 . . . 19 . . . 20 . . .

'Someone's coming,' Graham said.

A chill passed down her spine.

. . . 25 . . . 26 . . . 27 . . .

'Maybe it's the security guards,' she said.

He said nothing.

She wanted to turn and run, but she could not move. The numbers mesmerized her.

. . . 30 . . . 31 . . . 32 . . .

She thought of women lying in bloody bedclothes, women with their throats cut and their fingers chopped off and their ears cut off.

. . . 33 . . .

'The stairs!' Graham said, startling her.

'Stairs?'

'The emergency stairs.'

. . . 34 . . .

'What about them?'

'We've got to go down.'

'Hide out a few floors below?'

. . . 35 . . .

'No. All the way down to the lobby.'

'That's too far!'

'That's where there's help.'

. . . 36 . . .

'Maybe we don't need help.'

'We need it,' he said.

. . . 37 . . .

'But your leg –'

'I'm not a *complete* cripple,' he said sharply.

. . . 38 . . .

He grabbed her by the shoulder. His fingers hurt her, but she knew he wasn't aware of how fiercely he was gripping her. 'Come on, Connie!'

. . . 39 . . .

Frustrated with her hesitation, he gave her a shove, propelled her out of the alcove. She stumbled, and for an instant she thought she would fall. He kept her upright.

As they hurried down the dark corridor, she heard the elevator doors open behind them.

When Bollinger came out of the elevator alcove, he saw two people running away from him. They were nothing but ghostly shapes, vaguely silhouetted against the eerie glow of the red emergency light at the end of the corridor.

Harris and the woman? he wondered. Have they been alerted? Do they know who I am? How can they know?

'Mr. Harris?' Bollinger called.

They stopped two-thirds of the way down the hall, in front of the

444

open door to the Harris Publications suite. They turned toward him, but he could not see their faces even with the red light spilling over their shoulders.

'Mr. Harris, is that you?'

'Who are you?'

'Police,' Bollinger said. He took a step toward them, then another. As he moved he took the wallet with his badge from his inside coat pocket. With the elevator light behind him, he knew they could see more than he could.

'Don't come any closer,' Harris said.

Bollinger stopped. 'What's the matter?'

'I don't want you to come closer.'

'Why?'

'We don't know who you are.'

'I'm a detective. Frank Bollinger. We have an appointment for eight-thirty. Remember?' Another step. Then another.

'How did you get up here?' Harris's voice was shrill.

He's scared to death, Bollinger thought. He smiled and said, 'Hey, what's going on with you? Why are you so uptight? You were expecting me.' Bollinger took slow steps, easy steps, so as not to frighten the animals.

'How did you get up here?' Harris asked again. 'The elevators aren't working.'

'You're mistaken. I came up on an elevator.' He held the badge in front of him in his left hand, arm extended, hoping the light from behind would gleam on the gold finish. He had covered perhaps a fifth of the distance between them.

'The telephones are out,' Harris said.

'They are?' Step. Step.

He put his right hand in his coat pocket and gripped the butt of the pistol.

Connie couldn't take her eyes off the shadowy form moving steadily toward them. To Graham she said softly, 'You remember what you said on the Prine show?'

'What?' His voice cracked.

Don't let the fear take you, she thought. Don't break down and leave me to handle this alone.

She said, 'In your vision you saw that the police know the killer well.'

'What about it?'

'Maybe the Butcher is a cop.'

'Christ, that's it!'

He spoke so softly that she could barely hear him.

Bollinger kept coming, a big man, bearish. His face was in shadow. He had closed the distance between them by at least half.

'Stop right there,' Graham said. But there was no force in his voice, no authority.

Bollinger stopped anyway. 'Mr. Harris, you're acting very strange. I'm a *policeman*. You know . . . you're acting as if you've just done something that you want to hide from me.' He took a step, another, a third.

'The stairs?' Connie asked.

'No,' Graham said. 'We don't have enough of a lead. With my game leg, he'd catch us in a minute.'

'Mr. Harris?' Bollinger said. 'What are you two saying? Please don't whisper.'

'Where then?' Connie whispered.

'The office.'

He nudged her, and they ducked quickly into the Harris Publications suite, slammed and locked the reception room door.

A second later, Bollinger hit the outside of the door with his shoulder. It trembled in its frame. He rattled the knob violently.

'He's probably got a gun,' Connie said. 'He'll get in sooner or later.'

Graham nodded. 'I know.'

Part Three

FRIDAY
8:30–10:30 P.M.

·22·

Ira Preduski parked at the end of a string of three squad cars and two unmarked police sedans that blocked one half of the two-lane street. Although there was no one in any of the five vehicles, all the engines were running, headlights blazing; the trio of blue-and-whites were crowned with revolving red beacons. Preduski got out of his car and locked it.

A half inch of snow made the street look clean and pretty. As he walked toward the apartment house, Preduski scuffed his shoes against the sidewalk, sending up puffs of white flakes in front of him. The wind whipped the falling snow into his back, and cold flakes found their way past his collar. He was reminded of that February, in his fourth year, when his family moved to Albany, New York, where he saw his first winter storm.

A uniformed patrolman in his late twenties was standing at the bottom of the outside steps to the apartment house.

'Tough job you've got tonight,' Preduski said.

'I don't mind it. I like snow.'

'Yeah? So do I.'

'Besides,' the patrolman said, 'it's better standing out here in the cold than up there in all that blood.'

The room smelled of blood, excrement and dusting powder.

Fingers bent like claws, the dead woman lay on the floor beside the bed. Her eyes were open.

Two lab technicians were working around the body, studying it carefully before chalking its position and moving it.

Ralph Martin was the detective handling the on-scene investigation. He was chubby, completely bald, with bushy eyebrows and dark-rimmed glasses. He avoided looking at the corpse.

'The call from the Butcher came in at ten of seven,' Martin said.

449

'We tried your home number immediately, but we weren't able to get through until almost eight o'clock.'

'My phone was off the hook. I just got out of bed at a quarter past eight. I'm working graveyard.' He sighed and turned away from the corpse. 'What did he say – this Butcher?'

Martin took two folded sheets of paper from his pocket, unfolded them. 'I dictated the conversation, as well as I could recall it, and one of the girls made copies.'

Preduski read the two pages. 'He gave you no clue to who else he's going to kill tonight?'

'Just what's there.'

'This phone call is out of character.'

'And it's out of character for him to strike two nights in a row,' Martin said.

'It's also not like him to kill two women who knew each other and worked together.'

Martin raised his eyebrows. 'You think Sarah Piper knew something?'

'You mean, did she know who killed her friend?'

'Yeah. You think he killed Sarah to keep her from talking?'

'No. He probably just saw both of them at the Rhinestone Palace and couldn't make up his mind which he wanted the most. She didn't know who murdered Edna Mowry. I'd bet my life on that. Of course I'm not the best judge of character you'll ever meet. I'm pretty dense when it comes to people. God knows. Dense as stone. But this time I think I'm right. If she had known, she would have told me. She wasn't the kind of girl who could hide a thing like that. She was open. Forthright. Honest in her way. She was damned nice.'

Glancing at the dead woman's face, which was surprisingly unmarked and clear of blood in the midst of so much gore, Martin said, 'She was lovely.'

'I didn't mean just nice-looking,' Preduski said. 'She was a nice *person*.'

Martin nodded.

'She had a soft Georgia accent that reminded me of home.'

'Home?' Martin was confused. '*You're* from Georgia?'

'Why not?'

'Ira Preduski from Georgia?'

'They *do* have Jews and Slavs down there.'

'Where's your accent?'

'My parents weren't born in the South, so they didn't have an accent to pass on to me. And we moved North when I was four, before I had time to pick it up.'

For a moment they stared at the late Sarah Piper and at the pair of technicians who bent over her like Egyptian attendants of death.

Preduski turned away from the corpse, took a handkerchief from his pocket and blew his nose.

'The coroner's in the kitchen,' Martin said. His face was pale and greasy with sweat. 'He said he wanted to see you when you checked in.'

'Give me a few minutes,' Preduski said. 'I want to look around here a bit and talk with these fellows.'

'Mind if I wait in the living room?'

'No. Go ahead.'

Martin shuddered. 'This is a rotten job.'

'Rotten,' Preduski agreed.

·23·

The gunshot boomed and echoed in the dark corridor.

The lock shattered, and the wood splintered under the impact of the bullet.

Wrinkling his nose at the odor of burnt powder and scorched metal, Bollinger pushed open the ruined door.

The reception lounge was dark. When he found the light switch and flipped it up, he discovered that the room was also deserted.

Harris Publications occupied the smallest of three business suites on the fortieth floor. In addition to the hall door by which he had entered, two other doors opened from the reception area, one to the left and one to the right. Five rooms. Including the lounge. That didn't leave Harris and the woman with many places to hide.

First he tried the door to the left. It led to a private corridor that served three large offices: one for an editor and his secretary, one for an advertising space salesman, and one for the two man art department.

Neither Harris nor the woman was in any of those rooms.

Bollinger was cool, calm, but at the same time enormously excited. No sport could be half so dramatic and rewarding as hunting down people. He actually enjoyed the chase more than he did the kill. Indeed, he got an even greater kick out of the first few days immediately *after* a kill than he did from either the hunt or the murder itself. Once the act was done, once blood had been spilled, he had to wonder if he'd made a mistake, if he'd left behind a clue that would lead the police straight to him. The tension kept him sharp, made the juices bubble. Finally, when sufficient time had passed for him to be certain that he had gotten away with murder, a sense of well-being – of great importance, towering superiority, godhood – filled him like a magic elixir flowing into a long-empty pitcher.

The other door connected the reception room and Graham Harris's private office. It was locked.

He stepped back and fired two shots into the lock. The soft metal twisted and tore; chunks of wood spun into the air.

He still could not open it. They had pushed a heavy piece of furniture against the far side.

When he leaned on the door, pushed with all of his strength, he could not budge it; however, he *could* make the unseen piece of furniture rock back and forth on its base. He figured it was something high, at least as wide as the doorway, but not too deep. Perhaps a bookshelf. Something with a high center of gravity. He began to force the door rhythmically: push hard, relax, push hard, relax, push hard . . . The barricade tipped faster and farther each time he wobbled it – and suddenly it fell away from the door with a loud crash and the sound of breaking glass.

Abruptly the air was laden with whiskey fumes.

He squeezed through the door which remained partly blocked. He stepped over the antique bar they had used as a barrier and put his foot in a puddle of expensive Scotch.

The lights were on, but no one was there.

At the far end of the room there was another door. He went to it, opened it. Beyond lay the gloomy fortieth-floor corridor.

While he had wasted time searching the offices, they had slipped back into the hall by this circuitous route, gaining a few minutes lead on him.

Clever.

But not clever enough.

After all, they were nothing but ignorant game, while he was a master hunter.

He laughed softly.

Bathed in red light, Bollinger went to the nearer end of the hall and opened the fire door without making a sound. He stepped onto the landing in the emergency stairwell, closing the door quietly behind him. A dim white bulb burned above the exit on this side.

He heard their footsteps reverberating from below, amplified by the cold concrete walls.

He went to the steel railing and peered into the alternate layers of light and shadow: landings hung with bulbs, and stairs left dark. Ten or twelve flights down, five or six floors below, the woman's hand appeared on the railing, moving along less quickly than it should have. (If he had been in their place, he would have taken the steps two at a time, perhaps even faster.) Because the open core was so narrow – as long as a flight of stairs, but only one yard wide – Bollinger wasn't able to see at an angle into the tiers of steps beneath him. All he could see was the serpentine railing winding to infinity, and nothing of his prey except her white hand. A second later Harris's hand emerged from the velvety shadows, into the light that spilled out from a landing; he gripped the railing, followed the woman through the hazy light and into the darkness once again, descending.

For an instant Bollinger considered going down the steps behind them, shooting them in the back, but he rejected that thought almost as soon as it occurred to him. They would hear him coming. They would most likely scuttle out of the stairwell, seeking a place to hide or another escape route. He wouldn't know for certain at which floor they had left the stairs, and he couldn't run after them and watch their hands on the railing at the same time.

He didn't want to lose track of them. Although he wouldn't mind an interesting and complicated hunt, he didn't want it to drag on all night. For one thing, Billy would be waiting in the car, outside in the alley, at ten o'clock. For another, he wanted time with the woman, at least half an hour if she was at all good-looking.

Her pale hand slipped into sight on a light-swathed patch of railing.

Then Harris's hand.

They were still not moving as fast as they should have.

He tried to count flights of stairs. Twelve to fourteen. . . . They were six, maybe seven floors below.

Where did that put them?

Thirty-third floor?

Bollinger turned away from the railing, opened the door and left the stairwell. He ran down the fortieth-floor corridor to the elevator cab he was using. He switched it on with his key, hesitated, then put his thumb on the button for the twenty-sixth floor.

•24•

To Connie the stairwell seemed endless. As she passed through alternating levels of purple darkness and wan light, she felt as if she were following a long pathway to hell, the Butcher fulfilling the role of the grinning hellhound that harried her ever downward.

The stale air was cool. Nevertheless, she was perspiring.

She knew they should be going faster, but they were hampered in their flight by Graham's lame left leg. At one point she was almost overcome with anger, furious at him for being a hindrance to their escape. However, her fury vanished in the same instant, leaving her surprised by it and flushed with guilt. She had thought that no pressure, however great, could cause her to react to him so negatively. But filled with – nearly consumed by – the survival instinct, she clearly was capable of responses and attitudes that she would have criticized in others. Extreme circumstances could alter anyone's personality. That insight forced her to understand and appreciate Graham's fear to an extent she had never done before. After all, he had not *wanted* to fall on Everest; he hadn't *asked* for the injury. And indeed, considering the dull pain he suffered when he tried to climb or descend more than two flights of stairs, he was responding to this challenge damned well.

From behind her, Graham said, 'You go on ahead.' He had said it several times before. 'You move faster.'

'I'm staying,' she said breathlessly.

The echoes of their low-pitched voices were eerie, soft and sibilant.

She reached the landing at the thirty-first floor, waited for him to catch up, then went ahead. 'I won't leave you alone. Two of us . . . have a better chance against him . . . better than one of us would.'

'He's got a gun. We've *no* chance.'

She said nothing. She just kept taking the steps one at a time.

'Go on,' he said, sucking breath between phrases. 'You bring back . . . security guard . . . in time to keep . . . him from . . . killing me.'

'I think the guards are dead.'

'What?'

She hadn't wanted to say it, as if saying would make it so. 'How else . . . would he get past them?'

'Sign the registry.'

'And leave his name . . . for the cops to find?'

A dozen steps later he said, 'Christ!'

'What?'

'You're right.'

'No help . . . to be had,' she said. 'We've just got . . . to get out of . . . the building.'

Somehow he found new strength in his left leg. When she reached the thirtieth-floor landing, Connie didn't have to wait for him to catch up.

A minute later, a cannonlike sound boomed up from below, halting them within the fuzzy circle of light at the twenty-ninth floor.

'What was that?'

Graham said, 'A fire door. Someone slammed it . . . down there.'

'Him?'

'*Ssshh*.'

They stood perfectly still, trying to hear movement above the noise of their own labored breathing.

Connie felt as if the circle of light were shrinking around her, rapidly pulling back to a tiny point of brilliance. She was afraid of being blind and helpless, an easy target in pitch blackness. In her mind the Butcher had the quality of a mythical being; he could see in darkness.

As they got control of their breathing, the stairwell became silent.

Too silent.

Unnaturally silent.

Finally Graham said, 'Who's there?'

She jumped, startled by his voice.

The man below said, 'Police, Mr. Harris.'

Under her breath Connie said, 'Bollinger.'

She was at the outer edge of the steps; she looked down the open core. A man's hand was on the railing, four flights below, in the meager illumination just two or three steps up from the landing. She could also see the sleeve of his overcoat.

'Mr. Harris,' Bollinger said. His voice was cold, hollow, distorted by the shaft.

'What do you want?' Graham asked.

'Is she pretty?'

'What?'

'Is she *pretty*?'

'Who?'

'Your woman.'

With that, Bollinger started up. Not hurrying. Leisurely. One step at a time.

She was more frightened by his slow, casual approach than if he had rushed them. By *not* hurrying he was telling them that they were trapped, that he had the whole night to get them if he wished to stretch it out that long.

If only we had a gun, she thought.

Graham took hold of her hand, and they climbed the steps as fast as he was able. It wasn't easy for either of them. Her back and legs ached. With each step, Graham either gritted his teeth or moaned loudly.

When they had gone two floors, four flights, they were forced to stop and rest. He bent over, massaging his bum leg. She went to the railing, peered down.

Bollinger was four flights under them. Evidently he had run when he heard them running; but now he had stopped again. He was leaning over the railing, framed in a pool of light, the gun extended in his right hand.

He smiled at her and said, 'Hey now, you *are* pretty.'

She screamed, jerked back.

He fired.

The shot passed up the core, ricocheted off the top of the rail, smashed into the wall over their heads and ricocheted once more into the steps above them.

She grabbed Graham; he held her.

'I could have killed you,' Bollinger called to her. 'I had you dead on, sweetheart. But you and I are going to have a lot of fun later.'

Then he started up again. As before. Slowly. Shoes scraping ominously on the concrete: *shuss . . . shuss . . . shuss . . . shuss . . .* He began to whistle softly.

'He's not just chasing us,' Graham said angrily. 'The son of a bitch is playing with us.'

'What are we going to do?'

Shuss . . . shuss . . .

'We can't outrun him.'

'But we've got to.'

Shuss . . . shuss . . .

Harris pulled open the landing door. The thirty-first floor lay beyond. 'Come on.'

Not convinced that they gained anything by leaving the stairs, but having nothing better to suggest, she went out of the white light into the red.

Shuss . . . shuss . . .

Graham shut the door and stooped beside it. A collapsible door-stop was fixed to the bottom right-hand corner of the door. He pushed it all the way down, until the rubber-tipped shank was hard against the floor and the braces were locked in place. His hands were trembling, so that for a moment it looked as if he wouldn't be able to handle even a simple task like this.

'What are you doing?' she asked.

He stood up. 'It might not work if the stop didn't have locking hinges. But it does. See the doorsill? It's an inch higher than the floor on either side. When he tries to open the door, the stop will catch on the sill. It'll be almost as good as a bolt latch.'

'But he's got a gun.'

'Doesn't matter. He can't shoot through a heavy metal fire door.'

Although she was terrified, at the same time Connie was relieved that Graham had taken charge – for however brief a time – and was functioning in spite of his fear.

The door rattled as Bollinger depressed the bar handle on the far side. The stop caught on the sill; its hinges didn't fold up; the door refused to open.

'He'll have to go up or down a floor,' Harris said, 'and come at us by the stairs at the other end of the building. Or by the elevator. Which gives us a few minutes.'

Cursing, Bollinger shook the door, putting all his strength into it. It wouldn't budge.

'What good will a few minutes do us?' Connie asked.

'I don't know.'

'Graham, are we ever going to get out of here?'

'Probably not.'

·25·

Dr. Andrew Enderby, the medical examiner on the scene, was suave, even dashing, extremely fit for a man in his fifties. He had thick hair going white at the temples. Clear brown eyes. A long aristocratic nose, generally handsome features. His salt-and-pepper mustache was large but well kept. He was wearing a tailored gray suit with tastefully matched accessories that made Preduski's sloppiness all the more apparent.

'Hello, Andy,' Preduski said.

'Number eleven,' Enderby said. 'Unusual. Like numbers five, seven and eight.' When Enderby was excited, which wasn't often, he was impatient to express himself. He sometimes spoke in staccato bursts. He pointed at the kitchen table and said, 'See it? No butter smears. No jelly stains. No crumbs. Too damned neat. Another fake.'

A lab technician was disconnecting the garbage disposal unit from the pipes under the sink.

'Why?' Preduski said. 'Why does he fake it when he isn't hungry?'

'I know why. Sure of it.'

'So tell me,' Preduski said.

'First of all, did you know I'm a psychiatrist?'

'You're a coroner, a pathologist.'

'Psychiatrist too.'

'I didn't know that.'

'Went to medical school. Did my internship. Specialized in otolaryngology. Couldn't stand it. Hideous way to make a living. My family had money. Didn't have to work. Went back to medical school. Became a psychiatrist.'

'That must be interesting work.'

'Fascinating. But I couldn't stand it. Couldn't stand associating with the patients.'

'Oh?'

461

'All day with a bunch of neurotics. Began to feel that half of them should be locked up. Got out of the field fast. Better for me *and* the patients.'

'I should say so.'

'Kicked around a bit. Twenty years ago, I became a police pathologist.'

'The dead aren't neurotic.'

'Not even a little bit.'

'And they don't have ear, nose and throat infections.'

'Which they don't pass on to me,' Enderby said. 'No money in this job, of course. But I've got all the money I need. And the work is right for me. I'm perfect for the work, too. My psychiatric training gives me a different perspective. Insights. I have insights that other pathologists might not have. Like the one I had tonight.'

'About why the Butcher sometimes eats a hearty meal and sometimes *fakes* a hearty meal?'

'Yes,' Enderby said. He took a breath. Then: 'It's because there are two of him.'

Preduski scratched his head. 'Schizophrenia?'

'No, no. I mean . . . there isn't just one man running around killing women. There are *two*.' He smiled triumphantly.

Preduski stared at him.

Slamming his fist into his open hand, Enderby said, 'I'm right! I know I am. Butcher number one killed the first four victims. Killing them gave him an appetite. Butcher number two killed the fifth woman. Cut her up as Butcher number one had done. But he was ever so slightly more tender-hearted than the first Butcher. Killing *spoiled* his appetite. So he faked the meal.'

'Why bother to fake it?'

'Simple. He wanted to leave no doubt about who killed her. Wanted us to think it was the Butcher.'

Preduski was suddenly aware of how precisely Enderby's necktie had been knotted. He touched his own tie self-consciously. 'Pardon me. Excuse me. I don't quite understand. My fault. God knows. But, you see, we've never told the newspapers about the scene in the kitchens. We've held that back to check false confessions against real ones. If this guy, Butcher number two, wanted to imitate the real Butcher, how would he know about the kitchen?'

'You're missing my point.'

'I'm sure I am.'

'Butcher number one and Butcher number two know each other. They're in this together.'

462

Amazed, Preduski said, 'They're friends? You mean they go out and murder – like other men go out bowling?'

'I wouldn't put it like that.'

'They're killing women, trying to make it look like the work of one man?'

'Yes.'

'Why?'

'Don't know. Maybe they're creating a composite character in the Butcher. Giving us an image of a killer that isn't really like either of them. Throw us off the track. Protect themselves.'

Preduski started to pace in front of the littered table. 'Two psychopaths meet in a bar –'

'Not necessarily a bar.'

'They get chummy and sign a pact to kill all the women in Manhattan.'

'Not all,' Enderby said. 'But enough.'

'I'm sorry. Maybe I'm not very bright. I'm not well educated. Not a doctor like you. But I can't swallow it. I can't see psychopaths working together so smoothly and effectively.'

'Why not? Remember the Tate murders in California? There were several psychopaths in the Manson family, yet they all worked smoothly and efficiently together, committing a large number of murders.'

'They were caught,' Preduski said.

'Not for quite some time.'

·26·

Six business offices occupied the thirty-first floor of the Bowerton Building. Graham and Connie tried a few doors, all of which proved to be locked. They knew the others would be shut tight as well.

However, in the main hall near the elevator alcove, Connie discovered an unmarked, unlocked door. She opened it. Graham felt for the light switch, found it. They went inside.

The room was approximately ten feet deep and six or seven feet wide. On the left was a metal door that had been painted bright red; and to one side of the door, mops and brooms and brushes were racked on the wall. On the right, the wall was lined with metal storage shelves full of bathroom and cleaning supplies.

'It's a maintenance center,' Graham said.

Connie went to the red door. She took one step out of the room, holding the door behind her. She was surprised and excited by what she saw. 'Graham! Hey, look at this.'

He didn't respond.

She stepped back into the room, turned and said, 'Graham, look what –'

He was only a foot away, holding a large pair of scissors up to his face. He gripped the instrument in his fist, in the manner of a man holding a dagger. The blades gleamed, and, like polished gems, the sharp points caught the light.

'Graham?' she said.

Lowering the scissors, he said, 'I found these on the shelf over there. I can use them as a weapon.'

'Against a gun?'

'Maybe we can set up a trap.'

'What kind of trap?'

'Lure him into a situation where I can surprise him, where he won't have time enough to use the damned gun.'

'For instance?'

465

His hand was shaking. Light danced on the blades. 'I don't know,' he said miserably.

'It wouldn't work.' She said. 'Besides, I've found a way out of the building.'

He looked up. 'You have?'

'Come look. You won't need the scissors. Put them down.'

'I'll look,' he said. 'But I'll keep the scissors just in case.'

She was afraid that when he saw the escape route she'd found he would prefer to face the Butcher armed only with the scissors.

He followed her through the red door, onto a railed platform that was only eighteen inches wide and four feet long. A light glowed overhead; and other lights lay some distance away in a peculiar, at first unidentifiable void.

They were suspended on the side of one of the two elevator shafts that went from the ground floor to the roof. It served four cabs, all of which were parked at the bottom. Fat cables dangled in front of Connie and Graham. On this side and on the opposite wall of the cavernous well, from roof to basement at the odd-numbered floors, other doors opened onto other tiny platforms. There was one directly across from Graham and Connie, and the sight of it made them realize the precarious nature of their perch. On both sides of the shaft, metal rungs were bolted to the walls: ladders connecting the doors in each tier to other exits in the same tier.

The system could be used for emergency maintenance work or for moving people off stalled elevators in case of fire, power failure, or other calamity. A small white light burned above each door; otherwise, the shaft would have been in absolute darkness. When Connie looked up, and especially when she looked down from the thirty-first floor, the sets of farther lights appeared to be closer together than the sets of nearer lights. It was a long way to the bottom.

His voice wavered when he said, '*This* is a way out?'

She hesitated then said, 'We can climb down.'

'No.'

'We can't use the stairs. He'll be watching those.'

'Not this.'

'It won't be like mountain climbing.'

His eyes shifted quickly from left to right and back again. 'No.'

'We'll have the ladder.'

'And we'll climb down thirty-one floors?' he asked.

'Please. Graham. If we start now, we might make it. Even if he finds that the maintenance room is unlocked, and even if he sees this red door – well, he might not think we'd have enough nerve to climb down the shaft. And if he *did* see us, we could get off the ladder, leave the shaft at another floor. We'd gain more time.'

'I can't.' He was gripping the railing with both hands, and with such force that she would not have been surprised if the metal had bent like paper in his hands.

Exasperated, she said, 'Graham, what *else* can we do?'

He stared into the concrete depths.

When Bollinger found that Harris and the woman had locked the fire door, he ran down two flights to the thirtieth floor. He intended to use that corridor to reach the far end of the building where he could take the second stairwell back up to the thirty-first level and try the *other* fire door. However, at the next landing the words 'Hollowfield Land Management' were stenciled in black letters on the gray door: the entire floor belonged to a single occupant. That level had no public corridor; the fire door could be opened only from the inside. The same was true of the twenty-ninth and twenty-eight floors, which were the domain of Sweet Sixteen Cosmetics. He tried both entrances without success.

Worried that he would lose track of his prey, he rushed back to the twenty-sixth floor. That was where he had originally entered the stairwell, where he had left the elevator cab.

As he pulled open the fire door and stepped into the hall, he looked at his watch. 9:15. The time was passing too fast, unnaturally fast, as if the universe had become unbalanced.

Hurrying to the elevator alcove, he fished in his pocket for the dead guard's keys. They snagged on the lining. When he jerked them loose, they spun out of his hand and fell on the carpet with a sleighbell jingle.

He knelt and felt for them in the darkness. Then he remembered the pencil flashlight, but even with that he needed more than a minute to locate the keys.

As he got up, angry with himself, he wondered if Harris and the woman were waiting here for him. He put away the flashlight and snatched the pistol from his pocket. He stood quite still. He studied the darkness. If they were hiding there, they would have been silhouetted by the bright spot farther along at the alcove.

When he thought about it, he realized that they couldn't have known on which floor he'd left the elevator. Furthermore, they couldn't have gotten down here in time to surprise him.

The thirty-first floor was a different story. They might have time to set a trap for him up there. When the elevator doors slid open, they might be waiting for him; he would be most vulnerable at that moment.

Then again, *he* was the one with the pistol. So what if they were waiting with makeshift weapons? They didn't stand a chance of overpowering him.

At the elevator he put the key in the control board and activated the circuit.

He looked at his watch. 9:19.

If there were no more delays, he could kill Harris and still have twenty minutes or half an hour with the woman.

Whistling again, he pushed one of the buttons: 31.

•27•

The lab technician disconnected the garbage disposal, wrapped it in a heavy white plastic sheet, and carried it out of the apartment.

Preduski and Enderby were left alone in the kitchen.

In the foyer, a grandfather clock struck the quarter hour: two soft chimes, running five minutes late. In accompaniment, the wind fluted musically through the eaves just above the kitchen windows.

'If you find it hard to accept the idea of two psychopaths working so smoothly together,' Enderby said, 'then consider the possibility that they aren't psychopaths of any sort we've seen before.'

'Now you sound like Graham Harris.'

'I know.'

'The Butcher is mentally ill, Harris says. But you wouldn't know it to look at him, Harris says. Either the symptoms of his mania don't show, or he knows how to conceal them. He'd pass any psychiatric cxam, Harris says.'

'I'm beginning to agree with him.'

'Except you say there are two Butchers.'

Enderby nodded.

Preduski sighed. He went to the nearest window and drew the outline of a knife in the thin gray-white film of moisture that coated the glass. 'If you're right, I can't hold onto my theory. That he's just your ordinary paranoid schizophrenic. Maybe a lone killer could be operating in a psychotic fugue. But not two of them simultaneously.'

'They're not suffering any psychotic fugue,' Enderby agreed. 'Both of these men know precisely what they're doing. Neither of them suffers from amnesia.'

Turning from the window, from the drawing of the knife which had begun to streak as droplets of water slid down the pane, Preduski said, 'Whether this is a new type of psychotic or not, the crime is familiar. Sex murders are –'

'These aren't sex murders,' Enderby said.

Preduski cocked his head. 'Come again?'

'These aren't *sex* murders.'

'They only kill women.'

'Yes, but –'

'And they rape them first.'

'Yes. It's murder with sex *associated*. But these aren't *sex* murders.'

'I'm sorry. I'm lost. My fault. Not yours.'

'Sex isn't the motivating force. Sex isn't the whole or even the primary reason they have for attacking these women. The opportunity for rape is there. So they take it. Going to kill the women anyway. They aren't adding to their legal risks by raping them first. Sex is secondary. They aren't killing out of some psychosexual impulse.'

Shaking his head, Preduski said, 'I don't see how you can say that. You've never met them. What evidence do you have that their motives aren't basically sexual?'

'Circumstantial,' Enderby said. 'For instance, the way they mutilate the corpses.'

'What about it?'

'Have you studied the mutilations carefully?'

'I had no choice.'

'All right. Found any sign of anal mutilation?'

'No.'

'Mutilation of the genitalia?'

'No.'

'Mutilation of the breasts?'

'In some cases he's cut open the abdomen and chest cavity.'

'Mutilation of the breasts alone?'

'When he opens the chest –'

'I mean has he ever cut off a woman's nipples, or perhaps her entire breasts, as Jack the Ripper did?'

A look of loathing came over his face. 'No.'

'Has he ever mutilated the mouth of a victim?'

'The mouth?'

'Has he ever cut off the lips?'

'No. Never.'

'Has he ever cut out a tongue?'

'God, no! Andy, do we have to go on like this? It's morbid. And I don't see where it's leading.'

'If they were maniacal *sex* killers with a desire to cut their victims,' Enderby said, 'they'd have disfigured one of those areas.'

'Anus, breasts, genitalia, or mouth?'

'Unquestionably. At least one of them. Probably all of them. But they didn't. So the mutilation is an afterthought. Not a sexual compulsion. Window dressing.'

Preduski closed his eyes, pressed his fingertips to them, as if he were trying to suppress unpleasant images. 'Window dressing? I'm afraid I don't understand.'

'To impress us.'

'The police?'

'Yes. And the newspapers.'

Preduski went to the window where he had drawn the knife. He wiped away the film of moisture and stared at the snow sheeting through the glow around the street lamp. 'Why would he want to impress us?'

'I don't know. Whatever the reason, whatever the need behind his desire to impress – *that* is the true motivation.'

'If we knew what it was, we might be able to see a pattern in the killings. We might be able to anticipate him.'

Suddenly excited, Enderby said, 'Wait a minute. Another case. Two killers. Working together. Chicago. Nineteen twenty-four. Two young men were the murderers. Both sons of millionaires. In their late teens.'

'Leopold and Loeb.'

'You know the case?'

'Slightly.'

'They killed a boy, Bobby Franks. Fourteen years old. Son of another rich man. They had nothing against him. None of the usual reasons. No classic motive. Newspapers said it was for kicks. For thrills. Very bloody murder. But they killed Franks for other reasons. For more than kicks. For a philosophical ideal.'

Turning away from the window, Preduski said, 'I'm sorry. I must have missed something. I'm not making sense of this. *What* philosophical ideal?'

'They thought they were special. Supermen. The first of a new race. Leopold idolized Nietzsche.'

Frowning, Preduski said, 'One of the quotes in there on the bedroom wall is probably from Nietzsche's work, the other from Blake. There was a quote from Nietzsche written in blood on Edna Mowry's wall last night.'

'Leopold and Loeb. Incredible pair. They thought that committing the perfect crime was proof that they were supermen.

Getting away with murder. They thought that was *proof* of superior intelligence, superior cunning.'

'Weren't they homosexuals?'

'Yes. But that doesn't make Bobby Franks the victim of a sex killing. They didn't molest him. Never had any intention of molesting him. They weren't motivated by lust. Not at all. It was, as Loeb called it, ''an intellectual exercise.'' '

In spite of his excitement, Enderby noticed that his shirt cuffs were not showing beyond the sleeves of his suit jacket. He pulled them out, one at a time, until the proper half inch was revealed. Although he had worked for some time in the blood-splashed bedroom and then in the messy kitchen, he didn't have a stain on him.

His back to the window, leaning against the sill, conscious of his own scuffed shoes and wrinkled trousers, Preduski said, 'I'm having trouble understanding. You'll have to be patient with me. You know how I am. Dense sometimes. But if these two boys, Leopold and Loeb, thought that murder was an intellectual exercise, then they were crazy. Weren't they? Were they mad?'

'In a way. Mad with their own power. Both real and imagined power.'

'Would they have appeared to be mad?'

'Not at all.'

'How is that possible?'

'Remember, Leopold graduated from college when he was just seventeen. He had an IQ of two hundred or nearly so. He was a genius. So was Loeb. They were bright enough to keep their Nietzschean fantasies to themselves, to hide their grandiose self-images.'

'What if they'd taken psychiatric tests?'

'Psychiatric tests weren't very well developed in nineteen twenty-four.'

'But if there had been tests back then as sophisticated as those we have today, would Leopold and Loeb have passed them?'

'Probably with flying colors.'

'Have there been others like Leopold and Loeb since nineteen twenty-four?' Preduski asked.

'Not that I know of. Not in a pure sense, anyway. The Manson family killed for murky political and religious reasons. They thought Manson was Christ. Thought killing the rich would help the downtrodden. Unmitigated crazies, in my book. Think of some other killers, especially mass murderers. Charles Starkweather. Richard Speck. Albert DeSalvo. All of them were psychotic. All of them were driven by psychoses that had grown and festered in them, that had slowly corrupted them since childhood. In Leopold and Loeb, there were apparently no serious childhood traumas that could have led to psychotic behavior. No black seed to bear fruit later.'

'So if the Butcher is two men,' Preduski said forlornly, 'we've got a new Leopold and Loeb. Killing to prove their superiority.'

Enderby began to pace. 'Maybe. But then again, maybe it's more than that. Something more complex than that.'

'Like what?'

'I don't know. But I feel it's not *exactly* a Leopold and Loeb sort of thing.' He went to the table and stared at the remains of the meal that had never been eaten. 'Have you called Harris?'

Preduski said, 'No.'

'You should. He's been trying to get an image of the killer. Hasn't had any luck. Maybe that's because he's focusing on a single image, trying to envision just one face. Tell him there are *two* killers. Maybe that'll break it open for him. Maybe he'll finally get a handle on the case.'

'We don't *know* there are two. That's just a theory.'

'Tell him anyway,' Enderby said. 'What harm can it do?'

'I should tell him tonight. I really should. But I just can't,' Preduski said. 'He's gotten behind in his work because of this case. That's my fault. I'm always calling him, talking to him, pressuring him about it. He's working late, trying to get caught up. I don't want to disturb him.'

In the foyer by the front door, the grandfather clock chimed the half hour, five minutes late again.

Preduski glanced at his wristwatch and said, 'It'll soon be ten o'clock. I've got to be going.'

'Going? There's work to do here.'

'I'm not on duty yet.'

'Graveyard?'

'Yeah.'

'I never knew you to hesitate about a bit of overtime.'

'Well, I just got out of bed. I was cooking spaghetti when Head-quarters called me about this. Never got a chance to eat any of it. I'm starving.'

Enderby shook his head. 'As long as I've known you, I don't believe I've ever seen you eat a square meal. You're always grabbing sandwiches so you don't have to stop working to eat. And at home you're cooking spaghetti. You need a wife, Ira.'

'A wife?'

'Other men have them.'

'But me? Are you kidding?'

'Be good for you.'

'Andy, look at me.'

'I'm looking.'

'Look closer.'

'So?'

'You must be blind.'

'What should I see?'

'What woman in her right mind would marry me?'

'Don't give me your usual crap, Ira,' Enderby said with a smile. 'I know that under all of that self-deprecating chatter, you've got a healthy and proper respect for yourself.'

'You're the psychiatrist.'

'That's right. I'm not a suspect or a witness; you can't charm me with that blather.'

Preduski grinned.

'I'll bet there have been more than a few women who've fallen for that calculated little-boy look of yours.'

'A few,' Preduski admitted uncomfortably. 'But never the *right* woman.'

'Who said anything about the *right* one? Most men are happy to settle for half-right.'

'Not me.' Preduski looked at his watch again. 'I really have to be going. I'll come back around midnight. Martin probably won't even have finished questioning the other tenants by then. It's a big building.'

Dr Enderby sighed as if the troubles of the world were on his shoulders alone. 'We'll be here too. Dusting the furniture for prints, vacuuming the carpets for hairs and threads, finding nothing, but working hard. The same old circus.'

·28·

Graham's foot slipped off the rung.

Although he was still holding tightly with both hands, he panicked. He struck out at the ladder with his feet, scrabbling wildly, as if the ladder were alive, as if he had to kick it into submission before he could regain his foothold on it.

'Graham, what's wrong?' Connie asked from her position on the ladder above him. 'Graham?'

Her voice sobered him. He stopped kicking. He hung by his hands until he was breathing almost normally, until the vivid memories of Everest had faded.

'Graham?'

With his feet he probed for a rung, found one after several seconds that seemed like hours. 'I'm all right. My foot slipped. I'm okay now.'

'Don't look down.'

'I didn't. I won't.'

He sought the next rung, stepped to it, continued the descent.

He felt feverish. The hair was damp at the back of his neck. Perspiration beaded his forehead, jeweled his eyebrows, stung the corners of his eyes, filmed his cheeks, brought a salty taste to his lips. In spite of the perspiration, he was cold. He shivered as he moved down the long ladder.

He was as much aware of the void at his back as he would have been of a knife pressed between his shoulder blades.

On the thirty-first floor, Frank Bollinger entered the maintenance supply room.

He saw the red door. Someone had put down the doorstop that was fixed to it, so that it was open an inch or two. He knew immediately that Harris and the woman had gone through there.

But why was the door ajar?

It was like a signpost. Beckoning him.

475

Alert for a trap, he advanced cautiously. He held the Walther PPK in his right hand. He kept his left hand out in front of him, arm extended all the way, to stop the door in case they tried to throw it open in his face. He held his breath for those few steps, listening for the slightest sound other than the soft squeak of his own shoes.

Nothing. Silence.

He used the toe of his shoe to push up the doorstop; then he pulled open the door and walked onto the small platform. He had just enough time to realize where he was, when the door closed behind him and all the lights in the shaft went out.

At first he thought Harris had come into the maintenance room after him. But when he tried the door, it was not locked. And when he opened it, all the lights came on. The emergency lighting didn't burn twenty-four hours a day; it came on only when one of the service entrances was open, and that was why Harris had left the door ajar.

Bollinger was impressed by the system of lights and platforms and ladders. Not every building erected in the 1920s would have been designed with an eye toward emergencies. In fact, damned few skyscrapers built since the war could boast *any* safety provisions. These days, they expected you to wait in a stalled elevator until it was repaired, no matter if that took ten hours or ten days; and if the lift couldn't be repaired, you could risk a manually cranked descent, or you could rot in it.

The more time he spent in the building, the deeper he penetrated it, the more fascinating he found it to be. It was not on the scale of those truly gargantuan stadiums and museums and highrises that Hitler had designed for the 'super race' just prior to and during the first days of World War Two. But then Hitler's magnificent edifices had never been realized in stone and mortar, whereas this place *had* risen. He began to feel that the men who had designed and constructed it were Olympians. He found his appreciation strange, for he knew that had he been restricted to the halls and offices during the day, when the building was full of people and buzzing with commerce, he would not have noticed the great size and high style of the structure. One took for granted that which was commonplace; and to New Yorkers, there was nothing unusual about a forty-two-story office building. Now, however, abandoned for the night, the tower seemed incredibly huge and complex; in solitude and silence one had time to contemplate it and to see how magnificent and extraordinary it was. He was like a microbe wandering through the veins and bowels of a living creature, a behemoth almost beyond measurement.

He felt in league with the minds that could conceive of a monument

476

like this. He was one of them, a mover and shaker, a superior man. The Olympian nature of the building – and of the architects responsible for it – struck a responsive chord in him, made him reverberate with the knowledge of his own special godlike stature. Brimming with a sense of glory, he was more determined than ever to kill Harris and the woman. They were animals. Lice. Parasites. Because of Harris's freakish psychic gift, they posed a threat to Bollinger. They were trying to deny him his rightful place in this new and forceful current of history: the at first gradual but ever-quickening rise of the new men.

He pushed the doorstop against the floor to keep the door open and the lights burning. Then he went to the edge of the platform and peered down the ladder.

They were three floors under him. The woman on top, nearer by a few rungs. Harris below her, going first. Neither of them looked up. They certainly were aware of the momentary loss of light and understood the significance of it. They were hurrying toward the next platform, where they could get out of the shaft.

Bollinger knelt, tested the railing. It was strong. He leaned against it, using it like a safety harness to keep him from tumbling to his death.

He didn't want to kill them here. The place and method of murder were extremely important tonight. Here, they would drop to the bottom of the well, and that would ruin the scheme that he and Billy had come up with this afternoon. He wasn't here just to kill them any way he could; he had to dispose of them in a certain manner. If he brought it off just right, the police would be confused, misled; and the people of New York would begin to experience a spiraling reign of terror unlike anything in their worst nightmares. He and Billy had worked out a damned clever gambit, and he wouldn't abandon it so long as there was a chance of bringing it off as planned.

It was a quarter of ten. In fifteen minutes Billy would be in the alleyway outside, and he would wait only until ten-thirty. Bollinger saw that he probably wouldn't have time for the woman, but he was pretty sure he'd be able to carry out the plan in forty-five minutes.

Besides, he didn't know what Harris looked like, and he felt there was something cowardly about killing a man whose face he'd never seen. It was akin to shooting someone in the back. That sort of killing – even of an animal, even of a louse like Harris – didn't fit Bollinger's image of a superman. He liked to meet his prey head-on, to get close, so that there was at least a hint of danger.

477

The trick was to force them out of the shaft without killing them; to herd them to other ground where the plan could be carried out. He pointed the pistol down, aimed wide of the woman's head and squeezed the trigger.

The shot exploded; ear-splitting noise assaulted Connie from every side. Over the diminishing echoes, she could hear the bullet ricocheting from one wall to the other, farther down the shaft.

The situation was so unreal that she had to wonder if it was transpiring in her mind. She supposed it was possible that she was in a hospital and that all of this was the product of a fevered imagination, the delusions of madness.

Descending the ladder, she repeatedly caught herself murmuring softly: sometimes it was jumbled phrases that made little sense, sometimes strings of utterly meaningless sounds. Her stomach rolled over like a fish on a wet boat dock. Her bowels quivered. She felt as if a bullet had already ripped into her, already had torn apart her vital organs.

Bollinger fired again.

The shot seemed less sharp than the one before it. Her ears were desensitized, still ringing from the first explosion.

For a woman who had experienced little emotional – and *no* physical – terror in her life, she was handling herself surprisingly well.

When she looked down, she saw Graham let go of the ladder with one hand. He grabbed the railing that ringed the platform. He took one foot off the ladder; hesitated, leaning at a precarious angle; started to bring his foot back; suddenly found the courage to put it on the edge of the platform. For a moment, fighting his own terror, he stayed that way, crucified between the two points of safety. She was about to call to him, urge him on, when he finally freed himself of the ladder altogether, wobbled on the brink of the platform as if he would fall, then got his balance and climbed over the railing.

She descended the last dozen rungs much too fast and reached the platform as Bollinger fired a third shot. She hurried through the red door that Graham held open for her, into the maintenance supply room on the twenty-seventh level.

The first thing she saw was the blood on his trousers. A bright spot of it. As big as a silver dollar. Glistening on the gray fabric. 'What happened?'

'Had these in my pocket,' he said, holding up the scissors. 'A couple of floors back, when I almost fell, the blades tore through the lining and gouged my thigh.'

478

'Is it bad?'
'No.'
'Hurt?'
'Not much.'
'Better get rid of them.'
'Not just yet.'

Bollinger watched until they left the shaft. They had gotten out two platforms down. Because there was only a service entrance at every second floor, that put them on the twenty-seventh level.

He got up, hurried toward the elevator.

'Come on,' Graham said. 'Let's make a run for the stairs.'

'No. We've got to go back up the shaft.'

Incredulity showed on his face, anguish in his eyes. 'That's crazy!'

'He won't be looking for us in the shaft. At least not for a couple of minutes. We can go up two floors, then use the stairs when he comes back to check the shaft.' She opened the red door through which they'd come only seconds ago.

'I don't know if I can do it again,' he said.

'Of course you can.'

'You said *up* the shaft?'

'That's right.'

'We have to go down to escape.'

She shook her head; her hair formed a brief dark halo. 'You remember what I said about the night guards?'

'They might be dead.'

'If Bollinger killed them so he could have a free hand with us, wouldn't he also have sealed off the building? What if we get to the lobby, with Bollinger hot on our heels, and we find the doors are locked? Before we could break the glass and get out, he'd have killed us.'

'But the guards might not be dead. He might have gotten past them somehow.'

'Can we take that chance?'

He frowned. 'I guess not.'

'I don't want to get to the lobby until we're certain of having a long lead on Bollinger.'

'So we go up. How's that better?'

'We can't play cat and mouse with him for twenty-seven floors. The next time he catches us in the shaft or on the stairs, he won't

479

make any mistakes. But if he doesn't realize we're going *up*, we might be able to alternate between the shaft and the stairs for thirteen floors, long enough to get to your office.'

'Why there?'

'Because he won't expect us to backtrack.'

Graham's blue eyes were not as wide with fear as they had been; they had narrowed with calculation. In spite of himself, the will to survive was flowering in him; the first signs of the old Graham Harris were becoming visible, pushing through his shell of fear.

He said, 'Eventually, he'll realize what we've done. It'll buy us only fifteen minutes or so.'

'Time to think of another way out,' she said. 'Come on, Graham. We're wasting too much time. He'll be on this floor any second now.'

Less reluctantly than the first time, but still without enthusiasm, he followed her into the elevator shaft.

On the platform he said, 'You go first. I'll bring up the rear, so I won't knock you off the ladder if I fall.'

For the same reason, he had insisted on going first when they descended.

She put her arms around him, kissed him, then turned and started to climb.

As soon as he got off the elevator on the twenty-seventh floor, Bollinger investigated the stairs at the north end of the building. They were deserted.

He ran the length of the corridor and opened the door to the south stairs. He stood on the landing for almost a minute, listening intently for movement. He heard none.

In the corridor again, he searched for an unlocked office door until he realized they might have gone back into the elevator shaft. He located the maintenance supply room; the red door was ajar.

He approached it cautiously, as before. He was opening the door all the way when the shaft beyond was filled with the sound of another door closing on it.

On the platform, he bent over the railing. He stared down into the vertiginous depths, wondering which one of the doors they had used.

How many floors had they gained on him?

Dammit!

Cursing aloud, overcoat flapping around his legs, Bollinger went back to the south stairs to listen for them.

* * *

By the time they had climbed two flights on the north stairs, Graham was wincing with each step. From sole to hip, pain coruscated through his bad leg. In anticipation of each jolt, he tensed his stomach. Now his entire abdomen ached. If he had continued to work out and climb after his fall on Mount Everest, as the doctors had urged him to do, he would have been in shape for this. He had given his leg more punishment tonight than it ordinarily received in a year. Now he was paying in pain for five years of inactivity.

'Don't slow down,' Connie said.

'Trying not to.'

'Use the rail as much as you can. Pull yourself along.'

'How far are we going?'

'One more floor.'

'Eternity.'

'After that we'll switch back to the elevator shaft.'

He liked the ladder in the shaft better than he did the stairs. On the ladder he could use his good leg and pull with both hands to keep nearly all of his weight off the other leg. But on the stairs, if he didn't use the lame leg at all, he would have to hop from one step to the other; and that was too slow.

'One more flight,' she said encouragingly.

Trying to surprise himself, trying to cover a lot of ground before the pain transmitted itself from leg to brain, he put on a burst of speed, staggered up ten steps as fast as he could. That transformed the pain into agony. He had to slow down, but he kept moving.

Bollinger stood on the landing, listening for sound in the south stairwell.

Nothing.

He looked over the railing. Squinting, he tried to see through the layers of darkness that filled the space between the landings.

Nothing.

He went back into the hall and ran toward the north stairs.

•29•

Billy drove into the alley. His car made the first tracks in the new snow.

A forty-foot-long, twenty-foot-deep service courtyard lay at the back of the Bowerton Building. Four doors opened onto it. One of these was a big green garage door, where delivery could be taken on office furniture and other items too large to fit through the public entrance. A sodium vapor lamp glowed above the green door, casting a harsh light on the stone walls, on the rows of trash bins awaiting pickup in the morning, and on the snow; the shadows were sharply drawn.

There was no sign of Bollinger.

Prepared to leave at the first indication of trouble, Billy backed the car into the courtyard. He switched off the headlights but not the engine. He rolled down his window, just an inch, to keep the glass from steaming up.

When Bollinger didn't come out to meet him, Billy looked at his watch. 10:02.

Clouds of dry snow swirled down the alley in front of him. In the courtyard, out of the worst of the wind, the snow was relatively undisturbed.

Most nights, squad cars conducted random patrols of poorly lighted back streets like this one, always on the lookout for business-district burglars with half-filled vans, muggers with half-robbed victims, and rapists with half-subdued women. But not tonight. Not in this weather. The city's uniformed patrolmen would be occupied elsewhere. The majority of them would be busy cleaning up after the usual foul-weather automobile accidents, but as much as a third of the evening shift would be squirreled away in favorite hideouts, on a side street or in a park; they would be drinking coffee – in a few cases, something stronger – and talking about sports and women, ready to go to work only if the radio dispatcher insisted upon it.

Billy looked at his watch again. 10:04.

He would wait exactly twenty-six minutes. Not one minute less, and certainly not one more. That was what he had promised Dwight.

Once again, Bollinger reached the elevator shaft just as it was filled with the sound of another door closing on it.

He bent over the railing, looked down. Nothing but other railings, other platforms, other emergency light bulbs, and a lot of darkness. Harris and the woman had gone.

He was tired of playing hide-and-seek with them, of dashing from stairwell to stairwell to shaft. He was sweating profusely. Under his overcoat, his shirt clung to him wetly. He left the platform, went to the elevator, activated it with a key, pushed the button marked 'Lobby.'

On the ground level, he took off his heavy overcoat and dropped it beside the elevator doors. Sweat trickled down his neck, down the center of his chest. He didn't remove his gloves. With the back of his left hand and then with his shirt sleeve he wiped his dripping forehead.

Out of sight of anyone who might come to the street doors, he leaned against the marble wall at the end of the offset that contained the four banks of elevators. From that position, he could see two white doors with black stenciled letters on them, one at the north end and one at the south end of the lobby. These were the exits from the stairwells. When Harris and the woman came through one of them, he would blow their goddamned brains out. Oh, yes. With pleasure.

Hobbling along the fortieth-floor corridor toward the light that came from the open reception-room door of the Harris Publications suite, Harris saw the fire-alarm box. It was approximately nine inches on a side, set flush with the wall. The metal rim was painted red, and the face of it was glass.

He couldn't imagine why he hadn't thought of this before.

Ahead of him, Connie realized that he had stopped. 'What's the matter?'

'Look here.'

She came back.

'If we set it off,' Graham said, 'it'll bring the security guards up from downstairs.'

'If they aren't dead.'

'Even if they are dead, it'll bring the fire department on the double. Bollinger will have the crimps put to him.'

'Maybe he won't run when he hears the bells. After all, we know his name. He might hang on, kill us, sneak out past the firemen.'

'He might,' Graham agreed, unsettled by the thought of being stalked through dark halls full of clanging, banging bells.

They stared through the glass at the steel alarm lever that glinted in the red light.

He felt hope, like a muscle relaxant, relieve a fraction of the tension in his shoulders, neck and face. For the first time all night, he began to think they might escape.

Then he remembered the vision. The bullet. The blood. He was going to be shot in the back.

She said, 'The alarms will probably be so loud that we won't hear him if he comes after us.'

'But it works both ways,' he said eagerly. '*He* won't be able to hear *us*.'

She pressed her fingertips to the cool plate of glass, hesitated, then took her hand away. 'Okay. But there's no little hammer to break the glass.' She held up the chain that was supposed to secure a hammer to the side of the alarm. 'What do we use instead?'

Smiling, he took the scissors from his pocket and held them up as if they were a talisman.

'Applause, applause,' she said, beginning to feel just enough hope to allow herself a little joke.

'Thank you.'

'Be careful,' she said.

'Stand back.'

She did.

Graham held the scissors by the closed blades. Using the heavy handles as a hammer, he smashed the thin glass. A few pieces held stubbornly to the frame. So as not to cut himself, he broke out the jagged splinters before he put one hand into the shallow alarm box and jerked the steel lever from green to red.

No noise.

No bells.

Silence.

Christ!

'Oh, no,' she said.

Frantically, the flame of hope flickering in him, he pushed the lever up, back to the green safety mark, then slammed it down again.

Still nothing.

Bollinger had been as thorough with the fire alarm as he had been with the telephones.

The wipers swept back and forth, clearing the snow from the windshield. The rhythmic *thump-thump-thump* was getting on his nerves.

Billy glanced over his shoulder, through the rear window, at the green garage door, then at the other three doors.

The time was 10:15.

Where in the hell was Dwight?

Graham and Connie went to the magazine's art department in search of a knife and other sharp draftsmen's tools that would make better weapons than the scissors. He found a pair of razor-edged scalpel-like instruments in the center drawer of the art director's big metal desk.

When he looked up from the drawer, he saw that Connie was lost in thought. She was standing just inside the door, staring at the floor in front of a light blue photographic backdrop. Climbing equipment – coils of rope, pitons, étriers, carabiners, klettershoes, nylon jackets lined with down, and perhaps thirty other items – lay in a disordered heap before the screen.

'See what I found?' he said. He held up the blades.

She wasn't interested. 'What about this stuff?' she asked, pointing to the climbing equipment.

Coming from behind the desk, he said, 'This issue, we're running a buyer's guide. Each of those pieces was photographed for the article. Why'd you ask?' Then his face brightened. 'Never mind. I see why.' He hunkered in front of the equipment, picked up an ice ax. 'This makes a better weapon than any draftsman's tool.'

'Graham?'

He looked up.

Her expression was peculiar: a combination of puzzlement, fear and amazement. Although she clearly had thought of something interesting and important, her gray eyes gave no indication of what was going through her mind. She said, 'Let's not rush out to fight him. Can we consider all of our options?'

'That's why we're here.'

She stepped into the shor , private hallway, cocked her head and listened for Bollinger.

Graham stood up, prepared to use the ice ax.

486

When she was satisfied that there was nothing to listen for but more silence, she came back into the room.

He lowered the ax. 'I thought you heard something.'

'Just being cautious.' She glanced at the climbing equipment before she sat down on the edge of the desk. 'As I see it, there are five different things we can do. Number one, we can make a stand, try to fight Bollinger.'

'With this,' he said, hefting the ice ax.

'And with anything else we can find.'

'We can set a trap, surprise him.'

'I see two problems with that approach.'

'The gun.'

'That's sure one.'

'If we're clever enough, he won't have time to shoot.'

'More important,' she said, 'neither of us is a killer.'

'We could just knock him unconscious.'

'If you hit him on the head with an ax like that, you're bound to kill him.'

'If it's kill or be killed, I suppose I could do it.'

'Maybe. But if you hesitate at the last instant, we're dead.'

He didn't resent the limits of her faith in him; he knew that he didn't deserve her complete trust. 'You said there were five things we could do.'

'Number two, we can try to hide.'

'Where?'

'I don't know. Maybe look for an office that someone forgot to lock, go inside and lock it after us.'

'No one forgot.'

'Maybe we *can* continue to play cat and mouse with him.'

'For how long?'

'Until a new shift of guards finds the dead ones.'

'If he didn't kill the guards, then the new guards won't know what's going on up here.'

'That's right.'

'Besides, I think maybe they work twelve-hour shifts, four days a week. I know one of the night men. I've heard him curse the long shifts and at the same time praise the eight hours of overtime he gets each week. So if they come on duty at six, they won't be off until six in the morning.'

'Seven and a half hours.'

'Too long to play cat and mouse in the elevator shaft and on the stairs. Especially with this bum leg of mine.'

'Number three,' she said. 'We could open one of your office windows and shout for help.'

'From the fortieth floor? Even in good weather, they probably couldn't hear you on the sidewalk. With this wind, they wouldn't hear you even two floors away.'

'I know that. And on a night like this, there's not going to be anyone out walking anyway.'

'Then why'd you suggest it?'

'Number five is going to surprise you,' she said. 'When I get to it, I want you to understand that I've thought of every other possible way out.'

'What's number five?'

'Number four first. We open the office window and throw furniture into the street, try to catch the attention of anyone who's driving past on Lexington.'

'If anyone *is* driving in this weather.'

'Someone will be. A taxi or two.'

'But if we toss out a chair, we won't be able to calculate the effect of the wind on it. We won't be able to gauge where it'll land. What if it goes through the windshield of a car and kills someone?'

'I've thought of that.'

'We can't do it.'

'I know.'

'What's number five?'

She slid off the desk and went to the pile of climbing equipment. 'We've got to get rigged out in this stuff.'

'Rigged out?'

'Boots, jackets, gloves, ropes – the works.'

He was perplexed. 'Why?'

Her eyes were wide, like the eyes of a startled doe. 'For the climb down.'

'Down what?'

'Down the outside of the building. All the way to the street.'

Part Four

FRIDAY 10:30 P.M.– SATURDAY 4:00 A.M.

•30•

Promptly at ten-thirty, Billy drove out of the service courtyard behind the highrise.

The snowfall had grown heavier during the past half hour, and the wind had become downright dangerous. Roiling in the headlight beams, the sheets of powder-dry flakes were almost as dense as a fog.

At the mouth of the alley, as he was pulling onto the side street, the tires spun on the icy pavement. The car slewed toward the far curb. He turned the wheel in the direction of the slide and managed to stop just short of colliding with a panel truck parked at the curb.

He had been driving too fast, and he hadn't even been aware of it until he'd almost crashed. That wasn't like him. He was a careful man. He was never reckless. Never. He was angry with himself for losing control.

He drove toward the avenue. The traffic light was with him, and the nearest car was three or four blocks away, a lone pair of headlights dimmed and diffused by the falling snow. He turned the corner onto Lexington.

In three hundred feet, he came to the front of the Bowerton Building. Ferns and flowers, molded in a twenty-foot-long rectangular bronze plaque, crowned the stonework above the four revolving doors. Part of the enormous lobby was visible beyond the entrance, and it appeared to be deserted. He drove near the curb, in the parking lane, barely moving, studying the building and the sidewalks and the calcimined street, looking for some sign of trouble and finding none.

Nevertheless, the plan had failed. Something had gone wrong in there. Terribly, terribly wrong.

Will Bollinger talk if he's caught? Billy wondered uneasily. Will he implicate me?

He would have to go to work without knowing how badly Dwight

491

had failed, without knowing whether or not Bollinger would be – had been? – apprehended by the police. He was going to find it difficult to concentrate on his job tonight; but if he was going to construct an alibi to counter a possible confession from Dwight, it would help his case if he was calm tonight, as much like himself as he could be, as thorough and diligent as those who knew him expected him to be.

Franklin Dwight Bollinger was getting restless. He was bathed in a thin, oily sweat. His fingers ached from the tight grip he had kept on the Walther PPK. He'd been watching the stairwell exits for more than twenty minutes, but there was no sign of Harris or the woman.

Billy was gone by now, the schedule destroyed. Bollinger hoped he might salvage the plan. But at the same time he knew that wasn't possible. The situation had degenerated to this: slaughter them and get the hell out.

Where *is* Harris? he wondered. Has he sensed that I'm waiting here for him? Has he used his carnival act, his goddamned clairvoyance, to anticipate me?

He decided to wait five minutes more. Then he would be forced to go after them.

Staring out of the office window at an eerie panorama of gigantic, snow-swept buildings and fuzzy lights, Graham said, 'It's impossible.'

Beside him, Connie put one hand on his arm. '*Why* is it impossible?'

'It just is.'

'That's not good enough.'

'I can't climb it.'

'It's not a climb.'

'What?'

'It's a descent.'

'Doesn't matter.'

'Can it be done?'

'Not by me.'

'You climbed the ladder in the shaft.'

'That's different.'

'How?'

'Besides, you've never climbed.'

'You can teach me.'

'No.'

'Sure you can.'

'You can't learn on the sheer face of a forty-story building in the middle of a blizzard.'

'I'd have a damned good teacher,' she said.

'Oh, yeah. One who hasn't climbed in five years.'

'You still know how. You haven't forgotten.'

'I'm out of shape.'

'You're a strong man.'

'You forget my leg.'

She turned away from the window and went back to the door so that she could listen for Bollinger while she talked. 'Remember when Abercrombie and Fitch had a man scale their building to advertise a new line of climbing equipment?'

He didn't look away from the window. He was transfixed by the night. 'What about it?'

'At the time, you said what that man did wasn't really so difficult.'

'Did I?'

'You said a building, with all its ledges and setbacks, is an easy climb compared to almost any mountain.'

He said nothing. He remembered telling her that, and he knew he had been right. But when he'd said it he never thought he'd be called upon to *do* it. Images of Mount Everest and of hospital rooms filled his mind.

'This equipment you chose for the buyer's guide –'

'What about it?'

'It's the best, isn't it?'

'The best, or close to it.'

'We'd be perfectly outfitted.'

'If we try it, we'll die.'

'We'll die if we stay here.'

'Maybe not.'

'I think so. Absolutely.'

'There has to be an alternative.'

'I've outlined them already.'

'Maybe we *can* hide from him.'

'Where?'

'I don't know. But –'

'And we can't hide for seven hours.'

'This is crazy, dammit!'

'Can you think of anything better?'

'Give me time.'

493

'Bollinger will be here any minute.'

'The wind speed must be forty miles an hour at street level. At least when it's gusting. Fifty miles an hour up this high.'

'Will it blow us off?'

'We'd have to fight it every inch.'

'Won't we anchor the ropes?'

He turned away from the window. 'Yes, but –'

'And won't we be wearing those?' She pointed to a pair of safety harnesses that lay atop the pile of equipment.

'It'll be damned cold out there, Connie.'

'We've got the down-lined jackets.'

'But we don't have quilted, insulated pants. You're wearing ordinary jeans. So am I. For all the good they'll do us, we might as well be naked below the waist.'

'I can stand the cold.'

'Not for very long. Not cold as bitter as that.'

'How long will it take us to get to the street?'

'I don't know.'

'You must have *some* idea.'

'An hour. Maybe two hours.'

'That long?'

'You're a novice.'

'Couldn't we rappel?'

'Rappel?' He was appalled.

'It looks so easy. Swinging out and back, dropping a few feet with every swing, bouncing off the stone, dancing along the side of the building . . .'

'It looks easy, but it isn't.'

'But it's fast.'

'Jesus! You've never climbed before, and you want to rappel down.'

'I've got guts.'

'But no common sense.'

'Okay,' she said. 'We don't rappel.'

'We definitely don't rappel.'

'We go slow and easy.'

'We don't go at all.'

Ignoring him, she said, 'I can take two hours of the cold. I know I can. And if we keep moving, maybe it won't bother us so much.'

'We'll freeze to death.' He refused to be shaken from that opinion.

'Graham, we have a simple choice. Go or stay. If we make the climb, *maybe* we'll fall or freeze to death. If we stay here, we'll sure as hell be killed.'

'I'm not convinced it *is* that simple.'

'Yes, you are.'

He closed his eyes. He was furious with himself, sick of his inability to accept unpleasant realities, to risk pain, and to come face to face with his own fear. The climb would be dangerous. Supremely dangerous. It might even prove to be sheer folly; they could die in the first few minutes of the descent. But she was correct when she said they had no choice but to try it.

'Graham? We're wasting time.'

'You know the real reason why the climb isn't possible.'

'No,' she said. 'Tell me.'

He felt color and warmth come into his face. 'Connie, you aren't leaving me with any dignity.'

'I never took that from you. You've taken it from yourself.' Her lovely face was lined with sorrow. He could see that it hurt her to have to speak to him so bluntly. She came across the room, put one hand to his face. 'You've surrendered your dignity and your self-respect. Piece by piece.' Her voice was low, almost a whisper; it wavered. 'I'm afraid for you, afraid that if you don't stop throwing it away, you'll have nothing left. Nothing.'

'Connie . . .' He wanted to cry. But he had no tears for Graham Harris. He knew precisely what he had done to himself. He had no pity; he *despised* the man he'd become. He felt that, deep inside, he had always been a coward, and that his fall on Mount Everest had given him an excuse to retreat into fear. Why else had he resisted going to a psychiatrist? Every one of his doctors had suggested psychoanalysis. He suspected that he was comfortable in his fear; and that possibility sickened him. 'I'm afraid of my own shadow. I'd be no good to you out there.'

'You're not so frightened today as you were yesterday,' she said tenderly. 'Tonight, you've coped damned well. What about the elevator shaft? This morning, the thought of going down that ladder would have overwhelmed you.'

He was trembling.

'This is your chance,' she said. 'You can overcome the fear. I know you can.'

He licked his lips nervously. He went to the pile of gear in front of the photographic backdrop. 'I wish I could be half as sure of me as you are.'

Following him, she said, 'I understand what I'm asking of you. I know it'll be the hardest thing you've ever done.'

He remembered the fall vividly. He could close his eyes any time – even in a crowded room – and experience it again: his foot slipping, pain in the chest as the safety harness tightened around him, pain abruptly relieved as the rope snapped, breath caught like an unchewed lump of meat in his throat, then floating and floating and floating. The fall was only three hundred feet, and it had ended in a thick cushion of snow; it had seemed a mile.

She said, 'If you stay here, you'll die; but it'll be an easier death. The instant Bollinger sees you, he'll shoot to kill. He won't hesitate. It'll be over within a second for you.' She took hold of his hand. 'But it won't be like that for me.'

He looked up from the equipment. Her gray eyes radiated a fear as primal and paralyzing as his own.

'Bollinger will use me,' she said.

He was unable to speak.

'He'll cut me,' she said.

Unbidden, an image of Edna Mowry came to him. She had been holding her own bloody navel in her hand.

'He'll disfigure me.'

'Maybe –'

'He's the Butcher. Don't forget. Don't forget who he is. What he is.'

'God help me,' he said.

'I don't want to die. But if I *have* to die, I don't want it to be like that.' She shuddered. 'If we're not going to make the climb, if we're just going to wait for him here, then I want you to kill me. Hit me across the back of the head with something. Hit me very hard.'

Amazed, he said, 'What are you talking about?'

'Kill me before Bollinger can get to me. Graham, you owe me that much. You've got to do it.'

'I love you,' he said weakly. 'You're everything. There's nothing else for me.'

She was somber, a mourner at her own execution. 'If you love me, then you understand why you've got to kill me.'

'I couldn't do it.'

'We don't have much time,' she said. 'Either we get ready for the climb right now – or you kill me. Bollinger will be here any minute.'

Glancing at the main entrance to see if anyone was trying to get in, Bollinger crossed the marble floor and opened the white door. He stood at the bottom of the north stairs and listened for footsteps. There were none. No footsteps, no voices, no noise at all. He peered up the narrow, open core of the shaft, but he didn't see anyone moving alongside the switchback railing.

He went to the south stairs.

Those too were deserted.

He looked at his watch. 10:38.

Running some of Blake's verses through his mind to calm himself, he went to the elevator.

·31·

Well-made boots are essential to a serious climber. They should be five to seven inches high, crafted from the best grade of leather, lined with leather, preferably hand-sewn, with foam-padded tongues. Most important of all, the soles should be hard and stiff, with tough lugs made of Vibram.

Graham was wearing just such a pair of boots. They were a perfect fit, more like gloves than footwear. Although putting them on and lacing them up brought him closer to the act that he regarded with terror, he found the boots strangely comforting, reassuring. His familiarity with them, with climbing gear in general, seemed like a touchstone against which he could test for the old Graham Harris, test for a trace of the courage he'd once shown.

Both pairs of boots in the pile of equipment were four sizes too large for Connic. She couldn't wear either of them. If she stuffed paper into the toes and along the sides, she would feel as if she were wearing blocks of concrete; and she would surely misstep at some crucial point in the climb.

Fortunately, they found a pair of klettershoes that fitted well enough. The klettershoe – an anglicization of *Kletterschuh*, German for 'climbing shoe' – was lighter, tighter, more flexible, and not so high as standard climbing boots. The sole was of rubber, and the welt did not protrude, making it possible for the wearer to gain toeholds on even the narrowest ledges.

Although they would have to serve for want of something better, the klettershoes weren't suited for the climb that lay ahead. Because they were made of suede and were not waterproof, they should be used only in the fairest weather, never in a snowstorm.

To protect her feet from becoming wet and from the inevitable frostbite, Connie wore both socks and plastic binding. The socks were thick, gray, woolen; they came to mid-calf. The plastic was ordinarily used to seal up the dry food that a climber carried in his

499

rucksack. Graham had wrapped her feet in two sheets of plastic, securing the waterproof material at her ankles with rubber bands.

They were both wearing heavy, bright red nylon parkas with hoods that tied under the chin. Between the outer nylon surface and the inner nylon lining, his jacket was filled with man-made insulation, sufficient for autumn climbing but not for the cold that awaited them tonight. Her parka was much better – although he hadn't explained that to her for fear she would insist that *he* wear it – because it was insulated with one hundred percent goose down. That made it the warmest garment, for its size and weight, that she could have worn.

Over the parka, each of them was wearing a *Klettergürtel*, a climbing harness, for protection in the event of a fall. This piece of equipment was a great improvement over the waistband that climbers had once used, for in a fall the band sometimes jerked so tight that it damaged the heart and lungs. The simple leather harness distributed the pressure over the entire body trunk, reducing the risk of a severe injury and virtually guaranteeing the climber that he would not turn upside down.

Connie was impressed by the *Klettergürtel*. As he strapped her into it, she said. 'It's perfect insurance, isn't it? Even if you fall, it brings you up short.'

Of course, if she didn't just slip or misplace her foot, if instead the rope broke, and if she was on a single line, the harness would not stop her fall. However, Connie didn't have to worry about that, for he was taking extraordinary safety measures with her: she would be going down on two independent lines. In addition to the main rope, he intended to fix her to a second which he would belay all the way to the street.

He would not be so well looked after as she was. There was no one to belay him. He would be descending last – on a single line.

He didn't explain that to her. When she got outside, the less she had to worry about, the better her chances were of coming out of this alive. Tension was good for a climber; but too much tension could cause him to make mistakes.

Both harnesses had accessory loops at the waist. Graham was carrying pitons, carabiners, expansion bolts, a hammer, and a compact battery-powered drill the size of two packs of cigarettes. In her harness loops, Connie had a variety of extra pitons and carabiners.

Besides the equipment hung on their harnesses, they were both burdened with rope. Connie had hundred-foot lengths of it at each hip; it was heavy, but so tightly coiled that it did not restrict her movements. Graham had another hundred-foot coil at his right hip. They were left with two shorter lengths: and these they would use for the first leg of the descent.

Last of all, they put on their gloves.

At every floor, Bollinger got off the elevator. If the entire level was occupied by one business firm, he tried the locked doors at opposite ends of the alcove. If it was an 'open' floor, he stepped out of the alcove to make certain there was no one in the corridor.

At every fifth floor, he looked not only into the corridor but into the stairs and the elevator shafts as well. On the first twenty floors, four elevator shafts served the building; from the twentieth to the thirty-fifth floors, two shafts; and from the thirty-fifth to the forty-second, only one shaft. In the first half of his vertical search, he wasted far more time than he could afford, opening the emergency doors to all of those shafts.

At ten-fifty he was on the fifteenth floor.

He had not found a sign of them. He was beginning to wonder if he was conducting the search properly. However, at the moment he was unable to see any other way to go about it.

He went to the sixteenth floor.

Connie pulled on the heavy cord and drew back the office draperies.

Graham unlatched the center window. The two rectangular panes wouldn't budge at first, then abruptly gave with a squeal, opened inward like casement windows.

Wind exploded into the room. It had the voice of a living creature; its screams were piercing, demonic. Snowflakes swirled around him, danced across the top of the conference table and melted on its polished surface, beaded like dew on the grass-green carpet.

Leaning over the sill, he looked down the side of the Bowerton Building. The top five floors – and the four-story decorative pinnacle above them – were set back two yards from the bottom thirty-seven levels. Just three floors below, there was a six-foot-wide ledge that ringed the structure. The lower four-fifths of the building's face lay beyond the ledge, out of his line of sight.

The snow was falling so thickly that he could barely see the street lamps on the far side of Lexington Avenue. Under the lights, not even a small patch of pavement was visible.

In the few seconds he needed to survey the situation, the

wind battered his head, chilled and numbed his exposed face.

'That's damned cold!' As he spoke, breath pluming out of him, he turned from the window. 'We're bound to suffer at least *some* frostbite.'

'We've got to go anyway,' she said.

'I know. I'm not trying to back out.'

'Should we wrap our faces?'

'With what?'

'Scarves –'

'The wind would cut through any material we've got handy, then paste it to our faces so we'd have trouble breathing. Unfortunately, the magazine didn't recommend any face masks in that buyer's guide. Otherwise, we'd have exactly what we need.'

'Then what can we do?'

He had a sudden thought and went to his desk. He stripped off his bulky gloves. The center drawer contained evidence of the hypochondria that had been an ever-growing component of his fear: Anacin, aspirin, half a dozen cold remedies, tetracycline capsules, throat lozenges, a thermometer in its case . . . He picked up a small tube and showed it to her.

'Chap Stick?' she asked.

'Come here.'

She went to him. 'That stuff's for chapped lips. If we're going to be frostbitten, why worry about a little thing like chapped lips?'

He pulled the cap off the tube, twisted the base to bring up the waxy stick, and coated her entire face – forehead, temples, cheeks, nose, lips and chin. 'With even a thin shield of this, the wind will need more time to leech the warmth out of you. And it'll keep your skin supple. Loss of heat is two-thirds of the danger. But loss of moisture along with loss of heat is what causes severe frostbite. The moisture in bitterly cold air doesn't get to your skin; in fact, subzero wind can dry out your face almost as thoroughly as desert air.'

'I was right,' she said.

'Right about what?'

'There's some Nick Charles in you.'

At eleven o'clock, Bollinger entered the elevator, switched it on, and pressed the button for the twenty-second floor.

·32·

The window frame was extremely sturdy, not cold-pressed and not of aluminum as were most of the window frames in buildings erected during the past thirty years. The grooved, steel center post was almost an inch thick and appeared to be capable of supporting hundreds of pounds without bending or breaking loose from the sash.

Harris hooked a carabiner to the post.

This piece of hardware was one of the most important that a climber carried. Carabiners were made of steel or alloy and came in several shapes – oval D, offset D, and pear or keyhole – but the oval was used more often than any of the others. It was approximately three and a half inches by one and three-quarters inches, and it resembled nothing so much as an oversized key ring or perhaps an elongated chain link. A spring-loaded gate opened on one side of the oval, making it possible for the climber to connect the carabiner to the eye of a piton; he could also slip a loop of rope onto the metal ring. A carabiner, which was sometimes referred to as a 'snap link,' could be employed to join two ropes at any point along them, which was essential when the ends of those lines were secured above and below. A vital – but not the only – function of the highly polished snap links was to prevent ropes from chafing each other, to guard against their fraying through on the rough, unpolished eye of a piton or on the sharp edge of a rock; carabiners saved lives.

At Graham's direction, Connie had stripped the manufacturer's plastic bands from an eighty-foot coil of red and blue hawser-laid nylon rope.

'It doesn't look strong,' she said.

'It's got a breaking strength of four thousand pounds.'

'So thin.'

'Seven-sixteenths of an inch.'

'I guess you know what you're doing.'

Smiling reassuringly, he said, 'Relax.'

He tied a knot in one end of the rope. That done, he grasped the double loop that sprouted above the knot and slipped it through the gate of the carabiner that was attached to the window post.

He was surprised at how quickly he was working, and by the ease with which he had fashioned the complex knot. He seemed to be operating on instinct more than on knowledge. In five years he had not forgotten anything.

'This will be your safety line,' he told her.

The carabiner was one of those that came with a metal sleeve that fitted over the gate to guard against an accidental opening. He screwed the sleeve in place.

He picked up the rope and pulled it through his hands, quickly measuring eleven yards of it. He took a folding knife from a pocket of his parka and cut the rope, dropped one piece to the floor. He tied the cut end of the shorter section to her harness, so that she was attached to the window post by a thirty-foot umbilical. He took one end of the other piece of rope and tied it around her waist, using a bowline knot.

Patting the windowsill, he said, 'Sit up here.'

She sat facing him, her back to the wind and snow.

He pushed the thirty-foot rope out of the window; and the loop of slack, from the post to Connie's harness, swung in the wind. He arranged the forty-five-foot length on the office floor, carefully coiled it to be certain that it would pay out without tangling, and finally tied the free end around his waist.

He intended to perform a standing hip belay. On a mountain, it was always possible that a belayer might be jerked from his standing position if he was not anchored by another rope and a well-placed piton; he could lose his balance and fall, along with the person whom he was belaying. Therefore, a standing belay was considered less desirable than one accomplished from a sitting position. However, because Connie weighed sixty pounds less than he, and because the window was waist high, he didn't think she would be able to drag him out of the room.

Standing with his legs spread to improve his balance, he picked up the forty-five-foot line at a point midway between the neatly piled coil and Connie. He had knotted the rope at his navel; now, he passed it behind him and across the hips at the belt line. The rope that came from Connie went around his left hip and then around his right; therefore, his left hand was the guide hand, while the right was the braking hand.

From his anchor point six feet in front of her, he said, 'Ready?'

She bit her lip.

'The ledge is only thirty feet below.'

'Not so far,' she said weakly.

'You'll be there before you know it.'

She forced a smile.

She looked down at her harness and tugged on it, as if she thought it might have come undone.

'Remember what to do?' he asked.

'Hold the line with both hands above my head. Don't try to help. Look for the ledge, get my feet on it right away, don't let myself be lowered past it.'

'And when you get there?'

'First, I untie myself.'

'But only from this line.'

'Yes.'

'Not from the other.'

She nodded.

'Then, when you've untied yourself –'

'I jerk on this line twice.'

'That's right. I'll put you down as gently as I can.'

In spite of the stinging cold wind that whistled through the open window on both sides of her, her face was pale. 'I love you,' she said.

'And I love you.'

'You can do this.'

'I hope so.'

'I *know*.'

His heart was pounding.

'I trust you,' she said.

He realized that if he allowed her to die during the climb, he would have no right or reason to save himself. Life without her would be an unbearable passage through guilt and loneliness, a gray emptiness worse than death. If she fell, he might as well pitch himself after her.

He was scared.

All he could do was repeat what he had already said, 'I love you.'

Taking a deep breath, leaning backward, she said, 'Well . . . woman overboard!'

The corridor was dark and deserted.

Bollinger returned to the elevator and pressed the button for the twenty-seventh floor.

505

·33·

The instant that Connie slipped backward off the windowsill she sensed the hundreds of feet of open space beneath her. She didn't need to look down to be profoundly affected by that great, dark gulf. She was even more terrified than she had expected to be. The fear had a physical as well as a mental impact on her. Her throat constricted; she found it hard to breathe. Her chest felt tight, and her pulse rate soared. Suddenly acidic, her stomach contracted sickeningly.

She resisted the urge to clutch the windowsill before it was out of her grasp. Instead, she reached overhead and gripped the rope with both hands.

The wind rocked her from side to side. It pinched her face and stung the thin rim of ungreased skin around her eyes.

In order to see at all, she was forced to squint, to peer out through the narrowest of lash-shielded slits. Otherwise, the wind would have blinded her with her own tears. Unfortunately, the pile of climbing equipment in the art director's office had not contained snow goggles.

She glanced down at the ledge toward which she was slowly moving. It was six feet wide, but to her it looked like a tightrope.

His feet slipped on the carpet.

He dug in his heels.

Judging by the amount of rope still coiled beside him, she was not even halfway to the ledge. Yet he felt as if he had lowered her at least a hundred feet.

Initially, the strain on Graham's arms and shoulders had been tolerable. But as he payed out the line, he became increasingly aware of the toll taken by five years of inactivity. With each foot of rope, new aches sprang up like sparks in his muscles, spread toward each other, fanned into cracking fires.

Nevertheless, the pain was the least of his worries. More

507

important, he was facing away from the office doors. And he could not forget the vision: a bullet in the back, blood, and then darkness.

Where was Bollinger?

The farther Connie descended, the less slack there was in the line that connected her to the window post. She hoped that Graham had estimated its length correctly. If not, she might be in serious trouble. A too-long safety line posed no threat; but if it was too short, she would be hung up a foot or two from the ledge. She would have to climb back to the window so that Graham could rectify the situation – or she would have to give up the safety line altogether, proceed to the setback on just the belayer's rope. Anxiously, she watched the safety line as it gradually grew taut.

Overhead, the main rope was twisting and untwisting with lateral tension. As the thousands of nylon strands repeatedly tightened, relaxed, tightened, she found herself turning slowly in a semicircle from left to right and back again. This movement was in addition to the pendulumlike swing caused by the wind; and of course it made her increasingly ill.

She wondered if the rope would break. Surely, all of that twisting and untwisting began where the rope dropped away from the window. Was the thin line even now fraying at its contact point with the sill?

Graham had said there would be some dangerous friction at the sill. But he had assured her that she would be on the ledge before the nylon fibers had even been slightly bruised. Nylon was tough material. Strong. Reliable. It would not wear through from a few minutes – or even a quarter-hour – of heavy friction.

Still, she wondered.

At eight minutes after eleven, Frank Bollinger started to search the thirtieth floor.

He was beginning to feel that he was trapped in a surreal landscape of doors; hundreds upon hundreds of doors. All night long he had been opening them, anticipating sudden violence, overflowing with that tension that made him feel *alive*. But all of the doors opened on the same thing: darkness, emptiness, silence. Each door promised to deliver what he had been hunting for, but not one of them kept the promise.

It seemed to him that the wilderness of doors was a condition not merely of this one night but of his entire life. Doors. Doors that opened on darkness. On emptiness. On blind passages and dead ends of every sort. Each day of his life, he had expected to find a door that, when flung wide, would present him with all that he deserved. Yet that golden door eluded him. He had not been treated fairly. After all, he was one of the new men, superior to everyone he saw around him. Yet what had he become in thirty-seven years? Anything? Not a president. Not even a senator. Not famous. Not rich. He was nothing but a lousy vice detective, a cop whose working life was spent in the grimy subculture of whores, pimps, gamblers, addicts, and petty racketeers.

That was why Harris (and tens of millions like him) had to die. They were subhumans, vastly inferior to the new breed of men. Yet for every new man, there were a million old ones. Because there was strength in numbers, these pitiful creatures – risking thermonuclear destruction to satisfy their greed and their fondness for childish posturing – held on to the world's power, money and resources. Only through the greatest slaughter in history, only in the midst of Armageddon, could the new men seize what was rightfully theirs.

The thirtieth level was deserted, as were the stairs and the elevator shafts.

He went up onc floor.

Connie's feet touched the ledge. Thanks to the scouring wind, the stone was pretty much free of snow; therefore, there had been no chance for the snow to be pressed into ice. She wasn't in any danger of sliding off her perch.

She put her back to the face of the building, staying as far from the brink as she could.

Surprisingly, with stone under her feet, she was more impressed by the gulf in front of her than when she was dangling in empty space. Swinging at the end of the rope, she had not been able to see the void in the proper perspective. Now, with the benefit of secure footing, she found the thirty-eight-story drop doubly terrifying; it seemed a bottomless pit.

She untied the knot at her harness, freed herself of the main line. She jerked on the rope twice, hard.

Immediately Graham reeled it up.

In a minute he would be on his way to her.

Would he panic when he got out here?

I trust him, she told herself. I really do. I *have* to.

Nonetheless, she was afraid he would get only part of the way out of the window before he turned and fled, leaving her stranded.

·34·

Graham took off his gloves, leaned out of the window, and felt the stone below the sash. It was planed granite, a rock meant to withstand the ages. However, before the icy wind could numb his fingertips, he discovered a tiny horizontal fissure that suited his purpose.

Keeping one hand on the crack in order not to lose it, he took the hammer and a piton from the tool straps at his waist. Balanced on the sill, leaning out as far as he dared, he put the sharp tip of the steel peg into the crack and pounded it home.

The light he had to work by was barely adequate. It came from the aircraft warning lights that ringed the decorative pinnacle of the building just thirty feet above him; it alternated between red and white.

From his upside-down position, the work went more slowly than he would have liked. When he finished at last, he looked over his shoulder to see if Bollinger was behind him. He was still alone.

The piton felt as if it were well placed. He got a good grip on it, tried to wiggle it. It was firm.

He snapped a carabiner through the eye of the piton.

He snapped another carabiner to the center post of the window, above the one that secured Connie's safety line.

Next, he pulled the knots out of the belaying rope. He took it from around his waist and dropped it on the floor by the window.

He closed one of the tall, rectangular panes as best he could; the carabiners fixed to the center post would not permit it to close all the way. He would attempt to shut the other half of the window from the outside.

He hurried to the draw cords and pulled the green velvet drapes into place.

Eventually, Bollinger would come back to this office and would realize that they had gone out of the window. But Graham wanted to conceal the evidence of their escape as long as possible.

Stepping behind the drapes, he sidled along to the window. Wind roared through the open pane and billowed the velvet around him.

He picked up an eleven-yard line that he had cut from another hundred-foot coil. He tied it to his harness and to the free carabiner on the window post. There was no one here to belay him as he had done Connie, but he had worked out a way to avoid a single-line descent; he would have a safety tether exactly like Connie's.

He quickly tied a figure-eight knot in one end of the forty-five-foot-line. Leaning out of the window once more, he hooked the double loops of rope through the carabiner that was linked to the piton. Then he screwed the sleeve over the gate, locking the snap link. He tossed the rope into the night and watched to be sure that it hung straight and unobstructed from the piton. This would be his rappelling line.

He was not adhering strictly to orthodox mountain climbing procedure. But then this 'mountain' certainly was not orthodox either. The situation called for flexibility, for a few original methods.

After he had put on his gloves again, he took hold of the thirty-foot safety line. He wrapped it once around his right wrist and then seized it tightly with the same hand. Approximately four feet of rope lay between his hand and the anchor point on the window post. In the first few seconds after he went through the window, he would be hanging by his right arm, four feet under the sill.

He got on his knees on the window ledge, facing the lining of the office drapes. Slowly, cautiously, reluctantly, he went out of the room backward, feet first. Just before he overbalanced and slid all the way out, he closed the open half of the window as far as the carabiners would allow. Then he dropped four feet.

Memories of Mount Everest burst upon him, clamored for his attention. He shoved them down, desperately forced them deep into his mind.

He tasted vomit at the back of his mouth. But he swallowed hard, swallowed repeatedly until his throat was clear. He *willed* himself not to be sick, and it worked. At least for the moment.

With his left hand he plucked the rappelling line from the face of the building. Holding that loosely, he reached above his head and grabbed the safety rope that he already had in his right hand. Both hands on the shorter line, he raised his knees in a fetal position and planted his boots against the granite. Pulling hand over hand on the safety tether, he took three small steps up the sheer wall until he was balanced against the building at a forty-five-degree angle. The toes

512

of his boots were jammed into a narrow mortar seam with all the force he could apply.

Satisfied with his precarious position, he let go of the safety tether with his left hand.

Although he remained securely anchored, the very act of letting go of anything at that height made the vomit rise in his throat once more. He gagged, held it down, quickly recovered.

He was balanced on four points: his right hand on the shorter rope, now only two feet from the window post; his left hand on the line with which he would rappel down; his right foot; his left foot. He clung like a fly to the side of the highrise.

Keeping his eyes on the piton that thrust up between his spread feet, he jerked on the rappelling line several times. Hard. The piton didn't move. He shifted his weight to the longer line but kept his right-hand grip on the safety tether. Even with a hundred and fifty pounds of downward drag, the piton did not shift in the crack.

Convinced that the peg was well placed, he released the safety tether.

Now he was balanced on three points: left hand on the long line, both feet on the wall, still at a forty-five-degree angle to the building.

Although he would not be touching it again before he reached the ledge, the safety rope would nevertheless bring him up short of death if the longer line broke while he was rappelling down to Connie.

He told himself to remember that. Remember and stave off panic. Panic was the real enemy. It could kill him faster than Bollinger could. The tether was there. Linking his harness to the window post. He must remember . . .

With his free hand, he groped under his thigh, felt behind himself for the long rope that he already held in his other hand. After a maddening few seconds, he found it. Now, the line on which he would rappel came from the piton to his left hand in front of him, passed between his legs at crotch level to his right hand behind him. With that hand he brought the rope forward, over his right hip, across his chest, over his head, and finally over his left shoulder. It hung down his back, passed through his right hand, and ran on into empty space.

He was perfectly positioned.

The left hand was his guiding hand.

The right hand was his braking hand.

He was ready to rappel.

For the first time since he had come through the window, he took a good look around him. Dark monoliths, gigantic skyscrapers rose eerily out of the winter storm. Hundreds of thousands of points of light, made hazy and even more distant by the falling snow, marked the night on every side of him. Manhattan to his left. Manhattan to his right. Manhattan behind him. Most important – Manhattan *below* him. Six hundred feet of empty night waiting to swallow him. Strangely, for an instant he felt as if this were a miniature replica of the city, a tiny reproduction that was forever frozen in plastic; he felt as if he were also tiny, as if he were suspended in a paperweight, one of those clear hemispheres that filled with artificial snow when it was shaken. As unexpectedly as it came, the illusion passed: the city became huge again; the concrete canyon below appeared to be bottomless; however, while all else returned to normal, he remained tiny, insignificant.

When he first came out of the window, he had focused his attention on pitons, ropes and technical maneuvers. Thus occupied, he had been able to ignore his surroundings, to blunt his awareness of them.

That was no longer possible. Suddenly, he was *too* aware of the city and of how far it was to the street.

Inevitably, such awareness brought unwanted memories: *his foot slipping, harness jerking tight, rope snapping, floating, floating, floating, floating, striking, darkness, splinters of pain in his legs, darkness again, a hot iron in his guts, pain breaking like glass in his back, blood, darkness, hospital rooms. . . .*

Although the bitterly cold wind pummeled his face, sweat popped out on his brow and along his temples.

He was trembling.

He knew he couldn't make the climb.

Floating, floating . . .

He couldn't move at all.

Not an inch.

In the elevator, Bollinger hesitated. He was about to press the button for the twenty-third floor, when he realized that, after he lost track of them, Harris and the woman apparently had not continued down toward the lobby. They had vanished on the twenty-seventh level. He had searched that floor and all those below it; and he was as certain as he could be, short of shooting open every locked door, that they were not in the lower three-fourths of the building. They'd gone up. Back to Harris's office? As soon as that occurred to him, he knew it was true, and he knew why they had done it. They'd gone up because that was the last thing he would expect them to do. If they had continued down the stairs or elevator shaft, he would have nailed them in minutes. Sure as hell. But, in going up, they had confused him and gained time.

Forty-five minutes of time, he thought angrily. That bastard has made a fool out of me. Forty-five minutes. But not one goddamned minute more.

He pushed the button for the fortieth floor.

Six hundred feet.

Twice as far as he had fallen on Everest.

And this time there would be no miracle to save him, no deep snowdrift to cushion the impact. He would be a bloody mess when the police found him. Broken. Ruined. Lifeless.

Although he could see nothing of it, he stared intently at the street. The darkness and snow obscured the pavement. Yet he could not look away. He was mesmerized not by what he saw, but by what he didn't *need* to see, transfixed by what he *knew* lay below the night and below the shifting white curtains of the storm.

He closed his eyes. Thought about courage. Thought about how far he had come. Toes pressed into the shallow mortar-filled groove between two blocks of granite. Left hand in front. Right hand behind. Ready, get set . . . but he couldn't go.

When he opened his eyes, he saw Connie on the ledge.

She motioned for him to hurry.

If he didn't move, she would die. He would fail her utterly. She didn't deserve that after the eighteen months she'd given him, eighteen months of tender care and saintlike understanding. She hadn't once criticized him for whining, for his paranoia or his self-pity or his selfishness. She had put herself in emotional jeopardy that was no less terrifying than the physical risk demanded of him. He knew that mental anguish was every bit as painful as a broken leg. In return for those eighteen months, he had to make this climb for her. He owed her that much; hell, he owed her *everything*.

The perspiration had dissolved some of the coating of Chap Stick on his forehead and cheeks. As the wind dried the sweat, it chilled his face. He realized again how little time they could spend out here before the winter night sapped their strength.

He looked up at the piton that anchored him.

Connie will die if you don't do this.

515

He was squeezing the line too tightly with his left hand, which ought to be used only to guide him. He should hold the line *loosely*, using his right hand to pass rope and to brake.

Connie will die . . .

He relaxed his left-hand grip.

He told himself not to look down. Took a deep breath. Let it out. Started to count to ten. Told himself he was stalling. Pushed off the wall.

Don't panic!

As he swung backward into the night, he slid down the rope. When he glided back to the wall, both feet in front of him and firmly planted against the granite, pain zigzagged through his game leg. He winced, but he knew he could bear it. When he looked down, he saw that he had descended no more than two feet, but the fact that he had gotten anywhere at all made the pain seem unimportant.

He had intended to thrust away from the stone with all his strength and to cover two yards on each long arc. But he could not do it. Not yet. He was too scared to rappel as enthusiastically as he had done in the past; furthermore, a more vigorous descent would make the pain in his leg unbearable.

Instead, he pushed from the wall again, swung backward, dropped two feet along the line, swooped back to the wall. And again: just a foot or eighteen inches this time. Little mincing steps. A cautious dance of fear along the face of the building. Out, down, in; out, down, in; out, down, in . . .

The terror had not evaporated. It was in him yet, bubbling, thick as stew. A cancer that had fed upon him and grown for years was not likely to vanish through natural remission in a few minutes. However, he was no longer overwhelmed by fear, incapacitated by it. He could see ahead to a day when he might be cured of it; and that was a fine vision.

When he finally dared to look down, he saw that he was so near the ledge that he no longer needed to rappel. He let go of the rope and dropped the last few feet.

Connie pressed close to him. She had to shout to be heard above the wind. 'You did it.'

'I did it!'

'You've beaten it.'

'So far.'

'Maybe this is far enough.'

'What?'

She pointed to the window beside them. 'What if we break in here?'

'Why should we?'

'It's somebody's office. We could hide in it.'

'What about Bollinger?'

She raised her voice a notch to compensate for a new gust of wind. 'Sooner or later, he'll go to your office.'

'So?'

'He'll see the window. Carabiners and ropes.'

'I know.'

'He'll think we went all the way to the street.'

'Maybe he will. I doubt it.'

'Even if he doesn't think that, he won't know where we stopped. He can't blast open every door in the building, looking for us.'

The wind *whooshed* between them, rebounded from the building, rocked them as if they were toy figures. It wailed: a banshee.

Snowflakes sliced into Graham's eyes. They were so fine and cold that they affected him almost as grains of salt would have done. He squeezed his eyes shut, trying to force out the sudden pain. He had some success; but the pain was replaced by a copious flow of tears that temporarily blinded him.

They pressed their foreheads together, trying to get closer so they wouldn't have to yell at each other.

'We can hide until people come to work,' she said.

'Tomorrow's Saturday.'

'*Some* people will work. The custodial crews, at least.'

'The city will be paralyzed by morning,' he said. 'This is a blizzard! No one will go to work.'

'Then we hide until Monday.'

'What about water? Food?'

'A big office will have water coolers. Coffee and soda-vending machines. Maybe even a candy and cracker vendor.'

'Until Monday?'

'If we have to.'

'That's a long time.'

She jerked one hand to the void at her left side. 'And that's a long *climb*!'

'Agreed.'

'Come on,' she said impatiently. 'Let's smash in the window.'

Bollinger stepped over the fallen liquor cabinet and looked around Harris's office.

Nothing out of the ordinary. No sign of the prey.

Where in the name of God *were* they?

He was turning to leave when the green velvet drapes billowed out from the wall.

He brought up the Walther PPK, almost opened fire.

Before he could squeeze off the first shot, the drapes fell back against the wall. Nobody could be hiding behind them; there wasn't enough room for that.

He went to one end of the drapes and found the draw cords. The green velvet folded back on itself with a soft hiss.

As soon as the middle window was revealed, he saw that something was wrong with it. He went to it and opened the tall, rectangular panes.

The wind rushed in at him, fluttered his unbuttoned collar, mussed his hair, moaned to him. Hard-driven flakes of snow peppered his face.

He saw the carabiners on the center post, and the ropes leading from them.

He leaned out of the window, looked down the side of the building.

'I'll be damned!' he said.

Graham was trying to unhook the hammer from the accessory strap on his safety harness, but he was hampered by his heavy gloves. Without the gloves, it would have been an easy chore, but he didn't want to take them off out here for fear they would slip away from him and disappear over the edge. If something went wrong and they were forced to continue the climb, he would need gloves desperately.

Above him, the wind made a strange sound. *Whump!* A loud, blunt noise. Like a muffled crack of thunder.

He finally got the hammer off the strap.

Whump!

Connie grabbed his arm. 'Bollinger!'

At first he didn't know what she meant. He looked up only because she did.

Thirty feet above them, Bollinger was leaning out of the window.

To Connie, Graham said, 'Stand against the wall!'

She didn't move. She seemed stunned. This was the first time she had ever *looked* frightened.

'Don't make a target of yourself!' he shouted.

She pressed her back to the building.

'Untie yourself from the safety line,' he said.

518

Overhead, a tongue of flame licked out of the pistol's muzzle: *whump!*

Graham swung the hammer, struck the window.

Glass exploded inward.

Frantically, unable to forget the vision of himself being shot in the back, he smashed the stubborn, jagged shards that clung to the frame.

Whump!

The sharp sound of a ricochet made Graham jump. The bullet skipped off the stone inches from his face.

He was sweating again.

Bollinger shouted something.

The wind tore his words apart, transformed them into meaningless sounds.

Graham didn't look up. He kept working at the spiked edges of the window.

Whump!

'Go!' he shouted as he shattered the last dangerous piece of glass.

Connie scrambled over the windowsill, disappeared into the dark office.

He slipped the safety line knot at his harness.

Whump!

The shot was so close that he cried out involuntarily. The slug plucked at the sleeve of his parka. He was unbalanced by the surprise, and for an instant he thought he would fall off the ledge.

Whump!

Whump!

He plunged forward, through the broken window, expecting to be stopped at the last second by a bullet in the spine.

·35·

In the unlighted office on the thirty-eighth floor, the glass crunched under their feet.

Connie said, 'How could he miss us?'

As he patted the sweat from his face with the palm of his glove, Graham said, 'Wind's near gale force. Could have deflected the bullets slightly.'

'In just thirty feet?'

'Maybe. Besides, he was firing from a bad angle. Leaning out the window, shooting down and in. Light was bad. Wind was in his face. He'd have been damned lucky if he'd hit us.'

'We can't stay here as we planned,' she said.

'Of course not. He knows which floor we're on. He's probably running for the elevator right now.'

'We go back out?'

'I sure don't want to.'

'He'll keep popping up along the way, trying to shoot us off the side of the building.'

'Do we have a choice?'

'None,' she said. 'Ready to climb?'

'As I'll ever be.'

'You've done well.'

'I'm not all the way down yet.'

'You'll make it.'

'Are you the clairvoyant now?'

'You'll make it. Because you aren't afraid anymore.'

'Who? Me?'

'You.'

'I'm scared to death.'

'Not like you once were. Not that bad. Anyway, there's good reason to be afraid right now. It's a healthy fear you've got this time.'

'Oh, yeah. I'm brimming with healthy fear.'

'I was right.'

'About what?'

'You're the man I've always wanted.'

'Then you haven't wanted much.'

In spite of what he said, she detected pleasure in his voice. He didn't sound as if he were seriously denigrating himself; at worst, he was poking fun at the sort of inferiority complex he'd displayed before tonight. Already, he had regained some of his self-respect.

He pulled open the second half of the window and said, 'You wait here. I'll set another piton, tie up a new line.' He took off his gloves. 'Hold these for me.'

'Your hands will freeze.'

'Not in just a minute or two. I can work faster with bare hands.'

Cautiously he put his head out of the window, looked up.

'Is he still there?' she asked.

'No.'

He crawled onto the six-foot-wide ledge, stretched out on his stomach. His feet were toward her, his head and shoulders over the brink.

She took a few steps away from the window. Stood very still. Listened for Bollinger.

In the Harris Publications suite, Bollinger paused to reload the Walther PPK before going to the elevator.

Graham hammered the piton into the tight horizontal mortar line between two granite blocks. He tested it, found it to be secure, and snapped a carabiner to it.

Sitting up, he took the hundred-foot length of rope from his right hip and quickly arranged it in a coil that would unravel without a hitch. The wind had sufficient force to disturb the coil; he would have to watch it all the while he was belaying Connie. If it got fouled on itself, they would both be in trouble. He tied a knot in one end of the line, a knot with two small loops rising above it.

Lying down again, he reached over the brink and hooked the loops of rope through the carabiner. He shut the gate on the snap link and screwed the sleeve in place.

He sat up, his back to the wind. He felt as if strong hands were trying to shove him off the ledge.

Already, his fingers were numb with cold.

The two safety lines they had used during their descent from the fortieth floor were dangling beside him. He took hold of one.

Overhead, the line had been fixed to the carabiner in such a fashion that it could be tugged loose and retrieved from below. As long as there was heavy tension on the line, the knot remained tight and safe; in fact, the more tension there was – and the greater the climber's weight, the greater the tension – the firmer the knot. However, when the climber left the rope, releasing the tension, and when the rope was tugged in the proper manner, the knot would slip open. He jerked on the line, then again, and a third time. Finally it freed itself from the snap link and tumbled down into his lap.

He took a folding knife from a pocket of his parka, opened it. He cut two five-foot pieces from the eleven-yard safety line, then put the knife away.

He stood up, tottering slightly as pain shimmered through his bad leg.

One of the five-foot lines was for him. He tied an end of it to his harness. He tied the other end to a carabiner and snapped the carabiner to the window post.

Leaning in the window, he said, 'Connie?'

She stepped out of the shadows, into the wan fan of light. 'I was listening.'

'Hear anything?'

'Not yet.'

'Come out here.'

He wished Billy could be here for the kill. He felt that Billy was half of him, fifty percent of his flesh and blood and mind. Without Billy, he wasn't fully alive at moments like this. Without Billy, he could experience only a part of the thrill, half of the excitement.

On his way to the elevator, Bollinger thought about Billy, mostly about the first few nights they had known each other.

They had met on a Friday and spent nine hours in a private all-night club on Forty-fourth Street. They had left well after dawn, and they were amazed at how the time had flown. The bar was a favorite hangout for city detectives and was always busy; however, it seemed to Bollinger that he and Billy had been the only people in the place, all alone in their corner booth.

From the start they weren't awkward with each other. He felt as if they were twin brothers, as if they shared that mythical oneness of twins in addition to years of daily contact. They talked rapidly, eagerly. No chitchat or gossip. Conversation. Honest-to-God conversation. It was an exchange of ideas and sentiments that Bollinger had never enjoyed with anyone else. Nothing was taboo. Politics. Religion. Poetry. Sex. Self-appraisal. They found a phenomenal number of things about which they held the same unorthodox opinions. After nine hours, they knew each other better than either of them had ever known another human being.

The following night they met at the bar, talked, drank, picked up a good-looking whore and took her to Billy's apartment. The three of them had gone to bed together, but not in a bisexual sense. In fact, it would be more accurate to say that the two of them had gone to bed with her, for although they performed, sometimes separately and sometimes simultaneously, a wide variety of sex acts with and upon her, Billy did not touch Bollinger, nor did Bollinger touch Billy.

That night, sex was more dynamic, exhilarating, frenzied, manic, and ultimately more exhausting than Bollinger had ever imagined it could be. Billy certainly didn't look like a stud. Far from it. But he was precisely that, insatiable. He delighted in withholding his orgasm for hours, for he knew that the longer he denied himself, the more shattering the climax when it finally came. A sensualist, he preferred to refuse immediate satisfaction in favor of a far greater series of sensations later on. Bollinger realized from the moment he climbed into the bed that he was being tested. Rated. Billy was watching. He found it difficult to match the pace set by the older man, but he did. Even the girl complained of being worn out, used up.

He vividly recalled the position in which he'd been when he'd climaxed, because afterward he suspected that Billy had maneuvered him into it. The girl was on hands and knees in the center of the bed. Billy knelt in front of her. Bollinger knelt behind, stroking her dog-fashion. He faced Billy across her back; later, he knew that Billy had wanted to finish while confronting him.

He watched himself moving in and out of the girl, then looked up and saw Billy staring at him. Staring intently. Eyes wide, electric. Eyes that weren't entirely sane. Although he was frightened by it, he returned the stare – and was plunged into an hallucinogenic experience. He imagined he was rising out of his body, felt as if he were floating toward Billy. And as he floated, he shrank until he was so small he could tumble into those eyes. Knowing that it was an illusion in no way detracted from the impact of it; he could have sworn that he actually *was* sinking into Billy's eyes, sinking down, down . . .

His climax was considerably more than a biological function; it joined him to the whore on a physical level, but it also tied him to Billy on a much higher plane. He spurted deep into her vagina, and precisely at that moment Billy spilled seed into her mouth. In the throes of an intense orgasm, Bollinger had the odd notion that he and Billy had grown incredibly inside of the girl, had swelled and lengthened until they were touching at the center of her. Then he went one step further, lost all awareness of the woman; so far as he was concerned, he and Billy were the only people in the room. In his mind he saw them standing with the tips of their organs pressed together, ejaculating into each other's penis. The image was powerful but strangely asexual. There was certainly nothing *homosexual* about it. Absolutely nothing. He wasn't queer. He had no doubt about that. None at all. The imaginary act that preoccupied him was similar to the ritual by which members of certain American Indian tribes had once become blood brothers. The Indians cut their hands and pressed the cuts together; because they believed that the blood flowed from the body of one into that of the other, they felt that they would be part of each other forever. Bollinger's bizarre vision was like the Indians' blood-brother ceremony. It was an oath, a most sacred bond. And he knew that a metamorphosis had taken place; henceforth, they were not two men but one.

Now, feeling incomplete without Billy beside him, he reached the elevator cab and switched it on.

Connie clambered through the window, onto the thirty-eighth-floor setback.

Graham quickly tied the free end of the hundred-foot main line to her harness.

'Ready?' she asked.

'Not quite.'

His hands were getting numb. His fingertips stung, and his knuckles ached as if they were arthritic.

He tied carabiners to both ends of one of the five-foot pieces of rope he had cut. He snapped both carabiners to a metal ring on her harness. The rope between them looped all the way to her knees.

He clipped the hammer to the accessory strap on the waist belt of her harness.

'What's all this for?' she asked.

'The next setback is five stories down. Looks about half as wide as this one. I'll lower you the same way I got you here. I'll be anchored to the window post.' He tugged on his own five-foot tether. 'But we don't have time to rig a seventy-five-foot safety line for you. You'll have to go on just a single rope.'

She chewed her lower lip, nodded.

'As soon as you reach that ledge,' Graham said, 'look for a narrow, horizontal masonry seam between blocks of granite. The narrower the better. But don't waste too much time comparing cracks. Use the hammer to pound in a piton.'

'This short rope you just hooked onto me: is that to be my safety line when I get down there?'

'Yes. Unclip one end of it from your harness and snap the carabiner to the piton. Make sure the sleeve is screwed over the gate.'

'Sleeve?'

He showed her what he meant. 'As soon as you've got the sleeve in place, untie yourself from the main line so that I can reel it up and use it.'

She gave him his gloves.

He put them on. 'One more thing. I'll be letting the rope out much faster than I did the first time. Don't panic. Just hold on, relax, and keep your eyes open for the ledge coming up under you.'

'All right.'

'Any questions?'

'No.'

She sat on the edge of the setback, dangled her legs over the gulf.

He picked up the rope, flexed his cold hands several times to be certain he had a firm grip. A meager trace of warmth had begun to seep into his fingers. He spread his feet, took a deep breath, and said, 'Go!'

She slid off the ledge, into empty space.

Pain pulsated through his arms and shoulders as her full weight suddenly dragged on him. Gritting his teeth, he payed out the rope as fast as he dared.

In the thirty-eighth-floor corridor, Frank Bollinger had some difficulty deciding which business lay directly under Harris's office. Finally, he settled on two possibilities: Boswell Patent Brokerage and Dentonwick Mail Order Sales.

Both doors were locked.

He pumped three bullets into the lock on the Dentonwick office. Pushed open the door. Fired twice into the darkness. Leaped inside, crouched, fumbled for the wall switch, turned on the overhead lights.

The first of the three rooms was deserted. He proceeded cautiously to search the other two.

The tension went out of the line.

Connie had reached the ledge five stories below.

Nevertheless, he kept his hands on the rope and was prepared to belay her again if she slipped and fell before she had anchored her safety tether.

He heard two muffled shots.

The fact that he could hear them at all above the howling wind meant that they were frighteningly close.

But what was Bollinger shooting at?

The office behind Graham remained dark; but suddenly, lights came on beyond the windows of the office next door.

Bollinger was too damned close.

Is this where it happens? he wondered. Is this where I get the bullet in the back?

Sooner than he had expected, the signal came on the line: two sharp tugs.

He reeled in the rope, wondering if he had as much as a minute left before Bollinger found the correct office, the broken window – and him.

If he was going to reach that ledge five stories below before Bollinger had a chance to kill him, he would have to rappel much faster than he had done the first time.

Once more, the rope passed over regularly spaced windows. He would have to be careful not to put his feet through one of them. Because he'd have to take big steps rather than little ones, and because he'd have to descend farther on each arc and take less time to calculate his movements, avoiding the glass would be far more difficult than it had been from the fortieth to the thirty-eighth floor.

His prospects rekindled his terror. Perhaps it was fortunate that he needed to hurry. If he'd had time to delay, the fear might have grown strong enough to immobilize him again.

Harris and the woman were not in the offices of Dentonwick Mail Order Sales.

Bollinger returned to the corridor. He fired two shots into the door of the Boswell Patent Brokerage suite.

·36·

Boswell Patent Brokerage occupied three small rooms, all of them shabbily furnished – and all of them deserted.

At the broken window, Bollinger leaned out, looked both ways along the snow-swept six-foot-wide setback. They weren't there either.

Reluctantly, he brushed the shards of glass out of his way and crawled through the window.

The storm wind raced over him, pummeled him, stood his hair on end, dashed snowflakes in his face and shoved them down his shirt, under his collar, where they melted on his back. Shivering, he regretted having taken off his overcoat.

Wishing he had handholds of some sort, he stretched out on his belly. The stone was so cold that he felt as if he had lain down bare-chested on a block of ice.

He peered over the edge. Graham Harris was only ten feet below, swinging away from the building on a thin rope, slipping down the line as he followed his arc, swinging back to the building: rappelling.

He reached down, gripped the piton. It was so cold that his fingers almost froze to it. He tried to twist it loose but discovered it was well planted.

Even in the pale, almost nonexistent light, he could see that there was a gate in the snap link that was fixed to the piton. He fingered it, tried to open it, but couldn't figure out how it worked.

Although he was right on top of Harris, Bollinger knew he could not get off an accurate shot. The cold and the wind had brought tears to his eyes, blurring his vision. The light was poor. And the man was moving too fast to make a good target.

Instead, he put down the Walther PPK, rolled onto his side, and quickly extracted a knife from his trousers pocket. He flicked it open. It was the same razor-sharp knife with which he had murdered

529

so many women. And now, if he could cut the rappelling line before Harris got down to the ledge, he would have claimed his first male victim with it. Reaching to the piton, he began to saw through the loop of the knot that was suspended from the jiggling carabiner.

The wind struck the side of the building, rose along the stone, buffeted his face.

He was breathing through his mouth. The air was so cold that it made his throat ache.

Completely unaware of Bollinger, Harris pushed away from the building once more. Swung out, swung back, descended six or eight feet in the process. Pushed out again.

The carabiner was moving on the piton, making it difficult for Bollinger to keep the blade at precisely the same cutting point on the rope.

Harris was rappelling fast, rapidly approaching the ledge where Connie waited for him. In a few seconds he would be safely off the rope.

Finally, after Harris had taken several more steps along the face of the highrise, Bollinger's knife severed the nylon rope; and the line snapped free of the carabiner.

As Graham swooped toward the building, his feet in front of him, intending to take brief possession of a narrow window ledge, he felt the rope go slack.

He knew what had happened.

His thoughts accelerated. Long before the rope had fallen around his shoulders, before his forward momentum was depleted, even as his feet touched the stone, he had considered his situation and decided on a course of action.

The ledge was two inches deep. Just the tips of his boots fitted on it. It wasn't large enough to support him.

Taking advantage of his momentum, he flung himself toward the window and pushed in that direction with his toes – up and in, with all of his strength – the instant he made contact with the window ledge. His shoulder hit one of the tall panes. Glass shattered.

He had hoped to thrust an arm through the glass, then throw it around the center post. If he could do that, he might hold on long enough to open the window and drag himself inside.

However, even as the glass broke, he lost his toehold on the icy two-inch-wide sill. His boots skidded backward, sank through empty air.

He slid down the stonework. He pawed desperately at the window as he went.

His knees struck the sill. The granite tore his trousers, gouged his skin. His knees slipped off the impossibly shallow indention just as his feet had done.

He grabbed the sill with both hands as gravity drew him over it. He held on as best he could. By his fingers. Dangling over the street. Kicking at the wall with his feet. Trying to find a toehold where there was none. Gasping.

The setback where Connie waited was only fifteen feet from the sill to which he clung, just seven or eight feet from the bottoms of his boots. Eight feet. It looked like a mile to him.

As he contemplated the long fall to Lexington Avenue, he hoped to God that his vision of a bullet in the back had been correct.

His gloves were too thick to serve him well in a precarious position like this. He lost his grip on the ice-sheathed stone.

He dropped onto the yard-wide setback. Landed on his feet. Cried out in pain. Tottered backward.

Connie shouted.

With one foot he stepped into space. Felt death pulling at him. Screamed. Windmilled his arms.

Connie was tethered to the wall and willing to test the piton that she had hammered between the granite blocks. She jumped at Graham, clutched the front of his parka, jerked at him, tried to stagger to safety with him.

For what must have been only a second or two but seemed like an hour, they swayed on the brink.

The wind shoved them toward the street.

But at last she proved sufficiently strong to arrest his backward fall. He brought his foot in from the gulf. They stabilized on the last few inches of stone. Then he threw his arms around her, and they moved back to the face of the building, to safety, away from the concrete canyon.

•37•

'He may have cut the rope,' Connie said, 'but he isn't up there now.'

'He's coming for us.'

'Then he'll cut the rope again.'

'I guess he will. So we'll just have to be too damned fast for him.'

Graham stretched out on the yard-wide ledge, parallel to the side of the building.

His bad leg was filled with a steady almost crippling pain from ankle to hip. Considering all the rappelling he would have to do to reach the street, he was certain the leg would give out at some crucial point in the climb, probably just when his life most depended on surefootedness.

He took a piton from one of the accessory straps at his waist. He held out one hand to Connie. 'Hammer.'

She gave it to him.

He twisted around a bit, lay at an angle to the building, his head and one arm over the edge of the setback.

Far below, an ambulance moved cautiously on Lexington Avenue, its lights flashing. Even from the thirty-third floor, the street was not entirely visible. He could barely make out the lines of the ambulance in the wash of its own emergency beacons. It drew even with the Bowerton Building, then drove on into the snowy night.

He found a mortar seam even without removing his bulky gloves, and he started to pound in a piton.

Suddenly, to one side, two floors below, movement caught his eye. A window opened inward. One of two tall panes. No one appeared at it. However, he sensed the man in the darkness of the office beyond.

A chill passed along his spine; it had nothing to do with the cold or the wind.

Pretending that he had seen nothing, he finished hammering the piton in place. Then he slid away from the edge, stood up. 'We can't go down here,' he told Connie.

533

She looked puzzled. 'Why not?'

'Bollinger is below us.'

'What?'

'At a window. Waiting to shoot us – or at least you – as we go past him.'

Her gray eyes were wide. 'But why didn't he come here to get us?'

'Maybe he thought we'd already started down. Or maybe he thought we'd run out of his reach along this setback the moment he came into an office on this floor.'

'What now?'

'I'm thinking.'

'I'm scared.'

'Don't be.'

'Can't help it.'

Her eyebrows were crusted with snow, as was the fringe of fur lining that escaped her hood. He held her. The wind moaned incessantly.

He said, 'This is a corner building.'

'Does that matter?'

'It faces on another street besides Lexington.'

'So?'

'So we follow the setback,' he said excitedly. 'Turn the corner on the setback.'

'And climb down the other face, the one that overlooks the side street?'

'You've got it. That's no harder to climb than this wall.'

'And Bollinger can only see Lexington Avenue from his window,' she said.

'That's right.'

'Brilliant.'

'Let's do it.'

'Sooner or later, he'll figure out what we've done.'

'Later.'

'It had better be.'

'Sure. He'll wait right where he is for a few minutes, expecting to pick us off. Then he'll waste time checking this entire floor.'

'And the stairwells.'

'And the elevator shafts. We might get most of the way down before he finds us.'

'Okay,' she said. She unhooked her safety tether from the window post.

·38·

At the open window on the thirty-first floor, Frank Bollinger waited. Apparently they were preparing the rope which they would hook to the piton that Harris had just pounded into place.

He looked forward to shooting the woman as she came past him on the line. The image excited him. He would enjoy blowing her away into the night.

When that happened, Harris would be stunned, emotionally destroyed, unable to think fast, unable to protect himself. Then Bollinger could go after him at will. If he could kill Harris where he chose, kill him cleanly, he could salvage the plan that he and Billy had devised this afternoon.

As he waited for his prey, he thought again of that second night of his relationship with Billy. . . .

After the whore left Billy's apartment, they ate dinner in the kitchen. Between them they consumed two salads, four steaks, four rashers of bacon, six eggs, eight pieces of toast, and a large quantity of Scotch. They approached the food as they had the woman: with intensity, with single-mindedness, with appetites that were not those of men but those of supermen.

At midnight, over brandy, Bollinger had talked about the years when he had lived with his grandmother.

Even now he could remember any part of that conversation he wished. He was blessed with virtually total recall, a talent honed by years of memorizing complex poetry.

'So she called you Dwight. I like that name.'

'Why are you talking that way?'

'The Southern accent? I was born in the South. I had an accent until I was twenty. I made a concerted effort to lose it. Took voice lessons. But I can recall it when I want. Sometimes the drawl amuses me.'

'Why did you take voice lessons in the first place? The accent is nice.'

535

'*Nobody up North takes you seriously when you've got a heavy drawl. They think you're a redneck. Say, what if I call you Dwight?*'

'*If you want.*'

'*I'm closer to you than anyone's been since your grandmother. Isn't that true?*'

'*Yeah.*'

'*I should call you Dwight. In fact, I'm closer to you than your grandmother was.*'

'*I guess so.*'

'*And you know me better than anyone else does.*'

'*Do I? I suppose I do.*'

'*Then we need special names for each other.*'

'*So call me Dwight. I like it.*'

'*And you call me – Billy.*'

'*Billy?*'

'*Billy James Plover.*'

'*Where'd you get that?*'

'*I was born with it.*'

'*You changed your name?*'

'*Just like I did the accent.*'

'*When?*'

'*A long time ago.*'

'*Why?*'

'*I went to college up North. Didn't do as well as I should have done. Didn't get the grades I deserved. Finally dropped out. But by then I knew why I didn't make it. In those days, Ivy League professors didn't give you a chance if you spoke with a drawl and had a redneck name like Billy James Plover.*'

'*You're exaggerating.*'

'*How would you know? How in the hell would you know? You've always had a nice white Anglo-Saxon Protestant Northern name. Franklin Dwight Bollinger. What would you know about it?*'

'*I guess you're right.*'

'*At that time, all the Ivy League intellectuals were involved in a conspiracy of sorts against the South, against Southerners. They still are, except that the conspiracy isn't so broad or so vicious as it once was. Back then, the only way you could succeed in a Northern university or community was to have an Anglo-Saxon name like yours – or else one that was out-and-out Jewish. Frank Bollinger or Sol Cohen. You could be accepted with either name. But not with Billy James Plover.*'

'*So you stopped being Billy.*'

'As soon as I could.'

'And did your luck improve?'

'The same day I changed my name.'

'But you want me to call you Billy.'

'It wasn't the name *that was wrong. It was the people who reacted negatively to the name.'*

'Billy . . .'

'Shouldn't we have special names for each other?'

'Doesn't matter. If you want.'

'Aren't we special ourselves, Frank?'

'I think so.'

'Aren't we different from other people?'

'Quite different.'

'So we shouldn't use between us the names they call us by.'

'If you say so.'

'We're supermen, Frank.'

'What?'

'Not like Clark Kent.'

'I sure don't have X-ray vision.'

'Supermen as Nietzsche meant.'

'Nietzsche?'

'You aren't familiar with his work?'

'Not particularly.'

'I'll lend you a book by him.'

'Okay.'

'In fact, since Nietzsche should be read over and over again, I'll give you a book by him.'

'Thank you . . . Billy.'

'You're welcome, Dwight.'

At the half-open window, Bollinger glanced at his watch. The time was 12:30.

Neither Harris nor the woman had started down from the thirty-third-floor setback.

He couldn't wait any longer. He had squandered too much time already. He would have to go looking for them.

·39·

Connie hammered a piton into a horizontal mortar seam. She hooked the safety tether to the piton with a carabiner, then untied herself from the main line.

The moment it was free, Graham reeled up the rope.

Climbing this face of the building was proving easier than scaling the front on Lexington Avenue. Not that there was a greater number of setbacks, ledges or foot-holds here than there; the distribution of those was the same. However, the wind was much less fierce on the side street than it had been on Lexington. Here, the snowflakes that struck her face *felt* like snowflakes and not like tiny bullets. The cold air hugged her legs, but it did not press *through* her jeans; it didn't pinch her thighs and stab painfully into her calves as it had done earlier.

She had descended ten floors – and Graham five – since they had seen Bollinger waiting for them at the window. Graham had lowered her to the yard-wide twenty-eighth-floor setback and had rappelled down after her. Below that point there was only one other setback, this one at the sixth floor, three hundred and thirty feet down. At the twenty-third level, there was an eighteen-inch-wide decorative ledge – quintessential art deco; the stone was carved into a band of connected, abstract bunches of grapes – and they made that their next goal. Graham belayed her, and she found that the carved ledge was large and strong enough to support her. In less than a minute, powered by his new-found confidence, he would be beside her.

She had no idea what they would do after that. The sixth-floor setback was still a long way off; figuring five yards to a floor, that haven lay two hundred and fifty-five feet below. Their ropes were only one hundred feet long. Between this ledge of stone grapes and the sixth story, there was nothing but a sheer wall and impossibly narrow window ledges.

Graham had assured her that they were not at a dead end. Nevertheless, she was worried.

Overhead, he began to rappel through the falling snow. She was fascinated by the sight. He seemed to be creating the line as he went, weaving it out of his own substance; he resembled a spider that was swinging gracefully, smoothly on its own silk from one point to another on a web that it was constructing.

In seconds he was standing beside her.

She gave him the hammer.

He placed two pitons in the wall between the windows, in different horizontal mortar seams.

He was breathing hard; mist plumed from his open mouth.

'You all right?' she asked.

'So far.'

Without benefit of a safety line, he sidled along the ledge, away from her, his back to the street, his hands pressed against the stone. On this side of the building, the gentler wind had formed miniature drifts on the ledges and on the windowsills. He was putting his feet down in two or three inches of snow and, here and there, on patches of brittle ice.

Connie wanted to ask him where he was going, what he was doing; but she was afraid that if she talked she would distract him and he would fall.

Past the window, he stopped and pounded in another piton, then hung the hammer on the accessory strap at his waist.

He returned, inch by inch to where he had placed the first two pegs. He snapped his safety harness to one of those pitons.

'What was all that for?' she asked.

'We're going to rappel down a few floors,' he said. 'Both of us. At the same time. On two separate ropes.'

Swallowing hard, she said, 'Not me.'

'Yes, you.'

Her heart was thumping so furiously that she thought it might burst. 'I can't do it.'

'You can. You will.'

She shook her head: no.

'You won't rappel the way I've done.'

'That's for damned sure.'

'I've been doing a body rappel. You'll go down in a seat rappel. It's safer and easier.'

Although none of her doubts had been allayed, Connie said, 'What's the difference between a body rappel and a seat rappel?'

'I'll show you in a minute.'

'Take your time.'

He grabbed the hundred-foot line on which he had descended from the twenty-eighth-floor setback. He tugged on it three times, jerked it to the right. Five stories above them, the knot came loose; the rope snaked down.

He caught the line, piled it beside him.

He examined the end of it to see if it was worn, and was satisfied that it wasn't. He tied a knot in it, looped the rope through the gate of the carabiner. He snapped the carabiner to the free piton that was one mortar seam above the peg that anchored his safety tether.

'We can't rappel all the way to the street,' Connie said.

'Sure we can.'

'The ropes aren't long enough.'

'You'll rappel just five floors at a time. Brace yourself on a window ledge. Then let go of the rappelling line with your right hand –'

'Brace myself on a two-inch sill?'

'It can be done. Don't forget, you'll still be holding onto the line with your left hand.'

'Meanwhile, what will my right hand be doing?'

'Smashing in both panes of the window.'

'And then?'

'First, attach your safety tether to the window. Second, snap another carabiner to the center post. As soon as that's done, you take your weight off the main line and then –'

'Tug on it,' Connie said, 'pull apart the overhead knot like you did just a minute ago.'

'I'll show you how.'

'I catch the line as it falls?'

'Yes.'

'And tie it to the carabiner that I've linked to the window post.'

'That's right.'

Her legs were cold. She stamped her feet on the ledge. 'I guess then I unhook my safety line and rappel down five more floors.'

'And brace yourself in another window and repeat the entire routine. We'll go all the way to the street, but only five stories at a time.'

'You make it sound simple.'

'You'll manage better than you think. I'll show you how to use a seat rappel.'

'There's another problem.'

'What?'

'I don't know how to tie one of those knots that can be jerked loose from below.'

'It isn't difficult. I'll show you.'

He untied the main line from the carabiner in front of him.

She leaned close to him and bent over the rope that he held in both hands. The world-famous glow of Manhattan's millions of bright lights was screened by the storm. Below, the rimed pavement of the street reflected the light from the many street lamps; but that illumination scarcely affected the purple shadows twenty-three floors above. Nevertheless, if she squinted, she could see what Graham was doing.

In a few minutes, she learned how to attach the rope to the anchor point so that it could be retrieved. She tied it several times to make sure she would not forget how it was done.

Next, Graham looped a sling around her hips and through her crotch. He joined the three end-points of the rope with yet another carabiner.

'Now, about this rappelling,' she said as she gripped the main line. She manufactured a smile that he probably did not see, and she tried not to sound terrified.

Taking another snap link from the accessory strap at his waist, Graham said, 'First, I've got to link the main line to the sling. Then I'll show you how you should stand to begin the rappel. I'll explain –'

He was interrupted by the muffled report of a gun: *whump!*

Connie looked up.

Bollinger wasn't above them.

She wondered if she actually had heard a gun or whether the noise might have been produced by the wind.

Then she heard it again: *whump!* There was no doubt. A shot. Two shots. Very close. Inside the building. Somewhere on the twenty-third floor.

Frank Bollinger pushed open the broken door, went into the office, switched on the lights. He stepped around the receptionist's desk, around a typewriter stand and a Xerox copier. He hurried toward the windows that overlooked the side street.

When the lights came on behind the windows on both sides of them, Graham unhooked his safety tether from the piton and told Connie to unhook her own five-foot line.

There was a noise at the window on their right as Bollinger pushed up the rusty latch.

'Follow me,' Graham said.

542

He was perspiring again. His face was slick with sweat. Under the hood, his moist scalp itched.

He turned away from Connie, from the window that Bollinger was about to open, turned to his left, toward Lexington Avenue. Without benefit of a safety line, he walked the narrow ledge instead of sidling along it. He kept his right hand on the granite for what little sense of security it gave him. He had to place each foot directly in front of the other, as if he were on a tightrope, for the ledge was not wide enough to allow him to walk naturally.

He was fifty feet from the Lexington Avenue face of the highrise. When he and Connie turned the corner on the ledge, they would be out of the line of fire.

Of course, Bollinger would find an office with windows that had a view of Lexington. At most they would gain only a minute or two. But right now, an extra minute of life was worth any effort.

He wanted to look back to see if Connie was having any difficulty, but he didn't dare. He had to keep his eyes on the ledge ahead of him and carefully judge the placement of each boot.

Before he had gone more than ten feet, he heard Bollinger shouting.

He hunched his shoulders, remembering the psychic vision, anticipating the bullet.

With a shock he realized that Connie was shielding him. He should have sent her ahead, should have placed himself between her and the pistol. If she stopped a bullet that was meant for him, he didn't want to live. However, it was much too late for him to relinquish the lead. If they stopped they would make even better targets than they already were.

A shot cracked in the darkness.

Then another.

He began to walk faster than was prudent, aware that a misstep would plummet him to the street. His feet slipped on the snow-sheathed stone.

The corner was thirty feet away.

Twenty-five . . .

Bollinger fired again.

Twenty feet.

He felt the fourth shot before he heard it. The bullet ripped open the left sleeve of his parka, seared through the upper part of his arm.

The impact of the slug made him stumble a bit. He lumbered forward a few quick, unplanned steps. The street appeared to spin wildly below him. With his right hand he pawed helplessly at the side of the building. He put one foot down on the edge of the stone, his heel in empty air. He heard himself shouting but hardly knew what he was saying. His boots gripped in the drifted snow, but they skidded on a patch of ice. When he regained his balance within half a dozen steps, he was amazed that he hadn't fallen.

At first there was no pain in his arm. He was numb from the shoulder down. It was as if his arm had been blown off. For an instant he wondered if he had been mortally wounded; but he realized that a direct hit would have had more force, would have knocked him off his feet and pitched him off the ledge. In a minute or two the wound would begin to hurt like hell, but it wouldn't kill him.

Fifteen feet . . .

He was dizzy.

His legs felt weak.

Probably shock, he thought.

Ten feet.

Another shot. Not so loud as the ones that had come before it. Not as frighteningly close. Fifteen yards away.

At the corner, as he started to inch around onto the Lexington Avenue face of the highrise where a violent wind wrenched at him, he was able to glance back the way he had come. Behind him, the ledge was empty.

Connie was gone.

·40·

Connie was four or five yards below the twenty-third-floor ledge of stone grapes, swinging slightly, suspended over the street. She couldn't bear to look down.

Arms extended above her, she held the nylon rope with both hands. She had considerable difficulty maintaining her grip. Strain had numbed her fingers, and she could no longer be certain that she was clutching the line tightly enough to save herself. A moment ago, relaxing her hands without realizing what she was doing, she had slipped down the rope as if it were well greased, covering two yards in a split second before she was able to halt herself.

She had tried to find toeholds. There were none.

She fixed her gaze on the ledge overhead. She expected to see Bollinger.

Minutes ago, when he opened the window on her right and leaned out with the pistol in one hand, she had known at once that he was too close to miss her. She couldn't follow Graham toward the Lexington Avenue corner. If she tried that, she would be shot in the back. Instead, she gripped the main line and tried to anticipate the shot. If she had even the slimmest chance of escaping – and she was not convinced that she had – then she would have to act only a fraction of a second *before* the explosion came. If she didn't move until or after he fired, she might be dead, and she would certainly be too late to fool him. Fortunately, her timing was perfect; she jumped backward into the void just as he fired, so he must have thought he hit her.

She prayed he would think she was dead. If he had any doubt, he would crawl part of the way through the window, lean over the ledge, see her – and cut the rope.

Although her own plight was serious enough to require all of her attention, she was worried about Graham. She knew that he hadn't been shot off the ledge, for she would have seen him as he fell past her. He was still up there, but he might be badly wounded.

Whether or not he was hurt, her life depended on his coming back to look for her.

She was not a climber. She didn't know how to rappel. She didn't know how to secure her position on the rope. She didn't know how to do anything but hang there; and she wouldn't be able to do even that much longer.

She didn't want to die, *refused* to die. Even if Graham had been killed already, she didn't want to follow him into death. She loved him more than she had ever loved anyone else. At times she became frustrated because she could not find the words to express the breadth and depth of her feeling for him. The language of love was inadequate. She ached for him. But she cherished life as well. Getting up in the morning and making French toast for breakfast. Working in the antique shop. Reading a good book. Going out to an exciting movie. So many small delights. Perhaps it was true that the little joys of daily life were insignificant when compared to the intense pleasures of love, but if she was to be denied the ultimate, she would settle willingly for second best. She knew that her attitude in no way cheapened her love for Graham or made suspect the bonds between them. Her love of life was what had drawn him to her and made her so right for him. To Connie, there was but one obscenity, and that was the grave.

Fifteen feet above, someone moved in the light that radiated through the open window.

Bollinger?

Oh, Jesus, no!

But before she could give in to despair, Graham's face came out of the shadows. He saw her and was stunned. Obviously, he had expected her to be twenty-three stories below, a crumpled corpse on the snow-covered pavement.

'Help me,' she said.

Grinning, he began to reel her up.

In the twenty-third-floor corridor, Frank Bollinger stopped to reload his pistol. He was nearly out of ammunition.

'*So you read Nietzsche last night. What did you think?*'

'*I agree with him.*'

'*About what?*'

'*Everything.*'

'*Supermen?*'

'*Especially that.*'

'Why especially?'

'He has to be right. Mankind as we know it has to be an inter-mediate stage in evolution. Otherwise, everything is so pointless.'

'Aren't we the kind of men he was talking about?'

'It sure as hell seems to me that we are. But one thing bothers me. I've always thought of myself as a liberal. In politics.'

'So?'

'How do I reconcile liberal, left-of-center politics with a belief in a superior race?'

'No problem, Dwight. Pure, hard-core liberals believe in a superior race. They think they're it. They believe they're more intelligent than the general run of mankind, better suited than the little people are to manage the little people's lives. They think they have the one true vision, the ability to solve all the moral dilemmas of the century. They prefer big government because that is the first step to totalitarianism, toward unquestioned rule by the elite. And of course they see themselves as the elite. Reconcile Nietzsche with liberal politics? That's no more difficult than reconciling it with extreme right-wing philosophy.'

Bollinger stopped in front of the door to Opway Electronics, because that office had windows that overlooked Lexington Avenue. He fired the Walther PPK twice; the lock disintegrated under the bullets' impact.

Suggesting ways that she could help herself, favoring his injured left arm, Graham pulled Connie onto the ledge.

Weeping, he hugged her with both arms, squeezed her so tightly that he would have cut off her breath if they hadn't been wearing the insulated parkas. They swayed on the narrow ledge; and for the moment they were unaware of the long drop beside them, tem-porarily unimpressed by the danger. He didn't want to let go of her, not ever. He felt as if he had taken a drug, an upper, something to boost his spirits. Considering their circumstances, his mood was unrealistic. Although they were a long way, both in time and in distance, from safety, he was elated; she was alive.

'Where's Bollinger?' she asked.

Behind Graham, the office was full of light, the window open. But there was no sign of the killer.

'He probably went to look for me on the Lexington side,' Graham said.

'Then he *does* think I'm dead.'

'He must. *I* thought you were.'

'What's happened to your arm?'

'He shot me.'

'Oh, no!'

'It hurts. And it feels stiff, but that's all.'

'There's a lot of blood.'

'Not much. The bullet probably cauterized the wound; that's how shallow it is.' He held out his left hand, opened and closed it to show her that he wasn't seriously affected. 'I can climb.'

'You shouldn't.'

'I'll be fine. Besides, I don't have a choice.'

'We could go inside, use the stairs again.'

'As soon as Bollinger checks the Lexington side and doesn't find me, he'll come back. If I'm not here, he'll look on the stairs. He'd nail us if we tried to go that way.'

'Now what?'

'Same as before. We'll walk this ledge to the corner. By the time we get to Lexington, he'll have looked over that face of the building and be gone. Then we'll rappel.'

'With your arm like this?'

'With my arm like this.'

'The vision you had about being shot in the back –'

'What about it?'

She touched his left arm. 'Was this it?'

'No.'

Bollinger turned away from the window that opened onto Lexington Avenue. He hurried out of the Opway Electronics suite and down the hall toward the office from which he had shot at Harris a few minutes ago.

'Chaos, Dwight.'

'Chaos?'

'There are too damned many of these subhumans for the supermen to take control of things in ordinary times. Only in the midst of Armageddon will men like us ascend.'

'You mean . . . after a nuclear war?'

'That's one way it could happen. Only men like us would have the courage and imagination to lead civilization out of the ruins. But wouldn't it be ridiculous to wait until they've destroyed everything we should inherit?'

'Ridiculous.'

'So it's occurred to me that we could generate the chaos we need, bring about Armageddon in a less destructive form.'

'How?'

'Well . . . does the name Albert DeSalvo mean anything to you?'

'No.'

'He was the Boston Strangler.'

'Oh, yeah. He murdered a lot of women.'

'We should study DeSalvo's case. He wasn't one of us, of course. He was an inferior and a psychotic to boot. But I think we should use him as a model. Single-handedly, he created so much fear that he almost threw the city of Boston into a state of panic. Fear would be our basic tool. Fear can be stoked into panic. A handful of panic-stricken people can transmit their hysteria to the entire population of a city or country.'

'But DeSalvo didn't come close to creating the kind of – or the degree of – chaos that would lead to the collapse of society.'

'Because that wasn't his goal.'

'Even if it had been –'

'Dwight, suppose an Albert DeSalvo . . . better yet, suppose a Jack the Ripper were loose in Manhattan. Suppose he murdered not just ten women, not twenty, but a hundred. Two hundred. In a particularly brutal fashion. With clear evidence of aberrant sex in every case. So there was no doubt that they all died by the same hand. And what if he did all of this in a few months?'

'There would be fear. But –'

'It would be the biggest news story in the city, in the state, and probably in the country. Then suppose that after we murdered the first hundred women, we began to spend half our time killing men. Each time, we'd cut off the man's sex organ and leave behind a message attributing the murder to a fictitious militant feminist group.'

'What?'

'We'd make the public think the men were being murdered in retaliation for the murders of the hundred women.'

'Except women don't typically commit crimes like that.'

'Doesn't matter. We're not trying to create a typical situation.'

'I'm not sure I understand what sort of situation we are trying to create.'

'Don't you see? There are damned ugly tensions between men and women in this country. Hideous tensions. Year by year, as the women's liberation movement has grown, those tensions have become almost unbearable, because they're repressed, hidden. We'll make them boil to the surface.'

'It's not bad. You're exaggerating.'

'I'm not. Believe me. I know. And don't you see what else? There

are hundreds of potential psychotic killers out there. All they need is to be given some direction, a little push. They'll hear about and read about the killings so much that they'll get ideas of their own. Once we've cut up a hundred women and twenty or so men, pretending to be psychotic ourselves, we'll have a dozen imitators doing our work for us.'

'Maybe.'

'Definitely. All mass murderers have had their imitators. But none of them has ever committed crimes grand enough to inspire legions of mimics. We will. And then when we've turned out a squad of sex killers, we'll shift the direction of our own activities.'

'Shift to what?'

'We'll murder white people at random and use a fictitious black revolutionary group to claim credit. After a dozen killings of that sort –'

'We could knock off some blacks and leave everyone under the impression they were killed in retaliation.'

'You've got it. Fan the flames.'

'I'm beginning to see your point. In a city this size, there are countless factions. Blacks, whites, Puerto Ricans, Orientals, men, women, liberals, conservatives, radicals and reactionaries, Catholics and Jews, rich and poor, young and old. . . . We could try to turn each against its opposite and all of them against one another. Once factional violence begins, whether it's religious or political or economic, it usually escalates endlessly.'

'Exactly. If we planned carefully enough, we could do it. In six months, you'd have at least two thousand dead. Maybe five times that number.'

'And you'd have martial law. That would put an end to it before there was chaos on the scale you've talked about.'

'We might have martial law. But we'd still have chaos. In Northern Ireland they've had soldiers on street corners for years, but the killing goes on. Oh, there'd be chaos, Dwight. And it would spread to other cities as –'

'No. I can't swallow that.'

'All over the country, people would be reading and hearing about New York. They'd –'

'It wouldn't spread that easily, Billy.'

'All right. All right. But there would be chaos here, at least. The voters would be ready to elect a tough-talking mayor with new ideas.'

'Certainly.'

'We could elect one of us, one of the new race. The mayoralty of New York is a good political base for a smart man who wants the presidency.'

'The voters might elect a political strongman. But not every political strongman is going to be one of our people.'

'If we planned the chaos, we could also plan to run one of our men in the wake of it. He would know what was coming; he'd have an inside track.'

'One of our men? Hell, we don't know any but you and me.'

'I'd make an excellent mayor.'

'You?'

'I have a good base for a campaign.'

'Christ, come to think of it, you do.'

'I could win.'

'You'd have a fair chance, anyway.'

'It would be a step up the ladder of power for our kind, our race.'

'Jesus, the killing we'd have to do!'

'Haven't you ever killed?'

'A pimp. Two drug pushers who pulled guns on me. A whore that nobody knows about.'

'Did killing disturb you?'

'No. They were scum.'

'We'd be killing scum. Our inferiors. Animals.'

'Could we get away with it?'

'We both know cops. What would cops look for? Known mental patients. Known criminals. Known radicals. People with some sort of motive. We have a motive, but they'd never figure it in a million years.'

'If we worked out every detail, planned carefully – hell, we might do it.'

'Do you know what Leopold wrote to Loeb before they murdered Bobby Franks? "The superman is not liable for anything he may do, except for the one crime that it is possible for him to commit – to make a mistake." '

'If we did something like this –'

'If?'

'You're committed to it?'

'Aren't you, Dwight?'

'We'd start with women?'

'Yes.'

'Kill them'

'Yes.'

'Billy . . .?'
'Yes?'
'Rape them first?'
'Oh, yes.'
'It could even be fun.'

Bollinger leaned out of the window, looked both ways along the ledge. Harris was not on the face of the building that overlooked the side street.

Although the pitons were wedged in the stone beside the window, as they had been when he'd fired at Harris, the rope that had been attached to one of them was gone.

Bollinger crawled onto the windowsill, leaned out much too far, peered over the ledge. The woman's body should have been on the street below. But there was no corpse. Nothing but the smooth sheen of fresh snow.

Dammit, she hadn't fallen! He hadn't shot the bitch after all!

Why wouldn't these people *die*?

Furious, he stumbled back into the room, out of the wind-whipped snow. He left the office and followed the corridor to the nearest stairwell.

Connie wished that she could rappel with her eyes closed. Balanced on the side of the highrise, twenty-three stories above Lexington Avenue, without a safety tether, she was unnerved by the scene.

Right hand behind.

Left hand in front.

Right hand to brake.

Left hand to guide.

Feet spread and planted firmly on the wall.

Repeating to herself all that Graham had taught her, she pushed away from the building. And gasped. She felt as if she had taken a suicidal leap.

As she swung out, she realized that she was clenching the rope too tightly with her left hand. Left to guide. *Right* to brake. She relaxed her grip on the rope in front of her and slid down a few feet before braking.

She approached the building improperly. Her legs were not straight out in front of her, and they weren't rigid enough. They buckled. She twisted to the right, out of control, and struck the granite with her shoulder. The impact was not great enough to break a bone, but it was much too hard.

It dazed her, but she didn't let go of the rope. Got her feet against the stone once more. Got into position. Shook her head to clear it. Glanced to her left. Saw Graham three yards away on that side. Nodded so he would know that she was all right. Then pushed outward. Pushed hard. Slid down. Swung back. She didn't make any mistakes this time.

Grinning, Graham watched as Connie took a few more steps down the stone. Her endurance and determination delighted him. There really was some Nora Charles in her. And a hell of a lot of Nick too.

When he saw that she had pretty much gotten the knack of rappelling – her style was crude but adequate – he kicked away from the wall. He descended farther than she did on each arc and reached the eighteenth floor ahead of her.

He braced himself on the almost nonexistent window ledge. He smashed in the two tall panes of glass and fixed a snap link to the metal center post. When he had attached his safety tether to that carabiner, he released the main line, pulled it free of the overhead anchor. He caught the rope, tied it to the carabiner in front of him, and took up a rappelling position.

Beside him, nine feet away, Connie was also ready to rappel.

He flung himself into space.

He was amazed not only at how well he remembered the skills and techniques of a climber, but at how quickly the worst of his fear had vanished. He was still afraid, but not unnaturally so. Necessity and Connie's love had produced a miracle that no psychiatrist could have matched.

He was beginning to think they might escape. His left arm ached where the bullet had grazed it, and the fingers of that hand were stiff. The pain in his bad leg had subsided to a continuous dull throb that made him grit his teeth occasionally but which didn't interfere too much with his rappelling.

In a couple of steps he reached the seventeenth floor. In two more jumps he came to rest against the sixteenth-story window ledge – where Frank Bollinger had decided to set up an ambush.

The window was closed. However, the drapes had been drawn back. One desk lamp glowed dimly in the office.

Bollinger was on the other side of the glass, a huge silhouette. He was just lifting the latch.

No! Graham thought.

In the same instant that his boots touched the window ledge, he kicked away from it.

Bollinger saw him and pulled off a shot without bothering to open the rectangular panes. Glass sliced into the night.

Although Bollinger reacted fast, Graham was already out of his line of fire. He swung back to the wall seven or eight feet below Bollinger, rappelled again, stopped at the fifteenth-story window.

He looked up and saw flame flicker briefly from the muzzle of the pistol as Bollinger shot at Connie.

The gunfire threw her off her pace. She hit the wall with her shoulder again. Frantic, she got her feet under her and rappelled.

Bollinger fired again.

·41·

Bollinger knew that he hadn't scored a hit on either of them.

He left the office, ran to the elevator. He switched on the control panel and pushed the button for the tenth floor.

As the lift descended, he thought about the plan that he and Billy had formulated yesterday.

'*You'll kill Harris first. Do what you want with the woman, but be sure to cut her up.*'

'*I always cut them up. That was my idea in the first place.*'

'*You should kill Harris where it'll cause the least mess, where you can clean up after.*'

'*Clean up?*'

'*When you're done with the woman, you'll go back to Harris, wipe up every speck of blood around him, and wrap his body in a plastic tarp. So don't kill him on a carpet where he'll leave stains. Take him into a room with a tile floor. Maybe a bathroom.*'

'*Wrap him in a tarp?*'

'*I'll be waiting behind the Bowerton Building at ten o'clock. You'll bring the body to me. We'll put it in the car. Later, we can take it out of the city, bury it upstate someplace.*'

'*Bury it? Why?*'

'*We're going to try to make the police think that Harris has killed his own fiancée, that he's the Butcher. I'll disguise my voice and call Homicide. I'll claim to be Harris, and I'll tell them I'm the Butcher.*'

'*To mislead them?*'

'*You've got it.*'

'*Sooner or later they'll smell a trick.*'

'*Yes, they will. Eventually. But for a few weeks, maybe even for a few months, they'll be after Harris. There wouldn't be any chance whatsoever that they'd follow a good lead, one that might bring them to us.*'

'A classic red herring.'
'Precisely.'
'It'll give us time.'
'Yes.'
'To do everything we want.'
'Nearly everything.'

The plan was ruined.

The clairvoyant was too damned hard to kill.

The doors of the lift slid apart.

Bollinger tripped coming out of the elevator. He fell. The pistol flew out of his hand, clattered against the wall.

He got to his knees and wiped the sweat out of his eyes.

He said, 'Billy?'

But he was alone.

Coughing, sniffling, he crawled to the pistol, clutched it in his right hand and stood up.

He went into the dark hall, to the door of an office that would have a view of Lexington.

Because he was worried about running out of ammunition, he used only one shot on the door. He aimed carefully. The *boom!* echoed and reechoed in the corridor. The lock was damaged, but it wouldn't release altogether. The door rattled in its frame. Rather than use another bullet, he put his shoulder to the panel, pressed until it gave inward.

By the time he reached the Lexington Avenue windows, Harris and the woman had passed him. They were two floors below.

He returned to the elevator. He was going to have to go outside and confront them when they reached the street. He pushed the button for the ground floor.

•42•

Braced against the eighth-floor windows, they agreed to cover the final hundred and twenty feet in two equal rappels, using the fourth-floor window posts as their last anchor points.

At the fourth level, Graham smashed in both rectangular panes. He snapped a carabiner to the post, hooked his safety tether to the carabiner, and jerked involuntarily as a bullet slapped the stone a foot to the right of his head.

He knew at once what had happened. He turned slightly and looked down.

Bollinger, in shirt sleeves and looking harried, stood on the snow-shrouded sidewalk, sixty feet below.

Motioning to Connie, Graham shouted, 'Go in! Get inside! Through the window!'

Bollinger fired again.

A burst of light, pain, blood: a bullet in the back . . .

Is this where it happens? he wondered.

Desperately, Graham used his gloved fist to punch out the shards of glass that remained in the window frame. He grabbed the center post and was about to drag himself inside when the street behind him was suddenly filled with a curious rumbling.

A big yellow road grader turned the corner into Lexington Avenue. Its large black tires churned through the slush and spewed out an icy liquid behind. The plow on the front of the machine was six feet high and ten feet across. Emergency beacons flashed on the roof of the operator's cab. Two headlights the size of dinner plates popped up like the eyes of a frog, glared through the falling snow.

It was the only vehicle in sight on the storm-clogged street.

Graham glanced at Connie. She seemed to be having trouble disentangling herself from the lines and getting through the window. He turned away from her, waved urgently at the driver of the grader. The man could barely be seen behind the dirty windshield.

'Help!' Graham shouted. He didn't think the man could hear him over the roar of the engine. Nevertheless, he kept shouting. 'Help! Up here! Help us!'

Connie began to shout too.

Surprised, Bollinger did exactly what he should not have done. He whirled and shot at the grader.

The driver braked, almost came to a full stop.

'Help!' Graham shouted.

Bollinger fired at the machine again. The slug ricocheted off the steel that framed the windshield of the cab.

The driver shifted gears and gunned the engine.

Bollinger ran.

Lifted by hydraulic arms, the plow rose a foot off the pavement. It cleared the curb as the machine lumbered onto the sidewalk.

Pursued by the grader, Bollinger ran thirty or forty feet along the walk before he sprinted into the street. Kicking up small clouds of snow with each step, he crossed the avenue, with the plow close behind him.

Connie was rapt.

Bollinger let the grader close the distance between them. When only two yards separated him from the shining steel blade, he dashed to one side, out of its way. He ran past the machine, came back toward the Bowerton Building.

The grader didn't turn as easily as a sports car. By the time the driver had brought it around and was headed back, Bollinger was standing under Graham again.

Graham saw him raise the gun. It glinted in the light from the street lamp.

At ground level where the wind was a bit less fierce, the shot was very loud. The bullet cracked into the granite by Graham's right foot.

The grader bore down on Bollinger, horn blaring.

He put his back to the building and faced the mechanical behemoth.

Sensing what the madman would do, Graham fumbled with the compact, battery-powered rock drill that was clipped to his waist belt. He got it free of the strap.

The grader was fifteen to twenty feet from Bollinger, who aimed the pistol at the windshield of the operator's cab.

From his perch on the fourth floor, Graham threw the rock drill. It arced through sixty feet of falling snow and hit Bollinger – not a solid blow on the head, as Graham had hoped, but on the hip. It glanced off him with little force.

Nevertheless, the drill startled Bollinger. He jumped, put a foot on ice, pitched forward, stumbled off the curb, skidded with peculiar grace in the snow, and sprawled face-down in the gutter.

The driver of the grader had expected his quarry to run away; instead, Bollinger fell toward the machine, into it. The operator braked, but he could not bring the grader to a full stop within only eight feet.

The huge steel plow was raised twelve inches off the street; but that was not quite high enough to pass safely over Bollinger. The bottom of the blade caught him at the buttocks and gouged through his flesh, rammed his head, crushed his skull, jammed his body against the raised curb.

Blood sprayed across the snow in the circle of light beneath the nearest street lamp.

·43·

MacDonald, Ott, the security guards and the building engineer had been tucked into heavy plastic body bags supplied by the city morgue. The bags were lined up on the marble floor.

Near the shuttered newsstand at the front of the lobby, half a dozen folding chairs had been arranged in a semicircle. Graham and Connie sat there with Ira Preduski and three other policemen.

Preduski was in his usual condition: slightly bedraggled. His brown suit hung on him only marginally better than a sheet would have done. Because he had been walking in the snow, his trouser cuffs were damp. His shoes and socks were wet. He wasn't wearing galoshes or boots; he owned a pair of the former and two pairs of the latter, but he never remembered to put them on in bad weather.

'Now, I don't mean to mother you,' Preduski said to Graham. 'I know I've asked before. And you've told me. But I'm worried. I can't help it. I worry unnecessarily about a lot of things. That's another fault of mine. But what about your arm? Where you were shot. Is it all right?'

Graham lightly patted the bandage under his shirt. A paramedic with bad breath but sure hands had attended to him an hour ago. 'I'm just fine.'

'What about your leg?'

Graham grimaced. 'I'm no more crippled now than I was before all this happened.'

Turning to Connie, Preduski said, 'What about you? The doc with the ambulance says you've got some bad bruises.'

'Just bruises,' she said almost airily. She was holding Graham's hand. 'Nothing worse.'

'Well, you've both had a terrible night. Just awful. And it's my fault. I should have caught Bollinger weeks ago. If I'd had half a brain, I'd have wrapped up this case long before you two got involved.' He looked at his watch. 'Almost three in the morning.'

561

He stood up, tried unsuccessfully to straighten the rumpled collar of his overcoat. 'We've kept you here much too long. Much too long. But I'm going to have to ask you to hang around fifteen or twenty minutes more to answer any questions that the other detectives or forensics men might have. Is that too much to ask? Would you mind? I know it's a terrible, terrible imposition. I apologize.'

'It's all right,' Graham said wearily.

Preduski spoke to another plainclothes detective sitting with the group. 'Jerry, will you be sure they aren't kept more than fifteen or twenty minutes?'

'Whatever you say, Ira.' Jerry was a tall, chunky man in his late thirties. He had a mole on his chin.

'Make sure they're given a ride home in a squad car.'

Jerry nodded.

'And keep the reporters away from them.'

'Okay, Ira. But it won't be easy.'

To Graham and Connie, Preduski said, 'When you get home, unplug your telephones first thing. You'll have to deal with the press tomorrow. But that's soon enough. They'll be pestering you for weeks. One more cross to bear. I'm sorry. I really am. But maybe we can keep them away from you tonight, give you a few hours of peace before the storm.'

'Thank you,' Connie said.

'Now, I've got to be going. Work to do. Things that ought to have been done long ago. I'm always behind in my work. Always. I'm not cut out for this job. That's the truth.'

He shook hands with Graham and performed an awkward half bow in Connie's direction.

As he walked across the lobby, his wet shoes squished and squeaked.

Outside, he dodged some reporters and refused to answer the questions of others.

His unmarked car was at the end of a double line of police sedans, black-and-whites, ambulances and press vans. He got behind the wheel, buckled his safety belt, started the engine.

His partner, Detective Daniel Mulligan, would be busy inside for a couple of hours yet. He wouldn't miss the car.

Humming a tune of his own creation, Preduski drove onto Lexington, which had recently been plowed. There were chains on his tires; they crunched in the snow and sang on the few bare patches of pavement. He turned the corner, went to Fifth Avenue, and headed downtown.

Less than fifteen minutes later, he parked on a tree-lined street in Greenwich Village.

He left the car. He walked a third of a block, keeping to the shadows beyond the pools of light around the street lamps. With a quick backward glance to be sure he wasn't observed, he stepped into a narrow passageway between two elegant townhouses.

The roofless walkway ended in a blank wall, but there were high gates on both sides. He stopped in front of the gate on his left.

Snowflakes eddied gently in the still night air. The wind did not reach down here, but its fierce voice called from the rooftops above.

He took a pair of lock picks from his pocket. He had found them a long time ago in the apartment of a burglar who had committed suicide. Over the years there had been rare but important occasions on which the picks had come in handy. He used one of them to tease up the pins in the cheap gate lock, used the other pick to hold the pins in place once they'd been teased. In two minutes he was inside.

A small courtyard lay behind Graham Harris's house. A patch of grass. Two trees. A brick patio. Of course, the two flower beds were barren during the winter; however, the presence of a wrought-iron table and four wrought-iron chairs made it seem that people had been playing cards in the sun just that afternoon.

He crossed the courtyard and climbed three steps to the rear entrance.

The storm door was not locked.

As delicately, swiftly, and silently as he could manage, he picked the lock on the wooden door.

He was dismayed by the ease with which he had gained entry. Wouldn't people *ever* learn to buy good locks?

Harris's kitchen was warm and dark. It smelled of spice cake, and of bananas that had been put out to ripen and were now over-ripe.

He closed the door soundlessly.

For a few minutes he stood perfectly still, listening to the house and waiting for his eyes to adjust to the darkness. Finally, when he could identify every object in the kitchen, he went to the table, lifted a chair away from it, put the chair down again without making even the faintest noise.

He sat down and took his revolver from the shoulder holster under his left arm. He held the gun in his lap.

·44·

The squad car waited at the curb until Graham opened the front door of the house. Then it drove away, leaving tracks in the five-inch snowfall that, in Greenwich Village, had not yet been pushed onto the sidewalks.

He switched on the foyer light. As Connie closed the door, he went into the unlighted living room and located the nearest table lamp. He turned it on – and froze, unable to find the strength or the will to remove his fingers from the switch.

A man sat in one of the easy chairs. He had a gun.

Connie put one hand on Graham's arm. To the man in the chair, she said, 'What are *you* doing here?'

Anthony Prine, the host of *Manhattan at Midnight*, stood up. He waved the gun at them. 'I've been waiting for you.'

'Why are you talking like that?' Connie asked.

'The Southern accent? I was born with it. Got rid of it years ago. But I can recall it when I want. It was losing the accent that got me interested in mimicry. I started in show business as a comic who did imitations of famous people. Now I imitate Billy James Plover, the man I used to be.'

'How did you get in here?' Graham demanded.

'I went around the side of the house and broke a window.'

'Get out. I want you out of here.'

'You killed Dwight,' Prine said. 'I drove by the Bowerton Building after the show. I saw all the cops. I know what you did.' He was very pale. His face was lined with strain.

'Killed who?' Graham asked.

'Dwight. Franklin Dwight Bollinger.'

Perplexed, Graham said, 'He was trying to kill us.'

'He was one of the best people. One of the very best there ever was. I did a program about vice cops, and he was one of the guests. Within minutes we knew we were two of a kind.'

'He was the Butcher, the one who –'

Prine was extremely agitated. His hands were shaking. His left cheek was distorted by a nervous tic. He interrupted Connie and said, 'Dwight was *half* the Butcher.'

'Half the Butcher?' Connie said.

Graham lowered his hand from the switch and gripped the pillar of the brass table lamp.

'I was the other half,' Prine said. 'We were identical personalities, Dwight and I.' He took one step toward them. Then another. 'More than that. We were incomplete without each other. We were halves of the same organism.' He pointed the pistol at Graham's head.

'Get out of here!' Graham shouted. 'Run, Connie!' And as he spoke he threw the lamp at Prine.

The lamp knocked Prine back into the easy chair.

Graham turned to the foyer.

Connie was opening the front door.

As he followed her, Prine shot him in the back.

A terrible blow on the right shoulder blade, a burst of light, blood spattering the carpet all around him . . .

He fell and rolled onto his side in time to see Ira Preduski come out of the hallway that led to the kitchen.

He floated on a raft of pain in a sea that grew darker by the second. What was happening?

The detective shouted at Prine and then shot him in self-defense. Once. In the chest.

The talk-show host collapsed against a magazine rack.

Pain. Just the first twitches of pain.

Graham closed his eyes. Wondered if that was the wrong thing to do. If you go to sleep, you'll die. Or was that only with a head injury? He opened his eyes to be on the safe side.

Connie was wiping the sweat from his face.

Kneeling beside him, Preduski said, 'I called an ambulance.'

Some time must have passed. He seemed to fade out in the middle of one conversation and in on the middle of the next.

He closed his eyes.

Opened them.

'Medical examiner's theory,' Preduski said. 'Sounded crazy at first. But the more I thought about it . . .'

'I'm thirsty,' Graham said. He was hoarse.

'Thirsty? I'll bet you are,' Preduski said.

'Get me . . . drink.'

'That might be the wrong thing to do for you,' Connie said. 'We'll wait for the ambulance.'

The room spun. He smiled. He rode the room as if it were a carousel.

'I shouldn't have come here alone,' Preduski said miserably. 'But you see why I thought I had to? Bollinger was a cop. The other half of the Butcher might be a cop too. Who could I trust? Really. Who?'

Graham licked his lips and said, 'Prine. Dead?'

'I'm afraid not,' Preduski said.

'Me?'

'What about you?'

'Dead?'

'You'll live.'

'Sure?'

'Bullet wasn't near the spine. Didn't puncture any vital organ, I'll bet.'

'Sure?'

'*I'm* sure,' Connie said.

Graham closed his eyes.

Epilogue

SUNDAY

Ira Preduski stood with his back to the hospital window. The late afternoon sun framed him in soft gold light. 'Prine says they wanted to start racial wars, religious wars, economic wars . . .'

Graham was lying on his side in the bed, propped up with pillows. He spoke somewhat slowly because of the pain killers he had been given. 'So they could gain power in the aftermath.'

'That's what he says.'

From her chair at Graham's bedside, Connie said, 'But that's crazy. In fact, didn't Charles Manson's bunch of psychos kill all those people for the same reason?'

'I mentioned Manson to Prine,' Preduski said. 'But he tells me Manson was a two-bit con man, a cheap sleazy hood.'

'While Prine is a superman.'

Preduski shook his head sadly. 'Poor Nietzsche. He was one of the most brilliant philosophers who ever lived – and also the most misunderstood.' He bent over and sniffed at an arrangement of flowers that stood on the table by the window. When he looked up again, he said, 'Excuse me for asking. It's none of my business. I know that. But I'm a curious man. One of my faults. But – when's the wedding?'

'Wedding?' Connie said.

'Don't kid me. You two are getting married.'

Confused, Graham said, 'How could you know that? We just talked about it this morning. Just the two of us.'

'I'm a detective,' Preduski said. 'I've picked up clues.'

'For instance?' Connie said.

'For instance, the way the two of you are looking at each other this afternoon.'

Delighted at being able to share the news, Graham said, 'We'll be married a few weeks after I'm released from the hospital, as soon as I have my strength back.'

571

'Which he'll need,' Connie said, smiling wickedly.

Preduski walked around the bed, looked at the bandages on Graham's left arm and on the upper right quarter of his back. 'Every time I think of all that happened Friday night and Saturday morning, I wonder how you two came out of it alive.'

'It wasn't much,' Connie said.

'Not much?' Preduski said.

'No. Really. It wasn't so much, what we did, was it, Nick?'

Graham smiled and felt very good indeed. 'No, it wasn't much, Nora.'

THE MASK

This book is dedicated to
Willo and Dave Roberts
and to
Carol and Don McQuinn
who have no faults –
except that they live
too far away from us

A dirge for her, the doubly dead, in that
    she died so young.
                    – Edgar Allan Poe, "Lenore"

And much of Madness, and more of Sin,
And Horror the soul of the plot.
– Edgar Allan Poe, "The Conqueror Worm"

Extreme terror gives us back the
gestures of our childhood.
                                    – Chazal

Prologue

Laura was in the cellar, doing some spring cleaning and hating every minute of it. She didn't dislike the work itself; she was by nature an industrious girl who was happiest when she had chores to do. But she was afraid of the cellar.

For one thing, the place was gloomy. The four narrow windows, set high in the walls, were hardly larger than embrasures, and the dust-filmed panes of glass permitted only weak, chalky light to enter. Even brightened by a pair of lamps, the big room held on tenaciously to its shadows, unwilling to be completely disrobed. The flickering amber light from the lamps revealed damp stone walls and a hulking, coal-fired furnace that was cold and unused on this fine, warm May afternoon. On a series of long shelves, row upon row of quart jars reflected splinters of light, but their contents – home canned fruit and vegetables that had been stored here for the past nine months remained unilluminated. The corners of the room were all dark, and the low, open-beamed ceiling was hung with shadows like long banners of funeral crepe.

The cellar always had a mildly unpleasant odor, too. It was musty, rather like a limestone cave. In the spring and summer, when the humidity was high, a mottled gray-green fungus sometimes sprang up in the corners, a disgusting scablike growth, fringed with hundreds of tiny white spores that resembled insect eggs; that grotesquery added its own thin but nonetheless displeasing fragrance to the cellar air.

However, neither the gloom nor the offending odors nor the fungus gave rise to Laura's fears; it was the spiders that frightened her. Spiders ruled the cellar. Some of them were small, brown, and quick; others were charcoal gray, a bit bigger than the brown ones, but just as fast-moving as their smaller cousins. There were even a few blue-black giants as large as Laura's thumb.

As she wiped dust and a few cobwebs from the jars of home-

577

canned food, always alert for the scuttling movement of spiders, Laura grew increasingly angry with her mother. Mama could have let her clean some of the upstairs rooms instead of the cellar; Aunt Rachael or Mama herself could have cleaned down here because neither of them worried about spiders. But Mama knew that Laura was afraid of the cellar, and Mama was in the mood to punish her. It was a terrible mood, black as thunderclouds. Laura had seen it before. Too often. It descended over Mama more frequently with every passing year, and when she was in its thrall, she was a different person from the smiling, always singing woman that she was at other times. Although Laura loved her mother, she did not love the short-tempered, mean-spirited woman that her mother sometimes became. She did not love the hateful woman who had sent her down into the cellar with the spiders.

Dusting the jars of peaches, pears, tomatoes, beets, beans, and pickled squash, nervously awaiting the inevitable appearance of a spider, wishing she were grown up and married and on her own, Laura was startled by a sudden, sharp sound that pierced the dank basement air. At first it was like the distant, forlorn wail of an exotic bird, but it quickly became louder and more urgent. She stopped dusting, looked up at the dark ceiling, and listened closely to the eerie ululation that came from overhead. After a moment she realized that it was her Aunt Rachael's voice and that it was a cry of alarm.

Upstairs, something fell over with a crash. It sounded like shattering porcelain. It must have been Mama's peacock vase. If it was the vase, Mama would be in an *extremely* foul mood for the rest of the week.

Laura stepped away from the shelves of canned goods and started toward the cellar stairs, but she stopped abruptly when she heard Mama scream. It wasn't a scream of rage over the loss of the vase; there was a note of terror in it.

Footsteps thumped across the living room floor, toward the front door of the house. The screen door opened with the familiar singing of its long spring, then banged shut. Rachael was outside now, shouting, her words unintelligible but still conveying her fear.

Laura smelled smoke.

She hurried to the stairs and saw pale tongues of fire at the top. The smoke wasn't heavy, but it had an acrid stench.

Heart pounding, Laura climbed to the uppermost step. Waves of heat forced her to squint, but she could see into the kitchen. The wall of fire wasn't solid. There was a narrow route of escape, a corridor of cool safety; the door to the back porch was at the far end.

She lifted her long skirt and pulled it tight across her hips and thighs, bunching it in both hands to prevent it from trailing in the flames. She moved gingerly onto the fire-ringed landing, which creaked under her, but before she reached the open door, the kitchen exploded in yellow-blue flames that quickly turned orange. From wall to wall, floor to ceiling, the room was an inferno; there was no longer a path through the blaze. Crazily, the fire-choked doorway brought to Laura's mind the image of a glittering eye in a jack-o'-lantern.

In the kitchen, windows exploded, and the fire eddied in the sudden change of drafts, pushing through the cellar door, lashing at Laura. Startled, she stumbled backwards, off the landing. She fell. Turning, she grabbed at the railing, missed it, and stumbled down the short flight, cracking her head against the stone floor at the bottom.

She held on to consciousness as if it were a raft and she a drowning swimmer. When she was certain she wouldn't faint, she got to her feet. Pain coruscated across the top of her head. She raised one hand to her brow and found a trickle of blood, a small abrasion. She was dizzy and confused.

During the minute or less that she had been incapacitated, fire had spread across the entire landing at the head of the stairs. It was moving down onto the first step.

She couldn't keep her eyes focused. The rising stairs and the descending fire repeatedly blurred together in an orange haze.

Ghosts of smoke drifted down the stairwell. They reached out with long, insubstantial arms, as if to embrace Laura.

She cupped her hands around her mouth. 'Help!'

No one answered.

'Somebody help me! I'm in the cellar!'

Silence.

'Aunt Rachael! Mama! For God's sake, somebody help me!'

The only response was the steadily increasing roar of the fire.

Laura had never felt so alone before. In spite of the tides of heat washing over her, she felt cold inside. She shivered.

Although her head throbbed worse than ever, and although the abrasion above her right eye continued to weep blood, at least she was having less trouble keeping her eyes focused. The problem was that she didn't like what she saw.

She stood statue-still, transfixed by the deadly spectacle of the flames. Fire crawled lizardlike down the steps, one by one, and it slithered up the rail posts, then crept down the rail with a crisp, chuckling sound.

The smoke reached the bottom of the steps and enfolded her. She coughed, and the coughing aggravated the pain in her head, making her dizzy again. She put one hand against the wall to steady herself.

Everything was happening too fast. The house was going up like a pile of well-seasoned tinder.

I'm going to die here.

That thought jolted her out of her trance. She wasn't ready to die. She was far too young. There was so much of life ahead of her, so many wonderful things to do, things she had long dreamed about doing. It wasn't fair. She *refused* to die.

She gagged on the smoke. Turning away from the burning stairs, she put a hand over her nose and mouth, but that didn't help much.

She saw flames at the far end of the cellar, and for an instant she thought she was already encircled and that all hope of rescue was gone. She cried out in despair, but then she realized the blaze hadn't found its way into the other end of the room after all. The two points of fire that she was seeing were only the twin oil lamps that had provided her with light. The flames in the lamps were harmless, safely ensconced in tall glass chimneys.

She coughed violently again, and the pain in her head settled down behind her eyes. She found it difficult to concentrate. Her thoughts were like droplets of quicksilver, sliding over one another and changing shape so often and so fast that she couldn't make sense of some of them.

She prayed silently and fervently.

Directly overhead, the ceiling groaned and appeared to *shift*. For a few seconds she held her breath, clenched her teeth, and stood with her hands fisted at her sides, waiting to be buried in rubble. But then she saw that the ceiling wasn't going to collapse – not yet.

Trembling, whimpering softly, she scurried to the nearest of the four high-set windows. It was rectangular, approximately eight inches from sill to top and eighteen inches from sash to sash, much too small to provide her with a means of escape. The other three windows were identical to the first; there was no use even taking a closer look at them.

The air was becoming less breathable by the second. Laura's sinuses ached and burned. Her mouth was filled with the revulsive, bitter taste of the smoke.

For too long she stood beneath the window, staring up in frustration and confusion at the meager, milky light that came through the dirty pane and through the haze of smoke that pressed tightly against the glass. She had the feeling she was overlooking an obvious and convenient escape hatch; in fact she was sure of it. There *was* a way out, and it had nothing to do with the windows, but she couldn't get her mind *off* the windows; she was fixated on them, just as she had been fixated on the sight of the advancing flames a couple of minutes ago. The pain in her head and behind her eyes throbbed more powerfully than ever, and with each agonizing pulsation, her thoughts became more muddled.

I'm going to die here.

A frightening vision flashed through her mind. She saw herself afire, her dark hair turned blond by the flames that consumed it and standing straight up on her head as if it were not hair but the wick of a candle. In the vision, she saw her face melting like wax, bubbling and steaming and liquefying, the features flowing together until her face no longer resembled that of a human being, until it was the hideously twisted countenance of a leering demon with empty eye sockets.

No!

She shook her head, dispelling the vision.

She was dizzy and getting dizzier. She needed a draught of clean air to rinse out her polluted lungs, but with each breath she drew more smoke than she had drawn last time. Her chest ached.

Nearby, a rhythmic pounding began; the noise was even louder than her heartbeat, which drummed thunderously in her ears.

She turned in a circle, gagging and coughing, searching for the source of the hammering sound, striving to regain control of herself, struggling hard to *think*.

The hammering stopped.

'Laura . . .'

Above the incessant roar of the fire, she heard someone calling her name.

'Laura . . .'

'I'm down here . . . in the cellar!' she shouted. But the shout came out as nothing more than a whispered croak. Her throat was constricted and already raw from the harsh smoke and the fiercely hot air.

The effort required to stay on her feet became too great for her. She sank to her knees on the stone floor, slumped against the wall, and slid down until she was lying on her side.

'Laura . . .'

The pounding began again. A fist beating on a door.

Laura discovered that the air at floor level was cleaner than that which she had been breathing. She gasped frantically, grateful for this reprieve from suffocation.

For a few seconds the throbbing pain behind her eyes abated, and her thoughts cleared, and she remembered the outside entrance to the cellar, a pair of doors slant-set against the north wall of the house. They were locked from the inside, so that no one could get in to rescue her; in the panic and confusion she had forgotten about those doors. But now, if she kept her wits about her, she would be able to save herself.

'Laura!' It was Aunt Rachael's voice.

Laura crawled to the northwest corner of the room, where the doors sloped down at the top of a short flight of steps. She kept her head low, breathing the tainted but adequate air near the floor. The edges of the mortared stones tore her dress and scraped skin off her knees.

To her left, the entire stairwell was burning now, and flames were spreading across the wooden ceiling. Refracted and diffused by the smoky air, the firelight glowed on all sides of Laura, creating the illusion that she was crawling through a narrow tunnel of flames. At the rate the blaze was spreading, the illusion would soon be fact.

Her eyes were swollen and watery, and she wiped at them as she inched toward escape. She couldn't see very much. She used Aunt Rachael's voice as a beacon and otherwise relied on instinct.

'*Laura!*' The voice was near. Right above her.

She felt along the wall until she located the setback in the stone. She moved into that recess, onto the first step, lifted her head, but could see nothing: the darkness here was seamless.

'Laura, answer me. Baby, are you in there?'

Rachael was hysterical, screaming so loudly and pounding on the outside doors with such persistence that she wouldn't have heard a response even if Laura had been capable of making one.

Where was Mama? Why wasn't Mama pounding on the door, too? Didn't Mama care?

Crouching in that cramped, hot, lightless space, Laura reached up and put her hand against one of the two slant-set doors above her head. The sturdy barrier quivered and rattled under the impact of Rachael's small fists. Laura groped blindly for the latch. She put her hand over the warm metal fixture – and squarely over something else, too. Something strange and unexpected. Something that squirmed and was alive. Small but *alive*. She jerked convulsively and pulled her hand away. But the thing she touched had shifted its grip from the latch to her flesh, and it came away from the door when she withdrew her hand. It skittered out of her palm and over her thumb and across the back of her hand and along her wrist and under the sleeve of her dress before she could brush it away.

A *spider*.

She couldn't see it, but she knew what it was. A spider. One of the really big ones, as large as her thumb, a plump black body that glistened like a fat drop of oil, inky black and ugly. For a moment she froze, unable even to draw a breath.

She felt the spider moving up her arm, and its bold advance snapped her into action. She slapped at it through the sleeve of her dress, but she missed. The spider bit her above the crook of her arm, and she winced at the tiny nip of pain, and the disgusting creature scurried into her armpit. It bit her there, too, and suddenly she felt as though she was living through her worst nightmare, for she feared spiders more than she feared anything else on earth – certainly more than she feared fire, for in her desperate attempt to kill the spider, she had forgotten all about the burning house that was dissolving into ruin above her – and she flailed in panic, lost her balance, rolled backwards off the steps, into the main room of the cellar, cracking one hip on the stone floor. The spider tickled its way along the inside of her bodice until it was between her breasts. She screamed but could make no sound whatsoever. She put a hand to her bosom and pressed hard, and even through the fabric she could feel the spider squirming angrily against the palm of her hand, and she could feel its frenzied struggle even more directly on her bare breast, to which it was pressed, but she persisted until at last she crushed it, and she gagged again, but this time not merely because of the smoke.

For several seconds after killing the spider, she lay on the floor in a tight fetal position, shuddering violently and uncontrollably. The repulsive, wet mass of the smashed spider slid very slowly down the curve of her breast. She wanted to reach inside her bodice and pluck the foul wad from herself, but she hesitated because, irrationally, she was afraid it would somehow come to life again and sting her fingers.

She tasted blood. She had bitten her lip.

Mama . . .

Mama had done this to her. Mama had sent her down here, knowing there were spiders. Why was Mama always so quick to deal out punishment, so eager to assign penance?

Overhead, a beam creaked, sagged. The kitchen floor cracked open. She felt as though she were staring up into Hell. Sparks showered down. Her dress caught fire, and she scorched her hands putting it out.

Mama did this to me.

Because her palms and fingers were blistered and peeling, she couldn't crawl on her hands and knees any longer, so she got to her feet, although standing up required more strength and determination than she had thought she possessed. She swayed, dizzy and weak.

Mama sent me down here.

Laura could see only pulsing, all-encompassing orange luminescence, through which amorphous smoke ghosts glided and whirled. She shuffled toward the short flight of steps that led to the outside cellar doors, but after she had gone only two yards, she realized she was headed in the wrong direction. She turned back the way she had come – or back the way she *thought* she had come – but after a few steps she bumped into the furnace, which was nowhere near the outside doors. She was completely disoriented.

Mama did this to me.

Laura squeezed her ruined hands into raw, bloody fists. In a rage she pounded on the furnace, and with each blow she fervently wished that she were beating her mother.

The upper reaches of the burning house twisted and rumbled. In the distance, beyond an eternity of smoke, Aunt Rachael's voice echoed hauntingly: 'Laura . . . Laura . . .'

Why wasn't Mama out there helping Rachael break down the cellar doors? Where in God's name *was* she? Throwing coal and lamp oil on the fire?

Wheezing, gasping, Laura pushed away from the furnace and tried to follow Rachael's voice to safety.

A beam tore loose of its moorings, slammed into her back, and catapulted her into the shelves of home-canned food. Jars fell, shattered. Laura went down in a rain of glass. She could smell pickles, peaches.

Before she could determine if any bones were broken, before she could even lift her face out of the spilled food, another beam crashed down, pinning her legs.

There was so much pain that her mind simply blanked it out altogether. She was not even sixteen years old, and there was only so much she could bear. She sealed the pain in a dark corner of her mind; instead of succumbing to it, she twisted and thrashed hysterically, raged at her fate, and cursed her mother.

Her hatred for her mother wasn't rational, but it was so passionately felt that it took the place of the pain she could not allow herself to feel. Hate flooded through her, filled her with so much demonic energy that she was nearly able to toss the heavy beam off her legs.

Damn you to Hell, Mama.

The top floor of the house caved in upon the ground floor with a sound like cannons blasting.

Damn you, Mama! Damn you!

The first two floors of flaming rubble broke through the already weakened cellar ceiling.

Mama –

Part One

SOMETHING WICKED THIS WAY COMES . . .

By the pricking of my thumbs,
Something wicked this way comes.
  Open, locks,
  whoever knocks!

– Shakespeare, *Macbeth*

Chapter One

Across the somber gray clouds, lightning followed a jagged course like cracks in a china plate. In the unsheltered courtyard outside Alfred O'Brian's office, the parked cars glimmered briefly with hard-edged reflections of the storm light. The wind gusted, whipping the trees. Rain beat with sudden fury against the three tall office windows, then streamed down the glass, blurring the view beyond.

O'Brian sat with his back to the windows. While thunder reverberated through the low sky and seemed to hammer on the roof of the building, he read the application that Paul and Carol Tracy had just submitted to him.

He's such a neat little man, Carol thought as she watched O'Brian. When he sits very still like that, you'd almost think he was a mannequin.

He was exceedingly well groomed. His carefully combed hair looked as if it had received the attention of a good barber less than an hour ago. His mustache was so expertly trimmed that the halves of it appeared to be perfectly symmetrical. He was wearing a gray suit with trouser creases as tight and straight as blades, and his black shoes gleamed. His fingernails were manicured, and his pink, well-scrubbed hands looked sterile.

When Carol had been introduced to O'Brian less than a week ago, she had thought he was prim, even prissy, and she had been prepared to dislike him. She was quickly won over by his smile, by his gracious manner, and by his sincere desire to help her and Paul.

She glanced at Paul, who was sitting in the chair next to hers, his own tensions betrayed by the angular position of his lean, usually graceful body. He was watching O'Brian intently, but when he sensed that Carol was looking at him, he turned and smiled. His smile was even nicer than O'Brian's, and, as usual, Carol's spirits were lifted by the sight of it. He was neither handsome nor ugly, this

589

man she loved; you might even say he was plain, yet his face was enormously appealing because the pleasing, open composition of it contained ample evidence of his gentleness and sensitivity. His hazel eyes were capable of conveying amazingly subtle degrees and mixtures of emotions. Six years ago, at a university symposium entitled 'Abnormal Psychology and Modern American Fiction,' where Carol had met Paul, the first thing that had drawn her to him had been those warm, expressive eyes, and in the intervening years they had never ceased to intrigue her. Now he winked, and with that wink he seemed to be saying: *Don't worry; O'Brian is on our side; the application will be accepted; everything will turn out all right; I love you.*

She winked back at him and pretended to be confident, even though she was sure he could see through her brave front.

She wished that she could be certain of winning Mr. O'Brian's approval. She knew she ought to be overflowing with confidence, for there really was no reason why O'Brian would reject them. They were healthy and young. Paul was thirty-five, and she was thirty-one, and those were excellent ages at which to set out upon the adventure they were contemplating. Both of them were successful in their work. They were financially solvent, even prosperous. They were respected in their community. Their marriage was happy and trouble-free, stronger now than at any time in the four years since their wedding. In short, their qualifications for adopting a child were pretty much impeccable, but she worried nonetheless.

She loved children, and she was looking forward to raising one or two of her own. During the past fourteen years – in which she had earned three degrees at three universities and had established herself in her profession – she had postponed many simple pleasures and had skipped others altogether. Getting an education and launching her career had always come first. She had missed too many good parties and had foregone an unremembered number of vacations and getaway weekends. Adopting a child was one pleasure she did not want to postpone any longer.

She had a strong psychological need – almost a *physical* need – to be a mother, to guide and shape children, to give them love and understanding. She was intelligent enough and sufficiently self-aware to realize that this deep-seated need arose, at least in part, from her inability to conceive a child of her own flesh and blood.

The thing we want most, she thought, is always the thing we cannot have.

She was to blame for her sterility, which was the result of an unforgivable act of stupidity committed a long time ago; and of course her culpability made her condition harder to bear than it would have been if nature – rather than her own foolishness – had cursed her with a barren womb. She had been a severely troubled child, for she had been raised by violent, alcoholic parents who had frequently beaten her and who had dealt out large doses of psychological torture. By the time she was fifteen, she was a hellion, engaged in an angry rebellion against her parents and against the world at large. She hated everyone in those days, especially herself. In the blackest hours of her confused and tormented adolescence, she had gotten pregnant. Frightened, panicky, with no one to turn to, she tried to conceal her condition by wearing girdles, by binding herself with elastic cloth and tape, and by eating as lightly as possible to keep her weight down. Eventually, however, complications arose because of her attempts to hide her pregnancy, and she nearly died. The baby was born prematurely, but it was healthy. She had put it up for adoption and hadn't given it much thought for a couple of years, though these days she often wondered about the child and wished she could have kept it somehow. At the time, the fact that her ordeal had left her sterile did not depress her, for she didn't think she would ever want to be pregnant again. But with a lot of help and love from a child psychologist named Grace Mitowski, who did charity work among juvenile wards of the court, Carol had turned her life completely around. She had learned to like herself and, years later, had come to regret the thoughtless actions that had left her barren.

Fortunately, she regarded adoption as a more-than-adequate solution to her problem. She was capable of giving as much love to an adopted child as she would have given to her own offspring. She knew she would be a good and caring mother, and she longed to prove it – not to the world but to herself; she never needed to prove anything to anyone but herself, for she was always her own toughest critic.

Mr. O'Brian looked up from the application and smiled. His teeth were exceedingly white. 'This looks really fine,' he said, indicating the form he had just finished reading. 'In fact, it's splendid. Not everyone that applies to us has credentials like these.'

'It's kind of you to say so,' Paul told him.

O'Brian shook his head. 'Not at all. It's simply the truth. Very impressive.'

Carol said, 'Thank you.'

Leaning back in his chair, folding his hands on his stomach, O'Brian said, 'I *do* have a couple of questions. I'm sure they're the same ones the recommendations committee will ask me, so I might as well get your responses now and save a lot of back-and-forth later on.'

Carol stiffened again.

O'Brian apparently noticed her reaction, for he quickly said, 'Oh, it's nothing terribly serious. Really, it isn't. Believe me – I won't be asking you half as many questions as I ask most couples who come to see us.'

In spite of O'Brian's assurances, Carol remained tense.

Outside, the storm-dark afternoon sky grew steadily darker as the thunderheads changed color from gray to blue black, thickened, and pressed closer to the earth.

O'Brian swiveled in his chair to face Paul. 'Dr. Tracy, would you say you're an overachiever?'

Paul seemed surprised by the question. He blinked and said, 'I'm not sure what you mean.'

'You *are* the chairman of the department of English at the college, aren't you?'

'Yes. I'm on sabbatical this semester, and the vice-chairman is handling most things for the time being. Otherwise, I've been in charge of the department for the past year and a half.'

'Aren't you rather young to hold such a post?'

'Somewhat young,' Paul admitted. 'But that's no credit to me. You see, it's a thankless position, all work and no glory. My senior colleagues in the department craftily maneuvered me into it so that none of them would be stuck with the job.'

'You're being modest.'

'No, I'm really not,' Paul said. 'It's nothing much.'

Carol knew that he *was* being modest. The departmental chairmanship was a prized position, an honor. But she understood why Paul was playing it down; he had been unsettled by O'Brian's use of the word *overachiever*. She had been unsettled by it, too. Until this moment she had never thought that an unusually long list of achievements might count *against* them.

Beyond the tall windows, lightning zigzagged down the sky. The day flickered and, just for a second or two, so did the electric lights in O'Brian's office.

Still addressing Paul, O'Brian said, 'You're also an author.'

'Yes.'

'You've written a very successful textbook for use in American literature courses. You've turned out a dozen monographs on a variety of subjects, and you've done a local history of the county. *And* two children's books, *and* a novel. . . .'

'The novel was about as successful as a horse trying to walk a tightrope,' Paul said. 'The *New York Times* critic said it was "a perfect example of academic posturing, stuffed full of themes and symbols, utterly lacking in substance and narrative drive, infused with ivory-tower naivete." '

O'Brian smiled. 'Does every writer memorize his bad reviews?'

'I suppose not. But I have that one engraved on my cerebral cortex because there's an uncomfortable amount of truth in it.'

'Are you writing another novel? Is that why you've taken a sabbatical?'

Paul was not surprised by the question. Clearly he now understood what O'Brian was digging for. 'Yes, in fact I *am* writing a new novel. This one actually has a plot.' He laughed with easy self-deprecation.

'You're also involved in charity work.'

'Not much.'

'Quite a lot,' O'Brian disagreed. 'The Children's Hospital Fund, the Community Chest, the student scholarship program at the college – all of that in addition to your regular job and your writing. Yet you don't think you're an overachiever?'

'No, I really don't think I am. The charity work amounts to just a couple of meetings a month. It's no big thing. It's the least I can do, considering my own good fortune.' Paul edged forward on his chair. 'Maybe you're worried that I won't have time to give to a child, but if that's what's troubling you, then you can put your mind at rest. I'll *make* the time. This adoption is extremely important to us, Mr. O'Brian. We both want a child very badly, and if we are lucky enough to get one, we certainly won't ever neglect it.'

'Oh, I'm sure you won't,' O'Brian said quickly, raising his hands placatingly. 'That isn't at all what I meant to imply. Oh, certainly not. I'm on *your* side in this matter. I mean that very sincerely.' He swiveled to face Carol. 'Dr. Tracy – the *other* Dr. Tracy – what about you? Do you consider yourself an overachiever?'

Lightning slashed through the panoply of clouds again, nearer this time than before; it seemed to strike the ground no more than two blocks away. The ensuing crash of thunder rattled the tall windows.

Carol used the interruption provided by the thunderclap to consider her response, and she decided that O'Brian would appreciate

593

forthrightness more than modesty. 'Yes. I'd say I'm an overachiever. I'm involved in two of the three charities that Paul has his
hand in. And I know I'm a bit young to have established a psychiatric practice as successful as mine is. I'm also a guest lecturer at
the college on a fairly regular basis. And I'm doing post-doctoral
research on autistic children. During the summer I manage to keep
a little vegetable garden going, and I do some needle-point in the
winter months, and I even brush my teeth *three* times a day, every
day, without fail.'

O'Brian laughed. 'Three times a day, huh? Oh, you're most
definitely an overachiever.'

The warmth of his laughter reassured Carol, and with renewed
confidence she said, 'I believe I understand what you're concerned
about. You're wondering if Paul and I might expect too much of
our child.'

'Exactly,' O'Brian said. He noticed a speck of lint on his coat
sleeve and plucked it off. 'Parents who are overachievers tend to
push their kids too hard, too fast, too soon.'

Paul said, 'That's a problem that arises only when parents are
unaware of the danger. Even if Carol and I are overachievers –
which *I'm* not prepared to admit just yet – we wouldn't pressure
our kids to do more than they were capable of doing. Each of us has
to find his own pace in life. Carol and I realize that a child should be
guided, not hammered into a mold.'

'Of course,' Carol said.

O'Brian appeared to be pleased. 'I knew you'd say that – or
something very like it.'

Lightning flashed again. This time it seemed to strike even closer
than before, only a block away. Thunder cracked, then cracked
again. The overhead lights dimmed, fluttered, reluctantly came
back to full power.

'In my psychiatric practice, I deal with a wide variety of patients
who have all kinds of problems,' Carol told O'Brian, 'but I specialize in the mental disorders and emotional disturbances of children
and adolescents. Sixty or seventy percent of my patients are seventeen or younger. I've treated several kids who've suffered serious
psychological damage at the hands of parents who were too
demanding, who pushed them too hard in their schoolwork, in
every aspect of their intellectual and personal development. I've
seen the wounded ones, Mr. O'Brian, and I've nursed them as best I
could, and because of those experiences, I couldn't possibly turn
around and do to my children what I've seen some parents do to

theirs. Not that I won't make mistakes. I'm sure I will. My full share of them. But the one that you mentioned won't be among them.'

'That's valid,' O'Brian said, nodding. 'Valid and very well put. I'm sure that when I tell the recommendations committee what you've just said, they'll be quite satisfied on this point.' He spotted another tiny speck on his sleeve and removed it, frowning as if it were not merely lint, but offal. 'Another question they're bound to ask: Suppose the child you adopt turns out to be not only an under-achiever but . . . well . . . basically less intelligent than either of you. For parents as oriented toward an intellectual life as you are, wouldn't you be somewhat frustrated with a child of just average – or possibly slightly below average – intelligence?'

'Well, even if we were capable of having a child of our own,' Paul said, 'there wouldn't be any guarantee that he'd be a prodigy or any-thing of that sort. But if he was . . . slow . . . we'd still love him. Of course we would. And the same goes for any child we might adopt.'

To O'Brian, Carol said, 'I think you've got too high an opinion of us. Neither of us is a *genius*, for heaven's sake! We've gotten as far as we have primarily through hard work and perseverance, not because we were exceptionally bright. I wish it *had* come that easy, but it didn't.'

'Besides,' Paul said, 'you don't love a person merely because he's intelligent. It's his entire personality that counts, the whole package, and a lot of factors contribute to that package, a great many things other than just intellect.'

'Good,' O'Brian said. 'I'm glad to hear you feel that way. The committee will respond well to that answer, too.'

For the past few seconds, Carol had been aware of the distant wail of sirens. Fire engines. Now they were not as distant as they had been; they were rapidly growing nearer, louder.

'I think maybe one of those last two bolts of lightning caused some real damage when it touched down,' Paul said.

O'Brian swung his chair around toward the center window, which was directly behind his desk. 'It *did* sound as if it struck nearby.'

Carol looked at each of the three windows, but she couldn't see any smoke rising from behind the nearest rooftops. Then again, the view was blurred and visibility was reduced by the water-spotted panes of glass and by the curtains of mist and gray rain that wavered and whipped and billowed beyond the glass.

The sirens swelled.

'More than one truck,' O'Brian said.

The fire engines were right outside the office for a moment – at least two trucks, perhaps three – and then they passed, heading into the next block.

O'Brian pushed up from his chair and stepped to the window.

As the first sirens dwindled just a little, new ones shrieked in the street behind them.

'Must be serious,' Paul said. 'Sounds as if at least two engine companies are responding.'

'I see smoke,' O'Brian said.

Paul rose from his chair and moved toward the windows to get a better look.

Something's wrong here.

That thought snapped into Carol's mind, startling her as if a whip had cracked in front of her face. A powerful, inexplicable current of panic surged through her, electrified her. She gripped the arms of her chair so tightly that one of her fingernails broke.

Something . . . is . . . wrong . . . very wrong . . .

Suddenly the air was oppressively heavy – hot, *thick*, as if it were not air at all but a bitter and poisonous gas of some kind. She tried to breathe, couldn't. There was an invisible, crushing weight on her chest.

Get away from the windows!

She tried to shout that warning, but panic had short-circuited her voice. Paul and O'Brian were at different windows, but they both had their backs to her, so that neither of them could see she had been gripped by sudden, immobilizing fear.

Fear of what? she demanded of herself. What in the name of God am I so scared of?

She struggled against the unreasonable terror that had locked her muscles and joints. She started to get up from the chair, and that was when it happened.

A murderous barrage of lightning crashed like a volley of mortar fire, seven or eight tremendous bolts, perhaps more than that – she didn't count them, couldn't count them – one right after the other, without a significant pause between them, each fierce boom over-lapping the ones before and after it, yet each clearly louder than its predecessors, so loud that they made her teeth and bones vibrate, each bolt smashing down discernibly closer to the building than had the bolt before it, closer to the seven-foot-high windows – the gleaming, flashing, rattling, now-black, now-milky, now-shining, now-blank, now-silvery, now-coppery windows. . . .

The sharp bursts of purple-white light produced a series of jerky, stroboscopic images that were burned forever into Carol's memory:

Paul and O'Brian standing there, silhouetted against the natural fireworks, looking small and vulnerable; outside, the rain descending in an illusion of hesitation; wind-lashed trees heaving in a strobe-choppy rage; lightning blasting into one of those trees, a big maple, and then an ominous dark shape rising from the midst of the explosion, a torpedo-like thing, spinning straight toward the center window (all of this transpiring in only a second or two, but given a queer, slow-motion quality by the flickering lightning and, after a moment, by the overhead electric light as well, which began to flicker, too); O'Brian throwing one arm up in front of his face in what appeared to be half a dozen disconnected movements; Paul turning toward O'Brian and reaching for him, both men like figures on a motion picture screen when the film slips and stutters in the projector; O'Brian lurching sideways; Paul seizing him by a coat sleeve, pulling him back and down toward safety (only a fraction of a second after the lightning splintered the maple); a huge tree limb bursting through the center window even as Paul was pulling O'Brian out of the way; one leafy branch sweeping across O'Brian's head, ripping his glasses loose, tossing them into the air – his face, Carol thought, his *eyes*! – and then Paul and O'Brian falling to the floor, out of sight; the enormous limb of the shattered maple slamming down on top of O'Brian's desk in a spray of water, glass, broken mullions, and smoking chips of bark; the legs of the desk cracking and collapsing under the brutal impact of the ruined tree.

Carol found herself on the floor, beside her overturned chair. She couldn't remember falling.

The fluorescent tubes blinked off, stayed off.

She was lying on her stomach, one cheek pressed to the floor, staring in shock at the shards of glass and the torn maple leaves that littered the carpet. As lightning continued to stab down from the turbulent sky, wind roared through the missing window and stirred some of the loose leaves into a frantic, dervishlike dance; accompanied by the cacophonous music of the storm, they whirled and capered across the office, toward a row of green filing cabinets. A calendar flapped off the wall and swooped around on wings of January and December, darting and soaring and kiting as if it were a bat. Two paintings rattled on their wire hangers, trying to tear themselves free. Papers were everywhere – stationery, forms, small sheets from a note pad, bulletins, a newspaper – all rustling and skipping this way and that, floating up, diving down, bunching together and slithering along the floor with a snakelike hiss.

Carol had the eerie feeling that all of the movement in the room was not solely the result of the wind, that some of it was caused by a . . . *presence*. Something threatening. A bad poltergeist. Demonic spirits seemed to be at work in the office, flexing their occult muscles, knocking things off the walls, briefly taking up residence in a body composed only of leaves and rumpled sheets of newsprint.

That was a crazy idea, not at all the sort of thing she would ordinarily think of. She was surprised and disconcerted by a thrill of superstitious fear that coursed through her.

Lightning flared again. And again.

Wincing at the painfully sharp sound, wondering if lightning could get into a room through an open window, she put her arms over her head, for what little protection they provided.

Her heart was pounding, and her mouth was dry.

She thought about Paul, and her heartbeat grew even more frantic. He was over by the windows, on the far side of the desk, out of sight, under some of the maple tree's branches. She didn't think he was dead. He hadn't been directly in the path of the tree. O'Brian might be dead, yes, depending on how that small branch had struck his head, depending on whether he had been lucky or not, because maybe a pointed twig had been driven deep into his eye and his brain when his glasses had been knocked off, but Paul was surely alive. Surely. Nevertheless, he could be seriously injured, bleeding. . . .

Carol started to push herself up onto her hands and knees, anxious to find Paul and give him any first aid he might need. But another bolt of blinding, ear-shattering lightning spent itself just outside the building, and fear turned her muscles into wet rags. She didn't even have the strength to crawl, and she was infuriated by her weakness, for she had always been proud of her strength, determination and unflagging willpower. Cursing herself, she slumped back to the floor.

Something's trying to stop us from adopting a baby.

That incredible thought struck her with the same cold, hard force as had the forewarning of the window's implosion, which had come to her an instant before the impossible barrage of lightning had blasted into the courtyard.

Something's trying to stop us from adopting a baby.

No. That was ridiculous. The storm, the lightning – they were nothing more than acts of nature. They hadn't been directed against Mr. O'Brian just because he was going to help them adopt a child. Absurd.

Oh, yeah? she thought as the deafening thunder and the unholy light of the storm filled the room. Acts of nature, huh? When have you ever seen lightning like *this* before?

She hugged the floor, shaking, cold, more afraid than she had been since she was a little girl. She tried to tell herself that it was only the lightning that she was afraid of, for that was very much a legitimate, rational fear, but she knew she was lying. It was *not* just the lightning that terrified her. In fact, that was the least of it. There was something else, something she couldn't identify, something formless and nameless in the room, and the very presence of it, whatever the hell it was, pushed a panic button deep inside her, on a sub-subconscious, primitive level; this fear was gut-deep, instinctive.

A dervish of windblown leaves and papers whirled across the floor, directly toward her. It was a big one: a column about two feet in diameter, five or six feet high, composed of a hundred or more pieces of this and that. It stopped very near her, writhing, churning, hissing, changing shape, glimmering silver-dark in the flashing storm light, and she felt threatened by it. As she stared up at the whirlwind, she had the mad notion that it was staring down at her. After a moment it moved off to the left a few feet, then returned, paused in front of her again, hesitated, then scurried busily to the right, but came back once more, looming above her as if it were trying to make up its mind whether or not to pounce and tear her to shreds and sweep her up along with the leaves, newspaper pages, envelopes, and other flotsam by which it defined itself.

It's nothing more than a whirlwind of lifeless junk! she told herself angrily.

The wind-shaped phantom moved away from her.

See? she told herself scornfully. Just lifeless junk. What's wrong with me? Am I losing my mind?

She recalled the old axiom that was supposed to provide comfort in moments like this: If you think you're going mad, then you must be completely sane, for a lunatic never has doubts about his sanity. As a psychiatrist, she knew that hoary bit of wisdom was an over-simplification of complex psychological principles, but in essence it was true. So she must be sane.

Nevertheless, that frightening, irrational thought came to her again, unbidden, unwanted: *Something's trying to stop us from adopting a baby*.

If the maelstrom in which she lay was not an act of nature, then what *was* it? Was she to believe that the lightning had been sent with the conscious intent of transforming Mr. O'Brian into a smoking heap of charred flesh? That was a fruitcake notion, for sure. Who could use lightning as if it were a pistol? God? God wasn't sitting up in Heaven, aiming at Mr. O'Brian, popping away at him with lightning bolts, just to screw up the adoption process for Carol and Paul Tracy. The Devil? Blasting away at poor Mr. O'Brian from the depths of Hell? That *was* a looney idea. *Jesus!*

She wasn't even sure she believed in God, but she knew she definitely did not believe in the Devil.

Another window imploded, showering glass over her.

Then the lightning stopped.

The thunder decreased from a roar to a rumble, fading like the noise of a passing freight train.

There was a stench of ozone.

The wind was still pouring in through the broken windows, but apparently with less force than it had exerted a moment ago, for the whirling columns of leaves and papers subsided to the floor, where they lay in piles, fluttering and quivering as if exhausted.

Something . . .

Something . . .

Something's trying to stop us from –

She clamped off that unwanted thought as though it were a spurting artery. She was an educated woman, dammit. She prided herself on her levelheadedness and common sense. She couldn't permit herself to succumb to these disturbing, uncharacteristic, utterly superstitious fears.

Freaky weather – that was the explanation for the lightning. Freaky weather. You read about such things in the newspapers every once in a while. A half an inch of snow in Beverly Hills. An eighty-degree day in the middle of an otherwise frigid Minnesota winter. Rain falling briefly from an apparently cloudless blue sky. Although a lightning strike of this magnitude and intensity was undoubtedly a rare occurrence, it probably had happened before, sometime, somewhere, probably more than once. Of course it had. Of course. In fact, if you picked up one of those popular books in which the authors compiled all kinds of world records, and if you turned to the chapter on weather, and if you looked for a subsection entitled 'Lightning,' you would most likely find an impressive list of other serial lightning strikes that would put this one to shame. Freaky weather. That's what it was. That's *all* it was. Nothing stranger than that, nothing worse.

For the time being, at least, Carol managed to put aside all thoughts of demons and ghosts and malign poltergeists and other such claptrap.

In the relative quiet that followed in the wake of the fast-diminishing thunder, she felt her strength returning. She pushed up from the floor, onto her knees. With the clinking sound of mildly disturbed wind chimes, pieces of glass fell from her gray skirt and green blouse; she wasn't cut or even scratched. She was a bit dazed, however, and for a moment the floor appeared to roll sickeningly from side to side, as if this were a stateroom aboard a ship.

In the office next door, a woman began to cry hysterically. There were shouts of alarm, and someone began calling for Mr. O'Brian. No one had yet burst into the office to see what had happened, which meant that only a second or two had elapsed since the lightning had stopped, although it seemed to Carol as if a minute or two had passed.

Over by the windows, someone groaned softly.

'Paul?' she said.

If there was an answer, it was drowned out by a sudden gust of wind that briefly stirred the papers and leaves again.

She recalled the way that branch had whipped across O'Brian's head, and she shuddered. But Paul hadn't been touched. The tree had missed him. Hadn't it?

'Paul!'

With renewed fear, she got to her feet and moved quickly around the desk, stepping over splintered maple branches and an overturned wastebasket.

Chapter Two

That Wednesday afternoon, following a lunch of Campbell's vegetable soup and a grilled cheese sandwich, Grace Mitowski went into her study and curled up on the sofa to sleep for an hour or so. She never napped in the bedroom because that formalized it somehow, and though she had been taking naps three or four days a week for the past year, she still had not reconciled herself to the fact that she needed a midday rest. To her way of thinking, naps were for children and for old, used-up, burnt-out people. She wasn't in her childhood any more – neither the first nor the second, thank you – and although she *was* old, she certainly wasn't used up or burnt out. Being in bed in the middle of the day made her feel lazy, and she couldn't abide laziness in anyone, especially not in herself. Therefore, she took naps on the study sofa, with her back to the shuttered windows, lulled by the monotonous ticking of the mantel clock.

At seventy, Grace was still as *mentally* agile and energetic as she had ever been. Her gray matter hadn't begun to deteriorate at all; it was only her treacherous body that caused her grief and frustration. She had a touch of arthritis in her hands, and when the humidity was high – as it was today – she also suffered from a dull but unrelenting ache of bursitis in her shoulders. Although she did all of the exercises that her doctor recommended, and although she walked two miles every morning, she found it increasingly difficult to maintain her muscle tone. From the time she was a young girl, throughout most of her life, she had been in love with books, and she had been able to read all morning, all afternoon, and most of the evening without eyestrain; nowadays, usually after only a couple of hours of reading, her eyes felt grainy and hot. She regarded each of her infirmities with extreme indignation, and she struggled against them, even though she knew this was a war she was destined to lose.

603

That Wednesday afternoon she took a break from the battle, a brief period of R and R. Two minutes after she stretched out on the sofa, she was asleep.

Grace did not dream often, and she was even less often plagued by *bad* dreams. But Wednesday afternoon, in the book-lined study, her sleep was continuously disturbed by nightmares. Several times she stirred, came half awake, and heard herself gasping in panic. Once, drifting up from some hideous and threatening vision, she heard her own voice crying out wordlessly in terror, and she realized she was thrashing on the couch, twisting and torturing her aching shoulders. She tried to come fully awake, but she could not; something in the dream, something dark and menacing, reached up with icy, clammy hands and pulled her down into deep sleep again, down and down, all the way down into a lightless place where an unnameable creature gibbered and muttered and chuckled in a mucous-wet voice.

An hour later, when she finally woke up and managed to cast off the clutching dream, she was standing in the middle of the shadow-shrouded room, several steps away from the sofa, but she had no memory of getting to her feet. She was shaking, sheathed in sweat.

– *I've got to tell Carol Tracy.*
– *Tell her what?*
– *Warn her.*
– *Warn her about what?*
– *It's coming. Oh, God . . .*
– *What's coming?*
– *Just like in the dream.*
– *What about the dream?*

Already her memory of the nightmare had begun to dissolve; only fragments of it remained with her, and each of those disassociated images was evaporating as if it were a splinter of dry ice. All she could remember was that Carol had been a part of it, and had been in awful danger. And somehow she knew that the dream had been more than just an ordinary dream. . . .

As the nightmare receded, Grace became uncomfortably aware of how gloomy the study was. Before taking her nap, she had switched off the lamps. The shutters were all closed, and only thin blades of light were visible between the wooden slats. She had the irrational but unshakable feeling that something had followed her up from the dream, something vicious and evil that had undergone a magical metamorphosis from a creature of the imagination into one composed of solid flesh, something that was now crouched in a corner, watching, waiting.

    – *Stop it!*

    – *But the dream was . . .*

    – *Only a dream.*

Along the edges of the shutters, the taut threads of light abruptly brightened, then dimmed, then grew bright again as lightning flashed outside. A roof-rattling crash of thunder quickly followed, and more lightning, too, an unbelievable amount of it, one blue-white explosion after another, so that for at least half a minute the cracks in the shutters looked like sputtering electrical wires, white-hot with sparking current.

Still drugged with sleep and slightly confused, Grace stood in the middle of the unlighted room, rocking from side to side, listening to the thunder and the wind, watching the intense pulse of lightning. The extreme violence of the storm seemed unreal, and she concluded that she was still under the influence of the dream, mis-interpreting what she was seeing. It couldn't possibly be as savage outside as it appeared to be.

    '*Grace . . .*'

She thought she heard something call to her from over by the tallest set of bookshelves, directly behind her. Judging from its slurred, distorted pronunciation of her name, its mouth was severely malformed.

There's nothing behind me! Nothing.

Nevertheless, she did not turn around.

When the lightning finally stopped and the long-crescendo of thunder subsided, the air seemed thicker than it had been a minute ago. She had difficulty breathing. The room was darker, too.

    '*Grace . . .*'

A confining mantle of claustrophobia settled over her. The dimly visible walls appeared to ripple and move closer, as if the chamber might shrink around her until it was precisely the size and shape of a coffin.

    '*Grace . . .*'

She stumbled to the nearest window, banging her hip against the desk, nearly tripping over a lamp cord. She fumbled with the lever on the shutters, her fingers stiff and unresponsive. At last the slats opened wide; gray but welcome light poured into the study, forcing her to squint but gladdening her as well. She leaned against the shutters and stared out at the cloud-plated sky, resisting the insane urge to look over her shoulder to see if there really was something monstrous lurking there with a hungry grin on its face. She drew deep, gasping breaths, as if the daylight itself – rather than the air – sustained her.

Grace's house was atop a small knoll, at the end of a quiet street, sheltered by several large pine trees and by one enormous weeping willow; from her study window she could see the rain-swollen Susquehanna a couple of miles away. Harrisburg, the state capital, huddled solemnly, drearily along the river's banks. The clouds hung low over the city, trailing bedraggled beards of mist that obscured the upper floors of the tallest buildings.

When she'd blinked the last grains of sleep out of her eyes, when her nerves had stopped jangling, she turned around and surveyed the room. A quiver of relief swept through her, unknotting her muscles.

She was alone.

With the storm temporarily quiet, she could hear the mantel clock again. It was the only sound.

Hell, yes, you're alone, she told herself scornfully. What did you expect? A green goblin with three eyes and a mouthful of sharp teeth? You better watch yourself, Grace Louise Mitowski, or you'll wind up in a rest home, sitting all day in a rocking chair, happily chatting with ghosts, while smiling nurses wipe drool off your chin.

Having led an active life of the mind for so many years, she worried more about creeping senility than about anything else. She knew she was as sharp and alert as she had ever been. But what about tomorrow and the day after? Because of her medical training, and because she had kept up with her professional reading even after closing down her psychiatric practice, she was up to date on all the latest findings about senility, and she knew that only fifteen percent of all elderly people suffered from it. She also knew that more than half of those cases were treatable with proper nutrition and exercise. She knew her chances of becoming mentally incapacitated were small, only about one in eighteen. Nevertheless, although she was conscious of her excessive sensitivity regarding the subject, she still worried. Consequently, she was understandably disturbed by this uncharacteristic notion that something had been in the study with her a few moments ago, something hostile and . . . supernatural. As a lifelong skeptic with little or no patience for astrologers and psychics and their ilk, she could not justify even a fleeting belief in such superstitious nonsense; to her way of thinking, beliefs of that nature were . . . well . . . feeble-minded.

But good, sweet God, what a nightmare that had been!

She had never before experienced a dream even one-tenth as bad as that one. Although the grisly details had completely faded away, she could still clearly remember the mood of it – the terror, the gut-wrenching horror that had permeated every nasty image, every ticking sound.

She shivered.

The sweat that the dream had squeezed out of her was beginning to feel like a thin glaze of ice on her skin.

The only other thing she remembered from the nightmare was Carol. Screaming. Crying for help.

Until now, none of Grace's infrequent dreams had included Carol, and there was a temptation to view her appearance in this one with alarm, to see it as an omen. But of course it wasn't surprising that Carol should eventually have a role in one of Grace's dreams, for the loved-one-in-danger theme was common in nightmares. Any psychologist would attest to that, and Grace was a psychologist, a good one, although she was entering her third year of retirement. She cared deeply about Carol. If she'd had a child of her own, she couldn't have loved it any more than she loved Carol.

She had first met the girl sixteen years ago, when Carol had been an angry, obstinate, obstreperous fifteen-year-old delinquent who had recently given birth to a baby that had nearly killed her, and who, subsequent to that traumatic episode, had been remanded to a juvenile detention facility for possession of marijuana and for a host of other offenses. In those days, in addition to a private psychiatric practice, Grace had performed eight hours a week of free service to assist the overworked counseling staff at the reform school in which Carol was held. Carol was incorrigible, determined to kick you in the teeth if you smiled at her, but even then her intelligence and innate goodness were there, to be seen by anyone who looked closely enough, beneath the rough exterior. Grace had taken a very close look indeed, and had been intrigued, impressed. The girl's obsessively foul language, her vicious temper, and her amoral pose had been nothing more than defense mechanisms, shields with which she protected herself from the physical and psychological abuse dished out by her parents.

As Grace gradually unearthed the horrendous story of Carol's monstrous home life, she became convinced that reform school was the wrong place for the girl. She used her influence with the court to get Carol permanently removed from the custody of her parents. Later, she arranged to serve as Carol's foster parent. She had watched the girl respond to love and guidance, had watched her grow from a brooding, self-centered, self-destructive teenager into a warm, self-assured admirable young woman with hopes and dreams, a woman of character, a sensitive woman. Playing a part in that exciting transformation had been perhaps the most satisfying thing that Grace had ever done.

The only regret she had about her relationship with Carol was the role she had played in putting the baby up for adoption. But there had been no reasonable alternative. Carol simply hadn't been financially or emotionally or mentally capable of providing for the infant. With that responsibility to attend to, she would never have had an opportunity to grow and change. She would have been miserable all her life, and she would have made her child miserable, too. Unfortunately, even now, sixteen years later, Carol felt guilty about giving her baby away. Her guilt became overpowering on each anniversary of the child's birth. On that black day, Carol sank into a deep depression and became uncharacteristically uncommunicative. The excessive anguish that she suffered on that one day was evidence of the deep-seated, abiding guilt that she carried with her, to a lesser degree, during the rest of the year. Grace wished she had foreseen this reaction, wished she had done more to assuage Carol's guilt.

I'm a psychologist, after all, she thought. I should have anticipated it.

Perhaps when Carol and Paul adopted someone else's child, Carol would feel that the scales had at last been balanced. The adoption might relieve some of her guilt, in time.

Grace hoped it would. She loved Carol like a daughter and wanted only the best for her.

And of course she couldn't bear the thought of losing Carol. Therefore, Carol's appearance in a nightmare wasn't the least bit mysterious. It was certainly *not* an omen.

Clammy with stale sweat, Grace turned to the study window again, seeking warmth and light, but the day was ashen, chilly, forbidding. Wind pressed on the glass, soughed softly under the eaves one floor above.

In the city, near the river, a roiling column of smoke rose into the rain and mist. She had not noticed it a minute ago, but it must have been there; it was too much smoke to have appeared in only a few seconds. Even from this distance, she could see a glint of fire at the base of the dark column.

She wondered if lightning had done the dirty work. She recalled the storm flashing and roaring with extraordinary power in those first seconds after she had awakened. At the time, groggy and bleary-eyed, she had thought her sleep-dulled senses were misleading her and that the extreme violence of the lightning was largely illusory or even imaginary. Could that incredible, destructive barrage have been real after all?

She glanced at her wristwatch.

Her favorite radio station would carry its hourly newscast in less than ten minutes. Maybe there would be a story about the fire and the lightning.

After she'd straightened the throw pillows on the sofa, she stepped out of the study and spotted Aristophanes at the far end of the downstairs hall, near the front door. He was sitting up straight and tall, his tail curled forward and across his front paws, his head held high, as if he were saying, 'A Siamese cat is the very best thing on earth, and I am an exceedingly handsome example of the species, and don't you dare forget it.'

Grace held one hand toward him, rapidly rubbing her thumb against her forefinger. 'Kitty-kitty-kitty.'

Aristophanes didn't move.

'Kitty-kitty-kitty. Come here, Ari. Come on, baby.'

Aristophanes got up and went through the archway on his left, into the dark living room.

'Stubborn damn cat,' she said affectionately.

She went into the downstairs bathroom and washed her face and combed her hair. The mundane task of grooming herself took her mind off the nightmare. Gradually, she began to relax. Her eyes were watery and bloodshot. She rinsed them out with a few drops of Murine.

When she came out of the bathroom, Aristophanes was sitting in the hallway again, watching her.

'Kitty-kitty-kitty,' she coaxed.

He stared unblinkingly.

'Kitty-kitty-kitty.'

Aristophanes rose to his feet, cocked his head, and examined her with curious, shining eyes. When she took a step toward him, he turned and quickly slunk away, casting one backward glance, then disappeared into the living room again.

'Okay,' Grace said. 'Okay, buster. Have it your way. Snub me if you want. But just see if there's any Meow Mix in *your* bowl tonight.'

In the kitchen she snapped on the lights, then the radio. The

609

station came in clearly enough, though there was a continuous crackle of storm-generated static.

While she listened to tales of economic crises and breathless accounts of airplane hijackings and rumors of war, Grace put a clean paper filter in the coffee machine, filled the brewing basket with drip-ground Colombian, and added half a spoonful of chicory. The story of the fire came at the end of the newscast, and it was only a sketchy bulletin. The reporter knew nothing more than that lightning had struck a couple of buildings in the heart of the city and that one of them, a church, was afire. He promised more details on the half hour.

When the coffee was ready, Grace poured some for herself. She took her mug to the small table by the kitchen's only window, pulled out a chair, and sat down.

In the backyard, the myriad roses – red, pink, orange, white, yellow – looked preternaturally bright, almost phosphorescent, against the cinereous backdrop of the rain.

Two psychology journals had arrived in the morning mail. Grace opened one of them with pleasant anticipation.

Halfway through an article about new findings in criminal psychology, as she finished her first mug of coffee, there was a pause between songs on the radio, a few seconds of dead air, and in that brief quietude, she heard furtive movement behind her. She turned in her chair and saw Aristophanes.

'Come to apologize?' she asked.

Then she realized that he appeared to have been sneaking up on her, and that now, confronted, he was frozen; every lithe muscle in his small body was spring-taut, and the fur bristled along his arched back.

'Ari? What's wrong, you silly cat?'

He whirled and ran out of the kitchen.

Chapter Three

Carol sat in a chrome chair with shiny black vinyl cushions, and she slowly sipped whiskey from a paper cup.

Paul slumped in the chair next to hers. He didn't sip his whiskey; he gulped the stuff. It was an excellent bourbon, Jack Daniel's Black Label, thoughtfully provided by an attorney named Marvin Kwicker, who had offices down the hall from Alfred O'Brian and who realized that a restorative was urgently needed. Pouring bourbon for Carol, Marvin had said, 'Kwicker with liquor,' which he had probably said ten thousand times before, but he still enjoyed his own joke. 'Kwicker with liquor,' he repeated when dispensing a double shot to Paul. Although Paul wasn't much of a drinker, he needed every drop that the attorney gave him. His hands were still shaking.

The reception lounge that served O'Brian's office was not large, but most of the people who worked on the same floor had congregated here to talk about the lightning that had shaken the building, to marvel that the place hadn't caught fire, to express surprise that the electric power had been restored so quickly, and to wait their turns for a peek at the rubble and ruin in O'Brian's inner sanctum. The resultant roar of conversation did nothing to soothe Paul's nerves.

Every thirty seconds or so, a bleached blonde with a shrill voice repeated the same words of amazement: 'I can't believe nobody got killed in all that! I can't believe *nobody* got killed.' Each time she spoke, regardless of where she was in the room, her voice carried over the din and made Paul wince. 'I can't believe *nobody* got killed.' She sounded somewhat disappointed.

Alfred O'Brian was sitting at the reception desk. His secretary, a prim-looking woman whose hair was drawn back in a tight bun, was trying to apply Merthiolate to half a dozen scratches on her boss's face, but O'Brian seemed more concerned about the

611

condition of his suit than he was about himself. He plucked and brushed at the dirt, lint, and small fragments of tree bark that clung to his jacket.

Paul finished his whiskey and looked at Carol. She was still badly shaken. Contrasted with her glossy dark hair, her face was very pale.

Apparently, she saw the concern in his eyes, for she took his hand, squeezed it, and smiled reassuringly. However, the smile didn't set well on her lips; it was tremulous.

He leaned close to her, so that she could hear him above the excited chatter of the others. 'Ready to get out of here?'

She nodded.

Over by the window, a young executive type raised his voice. 'Hey! Hey, everybody! Better look sharp. The TV news people just drove up to the front door.'

'If we get trapped by reporters,' Carol said, 'we'll be here an hour or more.'

They left without saying goodbye to O'Brian. In the hall, as they headed toward a side entrance, they slipped into their raincoats. Outside, Paul opened his umbrella and put one arm around Carol's waist. They hurried across the slippery macadam parking lot, stepping gingerly around huge puddles. The gusting wind was chilly for early September, and it kept changing direction until it finally got under the umbrella and turned it inside out. The cold, wind-driven rain was falling so hard that it stung Paul's face. By the time they reached the car, their hair was plastered to their heads, and a lot of water had found its way down the backs of their necks, under the collars of their coats.

Paul half expected the Pontiac to be lightning-damaged, but it was just as they had left it. The engine turned over without protest.

Leaving the parking lot, he started to turn left but put his foot on the brake pedal when he saw that the street was sealed off by police cars and fire trucks just half a block away. The church was still ablaze, in spite of the pouring rain and in defiance of the big streams of water that the firemen directed onto it. Black smoke billowed into the gray day, and behind the blasted windows, flames spurted and churned. Clearly, the church was going to be a total loss.

He turned right, instead, and drove home through rain-choked streets, where the gutters overflowed and where every depression in the pavement had been transformed into a treacherous lake that had to be negotiated with utmost caution to avoid drowning the engine and stalling out.

Carol slouched in her seat and huddled against the passenger-side door, hugging herself. Although the heater was on, she was obviously cold.

Paul realized his teeth were chattering.

The trip home took ten minutes, and during that time neither of them said a word. The only sounds were the whispery hiss of the tires on the wet pavement and the metronomic thump of the windshield wipers. The silence was not uncomfortable or strained, but there was a peculiar intensity about it, an aura of tremendous, pent-up energy. Paul had the feeling that if he *did* speak, the surprise would send Carol straight through the roof of the car.

They lived in a Tudor-style house, which they had painstakingly restored, and as always, the sight of it – the stone walk, the big oak doors framed by carriage lamps, the leaded-glass windows, the gabled roofline – pleased Paul and gave him the warm feeling that this was where he belonged. The automatic garage door rolled up, and he pulled the Pontiac inside, next to Carol's red Volkswagen Rabbit.

In the house, they maintained their silence.

Paul's hair was wet, and the legs of his trousers clung damply to him, and the back of his shirt was still soaked. He figured he was going to come down with a nasty cold if he didn't get into some dry clothes right away. Apparently, Carol had the same thought, and they went straight upstairs to the master bedroom. She opened the closet doors, and he switched on a bedside lamp. Shivering, they stripped out of their wet clothes.

When they were nearly undressed, they glanced at each other. Their eyes locked.

Still, they didn't speak. They didn't need to.

He took her in his arms, and they kissed lightly at first, tenderly. Her mouth was warm and soft and vaguely flavored with whiskey.

She clutched him, pulled him closer, her fingertips digging into the muscles of his back. She pushed her mouth hard against his, scraped his lip with her teeth, thrust her tongue deep, and abruptly their kisses grew hot, demanding.

Something seemed to snap in him, and in her, too, for their desire was suddenly marked by animal urgency. They responded to each other in a hungry, almost frenzied fashion, hastily casting off the last of their clothes, pawing at each other, squeezing, stroking. She nipped his shoulder with her teeth. He gripped her buttocks and kneaded them with uncharacteristic crudity, but she didn't wince or try to pull away; indeed, she pressed even more insistently against him, rubbing her breasts over his chest and grinding her hips against his. The soft whimpers that escaped from her were not sounds of pain; they clearly expressed her eagerness and need. In bed, his energy was manic, and his staying power amazed him. He was insatiable, and so was she. They thrust and thrashed and flexed and tensed in perfect harmony, as if they were not only joined but *fused*, as if they were a single organism, shaken by only one set of stimuli instead of two. Every vestige of civilization slipped from them, and for a long while the only noises they made were animal sounds: panting; groaning; throaty grunts of pleasure; short, sharp cries of excitement. At last Carol uttered the first word to pass between them since they had left O'Brian's office: 'Yes.' And again, arching her slender, graceful body, tossing her head from side to side on the pillow: 'Yes, yes!' It was not merely an orgasm to which she was saying yes, for she'd already had a couple of those and had announced them with only ragged breathing and soft mewling. She was saying yes to life, yes to the fact that she still existed and was not just a charred and oozing lump of unanimated flesh, yes to the miraculous fact that they had both survived the lightning and the deadly, splintered branches of the toppling maple tree. Their unrestrained, fiercely passionate coupling was a slap in Death's face, a not wholly rational but nevertheless satisfying denial of the grim specter's very existence. Paul repeated the word as if chanting an incantation – 'Yes, yes, yes!' – as he emptied himself into her a second time, and it seemed as though his fear of death spurted out of him along with his seed.

Spent, they stretched out on their backs, side by side on the disheveled bed. For a long time they listened to the rain on the roof and to the persistent thunder, which was no longer loud enough to rattle the windows.

Carol lay with her eyes closed, her face completely relaxed. Paul studied her, and, as he had done on countless other occasions during the past four years, he wondered why she had ever consented to marry him. She was beautiful. He was not. Anyone putting together a dictionary could do worse than to use a picture of his face as the sole definition of the word *plain*. He had once jokingly expressed a similar opinion of his physical appearance, and Carol had been angry with him for talking about himself that way. But it was true, and it didn't really matter to him that he was not Burt Reynolds, just so long as Carol didn't notice the difference. It was not only his plainness of which she seemed unaware; she could not comprehend her own beauty, and she insisted *she* was actually rather plain, or at least no more than 'a little bit pretty, no, not even pretty, just sort of cute, but kind of funny-looking cute.' Her dark hair – even now, when it was matted and curled by rain and sweat – was thick, glossy, lovely. Her skin was flawless, and her cheekbones were so well sculpted that it was difficult to believe the clumsy hand of nature could have done the job. Carol was the kind of woman you saw on the arm of a tall, bronzed Adonis, not with the likes of Paul Tracy. Yet here she was, and he was grateful to have her beside him. He never ceased to be surprised that they were compatible in every respect – mentally, emotionally, physically.

Now, as rain began to beat on the roof and windows with renewed force, Carol sensed that he was staring at her, and she opened her eyes. They were so brown that, from a distance of more than a few inches, they looked black. She smiled. 'I love you.'

'I love you,' he said.

'I thought you were dead.'

'Wasn't.'

'After the lightning stopped, I called you, but you didn't answer for the longest time.'

'I was busy with a call to Chicago,' he said, grinning.

'Seriously.'

'Okay. It was San Francisco.'

'I was scared.'

'I *couldn't* answer you right away,' he said soothingly. 'In case you've forgotten, O'Brian fell on top of me. Knocked the wind right out. He doesn't look so big, but he's as solid as a rock. I guess he builds a lot of muscles by picking lint off his suits and shining his shoes nine hours a day.'

'That was a pretty brave thing you did.'

'Making love to you? Think nothing of it.'

Playfully, she slapped his face. 'You know what I mean. You saved O'Brian's life.'

'Nope.'

'Yes, you did. He thought so, too.'

'For God's sake, I didn't step in front of him and shield him from the tree with mine own precious bod! I just pulled him out of the way. Anyone would have done the same.'

She shook her head. 'Wrong. Not everyone thinks as fast as you do.'

'A fast thinker, huh? Yeah. That's something I'll admit to being.

I'm a fast thinker, but I'm sure no hero. I won't let you pin *that* label on me because then you'll expect me to live up to it. Can you just imagine what a hell on earth Superman's life would be if he ever married Lois Lane? Her expectations would be so high!'

'Anyway,' Carol said, 'even if you won't admit it, O'Brian knows you saved his life, and that's the important thing.'

'It is?'

'Well, I was pretty sure the adoption agency would approve us. But now there's not the slightest doubt about it.'

'There's always a slim chance –'

'No,' she said, interrupting him. 'O'Brian's not going to fail you after you saved his life. Not a chance. He's going to wrap the recommendations committee around his finger.'

Paul blinked, then slowly broke into a smile. 'I'll be damned. I didn't think of that.'

'So you're a hero, Papa.'

'Well . . . maybe I am, Mama.'

'I think I prefer "Mom." '

'And I prefer "Dad." '

'What about "Pop?" '

'Pop isn't a name. It's a sound a champagne cork makes.'

'Are you suggesting a celebration?' she asked.

'I thought we'd put on our robes, mosey down to the kitchen, and whip up an early dinner. If you're hungry, that is.'

'Famished.'

'You can make a mushroom salad,' he said. 'I'll whip up my famous fettuccine Alfredo. We've got a bottle or two of Mumm's Extra Dry we've been saving for a special occasion. We'll open that, pile our plates high with fettuccine Alfredo and mushrooms, come back up here, and have dinner in bed.'

'And watch the TV news while we eat.'

'Then pass the evening reading thrillers and sipping champagne until we can't keep our eyes open.'

'Sounds wonderfully, sinfully lazy,' she said.

More evenings than not, he spent two hours proofreading and polishing his novel. And it was an unusual night when Carol didn't have some paperwork to catch up on.

As they dressed in robes and bedroom slippers, Paul said, 'We've got to learn to take *most* evenings off. We'll have to spend plenty of time with the kid. We'll owe it to him.'

'Or her.'

'Or them,' he said.

Her eyes shone. 'You think they'll let us adopt more than one?'

'Of course they will – once we've proven we can handle the first. After all,' he said self-mockingly, 'am I not the hero who saved good old Al O'Brian's life?'

On their way to the kitchen, halfway down the stairs, she stopped and turned and hugged him. 'We're really going to have a family.'

'So it seems.'

'Oh, Paul, I don't remember when I've ever been so happy. Tell me this feeling's going to last forever.'

He held her, and it was very fine to have her in his arms. When you got right down to it, affection was even better than sex; being needed and loved was better than making love.

'Tell me nothing can go wrong,' she said.

'Nothing can go wrong, and that feeling you have will last forever, and I'm glad you're so happy. There. How's that?'

She kissed his chin and the corners of his mouth, and he kissed her nose.

'Now,' he said, 'can we please get some fettuccine before I start chewing my tongue?'

'Such a romantic.'

'Even romantics get hungry.'

As they reached the bottom of the steps, they were startled by a sudden, loud hammering sound. It was steady but arhythmic: *Thunk, thunk, thunk-thunk-thunk, thunk-thunk . . .*

Carol said, 'What the devil's that?'

'It's coming from outside . . . and above us.'

They stood on the last step, looking up and back toward the second floor.

Thunk, thunk-thunk, thunk, thunk . . .

'Damn,' Paul said. 'I'll bet one of the shutters came loose in the wind.' They listened for a moment, and then he sighed. 'I'll have to go out and fix it.'

'Now? In the rain?'

'If I don't do anything, the wind might tear it clean off the house. Worse yet, it might just hang there and clatter all night. We won't get any sleep, and neither will half the neighborhood.'

She frowned. 'But the lightning . . . Paul, after everything that's happened, I don't think you should risk climbing around on a ladder in the middle of a storm.'

He didn't like the idea, either. The thought of being high on a ladder in the middle of a thunderstorm made his scalp prickle.

She said, 'I don't want you to go out there if –'

The hammering stopped.

They waited.

Wind. The patter of rain. The branches of a tree scraping lightly against an outside wall.

At last, Paul said, 'Too late. If it was a shutter, it's been torn off.'

'I didn't hear it fall.'

'It wouldn't make much noise if it dropped in the grass or the shrubbery.'

'So you don't have to go out in the rain,' she said, crossing the foyer toward the short hall that led to the kitchen.

He followed her. 'Yeah, but now it's a bigger repair job.'

As they entered the kitchen, their footsteps echoing hollowly off the quarry-tile floor, she said, 'You don't have to worry about it until tomorrow or the day after. Right now, all you've got to worry about is the sauce for the fettuccine. Don't let it curdle.'

Taking a copper saucepan from a rack of gleaming utensils that hung over the center utility island, he pretended to be insulted by her remark. 'Have I *ever* curdled the sauce for the fettuccine?'

'Seems to me the last time you made it, the stuff was –'

'Never!'

'Yes,' she said teasingly. 'Yes, it definitely wasn't up to par the last time.' She took a plastic bag of mushrooms from the big, stainless-steel refrigerator. 'Although it breaks my heart to tell you this, the last time you made fettuccine Alfredo, the sauce was as lumpy as the mattress in a ten-dollar-a-night motel.'

'What a vile accusation! Besides, what makes you such an expert on ten-dollar-a-night motels? Are you leading a secret life I ought to know about?'

Together, they prepared dinner, chatting about this and that, bantering a lot, trying to amuse each other and to elicit a laugh now and then. For Paul, the world dwindled until they were the only two people in it. The universe was no larger than the warm, familiar kitchen.

Then lightning flickered, and the cozy mood was broken. It was soft lightning, nothing as dazzling and destructive as the bolts that had struck outside of O'Brian's office a few hours ago. Nevertheless, Paul stopped talking in midsentence, his attention captured by the flash, his eyes drawn to the long, many-paned window behind the sink. On the rear lawn, the trees appeared to writhe and shimmer and ripple in the fluttering storm light, so that it seemed he was looking not at the trees themselves but at their reflections in the surface of a lake.

Suddenly, another movement caught his eye, though he wasn't sure what he was seeing. The afternoon, which had been gray and dark to begin with, was now gradually giving away to an early night, and thin fog was drifting in. Shadows lay everywhere. The meager daylight was deceptive, muddy; it distorted rather than illuminated those things it touched. In that penumbral landscape, something abruptly darted out from behind the thick trunk of an oak tree, crossed a stretch of open grass, and quickly disappeared behind a lilac bush.

Carol said, 'Paul? What's wrong?'

'Someone's out on the lawn.'

'In this rain? Who?'

'I don't know.'

She joined him by the window. 'I don't see anybody.'

'Someone ran from the oak to the lilac bush. He was hunched over and moving pretty fast.'

'What's he look like?'

'I can't say. I'm not even sure it was a man. Might have been a woman.'

'Maybe it was just a dog.'

'Too big.'

'Could've been Jasper.'

Jasper was the Great Dane that belonged to the Hanrahan family, three doors down the street. He was a large, piercing-eyed, friendly animal with an amazing tolerance for small children and a liking for Oreo cookies.

'They wouldn't let Jasper out in weather like this,' Paul said. 'They pamper that mutt.'

Lightning pulsed softly again, and a violent gust of wind whipped the trees back and forth, and rain began to fall harder than before – and in the middle of that maelstrom, something rushed out from the lilac bush.

'There!' Paul said.

The intruder crouched low, obscured by the rain and the mist, a shadow among shadows. It was illuminated so briefly and strangely by the lightning that its true appearance remained tantalizingly at the edge of perception. It loped toward the brick wall that marked the perimeter of the property, vanished for a moment in an especially dense patch of fog, reappeared as an amorphous black shape, then changed direction, paralleling the wall now, heading toward the gate at the northwest corner of the rear lawn. As the darkening sky throbbed with lightning once more, the intruder fled through electric-blue flashes, through the open gate, into the street, and away.

'Just the dog,' Carol said.

Paul frowned. 'I thought I saw . . .'

'What?'

'A face. A woman looking back . . . just for a second, just as she went through the gate.'

'No,' Carol said. 'It was Jasper.'

'You saw him?'

'Yes.'

'Clearly?'

'Well, no, not clearly. But I could see enough to tell that it was a dog the size of a small pony, and Jasper's the only pooch around who fits that description.'

'I guess Jasper's a lot smarter than he used to be.'

Carol blinked. 'What do you mean?'

'Well, he had to unlatch the gate to get into the yard. He never used to be able to do that trick.'

'Oh, of course he didn't. We must have left the gate open.'

Paul shook his head. 'I'm sure it was closed when we drove up a while ago.'

'Closed, maybe – but not latched. The wind pushed it open, and Jasper wandered in.'

Paul stared out at the rain-slashed fog, which glowed dully with the last somber rays of the fading twilight. 'I guess you're right,' he said, though he was not entirely convinced. 'I better go latch the gate.'

'No, no,' Carol said quickly. 'Not while the storm's on.'

'Now look here, sugarface, I'm not going to jump into bed and pull the blankets over my head every time there's a little thunder – just because of what happened this afternoon.'

'I don't expect you to,' she said. 'But before you start dancing in the rain like Gene Kelly, you've got to let *me* get over what happened today. It's still too fresh in my mind for me to stand here watching you while you cavort across the lawn in the lightning.'

'It'll only take a moment and –'

'Say, are you trying to get out of making that fettuccine?' she asked, cocking her head and looking at him suspiciously.

'Certainly not. I'll finish making it as soon as I've gone and closed the gate.'

'I know what you're up to, mister,' she said smugly. 'You're hoping you *will* be struck by lightning because you *know* your sauce is going to turn out lumpy, and you simply can't take the humiliation.'

'That's a base canard,' he said, falling easily into their game again. 'I make the silkiest fettuccine Alfredo this side of Rome. Silkier than Sophia Loren's thighs.'

'All I know is, the last time you made it, the stuff was as lumpy as a bowl of oatmeal.'

'I thought you said it was as lumpy as a mattress in a ten-dollar-a-night motel.'

She lifted her head proudly. 'I'm not just a one-simile woman, you know.'

'How *well* I know.'

'So are you going to make fettuccine – or will you take the coward's way out and get killed by lightning?'

'I'll make you eat your words,' he said.

Grinning, she said, 'That's easier than eating your lumpy fettuccine.'

He laughed. 'All right, all right. You win. I can latch the gate in the morning.'

He returned to the stove, and she went back to the cutting board where she was mincing parsley and scallions for the salad dressing.

He knew she was probably right about the intruder. Most likely, it had been Jasper, chasing a cat or looking for an Oreo handout. The thing he'd thought he had seen – the slightly twisted, moon-white face of a woman, lightning reflected in her eyes, her mouth curled into a snarl of hatred or rage – had surely been a trick of light and shadow. Still, the incident left him uneasy. He could not entirely regain the warm, cozy feeling he'd had just before he'd looked out the window.

* * *

Grace Mitowski filled the yellow plastic bowl with Meow Mix and put it in the corner by the kitchen door.

'Kitty-kitty-kitty.'

Aristophanes didn't respond.

The kitchen wasn't Ari's favorite place in the house, for it was the only room in which he was not permitted to climb wherever he wished. He wasn't actually much of a climber anyway. He lacked the spirit of adventure that many cats had, and he usually stayed on the floor. However, even though he had no burning desire to scamper up on the kitchen counters, he didn't want anyone telling him he *couldn't* do it. Like most cats, he resisted discipline and despised all rules. Nevertheless, as little as he liked the kitchen, he never failed to put in an appearance at mealtime. In fact, he was often waiting impatiently by his bowl when Grace came to fill it.

She raised her voice. 'Kitty-kitty-kitty.'

There was no answering meow. Aristophanes did not, as expected, come running, his tail curled up slightly, eager for his dinner.

'Ari-Ari-Ari! Soup's on, you silly cat.'

She put away the box of cat food and washed her hands at the sink.

Thunk, thunk-thunk!

The hammering sound – one hard blow followed by two equally hard blows struck close together – was so sudden and loud that Grace jerked in surprise and almost dropped the small towel on which she was drying her hands. The noise had come from the front of the house. She waited a moment, and there was only the sound of the wind and falling rain, and then –

Thunk! Thunk!

She hung the towel on the rack and stepped into the downstairs hallway.

Thunk-thunk-thunk!

She walked hesitantly down the hall to the front door and snapped on the porch light. The door had a peephole, and the fish-eye lens provided a wide view. She couldn't see anyone; the porch appeared to be deserted.

THUNK!

That blow was delivered with such force that Grace thought the door had been torn from its hinges. There was a splintering sound as she jumped back, and she expected to see chunks of wood exploding into the hall. But the door still hung firmly in place, though it vibrated noisily in its frame; the deadbolt rattled against the lock plate.

THUNK! THUNK! THUNK!

'Stop that!' she shouted. 'Who are you? Who's there?'

The pounding stopped, and she thought she heard adolescent laughter.

She had been on the verge of either calling the police or going for the pistol she kept in her nightstand, but when she heard the laughter, she changed her mind. She could certainly handle a few kids without help. She wasn't so old and weak and fragile that she needed to call the cops to deal with a bunch of ornery little pranksters.

Cautiously, she drew aside the curtain on the long, narrow window

622

beside the door. Tense, ready to step away quickly if someone made a threatening move toward the glass, she looked out. There was no one on the porch.

She heard the laughter again. It was high-pitched, musical, girlish.

Letting the curtain fall back into place, she turned to the door, unlocked it, and stepped onto the threshold.

The night wind was raw and wet. Rain drizzled off the scalloped eaves of the porch.

The immediate area in front of the house offered at least a hundred hiding places for the hoaxers. Bristling shrubbery rustled in the wind, just the other side of the railing, and the yellowish glow from the insect-repelling bulb in the porch ceiling illuminated little more than the center of the porch. The walkway that led from the bottom of the porch steps to the street was flanked by hedges that looked blue black in the darkness. Among the many shades of night, none of the pranksters was visible.

Grace waited, listened.

Thunder rumbled in the distance, but there was no laughter, no giggling in the darkness.

– *Maybe it wasn't kids.*

– *Who else?*

– *You see them on TV news all the time. The iron-eyed ones who shoot and stab and strangle people for the fun of it. They seem to be everywhere these days, the misfits, the psychopaths.*

– *That was not adult laughter. This is kids' work.*

– *Still, maybe I better get inside and lock the door.*

– *Stop thinking like a frightened old lady, dammit!*

It *was* odd that any of the neighborhood children would harass her, for she was on excellent terms with all of them. Of course, maybe these weren't kids from the immediate neighborhood. Just a couple of streets away, everyone was a stranger to her.

She turned and examined the outer face of the front door. She could find no indication that it had been struck repeatedly and violently only moments ago. The wood was not chipped or cracked; it wasn't even slightly marred.

She was amazed because she was certain she had heard the wood splintering. What would kids use that would make a lot of noise while leaving absolutely no marks on the door? Bean bags or something of that nature? No. A bean bag wouldn't have made such a horrendous racket; the impact of the bag against the door might have been loud, yes, very loud indeed, if it had been swung with sufficient force, but the sound wouldn't have been so hard, so sharp.

Again, she slowly scanned the yard. Nothing moved out there except the wind-stirred foliage.

For nearly a minute she watched and listened. She would have waited longer, if only to prove to any mischievous young observers that she was not a frightened old lady who could be easily intimidated; but the air was damp and chilly, and she began to worry about catching a cold.

She went inside and closed the door.

She waited with her hand on the knob, expecting the kids to return shortly. The first time they hit the door, she would jerk it open and catch them red-handed, before they could dart off the porch and hide.

Two minutes passed. Three minutes. Five.

No one hammered on the door, which was distinctly strange. To pranksters, the fun wasn't in the first assault so much as in the second and third and fourth; their intent was not to startle but to torment.

Apparently, the defiant stance she had taken in the doorway had discouraged them. Very likely, they were on their way to another house, seeking a more excitable victim.

She snapped the lock into place.

What kind of parents would allow their children to be out playing in an electrical storm like this?

Shaking her head in dismay at the irresponsibility of some parents, Grace headed back the hall, and with each step she half expected the hammering to start again. But it didn't.

She had planned to have a light, nutritious dinner of steamed vegetables covered with Cheddar cheese, accompanied by a slice or two of home-baked cornbread, but she wasn't hungry yet. She decided to watch the ABC evening news before preparing dinner – although she knew that, with the world in the state it was, the news might put her off her dinner altogether.

In the study, before she had a chance to turn on the television set and hear the latest atrocity stories, she found a mess on the seat of her big armchair. For a moment she could do nothing but stare at the ruin in disbelief: hundreds of feathers; shreds of cloth; colorful, unraveled threads that had once constituted a needlework pattern, but which now lay in a bright, meaningless tangle amidst drifts of goosedown. A couple of years ago, Carol Tracy had given her a set of three small, exceedingly lovely, handmade needlework throw pillows. It was one of those gifts that had been clawed to pieces and left on the armchair.

Aristophanes.

Ari hadn't ripped up anything important since he was a kitten. An act as destructive as this was quite out of character for him, but he was surely the culprit. There was not really another suspect to be seriously considered.

'Ari! Where are you hiding, you sneaky Siamese?'

She went to the kitchen.

Aristophanes was standing at the yellow bowl, eating his Meow Mix. He glanced up as she entered the room.

'You fur-footed menace,' she said. 'What in the world has gotten into you today?'

Aristophanes blinked, sneezed, rubbed his muzzle with one paw, and returned to his dinner with lofty, catlike indifference to her exasperation and puzzlement.

*　　*　　*

Later that night, in her darkened bedroom, Carol Tracy stared at the adumbral ceiling and listened to her husband's soft, steady breathing. He had been asleep for only a few minutes.

The night was quiet. The rain had stopped, and the sky was no longer shaken by thunder. Occasionally, wind brushed across the shingled roof and sighed wearily at the windows, but the fury had gone out of it.

Carol teetered pleasantly on the edge of sleep. She was a bit lightheaded from the champagne she had been slowly sipping throughout the evening, and she felt as if she were floating in warm water, with gentle waves lapping at her sides.

She thought dreamily about the child they would adopt, tried to envision its appearance. A gallery of sweet young faces filled her imagination. If it was an infant, rather than a three- or four-year-old, they would name it themselves: Jason, if a boy; Julia, if a girl. Carol rocked herself on the thin line between wakefulness and dreams by rolling those two names back and forth in her mind: *Jason, Julia, Jason, Julia, Jason . . .*

Falling off the edge, dropping into a well of sleep, she had the ugly, unwelcome thought she had resisted so strenuously earlier in the day: *Something's trying to stop us from adopting a baby.*

Then she was in a strange place where there was not much light, where something hissed and murmured sullenly just out of sight, where the purple-amber shadows had substance and crowded close with menacing intent. In that unknown place, the nightmare unrolled with the frantic, nerve-jarring rhythm of player-piano music.

At first she was running in utter lightlessness, and then she was suddenly running from one room to another in a large house, weaving through a forest of furniture, knocking over a floor lamp, banging one hip against the sharp corner of a credenza, stumbling and nearly falling over the loose edge of an oriental carpet. She plunged through an archway, into a long hall, and turned and looked back into the room from which she had come, but the room wasn't there any longer. The house existed only in front of her; behind, there was perfect, featureless blackness. Blackness . . . and then a glimmer of something. A glint. A splinter of light. A silvery, moving object. The thing swung from side to side, vanishing into darkness, reappearing with a gleam a second later, vanishing again, back and forth, back and forth, rather like a pendulum, never visible long enough to be identified. Although she couldn't quite see what the silvery thing was, she could tell that it was moving toward her, and she knew she must get away from it or die. She ran along the hall to the foot of the stairs, climbed quickly to the second floor. She glanced back and down, but the stairs were not there any more. Just an inky pit. And then the brief flash of something swinging back and forth in that pit . . . again . . . again . . . like a ticking metronome. She rushed into the bedroom, slammed the door, grabbed a chair with the intention of bracing it under the knob – and discovered that, while her back was turned, the door had disappeared, as had the wall in which it had been set. Where the wall had been, there was subterranean gloom. And a silvery flicker. Very close now. Closer still. She screamed but made no sound, and the mysteriously gleaming object arced over her head and –

(Thunk!)

– This is more than just a dream, she thought desperately. Much more than that. This is a memory, a prophecy, a warning. This is a –

(Thunk!)

– She was running in another house that was altogether different from the first. This place was smaller, the furnishings less grand. She did not know where she was, yet she knew she had been here before. The house was familiar, just as the first place had been. She hurried through a doorway, into a kitchen. Two bloody, severed heads were on the kitchen table. One of them was a man's head, and the other was a woman's. She recognized them, felt that she knew them well, but was unable to think of their names. The four dead eyes were wide but sightless; the two mouths gaped, the swollen tongues protruding over the purple lips. As Carol stood transfixed by that grisly sight, the dead eyes rolled in their sockets and focused on her. The cold lips twisted into icy smiles. Carol turned, intending to flee, but there was only a void behind her and a glint of light off the hard surface of something silvery and then –

(Thunk!)

– She was running through a mountain meadow in reddish, late-afternoon light. The grass was knee-high, and the trees loomed ahead of her. When she looked over her shoulder, the meadow was no longer back there. Only blackness, as before. And the rhythmically swinging, shimmering, steadily approaching *thing* to which she was unable to fix a name. Gasping, her heart racing, she ran faster, reached the trees, glanced back once more, saw that she had not run nearly fast enough to escape, cried out and –

(Thunk!)

For a long time the nightmare shifted from one of those three dreamscapes to the other – from the first house to the meadow to the second house to the meadow to the first house again – until at last she woke with an unvoiced scream caught in her throat. She sat straight up, shuddering. She was cold and yet slick with sweat; she slept in just a T shirt and panties, and both garments clung to her skin, unpleasantly sticky. The frightening sound from the nightmare continued to echo in her mind – *thunk, thunk, thunk-thunk, thunk* – and she realized that her subconscious had borrowed that noise from reality, from the wind-loosened shutter that had startled her and Paul earlier. Gradually, the pounding noise faded and blended with the thumping of her heart.

She drew back the covers and swung her bare legs out of bed. She sat on the edge of the mattress, hugging herself.

Dawn had come. Gray light seeped in around the drapes; it was too dim to reveal the details of the furniture, but it was just bright enough to deepen the shadows and distort the shapes of everything, so that the room seemed like an alien place.

The rain had stopped a couple of hours before she'd gone to bed, but the storm had returned while she'd been sleeping. Rain pattered on the roof and gurgled through the gutters and the downspouts. Low thunder rumbled like a distant cannonade.

Paul was still asleep, snoring softly.

Carol knew she wouldn't be able to get back to sleep. Like it or not, rested or not, she was up for the day.

Without turning on a light, she went into the master bathroom. In the weak glow of dawn, she stripped out of her damp T-shirt and panties. While soaping herself in the shower, she thought about the nightmare, which had been considerably more vivid than any dream she'd ever had before.

That strange, jarring sound – *thunk, thunk* – had been the most frightening thing in the dream, and the memory of it still nagged her. It wasn't just an ordinary hammering noise; there was an odd echo to it, a hardness and sharpness she couldn't quite define. She decided it was not *only* a case of her subconscious mind borrowing the noise the shutter had made earlier. The terrifying sound in the dream was caused by something considerably more disturbing than the mere banging of an unmoored shutter. Furthermore, she was sure she had heard *precisely* that sound on another occasion, too. Not in the nightmare. In real life. In another place . . . a long time ago . . .

As she let the hot water stream over her, sluicing away the soap, she tried to recall where and when she had heard exactly that same unsettling sound, for it suddenly seemed important for her to identify it. Without understanding why, she felt vaguely threatened as long as she could not recall the source of the sound. But remembrance hung tantalizingly beyond the limits of her reach, like the title of a hauntingly familiar but unnameable piece of music.

Chapter Four

At 8:45, after breakfast, Carol left for work, and Paul went upstairs to the rear bedroom that he had converted into an office. He had created a Spartan atmosphere in which to write without distraction. The off-white walls were bare, unadorned by even a single painting. The room contained only an inexpensive desk, a typist's chair, an electric typewriter, a jar bristling with pens and pencils, a deep letter tray that now contained nearly two hundred manuscript pages of the novel he had started at the beginning of his sabbatical, a telephone, a three-shelf bookcase filled with reference works, a bottled-water dispenser in one corner, and a small table upon which stood a Mr. Coffee machine.

This morning, as usual, he prepared a pot of coffee first thing. Just as he pressed the switch labeled BREWER and poured water into the top of the Mr. Coffee, the telephone rang. He sat on the edge of the desk, picked up the receiver. 'Hello.'

'Paul? Grace Mitowski.'

'Good morning, love. How are you?'

'Well, these old bones don't like rainy weather, but otherwise I'm coping.'

Paul smiled. 'Listen, I know you can still run circles around me any time.'

'Nonsense. You're a compulsive worker with a guilt complex about leisure. Not even a nuclear reactor has your energy.'

He laughed. 'Don't psychoanalyze me, Grace. I get enough of that from my wife.'

'Speaking of whom . . .'

'Sorry, but you just missed her. You ought to be able to catch her at the office in half an hour.'

Grace hesitated.

Hot coffee began to drizzle into the Pyrex pot, and the aroma of it swiftly filled the room.

Sensing tension in Grace's hesitation, Paul said, 'What's wrong?'

'Well . . .' She cleared her throat nervously. 'Paul, how *is* she? She's not ill or anything?'

'Carol? Oh, no. Of course not.'

'You're sure? I mean, you know that girl's like a daughter to me. If anything was wrong, I'd want to know.'

'She's fine. Really. In fact she had a physical exam last week. The adoption agency required it. Both of us passed with flying colors.'

Grace was silent again.

Frowning, Paul said, 'Why are you worried all of a sudden?'

'Well . . . you'll think old Gracie is losing her marbles, but I've had two disturbing dreams, one during a nap yesterday, the other last night, and Carol was in both. I seldom dream, so when I have *two* nightmares and wake up both times feeling I've got to warn Carol . . .'

'Warn her about what?'

'I don't know. All I remember about the dreams is that Carol was in them. I woke up thinking: *It's coming. I've got to warn Carol that it's coming*. I know that sounds silly. And don't ask me what "it" might be. I can't remember. But I feel Carol's in danger. Now Lord knows, I don't believe in dream prophecies and garbage like that. I *think* I don't believe in them – yet here I am calling you about this.'

The coffee was ready. Paul leaned over, turned off the brewer. 'The strange thing is – Carol and I were nearly hurt in a freak accident yesterday.' He told her about the damage at O'Brian's office.

'Good God,' she said, 'I saw that lightning when I woke up from my nap, but it never occurred to me that you and Carol . . . that the lightning might be the very thing I was . . . the very thing my *dream* oh, hell! I'm afraid to say it because I might sound like a superstitious old fool, but here goes anyway: *Was* there actually something prophetic about that dream? Did I foresee the lightning strike a few minutes before it happened?'

'If nothing else,' Paul said uneasily, 'it's at least a remarkable coincidence.'

They were silent for a moment, wondering, and then she said, 'Listen, Paul, I don't recall that we've ever discussed this subject much before, but tell me – do *you* believe in dream prophecies, clairvoyance, things of that nature?'

'I don't believe, and I don't disbelieve. I've never really made up my mind.'

'I've always been so smug about it. Always considered it a pack of lies, delusions, or just plain nonsense. But after this –'

'You're reconsidering.'

'Let's just say a tiny doubt has cropped up. And now I'm more worried about Carol than I was when I called you.'

'Why? I told you she wasn't even scratched.'

'She escaped once,' Grace said, 'but I had *two* dreams, and one of them came to me hours after the lightning. So maybe the "it" is something else. I mean, if the first dream had some truth in it, then maybe the second does, too. God, isn't this crazy? If you start believing in just a little bit of this nonsense, you get carried away with it real fast. But I can't help it. I'm still concerned about her.'

'Even if your first dream was prophetic,' Paul said, 'the second one was probably just a repeat of it, an echo, not a whole new dream.'

'You think so?'

'Sure. This never happened to you before, so why should it happen again? Most likely, it was just a freak thing . . . like the lightning yesterday.'

'Yeah, I guess you're probably right,' she said, sounding somewhat relieved. 'Maybe it could happen once. Maybe I can accept that. But I'm not Edgar Cayce or Nostradamus. And I can guarantee you I'm never going to be writing a weekly column of predictions for the *National Enquirer*.'

Paul laughed.

'Still,' she said, 'I wish I could remember exactly what happened in *both* those nightmares.'

They talked a while longer, and when Paul finally hung up, he stared at the receiver for a moment, frowning. Although he was pretty much convinced that the timing of Grace's dream had been merely a strange coincidence, he was nonetheless affected by it, more profoundly affected than seemed reasonable.

It's coming.

The moment Grace had voiced those two words, Paul had felt a gut-deep, bone-deep chill.

It's coming.

Coincidence, he told himself. Sheer coincidence and nonsense. Forget about it.

Gradually he became aware, once again, of the rich aroma of hot coffee. He rose from the edge of the desk and filled a mug with the steaming brew.

For a minute or two he stood at the window behind the desk, sipping coffee, staring out at the dirty, scudding clouds and at the incessant rain. Eventually he lowered his gaze and looked down into the rear yard, instantly recalling the intruder he had seen last evening while he and Carol had been making dinner: that briefly glimpsed, pale, distorted, lightning-illuminated face; a woman's face; shining eyes; mouth twisted into a snarl of rage or hatred. Or perhaps it had just been Jasper, the Great Dane, and a trick of light.

THUNK!

The sound was so loud and unexpected that Paul jumped in surprise. If his mug hadn't been half empty, he would have spilled coffee all over the carpet.

THUNK! THUNK!

It couldn't be the same shutter they'd heard last evening, for it would have continued banging all night. Which meant there were now two of them to repair.

Jeez, he thought, the old homestead is falling down around my ears.

THUNK!

The source of the sound was nearby; in fact it was so close that it seemed to originate within the room.

Paul pressed his forehead against the cool window glass, peered out to the left, then to the right, trying to see if that pair of shutters was in place. As far as he could see, they were both properly anchored.

Thunk, thunk-thunk, thunk, thunk . . .

The noise grew softer but settled into a steady, arhythmical beat that was more irritating than the louder blows had been. And now it seemed to be coming from another part of the house.

Although he didn't want to get up on a ladder and fix a shutter in the rain, that was exactly what had to be done, for he couldn't get any writing accomplished with that constant clattering to distract him. At least there hadn't been any lightning this morning.

He put his mug on the desk and started out of the room. Before he reached the door, the telephone rang.

So it's going to be one of *those* days, he thought wearily.

Then he realized that the shutter had stopped banging the moment the phone had rung. Maybe the wind had wrenched it loose of the house, in which case repairs could wait until the weather improved.

He returned to his desk and answered the telephone. It was Alfred O'Brian, from the adoption agency. Initially, the conversation was awkward, and Paul was embarrassed by it. O'Brian insisted on expressing his gratitude: 'You saved my life; you really did!' He was equally insistent about repeatedly and quite unnecessarily apologizing for his failure to express that gratitude yesterday, immediately following the incident in his office: 'But I was so shaken, stunned, I just wasn't thinking clearly enough to thank you, which was unforgivable of me.' Each time Paul protested at the mention of words like 'heroic,' and 'brave,' O'Brian became even more vociferous than before. At last, Paul stifled his objections and allowed the man to get it out of his system; O'Brian was determined to cleanse his conscience in much the same way that he fussed with the minute specks of lint on his suit jacket. Finally, however, he seemed to feel he had atoned for his (largely imaginary) thoughtlessness, and Paul was relieved when the conversation changed directions.

O'Brian had a second reason for calling, and he got straight to it now, as if he, too, was suddenly embarrassed. He could not (he explained with more apologies) locate the application form that the Tracys had brought to his office the previous day. 'Of course, when that tree crashed through the window, it scattered a lot of papers all over the floor. A terrible mess. Some of them were rumpled and dirty when we gathered them up, and a great many of them were damp from the rain. In spite of that, Margie, my secretary, was able to put them in order – except, of course, for your application. We can't find it anywhere. I suppose it might have blown out through one of the broken windows. I don't know why your papers should be the only ones we've lost, and of course we must have a completed, signed application before we can present your names to the recommendations committee. I'm extremely sorry about this inconvenience, Mr. Tracy, I truly am.'

'It wasn't your fault,' Paul said. 'I'll just stop in later today and pick up another form. Carol and I can fill it out and sign it tonight.'

'Good,' O'Brian said. 'I'm glad to hear that. It has to be back in my hands early tomorrow morning if we're going to make the next meeting of the committee. Margie needs three full business days to run the required verifications on the information in your application, and that's just about how much time we have before next Wednesday's committee meeting. If we miss that session, there's not another one for two weeks.'

'I'll be in to pick up the form before noon,' Paul assured him. 'And I'll have it back to you first thing Friday morning.'

They exchanged goodbyes, and Paul put down the phone.

THUNK!

When he heard that sound, he sagged, dispirited. He was going to have to fix a shutter after all. And then drive into the city to pick up the new application. And then drive home. And by the time he did all of that, half the day would be shot, and he wouldn't have written a single word.

THUNK! THUNK!

'Dammit,' he said.

Thunk, thunk-thunk, thunk-thunk . . .

It definitely was going to be one of *those* days.

He went downstairs to the hall closet where he kept his raincoat and galoshes.

*   *   *

The windshield wipers flogged back and forth, back and forth, with a short, shrill squeak that made Carol grit her teeth. She hunched forward a bit, over the steering wheel, squinting through the streaming rain.

The streets glistened; the macadam was slick, greasy looking. Dirty water raced along the gutters and formed filthy pools around clogged drainage grids.

At ten minutes past nine, the morning rush hour was just over. Although the streets were still moderately busy, traffic was moving smoothly and swiftly. In fact everyone was driving too fast to suit Carol, and she hung back a little, watchful and cautious.

Two blocks from her office, her caution proved justified, but it still wasn't enough to avert disaster altogether. Without bothering to look for oncoming traffic, a young blond woman stepped out from between two vans, directly into the path of the VW Rabbit.

'Christ!' Carol said, ramming her foot down on the brake pedal so hard that she lifted herself up off the seat.

The blonde glanced up and froze, wide-eyed.

Although the VW was moving at only twenty miles an hour, there was no hope of stopping it in time. The brakes shrieked. The tires bit – but also skidded – on the wet pavement.

God, no! Carol thought with a sick, sinking feeling.

The car hit the blonde and lifted her off the ground, tossed her backwards onto the hood, and then the rear end of the VW began to slide around to the left, into the path of an oncoming Cadillac, and the Caddy swerved, brakes squealing, and the other driver hit his horn as if he thought a sufficient volume of sound might magically push Carol safely out of his way, and for an instant she was certain they would collide, but the Caddy slid past without scraping, missing her by only an inch or two – all of this in two or three or four seconds – and at the same time the blonde rolled off the hood, toward the right side, the curb side, and the VW came to a full stop, sitting aslant the street, rocking on its springs as if it were a child's hobby horse.

*　　*　　*

None of the shutters was missing. Not one. None of them was loose and flapping in the wind, as Paul had thought.

Wearing galoshes and a raincoat with a hood, he walked all the way around the house, studying each set of shutters on the first and second floors, but he couldn't see anything amiss. The place showed no sign of storm damage.

Perplexed, he circled the house again, each step resulting in a squishing noise as the rain-saturated lawn gave like a sodden sponge beneath him. This time around, he looked for broken tree limbs that might be swinging against the walls when the wind gusted. The trees were all intact.

Shivering in the unseasonably chilly autumn air, he just stood on the lawn for a minute or two, cocking his head to the right and then to the left, listening for the pounding that had filled the house moments ago. He couldn't hear it now. The only sounds were the soughing wind, the rustling trees, and the rain driving into the grass with a soft, steady hiss.

At last, his face numbed by the cold wind and by the heat-leaching rain, he decided to halt his search until the pounding started again and gave him something to get a fix on. Meanwhile, he could drive downtown and pick up the application form at the adoption agency. He put one hand to his face, felt his beard stubble, remembered Alfred O'Brian's compulsive neatness, and figured he ought to shave before he went.

He reentered the house by way of the screened-in rear porch, leaving his dripping coat on a vinyl-upholstered glider and shedding his galoshes before going into the kitchen. Inside, he closed the door behind him and basked for a moment in the warm air.

THUNK! THUNK! THUNK!

The house shuddered as if it had received three extremely hard, rapid blows from the enormous fist of a giant. Above the kitchen's central utility island, where a utensil rack was suspended from the ceiling, copper pots and pans swung on their hooks and clattered against one another.

THUNK!

The wall clock rattled on its hook; if it had been any less firmly attached than it was, it would have flung itself off the wall, onto the floor.

Paul moved toward the middle of the room, trying to ascertain the direction from which the pounding was coming.

THUNK! THUNK!

The oven door fell open.

The two dozen small jars nestled in the spice rack began to clink against one another.

What the hell is happening here? he wondered uneasily.

THUNK!

He turned slowly, listening, seeking.

The pots and pans clattered again, and a large ladle slipped from its hook and fell with a clang to the butcher-block work surface that lay under it.

Paul looked up at the ceiling, tracking the sound.

THUNK!

He expected to see the plaster crack, but it didn't. Nevertheless, the source of the sound was definitely overhead.

Thunk, thunk-thunk, thunk . . .

The pounding suddenly grew quieter than it had been, but it didn't fade away altogether. At least the house stopped quivering, and the cooking utensils stopped banging together.

Paul headed for the stairs, determined to track down the cause of the disturbance.

*   *   *

The blonde was in the gutter, flat on her back, one arm out at her side with the palm up and the hand slack, the other arm draped across her belly. Her golden hair was muddy. A three-inch-deep stream of water surged around her, carrying leaves and grit and scraps of paper litter toward the nearest storm drain, and her long hair fanned out around her head and rippled silkily in those filthy currents.

Carol knelt beside the woman and was shocked to see that the victim wasn't actually a woman at all. She was a girl, no older than fourteen or fifteen. She was exceptionally pretty, with delicate features, and at the moment she was frighteningly pale.

She was also inadequately dressed for inclement weather. She wore white tennis shoes, jeans, and a blue and white checkered blouse. She had neither a raincoat nor an umbrella.

With trembling hands, Carol lifted the girl's right arm and felt the wrist for a pulse. She found the beat at once; it was strong and steady.

'Thank God,' Carol said shakily. 'Thank God, thank God.'

She began to examine the girl for bleeding. There did not seem to be any serious injuries, no major blood loss, just a few shallow cuts and abrasions. Unless, of course, the bleeding was internal.

The driver of the Cadillac, a tall man with a goatee, stepped around the end of the VW Rabbit and looked down at the injured girl. 'Is she dead?'

'No,' Carol said. She gently thumbed back one of the girl's eyelids, then the other. 'Just unconscious. Probably a mild concussion. Is anyone calling an ambulance?'

'I don't know,' he said.

'Then you can call one. Quickly.'

He hurried away, splashing through a puddle that was deeper than the tops of his shoes.

Carol pressed down on the girl's chin; the jaw was slack, and the mouth fell open easily. There was no visible obstruction, no blood, nothing that might choke her, and her tongue was in a safe position.

A gray-haired woman in a transparent plastic rain coat, carrying a red and orange umbrella, appeared out of the rain. 'It wasn't your fault,' she told Carol. 'I saw it happen. I saw it all. The child darted out in front of you without looking. There wasn't a thing you could have done to prevent it.'

'I saw it, too,' said a portly man who didn't quite fit under his black umbrella. 'I saw the kid walking down the street like she was in a trance or something. No coat, no umbrella. Eyes kind of blank. She stepped off the curb, between those two vans, and just stood there for a few seconds, like she was just waiting for someone to come along so she could step out and get herself killed. And by God, that's what happened.'

'She's not dead,' Carol said, unable to keep a tremor out of her voice. 'There's a first-aid kit on the back seat of my car. Will one of you get it for me?'

'Sure,' the portly man said, turning toward the VW.

The first-aid kit contained, among other things, a packet of tongue depressors, and Carol wanted to have those handy. Although the unconscious girl didn't appear to be headed for imminent convulsions, Carol intended to be prepared for the worst.

A crowd had begun to gather.

A siren sounded a couple of blocks away, approaching fast. It was probably the police; the ambulance couldn't have made it so fast.

'Such a pretty child,' the gray-haired woman said, staring down at the stricken girl.

Other onlookers murmured in agreement.

Carol stood up and stripped out of her raincoat. There was no point in covering the girl, for she was already as wet as she could get. Instead, Carol folded the coat, knelt down again, and carefully slipped the makeshift pillow under the victim, elevating her head just a bit above the gushing water.

The girl didn't open her eyes or stir in any way whatsoever. A tangled strand of golden hair had fallen across her face, and Carol carefully pushed it aside for her. The girl's skin was hot to the touch, fevered, in spite of the cold rain that bathed it.

Suddenly, while her fingers were still touching the girl's cheek, Carol felt dizzy and was unable to get her breath. For a moment she thought she was going to pass out and collapse on top of the unconscious teenager. A black wave rose behind her eyes, and then in that darkness there was a brief flash of silver, a glint of light off a moving object, the mysterious thing from her nightmare.

She gritted her teeth, shook her head, and refused to be swept away in that dark wave. She pulled her hand away from the girl's cheek, put it to her own face; the dizzy spell passed as abruptly as it had come. Until the ambulance arrived, she was responsible for the injured girl, and she was determined not to fail in that responsibility.

Huffing slightly, the portly man hurried back with the first-aid kit. Carol took one of the tongue depressors out of its crisp cellophane wrapper – just in case.

A police car rounded the corner and stopped behind the Volkswagen. Its revolving emergency beacons splashed red light across the wet pavement and appeared to transform the puddles of rainwater into pools of blood.

As the squad car's siren died with a growl, another, more distant siren became audible. To Carol, that warbling, high-pitched wail was the sweetest sound in the world.

The horror is almost over, she thought.

But then she looked at the girl's chalk-white face, and her relief was clouded with doubt. Perhaps the horror wasn't over after all; perhaps it had only just begun.

* * *

Upstairs, Paul walked slowly from room to room, listening to the hammering sound.

Thunk . . . thunk . . .

The source was still overhead. In the attic. Or on the roof.

The attic stairs were behind a paneled door at the end of the second-floor hallway. They were narrow, unpainted, and they creaked as Paul climbed them.

Although the attic had full flooring, it was not otherwise a finished room. The construction of the walls was open for inspection; the pink fiberglass insulation, which somewhat resembled raw meat, and the regularly spaced supporting studs, like ribs of bone, were visible. Two naked, hundred-watt bulbs furnished light, and shadows coiled everywhere, especially toward the eaves. For all of its length and for half of its width, the attic was high enough to allow Paul to walk through it without stooping.

The patter of rain on the roof was more than just a patter up here. It was a steady hissing, a soft, all-encompassing roar.

Nevertheless, the other sound was audible above the drumming of the rain: *Thunk . . . thunk-thunk . . .*

Paul moved slowly past stacks of cardboard cartons and other items that had been consigned to storage: a pair of large touring trunks; an old six-pronged coat rack; a tarnished brass floor lamp; two busted-out, cane-bottomed chairs that he intended to restore some day. A thin film of whitish dust draped shroudlike over all the contents of the room.

Thunk . . . thunk . . .

He walked the length of the attic, then slowly returned to the center of it and stopped. The source of the sound seemed to be directly in front of his face, only inches away. But there was nothing here that could possibly be the cause of the disturbance; nothing moved.

Thunk . . . thunk . . . thunk . . . thunk . . .

Although the hammering was softer now than it had been a few minutes ago, it was still solid and forceful; it reverberated through the frame of the house. The pounding had acquired a monotonously simple rhythm, too; each blow was separated from the ones before and after it by equal measures of time, resulting in a pattern not unlike the beating of a heart.

Paul stood in the attic, in the dust, smelling the musty odor common to all unused places, trying to get a fix on the sound, trying to understand how it could be coming out of thin air, and gradually his attitude toward the disturbance changed. He had been thinking of it as nothing more than the audible evidence of storm damage to

639

the house, as nothing more than tedious and perhaps expensive repairs that might have to be made, an interruption in his writing schedule, an inconvenience, nothing more. But as he turned his head from side to side and squinted into every shadow, as he listened to the relentless thudding, he suddenly perceived that there was something ominous about the sound.

Thunk . . . thunk . . . thunk . . .

For reasons he could not define, the noise now seemed threatening, malevolent.

He felt colder in this sheltered place than he had felt outside in the wind and rain.

*   *   *

Carol wanted to ride to the hospital in the ambulance with the injured girl, but she knew she would only be in the way. Besides, the first police officer on the scene, a curly-headed young man named Tom Weatherby, needed to get a statement from her.

They sat in the front seat of the patrol car, which smelled like the peppermint lozenges on which Weatherby was sucking. The windows were made opaque by shimmering streams of rain. The police radio sputtered and crackled.

Weatherby frowned. 'You're soaked to the skin. I've got a blanket in the trunk. I'll get it for you.'

'No, no,' she said. 'I'll be fine.' Her green knit suit had become saturated. Her rain-drenched hair was pasted to her head and hung slackly to her shoulders. At the moment, however, she didn't care about her appearance or about the goosebumps that prickled her skin. 'Let's just get this over with.'

'Well . . . if you're sure you're okay.'

'I'm sure.'

As he turned up the thermostat on the car heater, Weatherby said, 'By any chance, do you know the kid who stepped in front of your car?'

'Know her? No. Of course not.'

'She didn't have any ID on her. Did you notice if she was carrying a purse when she walked into the street?'

'I can't say for sure.'

'Try to remember.'

'I don't think she was.'

'Probably not,' he said. 'After all, if she goes walking in a storm like this without a raincoat or an umbrella, why would she bother to take a purse? We'll search the street anyway. Maybe she dropped it somewhere.'

'What happens if you can't find out who she is? How will you get in touch with her parents? I mean, she shouldn't be alone at a time like this.'

'No problem,' Weatherby said. 'She'll tell us her name when she regains consciousness.'

'*If* she does.'

'Hey, she will. There's no need to be concerned about that. She didn't seem seriously injured.'

Carol worried about it nonetheless.

For the next ten minutes, Weatherby asked questions, and she answered them. When he finished filling out the accident report, she quickly read over it, then signed at the bottom.

'You're in the clear,' Weatherby said. 'You were driving under the speed limit, and three witnesses say the girl stepped out of a blind spot right in front of you, without bothering to look for traffic. It wasn't your fault.'

'I should have been more careful.'

'I don't see what else you could have done.'

'Something. Surely I could have done something,' she said miserably.

He shook his head. 'No. Listen, Dr. Tracy, I've seen this sort of thing happen before. There's an accident, and somebody's hurt, and nobody's really to blame – yet one of the people involved has a misplaced sense of responsibility and insists on feeling guilty. And in this case, if there *is* anybody to blame, it's the kid herself, not you. According to the witnesses, she was behaving strangely just before you turned the corner, almost as if she *intended* to get herself run down.'

'But why would such a pretty girl want to throw herself in front of a car?'

Weatherby shrugged. 'You told me you were a psychiatrist. You specialize in children and teenagers, right?'

'Yes.'

'So you must know all the answers better than I do. Why would she want to kill herself? Could be trouble at home – a father who drinks too much and makes heavy passes at his own little girl, a mother who doesn't want to hear about it. Or maybe the kid was just jilted by her boyfriend and thinks the world is coming to an end. Or just discovered she was pregnant and decided she couldn't face her folks with the news. There must be hundreds of reasons, and I'm sure you've heard most of them in your line of work.'

What he said was true, but it didn't make Carol feel better.

If only I'd been driving slower, she thought. If only I'd been quicker to react, maybe that poor girl wouldn't be in the hospital now.

'She might have been on drugs, too,' Weatherby said. 'Too damned many kids fool around with dope these days. I swear, some of them'll swallow any pill they're given. If it isn't something that can be swallowed, they'll sniff it or stick it in a vein. This kid you hit might have been so high she didn't even know where she was when she stepped in front of your car. Now, if that's the case, are you going to tell me it's *still* somehow your fault?'

Carol leaned back in the seat, closed her eyes, and let her breath out with a shudder. 'God, I don't know *what* to tell you. All I know is . . . I feel wrung out.'

'That's perfectly natural, after what you've just been through. But it isn't natural to feel guilty about this. It wasn't your fault, so don't dwell on it. Put it behind you and get on with your life.'

She opened her eyes, looked at him, and smiled. 'You know, Officer Weatherby, I have a hunch you'd make a pretty good psychotherapist.'

He grinned. 'Or a terrific bartender.'

Carol laughed.

'Feeling better?' he asked.

'A little bit.'

'Promise me you won't lose any sleep over this.'

'I'll try not to,' she said. 'But I'm still concerned about the girl. Do you know which hospital they've taken her to?'

'I can find out,' he said.

'Would you do that for me? I'd like to go talk to the doctor who's handling her case. If he tells me she's going to be all right, I'll find it a whole lot easier to take your advice about getting on with my life.'

Weatherby picked up the microphone and asked the police dispatcher to find out where the injured girl had been taken.

* * *

The television antenna!

Standing in the attic, staring up at the roof above his head, Paul laughed out loud when he realized what was causing the pounding noise. The sound wasn't coming out of the empty air in front of his face, which was what he had thought for one unsettling moment. It was coming from the roof, where the television antenna was anchored. They had subscribed to cable TV a year ago, but they hadn't removed the old antenna. It was a large, directional, remote-control model affixed to a heavy brace-plate; the plate was bolted through the shingles and attached directly to a roof beam. Apparently, a nut or some other fastener had loosened slightly, and the wind was tugging at the antenna, rocking the brace-plate up and down on one of its bolts, slamming it repeatedly against the roof. The solution to the big mystery was amusingly mundane.

Or was it?

Thunk . . . thunk . . . thunk . . .

The sound was softer now than ever before, barely audible above the roar of the rain on the roof, and it was easy to believe that the antenna could be the cause of it. Gradually, however, as Paul considered this answer to the puzzle, he began to doubt if it was the *correct* answer. He thought about how loud and violent the pounding had been a few minutes ago when he had been in the kitchen: the entire house quivering, the oven door falling open, bottles rattling in the spice rack. Could a loose antenna really generate so much noise and vibration?

Thunk . . . thunk . . .

As he stared up at the ceiling, he tried to make himself believe unequivocally in the antenna theory. If it was striking a roof beam in precisely the right way, at a very special angle, so that the impact was transmitted through the entire frame of the house, perhaps a loose antenna *could* cause the pots and pans to clatter against one another in the kitchen and could make it seem as if the ceilings were about to crack. After all, if you set up exactly the right vibrations in a steel suspension bridge, you could bring it to ruin in less than a minute, regardless of the number of bolts and welds and cables holding it together. And although Paul didn't believe there was even a remote danger of a loose antenna causing that kind of apocalyptic destruction to a wood-frame house, he knew that moderate force, applied with calculation and pin-point accuracy, could have an effect quite out of proportion to the amount of energy expended. Besides, the TV antenna *had* to be the root of the disturbance, for it was the only explanation he had left.

The hammering noise became even softer and then faded altogether. He waited for a minute or two, but the only sound was the rain on the shingles overhead.

The wind must have changed direction. In time it would change back again, and the antenna would begin to rock on its brace-plate, and the pounding would start once more.

As soon as the storm was over, he would have to get the extension ladder out of the garage, go up onto the roof, and dismantle the antenna. He should have taken care of that chore shortly after they had subscribed to the cable television service. Now, because he had delayed, he was going to lose precious writing time – and at one of the most difficult and crucial points in his manuscript. That prospect frustrated him and made him nervous.

He decided to shave, drive downtown, and pick up the new set of application papers at the adoption agency. The storm might pass by the time he got home again. If it did, if he could be on the roof by eleven-thirty, he ought to be able to tear down the antenna, then have a bite of lunch, and work on his book all afternoon, barring further interruptions. But he suspected there *would* be further interruptions. He had already resigned himself to the fact that it was one of those days.

As he left the attic and turned out the lights, the house quivered under another blow.

THUNK!

Just one this time.

Then all was quiet again.

* * *

The visitors' lounge at the hospital looked like an explosion in a clown's wardrobe. The walls were canary yellow; the chairs were bright red; the carpet was orange; the magazine racks and end tables were made of heavy purple plastic; and the two large abstract paintings were done primarily in shades of blue and green.

The lounge – obviously the work of a designer who had read too much about the various psychological mood theories of color – was supposed to be positive, life-affirming. It was supposed to lift the spirits of visitors and take their minds off sick friends and dying relatives. In Carol, however, the determinedly cheery decor elicited the opposite reaction from that which the designer had intended. It was a frenetic room; it abraded the nerves as effectively as coarse sandpaper would abrade a stick of butter.

She sat on one of the red chairs, waiting for the doctor who had treated the injured girl. When he came, his stark white lab coat contrasted so boldly with the flashy decor that he appeared to radiate a saintlike aura.

Carol rose to meet him, and he asked if she was Dr. Tracy, and he said his name was Sam Hannaport. He was tall, very husky, square-

faced, florid, in his early fifties. He looked as if he would be loud
and gruff, perhaps even obnoxious, but in fact he was soft-spoken
and seemed genuinely concerned about how the accident had
affected Carol both physically and emotionally. It took her a couple
of minutes to assure him that she was all right on both counts, and
then they sat down on facing red chairs.

Hannaport raised his bushy eyebrows and said, 'You look as if
you could use a hot bath and a big glassful of warm brandy.'

'I was soaked to the skin,' she said, 'but I'm pretty well dried out
now. What about the girl?'

'Cuts, contusions, abrasions,' he said.

'Internal bleeding?'

'Nothing showed up on the tests.'

'Fractures?'

'Not a broken bone in her body. She came through it amazingly
well. You couldn't have been driving very fast when you hit her.'

'I wasn't. But considering the way she slipped up onto the hood
and then rolled off into the gutter, I thought maybe . . .' Carol
shuddered, unwilling to put words to what she had thought.

'Well, the kid's in good condition now. She regained consciousness in the ambulance, and she was alert by the time I saw her.'

'Thank God.'

'There's no indication that she's even mildly concussed. I don't
foresee any lasting effects.'

Relieved, Carol sagged back in the red chair. 'I'd like to see her,
talk to her.'

'She's resting now,' Dr. Hannaport said. 'I don't want her disturbed at the moment. But if you'd like to come back this evening,
during visiting hours, she'll be able to see you then.'

'I'll do that. I'll definitely do that.' She blinked. 'Good heavens,
I haven't even asked you what her name is.'

His bushy eyebrows rose again. 'Well, we've got a small problem
about that.'

'Problem?' Carol tensed up again. 'What do you mean? Can't
she remember her name?'

'She hasn't remembered it yet, but –'

'Oh, God.'

'– she will.'

'You said no concussion –'

'I swear to you, it *isn't* serious,' Hannaport said. He took her left
hand in his big hard hands and held it as if it might crack and
crumble at any moment. 'Please don't excite yourself about this.

The girl is going to be fine. Her inability to remember her name isn't a symptom of severe concussion or any serious brain injury; not in her case, anyway. She isn't confused or disoriented. Her field of vision is normal, and she has excellent depth perception. We tested her thought processes with some math problems – addition, sub-traction, multiplication – and she got them all correct. She can spell any word you throw at her; she's a damn good speller, that one. So she's not severely concussed. She's simply suffering from mild amnesia. It's selective amnesia, you understand, just a loss of per-sonal memories, not a loss of skills and education and whole blocks of social concepts. She hasn't forgotten how to read and write, thank God; she's only forgotten who she is, where she came from, and how she got to this place. Which sounds more serious than it really is. Of course, she's disconcerted and apprehensive. But selec-tive amnesia is the easiest kind to recover from.'

'I know,' Carol said. 'But somehow that doesn't make me feel a whole hell of a lot better.'

Hannaport squeezed her hand firmly and gently. 'This kind of amnesia is only very, very rarely permanent or even long-lasting. She'll most likely remember who she is before dinnertime.'

'If she doesn't?'

'Then the police will find out who she is, and the minute she hears her name, the mists will clear.'

'She wasn't carrying any ID.'

'I know,' he said. 'I've talked to the police.'

'So what happens if they can't find out who she is?'

'They will.' He patted her hand one last time, then let go.

'I don't see how you can be so sure.'

'Her parents will file a missing-persons report. They'll have a photograph of her. When the police see the photograph, they'll make a connection. It'll be as simple as that.'

She frowned. 'What if her parents *don't* report her missing?'

'Why wouldn't they?'

'Well, what if she's a runaway from out of state? Even if her folks did file a missing-persons report back in her hometown, the police here wouldn't necessarily be aware of it.'

'The last time I looked, runaway kids favored New York City, California, Florida – just about any place besides Harrisburg, Pennsylvania.'

'There's always an exception to any rule.'

Hannaport laughed softly and shook his head. 'If pessimism were a competitive sport, you'd win the world series.'

She blinked in surprise, then smiled. 'I'm sorry. I guess I am being excessively gloomy.'

Glancing at his watch, getting up from his chair, he said, 'Yes, I think you are. Especially considering how well the girl came through it all. It could have been a lot worse.'

Carol got to her feet, too. In a rush, the words falling over one another, she said, 'I guess maybe the reason it bothers me so much is because I deal with disturbed children every day, and it's my job to help them get well again, and that's all I ever wanted to do since I was in high school – work with sick kids, be a healer – but now I'm responsible for all the pain this poor girl is going through.'

'You mustn't feel that way. You didn't *intend* to harm her.'

Carol nodded. 'I know I'm not being entirely rational about the situation, but I can't help feeling the way I feel.'

'I have some patients to see,' Hannaport said, glancing at his watch again. 'But let me leave you with one thought that might help you handle this.'

'I'd like to hear it.'

'The girl suffered only minor physical injuries. I won't say they were negligible injuries, but they were damned close to it. So you've got nothing to feel guilty about on that score. As for her amnesia . . . , well, maybe the accident had nothing to do with it.'

'Nothing to do with it? But I assumed that when she hit her head on the car or on the pavement –'

'I'm sure you know a blow on the head isn't the only cause of amnesia,' Dr. Hannaport said. 'It's not even the most common factor in such cases. Stress, emotional shock – they can result in loss of memory. In fact we don't yet understand the human mind well enough to say for sure exactly what causes most cases of amnesia. As far as this girl is concerned, everything points to the conclusion that she was in her current state even before she stepped in front of your car.' He emphasized each argument in favor of his theory by raising fingers on his right hand. 'One: She wasn't carrying any ID. Two: She was wandering around in the pouring rain without a coat or an umbrella, as if she was in a daze. Three: From what I understand, the witnesses say she was acting very strange before you ever came on the scene.' He waggled his three raised fingers. 'Three very good reasons why you shouldn't be so eager to blame yourself for the kid's condition.'

'Maybe you're right, but I still –'

'I *am* right,' he said. 'There's no maybe about it. Give yourself a break, Dr. Tracy.'

A woman with a sharp, nasal voice paged Dr. Hannaport on the hospital's tinny public address system.

'Thank you for your time,' Carol said. 'You've been more than kind.'

'Come back this evening and talk to the girl if you want. I'm sure you'll find she doesn't blame you one bit.'

He turned and hurried across the gaudy lounge, in answer to the page's call; the tails of his white lab coat fluttered behind him.

Carol went to the pay phones and called her office. She explained the situation to her secretary, Thelma, and arranged for the rescheduling of the patients she had intended to see today. Then she dialed home, and Paul answered on the third ring.

'You just caught me as I was going out the door,' he said. 'I've got to drive down to O'Brian's office and pick up a new set of application papers. Ours were lost in the mess yesterday. So far, this has been a day I should have slept through.'

'Ditto on this end,' she said.

'What's wrong?'

She told him about the accident and briefly summarized her conversation with Dr. Hannaport.

'It could have been worse,' Paul said. 'At least we can be thankful no one was killed or crippled.'

'That's what everyone keeps telling me: "It could have been worse, Carol." But it seems plenty bad enough to me.'

'Are you all right?'

'Yeah. I told you. I wasn't even scratched.'

'I don't mean physically. I mean, are you together emotionally? You sound shaky.'

'I am. Just a little.'

'I'll come to the hospital,' he said.

'No, no. That's not necessary.'

'Are you sure you should drive?'

'I drove here after the accident without trouble, and I'm feeling better now than I did then. I'll be okay. What I'm going to do is, I'm going over to Grace's house. She's only a mile from here; it's easier than going home. I have to sponge off my clothes, dry them out, and press them. I need a shower, too. I'll probably have an early dinner with Grace, if that's all right by her, and then I'll come back here during visiting hours this evening.'

'When will you be home?'

'Probably not until eight or eight-thirty.'

'I'll miss you.'

'Miss you, too.'

'Give my best to Grace,' he said. 'And tell her I think she *is* the next Nostradamus.'

'What's that supposed to mean?'

'Grace called a while ago. Said she had two nightmares recently, and you figured in both. She was afraid something was going to happen to you.'

'Seriously?'

'Yeah. She was embarrassed about it. Afraid I'd think she was getting senile or something.'

'You told her about the lightning yesterday?'

'Yeah. But she felt something else would happen, something bad.'

'And it did.'

'Creepy, huh?'

'Decidedly,' Carol said. She remembered her own nightmare: the black void; the flashing, silvery object drawing nearer, nearer.

'I'm sure Grace'll tell you all about it,' Paul said. 'And I'll see you this evening.'

'I love you,' Carol said.

'Love you, too.'

She put down the phone and went outside to the parking lot.

Gray-black thunderheads churned across the sky, but only a thin rain was falling now. The wind was still cold and sharp; it sang in the power lines overhead, sounding like a swarm of angry wasps.

* * *

The semiprivate room had two beds, but the second one was not currently in use. At the moment, no nurse was present either. The girl was alone.

She lay under a crisp white sheet and a cream-colored blanket, staring at the acoustic-tile ceiling. She had a headache, and she could feel each dully throbbing, burning cut and abrasion on her battered body, but she knew she was not seriously hurt.

Fear, not pain, was her worst enemy. She was frightened by her inability to remember who she was. On the other hand, she was plagued by the inexplicable yet unshakable feeling that it would be foolish and exceedingly dangerous to remember her past. Without knowing why, she suspected that full remembrance would be the death of her – an odd notion that she found more frightening than anything else.

649

She knew her amnesia wasn't the result of the accident. She had a misty recollection of walking along the street in the rain a minute or two before she had blundered in front of the Volkswagen. Even then, she had been disoriented, afraid, unable to remember her name, utterly unfamiliar with the strange city in which she found herself and unable to recall how she had gotten there. The thread of her memory definitely had begun unraveling prior to the accident.

She wondered if it was possible that her amnesia was like a shield, protecting her from something horrible in the past. Did forgetfulness somehow equal safety?

Why? Safety from what?

What could I be running from? she asked herself.

She sensed that recovery of her identity was possible. In fact her memories seemed almost within her grasp. She felt as though the past lay at the bottom of a dark hole, close enough to touch; all she had to do was summon sufficient strength and courage to poke her hand into that lightless place and grope for the truth, without fear of what might bite her.

However, when she tried hard to remember, when she probed into that hole, her fear grew and grew until it was no longer just ordinary fear; it became incapacitating terror. Her stomach knotted, and her throat swelled tight, and she broke out in a greasy sweat, and she became so dizzy that she nearly fainted.

On the edge of unconsciousness, she saw and heard something disturbing, alarming – a fuzzy fragment of a dream, a vision – which she couldn't quite identify but which frightened her nonetheless. The vision was composed of a single sound and a single, mysterious image. The image was hypnotic but simple: a quick flash of light, a silvery glimmer from a not-quite-visible object that was swinging back and forth in deep shadows; a gleaming pendulum, perhaps. The sound was hard-edged and threatening but not identifiable, a loud hammering noise, yet more than that.

Thunk! Thunk! Thunk!

She jerked, quivered, as if something had struck her.

Thunk!

She wanted to scream, couldn't.

She realized that her hands were fisted and that they were full of twisted, sweat-soaked sheets.

Thunk!

She stopped trying to remember who she was.

Maybe it's better that I don't know, she thought.

650

Her heartbeat gradually slowed to normal, and she was able to draw her breath without wheezing. Her stomach unknotted.

The hammering sound faded.

After a while she looked at the window. A flock of large, black birds reeled across the turbulent sky.

What's going to happen to me? she wondered.

Even when the nurse came in to see how she was doing, and even when the doctor joined the nurse a moment later, the girl felt utterly, dishearteningly alone.

Chapter Five

Grace's kitchen smelled of coffee and warm spice cake. Rain washed down the window, obscuring the view of the rose garden that lay behind the house.

'I've never believed in clairvoyance or premonitions.'

'Neither have I,' Grace said. 'But now I wonder. After all, I have two nightmares about you getting hurt, and the next thing I hear is that you've had two close calls, just as if you were acting out a script or something.'

They sat at the small table by the kitchen window. Carol was wearing one of Grace's robes and a pair of Grace's slippers while her own clothes finished drying out.

'Only *one* close call,' she told Grace. 'The lightning. That was a gut-wrencher, all right. But I wasn't really in any danger this morning. That poor girl was the one who nearly got killed.'

Grace shook her head. 'No. It was a close call for you, too. Didn't you tell me you slid toward the oncoming traffic when you braked to avoid the girl? And didn't you say the Cadillac missed you by an inch or less? Well, what if it *hadn't* missed? If that Caddy had rammed your little VW, you certainly wouldn't have walked away without a scratch.'

Frowning, Carol said, 'I hadn't looked at it that way.'

'You've been so busy worrying about the girl that you haven't had a chance to think about yourself.'

Carol ate a bite of spice cake and washed it down with coffee. 'You're not the only one having nightmares.' She summarized her own dream: the severed heads, the houses that dissolved behind her as she passed through them, the flickering, silvery object.

Grace clasped her hands around her coffee cup and hunched over the table. There was worry in her blue eyes. 'That's one nasty dream. What do you make of it?'

'Oh, I don't think it's prophetic.'

'Why couldn't it be? Mine appear to have been.'

'Yes, but it doesn't follow that both of us are turning into sooth-sayers. Besides, my dream didn't make a whole lot of sense. It was just too wild to be taken seriously. I mean, severed heads that suddenly come to life – that sort of thing isn't really going to happen.'

'It could be prophetic without being *literally* prophetic. I mean, it might be a symbolic warning.'

'Of what?'

'I don't see any easy interpretation of it. But I really think you ought to be extra careful for a while. God, I know I'm starting to sound like a phony gypsy fortune-teller, like Maria Ouspenskya in all those old monster movies from the thirties, but I still don't think you should dismiss it as just an ordinary dream. Especially not after what's already happened.'

* * *

Later, after lunch, as Grace squirted some liquid soap into the sinkful of dirty dishes, she said, 'How's the situation with the adoption agency? Does it look like they'll give you and Paul a child soon?'

Carol hesitated.

Grace glanced at her. 'Something wrong?'

Taking the dish towel from the rack and unfolding it, Carol said, 'No. Not really. O'Brian says we'll be approved. It's a sure thing, he says.'

'But you're still worried about it.'

'A little,' Carol admitted.

'Why?'

'I'm not sure. It's just that . . . I've had this feeling. . . .'

'What feeling?'

'That it won't work out.'

'Why shouldn't it?'

'I can't shake the idea that somebody's trying to stop us from adopting.'

'Who?'

Carol shrugged.

'O'Brian?' Grace asked.

'No, no. He's on our side.'

'Someone on the recommendations committee?'

'I don't know. I don't actually have any evidence of ill will

654

toward Paul and me. I can't point my finger at anyone.'

Grace washed some silverware, put it in the drainage rack, and said, 'You've wanted to adopt for so long that you can't believe it's finally happening, so you're looking for boogeymen where there aren't any.'

'Maybe.'

'You're just spooked because of the lightning yesterday and the accident this morning.'

'Maybe.'

'That's understandable. It spooks me, too. But the adoption will go through as smooth as can be.'

'I hope so,' Carol said. But she thought about the lost set of application forms, and she wondered.

*   *   *

By the time Paul got back from the adoption agency, the rain had stopped, though the wind was still cold and damp.

He got the ladder out of the garage and climbed onto the least slanted portion of the many-angled roof. The wet shingles squeaked under his feet as he moved cautiously across the slope toward the television antenna, which was anchored near a brick chimney.

His legs were rubbery. He suffered from a mild case of acrophobia, a fear that had never become incapacitating because he occasionally forced himself to challenge and overcome it, as he was doing now.

When he reached the chimney, he put a hand against it for support and looked out across the roofs of the neighboring homes. The storm-dark September sky had settled lower, lower, until it appeared to be only six or eight feet above the tallest houses. He felt as if he could raise his arm and rap his knuckles on the bellies of the clouds, eliciting a hard, ironlike *clank*.

He crouched with his back to the chimney and inspected the TV antenna. The brace-plate was held down by four bolts that went through the shingles, either directly into a roof beam or into a stud linking two beams. None of the bolts was missing. None of them was loose. The plate was firmly attached to the house, and the antenna was anchored securely to the plate. The antenna could not possibly have been responsible for the hammering sound that had shaken the house.

*   *   *

After washing the dishes, Grace and Carol went into the study. The room reeked of cat urine and feces. Aristophanes had made his toilet on the seat of the big easy chair.

Stunned, Grace said, 'I don't believe it. Ari *always* uses the litter box like he's supposed to do. He's never done anything like this before.'

'He's always been a fussy cat, hasn't he? Fastidious.'

'Exactly. But now look what he's done. That chair'll have to be reupholstered. I guess I'd better find the silly beast, put his nose to this mess, and give him a good scolding. I don't want this to become a habit, for God's sake.'

They looked in every room, but they couldn't find Aristophanes. Apparently, he had slipped out of the house by way of the pet door in the kitchen.

Returning to the study with Grace, Carol said, 'Earlier, you mentioned something about Ari tearing up a few things.'

Grace winced. 'Yes. I didn't want to have to tell you – but he shredded two of those lovely little needlepoint pillows you made for me. I was sick about it. After all the work you put into those, and then he just –'

'Don't worry about it,' Carol said. 'I'll make you a couple of new pillows. I enjoy doing it. Needlepoint relaxes me. I only asked because I thought maybe, if Ari's been doing a lot of things that're out of character, it might be a sign that he isn't well.'

Grace frowned. 'He *looks* healthy. His coat's glossy, and he's certainly as spry as ever.'

'Animals are like people in some ways. And when a person suddenly starts behaving strangely, that *can* be an indication of a physical malady, anything from a brain tumor to an imbalanced diet.'

'I suppose I ought to take him to the vet.'

Carol said, 'While there's a break in the rain, why don't we go outside and see if we can find him?'

'Wasted effort. When a cat doesn't want to be found, it *won't* be found. Besides, he'll come back by dinnertime. I'll keep him in all night, and take him to the vet's in the morning.' Grace looked at the mess on the easy chair, grimaced, and shook her head. 'This isn't like my Ari,' she said worriedly. 'It's just not like him at all.'

* * *

The number on the open door was 316.

Hesitantly, Carol stepped into the white and blue hospital room and stopped just past the threshold. The place smelled vaguely of Lysol.

The girl was sitting up in the bed nearer the window, her face averted from the door, staring out at the twilight-shrouded hospital grounds. She turned her head when she realized she was no longer alone, and when she looked at Carol there was no recognition in her blue-gray eyes.

'May I come in?' Carol asked.

'Sure.'

Carol went to the foot of the bed. 'How are you feeling?'

'Okay.'

'With all the scrapes and cuts and bruises, it must be hard to get comfortable.'

'Gee, I'm not banged up all that bad. I'm just a little sore. It's nothing that's going to kill me. Everyone's so nice; you're all making too much of a fuss about me.'

'How's your head feel?'

'I had a headache when I first came to, but it's been gone for hours.'

'Double vision?'

'Nothing like that,' the girl said. A strand of golden hair slipped from behind her ear and fell across her cheek; she tucked it back in place. 'Are you a doctor?'

'Yes,' Carol said. 'My name's Carol Tracy.'

'You can call me Jane. That's the name on my chart. Jane Doe. I guess it's as good as any. It might even turn out to be a lot nicer than my real name. Maybe I'm actually Zelda or Myrtle or something like that.' She had a lovely smile. 'You're the umpteenth doctor who's been in to see me. How many do I have, anyway?'

'I'm not one of yours,' Carol said. 'I'm here because . . . well . . . it was my car you stepped in front of.'

'Oh. Hey, gee, I'm awfully sorry. I hope there wasn't a lot of damage.'

Surprised by the girl's statement and by the genuine look of concern on her face, Carol laughed. 'For heaven's sake, honey, don't worry about my car. It's your health that's important, not the VW. And *I'm* the one who should be apologizing. I feel terrible about this.'

'You shouldn't,' the girl said. 'I still have all my teeth, and none of my bones are broken, and Dr. Hannaport says the boys will still be interested in me.' She grinned self-consciously.

'He's certainly right about the boys,' Carol said. 'You're a very pretty girl.'

The grin became a shy smile, and the girl looked down at the covers on her lap, blushing.

Carol said, 'I was hoping I'd find you here with your folks.'

The girl tried to maintain a cheerful facade, but when she looked up, fear and doubt showed through the mask. 'I guess they haven't filed a missing-persons report yet. But it's only a matter of time.'

'Have you remembered anything at all about your past?'

'Not yet. But I will.' She straightened the collar of her hospital gown and smoothed the covers over her lap as she talked. 'Dr. Hannaport says everything'll probably come back to me if I just don't push too hard at remembering. He says I'm lucky I don't have global amnesia. That's when you even forget how to read and write. I'm not *that* bad off! Heck, no. Boy, wouldn't that be something? What if I had to learn to read, write, add, subtract, multiply, divide, and spell all over again? What a bore!' She finished smoothing her covers and looked up again. 'Anyway, I'll most likely have my memory back in a day or two.'

'I'm sure you will,' Carol said, though she wasn't sure at all. 'Is there anything you need?'

'No. They supply everything. Even tiny tubes of toothpaste.'

'What about books, magazines?'

The girl sighed. 'I was bored out of my skull this afternoon. You think they might keep a pile of old magazines for the patients?'

'Probably. What do you like to read?'

'Everything. I *love* to read; I remember that much. But I can't remember the titles of any books or magazines. This amnesia sure is funny, isn't it?'

'Hilarious,' Carol said. 'Sit tight. I'll be right back.'

At the nurses' station at the end of the hall, she explained who she was and arranged to rent a small television set for Jane Doe's room. An orderly promised to hook it up right away.

The chief RN on duty – a stocky, gray-haired woman who wore her glasses on a chain around her neck – said, 'She's such a sweet girl. She's charmed everyone. Hasn't complained or uttered a cross word to a soul. There aren't many teenagers with her composure.'

Carol took the elevator down to the ground-floor lobby and went to the newsstand. She bought a Hershey bar, an Almond Joy, and six magazines that looked as if they would appeal to a young girl. By the time she got back to room 316, the orderly had just finished installing the TV.

'You shouldn't have done all this,' the girl said. 'When my parents show up, I'll make sure they pay you back.'

'I won't accept a dime,' Carol said.

'But –'

'No buts.'

'I don't need to be pampered. I'm fine. Really. If you –'

'I'm not pampering you, honey. Just think of the magazines and the television as forms of therapy. In fact, they might be precisely the tools you need to break through this amnesia.'

'What do you mean?'

'Well, if you watch enough television, you might see a show you remember seeing before. That might spark a sort of chain reaction of memories.'

'You think so?'

'It's better than just sitting and staring at the walls or out the window. Nothing in this place is going to spark a memory because none of it is related to your past. But there's a chance the TV will do the trick.'

The girl picked up the remote-control device that the orderly had given her, and she switched on the television set. A popular situation comedy was on.

'Familiar?' Carol asked.

The girl shook her head: no. Tears glistened in the corners of her eyes.

'Hey, don't get upset,' Carol said. 'It would be amazing if you remembered the first thing you saw. It's bound to take time.'

She nodded and bit her lip, trying not to cry.

Carol moved close, took the girl's hand; it was cool.

'Will you come back tomorrow?' Jane asked shakily.

'Of course I will.'

'I mean, if it's not out of your way.'

'It's no trouble at all.'

'Sometimes . . .'

'What?'

The girl shuddered. 'Sometimes I'm so afraid.'

'Don't be afraid, honey. Please don't. It'll all work out. You'll see. You're going to be back on the track in no time,' Carol said, wishing she could think of something more reassuring than those few hollow platitudes. But she knew her inadequate response was occasioned by her own nagging doubts.

The girl pulled a tissue out of the Kleenex dispenser that was built into the side of the tall metal nightstand. She blew her nose, used another tissue to daub at her eyes. She had slumped down in the bed; now she sat up straight, lifted her chin, squared her slender shoulders, and readjusted her covers. When she looked up at Carol, she was smiling again. 'Sorry,' she said. 'I don't know what got into me. Being a crybaby isn't going to solve anything. Anyway, you're right. My folks will probably show up tomorrow, and everything'll work out for the best. Look, Dr. Tracy, if you come to see me tomorrow –'

'I will.'

'If you do, promise not to bring me any more candy or magazines or anything. Okay? There's no reason for you to spend your money like that. You've already done too much for me. Besides, the best thing you could do is just come. I mean, it's nice to know someone outside the hospital cares about me. It's nice to know I haven't been lost or forgotten in here. Oh, sure, the nurses and the doctors are swell. They really are, and I'm grateful. They care about me, but it's sort of their job to care. You know? So that's not exactly the same thing, is it?' She laughed nervously. 'Am I making sense?'

'I know exactly what you're feeling,' Carol assured her. She was achingly aware of the girl's profound loneliness, for she had been lonely and frightened when she was the same age, before Grace Mitowski had taken custody of her and had given her large measures of guidance and love.

She stayed with Jane until visiting hours were over. Before she left, she planted a motherly kiss on the girl's forehead, and it seemed like a perfectly natural thing to do. A bond had formed between them in a surprisingly short time.

Outside, in the hospital parking lot, the sodium-vapor lights leached the true colors from the cars and made them all look yellowish.

The night was chilly. No rain had fallen during the afternoon or evening, but the air was heavy, damp. Thunder rumbled in the distance, and a new storm appeared to be on the way.

She sat for a moment behind the wheel of the VW, staring up at the third-floor window of the girl's room.

'What a terrific kid,' she said aloud.

She felt that someone quite special had come unexpectedly into her life.

* * *

Near midnight, a river-cold wind came out of the west and made the trees dance. The starless, moonless, utterly lightless night pressed close around the house and seemed to Grace to be a living thing; it snuffled at the doors and windows.

Rain began to fall.

She went to bed as the hall clock was striking twelve, and twenty minutes later she began to drift over the edge of sleep as if she were a leaf borne by cool currents toward a great waterfall. On the brink, with only darkness churning under her, she heard movement in the bedroom and instantly came awake again.

A series of stealthy sounds. A soft scrape. A rattle that died even as it began. A silken rustle.

She sat up, heart quickening, and opened the nightstand drawer. With one hand she felt blindly for the .22 pistol she kept in the drawer, and with the other hand she groped silently for the lamp switch. She touched the gun and lamp at the same moment.

With light, the source of the noise was clearly visible. Ari was crouched atop the highboy, staring down at her, as if he had been about to spring onto the bed.

'What are you doing in here? You know the rules.'

He blinked but didn't move. His muscles were bunched and taut; his fur was standing up on the back of his neck.

For sanitary reasons, she would allow him to climb neither onto the kitchen counters nor into her bed; generally, she kept the master bedroom door firmly shut, day and night, rather than tempt him. Already, housecleaning required extra hours each week because of him, for she was determined that the air should not contain even the slightest trace of cat odor; likewise, she was not about to subject her visitors to furniture covered with loose animal hairs. She loved Ari, and she thought him fine company, and for the most part she gave him the run of the house in spite of the extra work he caused her. But she was not prepared to live with cat hairs in her food or in her sheets.

She got out of bed, stepped into her slippers.

Ari watched.

'Come down from there this instant,' Grace said, looking up at him with her sternest expression.

His shining eyes were gas-flame blue.

Grace went to the bedroom door, opened it, stepped out of the way, and said, 'Shoo.'

The cat's muscles relaxed. He slumped in a furry puddle atop the highboy, as if his bones had melted. He yawned and began to lick one of his black paws.

'Hey!' she said.

Aristophanes raised his head languidly, peered down at her.

'Out,' she said gruffly. 'Now.'

When he still didn't move, she started toward the highboy, and he was at last encouraged to obey. He jumped down and darted past her so fast she didn't have time to swat him. He went into the hall, and she closed the door.

In bed again, with the lights out, she remembered the way he had looked as he perched atop the highboy: facing her, *aimed* at her, shoulders drawn up, head held low, haunches tense, his fur electrified, his eyes bright and slightly demented. He had intended to jump onto the bed and scare the bejesus out of her; there was no doubt about that. But such schemes were a kitten's games; Ari had not been playful in that fashion for the past three or four years, ever since he had attained a rather indolent maturity. What on earth had gotten into him?

That settles it, she told herself. We'll pay a visit to the veterinarian first thing in the morning. Good Lord, I might have a schizophrenic cat on my hands!

Seeking rest, she let the night embrace her again. She allowed herself to be carried along by the riverlike sound of the soughing wind. Within a few minutes she was once more being borne toward the waterfall of sleep. She trembled on the edge of it, and a quiver of uneasiness passed through her, a chill that nearly broke the spell, but then she dropped down into darkness.

She dreamed that she was trekking across a vast underwater landscape of brilliantly colored coral and seaweed and strange, undulating plants. A cat lurked among the plants, a big one, much bigger than a tiger, but with the coloring of a Siamese. It was stalking her. She could see its saucer eyes peering at her through the murky sea, from among wavering stalks of marine vegetation. She could hear and feel its low purr transmitted by the water. She paused repeatedly during her suboceanic trek so that she could fill a series of yellow bowls with generous portions of Meow Mix in the hope of pacifying the cat, but she knew in her heart that the beast would not be content until it had sunk its claws into her. She moved steadily past towers of coral, past grottoes, across wide aquatic plains of shifting sand, waiting for the cat to snarl and lunge from concealment, waiting for it to rip open her face and gouge out her eyes. . . .

Once, she woke and thought she heard Aristophanes scratching insistently on the other side of the closed bedroom door. But she was groggy and couldn't trust her senses; she wasn't able to wrench herself fully awake, and in a few seconds she sank down into the dream once more.

*   *   *

At one o'clock in the morning, the third floor of the hospital was so quiet that Harriet Gilbey, the head nurse on the graveyard shift, felt as though she was deep underground, in some kind of military complex, tucked into the stony roots of a mountain, far from the real world and the background noises of real life. The only sounds were the whisper of the heating system and the occasional squeak of the nurses' rubber-soled shoes on the highly polished tile floors.

Harriet – a small, pretty, neatly uniformed black woman – was at the nurses' station, around the corner from the bank of elevators, entering data on patients' charts, when the tranquility of the third floor was abruptly shattered by a piercing scream. She moved out from behind the reception desk and hurried along the hall, following the shrill cry. It came from room 316. When Harriet pushed open the door, stepped into the room, and snapped on the overhead lights, the screaming stopped as suddenly as it had begun.

The girl they called Jane Doe was in bed, flat on her back, one arm raised and angled across her face as if she were warding off a blow, the other hand hooked on to one of the safety rails. She had kicked the sheets and the blanket into a tangled wad at the foot of the bed, and her hospital gown was rucked up over her hips. She tossed her head violently from side to side, gasping, pleading with an imaginary assailant: 'No . . . no . . . no. Don't! Please don't kill me! *No!*'

With gentle hands, a gentle voice, and patient insistence, Harriet tried to quiet the girl. At first Jane resisted all ministrations. She had been given a sedative earlier. Now she was having trouble waking up. Gradually, however, she shook off the nightmare and calmed down.

Another nurse, Kay Hamilton, appeared at Harriet's side. 'What happened? Must've woke up half the floor.'

'Just a bad dream,' Harriet said.

Jane blinked sleepily at them. 'She was trying to kill me.'

'Hush now,' Harriet said. 'It was only a dream. No one here will hurt you.'

'A dream?' Jane asked, her voice slurred. 'Oh. Yeah. Just a dream. Whew! What a dream.'

The girl's thin white gown and the tangled sheets were damp with perspiration. Harriet and Kay replaced them with fresh linens.

As soon as the bed had been changed, Jane succumbed to the lingering tug of the sedative. She turned onto her side and murmured happily in her sleep; she even smiled.

'Looks like she switched to a better channel,' Harriet said.

'Poor kid. After what she's been through, the least she deserves is a good night's sleep.'

They watched her for a minute, then left the room, turning off the lights and closing the door.

*　　*　　*

Alone, deep in sleep, transported into a different dream from the one that had elicited her screams, Jane sighed, smiled, giggled quietly.

'The ax,' she whispered in her sleep. 'The ax. Oh, the ax. Yes. Yes.'

Her hands curled slightly, as if she were clutching a solid but invisible object.

'The ax,' she whispered, and the second of those two words reverberated softly through the dark room.

*　　*　　*

Thunk!

Carol ran through the huge living room, across the oriental carpet, banging her hip against the edge of the credenza.

Thunk! Thunk!

She dashed through the archway, into a long hall, headed toward the stairs that led to the second floor. When she glanced behind her, she saw that the house had vanished in her wake and had been replaced by a pitch-black void in which something silvery flickered back and forth, back and forth. . . .

Thunk!

Understanding came with a flash; she knew what the glimmering object was. An ax. The blade of an ax. Glinting as it swung from side to side.

Thunk . . . thunk-thunk . . .

Whimpering, she climbed the stairs toward the second floor.

Thunk . . . thunk . . .

At times the blade seemed to be biting into wood; the sound of it was dry, splintery. But at other times the sound had a subtly different quality, as if the blade were slicing brutally into a substance much softer than wood, into something wet and tender.

Into flesh?

Thunk!

Carol groaned in her sleep, turned restlessly, flinging off the sheets.

Then she was running across the high meadow. The trees ahead. The void behind. And the ax. The ax.

Chapter Six

Friday morning, there was another break in the rain, but the day was dressed in fog. The light coming through the hospital window was wintry, bleak.

Jane had only a hazy recollection of the nurses changing her sheets and her sweat-soaked bed gown during the night. She vaguely recalled having a frightening dream, too, but she couldn't bring to mind a single detail of it.

She was still unable to remember her name or anything else about herself. She could cast her mind back as far as the accident yesterday morning, perhaps even to a point a minute or so on the other side of the accident, but beyond that there was only a blank wall where her past should have been.

During breakfast, she read an article in one of the magazines that Carol Tracy had bought for her. Although there were no visiting hours until this afternoon, Jane was already looking forward to seeing the woman again. Dr. Hannaport and the nurses were nice, every one of them, but none of them affected her as positively as Carol Tracy did. For reasons she could not understand, she felt more secure, more at ease, less frightened by her amnesia when she was with Dr. Tracy than when she was with the others. Maybe that was what people meant when they said a doctor had a good bedside manner.

* * *

Shortly after nine o'clock, when Paul was on the freeway, headed downtown to deliver the new set of application papers to Alfred O'Brian's office, the Pontiac's engine cut out. It didn't sputter or cough; the pistons simply stopped firing while the car was hurtling along at nearly fifty miles an hour. As the Pontiac's speed plummeted, its power steering began to freeze up. Traffic whizzed

667

past on both sides at sixty and sixty-five, faster than the speed limit, too fast for the misty weather. Paul maneuvered the car across two lanes, toward the right-hand shoulder of the road. Second by second, he expected to hear a short squeal of brakes and feel the sickening impact of another car against his, but amazingly, he was able to avoid a collision. Wrestling with the stiffening steering wheel, he brought the Pontiac to a full stop on the berm.

He leaned back in his seat and closed his eyes until he had regained his composure. When at last he leaned forward and twisted the key in the ignition, the starter didn't make the slightest response; the battery had no juice to offer. He tried a few more times, then gave up.

A freeway exit was just ahead, and there was a service station less than a block from the off-ramp. Paul walked to it in ten minutes.

The station was busy, and the owner couldn't spare his young assistant – a big, redheaded, open-faced kid named Corky – until the stream of customers subsided to a trickle shortly before ten o'clock. Then Paul and Corky rode back to the crippled Pontiac in a tow truck.

They tried jump-starting the car, but the battery wouldn't hold a charge. The Pontiac had to be towed back to the station.

Corky intended to replace the battery and have the car running in half an hour. But it wasn't the battery after all, and the estimated time for completion of the repairs was extended again and again. Finally, Corky found a problem with the electrical system and fixed it.

Paul was stranded for three hours, always sure he would be on his way in just another twenty or thirty minutes. But it was one-thirty when he finally parked the revitalized Pontiac in front of the adoption agency's offices.

Alfred O'Brian came out to the reception lounge to greet Paul. He was wearing a well-tailored brown suit, a neatly pressed, cream-colored shirt, a neatly arranged, beige display handkerchief in the breast pocket of his suit jacket, and a pair of neatly shined, brown wing-tip shoes. He accepted the application, but he wasn't optimistic about the possibility of making all the required verifications prior to the recommendations committee's meeting next Wednesday morning.

'We'll try to do a rush job on your papers,' he told Paul. 'I owe you that much at least! But in getting these verifications, we have to deal with people outside this office, and some of them won't get back to us right away or won't like being hurried. It always takes a minimum of three full business days to run a complete verification, sometimes four or five days, sometimes even longer, so I very much doubt that we'll be ready for this session of the recommendations committee, even though I want to be. We'll probably have to submit your application at the second September meeting, at the end of the month. I feel terrible about that, Mr. Tracy. I'm more sorry than I can say. I truly am. If we hadn't lost those papers in the turmoil yesterday –'

'Don't worry about it,' Paul said. 'The lightning wasn't your doing, and neither was the problem with my car. Carol and I have waited a long, long time to adopt a child. Another two weeks isn't much in the scheme of things.'

'When your papers *are* presented to the committee, you'll be approved quickly,' O'Brian said. 'I've never been more sure about a couple than I am about you. That's what I'm going to tell them.'

'I appreciate that,' Paul said.

'If we can't make Wednesday's meeting – and I assure you we'll try our best – then it's only a minor, temporary setback. Nothing to be concerned about. Just a bit of bad luck.'

*   *   *

Dr. Brad Templeton was a fine veterinarian. However, to Grace, he always looked out of place when he was ministering to a cat or dog. He was a big man who would have looked more at home treating horses and farm animals in a country practice, where his massive shoulders and muscular arms would be of more use. He stood six-five, weighed about two hundred and twenty pounds, and had a ruddy, rugged, but pleasing face. When he plucked Aristophanes out of the padded travel basket, the cat looked like a toy in his enormous hands.

'He looks fit,' Brad said, putting Ari on the stainless-steel table that stood in the middle of the sparkling clean surgery.

'He's never been one to tear up the furniture, not since he was just a kitten,' Grace said. 'He's never been a climber, either. But now, every time I turn around, he's perched on top of something, peering down at me.'

Brad examined Ari, feeling for swollen glands and enlarged joints. The cat cooperated docilely, even when Brad used a rectal thermometer on him. 'Temperature's normal.'

'*Something's* wrong,' Grace insisted.

669

Aristophanes purred, rolled onto his back, asking for his belly to be rubbed.

Brad rubbed him and was rewarded with an even louder purr. 'Is he off his food?'

'No,' Grace said. 'He stills eats well.'

'Vomiting?'

'No.'

'Diarrhea?'

'No. He hasn't shown any symptoms like those. It's just that he's . . . different. He's not at all like he was. Every symptom I can point to is a symptom of a *personality* change, not an indication of physical deterioration. Like destroying the pillows. Leaving the mess on the armchair. The sudden interest he's taken in climbing. And he's gotten very sneaky lately, always creeping around, hiding from me, watching me when he thinks I don't see him.'

'All cats are a bit sneaky,' Brad said, frowning. 'That's the nature of the beast.'

'Ari didn't used to sneak,' Grace said. 'Not like he's been doing the last couple of days. And he's not as friendly as he used to be. The last two days, he hasn't wanted to be petted or cuddled.'

Still frowning, Brad lifted his gaze from the cat and met Grace's eyes. 'But, dear, look at him.'

Ari was still on his back, getting his belly rubbed, and clearly relishing all the attention being directed at him. His tail swished back and forth across the steel table. He raised one paw and batted playfully at the doctor's large, leathery hand.

Sighing, Grace said, 'I know what you're thinking. I'm an old woman. Old women get funny ideas.'

'No, no, no. I wasn't thinking any such thing.'

'Old women become obsessively attached to their pets because sometimes their pets are the only company they have, their only real friends.'

'I am perfectly aware that doesn't apply to you, Grace. Not with all the friends you've got in this town. I merely –'

She smiled and patted his cheek. 'Don't protest too strongly, Brad. I know what's going through your mind. Some old women are so afraid of losing their pets that they think they see signs of illness where there are none. Your reaction is understandable. It doesn't offend me. It *does* frustrate me because I know something *is* wrong with Ari.'

Brad looked down at the cat again, continued stroking its

belly, and said, 'Have you changed his diet in any way?'

'No. He gets the same brand of cat food, at the same times of day, in the same quantities he's always gotten it.'

'Has the company changed the product recently?'

'How do you mean?'

'Well, does the package say "new, improved," or "richer flavor," or anything like that?'

She thought about it for a moment, then shook her head. 'I don't think so.'

'Sometimes, when they change a formula, they add a new preservative or a new artificial flavoring or coloring agent, and some pets have an allergic reaction to it.'

'But wouldn't that be a physical reaction? Like I said, this seems to be strictly a personality change.'

Brad nodded. 'I'm sure you know food additives can cause behavioral problems in some children. A lot of hyperactive kids calm down when they're put on a diet free of the major additives. Animals can be affected by these things, too. From what you've told me, it sounds like Aristophanes is intermittently hyperactive and may be responding to a subtle change in the formulation of his cat food. Switch him to another brand, wait a week for his system to purge itself of whatever additives have offended it, and he'll probably be the old Ari again.'

'If he isn't?'

'Then bring him in, leave him with me for a couple of days, and I'll give him a really thorough going over. But I strongly recommend that we try changing his diet first, before we go to all that trouble and expense.'

You *are* humoring me, Grace thought. Just coddling an old lady.

'Very well,' she said. 'I'll try changing his food. But if he's still not himself a week from now, I'll want you to give him a complete battery of tests.'

'Of course.'

'I'll want an answer.'

On the stainless-steel table, Aristophanes purred, happily twitched his long tail, and looked infuriatingly *normal*.

*　　*　　*

Later, at home, just inside the front door, when Grace slipped the latch on the padded travel basket and opened the lid, Aristophanes exploded out of confinement with a hiss and a snarl, his fur bristling, his ears laid back against his head, eyes wild. He clawed her hand and squealed as she thrust him away from her. He sprinted down the hall, disappeared into the kitchen, where the pet door gave him access to the rear yard.

Shocked, Grace stared at her hand. Ari's claws had made three short furrows in the meaty edge of her palm. Blood welled up and began to trickle down her wrist.

*　　*　　*

Carol's last appointment on Friday was at one o'clock: a fifty-minute session with Kathy Lombino, a fifteen-year-old girl who was gradually recovering from anorexia nervosa. Five months ago, when she had first been brought to Carol, Kathy had weighed only seventy-five pounds, at least thirty pounds below her ideal weight. She had been teetering on the edge of starvation, repelled by the sight and even the thought of food, stubbornly refusing to eat more than an occasional soda cracker or slice of bread, often gagging on even those bland morsels. When she was put in front of a mirror and forced to confront the pathetic sight of her emaciated body, she still berated herself for being fat and could not be convinced that she was, in fact, frighteningly thin. Her prospects for survival had seemed slight. Now she weighed ninety pounds, up fifteen, still well below a healthy weight for a girl of her height and bone structure, but at least she was no longer in danger of dying. A loss of self-respect and self-confidence was nearly always the seed from which anorexia nervosa grew, and Kathy was beginning to like herself again, a sure sign that she was on her way back from the brink. She hadn't yet regained a normal appetite; she still experienced mild revulsion at the sight and taste of food; but her attitude was far better than it had been, for now she recognized the *need* for food, even though she didn't have any desire for it. The girl had a long way to go before she would be fully recovered, but the worst was past for her; in time she would learn to enjoy food again, and she would gain weight more rapidly than she had done thus far, stabilizing around a hundred and five or a hundred and ten pounds. Kathy's progress had been immensely satisfying to Carol, and today's session only added to that satisfaction. As had become customary, she and the girl hugged each other at the end of the session, and Kathy held on tighter and longer than usual. When the girl left the office, she was smiling.

A few minutes later, at two o'clock, Carol went to the hospital. In the gift shop off the lobby, she bought a deck of playing cards and a miniature checkerboard with nickle-sized checkers that all fit neatly into a vinyl carrying case.

Upstairs, in 316, the television was on, and Jane was reading a magazine. She looked up when Carol entered, and she said, 'You really came.'

'Said I would, didn't I?'

'What've you got?'

'Cards, checkers. I thought maybe they'd help you pass the time.'

'You promised you wouldn't buy me anything else.'

'Hey, did I say I was *giving* these to you? No way. You think I'm a soft touch or something? I'm *lending* them, kid. I expect them back. And whenever you return them, they'd better be in as good condition as they are now, or I'll take you all the way to the Supreme Court to get compensated for the damage.'

Jane grinned. 'Boy, you're tough.'

'I eat nails for breakfast.'

'Don't they get stuck in your teeth?'

'I pluck 'em out with pliers.'

'Ever eat barbed wire?'

'Never for breakfast. I have it for lunch now and then.'

They both laughed, and Carol said, 'So do you play checkers?'

'I don't know. I don't remember.'

'Cards?'

The girl shrugged.

'Nothing's come back yet?' Carol asked.

'Not a thing.'

'Don't worry. It will.'

'My folks haven't shown up, either.'

'Well, you've only been missing for one day. Give them time to find you. It's too soon to start worrying about that.'

They played three games of checkers. Jane remembered all of the rules, but she couldn't recall where or with whom she had played before.

The afternoon passed quickly, and Carol enjoyed every minute of it. Jane was charming, bright, and blessed with a good sense of humor. Whether the game was checkers, hearts, or five-hundred rummy, she played to win, but she never pouted when she lost. She was very good company.

The girl's charm and pleasing personality made it highly

unlikely that she would go unclaimed for long. Some teenagers are so self-centered, spaced out on drugs, bullheaded, and destructive that when one of them decides to run away from home, his decision often elicits only a sigh of relief from his mother and father. But when a good kid like Jane Doe disappears, a lot of people start sounding alarms.

There must be a family that loves her, Carol thought. They're probably crazy with worry right now. Sooner or later they'll turn up, crying and laughing with relief that their girl has been found alive. So why not sooner? Where *are* they?

* * *

The doorbell rang at precisely three-thirty. Paul answered it and found a pallid, gray-eyed man of about fifty. He wore gray slacks, a pale gray shirt, and a dark gray sweater.

'Mr. Tracy?'

'Yes. Are you from Safe Homes?'

'That's right,' the gray man said. 'Name's Bill Alsgood. I *am* Safe Homes. Started the company two years ago.'

They shook hands, and Alsgood entered the foyer, looking with interest at the interior of the house. 'Lovely place. You're lucky to get same-day service. Usually, I'm scheduled three days in advance. But when you called this morning and said it was an emergency, I'd just had a cancellation.'

'You're a building inspector?' Paul asked, closing the door.

'Structural engineer, to be precise. What our company does is inspect the house before it's sold, usually on behalf of the buyer, at his expense. We tell him if he's buying into a heartache of any sort – a leaky roof, a cellar that floods, a crumbling foundation, faulty wiring, bad plumbing, that kind of thing. We're fully bonded, so even if we overlook something, our client is protected. Are you the buyer or the seller?'

'Neither,' Paul said. 'My wife and I own the place, but we aren't ready to sell it. We're having a problem with the house, and I can't pinpoint the cause of it. I thought you might be able to help.'

Alsgood raised one gray eyebrow. 'May I suggest that what you need is a good handyman. He'd be considerably cheaper, and once he'd found the trouble, he could fix it, too. We don't do any repair work, you know. We only inspect.'

'I'm aware of that. I'm pretty handy myself, but I haven't

figured out what's wrong or how to fix it. I think I need the kind of expert advice that no handyman can give me.'

'You *do* know we charge two hundred and fifty dollars for an inspection?'

'I know,' Paul said. 'But this is an extremely annoying problem, and it might be causing serious structural damage.'

'What is it?'

Paul told him about the hammering sounds that occasionally shook the house.

'That's peculiar as hell,' Alsgood said. 'I've never heard a complaint like it before.' He thought for a moment, then said, 'Where's your furnace?'

'In the cellar.'

'Maybe it's a heating duct problem. Unlikely. But we can start down there and work our way up to the roof until we've found the cause.'

For the next two hours, Alsgood looked into every cranny of the house, poked and probed and rapped and visually inspected every inch of the interior, then every inch of the roof, while Paul tagged along, assisting wherever he could. A light rain began to fall when they were still on the roof, and they were both soaked by the time they finished the job and climbed down. Alsgood's left foot slipped off the last rung of the ladder, just as he was about to step onto the water-logged lawn, and he twisted his ankle painfully. All that risk and inconvenience was for nothing because Alsgood didn't find anything out of the ordinary.

At five-thirty, in the kitchen, they warmed up with coffee while Alsgood filled out his report. Wet and bedraggled, he looked even more pallid than when Paul had first seen him. The rain had transformed his gray clothes – once a variety of shades – into a single, dull hue, so that he appeared to be wearing a drab uniform. 'It's basically a solid house, Mr. Tracy. The condition is really topnotch.'

'Then where the devil did that sound come from? And why was the whole house shaken by it?'

'I wish I'd heard it.'

'I was sure it'd start up at least once while you were here.'

Alsgood sipped his coffee, but the warm brew added no color to his cheeks. 'Structurally, there's not a thing wrong with this house. That's what my report will say, and I'd stake my reputation on it.'

'Which puts me right back at square one,' Paul said, folding his hands around his coffee cup.

'I'm sorry you spent all this money without getting an answer,' Alsgood said. 'I really feel bad about that.'

'It isn't your fault. I'm convinced you did a thorough job. In fact, if I ever buy another house, I'll definitely want you to inspect it first. At least I now know the trouble isn't structural, which rules out possibilities and narrows the field of inquiry.'

'Maybe you won't even hear it again. It might stop just as suddenly as it started.'

'Somehow, I suspect you're wrong about that,' Paul said.

Later, at the front door, as Alsgood was leaving, he said, 'One thought has occurred to me, but I hesitate to mention it.'

'Why?'

'You might think it's off the wall.'

'Mr. Alsgood, I'm a desperate man. I'm willing to consider anything, no matter how farfetched it might be.'

Alsgood looked at the ceiling, then at the floor, then back along the hall that lay behind Paul, then down at his own feet. 'A ghost,' he said quietly.

Paul stared at him, surprised.

Alsgood cleared his throat nervously, shifted his eyes to the floor again, then finally raised them and met Paul's gaze. 'Maybe you don't believe in ghosts.'

'Do you?' Paul asked.

'Yes. I've been interested in the subject most of my life. I have a large collection of publications dealing with spiritualism of all sorts. I've had some personal experiences in haunted houses, too.'

'You've seen a ghost?'

'I believe I have, yes, on four occasions. Ectoplasmic apparitions. Insubstantial, manlike shapes drifting in the air. I've also twice witnessed poltergeist phenomena. As far as this house is concerned . . .' His voice trailed away, and he licked his lips nervously. 'If you find this boring or preposterous, I don't want to waste your time.'

'Quite frankly,' Paul said, 'I can't picture myself calling an exorcist in to deal with this. But I'm not entirely close-minded where ghosts are concerned. I find it hard to accept, but I'm certainly willing to listen.'

'Reasonable enough,' Alsgood said. For the first time since he had rung the doorbell more than two hours ago, color rose into his milky complexion, and his watery eyes brightened with a spark of enthusiasm. 'All right. Here's something to consider. From what you've told me, I'd say there might be a poltergeist at work here. Of course, no objects have been hurled around by an unseen presence; there's been no breakage, and poltergeists dearly love to break things. But the shaking of the house, the clattering pots and pans, the little bottles clinking against one another in the spice rack – those are all indications of a poltergeist at work, one that's just beginning to test its powers. If it *is* a poltergeist, then you can expect worse to come. Oh, yes. Definitely. Furniture moving across the floor all by itself. Pictures flung off the walls, lamps knocked down and broken. Dishes flying around the room as if they were birds.' His wan countenance flushed with excitement as he considered the supernatural destruction. 'Levitations of heavy objects like sofas and beds and refrigerators. Now mind you, there *are* some recorded cases of people being plagued by *benign* poltergeists that don't break much of anything, but the overwhelming number of them are malign, and that's what you'll most likely have to deal with – if indeed you've got one here at all.' Having warmed to his subject, he finished in an almost breathless rush of words: 'In its most active form, even a benign poltergeist can completely disrupt a household, interfere with your sleep, and keep you so on edge that you don't know whether you're coming or going.'

Startled by Alsgood's passionately delivered speech and by the odd new light in the man's eyes, Paul said, 'Well . . . uh . . . it's really not that bad. Not nearly that bad. Just a hammering sound and –'

'It's not that bad *yet*,' Alsgood said somberly. 'But if you have a poltergeist here, the situation could deteriorate rapidly. If you've never seen one in action, Mr. Tracy, you simply can't understand what it's like.'

Paul was disconcerted by the change in the man. He felt as if he had opened the door to one of those wholesome-looking types who turned out to be pushing crackpot religious pamphlets and who proclaimed the imminence of Judgment Day in the same bubbly, upbeat tone of voice that Donny Osmond might use to introduce his cute little sister, Marie, to a panting audience of Osmond fans. There was a disquieting zeal in Alsgood's manner.

'If it *does* turn out to be a poltergeist,' Alsgood said, 'if things *do* get a lot worse, will you call me right away? I've been fortunate enough to observe two poltergeists, as I said. I'd like nothing better than to see a third going through its tricks. The opportunity doesn't arise very often.'

'I guess not,' Paul said.

'So you'll call me?'

'I very much doubt there's a poltergeist involved here, Mr. Alsgood. If I keep looking long enough and hard enough, I'll find a perfectly logical explanation for what's been happening. But on the off-chance that it *is* a malign spirit, rest assured I'll give you a call the moment the first refrigerator or chiffonier levitates.'

Alsgood wasn't able to see anything amusing about their conversation. He frowned when he detected levity in Paul's voice, and he said, 'I didn't really expect you to take me seriously.'

'Oh, please don't think I'm not grateful for –'

'No, no,' Alsgood said, waving him to silence. 'I understand. No offense taken.' The excitement had gone out of his watery eyes. 'You've been raised to believe strictly in science. You've been taught to put your faith only in things that can be seen and touched and measured. That's the modern way.' His shoulders slumped. The color in his face faded, and his skin became pale, grayish, and slack, as it had been a few minutes ago. 'Asking you to be open-minded about ghosts is as pointless as trying to convince a deep-sea creature that there are such things as birds. It's sad but true, and I have no reason to be angry about it.' He opened the front door, and the sound of the rain grew louder. 'Anyway, for your sake, I hope it isn't a poltergeist you've got here. I hope you find that logical explanation you're looking for. I really do, Mr. Tracy.'

Before Paul could respond, Alsgood turned and walked out into the rain. He no longer seemed like a zealot; there was no trace of passion in him. He was just a thin, gray man, shuffling through the gray mist, head slightly bowed against the gray rain, illuminated by the gray light of the storm; he almost seemed like a ghost himself.

Paul closed the door, put his back against it, and looked around the hall, through the nearest archway, which opened onto the living room. Poltergeist? Not very damned likely.

He preferred Alsgood's other suggestion: that the hammering might simply stop as suddenly and inexplicably as it had started, without the cause ever being known.

He glanced at his watch. 6:06.

Carol had said she would remain at the hospital until eight o'clock and would then come home for a late meal. That gave him an hour or so to work on his novel before he had to start cooking dinner – broiled chicken breasts, steamed vegetables, and rice with bits of green pepper.

He went upstairs to his office and sat down at the typewriter. He picked up the last page he had written, intending to reread it a few times and get back into the mood and tone of the story he was telling.

THUNK! THUNK!

The house shook. The windows rattled.

He bolted up from his chair.

THUNK!

On his desk, the jar full of pens and pencils toppled over, cracked into several pieces, and spilled its contents onto the floor.

Silence.

He waited. One minute. Two minutes.

Nothing.

There was no sound except the snapping of the rain against the windows and the drumming of it on the roof.

Only three hammer blows this time. Harder than any that had come before. But only three. Almost as if someone were playing games with him, taunting him.

* * *

Shortly before midnight, in room 316, the girl laughed softly in her sleep.

Outside her window, lightning pulsed, and the night flickered, and the darkness seemed to gallop for a moment, as if it were a huge and eager beast.

The girl turned onto her stomach without waking, murmured into her pillows. 'The ax,' she said with a wistful sigh. 'The ax . . .'

* * *

On the stroke of midnight, just forty minutes after she had fallen asleep, Carol bolted up from her pillows, trembling violently. As she struggled out of the grip of her nightmare, she heard someone say, 'It's coming! It's coming!' She stared wildly, blindly into the lightless room until she realized the panic-stricken voice had been her own.

Suddenly she could not tolerate the darkness one second longer. She fumbled desperately for the switch on the bedside lamp, found it, and sagged with relief.

The light didn't disturb Paul. He mumbled in his sleep but didn't wake.

Carol leaned back against the headboard and listened to her racing heart as it gradually slowed to a normal beat.

Her hands were icy. She put them under the covers and curled them into warming fists.

The nightmares have got to stop, she told herself. I can't go through this every night. I need my sleep.

Perhaps a vacation was called for. She had been working too hard for too long. The accumulated weariness was probably partly to blame for her bad dreams. She had also been under a great deal of unusual stress lately: the pending adoption, the near-tragic events in O'Brian's office on Wednesday, the accident just yesterday morning, the girl's amnesia for which she felt responsible. . . . Living with too much tension could cause exceptionally vivid nightmares of the sort she was experiencing. A week in the mountains, away from everyday problems, seemed like the perfect medicine.

In addition to all the other sources of stress, *that* day was approaching, the birthday of the child she had put up for adoption. A week from tomorrow, the Saturday after next, would mark sixteen years since she had relinquished the baby. Already, eight days in advance of that anniversary, she was burdened by a heavy mantle of guilt. By the time next Saturday rolled around, she would most likely be thoroughly depressed, as usual. A week in the mountains, away from everyday problems, might be the perfect medicine for *that* ailment, too.

Last year, she and Paul had purchased a vacation cabin on an acre of timbered land in the mountains. It was a cozy place – two bedrooms, one bath, a living room with a big stone fireplace, and a complete kitchen – a retreat that combined all the comforts of civilization with the clean air, marvelous scenery, and tranquility that could not be found in the city.

They had planned to get away to the cabin at least two weekends every month during the summer, but they had made the trip only three times in the past four months, less than half as often as they had hoped. Paul had labored hard to meet a series of self-imposed deadlines on his novel, and she had taken on more patients – a couple of really troubled kids who simply could not be turned away – and for both herself and Paul, work had expanded to fill every spare moment. Perhaps they were the over-achievers that Alfred O'Brian had thought they might be.

But we'll change when we have a child, Carol told herself. We'll make lots of time for leisure and for family outings because creating the best environment for our child is the job we're looking forward to more than any other.

Now, sitting up in bed, the grisly nightmare still chillingly fresh in her mind, she decided to start changing her life from this moment on. They *would* take off a few days, maybe a whole week, and go to the mountains before the recommendations committee's meeting at the end of the month, so they would be rested and composed when at last they met the child who would be theirs. They couldn't take off this coming week, of course. She would need time to reschedule her appointments. Besides, she didn't want to leave town until Jane Doe's parents showed up and properly identified the girl; that might take a few more days. But they ought to be able to carve a large chunk of time out of the week after next, and she made up her mind to start nudging Paul about it first thing in the morning.

Having reached that decision, she felt better. The mere prospect of a vacation, even a brief one, relieved much of her tension.

She looked at Paul and said, 'I love you.'

He continued to snore softly.

Smiling, she clicked off the light and settled under the covers again. For a couple of minutes she listened to the rain and to her husband's rhythmic breathing; then she drifted into a sound, satisfying sleep.

*　　*　　*

Rain fell throughout Saturday, rounding out a monotonously watery, sunless week. The day was cool, too, and the wind had teeth.

Carol visited Jane in the hospital on Saturday afternoon. They played cards and talked about some of the articles the girl had read in the magazines Carol had bought for her. Through every conversation, regardless of the subject, Carol probed continuously but subtly at the girl's amnesia, prodded her memory without letting her see that she was being prodded. But it was all wasted effort, for Jane's past remained beyond her grasp.

At the end of the afternoon visiting hours, as Carol was heading toward the elevators on the third floor, she encountered Dr. Sam Hannaport in the corridor.

'Haven't the police come up with any leads at all?' she asked.

He shrugged his burly shoulders. 'Not yet.'

'It's been over two days since the accident.'

'Which isn't all that long.'

'It seems like an eternity to that poor kid in there,' Carol said, gesturing toward the door of 316.

'I know,' Hannaport said. 'And I feel just as bad about it as you do. But it's still too soon to be pessimistic.'

'If *I* had a girl like her, and if *my* kid turned up missing for even one day, I'd be pushing the police hard, and I'd make damned sure the story was in all the papers, and I'd be pounding on doors and making a nuisance of myself all over the city.'

Hannaport nodded. 'I know you would. I've seen how you operate, and I admire your style. And listen, I think your visits with the girl have an awful lot to do with keeping her spirits up. It's good of you to take all this time with her.'

'Well, I'm not angling for a testimonial dinner,' Carol said. 'I don't think I'm doing any more than I have to do. I mean, I've got a responsibility here.'

A nurse came along, pushing a patient in a wheelchair. Carol and Hannaport stepped out of the way.

'At least Jane seems to be in good physical shape,' Carol said.

'Like I told you on Wednesday – there were no serious injuries. In fact, because she *is* in such good condition, she presents us with a problem. She doesn't really belong in a hospital. I just hope her parents show up before I'm forced to discharge her.'

'Discharge her? But you can't do that if she has nowhere to go. She can't cope outside. For God's sake, she doesn't even know who she is!'

'Naturally, I'll keep her here as long as I possibly can. But by late tonight or tomorrow morning, all of our beds are probably going to be full. Then, if the number of emergency admissions is greater than the number of discharges already scheduled, we'll have to look around for a few other patients who can be safely released. Jane's bound to be one of them. If some guy's brought in here with a cracked skull from an auto accident, or if an ambulance delivers a woman who's been stabbed by a jealous boyfriend, I can't justify turning away seriously injured people while I'm keeping a perfectly healthy girl whose worst physical problem is a contusion on her left shoulder.'

'But her amnesia –'

'Is something we can't treat anyway.'

'But she has nowhere to go,' Carol said. 'What would happen to her?'

In his calm, soft, reassuring voice, Hannaport said, 'She'll be okay. Really. We're not going to just abandon her. We'll petition to have her declared a ward of the court until her parents show up. In the meantime, she'll do just as well at some minimal-care facility as she would do here.'

'What facility are you talking about?'

'Just three blocks from here, there's a home for runaway and pregnant teenage girls, and it's far cleaner and better managed than the average state institution.'

'The Polmar Home,' Carol said. 'I know it.'

'Then you know it's not a dungeon or a dump.'

'I still don't like moving her out of here,' Carol said. 'She's going to feel as if she's being shunted aside, forgotten, and left to rot. She's on very shaky ground already. This'll scare her half to death.'

Frowning, Hannaport said, 'I don't like it much myself, but I truly don't have an option. If we're short on bed space, the law says we've got to consider degrees of need and take in those patients who have the most to lose by being denied care or by having treatment delayed. I'm in a bind.'

'I understand. I'm not blaming you. Dammit, if someone would just come forward to claim her!'

'Someone might, any minute.'

Carol shook her head. 'No. I've got a feeling it's not going to be that easy. Have you told Jane yet?'

'No. We won't make the petition to the court sooner than Monday morning, so I might as well wait until tomorrow to explain it to her. Maybe something'll happen between now and then to make it unnecessary. No use worrying her until we have to.'

Carol was depressed, remembering her own days in a staterun institution, before Grace had come along to rescue her. She had been a tough kid, street-smart, but the experience had nevertheless scarred her. Jane was bright and spunky and strong and sweet, but she wasn't *tough*, not like Carol had been at her age. What would institutional living do to her if she had to endure it for more than a day or two? If she was simply dropped in among kids who *were* street-smart, among kids who had drug and behavioral problems, she would most likely be victimized, perhaps even violently. What she needed was a real home, love, guidance –

'Of course!' Carol said. She grinned.

Hannaport looked at her questioningly.

'Why can't she come with *me*?' Carol asked.

'What?'

'Look, Dr. Hannaport, if it's all right with Paul, my husband, why couldn't you recommend to the court that I be awarded temporary custody of Jane until someone shows up who can identify her?'

'You really better think twice about that,' Hannaport said. 'Taking her in, disrupting your lives –'

'It won't be a disruption,' Carol said. 'It'll be a pleasure. She's a delightful kid.'

Hannaport stared at her a long moment, searching her face and her eyes.

'After all,' Carol argued as persuasively as she could, 'the only kind of doctor who might be able to cure Jane's amnesia is a psychiatrist. And in case you've forgotten, that's what I am. I'd not only be able to provide a decent home for her; I'd also be able to treat her rather intensively.'

Finally, Hannaport smiled. 'I think it's a grand and generous offer, Dr. Tracy.'

'Then you'll make the recommendation to the court?'

'Yes. Of course, you never can be sure what a judge will do. But I think there's a pretty good chance he'll see where the best interests of the girl lie.'

* * *

A few minutes later, in the hospital lobby, Carol used a pay phone to call Paul. She recounted the conversation she'd had with Dr. Hannaport, but before she got to the big question, Paul interrupted her. 'You want to make a place for Jane,' he said.

Surprised, Carol said, 'How'd you guess?'

He laughed. 'I know you, sugarface. When it comes to kids, you've got a heart the consistency of vanilla pudding.'

'She won't be in your way,' Carol said quickly. 'She won't distract you from your writing. And now that O'Brian won't be able to present our application for the adoption until the end of the month, there's no chance we'll have *two* kids to take care of. In fact maybe the delay at the agency was meant to be – so we'd have a place for Jane until her folks show up. It's only temporary, Paul. Really. And we –'

'Okay, okay,' he said. 'You don't have to sell me on it. I approve of the plan.'

'If you'd like to come here and meet Jane first, that's –'

'No, no. I'm sure she's everything you've said she is. Don't forget, though, you were planning to go to the mountains in a week or so.'

'We might not even have Jane that long. And if we do, we can probably take her with us, so long as we let the court know where we're going.'

'When do we have to appear in court?'

'I don't know. Probably Monday or Tuesday.'

'I'll be on my best behavior,' Paul said.

'Scrub behind your ears?'

'Okay. And I'll also wear shoes.'

Grinning, Carol said, 'Don't pick your nose in front of the judge.'

'Not unless he picks his first.'

She said, 'I love you, Dr. Tracy.'

'I love *you*, Dr. Tracy.'

When she put down the receiver and turned away from the pay phone, she felt wonderful. Not even the gaudy decor of the visitors' lounge could get on her nerves now.

*　　*　　*

That night, there was no hammering sound in the Tracy house, no evidence of the poltergeist that Mr. Alsgood had warned Paul about. There was no disturbance the following day, either, and none the day after that. The strange noise and the vibrations had ceased as inexplicably as they had begun.

Carol stopped having nightmares, too. She slept deeply,

peacefully, without interruption. She quickly forgot about the flickering, silvery blade of the ax swinging back and forth in the strange void.

The weather improved, too. The clouds dissipated on Sunday. Monday was summery, blue.

* * *

Tuesday afternoon, while Paul and Carol were in court trying to obtain temporary custody of Jane Doe, Grace Mitowski was cleaning her kitchen. She had just finished dusting the top of the refrigerator when the telephone rang.

'Hello.'

No one answered her.

'Hello,' she said again.

A thin, whispery, male voice said, 'Grace . . .'

'Yes?'

His words were muffled, and there was an echo on the line, as if he were talking into a tin can.

'I can't understand you,' she said. 'Can you speak up?'

He tried, but again the words were lost. They seemed to be coming from an enormous distance, across an unimaginably vast chasm.

'We have a terrible connection,' she said. 'You'll have to speak up.'

'Grace,' he said, his voice only slightly louder. 'Gracie . . . it's almost too late. You've got to . . . move fast. You've got to stop it . . . from happening . . . again.' It was a dry, brittle voice; it cracked repeatedly, with a sound like dead autumn leaves underfoot. 'It's almost . . . too late . . . too late. . . .'

She recognized the voice, and she froze. Her hand tightened on the receiver, and she couldn't get her breath.

'Gracie . . . it can't go on forever. You've got . . . to put an end to it. Protect her, Gracie. Protect her. . . .'

The voice faded away.

There was only silence. But not the silence of an open phone line. There was no hissing. No electronic beeping in the background. This was perfect silence, utterly unmarred by even the slightest click or whistle of electronic circuitry. Vast silence. Endless.

She put the phone down.

She started to shake.

She went to the cupboard and got down the bottle of Scotch she kept for visitors. She poured herself a double shot and sat down at the kitchen table.

The liquor didn't warm her. Chills still shook her.

The voice on the phone had belonged to Leonard. Her husband. He had been dead for eighteen years.

Part Two

EVIL WALKS AMONG US . . .

Evil is no faceless stranger,
living in a distant neighborhood.
Evil has a wholesome, hometown face,
with merry eyes and an open smile.
Evil walks among us, wearing a mask
which looks like all our faces.

– The Book of Counted Sorrows

Chapter Seven

Tuesday, after winning temporary custody of Jane Doe, Paul went home to work on his novel, and Carol took the girl shopping. Because Jane had no clothes except those she'd been wearing when she'd stepped in front of the Volkswagen last Thursday morning, she needed a lot of things, even for just a few days. She was embarrassed about spending Carol's money, and at first she was reluctant to admit that she liked anything she saw or that anything fit her well enough to buy it.

At last Carol said, 'Honey, you *need* this stuff, so please just relax and let me buy it for you. Okay? In the long run, it won't be coming out of my pocket anyway. I'll most likely be reimbursed either by your parents, by the foster children program, or by some other county agency.'

That argument worked. They quickly purchased a couple of pairs of jeans, a few blouses, underwear, a good pair of sneakers, socks, a sweater, and a windbreaker.

When they got home, Jane was impressed by the Tudor house with its leaded-glass windows, gabled roof, and stonework. She fell in love with the guest room in which she was to stay. It had a cove ceiling, a long window seat inset in a bay window, and a wall of mirrored closet doors. It was done in deep blue and pale beige, with Queen Anne furniture of lustrous cherrywood. 'It's really just a guest room?' Jane asked, incredulous. 'You don't use it regularly? Boy, if this were my house, I'd come in here all the time! I'd just sit and read for a little while every day – read and sit there in the window and soak up the atmosphere.'

Carol had always liked the room, but through Jane's eyes she achieved a new perception and appreciation of it. As she watched the girl inspecting things – sliding open the closet doors, checking the view from each angle of the bay window, testing the firmness of the mattress on the queen-sized bed – Carol realized that one advantage of having children was that their innocent, fresh reactions to everything could keep their parents young and open-minded, too.

That evening, Carol, Paul, and Jane prepared dinner together. The girl fit in comfortably and immediately, in spite of the fact that she was somewhat shy. There was a lot of laughter in the kitchen and at the dinner table.

After dinner, Jane started washing dishes while Carol and Paul cleared the table. When they were separated from the girl for a moment, alone in the dining room, Paul said quietly, 'She's a terrific kid.'

'Didn't I tell you so?'

'Funny thing, though.'

'What?'

'Ever since I saw her this afternoon, outside the courtroom,' Paul said, 'I've had the feeling that I've seen her somewhere before.'

'Where?'

He shook his head. 'I'll be damned if I know. But there's something familiar about her face.'

*   *   *

Throughout Tuesday afternoon, Grace expected the phone to ring again.

She dreaded having to answer it.

She tried to work off her nervous energy by cleaning the house. She scrubbed the kitchen floor, dusted the furniture in every room, and swept all the carpets.

But she couldn't stop thinking about the call: the paper-dry, echo-distorted voice that had sounded like Leonard; the odd things he had said; the eerie silence when he had finished speaking; the disquieting sense of vast distances, an unimaginable gulf of space and time. . . .

It had to be a hoax. But who could be responsible for it? And why torment her with an imitation of Leonard's voice, eighteen years after the man had died? What was the point of playing games like this *now*, after so much time had passed?

She tried to get her mind off the call by baking apple dumplings. Thick, crusty dumplings – served with cinnamon, milk, and just a bit of sugar – were a suppertime favorite of hers, for she had been born and raised in Lancaster, the heart of the Pennsylvania Dutch country, where that dish was considered a meal in itself. But Tuesday evening, she had no appetite, not even for dumplings. She ate a few bites, but she couldn't even finish half of one dumpling, though she usually ate two whole ones in a single meal.

She was still picking disinterestedly at her food when the telephone rang.

Her head jerked up. She stared at the wall phone that was above the small, built-in desk beside the refrigerator.

It rang again. And again.

Trembling, she got up, went to the phone, and lifted the receiver.

'Gracie . . .'

The voice was faint but intelligible.

'Gracie . . . it's almost too late.'

It was him. Leonard. Or someone who sounded exactly like Leonard had sounded.

She couldn't respond to him. Her throat clutched tight.

'Gracie . . .'

Her legs seemed to be melting under her. She pulled out the chair that was tucked into the kneehole of the desk, and she sat down quickly.

'Gracie . . . stop it from happening again. It mustn't . . . go on forever . . . time after time . . . the blood . . . the murder . . .'

She closed her eyes, forced herself to speak. Her voice was weak, quavery. She didn't even recognize it as her own. It was the voice of a stranger – a weary, frightened, frail old woman. 'Who is this?'

The whispery, vibrative voice on the telephone said, 'Protect her, Gracie.'

'What do you want from me?'

'Protect her.'

'Why are you doing this?'

'Protect her.'

'Protect who?' she demanded.

'Willa. Protect Willa.'

She was still frightened and confused, but she was beginning to be angry, too. 'I don't *know* anyone named Willa, dammit! Who is this?'

'Leonard.'

'No! Do you think I'm a doddering, senile old fool? Leonard's dead. Eighteen years! You're not Leonard. What kind of game are you playing?'

She wanted to hang up on him, and she knew that was the best thing to do with a crank like this, but she couldn't make herself put down the receiver. He sounded so much like Leonard that she was mesmerized by his voice.

He spoke again, much softer than before, but she could still hear him. 'Protect Willa.'

'I tell you, I don't know her. And if you keep calling me with this nonsense, I'm going to tell the police that some sick practical joker is –'

'Carol . . . Carol,' the man said, his voice fading syllable by syllable. 'Willa . . . but you call her . . . Carol.'

'What the hell is going on here?'

'Beware . . . the . . . cat.'

'What?'

The voice was so distant now that she had to strain to hear it. 'The . . . cat . . .'

'Aristophanes? What about him? Have you done something to him? Have you poisoned him? Is that what's been wrong with him lately?'

No response.

'Are you there?'

Nothing.

'What about the cat?' she demanded.

No answer.

She listened to the pure, pure silence, and she began to tremble so violently that she had trouble holding the phone. 'Who are you? Why do you want to torment me like this? Why do you want to hurt Aristophanes?'

Far, far away, the achingly familiar voice of her long-dead husband uttered a few final, barely audible words. 'Wish . . . I was there . . . for the . . . apple dumplings.'

*   *   *

They had forgotten to buy pajamas for Jane. She went to bed in knee socks, panties, and one of Carol's T-shirts, which was a bit large for her.

'What happens tomorrow?' she asked when she was tucked in, her head raised on a plump pillow.

Carol sat on the edge of the bed. 'I thought we might start a program of treatment designed to pry open your memory.'

'What kind of treatment?'

694

'Do you know what hypnotic regression therapy is?'

Jane was suddenly frightened. Several times since the accident, she had made a conscious, concerted effort to remember who she was, but on each occasion, as she felt herself coming close to a disturbing revelation, she had become dizzy, disoriented, and panicky. When she pressed her mind back, back, back toward the truth, a psychological defense mechanism cut off her curiosity as abruptly as a strangler's garrotte might have cut off her air supply. And every time, on the edge of unconsciousness, she saw a strange, silvery object swinging back and forth through blackness, an utterly indecipherable yet blood-chilling vision. She sensed there was something hideous in her past, something so terrible that she would be better off *not* remembering. She had just about made up her mind not to seek what had been lost, to accept her new life as a nameless orphan, even though it might be filled with hardships. But through hypnotic regression therapy, she could be forced to confront the specter in her past, whether she wanted to or not. That prospect filled her with dread.

'Are you all right?' Carol asked.

The girl blinked, licked her lips. 'Yeah. I was just thinking about what you said. Hypnotic regression. Does that mean you're going to put me in a trance and make me remember everything?'

'Well, it isn't that easy, honey. There's no guarantee it'll work. I'll hypnotize you and ask you to think back to the accident on Thursday morning; then I'll nudge you further and further into the past. If you're a good subject, you might remember who you are and where you come from. Hypnotic regression is a tool that comes in handy sometimes when I'm trying to get a patient to relive a deeply hidden, severely regressed trauma. I've never used the technique on an amnesia victim, but I know it's applicable to a case like yours. Of course, it only works about half the time. And when it does work, it takes more than one or two sessions. It can be a tedious, frustrating process. We're not going to get much of anywhere tomorrow, and in fact your parents will probably show up before I've been able to help you remember. But we might as well make a start. That is, if it's all right with you.'

She didn't want Carol to know that she was afraid to remember, so she said, 'Oh, sure! It sounds fascinating.'

'I've got four patients scheduled for tomorrow, but I can work you in at eleven o'clock. You'll have to spend a lot of time in the waiting room, before and after your session, so first thing in the morning, we'll find a book for you to take along. Do you like to read mystery stories?'

'I guess so.'

'Agatha Christie?'

'The name's familiar, but I don't know whether I've ever read any of her books.'

'You can try one tomorrow. If you were a big fan of mysteries, maybe Agatha Christie will open your memory for you. Any stimulus, any connection whatsoever with your past can act like a doorway.' She leaned down, kissed Jane's forehead. 'But don't worry about it now. Just get a good night's sleep, kiddo.'

After Carol left the room, closing the door behind her, Jane didn't immediately switch off the light. She let her gaze travel slowly around the room and then slowly back again, her eyes resting on each point of beauty.

Please, God, she thought, let me stay here. Somehow, some way, let me stay in this house forever and ever. Don't make me go back where I came from, wherever that might be. This is where I want to live. This is where I want to *die*, it's so pretty.

Finally, she reached out and snapped off the bedside lamp.

Darkness folded in like bat wings.

*   *   *

Using a piece of Masonite and four nails, Grace Mitowski fixed a temporary seal over the inside of the pet door.

Aristophanes stood in the center of the kitchen, his head cocked to one side, watching her with bright-eyed interest. Every few seconds, he meowed in what seemed to be an inquisitive tone.

When the last nail was in place, Grace said, 'Okay, cat. For the time being, your license to roam has been suspended. There might be a man out there who's been feeding you small amounts of drugs or poison of some sort, and maybe that's been the cause of your bad behavior. We'll just have to wait and see if you improve. Have you been flying high on drugs, you silly cat?'

Aristophanes meowed questioningly.

'Yes,' Grace said. 'I know it sounds bizarre. But if it's not some kook I've got to deal with, then it really must've been Leonard on the phone. And that's even *more* bizarre, don't you think?'

The cat turned his head from one side to the other, as if he really were trying to make sense of what she was saying.

Grace stopped, held out her hand, and rubbed her thumb and

forefinger together. 'Here, kitty. Here, kitty-kitty-kitty.'

Aristophanes hissed, spat, turned, and ran.

* * *

For a change, they made love with the lights off. Carol's breath was hot against his neck. She pressed close, rocked and tensed and twisted and flexed in perfect harmony with him; her exquisite, pneumatic movements were as fluid as currents in a warm river. She arched her elegant back, lifted and subsided in tempo with his measured strokes. She was as pliant, as silken, and eventually as all-encompassing as the darkness.

Afterwards, they held hands and talked about inconsequential things, steadily growing drowsy. Carol fell asleep while Paul was talking. When she failed to respond to one of his questions, he gently disentangled his hand from hers.

He was tired, but he couldn't find sleep as quickly as she had found it. He kept thinking about the girl. He was certain he had seen her prior to their meeting outside the courtroom this morning. During dinner, her face had grown more and more familiar. It continued to haunt him. But no matter how hard he tried, he couldn't recall where else he had seen her.

As he lay in the dark bedroom, paging through his memory, he gradually became uneasy. He began to feel – utterly without reason – that his previous encounter with Jane had been strange, perhaps even unpleasant. Then he wondered if the girl might actually pose some sort of threat to Carol and himself.

But that's absurd, he thought. Doesn't make any sense at all. I must be even more tired than I thought. Logic seems to be slipping out of my grasp. What possible threat could Jane pose? She's such a nice kid. An exceptionally nice kid.

He sighed, rolled over, and thought about the plot of his first novel (the failed one), and that quickly put him to sleep.

* * *

At one o'clock in the morning, Grace Mitowski was sitting up in bed, watching a late movie on the Sony portable. She was vaguely aware that Humphrey Bogart and Lauren Bacall were engaged in witty repartee, but she didn't really hear anything they said. She had lost track of the film's plot only minutes after she had turned it on.

She was thinking about Leonard, the husband she had lost to cancer eighteen years ago. He had been a good man, hard-working, generous, loving, a grand conversationalist. She had loved him very much.

But not *everyone* had loved Leonard. He had had his faults, of course. The worst thing about him had been his impatience – and the sharp tongue that his impatience had encouraged. He couldn't tolerate people who were lazy or apathetic or ignorant or foolish. 'Which includes two-thirds of the human race,' he had often said when he was feeling especially curmudgeonly. Because he was an honest man with precious little diplomacy in his bones, he had told people exactly what he thought of them. As a result, he had led a life remarkably free of deception but rich in enemies.

She wondered if it had been one of those enemies who had called her, pretending to be Leonard. A sick man might get as much pleasure from tormenting Leonard's widow as he would have gotten from tormenting Leonard himself. He might get a thrill from poisoning her cat and from harassing her with weird phone calls.

But after *eighteen years*? Who would have remembered Leonard's voice so well as to be able to imitate it perfectly such a long time later? Surely she was the only person in the world who could still recognize that voice upon hearing it speak only a word or two. And why bring Carol into it? Leonard had died three years before Carol had entered Grace's life; he had never known the girl. His enemies couldn't possibly have anything against Carol. What had the caller meant when he'd referred to Carol as 'Willa'? And, most disturbing of all, how did the caller know she had just made apple dumplings?

There *was* another explanation, though she was loath to consider it. Perhaps the caller hadn't been an old enemy of Leonard's. Maybe the call actually had come from Leonard himself. From a dead man.

– No. Impossible.

– A lot of people believe in ghosts.

– Not me.

She thought about the strange dreams she'd had last week. She hadn't believed in dream prophecies then. Now she did. So why not ghosts, too?

No. She was a level-headed woman who had lived a stable, rational life, who had been trained in the sciences, who had always believed that science held all the answers. Now, at seventy years of age, if she made room for the existence of ghosts within her otherwise rational philosophy, she might be opening the floodgates on madness. If you truly believed in ghosts, what came next? Vampires? Did you have to start carrying a sharp wooden stake and a crucifix everywhere you went? Werewolves? Better buy a box of silver bullets! Evil elves who lived in the center of the earth and caused quakes and volcanoes? Sure! Why not?

Grace laughed bitterly.

She couldn't suddenly become a believer in ghosts, because acceptance of that superstition might require the acceptance of countless others. She was too old, too comfortable with herself, too accustomed to her familiar ways to reconsider her entire view of life. And she certainly wasn't going to contemplate such a sweeping reevaluation merely because she had received two bizarre phone calls.

That left only one thing to be decided: whether or not she should tell Carol that someone was harassing her and had used Carol's name. She tried to hear how she would sound when she explained the telephone calls and when she outlined her theory about Aristophanes being drugged or poisoned. She couldn't hope to sound like the Grace Mitowski that everyone knew. She'd come off like an hysterical old woman who was seeing nonexistent conspirators behind every door and under every bed.

They might even think she was going senile.

Am I? she wondered. Did I imagine the telephone calls? No. Surely not.

She wasn't imagining Aristophanes's changed personality, either. She looked at the claw marks on the palm of her hand; although they were healing, they were still red and puffy. Proof. Those marks were proof that *something* was wrong.

I'm not senile, she told herself. Not even a little bit. But I sure don't want to have to convince Carol or Paul that I've got all my marbles, once I've told them that I'm getting phone calls from Leonard. Better go easy for the time being. Wait. See what happens next. Anyway, I can figure this out on my own. I can handle it.

On the Sony, Bogart and Bacall grinned at each other.

* * *

When Jane woke up in the middle of the night, she discovered she had been sleepwalking. She was in the kitchen, but she couldn't recall getting out of bed and coming downstairs.

The kitchen was silent. The only sound was from the softly purring refrigerator. The only light was from the moon, but because the moon was full and because the kitchen had quite a few windows, there was enough light to see by.

Jane was standing at a counter near the sink. She had opened one of the drawers and had taken a butcher knife out of it.

She stared down at the knife, startled to find it in her hand.

Pale moonlight glinted on the cold blade.

She returned the knife to the drawer.

Closed the drawer.

She had been gripping the knife so tightly that her hand ached.

Why did I want a knife?

A chill skittered like a centipede along her spine.

Her bare arms and legs broke out in gooseflesh, and she was suddenly very aware that she was wearing only a T-shirt, panties, and knee socks.

The refrigerator motor shut off with a dry rattle that made her jump and turn.

Now the house was preternaturally silent. She could almost believe that she had gone deaf.

What was I doing with the knife?

She hugged herself to ward off the chills that kept wriggling through her.

Maybe she had dreamed about food and had come down here in her sleep to make a sandwich. Yes. That was probably what had happened. In fact she *was* a bit hungry. So she had gotten the knife out of the drawer in order to slice some roast beef for a sandwich. There was a butt end of a roast in the refrigerator. She had seen it earlier, when she had been helping Carol and Paul make dinner.

But now she didn't think she could eat a sandwich or anything else. Her bare legs were getting colder by the moment, and she felt immodestly exposed in just flimsy panties and a thin T-shirt. All she wanted now was to get back to bed, under the covers.

Climbing the steps in the darkness, she stayed close to the wall, where the treads were less likely to creak. She returned to her room without waking anyone.

Outside, a dog howled in the distance.

Jane burrowed deeper in her blankets.

For a while she had trouble getting to sleep because she felt guilty about prowling through the house while the Tracys slept. She felt sneaky. She felt as if she had been taking advantage of their hospitality.

Of course, that was silly. She hadn't been nosing around on purpose. She had been sleepwalking, and there was no way a person could control something like that.

Just sleepwalking.

Chapter Eight

The focal point of Carol Tracy's office was Mickey Mouse. One long wall of the room was fitted with shelves on which were displayed Mickey Mouse memorabilia. There were Mickey Mouse buttons, Mickey Mouse pins, a wristwatch, belt buckles, a Mickey Mouse phone, drinking glasses bearing the famous mouse's countenance, a beer mug on which there was a likeness of Mickey dressed in lederhosen and a Tyrolean hat. But mostly there were statuettes of the cartoon star: Mickey standing beside a little red car; Mickey curled up in striped pajamas sleeping; Mickey dancing a jig; Mickey with Minnie: Mickey with Goofy; Mickey holding barbells; Mickey with Pluto; Mickey and Donald Duck with their arms around each other's shoulders, looking like the best of friends; Mickey riding a horse, with a cowboy hat raised in one white-gloved, four-fingered hand; Mickey dressed like a soldier, a sailor, a doctor; Mickey in swimming trunks, clutching a surfboard. There were wooden, metal, chalk, porcelain, plastic, glass, and clay statuettes of Mickey; some of them were a foot high, and some were no more than one inch tall, though most were in between. The only thing those hundreds of Mickeys had in common was the fact that every one of them was smiling broadly.

The collection was an icebreaker with patients of all ages. No one could resist Mickey Mouse.

Jane responded as scores of patients had done before her. She said 'oooh' and 'aaah' a lot, and she laughed happily. By the time she had finished admiring the collection and had sat down in one of the big leather armchairs, she was ready for the therapy session; her tension and apprehension had disappeared. Mickey had worked his usual magic.

Carol didn't have an analyst's couch in her office. She preferred to conduct sessions from a large wing chair, with the patient seated in an identical chair on the other side of the octagonal coffee table.

The drapes were always kept tightly shut; soft, golden light was provided by shaded floor lamps. Except for the wall of Mickey Mouse images, the room had a nineteenth-century air.

They chatted about the collection for a couple of minutes, and then Carol said, 'Okay, honey. I think we ought to begin.'

Worry lines appeared on the girl's forehead. 'You really think this hypnosis is a good idea?'

'Yes. I think it's the best tool we have for restoring your memory. Don't worry. It's a simple process. Just relax and flow with it. Okay?'

'Well . . . okay.'

Carol got up and stepped around the coffee table, and Jane started to get up, too. 'No, you stay there,' Carol said. She moved behind the wing chair and put her fingertips against the girl's temples. 'Relax, honey. Lean back. Hands in your lap. Palms up, fingers slack. That's fine. Now close your eyes. Are they closed?'

'Yes.'

'Good. Very good. Now I want you to think of a kite. A large, diamond-shaped kite. Picture it in your mind. It's an enormous, blue kite sailing high in the blue sky. Can you see it?'

After a brief hesitation, the girl said, 'Yes.'

'Watch the kite, honey. See how gently it rises and falls on the currents of air. Rises, falls, up and down, up and down, side to side, sailing so gracefully, far above the earth, halfway between the earth and the clouds, far above your head,' Carol said in a mellow, soothing, rhythmic voice as she stared down at the girl's thick blond hair. 'While you're watching the kite, you'll gradually become as light and as free as it is. You'll learn to soar up and up into the blue sky, just like the kite.' With her fingertips, she lightly traced circles on the girl's temples. 'All the tension is leaving you, all the worries and cares are floating away, away, until the only thought in your head is the kite, the sailing kite in the blue sky. A great weight has been removed from your skull, from your forehead and your temples. Already, you feel much lighter.' She moved her hands down to the girl's neck. 'The muscles in your neck are relaxing. Tension is dropping away. A great weight is dropping away. You are so much lighter now that you can almost feel yourself rising up toward the kite . . . almost . . . almost . . .' She moved her hands down, touched the girl's shoulders. 'Relax. Let the tension fall away. Like blocks of concrete. Making you lighter, lighter. A weight is falling off your chest, too. And now you're floating. Just a few inches off the ground, but you *are* floating.'

'Yes . . . floating . . .' she said, her voice thick.

'The kite is gliding far above, but you are slowly, slowly moving up to join it . . .'

She went on like that for a minute, then returned to her own chair and sat down.

Jane was slumped in the other wing chair, head tilted to one side, eyes closed, face soft and slack, breathing softly.

'You are in a very deep sleep,' Carol told her. 'A very relaxed, very deep, deep sleep. Do you understand?'

'Yes,' the girl murmured.

'You will answer a few questions for me.'

'Okay.'

'You will remain in your deep sleep, and you will answer my questions until I tell you it's time to wake up. Understood?'

'Yes.'

'Good. Very good. Now tell me – what is your name?'

The girl was silent.

'What is your name, honey?'

'Jane.'

'Is that your real name?'

'No.'

'What is your real name?'

Jane frowned. 'I . . . don't remember.'

'Where did you come from?'

'The hospital.'

'Before that?'

'Nowhere.'

A bead of saliva glistened at the corner of the girl's mouth. Languorously, she licked it away before it could drool down her chin.

Carol said, 'Honey, do you remember the Mickey Mouse watch you saw a few minutes ago?'

'Yes.'

'Well, I've taken that watch from the shelf,' Carol said, though she hadn't moved from her chair. 'And now I'm turning the hands on it backwards, around and around the dial, always backwards. Can you see the hands moving backwards on that Mickey Mouse watch?'

'Yes.'

'Now something amazing is happening. As I turn those hands backwards and backwards, time itself begins to flow in reverse. It isn't a quarter past eleven any more. It's now eleven o'clock. This is

705

a magic watch. It governs the flow of time. And now it's ten o'clock in the morning . . . nine o'clock . . . eight o'clock. . . . Look around you. Where are you now?'

The girl opened her eyes. They were fixed on a distant point. She said, 'Ummm . . . the kitchen. Yeah. The breakfast nook. Boy, the bacon's nice and crisp.'

Gradually, Carol moved her back in time, back through the days she had spent in the hospital, finally regressing to the accident last Thursday morning. The girl winced as she relived the moment of impact, and cried out, and Carol soothed her, and then they went back a few minutes further.

'You're standing on the sidewalk,' Carol said. 'You're dressed only in a blouse and jeans. It's raining. Chilly.'

The girl closed her eyes again. She shivered.

'What's your name?' Carol asked.

Silence.

'What's your name, honey?'

'I don't know.'

'Where have you just come from?'

'Nowhere.'

'You mean you have amnesia?'

'Yes.'

'Even before the accident?'

'Yes.'

Although she was still very concerned about the girl, Carol was relieved to hear that she wasn't responsible for Jane's condition. For a moment she felt like that blue kite, capable of soaring up and away. Then she said, 'Okay. You're about to step into the street. Do you just want to cross it, or do you intend to walk in front of a car?'

'I . . . don't . . . know.'

'How do you feel? Happy? Depressed? Indifferent?'

'Scared,' the girl said in a small, shaky voice.

'What are you scared of?'

Silence.

'What are you scared of?'

'It's coming.'

'What's coming?'

'Behind me!'

'What's behind you?'

The girl opened her eyes again. She was still staring at a distant point, but now there was stark terror in her eyes.

'What's behind you?' Carol asked again.

'Oh God,' the girl said miserably.

'What is it?'

'No, no.' She shook her head. Her face was bloodless.

Carol leaned forward in her chair. 'Relax, honey. You will relax and be calm. Close your eyes. Calm . . . like the kite . . . far above everything . . . floating . . . warm.'

The tension went out of Jane's face.

'All right,' Carol said. 'Staying calm, always relaxed and calm, you will tell me what you're afraid of.'

The girl said nothing.

'Honey, what are you scared of? What's behind you?'

'Something . . .'

'What?'

'Something . . .'

Patiently, Carol said, 'Be specific.'

'I . . . don't know what it is . . . but it's coming . . . and it scares me.'

'Okay. Let's go back a bit further.' Using the image of the backwards-moving hands on the Mickey Mouse wristwatch, she regressed the girl another full day into the past. 'Now look around. Where are you?'

'Nowhere.'

'What do you see?'

'Nothing.'

'You must see something, honey.'

'Darkness.'

'Are you in a dark room?'

'No.'

'Are there walls in the darkness?'

'No.'

'Are you outdoors at night?'

'No.'

She regressed the girl another day. 'Now what do you see?'

'Just the darkness.'

'There must be something else.'

'No.'

'Open your eyes, honey.'

The girl obeyed. Her blue eyes were vacant, glassy. 'Nothing.'

Carol frowned. 'Are you sitting or standing in that dark place?'

'I don't know.'

'What do you feel under you? A chair? A floor? A bed?'

'Nothing.'

'Reach down. Touch the floor.'

'There isn't a floor.'

Uneasy about the direction the session was taking, Carol shifted in her chair and stared at the girl for a while, wondering what to try next.

After a few seconds, Jane's eyes fluttered and went shut.

Finally, Carol said, 'All right. I'm turning the hands of the watch counterclockwise again. Time is flowing in reverse. It will continue to flow backwards, hour by hour, day by day, faster and faster, until you stop me. I want you to stop me only when you come out of the darkness and can tell me where you are. I'm turning the hands now. Backwards . . . backwards . . .'

Ten seconds passed in silence. Twenty. Thirty.

After a full minute, Carol said, 'Where are you?'

'Nowhere yet.'

'Keep going. Backwards . . . back in time . . .'

After another minute, Carol began to think something was wrong. She had the disquieting feeling that she was losing control of the situation and placing her patient in some kind of danger that could not be foreseen. But as she was about to call a halt to the regression and bring the girl forward again, Jane spoke at last.

The girl shot up out of the chair, onto her feet, flailing and screaming. 'Somebody help me! Mama! Aunt Rachael! For God's sake, help me!'

The voice wasn't Jane's. It came from her mouth, through her tongue and lips, but it didn't sound at all like her. It wasn't merely distorted by panic. It was an entirely different voice from Jane's. It had its own character, its own accent and tone.

'I'm going to die here! Help! *Get me out of here!*'

Carol was on her feet, too. 'Honey, stop it. Calm down.'

'I'm on fire! I'm on fire!' the girl screamed, and she slapped at her clothes as if trying to put out the flames.

'No!' Carol said sharply. She stepped around the coffee table and managed to seize the girl's arm, taking several glancing blows in the process.

Jane thrashed, tried to break loose.

Carol held on and began to talk softly but insistently to her, calming her down.

Jane stopped struggling, but she began to gasp and wheeze. 'Smoke,' she said, gagging. 'So much smoke.'

Carol talked her out of that, too, and gradually brought her down from the peak of hysteria.

At last Jane sank back into the wing chair. She was wan, and her forehead was strung with beads of sweat. Her blue eyes, staring into a distant place and time, looked haunted.

Carol knelt beside the chair and held the girl's hand. 'Honey, can you hear me?'

'Yes.'

'Are you okay?'

'I'm afraid. . . .'

'There is no fire.'

'There was. Everywhere,' the girl said, still speaking with the unfamiliar voice.

'There isn't any more. No fire anywhere.'

'If you say so.'

'I do. I say so. Now tell me your name.'

'Laura.'

'Do you remember your last name?'

'Laura Havenswood.'

Carol flushed with triumph. 'Very good. That's just fine. Where's your home, Laura?'

'Shippensburg.'

Shippensburg was a small town less than an hour from Harrisburg. It was a quiet, pleasant place that existed to serve a flourishing state college and a large number of surrounding farms.

'Do you know the address where you live in Shippensburg?' Carol asked.

'There's no street name. It's a farm. Just outside of town, off Walnut Bottom Road.'

'So you could take me there if you had to?'

'Oh, yes. It's a pretty place. There are a pair of stone gateposts by the verge of the county lane; they mark the entrance to our land. And there's a long drive flanked by maples, and there are big oaks around the house. It's cool and breezy in the summer with all those shade trees.'

'What's your father's first name?'

'Nicholas.'

'And his phone number?'

The girl frowned. 'His what?'

'What's the telephone number at your house?'

The girl shook her head. 'I don't know what you mean.'

'Don't you have a telephone?'

'What *is* a telephone?' the girl asked.

Carol stared at her, puzzled. It wasn't possible for a person under hypnosis to be coy or to make jokes of this sort. As she considered her next move, she saw that Laura was becoming agitated again. The girl's brow furrowed, and her eyes widened. She started breathing hard again.

'Laura, listen to me. You will be calm. You will relax and –'

The girl writhed uncontrollably in her chair. Squealing and gasping, she slid off the chair, rolled onto the floor, bumping the coffee table and pushing it aside. She twisted and shuddered and wriggled as if she were having a severe epileptic fit, though she was not; she brushed frantically at herself, for again she seemed to believe she was on fire. She called for someone named Rachael and choked on nonexistent smoke.

Carol required almost a minute to talk her down, which was a serious loss of control; a hypnotist could usually calm a subject in only seconds. Apparently, Laura had lived through an extremely traumatic fire or had lost a loved one in a blaze. Carol wanted to pursue the matter and learn what was at the root of it, but this wasn't the right time. After taking so long to quiet her patient, she knew the session should be ended quickly.

When Laura was seated in the wing chair again, Carol crouched beside her and instructed her to remember everything that had happened and everything that had been said during the session. Then she led the girl forward through time to the present and brought her out of the trance.

The girl wiped at the moist corner of one eye, shook her head, cleared her throat. She looked at Carol and said, 'I guess it didn't work, huh?' She sounded like Jane again; the Laura voice was gone.

But why the hell had her voice changed in the first place? Carol wondered.

'You don't remember what happened?' Carol asked.

'What's to remember? All that talk about a blue kite? I could see what you were trying to do, how you were trying to lull me into a trance, so I guess that's why it didn't work.'

'But it *did* work,' Carol assured her. 'And you should be able to recall all of it.'

The girl looked skeptical. 'All of what? What happened? What did you find out?'

Carol stared at her. 'Laura.'

The girl didn't even blink. She merely looked perplexed.

'Your name is Laura.'

'Who said?'

'You did.'

'Laura? No. I don't think so.'

'Laura Havenswood,' Carol said.

The girl frowned. 'It doesn't ring any bells at all.'

Surprised, Carol said, 'You told me you live in Shippensburg.'

'Where's that?'

'About an hour from here.'

'I never heard of it.'

'You live on a farm. There are stone gateposts to mark the entrance to your father's property, and there's a long driveway flanked by maple trees. That's what you told me, and I'm sure it'll turn out to be just like you said. It's virtually impossible to answer questions incorrectly or deceptively while you're hypnotized. Besides, you don't have any reason to deceive me. You have nothing to lose and everything to gain if we break through this memory block.'

'Maybe I *am* Laura Havenswood,' the girl said. 'Maybe what I told you in the trance was true. But I can't remember it, and when you tell me who I am, it doesn't mean a thing to me. Boy, I thought if I could just remember my name, then everything would fall into place. But it's still a blank. Laura, Shippensburg, a farm – I can't *connect* with any of it.'

Carol was still crouched beside the girl's chair. She rose and flexed her stiff legs. 'I've never encountered anything quite like this. And so far as I know, a reaction like yours hasn't ever been reported in any of the psychology journals. Whenever a patient *is* susceptible to hypnosis, and whenever a patient *can* be regressed to a moment of trauma, there's always a profound effect. Yet you weren't touched at all by it. Very odd. If you remembered while you were under hypnosis, you ought to be able to remember now. And just hearing your name ought to open doors for you.'

'But it doesn't.'

'Strange . . .'

The girl looked up from the wing chair. 'What now?'

Carol thought for a moment, then said, 'I suppose we ought to have the authorities check out the Havenswood identity.'

She went to her desk, picked up the phone, and called the Harrisburg police.

The police operator referred her to a detective named Lincoln Werth, who was in charge of a number of conventional missing-persons files as well as the Jane Doe case. He listened to Carol's story with interest, promised to check it out right away, and said he would call her back the instant he obtained confirmation of the Havenswood identity.

* * *

Four hours later, at 3:55, after Carol's last appointment for the day, as she and the girl were about to leave the office and go home, Lincoln Werth rang back as promised. Carol took the call at her desk, and the girl perched on the edge of the desk, watching, clearly a bit tense.

'Dr. Tracy,' Werth said, 'I've been back and forth on the phone all afternoon with the police in Shippensburg and with the county sheriff's office up there. I'm afraid I have to report it's all been a wild-goose chase.'

'There must be some mistake.'

'Nope. We can't find anyone in Shippensburg or the surrounding county with the name Havenswood. There's no telephone listed for anyone of that name, and –'

'Maybe they just don't have a phone.'

'Of course, we considered that possibility,' Werth said. 'We didn't jump to conclusions, believe me. For instance, when we checked with the power company, we discovered they don't have a customer named Havenswood anywhere in Cumberland County, but that didn't discourage us either. We figured these people we're looking for might be Amish. Lots of Amish in that neck of the woods. If they were Amish, of course, they wouldn't have electricity in their house. So next we went to the property-tax rolls at the county offices up there. What we found was that nobody named Havenswood owns a house, let alone a farm, in that whole area.'

'They could be tenants,' Carol said.

'Could be. But what I really think they are is nonexistent. The girl must've been lying.'

'Why would she?'

'I don't know. Maybe the whole amnesia thing is a hoax. Maybe she's just an ordinary runaway.'

'No. Definitely not.' Carol looked up at Laura – no, her name was still Jane – looked into those clear, bottomless blue eyes. To Werth, she said, 'Besides, it just isn't possible to lie that well or that blatantly when you're hypnotized.'

Although Jane could hear only half of the conversation, she had begun to perceive that the Havenswood name wasn't going to check out. Her face clouded. She got up and went to the display shelves to study the statuettes of Mickey Mouse.

'There *is* something damned odd about the whole thing,' Lincoln Werth said.

'Odd?' Carol asked.

'Well, when I passed along the description of the farm that the girl gave – those stone gateposts, the long driveway with the maples – and when I said it was off Walnut Bottom Road, the Cumberland County sheriff and the various Shippensburg policemen I talked to all recognized the place right off the bat. It actually does exist.'

'Well, then –'

'But nobody named Havenswood lives there,' Detective Werth said. 'The Ohlmeyer family owns that spread. Really well known around those parts. Highly thought of, too. Oren Ohlmeyer, his wife, and their two sons. Never had a daughter, so I'm told. Before Oren owned the farm, it belonged to his daddy, who bought it seventy years ago. One of the sheriff's men went out there and asked the Ohlmeyers if they'd ever heard of a girl named Laura Havenswood or anything even similar to that. They hadn't. Didn't know anyone fitting our June Doe's description, either.'

'Yet the farm *is* there, just like she told us it was.'

'Yeah,' Werth said. 'Funny, isn't it?'

*   *   *

In the Volkswagen, on the way home from the office, as they drove along the sun-splashed autumn streets, the girl said, 'Do you think I was faking the trance?'

'Heavens, no! You were *very* deeply under. And I'm quite sure you aren't a good enough actress to fake that business about the fire.'

'Fire?'

'I guess you don't remember that, either.' Carol told her about Laura's screaming fit, the desperate cries for help. 'Your terror was genuine. It came from experience. I'd bet anything on that.'

'I don't remember any of it. You mean I really was in a fire once?'

'Could be.' Ahead, a traffic light turned red. Carol stopped the car and looked at Jane. 'You don't have any physical scars, so if you were in a fire, you escaped unharmed. Of course, it might be that you *lost* someone in a fire, someone you loved very much, and maybe you weren't actually in a fire yourself. If that's the case, then when you were hypnotized, you might have confused your fear for that person with fear for your own life. Am I making myself clear?'

'I think I get what you mean. So maybe the fire – the *shock* of it – is responsible for my amnesia. And maybe my parents haven't shown up to claim me because . . . they're dead, burned to death.'

Carol took the girl's hand. 'Don't worry about it now, honey. I may be all wrong. I probably am. But I think it's a possibility you ought to be prepared for.'

The girl bit her lip, nodded. 'The idea scares me a little. But I don't exactly feel sad. I mean, I don't remember my folks at all, so losing them would almost be like losing strangers.'

Behind them, the driver of a green Datsun blew his horn.

The light had changed. Carol let go of the girl's hand and touched the accelerator. 'We'll probe into the fire during tomorrow's session.'

'You still think I *am* Laura Havenswood?'

'Well, for the time being, we'll keep calling you Jane. But I don't see why you'd come up with the name Laura if it wasn't yours.'

'The identity didn't check out,' the girl reminded her.

Carol shook her head. 'That's not exactly true. We haven't proved or disproved the Havenswood identity. All we know for sure is that you never lived in Shippensburg. But you must have been there at least once because the farm exists; you've seen it, if only in passing. Apparently, even under hypnosis, even regressed beyond the onset of your amnesia, your memories are tangled. I don't know how that's possible or why. I've never encountered anything quite like it. But we'll work hard at untangling them for you. The problem might lie in the questions I asked and the way I asked them. We'll just have to wait and see.'

They rode in silence for a moment, and then the girl said, 'I half hope we don't get things untangled too quickly. Ever since you told me about your cabin in the mountains, I've really been looking forward to going up there.'

'Oh, you'll get to go. Don't worry about that. We're leaving on Friday, and even if tomorrow's session goes well, we won't be able to untangle this Laura Havenswood thing *that* fast. I warned you, this could be a slow, complicated, frustrating process. I'm surprised we made any progress at all today, and I'll be twice as surprised if we make even half as much headway tomorrow.'

'I guess you'll be stuck with me for a while.'

Carol sighed and pretended weariness. 'Looks that way. Oh, you're such a terrible, terrible, terrible burden. You're just too much to bear.' She took one hand off the steering wheel long enough to clutch her heart in a melodramatic gesture that made Jane giggle. 'Too much! Oh, oh!'

'You know what?' the girl asked.

'What?'

'I like you, too.'

They looked at each other and grinned.

At the next red light, Jane said, 'I've got a feeling about the mountains.'

'What's that?'

'I have this strong feeling that it's going to be a lot of fun up there. Really exciting. Something special. A real adventure.' Her blue eyes were even brighter than usual.

*   *   *

After dinner, Paul suggested they play Scrabble. He set up the board on the game table in the family room, while Carol explained the rules to Jane, who couldn't remember whether or not she had ever played it before.

After winning the starting lottery, Jane went first with a twenty-two-point word that took advantage of a double-count square and the automatic double score for the first word of the game.

BLADE

'Not a bad start,' Paul said. He hoped the girl would win, because she got such a kick out of little things like that. The smallest compliment, the most modest triumph delighted her. But he wasn't going to throw the game just to please her; she would have to earn it, by God. He was incapable of giving the match away to anyone; regardless of the kind of game he was playing, he always put as much effort and commitment into it as he put into his work. He didn't *indulge* in leisure activities; he *attacked* them. To Jane, he said, 'I have a hunch you're the kind of kid who says she's never played poker before – and quickly proceeds to win every pot in the game.'

'Can you bet on Scrabble?' Jane asked.

'You can, but we won't,' Paul said.

'Scared?'

'Terrified. You'd wind up with the house.'

'I'd let you stay.'

'How decent of you.'

'For very low rent.'

'Ah, this child truly has a heart of gold!'

While he bantered with Jane, Carol studied her own group of letters. 'Hey,' she said, 'I've got a word that ties right in with Jane's.' She added LOOD to the B in BLADE, forming BLOOD.

'Judging from your words,' Paul said, 'I guess you two intend to play a cut-throat game.'

Carol and Jane groaned dutifully at his bad joke and refilled their letter trays from the stock in the lid of the game box.

To Paul's surprise, when he looked at his own seven letters, he saw that he had a word with which to continue the morbid theme that had been established. He added EATH to the D at the end of BLOOD, creating DEATH.

'Weird,' Carol said.

'Here's something weirder still,' Jane said, taking her second turn by adding OMB to the T in DEATH.

```
B L A D E
L
O
O
D E A T H
      O
      M
      B
```

Paul stared at the board. He was suddenly uneasy.

What were the odds that the first four words in a game would be so closely related in theme? Ten thousand to one? No. It had to be much higher than that. A hundred thousand to one? A million to one?

Carol looked up from her unusual letters. 'You aren't going to *believe* this.' She added three letters to the board.

716

```
        B L A D E
K I L L
      O
      O
      D E A T H
          O
          M
          B
```

' "Kill"?' Paul said. 'Oh, come on. Enough's enough. Take it away and make another word.'

'I can't,' Carol said. 'That's all I have. The rest of my letters are useless.'

'But you could have put "lik" above the "e" in "blade," ' Paul said. 'You could have spelled "like" instead of "kill." '

'Sure, I could have done that, but I'd have gotten fewer points if I had. You see? There's no square with a double-letter score up there.'

As he listened to Carol's explanation, Paul felt strange. Bitterly cold inside. Hollow. As if he were balancing on a tightrope and knew he was going to fall and fall and fall . . .

He was gripped by déjà vu, by such a strikingly powerful awareness of having lived through this scene before that, for a moment, his heart seemed to stop beating. Yet nothing like this had ever happened in any other Scrabble game he'd ever played. So why was he so certain he had witnessed this very thing on a previous occasion? Even as he asked himself that question, he realized what the answer was. The seizure of déjà vu wasn't in reference to the words on the Scrabble board; not directly anyway. The thing that was so frighteningly familiar to him was the unusual, soul-shaking *feeling* that the coincidental appearance of those words aroused in him; the iciness that came from within rather than from without; the awful hollowness deep in his guts; the sickening sensation of teetering on a high wire, with only infinite darkness below. He had felt exactly the same way in the attic last week, when the mysterious hammering sound had seemed to issue out of the thin air in front of his face, when each *thunk!* had sounded as if it were coming from a sledge and anvil in another dimension of time and space. That was how he felt now, at the Scrabble board: as if he were confronted with something extraordinary, unnatural, perhaps even supernatural.

717

To Carol, he said, 'Listen, why don't you just take those last three letters off the board, put them back in the box, choose three brand-new letters, and make some other word besides "kill." '

He could see that his suggestion startled her.

She said, 'Why should I do that?'

Paul frowned. 'Blade, blood, death, tomb, kill – what kind of words are they for a nice, friendly, peaceable game of Scrabble?'

She stared at him for a moment, and her piercing eyes made him a bit uncomfortable. 'It's only coincidence,' she said, clearly puzzled by his tenseness.

'I *know* it's only coincidence,' he said, though he didn't know anything of the sort. He was simply unable to explain rationally the eerie feeling that the words on the board were the work of some force far stronger than mere coincidence, something worse. 'It still gives me the creeps,' he said lamely. He turned to Jane, seeking an ally. 'Doesn't it give you the creeps?'

'Yeah. It does. A little,' the girl agreed. 'But it's also kind of fascinating. I wonder how long we can keep going with words that fit this pattern.'

'I wonder, too,' Carol said. Playfully, she slapped Paul's shoulder. 'You know what your trouble is, babe? You don't have any scientific curiosity. Now come on. It's your turn.'

After putting DEATH on the board, he hadn't replenished his supply of letter tiles. He drew four of the small wooden squares from the lid of the game box, put them on the rack in front of him.

And froze.

Oh God.

He was on that tightrope again, teetering over a great abyss.

'Well?' Carol asked.

Coincidence. It *had* to be just coincidence.

'Well?'

He looked up at her.

'What have you got?' she asked.

Numb, he shifted his eyes to the girl.

She was hunched over the table, as eager as Carol to hear his response, anxious to see if the macabre pattern would continue.

Paul lowered his eyes to the row of letters on the wooden rack. The word was still there. Impossible. But it was there anyway, possible or not.

'Paul?'

He moved so quickly and unexpectedly that Carol and Jane jumped. He scooped up the letters on his rack and nearly flung them back into the lid of the box. He swept the five offensive words off the board before anyone could protest, and he returned those nineteen tiles to the box with all the others.

'Paul, for heaven's sake!'

'We'll start a new game,' he said. 'Maybe those words didn't bother you, but they bothered me. I'm here to relax. If I want to hear about blood and death and killing, I can switch on the news.'

Carol said, 'What word did you have?'

'I don't know,' he lied. 'I didn't work with the letters to see. Come on. Let's start all over.'

'You *did* have a word,' she said.

'No.'

'It looked to me like you did,' Jane said.

'Open up,' Carol said.

'All right, all right. I had a word. It was obscene. Not something a gentleman like me would use in a refined game of Scrabble, with ladies present.'

Jane's eyes sparkled mischievously. 'Really? Tell us. Don't be stuffy.'

'Stuffy? Have you no manners, young lady?'

'None!'

'Have you no modesty?'

'Nope.'

'Are you just a common *broad*?'

'Common,' she said, nodding rapidly. 'Common to the core. So tell us what word you had.'

'Shame, shame, shame,' he said. Gradually, he cajoled them into dropping their inquiry. They started a new game. This time all the words were ordinary, and they did not come in any unsettling, related order.

* * *

Later, in bed, he made love to Carol. He wasn't particularly horny. He just wanted to be as close to her as he could get.

Afterwards, when the murmured love talk finally faded into a companionable silence, she said, 'What *was* your word?'

'Hmmmm?' he said, pretending not to know what she meant.

'Your obscene word in the Scrabble game. Don't try to tell me you've forgotten what it was.'

'Nothing important.'

719

She laughed. 'After everything we just did in this bed, surely you don't think I need to be sheltered!'

'I didn't have an obscene word.' Which was the truth. 'I didn't really have any word at all.' Which was a lie. 'It's just that . . . I thought those first five words on the board were bad for Jane.'

'Bad for her?'

'Yes. I mean, you told me it's quite possible she lost one or both of her parents in a fire. She might be on the brink of learning about or remembering a terrible tragedy in her recent past. Tonight she just needed to relax, to laugh a bit. How could the game have been fun for her if the words on the board started to remind her that her parents might be dead?'

Carol turned on her side, raised herself up a bit, leaned over him, her bare breasts grazing his chest, and stared into his eyes. 'Is that really the only reason you were so upset?'

'Don't you think I was right? Did I overreact?'

'Maybe you did. Maybe you didn't. It *was* creepy.' She kissed his nose. 'You know why I love you so much?'

'Because I'm such a great lover?'

'You are, but that's not why I love you.'

'Because I have tight buns?'

'Not that.'

'Because I keep my fingernails so neat and clean?'

'Not that.'

'I give up.'

'You're so damned sensitive, so caring about other people. How typical of my Paul to worry about the Scrabble game being fun for Jane. *That's* why I love you.'

'I thought it was my hazel eyes.'

'Nah.'

'My classic profile.'

'Are you kidding?'

'Or the way my third toe on my left foot lays half under the second toe.'

'Oh, I'd forgotten about that. Hmmmmm. You're right. *That's* why I love you. Not because you're sensitive. It's your *toes* that drive me wild.'

Their teasing led to cuddling, and the cuddling led to kissing, and the kissing led to passion again. She reached her peak only a few seconds before he spurted deep within her, and when they finally parted for the night, he felt pleasantly wrung out.

Nevertheless, she was asleep before he was. He stared at the dark ceiling of the dark bedroom and thought about the Scrabble game.

BLADE, BLOOD, DEATH, TOMB, KILL . . .

He thought about the word he had hidden from Carol and Jane, the word that had compelled him to end the game and start another. After adding EATH to the D in BLOOD, he'd been left with just three letter tiles on his rack: X, U, and C. The X and the U had played no part in what was to follow. But when he had drawn four new letters, they had gone disconcertingly well with the C. First he'd picked up an A, then an R. And he had known what was going to happen. He hadn't wanted to continue; he'd considered throwing all the tiles back into the box at that moment, for he dreaded seeing the word that he knew the last two letters would spell. But he hadn't ended it there. He had been too curious to stop when he should have stopped. He had drawn a third tile, which had been an O, and then a fourth, L.

C . . . A . . . R . . . O . . . L . . .

BLADE, BLOOD, DEATH, TOMB, KILL, CAROL.

Of course, even if he was able to fit it in, he couldn't put CAROL on the board, for it was a proper name, and the rules didn't allow the use of proper names. But that was a moot point. The important thing was that her name had been spelled out so neatly, so boldly on his rack of letters that it was uncanny. He had drawn the letters in their proper order, for God's sake! What were the odds against *that*?

It seemed to be an omen. A warning that something was going to happen to Carol. Just as Grace Mitowski's two nightmares had turned out to be prophetic.

He thought about the other strange events that had transpired recently: the unnaturally violent lightning strikes at Alfred O'Brian's office; the hammering sound that had shaken the house; the intruder on the rear lawn during the thunderstorm. He sensed that all of it was tied together. But for Christ's sake, *how*?

BLADE, BLOOD.
DEATH, TOMB.
KILL, CAROL.

If the series of words on the Scrabble tiles had constituted a prophetic warning, what was he supposed to do about it? The omen, if it *was* an omen, was too vague to have any value. There was nothing specific to guard against. He couldn't protect Carol until he knew from which direction the danger was coming. A car wreck? A plane crash. A mugger? Cancer? It could be anything. He could see nothing to be gained by telling Carol that her name had turned up on his rack of Scrabble tiles; there was nothing she could do, either, nothing except worry about it.

He didn't want to worry her.

Instead, lying in the darkness, feeling icy even under the covers, he worried *for* her.

* * *

At two o'clock in the morning, Grace was still reading in the study. There wasn't any point in going to bed for at least another hour or two. The events of the last week had turned her into an insomniac.

The day just past had been relatively uneventful. Aristophanes was still behaving oddly – hiding from her, sneaking about, watching her when he thought she didn't know he was there – but he hadn't torn up any more pillows or furniture, and he had used his litter box as he was supposed to do, which were encouraging signs. She hadn't received any more telephone calls from the man who had pretended to be Leonard, and for that she was grateful. Yes, it had been pretty much an ordinary day.

And yet . . .

She was still tense and unable to sleep because she sensed that she was in the eye of the hurricane. She sensed that the peace and quiet in her house were deceptive, that thunder and lightning raged on all sides of her, just beyond the range of her hearing and just out of sight. She expected to be plunged back into the storm at any moment, and that expectation made it impossible for her to relax.

She heard a furtive sound and glanced up from the novel she was reading.

Aristophanes appeared at the open study door, peering in from the hallway. Only his elegant Siamese head was visible as he craned it cautiously around the doorframe.

Their eyes met.

For an instant, Grace felt that she was not looking into the eyes of a dumb animal. They seemed to contain intelligence. Wisdom. Experience. More than mere animal intent and purpose.

Aristophanes hissed.

His eyes were cold. Twin balls of crystal-clear, blue-green ice.

'What do you want, cat?'

He broke the staring contest. He turned away from her with haughty indifference, padded past the doorway, and went softly down the hall, pretending that he hadn't been spying on her, even though they both knew he had been doing exactly that.

Spying? she thought. Am I crazy? Who would a cat be spying for? Catsylvania? Great Kitten? Purrsia?

She could think of other puns, but none of them brought a smile to her lips.

Instead, she sat with the book on her lap, wondering about her sanity.

Chapter Nine

Thursday afternoon.

The office drapes were tightly closed as usual. The light from the two floor lamps was golden, diffuse. Mickey Mouse was still smiling broadly in all his many incarnations.

Carol and Jane sat in the wing chairs.

The girl slipped into a trance with only a little assistance from Carol. Most patients were more susceptible to hypnosis the second time than they had been the first, and Jane was no exception.

Again using the imaginary wristwatch, Carol turned the hands of time backwards and regressed Jane into the past. This time the girl didn't need two minutes to get beyond her amnesia. In only twenty or thirty seconds, she reached a point at which memories existed for her.

She twitched and suddenly sat up ramrod-straight in her chair. Her eyes popped open like the eyes on a doll; she was looking *through* Carol. Her face was twisted with terror.

'Laura?' Carol asked.

Both of the girl's hands flew up to her throat. She clutched herself, gasping, gagging, grimacing in pain. She appeared to be reliving the same traumatic experience that had panicked her during yesterday's sessions, but today she did not scream.

'You can't feel the fire,' Carol told her. 'There is no pain, honey. Relax. Be calm. You can't smell the smoke, either. It doesn't bother you at all. Breathe easily, normally. Be calm and relax.'

The girl didn't obey. She quivered and broke out in a sweat. She retched repeatedly, dryly, violently, yet almost silently.

Afraid that she had lost control again, Carol redoubled her efforts to soothe her patient, without success.

Jane began to gesture wildly, her hands cutting and stabbing and tugging and hammering at the air.

Abruptly, Carol realized the girl was trying to talk, but for some reason had lost her voice.

Tears welled up and slid down Jane's face. She was moving her mouth without the slightest result, desperately trying to force out words that refused to come. In addition to the terror in her eyes, there was now frustration.

Carol quickly fetched a notebook and a felt-tipped pen from her desk. She put the notebook on Jane's lap and pressed the pen into her hand.

'Write it for me, honey.'

The girl squeezed the pen so hard that her knuckles were white and nearly as sharp as the knuckles on a skeleton's fleshless hand. She looked down at the notebook. She stopped retching, but she continued to quiver.

Carol crouched beside the wing chair, where she could see the notebook. 'What is it you want to say?'

Her hand shaking like that of a palsied old woman, Jane hurriedly scrawled two words that were barely legible: *Help me.*

'Why do you need help?'

Again: *Help me.*

'Why can't you speak?'

Head.

'Be more specific.'

My head.

'What about your head?'

The girl's hand began to form a letter, then jumped down one line and made another false start, jumped to a third line – as if she couldn't figure out how to express what she wanted to say. At last, in a frenzy, she started slashing at the paper with the felt-tipped pen, making a meaningless cross-hatching of black lines.

'Stop it!' Carol said. 'You *will* relax, dammit. Be calm.'

Jane stopped slashing at the paper. She was silent, staring down at the notebook on her lap.

Carol tore off the smeared page and threw it on the floor. 'Okay. Now you're going to answer my questions calmly and as fully as you can. What is your name?'

Millie.

Carol stared at the handwritten name, wondering what had happened to Laura Havenswood. 'Millie? Are you sure that's your name?'

Millicent Parker.

'Where is Laura?'

Who's Laura?

Carol stared at the girl's drawn face. The perspiration was beginning to dry on her porcelain-smooth skin. Her blue eyes were blank, unfocused. Her mouth was slack.

Carol abruptly flashed a hand past the girl's face. Jane didn't flinch. She wasn't faking the trance.

'Where do you live, Millicent?'

Harrisburg.

'Right here in town. What's your address?'

Front Street.

'Along the river? Do you know the number?'

The girl wrote it down.

'What's your father's name?'

Randolph Parker.

'What's your mother's name?'

The pen made a meaningless squiggle on the notebook page.

'What's your mother's name?' Carol repeated.

The girl surrendered to a new series of spasmic tremors. She retched soundlessly and put her hands to her throat once more. The felt-tipped pen made a black mark on the underside of her chin.

Apparently, the mere mention of her mother frightened her. That was territory that would have to be explored, though not right now.

Carol talked her down, calmed her, and asked a new question. 'How old are you, Millie?'

Tomorrow's my birthday.

'Is it really? How old will you be?'

I won't make it.

'What won't you make?'

Sixteen.

'Are you fifteen now?'

Yes.

'And you think you won't live to be sixteen? Is that it?'

Won't live.

'Why not?'

The sheen of sweat had nearly evaporated from the girl's face, but again perspiration popped out along her hairline.

'Why won't you live to see your birthday?' Carol persisted.

As before, the girl used the felt-tipped pen to slash angrily at the notebook.

'Stop that,' Carol said firmly. 'Relax and be calm and answer my question.' She tore the ruined page out of the book and tossed it aside, then said, 'Why won't you live to see your sixteenth birthday, Millie?'

Head.

So we're back to this, Carol thought. She said, 'What about your head? What's wrong with it?'

Cut off.

Carol stared at those two words for a moment, then looked up at the girl's face.

Millie-Jane was struggling to remain calm, as Carol had told her she must. But her eyes jiggled nervously, and there was horror in them. Her lips were utterly colorless, tremulous. Beneath the rivulets of sweat that coursed down her forehead, her skin was waxy and mealy white.

She continued to scribble frantically in the notebook, but all she wrote was the same thing over and over again: *Cut off, cut off, cut off, cut off* . . . She was bearing down on the page with such great pressure that the head of the felt-tipped pen was squashed into shapeless mush.

My God, Carol thought, this is like a live report from the bottom of Hell.

Laura Havenswood. Millicent Parker. One girl screaming in pain as fire consumed her, the other a victim of decapitation. What did either of those girls have to do with Jane Doe? She couldn't be *both* of them. Perhaps she wasn't either of them. Were they people she had known? Or were they only figments of her imagination?

What in Christ's name is happening here? Carol wondered.

She put her own hand over the girl's writing hand and stilled the squeaking pen. Speaking gently, rhythmically, she told Millie-Jane that everything was all right, that she was perfectly safe, and that she must relax.

The girl's eyes stopped jiggling. She sagged back in her chair.

'All right,' Carol said. 'I think that's enough for today, honey.'

Employing the imaginary wristwatch, she brought the girl forward in time.

For a few seconds everything went well, but then, without warning, the girl erupted from her chair, knocking the notebook off her lap and flinging the pen across the room. Her pale face flushed red, and her placid expression gave way to a look of pure rage.

Carol rose from beside the girl's chair and stepped in front of her. 'Honey, what's wrong?'

The girl's eyes were wild. She began to shout with such force that she sprayed Carol with spittle. 'Shit! The bitch did it! The rotten, goddamn bitch!'

The voice wasn't Jane's.

It wasn't Laura's either.

It was a new voice, a third one, with its own special character, and Carol had a hunch it didn't belong to Millicent Parker, the mute. She suspected that an entirely new identity had surfaced.

The girl stood very stiff and straight, her hands fisted at her sides, staring off into infinity. Her face was distorted by anger. 'The stinking bitch did it! She did it to me *again*!'

The girl continued to shout at the top of her voice, and half of the words she blurted out were obscene. Carol tried to soothe her, but this time it wasn't easy. For at least a minute the girl continued to wail and curse. At last, however, at Carol's urging, she got control of herself. She stopped shouting, but there was still anger in her face.

Holding the girl by the shoulders, face to face with her, Carol said, 'What's your name?'

'Linda.'

'What's your last name?'

'Bektermann.'

It was yet another identity, as Carol had thought. She had the girl spell the name.

Then: 'Where do you live, Linda?'

'Second Street.'

'In Harrisburg?'

'Yes.'

Carol asked for the exact address, and the girl responded. It was only a few blocks from the Front Street address that Millicent Parker had provided.

'What's your father's name, Linda?'

'Herbert Bektermann.'

'What's your mother's name?'

That question had the same effect on Linda as it had had on Millie. She rapidly became agitated and began to shout again. 'The bitch! Oh, God, what she *did* to me. The slimy, rotten bitch! I hate her. I hate her!'

Chilled by the combination of fury and agony in the girl's tortured voice, Carol quickly quieted her.

Then: 'How old are you, Linda?'

'Tomorrow's my birthday.'

Carol frowned. 'Am I talking to Millicent now?'

'Who's Millicent?'

'Is this still Linda I'm talking to?'

'Yes.'

'And your birthday is tomorrow?'

'Yes.'

'How old will you be?'

'I won't make it.'

Carol blinked. 'You mean you won't live to see your birthday?'

'That's right.'

'Is it your sixteenth birthday?'

'Yes.'

'You're fifteen now?'

'Yes.'

'Why are you worried about dying?'

'Because I know I will.'

'How do you know?'

'Because I already am.'

'You're already dying?'

'Dead.'

'You're already dead?'

'I will be.'

'Please be specific. Are you telling me that you're already dead? Or are you saying that you're merely afraid you're *going* to die sometime soon?'

'Yes.'

'Which is it?'

'Both.'

Carol felt as if she were in the middle of a tea party at the Mad Hatter's house.

'How do you think you're going to die, Linda?'

'She'll kill me.'

'Who?'

'The bitch.'

'Your mother?'

The girl doubled over and clutched at her side, as if she had been struck. She screamed, turned, staggered two steps, and fell with a crash. On the floor she still clutched her side, and she kicked her legs, writhed. She was obviously in unendurable pain. It was only imaginary pain, of course, but to the girl it was indistinguishable from the real thing.

Frightened, Carol knelt beside her, held her hand, and urged her to be calm. When the girl eventually relaxed, Carol quickly brought her all the way back to the present and out of the trance.

Jane blinked, stared up at Carol, and put one hand on the floor beside her, as if testing the truth of what her eyes told her. 'Wow, what am I doing down here?'

Carol helped her to her feet. 'I suppose you don't remember?'

'No. Did I tell you anything more about myself?'

'No. I don't think so. You told me you were a girl named Millicent Parker, and then you told me you were a girl named Linda Bektermann, but obviously you can't be *both* of them *and* Laura, too. So I suspect that you aren't any of them.'

'I don't think so, either,' Jane said. 'Those two new names don't mean anything more to me than Laura Havenswood did. But who *are* those people? Where did I get their names, and why did I tell you I was any of them?'

'I'll be damned if I know,' Carol said. 'But sooner or later, we'll figure it out. We'll get to the bottom of all this, kiddo. I promise you that.'

But what in God's name will we find at the bottom, down there in the dark? Carol wondered. Will it be something we'll wish we'd left buried forever?

* * *

Thursday afternoon, Grace Mitowski worked in the rose garden behind her house. The day was warm and clear, and she felt the need for some exercise. Besides, in the garden she wouldn't be able to hear the telephone ringing and wouldn't be tempted to answer it. Which was fine, because she wasn't psychologically prepared to answer the phone just yet; she hadn't decided how to deal with the hoaxer the next time he called and pretended that he was her long-dead husband.

Because of last week's torrential rains, the roses were past their prime. The last flowers of the season should have been at the peak of their beauty right now, but many of the big blooms had lost a fifth or even a fourth of their petals under the lashing of the wind-whipped rain. Nevertheless, the garden was still a colorful, cheery sight.

She had let Aristophanes out for some exercise. She kept an eye on him, intending to call him back the moment he headed off the property. She was determined to keep him away from whoever had poisoned or drugged him. But he didn't seem to be in a rambling mood; he stayed nearby, creeping among the roses, stirring up a moth or two and chasing them with catlike single-mindedness.

Grace was on her hands and knees in front of a row of inter-mingled yellow and crimson and orange flowers, hand-spading the earth with a trowel, when someone said, 'You have a magnificent garden.'

Startled, she looked up and saw a thin, jaundice-skinned man in a rumpled blue suit that hadn't been in fashion for many years. His shirt and tie were hopelessly out of style, too. He looked as if he had stepped out of a photograph taken in the 1940s. He had thinning hair the color of summer dust, and his eyes were an unusual shade of soft brown, almost beige. His face was com-posed entirely of narrow features and sharp angles that gave him a look halfway between that of a hawk and that of a parsimonious moneylender in a Charles Dickens novel. He appeared to be in his early or middle fifties.

Grace glanced at the gate in the white board fence that separated her property from the street. The gate was standing wide open. Evidently, the man had been strolling by, had seen the roses through a gap in the poplar-tree hedge that stood on the outside of the fence, and had decided to come in and have a closer look.

His smile was warm, and there was kindness in his eyes, and he seemed not to be intruding, even though he was. 'You must have two dozen varieties of roses here.'

'Three dozen,' she said.

'Truly magnificent,' he said, nodding approval. His voice wasn't thin and sharp like the rest of him. It was deep, mellow, friendly, and would have seemed more fitting if it had issued from a brawny, hearty fellow half again this man's size. 'You take care of the entire garden yourself?'

Grace sat back on her heels, still holding the trowel in one gloved hand. 'Sure. I enjoy it. And somehow . . . it just wouldn't be *my* garden if I hired someone to help me with it.'

'Exactly!' the stranger said. 'Yes, I can understand how you feel.'

'Are you new in the neighborhood?' Grace asked.

'No, no. Used to live just a block from here, but that was a long, long time ago.' He took a deep breath and smiled again. 'Ah, the wonderful aroma of roses! Nothing else smells half so pretty. Yes, you've got a superb garden. Really superb.'

'Thank you.'

He snapped his fingers as a thought occurred to him. 'I ought to write something about this. It might make a first-rate human-interest piece. This fantasyland tucked away in an ordinary back-yard. Yes, I'm sure it would be just the thing. A nice change of pace for me.'

'Are you a writer?'

'Reporter,' he said, still taking deep breaths and savoring the aroma of the blooms.

'Are you with a local paper?'

'The *Morning News*. Name's Palmer Wainwright.'

'Grace Mitowski.'

'I hoped you might recognize my byline,' Wainwright said, grinning.

'Sorry. I don't read the *Morning News*. I take the *Patriot-News* from the delivery boy every morning.'

'Ah, well,' he said, shrugging, 'that's a good paper, too. But of course, if you don't read the *Morning News*, you never saw my story about the Bektermann case.'

As Grace realized that Wainwright intended to hang around awhile, she got off her haunches, stood up, and flexed her rapidly stiffening legs. 'The Bektermann case? That sounds familiar.'

'All the papers reported it, of course. But I did a five-part series. Good stuff, even if I do say so myself. I got a Pulitzer nomination for it. Did you know that? An honest-to-God Pulitzer nomination.'

'Really? Why, that's something,' Grace said, not sure if she should take him seriously but not wanting to offend him. 'That is *really* something. Imagine. A Pulitzer nomination.'

It seemed to her that the conversation had suddenly taken an odd turn. It wasn't casual any longer. She sensed that Wainwright had come into the yard not to admire her roses and not to have a friendly chat, but to tell her, a complete stranger, about his Pulitzer nomination.

'Didn't win,' Wainwright said. 'But the way I look at it, a nomination is almost as good as the prize itself. I mean, out of the tens of thousands of newspaper articles that're published in a year, only a handful are up for the prize.'

'Refresh my memory, if you will,' Grace said. 'What was the Bektermann case about?'

He laughed good-naturedly and shook his head. 'Wasn't about what I *thought* it was about. That's for damned sure. I wrote it up as a tangled, Freudian puzzle. You know – the iron-willed father, with perhaps an unnatural attraction for his own daughter, the mother with a drinking problem, the poor girl caught in the middle. The victimized young girl subjected to hideous psychological pressures beyond her understanding, beyond her tolerance, until at last she simply – *snapped*. That's how I saw it. That's how I wrote it up. I thought I was a brilliant detective, digging to the deepest roots of the Bektermann tragedy. But all I ever saw was the window-dressing. The real story was far stranger than anything I ever imagined. Hell, it was too strange for any serious reporter to risk handling it. No reputable paper would have printed it as news. If I *had* known the truth, and if I *had* somehow gotten it published, I'd have destroyed my career.'

What the devil's going on? Grace wondered. He seems obsessed with telling me about this in detail, *compelled* to tell me, even though he's never even seen me before. Is this life imitating art – Coleridge's poem reset in a rose garden? Am I the partygoer and Wainwright the Ancient Mariner?

As she looked into Wainwright's beige eyes, she suddenly realized how alone she was, even here in the yard. Her property was ringed by trees, sheltered, private.

'Was it a murder case?' she asked.

'Was and is,' Wainwright said. 'It didn't end with the Bektermanns. It's still going on. This damned, endless pursuit. It's still going on, and it's got to be stopped this time around. That's why I'm here. I've come to tell you that your Carol is in the middle of it. Caught in the middle. You've got to help her. Get her out of the girl's way.'

Grace gaped at him, reluctant to believe that she had heard what she knew she had heard.

'There are certain forces, dark and powerful forces,' Wainwright said calmly, 'that want to see –'

Shrieking angrily, Aristophanes sprang at Wainwright with berserk passion. He landed on the man's chest and scrambled onto his face.

Grace screamed and jumped back in fright.

Wainwright staggered to one side, grabbed the cat with both hands, and tried unsuccessfully to wrench it off his face.

'Ari!' Grace cried. 'Stop it!'

Aristophanes had his claws in the man's neck and was biting his cheek.

Wainwright wasn't screaming as he ought to have been. He was eerily silent as he wrestled with the cat, even though the creature seemed determined to tear off his face.

Grace moved toward Wainwright, wanting to help, not knowing what to do.

The cat was squealing. It bit off a gobbet of flesh from Wainwright's cheek.

Oh Jesus, no!

Grace moved in quickly, raising the trowel, but hesitated. She was afraid of hitting the man instead of the cat.

Wainwright suddenly turned away from her and stumbled through the rose bushes, past white and yellow blooms, the cat still clinging to him. He walked into a waist-high hedge, fell through it, onto the lawn on the other side, out of sight.

Grace hurried to the end of the hedgerow, stepped around it, heart hammering, and discovered that Wainwright had vanished. Only the cat was there, and it bolted past her, sprinted across the garden, up the back porch steps, and into the house through the half-open rear door.

Where was Wainwright? Had he crawled away, dazed, wounded? Had he passed out in some sheltered corner of the garden, bleeding to death?

The yard contained half a dozen shrubs large and dense enough to conceal the body of a man Wainwright's size. She looked around all of them, but she could find no trace of the reporter.

She looked toward the garden gate that led to the street. No. He couldn't have gone that far without drawing her attention.

Frightened, confused, Grace blinked at the sun-dappled garden, trying to understand.

*　　*　　*

The Harrisburg telephone book contained neither a listing for Mr. Randolph Parker nor one for Herbert Bektermann. Carol was perplexed but not surprised.

After she saw her final patient of the day, she and Jane drove to the address on Front Street where Millicent Parker had claimed to live. It was a huge, impressive Victorian mansion, but it hadn't been anyone's home for a long time. The front lawn had been paved over for a parking lot. There was a small, tasteful sign by the entrance drive:

MAUGHAM & CRICHTON, INC.
A MEDICAL CORPORATION

Many years ago, this portion of Front Street had been one of the most elegant neighborhoods in Pennsylvania's capital city. During the past couple of decades, however, many of the riverfront boulevard's grand old houses had been razed to make room for sterile, modern office buildings. A few of the rambling houses had been preserved, at least after a fashion – the exteriors beautifully restored, the interiors gutted and converted to various commercial uses. Farther north, there was still a section of Front Street that was a desirable residential area, but not here, not where Millicent Parker had sent them.

Maugham & Crichton was a group medical practice that included seven physicians: two general internists and five specialists. Carol had a chat with the receptionist, a henna-haired woman named Polly, who told her that none of the doctors was named Parker. Likewise, no one of that name was employed as a nurse or as a member of the clerical staff. Furthermore, Maugham & Crichton had been at their current address for nearly seventeen years.

It had occurred to Carol that Jane might once have been a patient of one of Maugham & Crichton's physicians, and that her subconscious mind had made use of the firm's address to flesh out the Millicent Parker identity. But Polly, who had worked for Maugham & Crichton ever since they'd opened their doors, was sure she had never seen the girl. However, intrigued by Jane's amnesia and sympathetic by nature, Polly agreed to check the files to see if Maugham & Crichton had ever treated anyone named Laura Havenswood, Millicent Parker, or Linda Bektermann. It was a fruitless search; none of those names appeared in the patient records.

*   *   *

Grace stepped through the gate, into the street, and looked both ways. There was no sign of Palmer Wainwright.

She returned to her own backyard, closed and latched the gate, and walked toward the house.

Wainwright was sitting on the porch steps, waiting for her.

She stopped fifteen feet from him, amazed, confused.

He got up from the steps.

'Your face,' she said numbly.

His face was unscarred.

He smiled as if nothing had happened and took two steps toward her. 'Grace –'

'The cat,' she said. 'I saw your cheek . . . your neck . . . its claws tore out . . .'

'Listen,' he said, taking another step toward her, 'there are certain forces, dark and powerful forces, that want to see this played out the wrong way. Dark forces that thrive on tragedy. They want to see it end in senseless violence and blood. That mustn't be allowed to happen, Grace. Not again. You've got to keep Carol out of the girl's way, for her sake and for the sake of the girl, too.'

Grace gaped at him. 'Who the hell are you?'

'Who are *you*?' Wainwright asked, raising one eyebrow quizzically. '*That* is the important question right now. You aren't only who you think you are. You aren't only Grace Mitowski.'

He's mad, she thought. Or I'm mad. Or we both are. Stark, raving mad.

She said, 'You're the one on the phone. You're the creep who imitates Leonard's voice.'

'No,' he said. 'I am –'

'No wonder Ari attacked you. You're the one who's been giving him drugs or poison or something like that. You're the one, and he *knew*.'

But what about the facial wounds, the gouged neck? she asked herself. How in the name of God did those injuries heal so quickly?

How?

She pushed those thoughts out of her mind, refused to think about such things. She must have been mistaken. She must have imagined that Ari had actually hurt the man.

'Yeah,' she said, 'you're the one who's behind all of these weird things that've been happening. Get off my property, you son of a bitch.'

'Grace, there are forces aligned . . .' He looked no different now from the way he had looked when he'd first spoken to her, several minutes ago. He hadn't looked crazed then; he didn't look crazed now. He didn't look dangerous, and yet he continued to babble about dark forces. '. . . good and evil, right and wrong. You're on the right side, Grace. But the cat – ah, the cat's a different story. At all times, you must be wary of the cat.'

'Get out of my way,' she said.

He took a step toward her.

She slashed at him with the gardening trowel, missing his face by just an inch or two. She slashed again and again and again, cutting only empty air, not really wanting to cut anything else unless she had no choice, just hoping to keep him at bay until she could slip around him, for he was between her and the house. And then she *was* around him; she turned and ran for the kitchen door, painfully aware that her legs were old and arthritic. She went only a few steps before she realized she shouldn't have turned her back on the lunatic, and she wheeled to confront him, gasping, certain that he was leaping toward her, perhaps with a knife in his hand –

But he was gone.

Vanished. Again.

He hadn't had time to reach any of the shrubs that were large enough to conceal a man, not during the split second her back had been turned. Even if he had been a much younger man than he was, in the very best condition, a trained runner – even then he couldn't have gone more than halfway to the gate in such a short time.

So where was he?

Where was he?

* * *

From the offices of Maugham & Crichton on Front Street, Carol and Jane drove a few blocks to the Second Street address that was supposed to be the home of Linda Bektermann. It was in a good neighborhood; a lovely French country house, at least fifty years old, in fine condition. No one was at home, but the name on the mailbox was Nicholson, not Bektermann.

They rang the bell at the house next door and talked to a neighbor, Jean Gunther, who confirmed that the French country place was owned and occupied by the Nicholson family.

'My husband and I have lived here for six years,' Mrs. Gunther said, 'and the Nicholsons were next door when we moved in. I think I once heard them say they'd lived in that house since 1965.'

The name Bektermann meant nothing to Jean Gunther.

In the car again, on the way home, Jane said, 'I'm really a lot of trouble for you.'

'Nonsense,' Carol said. 'I kind of enjoy playing detective. Besides, if I can help you break through your memory block, if I can uncover the truth behind all the sleight-of-hand tricks that your subconscious is playing, then I'll be able to write about this case for any psychology journal I choose. It'll definitely make my name in the profession. I might even wind up with a book out of it. So you see, because of you, kiddo, I could become rich and famous some day.'

'When you're rich and famous, will you still talk to me?' the girl teased.

'Certainly. Of course, you'll have to make an appointment a week in advance.'

They grinned at each other.

*   *   *

Using the kitchen phone, Grace called the offices of the *Morning News*.

The switchboard operator at the newspaper didn't have an extension number listed for Palmer Wainwright. She said, 'So far as I know, he don't even work here. And I'm sure he's no reporter. Maybe one of the new copy editors or somebody like that.'

'Could you connect me with the managing editor's office?' Grace asked.

'That would be Mr. Quincy,' the operator said. She buzzed the proper extension.

Quincy wasn't in his office, and his secretary didn't know whether or not the paper employed a man named Palmer Wainwright. 'I'm new here,' she said apologetically. 'I've only been Mr. Quincy's secretary since Monday, so I don't know everybody yet. If you'll leave your name and number, I'll have Mr. Quincy return your call.'

Grace gave her the number and said, 'Tell him Dr. Grace Mitowski wishes to speak with him and that I'll only need a few minutes of his time.' She seldom used the honorific in front of her name, but it came in handy in cases like this, for a doctor's phone calls were *always* returned.

'Is this an emergency, Dr. Mitowski? I don't think that Mr. Quincy's going to be back until tomorrow morning.'

'That'll be good enough,' she said. 'Have him call me first thing, no matter how early he gets in.'

After she hung up, she went to the kitchen and stared out at the rose garden.

How could Wainwright vanish like that?

*   *   *

For the third evening in a row, Paul and Carol and Jane prepared dinner together. The girl was fitting in better day by day.

If she stays with us just another week, Paul thought, it'll seem like she's *always* been here.

739

The salad consisted of hearts of palm and iceberg lettuce. That was followed by eggplant Parmigiana with spaghetti on the side.

As they were starting dessert – small dishes of richly flavored spumoni – Paul said, 'Any chance we could postpone the trip to the mountains for two days?'

'Why?' Carol asked

'I'm a bit behind in my writing schedule, and I'm at a very critical point in the book,' he said. 'I've written two-thirds of the toughest scene in the story, and I hate to leave it unfinished just to go on vacation. I won't enjoy myself. If we left Sunday instead of tomorrow, that would give me time to polish off the end of the chapter. And we'd still have eight days at the cabin.'

'Don't look at me,' Jane said. 'I'm just excess baggage. I'll go wherever you take me, whenever you take me.'

Carol shook her head. 'Just last week, when Mr. O'Brian said we were compulsive overachievers, we made up our minds to change our ways, didn't we? We've *got* to learn to make time for leisure and not let our work encroach on that.'

'You're right,' Paul said. 'But just this once –' He broke off in midsentence because he saw that Carol was determined. She was rarely intractable, but when she *did* decide not to compromise on an issue, she was about as movable as Gibraltar. He sighed. 'Okay. You win. We'll leave tomorrow morning. I'll just bring along the typewriter and the manuscript. I can finish the scene up at the cabin and –'

'Nothing doing,' Carol said, emphasizing each word by tapping her spoon against her ice cream dish. 'If you bring it along, you won't stop when you've reached the end of the scene you're working on. You'll keep going. You *know* you will. Having the typewriter within easy reach will just be too much of a temptation. You won't be able to resist it. The whole vacation will go down the drain.'

'But I just *can't* put that scene on hold for ten days,' he said pleadingly. 'By the time I get back to it, the tone and the spontaneity will be lost.'

Carol ate a spoonful of spumoni and said, 'All right. Here's what we'll do. Jane and I will leave for the mountains first thing in the morning, just as we planned. You stay here, finish your scene, and then drive up to join us whenever you're ready.'

He frowned. 'I'm not sure that's a good idea.'

'Why not?'

'Well, is it really wise for the two of you to go up there alone? I mean, the summer season is over. There aren't going to be many campers in the woods now, and most of the other cabins will be deserted.'

'For heaven's sake,' Carol said, 'there's no Abominable Snowman lurking around in *those* mountains, Paul. We're in Pennsylvania, not Tibet.' She smiled. 'It's nice to know you're so concerned about us, darling. But we'll be perfectly safe.'

* * *

Later, after Jane had gone to bed, Paul made one last attempt to change Carol's mind, although he knew the effort would be wasted.

He leaned against the frame of the closet door and watched as Carol selected clothes for the suitcases. 'Listen, be straight with me, okay?'

'Aren't I always? Straight about what?'

'The girl. Is there any chance she's dangerous?'

Carol turned from the clothes rack and stared at him, obviously surprised by his question. 'Jane? Dangerous? Well, a girl as pretty as she is will probably break a lot of hearts over the years. And if cuteness could kill, she'd leave the streets littered with bodies behind her.'

He refused to be amused. 'I don't want you to be flippant about this. I think it's important. I want you to give it careful thought.'

'I don't *need* to give it a lot of thought, Paul. She's lost her memory, sure. But she's a stable, mentally healthy kid. In fact, it takes an *amazingly* stable personality to handle amnesia the way she's handled it. I don't know that I'd do half as well if I were in her shoes right now. I'd either be a nervous wreck or sunk neck-deep in depression. She's resilient, flexible. Resilient and flexible people aren't dangerous.'

'Never?'

'Hardly ever. It's the rigid ones who crack.'

'But after what's happened in your therapy sessions with her, isn't it reasonable to wonder about what she might be capable of doing?' he asked.

'She's a tortured girl. I believe she's been through a truly terrifying experience, something so awful that she refuses to relive it, even under hypnosis. She obfuscates, misdirects, and holds back vital information, but that doesn't mean she's the least bit dangerous. Just scared. It seems evident to me that she was the victim of either physical or psychological violence at some time in her life. The *victim*, Paul, not the perpetrator.'

She carried a few pairs of jeans to the suitcases that were open on the bed.

Paul followed her. 'Are you going to continue her therapy while you're at the cabin?'

'Yes. I think it's best to keep chipping away at the wall of confusion she's thrown up.'

'Not fair.'

'Huh?'

'That's work,' he said. 'I'm not allowed to take *my* work up to the cabin, but *you're* going to work. That's a double standard, Dr. Tracy.'

'Double standard, my ass, Dr. Tracy. I'll need only half an hour a day for Jane's therapy. That's a lot different than lugging an IBM Selectric into the piny woods and pounding on the keys ten hours a day. Don't you realize that all the squirrels and deer and bunny rabbits would complain about the noise?'

* * *

Later still, when they were in bed and the lights were out, he said, 'Hell, I'm letting this book take possession of me. Why *can't* I let the scene lie unfinished for ten days? I might even do a better job with it if I take the time to think about it. I'll come along with you and Jane tomorrow, and I won't bring the typewriter. Okay? I won't even bring a pencil.'

'No,' Carol said.

'No?'

'When you *do* get to the mountains, I want you to be able to put the book completely out of your mind. I want us to take long walks in the forest. I want us to go boating on the lake and do some fishing and read a couple of books and act like bums who never even heard the word "work." If you don't finish that scene before you go, you'll just brood about it during the entire vacation. You won't have a moment's real peace, which means *I* won't have a moment's peace, either. And don't tell me I'm wrong. I know you better than I know myself, buster. You stay here, write the end of that scene, and then join us on Sunday.'

She kissed him goodnight, fluffed her pillows, and settled down to sleep.

He lay in the dark, thinking about the words in yesterday's Scrabble game.

```
                    B L A D E
          K I L L   L
                    O
                    O
                    D E A T H
                        O
                        M
                        B
```

And the one word he had refused to reveal: CAROL . . .

He still didn't think anything would be gained by telling her what the last of those six words had been. What could she do about it other than worry? Nothing. She could do nothing, and he could do nothing. Except wait and see. A threat – if one actually arose – could come from any of ten thousand or a hundred thousand sources. It could come anytime, anywhere. At home or in the mountains. One place was as safe – or as dangerous – as the other.

Anyway, maybe the appearance of those six words *had* been merely coincidence. An incredible but meaningless coincidence.

He stared into the darkness, trying hard to convince himself that there were no such things as spirit messages, omens, and clairvoyant prophecies. Only a week ago, he wouldn't have *needed* convincing.

*   *   *

Blood.

Get it off, scrub it off, every sticky drop of it, wash it off, quickly, quickly, down the drain, every incriminating drop of it, off, before someone finds out, before someone sees and knows what's been done, wash it off, off. . . .

The girl woke in the bathroom, in a fluorescent glare. She had been sleepwalking again.

She was surprised to find that she was nude. Her knee socks, panties, and T-shirt were scattered on the floor around her.

She was standing in front of the sink, scrubbing herself with a wet washcloth. When she looked at her reflection in the mirror, she was briefly paralyzed by what she saw.

Her face was smeared with blood.

Her arms were spattered with blood.

743

Her sweetly uptilted, bare breasts glistened with blood.

And she knew instantly that it wasn't her own. She had not been slashed or stabbed. *She* was the one who had done the slashing, the stabbing.

Oh God.

She stared at her gruesome reflection, morbidly fascinated by the sight of her blood-moistened lips.

What have I done?

She slowly lowered her gaze along her crimsoned neck, looked down at the reflection of her right nipple, on which hung a very fat, carmine droplet of gore. The gleaming pearl of blood quivered for an instant on the tip of her erect nipple; then it succumbed to gravity and fell away from her.

She pulled her gaze from the mirror, lowered her head to see where the droplet had struck the floor.

There was no blood.

When she looked directly at herself, rather than at her reflection, she discovered that her body was not covered with blood after all. She touched her bare breasts. They were damp because she had been scrubbing them with the washcloth, but the dampness was nothing more than water. Her arms weren't spattered with blood, either.

She squeezed the washcloth. Clear water dripped from it; the cloth bore no grisly stains.

Confused, she raised her eyes to the mirror once more and saw the blood, as before.

She held out her hand. In reality it was not bloody, but in the mirror it was sheathed in a glove of gore.

A vision, she thought. A weird illusion. That's all. I didn't hurt anyone. I didn't spill anyone's blood.

As she struggled to understand what was happening, her mirror image faded, and the glass in front of her turned black. It seemed to have been transformed into a window that looked out onto another dimension, for it reflected nothing that was in the bathroom.

This is a dream, she thought. I'm really snug in bed, where I belong. I'm only dreaming that I'm in the bathroom. I can put a stop to this just by waking up.

On the other hand, if it was a dream, would she be able to feel the cold ceramic floor beneath her bare feet as vividly as she could feel it now? If it was really only a dream, would she be aware of the cold water on her bare breasts?

She shivered.

In the lightless void on the other side of the mirror, something flickered far off in the darkness.

Wake up!

Something silvery. It flashed again and again, back and forth, the image growing steadily larger.

For God's sake, wake up!

She wanted to run. Couldn't.

She wanted to scream. Didn't.

In seconds the flickering object filled the mirror, pushing back the darkness out of which it had come, and then somehow it burst out of the mirror without shattering the glass, exploded out of the void and into the bathroom with one final, murderous swing, and she saw that it was an ax, bearing down on her face, the steel blade gleaming like the finest silver under the fluorescent lights. As the wickedly sharp edge of the ax swept inexorably toward her head, her knees buckled, and she fainted.

* * *

Near dawn, Jane woke again.

She was in bed. She was nude.

She threw the covers back, sat up, and saw her T-shirt, panties, and knee socks on the floor beside the bed. She dressed quickly.

The house was silent. The Tracys weren't up yet.

Jane hurried quietly down the hallway to the guest bathroom, hesitated on the threshold, then stepped inside and snapped on the lights.

There was no blood, and the mirror above the sink was only an ordinary mirror, reflecting her worried face but contributing no bizarre images of its own.

Okay, she thought, maybe I *was* sleepwalking. And maybe I *was* actually here without any clothes on, trying to scrub nonexistent blood off my body. But the rest of it was just part of the nightmare. It didn't happen. It couldn't. Impossible. The mirror couldn't really *change* like that.

She stared into her own blue eyes. She wasn't sure what she saw in them.

'Who *am* I?' she asked softly.

* * *

745

All week, Grace's sleep – what little she had managed to get between bouts of insomnia – had been dreamless. But tonight she thrashed for hours in the sheets, trying to fight her way out of a nightmare that seemed to last an eternity.

In the dream, a house was on fire. A big, beautifully ornamented Victorian house. She was standing outside the blazing structure, pounding on a pair of slant-set cellar doors and calling a name over and over again. 'Laura! Laura!' She knew that Laura was trapped in the cellar of the burning house and that these doors were the only way out, but the doors were latched on the inside. She hammered on the wood with her bare hands until each blow sent a cruel bolt of pain the length of her arms, through her shoulders, and up the back of her neck. She wished desperately that she had an ax or a pry-bar or some other tool with which she could smash through the cellar doors, but she had nothing other than her fists, so she pounded and pounded until her flesh bruised and split and bled, and she kept on pounding even then, all the while screaming for Laura. Windows exploded on the second floor, showering glass down over her, but she didn't turn away from the slant-set cellar doors; she didn't run. She continued to slam her bloodied fists into the wood, praying that the girl would answer at any moment. She ignored the sparks that showered down on her and threatened to set her gingham dress afire. She wept, and she coughed when the wind blew the acrid smoke in her direction, and she cursed the wood that so easily resisted her fierce but ineffectual attack.

The nightmare had no climax, no peak of terror. It simply went on all night long at a continuously breathless pace until, a few minutes after dawn, Grace finally wrenched herself out of the hot, clutching arms of sleep and woke with a wordless cry, flailing at the mattress.

She sat up on the edge of the bed and held her throbbing head in her hands.

Her mouth was filled with the taste of ashes and bile.

The dream had been so vivid that she had even felt the high-necked, long-sleeved, blue and white gingham dress binding at her shoulders and across her bust as she had hammered on the cellar doors. Now, wide awake, she could *still* feel the dress binding her, even though she was wearing a loose nightgown, and even though she had never worn such a dress in her entire life.

Worse, she could smell the house burning.

The smoke odor lingered so long after she had awakened that

she became convinced that her own house was ablaze. Quickly, she pulled on a robe, stepped into her slippers, and went from one room to another, searching for the fire.

There was no fire.

Yet for almost an hour, the stench of burning wood and tar stayed with her.

Chapter Ten

Friday morning at nine o'clock, Paul sat down at his writing desk, picked up the phone, and called Lincoln Werth, the police detective in charge of the Jane Doe case. He told Werth that Carol was taking the girl out of town for a few days of rest and recreation.

'Might as well,' Werth said. 'We don't have any leads, and I sure don't think this is going to break wide open anytime soon. We keep expanding the search area, of course. At first we just put the kid's photo and description out to authorities in the surrounding counties. When that didn't do us any good, we put it on the wire to police agencies all over the state. Yesterday morning we took another step and wired the same data to seven neighboring states. But I'll tell you something, just between you and me. Even if we expand the search area all the way to Hong Kong, I got a feeling we ain't never going to find anyone who knows the kid. I just have a hunch. We're going to keep coming up empty-handed.'

After talking to Werth, Paul went down to the garage, where Carol and Jane were putting their gear in the trunk of the Volkswagen. To spare the girl grief, Paul didn't pass along Werth's pessimistic assessment of the situation. 'He said it's all right to leave town for a few days. The court didn't restrict you to Harrisburg. I told him where the cabin is, so if anyone turns up to claim our girl here, the Harrisburg police will contact the county sheriff out that way, and he or one of his deputies will drop by the cabin and let you know you've got to come back.'

Carol kissed him goodbye. Jane kissed him, too; hers was a shy, chaste kiss, lightly planted on his cheek, and when she got into the car, she was blushing brightly.

He stood in front of the house and watched them drive away until the red Volkswagen Rabbit was out of sight.

After almost a week of blue skies, clouds had drifted in again. They were flat, slate gray. They matched Paul's mood.

* * *

When the kitchen phone rang, Grace steeled herself for the sound of Leonard's voice. She sat down in the chair at the small built-in desk, reached up, put her hand on the receiver that hung on the wall, let it ring once more, then picked it up. To her relief, it was Ross Quincy, the managing editor of the *Morning News*, returning the call she'd made late yesterday afternoon.

'You were inquiring about one of our reporters, Dr. Mitowski?'

'Yes. Palmer Wainwright.'

Quincy was silent.

'He does work for you, doesn't he?' Grace asked.

'Uh . . . Palmer Wainwright has been an employee of the *Morning News*, yes.'

'I believe he nearly won a Pulitzer Prize.'

'Yes. But of course . . . that was quite a while back.'

'Oh?'

'Well, if you know about the Pulitzer nomination, you must know it was for the series he did on the Bektermann murders.'

'Yes.'

'Which was back in 1943.'

'That long ago?'

'Uh . . . Dr. Mitowski, exactly what is it you wanted to know about Palmer Wainwright?'

'I'd like to talk with him,' she said. 'We've met, and we have some unfinished business that I'm rather anxious to take care of. It's a . . . personal matter.'

Quincy hesitated. Then: 'Are you a long-lost relative?'

'Of Mr. Wainwright's? Oh, no.'

'A long-lost friend?'

'No. Not that either.'

'Well, then, I guess I don't have to be delicate about this. Dr. Mitowski, I'm afraid that Palmer Wainwright is dead.'

'Dead!' she said, astounded.

'Well, surely you realized there was that possibility. He was never a well man, downright sickly. And you've obviously been out of touch with him for a long time.'

'Not all that long,' she said.

'Must be at least thirty-five years,' Quincy said. 'He died back in 1946.'

The air at Grace's back seemed suddenly colder than it had been an instant ago, as if a dead man had expelled his icy breath against the nape of her neck.

'Thirty-one years,' she said numbly. 'You must be wrong.'

'Not a chance. I was just a green kid back then, a copyboy. Palmer Wainwright was one of my heroes. I took it pretty hard when he went.'

'Are we talking about the same man?' Grace asked. 'He was quite thin, with sharp features, pale brown eyes, and a rather sallow complexion. His voice was several notes deeper than you'd expect from just looking at him.'

'That was Palmer, all right.'

'About fifty-five?'

'He was thirty-six when he died, but he did *look* twenty years older,' Quincy said. 'It was that string of illnesses, one thing right after another, with cancer at the end. It just wore him down, aged him fast. He was a fighter, but he just couldn't hold on any longer.'

Thirty-one years in the grave? she thought. But I saw him yesterday. We had a strange conversation in the rose garden. What do you say to that, Mr. Quincy?

'Dr. Mitowski? Are you still there?'

'Yes. Sorry. Listen, Mr. Quincy, I hate to take your valuable time, but this is really important. I believe the Bektermann case had a lot to do with the personal business I wanted to discuss with Mr. Wainwright. But I don't really know anything about those murders. Would you mind telling me what it was all about?'

'Family tragedy,' Quincy said. 'The Bektermanns' daughter went berserk the day before her sixteenth birthday. Her mind just snapped. Apparently, she got it in her head that her mother intended to kill her before she turned sixteen, which was not true, of course. But she *thought* it was true, and she went after her mother with an ax. Her father and a visiting cousin got in the way, and she killed them. Her mother actually managed to wrench the ax out of the girl's hands. But that didn't stop the kid. She just picked up a fireplace poker and kept coming. When the mother, Mrs. Bektermann, was backed into a corner and was about to have her skull cracked open with the poker, she didn't have any choice but to swing the ax at her daughter. She hit the girl once, in the side. A pretty deep cut. The kid died in the hospital the next day. Mrs. Bektermann only killed in self-defense, and no charges were brought against her, but she felt so guilty about killing her own child that she had a complete breakdown and eventually wound up in an institution.'

'And that's the story that won Mr. Wainwright his Pulitzer nomination?'

'Yeah. In the hands of a lot of reporters, the piece would have been nothing but sensationalistic garbage. But Palmer was good. He wrote a sensitive, well-researched study of a family with serious emotional, interpersonal problems. The father was a domineering man who set extremely high standards for his daughter and very likely had an unnatural attraction to her. The mother was always competing with the father for the girl's heart, mind, and loyalty, and when she saw she was losing that battle, she turned to drink. There were extraordinary psychological pressures brought to bear on the daughter, and Palmer made the reader feel and understand those pressures.'

She thanked Ross Quincy for his time and consideration. She hung up the phone.

For a while she just sat there, staring at the softly humming refrigerator, trying to make sense of what she had been told. If Wainwright had died in 1946, whom had she talked to in the garden yesterday?

And what did the Bektermann murders have to do with her? With Carol?

She thought of what Wainwright had told her: *This damned, endless pursuit. It's still going on, and it's got to be stopped this time around. . . . I've come to tell you that your Carol is in the middle of it. . . . You've got to help her. Get her out of the girl's way.*

She felt she was on the verge of understanding what he had meant. And she was scared.

Even though a number of impossible things had transpired within the past twenty-four hours, she no longer questioned either her sanity or her perceptions. She was sane, perfectly sane, and in command of all her faculties. Senility was not even a remote possibility any longer. She sensed that the explanation for these events was far more frightening, more soul-shattering even than the prospect of senility, which had once terrified her.

She recalled something else that Palmer Wainwright had said yesterday in the garden: *You aren't only who you think you are. You aren't only Grace Mitowski.*

She knew the solution to the puzzle was within her grasp. She sensed a dark knowledge within her, long-forgotten memories waiting to be tapped. She was afraid to tap them, but she knew she must do precisely that, for Carol's sake, and perhaps for her own sake as well.

Suddenly, the air in the kitchen, though still quite clear, reeked of wood and tar smoke. Grace could hear the crackle of fire, although there were no flames here, now, in this place and time.

Her heart pounded frantically, and her mouth turned dry and sour.

She closed her eyes and could see the burning house as vividly as she had seen it in the dream. She could see the cellar doors, and she could hear herself screaming, calling Laura.

She knew it hadn't been only a dream. It had been a memory, lost for ages, surfacing now, reminding her that, indeed, she was not only Grace Mitowski.

She opened her eyes.

The kitchen was hot, stifling.

She felt herself being pulled along by forces she could not comprehend, and she thought: Is this what I want? Do I really want to flow with this and discover the truth and turn my little world upside down? Can I handle it?

The stench of nonexistent smoke grew stronger.

The roar of nonexistent flames grew louder.

I guess there's no turning back now, she thought.

She held her hands up in front of her face and stared at them, amazed. Her flesh had been miraculously disfigured by stigmata. Her hands were bruised, abraded, bloody. There were splinters of wood embedded in her palms, splinters from the cellar doors on which she had pounded such a long, long time ago.

*   *   *

At ten o'clock, when the phone rang, Paul had been at his desk, writing, for almost an hour. The work had just begun to flow smoothly. He snatched up the receiver and said, a bit impatiently, 'Yes?'

An unfamiliar female voice said, 'Could I speak to Dr. Tracy, please?'

'Speaking.'

'Oh. Uh . . . no . . . the Dr. Tracy I'm looking for is a woman.'

'It's my wife you want,' he said. 'She's out of town for a few days. Can I take a message?'

'Yes, please. Would you tell her that Polly called from Maugham & Crichton?'

He jotted the name down on a note pad. 'And what's this in reference to?'

'Dr. Tracy was here yesterday afternoon with a young girl who's suffering from amnesia. . . .'

753

'Yes,' Paul said, suddenly more interested than he had been. 'I know the case.'

'Dr. Tracy was asking if we'd ever heard of anyone named Millicent Parker.'

'That's right. She told me about it last evening. It was another dead end, I gather.'

'It seemed to be a dead end yesterday,' Polly said, 'but now it turns out that one of our doctors is familiar with the name. Dr. Maugham himself, in fact.'

'Listen, rather than waiting for my wife to call you back, why don't you just tell *me* what you've come up with, and I can pass the information along to her.'

'Well, sure, why not? See, Dr. Maugham is the senior partner in the practice. He bought this property eighteen years ago and personally oversaw the restoration of the outside and the renovation of the interior. He's a history bug, so it was natural for him to want to know the history of the building he purchased. He says this place was built in 1902 by a man named Randolph Parker. Parker had a daughter named Millicent.'

'1902?'

'That's right.'

'Interesting.'

'You haven't heard the best part,' Polly said, the eagerness of a gossip-monger in her voice. 'Seems that back in 1905, the night before Millie's sixteenth birthday party, Mrs. Parker was in the kitchen, decorating a big cake for the girl. Millie snuck in behind her and stabbed her in the back four times.'

Unthinking, Paul snapped the pencil he'd been holding ever since he'd written Polly's name on the note pad. One broken piece popped out of his hand, spun across the top of the desk, and fell to the floor.

'She stabbed her own mother?' he asked, hoping that he had not heard correctly.

'Isn't that something?'

'Kill her?' he asked numbly.

'No. Dr. Maugham says that according to the newspaper accounts at that time, the girl used a short-bladed knife. It didn't sink in far enough to do really major damage. No vital organs or blood vessels were affected. Louise Parker – that was the mother's name – managed to grab a meat cleaver from a kitchen rack. She tried to hold the girl off with that. But I guess Millie must have been completely off her rocker, 'cause she charged straight at Mrs. Parker again, and Mrs. Parker had to use that cleaver.'

'Jesus.'

'Yeah,' Polly said, obviously enjoying his shocked reaction. 'Dr. Maugham says she put that cleaver right into her daughter's throat. Pretty much cut the girl's head clear off. Isn't that a terrible thing? But what else could she do? Just let the kid go on jabbing that knife into her?'

Stunned, Paul thought about yesterday's hypnotic regression therapy session, which Carol had recounted for him in some detail. He remembered the part about how Jane had claimed to be Millicent Parker and had insisted on writing out her answers to questions and had written that she was unable to talk because her head had been cut off.

'Are you still there?' Polly asked.

'Oh. Uh . . . sorry. Is there more to the story?'

'More?' Polly asked. 'Wasn't that *enough*?'

'Yes,' he said. 'You're absolutely right. That was enough. More than enough.'

'I don't know if this information is of any help to Dr. Tracy.'

'I'm sure it will be.'

'I don't see how it could have anything to do with the girl she brought in here with her yesterday.'

'Neither do I,' Paul said.

'I mean, that girl can't be Millicent Parker. Millicent Parker has been dead for seventy-six years.'

*　　*　　*

In the study, Grace stood at her desk, looking down at the open dictionary.

REINCARNATION (rē-in-kär-nā́-shen), *n.* 1. the doctrine that the soul, upon death of the body, comes back to earth in another body or form. 2. rebirth of the soul in a new body. 3. a new incarnation or embodiment, as of a person.

Bunk? Nonsense? Superstition? Bullshit?

At one time, not long ago, those were all the words she would have used to write her own irreverent definition of reincarnation. But not now. Not any longer.

She closed her eyes, and with only the slightest effort, she was able to bring back the image of the burning house. She wasn't just envisioning it; she was *there*, hammering with her fists on the cellar door. She was not Grace Mitowski now; she was Rachael Adams, Laura's aunt.

The fire scene was not the only part of Rachael's life that she could recall with perfect clarity. She knew the woman's most intimate thoughts, her hopes and dreams and hates and fears, shared her most closely held secrets, for those thoughts and hopes and dreams and fears and secrets had been her own.

She opened her eyes and needed a moment to refocus them on the present-day world.

REINCARNATION

She closed the dictionary.

God help me, she thought, do I really believe it?

Can it be true that I've lived before? And that Carol's lived before? And the girl they're calling Jane Doe? If it *was* true – if she had been permitted to recall her previous existence as Rachael Adams in order to save Carol's life in this incarnation – then she was wasting valuable time.

She picked up the phone to call the Tracys, wondering how in God's name she was going to make them believe her.

There was no dial tone.

She jiggled the receiver-cradle buttons.

Nothing.

She put the receiver down and followed the cord around the side of the desk to the wall, to see if it had come unplugged. It wasn't unplugged; it was *chewed*. Bitten in two.

Aristophanes.

She remembered other things that Palmer Wainwright had said in the garden: *There are certain forces, dark and powerful forces, that want to see this played out the wrong way. Dark forces that thrive on tragedy. They want to see it end in senseless violence and blood . . . There are forces aligned . . . good and evil, right and wrong. You're on the right side, Grace. But the cat – ah, the cat's a different story. At all times, you must be wary of the cat.*

She also remembered when the series of paranormal events had begun, and she realized that the cat had been an integral part of it all, from the very start. Wednesday of last week. When she had suddenly awakened from her afternoon nap that day – catapulted out of a nightmare about Carol – there had been an incredibly brilliant and violent barrage of lightning beyond the study windows. She had staggered to the nearest window, and while she had stood there on unsteady, arthritic legs, half-awake and half-asleep, she'd had the eerie feeling that something monstrous had followed her up from the world of her nightmare, something demonic with a hungry grin on its face. For a few seconds that feeling had been so strong, so real, that she had been afraid to turn around and look into the shadowy room behind her. But then she had dismissed that weird thought as nothing more than the cold residue of the nightmare. Now, of course, she knew she shouldn't have dismissed it so quickly. Something strange *had* been in the room with her – a spirit; a presence; call it what you will. It had been there. And now it was in the cat.

She left the study and hurried down the hall.

In the kitchen, she found that phone cord also chewed apart.

There was no sign of Aristophanes.

Nevertheless, Grace knew he was nearby, perhaps even close enough to be watching her. She sensed his – or *its* – presence.

She listened. The house was too silent.

She wanted to cross the few feet of open floor to the kitchen door, open it boldly, and walk away from the house. But she strongly suspected that any attempt to leave would trigger an immediate and vicious attack.

She thought about the cat's claws, teeth, fangs. It wasn't merely a house pet, not just an amusing Siamese with a cute, furry face. It was actually a tough little killing machine, too; its feral impulses lay beneath a thin veneer of domestication. It was both respected and dreaded by mice and birds and squirrels. But could it kill a grown woman?

Yes, she thought uneasily. Yes, Aristophanes could kill me if he caught me by surprise and if he went for either my throat or my eyes.

The best thing she could do was stay within the house and not antagonize the cat until she had armed herself and could feel confident of winning any battle.

The only other telephone was in the second-floor bedroom. Wary, she went upstairs, even though she knew the third extension would be out of order, too.

It was.

But there was something in the bedroom that made the journey up the stairs worthwhile. The gun. She pulled open the top drawer of her nightstand and took out the loaded pistol she kept there. She had a hunch she would need it.

A hiss. A rustle.

Behind her.

Before she could swing around and confront her adversary, he was on her. He vaulted from the floor to the bed, sprang from the bed to her back, landing with nearly enough force to knock her off balance. She tottered for a moment and almost fell forward into the bedside lamp.

Aristophanes hissed and spat and scrambled for purchase on her back.

Fortunately, she kept her feet under her. She spun around and shook herself, frantically attempting to throw him off before he could do any damage.

His claws were hooked in her clothes. Although she was wearing both a blouse and a sweater, she felt a couple of his razor-tipped nails puncturing her skin – hot little points of pain. He wouldn't let go.

She drew her shoulders up and tucked her head down, pulling her chin in tight against her chest, protecting her neck as best she could. She swung one fist up behind her back, struck only air, tried again, and hit the cat with a blow that was too weak to have done any harm.

Nevertheless, Aristophanes squealed with rage and snapped at her neck. He was foiled by her hunched shoulders and by her thick hair, which got in his mouth and gagged him.

She had never wanted anything half so much as she wanted to kill the little bastard. He was no longer the familiar pet she had loved; he was a strange and hateful beast, and she harbored no ghost of affection for him.

She wished she could use the gun she was clutching in her right hand, but there was no way she could shoot him without shooting herself, too.

She struck at him repeatedly with her left hand, her arthritic shoulder protesting sharply, painfully when she twisted her arm up and backwards at such an unnatural angle.

At least for a moment, the cat abandoned its relentless but thus far ineffective attack on her neck. It slashed its claws across her flailing fist, slicing open the skin on her knuckles.

Her fingers were instantly slick with blood. They stung so badly that her eyes started to water.

Either the sight or the odor of the blood encouraged the cat. It shrieked with savage glee.

Grace began to think the unthinkable – that she was going to lose this fight.

No!

She struggled against the grip of fear that threatened to incapacitate her, tried to clear her panic-befuddled mind, and suddenly had an idea that she thought might save her life. She stumbled toward the nearest stretch of open wall, to the left of the dresser.

The cat clung tenaciously to her back, insistently pressing its snout against the base of her skull, hissing and snarling. It was determined to force its way to her sheltered neck and rip open her jugular vein.

When Grace reached the wall, she turned her back to it, then fell against it with all her weight, slamming the cat into the plaster behind her, pinning it hard between her body and the wall, hoping to break its spine. The jolt brought a flash of pain through her shoulders and drove the animal's claws deeper into her back muscles. The cat's scream was nearly shrill enough to shatter fine crystal, and it sounded almost like the wail of a human infant. But its grip on her didn't weaken. Grace pushed away from the wall, then slammed into it a second time, and the cat wailed as before, but still held fast. She thrust herself off the wall, intending to make a third attempt to crush her adversary, but before she could fall back on him, the cat let go of her. He dropped to the floor, rolled, sprang to his feet, and scurried away from her, favoring his right foreleg.

Good. She had hurt him.

She sagged against the wall, raised the .22 pistol that was still in her right hand, and squeezed the trigger.

Nothing.

She had forgotten to switch off the safeties.

The cat hurried through the open door and disappeared into the upstairs hall.

Grace went to the door, closed it, leaned wearily against it. Gasping.

Her left hand was scratched and bleeding, and her back bore half a dozen claw punctures, but she had won the first round. The cat was limping; he was injured, perhaps as badly as she was, and *he* was the one who had retreated.

No celebration, though. Not yet.

Not until she had gotten out of the house alive. And not until she was certain that Carol was safe, too.

* * *

After the unsettling telephone conversation he'd had with the receptionist at Maugham & Crichton, Paul didn't know what the hell to do.

He couldn't write. That was for sure. He couldn't get his mind off Carol long enough to advance the plot of his novel by so much as even one sentence.

He wanted to call Lincoln Werth, at police headquarters, and arrange to have a sheriff's deputy waiting at the cabin when Carol and Jane arrived up there. He wanted them brought home. But he could imagine the conversation he would have with Detective Werth, and the thought of it daunted him:

'*You want a deputy to meet them at the cabin?*'

'*That's right.*'

'*Why?*'

'*I think my wife's in danger.*'

'*What kind of danger?*'

'*I think the girl, Jane Doe, might be violent. Maybe even homicidal.*'

'*Why do you think that?*'

'*Because under hypnosis she claimed to be Millie Parker.*'

'*Who's that?*'

'*Millie Parker once tried to kill her mother.*'

'*She did? When was that?*'

'*Back in 1905.*'

'*Then she'd be a little old lady today, for Christ's sake. The kid's only fourteen or fifteen.*'

'*You don't understand. Millie Parker's been dead for about seventy-six years and –*'

'*Wait a minute, wait a minute! What the hell are you saying? That your wife might be murdered by some kid who's been dead for most of the century?*'

'*No. Of course not.*'

'*Then what do you mean?*'

'*I . . . don't know.*'

Werth would think that he had been out boozing all night, or that he had started the morning with a couple of joints of good grass.

Besides, it wasn't fair to Jane to accuse her publicly of being a potential killer. Perhaps Carol was right. Maybe the kid was just a victim. Except for what she said under hypnosis, she certainly *seemed* to be incapable of violence.

On the other hand, of all the people she could have claimed to be, why had she said that she was Millicent Parker, the would-be murderess? Where had she heard that name before. Didn't the use of it indicate latent hostility?

Paul swiveled his typing chair away from the desk and stared out the window at the gray sky. The wind was picking up by the minute. The clouds were racing westward across the sky, as if they were enormous, swift, dark ships with billowing sails the color of thunderstorms.

BLADE, BLOOD, DEATH, TOMB, KILL, CAROL.

I've got to go to the cabin, he thought with sudden decisiveness, and he got to his feet.

Maybe he was overreacting to this Millicent Parker business, but he couldn't just sit here, wondering. . . .

He went into the master bedroom to throw some things into a suitcase. After only a brief hesitation, he decided to pack his .38 revolver.

*   *   *

The girl said, 'How much farther to the cabin?'

'Another twenty minutes,' Carol said. 'The whole drive usually takes just about two hours and fifteen minutes, and we're pretty much on schedule.'

The mountains were cool and green. Some trees had already been touched by the artful hand of autumn, and most – all but the evergreens – would change the color of their leaves during the next few weeks. Today, however, the predominant shade was still green, with a smattering of gold here and there, an occasional touch of red. The edge of the forest – wherever the meadow or the roadway met the trees – was decorated with a few end-of-the-season wildflowers, blue and white and purple.

'It's beautiful up here,' Jane said as they followed the two-lane county road around a curve. The right-hand bank, which sloped down to the macadam, was covered with vividly green clusters of rhododendron shrubs.

'I love the Pennsylvania mountains,' Carol said. She felt more relaxed now than she had in weeks. 'It's so peaceful here. Wait till you've been at the cabin a day or two. You'll forget the rest of the world exists.'

They came out of the curve onto an ascending straightaway, where the interlocking branches of the trees formed a tunnel over portions of the lane. At those points where the trees parted sufficiently to provide a glimpse of the sky, there was nothing to be seen but massive, gray-black clouds clotted together in surging, ugly, threatening formations.

'I sure hope it doesn't rain and spoil our first day here,' Jane said.

'Rain won't spoil anything,' Carol assured her. 'If we're forced to stay inside, we'll just throw a whole bunch of logs in the big stone fireplace and roast some hot dogs *in*doors. And we have a closetful of games to help us pass rainy days. Monopoly, Scrabble, Clue, Risk, Battleship, and at least a dozen others. I think we'll be able to avoid cabin fever.'

'It's going to be *fun*,' Jane said enthusiastically.

The canopy of trees parted overhead, and the September sky churned darkly.

Chapter Eleven

Grace sat on the edge of the bed, holding the .22 pistol, considering her options. She didn't have many.

In fact, the more she thought about it, the more it seemed to her that the cat had a better chance of winning this duel than she did.

If she attempted to leave the house by way of the bedroom window, she would surely break a leg and probably her neck as well. If she had been only twenty years younger, she might have tried it. But at seventy, with her swollen joints and brittle bones, jumping from a second-floor window onto a concrete patio could only end in misery. Anyway, the point wasn't just to get out of the house, but to get out in one piece, so she could make it across town to Carol's and Paul's place.

She could open the window and start screaming for help. But she was afraid that Aristophanes – or the thing using Aristophanes's body – would attack anyone who showed up and tried to assist her, and she didn't want a neighbor's death on her conscience.

This was her battle. No one else's. She would have to fight it alone.

She considered all the routes by which she might possibly leave the house once she had reached the bottom floor – if she reached the bottom floor – but no particular route seemed less dangerous than any other. The cat could be anywhere. Everywhere. The bedroom was the only safe place in the house. If she ventured out of this sanctuary, the cat would be waiting for her and would attack her, regardless of whether she tried to exit the house by the front door, the kitchen door, or one of the ground-floor windows. It would be crouched in one shadow or another, perhaps perched atop a bookcase or cupboard or hutch, tensed and ready to launch itself down onto her startled, upturned face.

She had the gun, of course. But the cat, stealthy by nature, would always have the advantage of surprise. If it got just a two- or three-second lead on her, if she was only that little bit slower to react than was the cat, it would have ample time to fasten onto her face, tear open her throat, or gouge her eyes out with its quick, stiletto claws.

Strangely, though she had accepted the doctrine of reincarnation, though she now knew beyond doubt that there was some kind of life after death, she nevertheless feared dying. The certainty of eternal life in no way diminished the value of *this* life. Indeed, now that she could discern godlike machinery just below the visible surface of the world, her life seemed to have more meaning and purpose than ever before.

She didn't want to die.

However, although the odds of her leaving the house alive were, at best, only fifty-fifty, she couldn't stay in the bedroom indefinitely. She had no water, no food. Besides, if she didn't get out of here in the next few minutes, she might be too late to be of any help to Carol.

If Carol is killed simply because I lack the courage to face that damned cat, she thought, then I might as well be dead anyway.

She switched off the two safeties on the pistol.

She got up and went to the door.

For nearly a minute she stood with one ear pressed to the door, listening for scratching noises or other indications that Aristophanes was nearby. She heard nothing.

Holding the pistol in her right hand, she used her bloody, claw-torn left hand to turn the knob. She opened the door with the utmost caution, half an inch at a time, expecting the cat to dart through the opening the instant it was wide enough to admit him. But he didn't.

Finally, reluctantly, she poked her head out into the hall. Looked left. Right.

The cat wasn't anywhere in sight.

She stepped into the hall and paused, afraid to move away from the bedroom door.

Go! she told herself angrily. Move your ass, Gracie!

She took a step toward the head of the stairs. Then another step. Trying to be quiet.

The stairs appeared to be a mile away.

She looked behind her.

Still no Aristophanes.

Another step.

This was going to be the longest walk she had ever taken.

764

*   *   *

Paul latched his suitcase, picked it up, turned away from the bed –
and jumped, startled, when the entire house shook as if a wrecker's
ball had struck the side of it.

THUNK!

He looked up at the ceiling.

THUNK! THUNK! THUNK!

During the past five days there had been no hammering to disturb
the peace. He hadn't entirely forgotten about it, of course; he still
occasionally wondered where that mysterious sound had come
from. For the most part, however, he had put it out of his mind;
there had been other things to worry about. But now –

THUNK! THUNK! THUNK!

The nerve-fraying noise reverberated in the windows and
bounced off the walls. It seemed to vibrate in Paul's teeth and
bones, too.

THUNK!

After spending days trying to identify the source of that sound,
understanding came to him unexpectedly, in a flash. *It was an ax.* It
was not a hammering, which was how he had been thinking of it.
No. There was a sharp edge to it, a brittle, cracking quality at the
end of each blow. It was a *chopping* sound.

THUNK!

Being able to identify the noise did absolutely nothing to help
him understand where it was coming from. So it was an ax instead
of a hammer. So what? He still couldn't make sense of it. Why
were the blows shaking the entire house? It would have to be the
mythical Paul Bunyan's ax to have such a tremendous impact.
And regardless of whether it was a hammer or an ax or even, for
Christ's sake, a *salami*, how could the sound of it issue from thin
air?

Suddenly, inexplicably, he thought of the meat cleaver that
Louise Parker had buried in the throat of her maniacal daughter
back in 1905. He thought about the freakish lightning strikes at
Alfred O'Brian's office; the strange intruder he had seen on the rear
lawn during the thunderstorm that evening; the Scrabble game two
nights ago (BLADE, BLOOD, DEATH, TOMB, KILL, CAROL);
Grace's two prophetic dreams. And he knew beyond doubt – without understanding *how* he knew – that the sound of the ax was the
thread that sewed together all these recent extraordinary events.
Intuitively, he knew that an ax would be the instrument by which

Carol's life would be endangered. He didn't know how. He didn't know why. But he *knew*.

THUNK! THUNK!

A painting popped off its wall hook and clattered to the floor.

The river of blood in Paul's veins turned winter-cold.

He had to get to the cabin. Fast.

He started toward the bedroom door, and it slammed shut in front of him. No one had touched it. There had been no sudden draft that might have moved it. One moment the door was standing wide open, and the next instant it was flung shut as if it had been shoved hard by an invisible hand.

Out of the corner of his eye, Paul saw something move. Heart banging, breath trapped in his constricted throat, he twisted around toward the movement and instinctively raised his suitcase to partially shield himself.

One of the two heavy, mirrored closet doors was sliding open. He expected someone to step out of the closet, but when the door was all the way open, he could see nothing in there except clothes on hangers. Then it slid shut, and the other door slid open. Then both of them started sliding at the same time, one crossing behind the other, back and forth, back and forth on their silent plastic wheels.

THUNK! THUNK!

A lamp crashed over on one of the nightstands.

Another painting fell off the wall.

THUNK!

On the dresser, two porcelain figurines – a ballerina and her male dancing partner – began to circle one another, almost as if they had come to life and were performing for Paul. They moved slowly at first, then faster, faster, until they were swept into the air and tossed halfway across the room and dashed to the floor.

*   *   *

The cabin was constructed of logs and was nestled in the cool shadows beneath the trees. It had a long, covered, screened porch out front and an excellent view of the lake.

It was one of ninety vacation cabins tucked into the scenic mountain valley, each on an acre or half-acre of its own. They were all built along the south shore of the lake and were reachable only by way of a private, gated, gravel-surfaced road that curved around the water. Some of the cabins were made of logs, like the one Paul and Carol had bought, but there were also white clapboard New

England models, modern A-frames, and a few that resembled small Swiss chalets.

At the end of her own graveled drive, which branched off the community road, Carol parked the car near the front door of the cabin. She and Jane got out and stood for a moment in companionable silence, listening to the stillness, breathing the wonderfully fresh air.

'It's lovely,' Jane said at last.

'Isn't it, though?'

'So quiet.'

'It isn't always. Not when most of the cabins are in use. But right now there's probably no one here except Peg and Vince Gervis.'

'Who're they?' Jane asked.

'The caretakers. The homeowner's association pays their salaries. They live year-round in the last cabin, out at the end of the lake. In the off season, they run a couple of inspection tours every day, just keeping a lookout for fire and vandals and whatnot. Nice people.'

Above the distant north shore of the lake, lightning blazed across the malevolent sky. A clap of thunder fell from the clouds and rolled across the water.

'We better get the suitcases and the food out of the car before we have to unload everything in the rain,' Carol said.

*　　*　　*

Grace expected to be attacked on the stairs, for that was where she would find it most difficult to defend herself. If the cat frightened her and caused her to lose her balance, she might fall. If she fell, she would probably break a leg or a hip, and while she was temporarily stunned by the shock and pain of the fall, the cat would be all over her, tearing, biting. Therefore, she descended the stairs sideways, with her back against the wall, so she could look both ahead and behind.

But Aristophanes did not show up. Grace reached the downstairs hall without incident.

She looked both ways along the hall.

To reach the front door, she had to pass the open door of the study and the archway that led to the living room. The cat could bolt out of either place as she was passing by and could leap for her face before she would have time to spot him, aim the pistol, and pull the trigger.

To reach the other door, the one at the back of the house, she had to go right, along the hallway, past the open dining room door, into the kitchen. That route didn't look any less dangerous.

The rock and the hard place, she thought unhappily. The devil and the deep blue sea.

Then she remembered that her car keys were in the kitchen, hanging on the pegboard beside the back door, and that settled it. She would have to leave through the kitchen.

She moved cautiously along the hall until she came to a wall mirror, beneath which stood a narrow, decorative table. There were two tall vases on the table, bracketing the mirror. She picked up one of them in her injured left hand and sidled toward the open dining room door.

She paused before reaching the doorway, listened.

Silence.

She leaned forward and risked her eyes by peering into the dining room. She could not see any sign of the cat. That didn't mean it wasn't in there. The drapes were half drawn, and the day was gloomy; there were lots of shadows, many places where a cat could hide.

For the purpose of creating a diversion in the event that Aristophanes *was* in one of those shadows, Grace pitched the vase inside. As it landed with a loud crash, she stepped across the threshold just far enough to grasp the doorknob, then pulled the door shut as she backed quickly into the hallway again. Now, if the cat was in there, it would bloody well have to *stay* in there.

She heard no noise from the dining room, which probably meant she hadn't managed to trap the elusive beast. If he'd been in there, he would have been squealing with rage and scratching at the inside of the closed door by now. Most likely, she had only wasted time and energy with her little trick. But at least there was now one downstairs room to which she could turn her back with impunity.

Repeatedly glancing left and right, forward and back, she crept to the kitchen door, hesitated, then stepped through it, the gun thrust out in front of her. She looked the room over slowly, thoroughly, before venturing farther. The small table and chairs. The humming refrigerator. The dangling, cat-chewed phone cord. The gleaming chrome fixtures on the oven. The double sinks. The white countertops. The small countertop wine rack. The cookie jar and the breadbox lined up beside the wine.

Nothing moved.

The refrigerator motor shut off, and the subsequent quiet was deep, unbroken.

Okay, she thought. Grit your teeth and move, Gracie.

She walked silently across the room, her eyes sweeping every niche, every nook: the opening under the built-in writing desk, the narrow space beside the refrigerator, the blind spot beyond the end of one row of cabinets. No cat.

Maybe I hurt him worse than I thought I did, she told herself hopefully. Maybe I didn't just lame the bastard. Maybe he crawled away and died.

She reached the back door.

She didn't dare breathe for fear her own breathing would mask whatever furtive sounds the cat might make.

A ring of keys, including those for the car, hung on a small oval pegboard beside the door. She slipped it off the hook.

She reached for the doorknob.

The cat hissed.

Grace cried out involuntarily and swung her head to the right, in the direction of the sound.

She was standing at one end of the long row of cabinets. At the far end, the wine rack and the breadbox and the cookie jar were lined up side by side; she had seen them from a front-on angle when she had first come into the room. Now she had a side view. From this angle she saw something she couldn't have seen from in front: The cookie jar and breadbox, which usually rested snug against the wall behind the counter, had been moved out a few inches. The cat had squeezed in behind those two objects, muscling them slowly out of its way. It had crouched in that hiding place, its butt against the wine rack, facing out toward the kitchen door. It was approximately twelve feet from her, and then it wasn't even that far away because it launched itself across the counter, hissing.

The confrontation was over in a few seconds, but during those seconds, time seemed to slow to a crawl, and Grace felt as if she were trapped in a slow-motion film. She stumbled backwards, away from the counter and the cat, but she didn't get far before she collided with a wall; as she moved, she raised the gun and fired two rounds in quick succession. The cookie jar exploded, and wood chips flew off one of the cabinet doors. But the cat kept coming, coming, in slow-motion strides across the slippery tile countertop, its mouth gaping and its fangs bared. She realized that hitting such a small, quick target was not easy, even at such short range as this. She fired again, but she knew the gun was wavering in her hand, and she wasn't surprised when she heard the bullet ricochet – making a high, piercing *eeeee* – off something wide of the mark. To her terror-heightened perceptions, the echoes of the

769

ricochet continued to infinity: *eeeee, eeeee, eeeee, eeeee, eeeee.* . . . Then the cat reached the end of the counter and leapt into the air, and Grace fired again. This time she hit the mark. The cat yelped. The bullet had sufficient impact to deflect the animal only an instant before it would have landed, scratching and biting, on her face. It was pitched back and to the left as if it were a bundle of rags. It slammed into the kitchen door and dropped stonelike to the floor, where it lay silent and motionless.

*   *   *

Paul couldn't decide what the poltergeist intended to accomplish by its impressive displays of power. He didn't know whether or not he had anything to fear from it. Was it trying to delay him, trying to keep him here until it was too late for him to help Carol? Or perhaps it was urging him on, trying its best to convince him that he must go to the cabin immediately.

Still holding the suitcase in one hand, he approached the bed-room door that had been flung shut by the unseen presence. As he reached for the knob, the door began to rattle in its frame – gently at first, then fiercely.

Thunk . . . thunk . . . thunk . . . THUNK!

He jerked his hand back, unsure what he ought to do.

THUNK!

The sound of the ax was coming from the door now, not from overhead, as it had been. Although the solid-core, raised-panel, fir door was a formidable barrier rather than just a flimsy Masonite model, it shook violently and then cracked down the middle as if it were constructed of balsa wood.

Paul backed away from it.

Another crack appeared, parallel to the first, and chips of wood flew into the room.

Sliding closet doors and flying porcelain figurines might be the work of a poltergeist, but this was something else again. Surely no spirit could chop apart a heavy door like this. There *had* to be some-one swinging a very real ax against the other side.

Paul felt defenseless. He scanned the room for makeshift weapons, but he saw nothing useful.

The .38 revolver was in the suitcase. He wouldn't be able to get to it in time to defend himself with it, and he wished fervently that he had kept the gun in his hand.

THUNKTHUNKTHUNKTHUNK!

770

The bedroom door exploded inward in half a dozen large pieces and countless smaller chunks and scraps.

He threw one arm over his face to protect his eyes. Wood rained down on all sides of him.

When he lowered his arm, he saw there was no one standing beyond the doorway, no man with an ax. The chopper-of-doors was, after all, the unseen presence.

THUNK!

Paul stepped over a shattered section of the door and went out into the hallway.

* * *

The fuse box was in the kitchen pantry. Carol engaged all the breaker switches, and the lights came on.

There was no telephone. That was virtually the only modern convenience the cabin lacked.

'Do you think it's chilly in here?' Carol asked.

'A little.'

'We have a bottled-gas furnace, but unless it's *really* cold, the fireplace is nicer. Let's bring in some firewood.'

'You mean we've got to cut down a tree?'

Carol laughed. 'That won't be necessary. Come see.'

She led the girl outside, to the rear of the cabin, where an open porch ended in steps leading down to a short rear yard. The yard met the edge of a small meadow where the grass was knee-deep, and the meadow climbed up toward a wall of trees fifty yards away.

When Carol saw that familiar landscape, she stopped, surprised, remembering the dream that had spoiled her sleep several nights last week. In the nightmare, she had been running through one house, then through another house, then across a mountain meadow, while something silvery flickered in the darkness behind her. At the time, she had not realized that the meadow in the dream was *this* meadow.

'Something wrong?' Jane asked.

'Huh? Oh. No. Let's get that firewood.'

She led the girl down the porch steps and to the left, to where a woodshed was attached to the south-west corner of the cabin.

Thunder rumbled in the distance. The rain hadn't begun to fall yet.

Carol keyed open the heavy-duty padlock on the woodshed, took it off the hasp, and slipped it in her jacket pocket. There would be

771

no need to replace it until they were ready to return to Harrisburg, nine or ten days from now.

The woodshed door creaked open on unoiled hinges. Inside, Carol tugged on the chain-pull light, and a bare hundred-watt bulb revealed stacks of dry cordwood being protected from inclement weather.

A scuttle for carrying firewood hung from a ceiling hook. Carol got it down and handed it to the girl. 'If you fill it up four or five times, we'll have more than enough wood to last us until tomorrow morning.'

By the time Jane returned from taking the first scuttle-load into the cabin, Carol was at the chopping block, using an ax to split a short log into four sticks.

'What're you doing?' the girl asked, stopping well out of the way and staring warily at the ax.

'When I build a fire,' Carol said, 'I put kindling on the bottom, a layer of these splits on top of that, and then the full logs to crown it off. It never fails to burn well that way. See? I'm a regular Daniel Boone.'

The girl scowled. 'That ax looks awful sharp.'

'Has to be.'

'Are you sure it's safe?'

'I've done it lots of times before, here and at home,' Carol said. 'I'm an expert. Don't worry, honey. I'm not going to accidentally amputate my toes.'

She picked up another short log and started to split it into quarters.

Jane went to the woodshed, giving the chopping block a wide berth. When she returned, carrying her second scuttle-load to the house, she repeatedly glanced over her shoulder, frowning.

Carol began quartering another log.

THUNK!

*   *   *

Carrying his suitcase, Paul walked down the second-floor hall to the stairway, and the poltergeist went with him. On both sides, doors opened and slammed shut, opened and slammed shut, again and again, all by themselves and with such tremendous force that it sounded as if he were walking through a murderous barrage of cannon fire.

As he descended the stairs, the chandelier at the top of the well began describing wide circles on the end of its chain, stirred by a breeze that Paul could not feel or moved by a hand that had no substance.

On the first floor, paintings were flung off walls as he passed by. Chairs toppled over. The living room sofa rocked wildly on its four graceful wooden legs. In the kitchen, the overhead utensil rack shook; pots and pans and ladles banged against one another.

By the time he reached the Pontiac in the garage, he knew he didn't have to bother taking the entire suitcase to the mountains. He hadn't wanted to go charging into the cabin with just a gun and the clothes on his back, for if nothing had been wrong, he would have looked like an idiot, and he would have done Jane a grave injustice. But now, because of the call from Polly at Maugham & Crichton, and because of the astounding display put on by the poltergeist, he knew that *everything* was wrong; there was no chance whatsoever that he would reach the cabin only to discover that all was peaceful. He would be walking into a nightmare of one kind or another. No doubt about it. So he opened the suitcase on the garage floor beside the car, took out the loaded revolver, and left the rest of his stuff behind.

As he was backing out of the driveway, he saw Grace Mitowski's blue Ford turn the corner, too fast. It angled toward the curb in front of the house, scraping its sidewalls so badly that blue-white smoke rose from them.

Grace was out of the car the instant it stopped. She rushed to the Pontiac, moving faster than Paul had seen her move in years. She pulled open the front, passenger-side door and leaned in. Her hair was in complete disarray. Her face was eggshell white and spattered with blood.

'Good God, Grace, what's happened to you?'

'Where's Carol?'

'She went to the cabin.'

'Already?'

'This morning.'

'Damn! Exactly when?'

'Three hours ago.'

Grace's eyes contained a haunted expression. 'The girl went with her?'

'Yes.'

She closed her eyes, and Paul could see she was on the edge of panic, trying to deal with it and calm herself. She opened her eyes and said, 'We've got to go after them.'

'That's where I'm headed.'

He saw her eyes widen as she noticed the revolver lying on the car seat beside him, the muzzle pointed forward, toward the dashboard.

She raised her eyes from the gun to his face. 'You know what's happening?' she asked, surprised.

'Not really,' he said, putting the gun in the glove compartment. 'All I know for sure is that Carol's in trouble. Damned serious trouble.'

'It's not just Carol we've got to worry about,' Grace said. 'It's both of them.'

'Both? The girl, you mean? But I think the girl's the one who's going to –'

'Yes,' Grace said. 'She's going to try to kill Carol. But she might be the one who ends up dead. Like before.'

She got in the car and pulled the door shut.

'Like before?' Paul said. 'I don't –' He saw her blood-crusted hand. 'That needs medical attention.'

'There's no time.'

'What the hell's happening?' he demanded, his fear for Carol briefly giving way to frustration. 'I know something strange is going on, but I don't know what in Christ's name it is.'

'I do,' she said. 'I know. In fact I know a lot more than maybe I want to know.'

'If you've got anything that makes sense, anything concrete,' he said, 'we should call the cops. They can put in a call to the sheriff's department up there and get help sent out to the cabin real fast, faster than we can get there.'

'What I've got, my information, is harder than concrete, so far as I'm concerned,' Grace said. 'But the police wouldn't see it the same way I do. They'd say I was just a senile old fool. They'd want to lock me up in a nice safe place for my own good. At best, they'd laugh at me.'

He thought about the poltergeist – the sound of the ax, the splintering door, the airborne ceramic figurines, the toppling chairs – and he said, 'Yeah. I know exactly what you mean.'

'We'll have to handle this ourselves,' Grace said. 'Let's get rolling. I can tell you everything I know on the way. Each minute we waste, I just get sicker and sicker, thinking about what might be happening in the mountains.'

Paul backed the car into the street and drove away from the house, heading for the nearest freeway entrance. When he was on the open highway, he floored the accelerator, and the car rocketed ahead.

'How long does it usually take to get there?' Grace asked.

'About two hours and fifteen minutes.'

'Too long.'

'We'll do better than that.'

The speedometer needle touched eighty.

Chapter Twelve

They had brought a lot of food in cardboard cartons and ice chests. They transferred all of those items to the cupboards and refrigerator, agreeing to forgo lunch altogether in order to indulge themselves guiltlessly in a glutton's dinner.

'All right,' Carol said, producing a list from one of the kitchen drawers, 'here's what we need to do to make this place livable.' She read from the list: 'Remove plastic dropcloths from furniture; dust everything; scrub the kitchen sink; clean the bathroom; and put sheets and blankets on the beds.'

'You call this a *vacation*?' Jane asked.

'What's wrong? Doesn't that sound like a fun agenda to you?'

'Thrilling.'

'Well, the cabin's not enormous. The two of us will go through the list of chores in an hour or an hour and a half.'

They had barely started when they were interrupted by a knock at the door. It was Vince Gervis, the colony's caretaker. He was a big, barrel-chested man with enormous shoulders, enormous biceps, enormous hands, and a smile to match the rest of him.

'Just makin' my rounds,' he said. 'Saw your car. Thought I'd say hello.' Carol introduced him to Jane and said she was a niece (a convenient white lie), and there was some polite chitchat, and then Gervis said, 'Dr. Tracy, where's the *other* Dr. Tracy? I'd like to give him my best, too.'

'Oh, he isn't with us right now,' Carol said. 'He's coming up on Sunday, after he finishes some important work he couldn't just put aside.'

Gervis frowned.

Carol said, 'Is something wrong?'

'Well . . . me and the missus was plannin' to go into town to do some shoppin', maybe see a movie, eat a restaurant meal. It's what we generally do on Friday afternoons, you see. But there isn't

777

another soul up here besides you and Jane. Will be tomorrow, bein'
as it's a Saturday, and seein' as if the weather don't get too bad so that
everybody stays to home. But there's no one else so far today except
you.'

'Don't worry about us,' Carol said. 'We'll be fine. You and Peg go
on into town like you planned.'

'Well . . . I'm not sure I like the idea of you two ladies out here all
by your lonesome, twenty miles from other folks. Nosir, I don't like
it much.'

'Nobody's going to bother us, Vince. The road's gated; you can't
even get in without a key card.'

'Anybody can *walk* in if he's willin' to go overland just a little
ways.'

Carol required several minutes and a lot of words to reassure him,
but at last he decided that he and his wife would keep to their usual
Friday schedule.

Shortly after Vince left, the rains came. The soft roar of a hundred
million droplets striking a hundred million rustling leaves was soothing to Carol.

But Jane found the noise somewhat unpleasant. 'I don't know
why,' she said, 'but the sound makes me think of fire. Hissing . . .
just like a lot of flames eating up everything in sight. Sizzle, sizzle,
sizzle . . .'

*   *   *

The rain forced Paul to slow down to sixty, which was still too fast for
highway conditions, but the situation called for the taking of some
risks.

The windshield wipers thumped metronomically, and the tires
sang softly on the wet macadam.

The day was dark and growing darker. It looked more like twilight
than like midday. The wind blew obscuring curtains of rain across the
treacherously wet pavement, and the gray-brown road spray flung
up by other traffic hung in the air, a thick and dirty mist.

It seemed almost as if the Pontiac were a tiny vessel sailing through
the deep currents of a vast, cold sea, the only pocket of warmth and
light within a million miles.

Grace said, 'You probably won't believe what I've got to tell you,
and that would be understandable.'

'After what's happened to me today,' Paul said, 'I'm ready to
believe anything.'

And maybe *that's* what the poltergeist meant to do, he thought. Maybe it meant to prepare me for whatever story Grace has to tell. In fact, if I hadn't been delayed by the poltergeist, I would have left the house before Grace arrived.

'I'll keep it as simple and straightforward as I can,' Grace said. 'But it's not a simple and straightforward matter.' She cradled her torn left hand in her right hand; the bleeding had stopped, and the cuts were all crusty, clotted. 'It starts in 1865, in Shippensburg. The family was named Havenswood.'

Paul glanced at her, startled by the name.

She looked straight ahead at the rain-sodden land through which they were rushing. 'The mother was Willa Havenswood, and the daughter's name was Laura. Those two didn't get along well. Not well at all. The fault was on both sides, and the reasons for their constant bickering aren't really important here. What's important is that one day in the spring of 1865, Willa sent Laura into the cellar to do some spring cleaning, even though she knew perfectly well that the girl was deathly afraid of the cellar. It was punishment, you see. And while Laura was down there in the cellar, a fire broke out upstairs. She was trapped and burned to death. She must have died blaming her mother for putting her in that trap in the first place. Maybe she even blamed Willa for starting the fire – which she didn't. It was accidentally started by Rachael Adams, Laura's aunt. It's even possible that Laura wondered if her mother had started the fire *on purpose*, just to get rid of her. The child had emotional problems; she was capable of melodramatic notions of that sort. The mother had emotional problems, too; she was capable of *inspiring* paranoia, for sure. Anyway, Laura died a gruesome death, and we can be pretty certain that her last thought was an ardent wish for revenge. There was no way she could have known that *her mother perished in that fire, too!*'

So that's why the Havenswood identity didn't check out when Carol put the police on to it, Paul thought. They'd have had to go all the way back to the 1800s in order to find the Havenswood family. County records for that period probably don't even exist any more.

A slow-moving truck appeared out of the mists ahead, and Paul passed it. For a moment the filthy spray from the truck's big tires drummed on the side of the Pontiac, and the noise was too loud for Grace to speak above it.

When they had passed the truck, she said, 'Since 1865, Laura has been pursuing revenge through at least two and probably three other lives. Reincarnation, Paul. Can you believe in that? Can you believe that in 1943, Laura Havenswood was a fifteen-year-old girl named Linda Bektermann and that the night before her sixteenth birthday she tried to kill her mother, who was Willa Havenswood reincarnated? It's a true case. Linda Bektermann went berserk and tried to ax her mother to death, but her mother turned the tables and killed the girl instead. *Laura didn't get her revenge.* And can you believe that Willa is now alive again and that she's our Carol this time? And that Laura is alive again, too?'

'Jane?'

'Yes.'

* * *

Together, Carol and Jane cleaned the cabin in an hour and fifteen minutes. Carol was delighted to see that the girl was an industrious worker who took great pleasure in doing even a menial job well.

When they were finished, they poured two glasses of Pepsi to reward themselves, and they sat in the two big easy chairs that faced the mammoth fireplace.

'It's too early to start cooking dinner,' Jane said. 'And it's too wet out there to go for a walk, so what game do you want to play?'

'Anything that looks good to you is fine with me. You can look over all the stuff in our game closet and take your pick. But first, I think we really should get the therapy session out of the way.'

'Are we going to keep that up even on vacation?' the girl asked. She was clearly uneasy about it, though she had not been noticeably uneasy before, even on the occasion of the first session, the day before yesterday.

'Of course we've got to keep on with it,' Carol said. 'Now that we've made a start, it's best to continue working at it, pushing and probing a little bit every day.'

'Well . . . all right.'

'Good. Let's turn these chairs around to face each other.'

The fire flickered off to one side, creating dancing shadows on the hearth.

Outside, the rain rattled ceaselessly through the trees and pattered on the roof, and Carol realized that it *did* sound like even more fire, as Jane had said, so that they seemed to be totally surrounded by the hiss and crackle of flames.

She needed only a few seconds to put Jane into a trance this time. But as had happened during the first session, the girl needed almost two minutes to regress to a period at which memories existed for her. This time the long silence didn't disturb Carol as it had done before.

When the girl spoke at last, she used the Laura voice. 'Mama? Is that you? Is that you, Mama?'

'Laura?'

The girl's eyes were squeezed shut. Her voice was tight, tense. 'Is that you? Is it you, Mama? Is it?'

'Relax,' Carol said.

Instead of relaxing, the girl became visibly more tense. She hunched her shoulders, fisted her hands in her lap. Lines of strain appeared in her forehead and at the corners of her mouth. She leaned away from the back of her chair, toward Carol.

'I want you to answer some questions,' Carol said. 'But you must be calm and relaxed first. Now, you will do exactly as I say. You will unclench your fists. You will –'

'I won't!'

The girl's eyes popped open. She leapt up out of her chair and stood before Carol, quivering.

'Sit down, honey.'

'I won't do what you say! I'm sick of doing what you tell me to do, sick of your punishments.'

'Sit down,' Carol said softly but forcefully.

The girl glared at her. 'You did it to me,' she said in the Laura voice. 'You put me down there in that awful place.'

Carol hesitated, then decided to flow with it. 'What place do you mean?'

'You *know*,' the girl said accusingly. 'I *hate* you.'

'Where is this awful place you spoke of?' Carol persisted.

'The cellar.'

'What's so awful about the cellar?'

Hatred seethed in the girl's eyes. Her lips were peeled back from her teeth in a feral snarl.

'Laura? Answer me. What's so awful about the cellar?'

The girl slapped her across the face.

The blow stunned Carol. It was sharp, painful, unexpected. For an instant she simply couldn't believe that she actually had been hit.

Then the girl hit her again. Backhanded.

And again. Harder than before.

Carol grabbed her adversary's slender wrists, but the girl wrenched loose. She kicked Carol in the shins, and when Carol cried out and sagged for an instant, the girl went for her throat.

Carol fended her off, though not easily, and attempted to get up from the armchair. Jane pushed her down and fell on top of her. She felt the girl bite her shoulder, and suddenly her shock and confusion turned to fear. The chair tipped over, and they both rolled onto the floor, flailing.

*   *   *

The flat land through which they had been driving began to rise and form itself into gently rolling hills, but the mountains were still a long way off.

If there had been any change in the weather during the last half hour, it had been for the worse. Rain was falling harder than ever; the hard, fat pellets of water shattered like glass on the roadway, and the amorphous fragments bounced high. Paul kept the speedometer needle at eighty.

'Reincarnation,' he said thoughtfully. 'Just a few minutes ago, I told you that I could believe anything today, but that's wild. Reincarnation? Where in the devil did you come by this theory?'

As the windshield wipers continued to thump, and as the tires sang a shrill dirge on the rain-puddled pavement, Grace told him about the telephone calls from Leonard, the visit from the long-dead reporter, the prophetic dreams; she told him about the grim battle with Aristophanes. 'I am Rachael Adams, Paul. That other life has been revealed to me so that I can stop this murderous cycle. Willa did not start the fire. *I* started it accidentally. There is no reason for the girl to seek revenge. It's all a mistake, a dark misunderstanding. If I can talk to the girl, Jane, while she's regressed to her Laura phase, I can persuade her of the truth. I know I can. I can stop all of this here, now, once and forever. Do you think I'm babbling? Senile? I don't believe I am. In fact, I *know* I'm not. And I suspect you've had some strange experiences recently that confirm what I'm telling you.'

'You hit that one on the head, all right,' he told her.

Nevertheless, reincarnation – being born again in a new body – it was a stunning, soul-shaking thing to accept. *There is no lasting death.* Yes, that was much harder to accept than the existence of poltergeists.

'Do you know about Millicent Parker?' he asked her.

'Never heard the name,' Grace said.

The rain started falling even harder. He turned the windshield wipers up to their highest speed.

'In 1905,' he told Grace, 'Millie Parker attempted to kill her mother – on the night before her sixteenth birthday. Like the Linda Bektermann case, the mother ended up killing Millie, instead of the other way around. Purely self-defense. And here's what you might not realize: Under hypnosis, Jane claimed to be Laura, Millie, and then Linda Bektermann. But the names meant nothing to us.'

'And again, in the Millicent Parker case,' Grace said, 'the girl's desire for revenge was frustrated. Yes. I knew there must be another life between Laura and Linda.'

'But why this night-before-the-birthday thing that keeps cropping up?'

'Laura was looking forward to *her* sixteenth birthday with great eagerness,' Grace-Rachael said. 'It was going to be the best day of her life, she said. She had all sorts of plans for it – and for how her life would be changed after she attained that magical age. I think, somehow, she felt her mother's treatment of her would change once she was "grown up." But she died in the fire before her birthday.'

'And in life after life, as her sixteenth birthday approaches, the fear of her mother and the hatred of her mother wells up from her subconscious.'

Grace nodded. 'From the subconscious of the girl she was in 1865, the girl – the identity – who is buried down at the bottom of Jane's psyche.'

They rode in silence for a minute or two.

Paul's hands were sweaty on the steering wheel.

His mind spun as he tried to absorb the story she had told, and he had that old feeling of balancing on a tightrope high above a deep, deep, dark chasm.

Then he said, 'But Carol isn't Jane's mother.'

'You've forgotten something,' Grace said.

'What?'

'Carol had a child out of wedlock when she was a teenager. I know she told you all about it. I'm giving away no secrets.'

Paul's stomach quivered. He was cold all the way into the marrow of his bones. 'My God. You mean . . . Jane is the child that Carol put up for adoption.'

'I have no proof of it,' Grace said. 'But I bet that when the police spread their search nets wide enough, when they finally locate the girl's parents in some other state, we'll learn that she's adopted. And that Carol is her natural mother.'

* * *

For what seemed like an eternity, they struggled on the floor by the hearth, grunting, twisting, the girl throwing punches, Carol trying to resist without hurting her. At last, when it became clear that Carol was unquestionably the stronger of the two and would eventually gain control of the situation, the girl shoved away from her, scrambled up, kicked her in the thigh, and ran out of the room, into the kitchen.

Carol was shocked and dazed both by the girl's unexpected violence and by the maniacal power of the blows. Her face stung, and she knew her cheeks were going to bruise. Her bitten shoulder was bleeding; a large, damp, red stain was spreading slowly down the front of her blouse.

She got up, swayed unsteadily for a moment. Then she went after the girl. 'Honey, wait!'

In the distance, outside the house, Laura's voice rose in a sharp, shrill scream: 'I *haaaaaate* you!'

Carol reached the kitchen, leaned against the refrigerator. The girl was gone. The back door was open.

The sound of the rain was very loud.

She hurried to the door and looked out at the rear lawn, at the small meadow, at the forest that crowded in at the edge of the meadow. The girl had disappeared.

'Jane! Laura!'

Millicent? She wondered. Linda? What on earth *should* I call her?

She crossed the porch and went down the steps into the yard, into the pelting, cold rain. She turned right, then left, not sure where to look first.

Then Jane appeared. The girl came out of the woodshed at the southwest corner of the cabin. She was carrying an ax.

*　　*　　*

'*. . . and Carol is her natural mother.*'

Grace's words echoed and reechoed in Paul's head.

For a moment he was incapable of speech.

He stared ahead, shocked, not really seeing the road, and he nearly ran up the back end of a sluggishly moving Buick. He jammed on his brakes. He and Grace were thrown forward, testing their seat belts. He slowed down until he could regain control of himself.

Finally, the words burst out of him like machine-gun fire: 'But how in the hell did the kid find out who her real mother was, they don't give out that kind of information to children her age, how did she get here from whatever state she was living in, how did she track us down and make it all happen like this? Good Christ, she *did* step in front of Carol's car on purpose. It was a setup. The whole damned thing was a setup!'

'I don't know how she found her way to Carol,' Grace said. 'Maybe her parents knew who the child's natural mother was, and kept the name around in the family records, in case the girl ever wanted to know it when she grew up. Perhaps not. Perhaps anything. Maybe she was simply drawn to Carol by the same forces that tried to get to me through Aristophanes. That might explain why she appeared to be in a daze before she stepped in front of the car. But I don't really know. Maybe we'll *never* know.'

'Oh, shit,' Paul said, and his voice wavered. 'Oh, no, no. Goddamn!'

'What?'

'You know how Carol is on *that* day,' he said shakily. 'The day her baby was born, the baby she gave up. She's different from the way she is every other day of the year. Depressed, withdrawn. It's always such a bad day for her that the date's engraved on my memory.'

'On mine, too,' Grace said.

'It's tomorrow,' he said. 'If Jane *is* Carol's child, she'll be sixteen tomorrow.'

'Yes.'

'And she'll try to kill Carol today.'

*   *   *

Sheets of dark rain rippled and flapped like wind-whipped canvas tents.

Carol stood on the soggy lawn, unable to move, numbed by fear, frozen by the cold rain.

Twenty feet away, the girl stood with the ax, gripping it in both hands. Her drenched hair hung straight to her shoulders, and her clothes were pasted to her. She appeared to be oblivious to the storm and the chilly air. Her eyes were owlish, as if she were high on amphetamine, and her face was distorted by rage.

'Laura?' Carol said at last. 'Listen to me. You will listen to me. You will drop the ax.'

'You stinking, rotten bitch,' the girl said through tightly clenched teeth.

Lightning cracked open the sky, and the falling rain glittered for a moment in the stroboscopic flashes that came through from the other side of the heavens.

When the subsequent thunder rolled away and Carol could be heard, she said, 'Laura, I want you to –'

'I hate you!' the girl said. She took one step toward Carol.

'Stop this right now,' Carol said, refusing to retreat. 'You will be calm. You will relax.'

The girl took another step.

'*Drop the ax*,' Carol insisted. 'Honey, listen to me. You *will* listen to me. You are only in a trance. You are –'

'I'm going to get you this time, Mama. This time I'm not going to lose.'

'I'm not your mother,' Carol said. 'Laura, you are –'

'I'm going to cut your goddamn head off this time, you bitch!'

The voice had changed.

It wasn't Laura's now.

It belonged to Linda Bektermann, the third identity.

'I'm going to cut your goddamn head off and put it on the kitchen table with Daddy's.'

With a jolt, Carol recalled last week's nightmare. There had been a moment in the dream when she had stepped into the kitchen and had encountered two severed heads on the table, a man's and a woman's. But how could Jane know what had been in that night-mare?

Carol finally took a step backwards, then another. Although the rain was cold, she began to sweat.

'I'm only going to tell you one more time, Linda. You must put the ax down and –'

'I'm going to cut your head off and chop you into a thousand little pieces,' the girl said.

And the voice now belonged to Jane.

It wasn't the voice of an identity heretofore only evident in a trance. This was *Jane*'s voice. She had come out of the trance on her own power. She knew who she was. She knew who Carol was. And she *still* wanted to use the ax.

Carol edged toward the back porch steps.

The girl quickly circled in that direction, blocking access to the cabin. Then she started toward Carol, moving fast, grinning.

Carol turned and ran toward the meadow.

* * *

In spite of the pounding rain, which snapped with bulletlike power into the windshield, in spite of the dirty mist that hung over the road, in spite of the treacherously greasy pavement, Paul slowly pressed the accelerator all the way to the floor and swung the Pontiac into the passing lane.

'It's a mask,' he said.

Grace said, 'What do you mean?'

'The Jane Doe identity, the Linda Bektermann and Millie Parker identities – each of them was just a mask. A very real, very convincing mask. But a mask nonetheless. Behind the mask there was always the same face, the same person. Laura.'

'And we've got to put an end to the masquerade once and for all,' Grace said. 'If I can just talk to her as her Aunt Rachael, I'll be able to stop this madness. I'm sure I will. She'll listen to me . . . to Rachael. That's who she was closest to. Closer than she was to her mother. I can make her understand that her mother, Willa, didn't intentionally or even accidentally start that fire back in 1865. At last she'll understand. She'll see that there's no justification for revenge. The cycle will come to an end.'

'If we're in time,' Paul said.

'If,' Grace said.

* * *

Carol ran through the stinging rain and through the knee-high grass. She ran up the sloping meadow, her arms tucked in close to her side, legs pumping high, gasping for breath, each stride jarring her to the bones.

Ahead lay the forest, which seemed to be her only salvation. There were thousand of places to hide in the wilderness, countless trails on which she could lose the girl. After all, she was somewhat familiar with the land, but to the girl it was a strange place.

Halfway across the meadow, she risked a glance behind her. The girl was only fifteen feet away.

Lightning slashed through the bellies of the clouds, and the blade of the ax flashed once, twice, with a brilliant reflection of that icy electric glow.

Carol looked straight ahead once more and redoubled her efforts to reach the trees. The meadow was wet, spongy, and in some places slippery. She expected to fall or at least twist an ankle, but she reached the perimeter of the forest without trouble. She plunged in among the trees, among the purple and brown and black shadows, into the lush undergrowth, and she began to think there was a chance – maybe only a very small chance, but a chance nonetheless – that she would come out of this alive.

*   *   *

Hunching over the steering wheel, squinting at the rain-swept highway, Paul said, 'I want one thing perfectly clear between us.'

Grace said, 'What's that?'

'Carol's my first concern.'

'Of course.'

'If we walk into the middle of a nasty situation at the cabin, I'll do whatever's necessary to protect Carol.'

Grace glanced at the glove compartment. 'You mean . . . the gun.'

'Yes. If I have to, if there's no other way, I'll use it, Grace. I'll shoot the girl if there's no other choice.'

'It's unlikely that we'll walk into the middle of a confrontation,' Grace said. 'Either it won't have begun yet – or it'll all be over with by the time we get there.'

'I won't let her hurt Carol,' he said grimly. 'And if worse comes to worst, I don't want you trying to stop me.'

'There are some things you should consider,' Grace said.

'What?'

'First of all, it'll be just as tragic if Carol kills the girl. And that's the pattern, after all. Both Millie and Linda attacked their mothers, but *they* were the ones killed. What if that happens this time? What if Carol is forced to kill the girl in self-defense? You know she's never stopped feeling guilty about putting the baby up for adoption. She carries that on her shoulders sixteen years after the fact. So what will happen when she discovers she's killed her own daughter?'

'It'll destroy her,' he said without hesitation.

'I think it very well might. And what'll it do to your relationship with Carol if *you* kill her daughter, even if you do it to save Carol's life?'

He thought about that for a moment. Then he said, 'It might destroy *us*,' and he shuddered.

*   *   *

For a while, no matter how tortuous the path she followed through the woods, Carol could not lose the girl. She switched from one natural trail to another, crossed a small stream, doubled back the way she had come. She moved in a crouch at all times, staying out of sight below the brush line. She made no sound that could be heard above the constant hissing of the rain. Most of the time she carefully stepped on old leaves or made her way from stone to stone, from log to log, leaving no footprints, in the damp, bare earth. Yet Jane pursued her with uncanny confidence, without hesitation, as if she were part bloodhound.

At last, however, Carol was certain she had lost the girl. She squatted under a huge pine, leaned back against the damp bark, and breathed deeply, rapidly, raggedly, while waiting for her heart to stop racing.

A minute passed. Two. Five.

The only sound was the rain drizzling down through the leaves and through the interlaced pine needles.

She became aware of the dank odor of heavy vegetation – moss and fungus and forest grass and more.

Nothing moved.

She was safe, at least for now.

But she couldn't just sit beneath the tall pine, waiting for help to arrive. Eventually, Jane would stop searching for her and would try to find a way back to the cabin. If the girl didn't get lost – which she most likely would do – if she somehow managed to return to the cabin, and if she was still in psychotic fugue when she got there, she might murder the first person she encountered. If she took Vince Gervis by surprise, even his great size and impressive muscles would be of no use against the blade of an ax.

Carol stood up, moved away from the tree, and began to circle back toward the cabin. The keys to the Volkswagen were in her purse, and her purse was in one of the bedrooms. She had to get the keys, drive into town, and ask the county sheriff for assistance.

What went wrong? she wondered. The girl shouldn't have become violent. There was no indication that she was capable of such a thing. The potential to kill simply was not a part of her psychological profile. Paul was right to be worried. But *why*?

Proceeding with utmost caution, expecting the girl to leap at her from behind every tree and bush, Carol needed fifteen minutes to reach the edge of the forest at a point not far from the place at which she had entered the trees with the girl in hot pursuit. The meadow was deserted. At the bottom of the slope, the cabin huddled in the pouring rain.

The kid's lost, Carol thought. All of that twisting and turning and doubling back through unfamiliar territory was too much for her. She'll never find the way home by herself.

The sheriff's men weren't going to like this one: a search in the rain, in the forest, for a violent girl who was armed with an ax. No, they weren't going to like this one at all.

Carol navigated the meadow at a run.

The rear door of the cabin was standing open, just as she had left it.

She hurried inside, slammed the door, and threw the bolt. Relief swept through her.

She swallowed a couple of times, caught her breath, and crossed the kitchen to the door that led into the living room. She was about to step across that threshold when she was stopped by a sudden, terrible certainty that she was not alone.

She jumped back, spurred by intuition more than anything else, and even as she moved, the ax swung in from the left, through the doorway. It sliced the air where she had been. If she hadn't moved, she would have been cut in half.

The girl stepped into the room, brandishing the ax. 'Bitch.'

Carol backed to the door that she had just latched. She fumbled behind her for the bolt. Couldn't find it.

The girl closed in.

Whimpering, Carol turned to the door, seized the latch. She sensed the ax rising into the air behind her and knew she wouldn't have time to open the door, and she jerked to one side, and the blade bit into the door just where her head would have been.

With superhuman strength, the girl wrenched the ax out of the wood.

Gasping, Carol ducked past her and ran into the living room. She looked for something with which to defend herself. The only thing available was a poker in the rack of fireplace tools. She grabbed it.

Behind her, Jane said, 'I hate you!'

Carol whirled.

The girl swung the ax.

Carol brought the poker up without any time to spare, and it rang against the gleaming, viciously sharp blade, deflecting the blow.

The impact rang back the length of the poker, into Carol's hands, numbing them. She couldn't maintain her grip on the iron rod; it fell from her tingling hands.

The impact did not ring back along the wooden handle of the ax, and Jane still held that weapon with firm determination.

Carol backed up onto the wide hearth of the stone fireplace. She could feel the heat against her legs.

She had nowhere else to run.

'Now,' Jane said. 'Now. At last.'

She lifted the ax high, and Carol cried out in anticipation of the pain, and the front door was flung open. It crashed against the wall. Paul was there. And Grace.

The girl glanced at them but was not going to be distracted; she brought the ax down toward Carol's face.

Carol collapsed onto the hearth.

The ax struck the stone mantel over her head; sparks flew.

Paul rushed at the girl, but she sensed him coming. She turned toward him, slashed with the ax, and drove him back.

Then turned on Carol again.

'Cornered rat,' she said, grinning.

The ax came up.

This time it won't miss, Carol thought.

Someone said, 'Spiders!'

The girl froze.

The ax was suspended in midair.

'Spiders!' It was Grace. 'There are spiders on your back, Laura. Oh God, they're all over your back. Spiders! Laura, look out for the spiders!'

Carol watched, bewildered, as a look of stark terror took possession of the girl's face.

'Spiders!' Grace shouted again. 'Big, black, hairy spiders, Laura. Get them off! Get them off your back. Quick!'

The girl screamed and dropped the ax, which clattered against the stone hearth. She brushed frantically at her back, twisting her arms up behind her. She was snuffling and squealing like a very small child. 'Help me!'

'Spiders,' Grace said again, as Paul picked up the ax and put it out of the way.

The girl tried to tear off her blouse. She dropped to her knees, then fell onto her side, gibbering in terror. She writhed on the floor, brushing imaginary spiders off her body. Within a minute she seemed to be in a state of shock; she lay shuddering, weeping.

'She was always afraid of spiders,' Grace said. 'That was why she hated the cellar.'

'The cellar?' Carol asked.

'Where she died,' Grace said.

Carol didn't understand. But at the moment she didn't care. She watched the girl writhing on the floor, and she suddenly felt overwhelming pity for her. She knelt beside Jane, lifted her up, hugged her.

'You okay?' Paul asked her.

She nodded.

'Spiders,' the girl said, quivering uncontrollably.

'No, honey,' Carol said. 'No spiders. There aren't any spiders on you. Not now. Not any more.' And she looked at Grace, wondering.